A truly exceptional collection of great stories

Short stories can be funny, pathetic, frightening, up-lifting, nostalgic, beautiful—and it is just this variety that makes them the popular and satisfying reading they are. Here, in one volume, have been brought together 35 of the best stories of our time, in an outstanding anthology that ranges in kind from the humor of James Thurber and Ring Lardner to the irony of Hemingway and Joyce. All the modern masters are here—Fitzgerald, Faulkner, Katherine Anne Porter, Maugham, and many more. Each story is different from every other—but each bears the stamp of unmistakable greatness.

ABOUT THE EDITORS: *Robert Penn Warren, winner of a Pulitzer Prize for fiction and one for poetry and of the National Book Award for Poetry, is the author of* ALL THE KING'S MEN, WORLD ENOUGH AND TIME, PROMISES, FLOOD, *and many other works of fiction, poetry and literary criticism. He died in 1989.*

Albert Erskine was a vice-president and executive editor at Random House in New York. He was also formerly on the staff of THE SOUTHERN REVIEW *and was associated with the Louisiana State University Press.*

OTHER LAUREL EDITIONS OF INTEREST

SHORT
STORY
MASTERPIECES

EDITED BY

ROBERT PENN WARREN

AND

ALBERT ERSKINE

A LAUREL BOOK
Published by
Dell Publishing
a division of
Bantam Doubleday Dell Publishing Group, Inc.
1540 Broadway
New York, New York 10036

COPYRIGHT NOTICES AND ACKNOWLEDGMENTS:

The following selections in this anthology are reproduced by permission of the authors, their publishers, or their agents.

"Impulse" from *The Short Stories of Conrad Aiken*, by Conrad Aiken, copyright, 1950, by Conrad Aiken. Reprinted by permission of Duell, Sloan & Pearce, Inc.

"A Bottle of Milk for Mother" from *Neon Wilderness*, by Nelson Algren, copyright, 1941, by Nelson Algren. Reprinted by permission of Doubleday & Company, Inc.

"The Egg" from *The Triumph of the Egg*, by Sherwood Anderson, copyright, 1921, by Eleanor Anderson. Reprinted by permission of Harold Ober Associates.

"Torch Song" from *The Enormous Radio and Other Stories*, by John Cheever, copyright, 1953, by John Cheever. Reprinted by permission of Funk & Wagnalls Company, New York. This story appeared originally in *The New Yorker*.

"Witch's Money," copyright, 1939, by John Collier, from *Fancies and Goodnights*, published by Doubleday & Company, Inc. Reprinted by permission of Harold Matson. This story appeared originally in *The New Yorker*.

"The Third Prize" reprinted from *The Collected Tales of A. E. Coppard*, by permission of Alfred A. Knopf, Inc. and A. D. Peters. Copyright, 1929, 1948, by A. E. Coppard.

"The Bride Comes to Yellow Sky" reprinted from *Stephen Crane: An Omnibus*, edited by Robert Wooster Stallman, by permission of Alfred A. Knopf, Inc. Copyright, 1925, by William H. Crane and 1952, by Alfred A. Knopf, Inc.

"Open Winter," copyright, 1939, by the Curtis Publishing Company. From *Team Bells Woke Me* by H. L. Davis, published by William Morrow & Company, Inc.

The trademark Laurel® is registered in the U.S. Patent and Trademark Office.

The trademark Dell® is registered in the U.S. Patent and Trademark Office.

ISBN: 0-440-37864-8

Printed in the United States of America

Published simultaneously in Canada

OPM 61   60   59   58   57

CONTENTS

Editors' Note

A good story gives pleasure and satisfaction to anyone who is curious about, and sympathetic with, his fellow men, anyone whose feelings are fresh and can respond to the funny, the pitiful, the noble, or the terrible, anyone who is concerned with the meaning of his own, or other people's experience, anyone whose imagination is strong and healthy enough to create, from the words put before him by the writer, people, things, and events—the movement and color of life.

We have chosen the stories in this book because we think that each one, in its own particular way, in its own scale, tonality, and self-imposed limitation, will give pleasure and satisfaction. It does not matter whether the movement and color of life are exhibited in the preposterous crazy farce of Thurber's "You Could Look It Up," with its hint of a folktale of the diamond and dugout, or in the mordant, sad irony of James Joyce's "The Boarding House," in the lyric nostalgia in Elizabeth Parsons's "The Nightingales Sing," or in the sardonic pathos of Ernest Hemingway's "Soldier's Home." What does matter is that the movement and color be delivered to us with force and freshness, and that the writer who delivers these to us make us feel, somehow, a significance in the process.

By significance, we don't mean moralizing, about either individuals or society. What we do mean is best indicated indirectly by saying that the pleasure we get from Ring Lardner's acidulous comedies would be much less if behind these comedies there were not an outraged hatred of sham and a love of common decency and honesty, and that the wire-drawn suspense and taut style of Hemingway's dramas have a close relation to his ethic of courage and honor. Behind the good story, no matter how light its tone, how trivial its subject matter, or how cranky its end, we feel that an interesting mind and temperament has made contact with life. Even though the point of the story, stated or implied, may be contrary to our personal conclusions about things, it enlarges our own sense of human possibility, for good or bad.

The really fine story is by a writer who has some characteristic slant on the world, some characteristic reading of human values. It is not just another moderately entertaining story that might just as well have been signed by some other writer. A story by Joyce isn't like a story by anybody else, nor is a story by Conrad. Even the most expert and sedulous imitator misses something in the work of the better writer whom he imitates.

Making an anthology is not only a process of selection; it is perhaps even more a process of setting limitations. There are thirty-five stories in this volume, by as many writers. All of them were written in English during what might roughly be called the last half-century—our own time; only six of the writers here represented—Anderson, Conrad, Crane, James, Maugham, and "Saki"—had reached their majority before 1900, but they are significantly identified with our time.

But the boundaries of date and language are only part of the problem. The title of this book has that imposing word "Masterpieces" in it, and it would be nice to be able to say that we feel that we have here the "best" thirty-five stories written in English in our time. Candor and caution forbid such a claim. For one thing, some "masterpieces"—such as Joseph Conrad's "Heart of Darkness" or F. Scott Fitzgerald's "The Rich Boy"—are too long to be included in a book of this plan. Furthermore, if we had got together within our available number of pages what we considered the best thirty-five stories there would be fewer authors. William Faulkner, for example, would have more than one, and, among others, Ernest Hemingway, James Joyce, Katherine Anne Porter, Eudora Welty, and Frank O'Connor. There are few such real masters of the short story, and they are masters because they have written a number of fine examples of the form. But there are other writers who have produced one or two stories so memorable that they must find a place in a book like this, which aims to give some representation to the considerable variety of good stories that have been written in our time.

In giving this spread of representation, we have tried to be unswayed by the distinction or power a writer may have achieved in some other literary form. It is always a hopeful temptation to see refracted in the short story of a poet or novelist some of the qualities that have made his poems or novels significant, but unless the story of the famous poet or novelist seemed good in itself, we have left it out. We have also passed over those stories in which the narrative interest is markedly subordinate to the lyrical or philosophical or symbolic intentions of the writer; exciting and significant work has been done in this kind, but the scale of this book has forced us to forgo the indulgence of our tastes in that direction.

—ROBERT PENN WARREN
—ALBERT ERSKINE

IMPULSE

Conrad Aiken

Michael Lowes hummed as he shaved, amused by the face he saw—the pallid, asymmetrical face, with the right eye so much higher than the left, and its eyebrow so peculiarly arched, like a "v" turned upside down. Perhaps this day wouldn't be as bad as the last. In fact, he knew it wouldn't be, and that was why he hummed. This was the bi-weekly day of escape, when he would stay out for the evening, and play bridge with Hurwitz, Bryant, and Smith. Should he tell Dora at the breakfast table? No, better not. Particularly in view of last night's row about unpaid bills. And there would be more of them, probably, beside his plate. The rent. The coal. The doctor who had attended to the children. Jeez, what a life. Maybe it was time to do a new jump. And Dora was beginning to get restless again—

But he hummed, thinking of the bridge game. Not that he liked Hurwitz or Bryant or Smith—cheap fellows, really—mere pick-up acquaintances. But what could you do about making friends, when you were always hopping about from one place to another, looking for a living, and fate always against you! They were all right enough. Good enough for a little escape, a little party—and Hurwitz always provided good alcohol. Dinner at the Greek's, and then to Smith's room—yes. He would wait till late in the afternoon, and then telephone to Dora as if it had all come up suddenly. Hello, Dora—is that you, old girl? Yes, this is Michael—Smith has asked me to drop in for a hand of bridge—you know—so I'll just have a little

snack in town. Home by the last car as usual. Yes. . . .
Gooo-bye! . . .

And it all went off perfectly, too. Dora was quiet, at
breakfast, but not hostile. The pile of bills was there, to be
sure, but nothing was said about them. And while Dora was
busy getting the kids ready for school, he managed to slip
out, pretending that he thought it was later than it really
was. Pretty neat, that! He hummed again, as he waited for
the train. Telooralooraloo. Let the bills wait, damn them! A
man couldn't do everything at once, could he, when bad
luck hounded him everywhere? And if he could just get a
little night off, now and then, a rest and change, a little
diversion, what was the harm in that?

At half-past four he rang up Dora and broke the news to
her. He wouldn't be home till late.

"Are you sure you'll be home at all?" she said, coolly.

That was Dora's idea of a joke. But if he could have
foreseen—!

He met the others at the Greek restaurant, began with a
couple of *araks*, which warmed him, then went on to red
wine, bad olives, *pilaf*, and other obscure foods; and considerably later they all walked along Boylston Street to
Smith's room. It was a cold night, the temperature below
twenty, with a fine dry snow sifting the streets. But Smith's
room was comfortably warm, he trotted out some gin and
the Porto Rican cigars, showed them a new snapshot of
Squiggles (his Revere Beach sweetheart), and then they
settled down to a nice long cozy game of bridge.

It was during an intermission, when they all got up to
stretch their legs and renew their drinks, that the talk
started—Michael never could remember which one of them
it was who had put in the first oar—about impulse. It might
have been Hurwitz, who was in many ways the only intel-
lectual one of the three, though hardly what you might call
a highbrow. He had his queer curiosities, however, and the
idea was just such as might occur to him. At any rate, it was
he who developed the idea, and with gusto.

"Sure," he said, "anybody might do it. Have you got

impulses? Of course, you got impulses. How many times you think—suppose I do that? And you don't do it, because you know damn well if you do it you'll get arrested. You meet a man you despise—you want to spit in his eye. You see a girl you'd like to kiss—you want to kiss her. Or maybe just to squeeze her arm when she stands beside you in the street car. You know what I mean."

"Do I know what you mean!" sighed Smith. "I'll tell the world. I'll tell the cock-eyed world! . . ."

"You would," said Bryant. "And so would I."

"It would be easy," said Hurwitz, "to give in to it. You know what I mean? So simple. Temptation is too close. That girl you see is too damn good-looking—she stands too near you—you just put out your hand it touches her arm—maybe her leg—why worry? And you think, maybe if she don't like it I can make believe I didn't mean it. . . ."

"Like these fellows that slash fur coats with razor blades," said Michael. "Just impulse, in the beginning, and only later a habit."

"Sure. . . . And like these fellows that cut off braids of hair with scissors. They just feel like it and do it. . . . Or stealing."

"Stealing?" said Bryant.

"Sure. Why, I often feel like it. . . . I see a nice little thing right in front of me on a counter—you know, a nice little knife, or necktie, or a box of candy—quick, you put it in your pocket, and then go to the other counter, or the soda fountain for a drink. What would be more human? We all want things. Why not take them? Why not do them? And civilization is only skin-deep. . . ."

"That's right. Skin-deep," said Bryant.

"But if you were caught, by God!" said Smith, opening his eyes wide.

"Who's talking about getting caught? . . . Who's talking about doing it? It isn't that we do it, it's only that we want to do it. Why, Christ, there's been times when I thought to hell with everything, I'll kiss that woman if it's the last thing I do."

"It might be," said Bryant.

Michael was astonished at this turn of the talk. He had often felt both these impulses. To know that this was a kind of universal human inclination came over him with something like relief.

"Of *course,* everybody has those feelings," he said smiling. "I have them myself. . . . But suppose you *did* yield to them?"

"Well, we don't," said Hurwitz.

"I know—but suppose you did?"

Hurwitz shrugged his fat shoulders, indifferently.

"Oh, well," he said, "it would be bad business."

"Jesus, yes," said Smith, shuffling the cards.

"Oy," said Bryant.

The game was resumed, the glasses were refilled, pipes were lit, watches were looked at. Michael had to think of the last car from Sullivan Square, at eleven-fifty. But also he could not stop thinking of this strange idea. It was amusing. It was fascinating. Here was everyone wanting to steal— toothbrushes, or books—or to caress some fascinating stranger of a female in a subway train—the impulse everywhere— why not be a Columbus of the moral world and really do it? . . . He remembered stealing a conch-shell from the drawing room of a neighbor when he was ten—it had been one of the thrills of his life. He had popped it into his sailor blouse and borne it away with perfect aplomb. When, later, suspicion had been cast upon him, he had smashed the shell in his back yard. And often, when he had been looking at Parker's collection of stamps—the early Americans—

The game interrupted his recollections, and presently it was time for the usual night-cap. Bryant drove them to Park Street. Michael was a trifle tight, but not enough to be unsteady on his feet. He waved a cheery hand at Bryant and Hurwitz and began to trudge through the snow to the subway entrance. The lights on the snow were very beautiful. The Park Street Church was ringing, with its queer, soft quarter-bells, the half-hour. Plenty of time. Plenty of time. Time enough for a visit to the drugstore, and a hot chocolate—he could see the warm lights of the windows falling on the snowed sidewalk. He zigzagged across the street and entered.

And at once he was seized with a conviction that his real reason for entering the drugstore was not to get a hot chocolate—not at all! He was going to steal something. He was going to put the impulse to the test, and see whether (*one*) he could manage it with sufficient skill, and (*two*) whether theft gave him any real satisfaction. The drugstore was crowded with people who had just come from the theatre next door. They pushed three deep round the soda fountain, and the cashier's cage. At the back of the store, in the toilet and prescription department, there were not so many, but nevertheless enough to give him a fair chance. All the clerks were busy. His hands were in the side pockets of his overcoat—they were deep wide pockets and would serve admirably. A quick gesture over a table or counter, the object dropped in—

Oddly enough, he was not in the least excited: perhaps that was because of the gin. On the contrary, he was intensely amused; not to say delighted. He was smiling, as he walked slowly along the right-hand side of the store toward the back; edging his way amongst the people, with first one shoulder forward and then the other, while with a critical and appraising eye he examined the wares piled on the counters and on the stands in the middle of the floor. There were some extremely attractive scent-sprays or atomizers— but the dangling bulbs might be troublesome. There were stacks of boxed letter-paper. A basket full of clothes-brushes. Green hot-water bottles. Percolators—too large, and out of the question. A tray of multicolored toothbrushes, bottles of cologne, fountain pens—and then he experienced love at first sight. There could be no question that he had found his chosen victim. He gazed, fascinated, at the delicious object—a *de luxe* safety-razor set, of heavy gold, in a snakeskin box which was lined with red plush. . . .

It wouldn't do, however, to stare at it too long—one of the clerks might notice. He observed quickly the exact

position of the box—which was close to the edge of the glass
counter—and prefigured with a quite precise mental picture
the gesture with which he would simultaneously close it and
remove it. Forefinger at the back—thumb in front—the
box drawn forward and then slipped down toward the
pocket—as he thought it out, the muscles in his forearm
pleasurably contracted. He continued his slow progress round
the store, past the prescription counter, past the candy
counter; examined with some show of attention the display
of cigarette lighters and blade sharpeners; and then, with a
quick turn, went leisurely back to his victim. Everything
was propitious. The whole section of counter was clear for
the moment—there were neither customers nor clerks. He
approached the counter, leaned over it as if to examine
some little filigreed "compacts" at the back of the showcase,
picking up one of them with his left hand, as he did so. He
was thus leaning directly over the box; and it was the
simplest thing in the world to clasp it as planned between
thumb and forefinger of his other hand, to shut it softly, and
to slide it downward to his pocket. It was over in an instant.
He continued then for a moment to turn the compact case
this way and that in the light, as if to see it sparkle. It
sparkled very nicely. Then he put it back on the little pile of
cases, turned, and approached the soda fountain—just as
Hurwitz had suggested.

He was in the act of pressing forward in the crowd to ask
for his hot chocolate when he felt a firm hand close round
his elbow. He turned, and looked at a man in a slouch hat
and dirty raincoat, with the collar turned up. The man was
smiling in a very offensive way.

"I guess you thought that was pretty slick," he said in a
low voice which nevertheless managed to convey the very
essence of venom and hostility. "You come along with me,
mister!"

Michael returned the smile amiably, but was a little frightened. His heart began to beat.

"I don't know what you're talking about," he said, still
smiling.

"No, of course not!"

The man was walking toward the rear of the store, and was pulling Michael along with him, keeping a paralyzingly tight grip on his elbow. Michael was beginning to be angry, but also to be horrified. He thought of wrenching his arm free, but feared it would make a scene. Better not. He permitted himself to be urged ignominiously along the shop, through a gate in the rear counter, and into a small room at the back, where a clerk was measuring a yellow liquid into a bottle.

"Will you be so kind as to explain to me what this is all about?" he then said, with what frigidity of manner he could muster. But his voice shook a little. The man in the slouch hat paid no attention. He addressed the clerk instead, giving his head a quick backward jerk as he spoke.

"Get the manager in here," he said.

He smiled at Michael, with narrowed eyes, and Michael, hating him, but panic-stricken, smiled foolishly back at him.

"Now, look here—" he said.

But the manager had appeared, and the clerk; and events then happened with revolting and nauseating speed. Michael's hand was yanked violently from his pocket, the fatal snakeskin box was pulled out by the detective, and identified by the manager and the clerk. They both looked at Michael with a queer expression, in which astonishment, shame, and contempt were mixed with vague curiosity.

"Sure that's ours," said the manager, looking slowly at Michael.

"I saw him pinch it," said the detective. "What about it?" He again smiled offensively at Michael. "Anything to say?"

"It was all a joke," said Michael, his face feeling very hot and flushed. "I made a kind of bet with some friends. . . . I can prove it. I can call them up for you."

The three men looked at him in silence, all three of them just faintly smiling, as if incredulously.

"Sure you can," said the detective, urbanely. "You can prove it in court. . . . Now come along with me, mister."

Michael was astounded at this appalling turn of events,

but his brain still worked. Perhaps if he were to put it to
this fellow as man to man, when they got outside? As he was
thinking this, he was firmly conducted through a back door
into a dark alley at the rear of the store. It had stopped
snowing. A cold wind was blowing. But the world, which
had looked so beautiful fifteen minutes before, had now lost
its charm. They walked together down the alley in six
inches of powdery snow, the detective holding Michael's
arm with affectionate firmness.

"No use calling the wagon," he said. "We'll walk. It ain't
far."

They walked along Tremont Street. And Michael couldn't
help, even then, thinking what an extraordinary thing this
was! Here were all these good people passing them, and
little knowing that he, Michael Lowes, was a thief, a thief
by accident, on his way to jail. It seemed so absurd as
hardly to be worth speaking of! And suppose they shouldn't
believe him? This notion made him shiver. But it wasn't
possible—no, it wasn't possible. As soon as he had told his
story, and called up Hurwitz and Bryant and Smith, it
would all be laughed off. Yes, laughed off.

He began telling the detective about it: how they had
discussed such impulses over a game of bridge. Just a friendly
game, and they had joked about it and then, just to see
what would happen, he had done it. What was it that made
his voice sound so insincere, so hollow? The detective neither slackened his pace nor turned his head. His businesslike grimness was alarming. Michael felt that he was paying
no attention at all; and, moreover, it occurred to him that
this kind of lowbrow official might not even understand such
a thing. . . . He decided to try the sentimental.

"And good Lord, man, there's my wife waiting for me—!'

"Oh, sure, and the kids too."

"Yes, and the kids!"

The detective gave a quick leer over the collar of his dirty
raincoat.

"And no Santy Claus *this* year," he said.

Michael saw that it was hopeless. He was wasting his time.

"I can see it's no use talking to you," he said stiffly. "You're so used to dealing with criminals that you think all mankind is criminal, *ex post facto.*"

"Sure."

Arrived at the station, and presented without decorum to the lieutenant at the desk, Michael tried again. Something in the faces of the lieutenant and the sergeant, as he told his story, made it at once apparent that there was going to be trouble. They obviously didn't believe him—not for a moment. But after consultation, they agreed to call up Bryant and Hurwitz and Smith, and to make inquiries. The sergeant went off to do this, while Michael sat on a wooden bench. Fifteen minutes passed, during which the clock ticked and the lieutenant wrote slowly in a book, using a blotter very frequently. A clerk had been dispatched, also, to look up Michael's record, if any. This gentleman came back first, and reported that there was nothing. The lieutenant scarcely looked up from his book, and went on writing. The first serious blow then fell. The sergeant, reporting, said that he hadn't been able to get Smith (of course—Michael thought—he's off somewhere with Squiggles) but had got Hurwitz and Bryant. Both of them denied that there had been any bet. They both seemed nervous, as far as he could make out over the phone. They said they didn't know Lowes well, were acquaintances of his, and made it clear that they didn't want to be mixed up in anything. Hurwitz had added that he knew Lowes was hard up.

At this, Michael jumped to his feet, feeling as if the blood would burst out of his face.

"The damned liars!" he shouted. "The bloody liars! By God—!"

"Take him away," said the lieutenant, lifting his eyebrows, and making a motion with his pen.

Michael lay awake all night in his cell, after talking for five minutes with Dora on the telephone. Something in Dora's cool voice had frightened him more than anything else.

*   *   *

And when Dora came to talk to him the next morning at
nine o'clock, his alarm proved to be well-founded. Dora was
cold, detached, deliberate. She was not at all what he had
hoped she might be—sympathetic and helpful. She didn't
volunteer to get a lawyer, or in fact to do anything—and when
she listened quietly to his story, it seemed to him that she
had the appearance of a person listening to a very improbable
lie. Again, as he narrated the perfectly simple episode—the
discussion of "impulse" at the bridge game, the drinks, and
the absurd tipsy desire to try a harmless little experiment—
again, as when he talked to the store detective, he heard his
own voice becoming hollow and insincere. It was exactly as
if he knew himself to be guilty. His throat grew dry, he
began to falter, to lose his thread, to use the wrong words.
When he stopped speaking finally, Dora was silent.

"Well, say something!" he said angrily, after a moment.
"Don't just stare at me. I'm not a criminal!"

"I'll get a lawyer for you," she answered, "but that's all I
can do."

"Look here, Dora—you don't mean you—"

He looked at her incredulously. It wasn't possible that
she really thought him a thief? And suddenly, as he looked
at her, he realized how long it was since he had really
known this woman. They had drifted apart. She was embittered, that was it—embittered by his non-success. All
this time she had slowly been laying up a reserve of resentment. She had resented his inability to make money for the
children, the little dishonesties they had had to commit in
the matter of unpaid bills, the humiliations of duns, the
too-frequent removals from town to town—she had more
than once said to him, it was true, that because of all this
she had never had any friends—and she had resented, he
knew, his gay little parties with Hurwitz and Bryant and
Smith, implying a little that they were an extravagance
which was to say the least inconsiderate. Perhaps they *had*
been. But was a man to have no indulgences? . . .

"Perhaps we had better not go into that," she said.

"Good Lord—you don't believe me!"

"I'll get the lawyer—though I don't know where the fees are to come from. Our bank account is down to seventy-seven dollars. The rent is due a week from today. You've got some salary coming, of course, but I don't want to touch my own savings, naturally, because the children and I may need them."

To be sure. Perfectly just. Women and children first. Michael thought these things bitterly, but refrained from saying them. He gazed at this queer cold little female with intense curiosity. It was simply extraordinary—simply astonishing. Here she was, seven years his wife, he thought he knew her inside and out, every quirk of her handwriting, inflection of voice; her passion for strawberries, her ridiculous way of singing; the brown moles on her shoulder, the extreme smallness of her feet and toes, her dislike of silk underwear. Her special voice at the telephone, too—that rather chilly abruptness, which had always surprised him, as if she might be a much harder woman than he thought her to be. And the queer sinuous cat-like rhythm with which she always combed her hair before the mirror at night, before going to bed—with her head tossing to one side, and one knee advanced to touch the chest of drawers. He knew all these things, which nobody else knew, and nevertheless, now, they amounted to nothing. The woman herself stood before him as opaque as a wall.

"Of course," he said, "you'd better keep your own savings." His voice was dull. "And you'll, of course, look up Hurwitz and the others? They'll appear, I'm sure, and it will be the most important evidence. In fact, *the* evidence."

"I'll ring them up, Michael," was all she said, and with that she turned quickly on her heel and went away. . . .

Michael felt doom closing in upon him; his wits went round in circles; he was in a constant sweat. It wasn't possible that he was going to be betrayed? It wasn't possible! He assured himself of this. He walked back and forth, rubbing his hands together, he kept pulling out his watch to see what time it was. Five minutes gone. Another five minutes gone. Damnation, if this lasted too long, this confounded business, he'd lose his job. If it got into the papers, he might

lose it anyway. And suppose it was true that Hurwitz and
Bryant had said what they said—maybe they were afraid of
losing their jobs too. Maybe that was it! Good God. . . .

This suspicion was confirmed, when, hours later, the
lawyer came to see him. He reported that Hurwitz, Bryant
and Smith had all three refused flatly to be mixed up in the
business. They were all afraid of the effects of the publicity.
If subpenaed, they said, they would state that they had
known Lowes only a short time, had thought him a little
eccentric, and knew him to be hard up. Obviously—and
the little lawyer picked his teeth with the point of his
pencil—they could not be summoned. It would be fatal.

The Judge, not unnaturally perhaps, decided that there
was a perfectly clear case. There couldn't be the shadow of a
doubt that this man had deliberately stolen an article from
the counter of So-and-so's drugstore. The prisoner had stubbornly maintained that it was the result of a kind of bet with
some friends, but these friends had refused to give testimony in his behalf. Even his wife's testimony—that he had
never done such a thing before—had seemed rather half-
hearted; and she had admitted, moreover, that Lowes was
unsteady, and that they were always living in a state of
something like poverty. Prisoner, further, had once or twice
jumped his rent and had left behind him in Somerville
unpaid debts of considerable size. He was a college man, a
man of exceptional education and origin, and ought to have
known better. His general character might be good enough,
but as against all this, here was a perfectly clear case of
theft, and a perfectly clear motive. The prisoner was
sentenced to three months in the house of correction.

By this time, Michael was in a state of complete stupor.
He sat in the box and stared blankly at Dora who sat very
quietly in the second row, as if she were a stranger. She was
looking back at him, with her white face turned a little to
one side, as if she too had never seen him before, and were
wondering what sort of people criminals might be. Human?

Sub-human? She lowered her eyes after a moment, and before she had looked up again, Michael had been touched on the arm and led stumbling out of the courtroom. He thought she would of course come to say goodbye to him, but even in this he was mistaken; she left without a word.

And when he did finally hear from her, after a week, it was in a very brief note.

"Michael," it said, "I'm sorry, but I can't bring up the children with a criminal for a father, so I'm taking proceedings for a divorce. This is the last straw. It was bad enough to have you always out of work and to have to slave night and day to keep bread in the children's mouths. But this is too much, to have disgrace into the bargain. As it is, we'll have to move right away, for the schoolchildren have sent Dolly and Mary home crying three times already. I'm sorry, and you know how fond I was of you at the beginning, but you've had your chance. You won't hear from me again. You've always been a good sport, and generous, and I hope you'll make this occasion no exception, and refrain from contesting the divorce. Goodbye—Dora."

Michael held the letter in his hands, unseeing, and tears came into his eyes. He dropped his face against the sheet of notepaper, and rubbed his forehead to and fro across it . . . Little Dolly! . . . Little Mary! . . . Of course. This was what life was. It was just as meaningless and ridiculous as this; a monstrous joke; a huge injustice. You couldn't trust anybody, not even your wife, not even your best friends. You went on a little lark, and they sent you to prison for it, and your friends lied about you, and your wife left you. . . .

Contest it? Should he contest the divorce? What was the use? There was the plain fact: that he had been convicted for stealing. No one had believed his story of doing it in fun, after a few drinks; the divorce court would be no exception. He dropped the letter to the floor and turned his heel on it, slowly and bitterly. Good riddance—good riddance! Let them all go to hell. He would show them. He would go west, when he came out—get rich, clear his name somehow. . . . But how?

He sat down on the edge of his bed and thought of Chicago. He thought of his childhood there, the Lake Shore Drive, Winnetka, the trip to Niagara Falls with his mother. He could hear the Falls now. He remembered the Fourth of July on the boat; the crowded examination room at college; the time he had broken his leg in baseball, when he was fourteen; and the stamp collection which he had lost at school. He remembered his mother always saying, "Michael, you *must* learn to be orderly"; and the little boy who had died of scarlet fever next door; and the pink conch-shell smashed in the back yard. His whole life seemed to be composed of such trivial and infinitely charming little episodes as these; and as he thought of them, affectionately and with wonder, he assured himself once more that he had really been a good man. And now, had it all come to an end? It had all come foolishly to an end.

◆ ────────────────────────────────── ◆

A BOTTLE OF MILK FOR MOTHER

Nelson Algren

I feel I am of them—
I belong to those convicts and prostitutes myself,
And henceforth I will not deny them—
For how can I deny myself?

WHITMAN

Two months after the Polish Warriors S.A.C. had had their heads shaved, Bruno Lefty Bicek got into his final difficulty with the Racine Street police. The arresting officers and a reporter from the *Dziennik Chicagoski* were grouped about the captain's desk when the boy was urged forward into the room by Sergeant Adamovitch, with two fingers wrapped about the boy's broad belt: a full-bodied boy wearing a worn and sleeveless blue work shirt grown too tight across the shoulders; and the shoulders themselves with a loose swing to them. His skull and face were shining from a recent scrubbing, so that the little bridgeless nose glistened between the protective points of the cheekbones. Behind the desk sat Kozak, eleven years on the force and brother to an alderman. The reporter stuck a cigarette behind one ear like a pencil.

"We spotted him followin' the drunk down Chicago—" Sergeant Comiskey began.

Captain Kozak interrupted. "Let the jackroller tell us how he done it hisself."

"I ain't no jackroller."

"What you doin' here, then?"

Bicek folded his naked arms.

"Answer me. If you ain't here for jackrollin' it must be for strong-arm robb'ry—'r you one of them Chicago Av'noo moll-buzzers?"

"I ain't that neither."

"C'mon, c'mon, I seen you in here before—what were you up to, followin' that poor old man?"

"I ain't been in here before."

Neither Sergeant Milano, Comiskey, nor old Adamovitch moved an inch; yet the boy felt the semicircle about him drawing closer. Out of the corner of his eye he watched the reporter undoing the top button of his mangy raccoon coat, as though the barren little query room were already growing too warm for him.

"What were you doin' on Chicago Av'noo in the first place when you live up around Division? Ain't your own ward big enough you have to come down here to get in trouble? What do you *think* you're here for?"

"Well, I was just walkin' down Chicago like I said, to get

a bottle of milk for Mother, when the officers jumped me. I didn't even see 'em drive up, they wouldn't let me say a word, I got no idea what I'm here for. I was just doin' a errand for Mother 'n—"

"All right, son, you want us to book you as a pickup 'n hold you overnight, is that it?"

"Yes sir."

"What about this, then?"

Kozak flipped a spring-blade knife with a five-inch blade onto the police blotter; the boy resisted an impulse to lean forward and take it. His own double-edged double-jointed spring-blade cuts-all genuine Filipino twisty-handled all-American gut-ripper.

"Is it yours or ain't it?"

"Never seen it before, Captain."

Kozak pulled a billy out of his belt, spread the blade across the bend of the blotter before him, and with one blow clubbed the blade off two inches from the handle. The boy winced as though he himself had received the blow. Kozak threw the broken blade into a basket and the knife into a drawer.

"Know why I did that, son?"

"Yes sir."

"Tell me."

" 'Cause it's three inches to the heart."

"No. 'Cause it's against the law to carry more than three inches of knife. C'mon, Lefty, tell us about it. 'N it better be good."

The boy began slowly, secretly gratified that Kozak appeared to know he was the Warriors' first-string left-hander: maybe he'd been out at that game against the Knothole Wonders the Sunday he'd finished his own game and then had relieved Dropkick Kodadek in the sixth in the second. Why hadn't anyone called him "Iron-Man Bicek" or "Fireball Bruno" for that one?

"Everythin' you say can be used against you," Kozak warned him earnestly. "Don't talk unless you want to." His lips formed each syllable precisely.

Then he added absently, as though talking to someone unseen, "We'll just hold you on an open charge till you do."

And his lips hadn't moved at all.

The boy licked his own lips, feeling a dryness coming into his throat and a tightening in his stomach. "We seen this boobatch with his collar turned inside out cash'n his check by Konstanty Stachula's Tonsorial Palace of Art on Division. So I followed him a way, that was all. Just break'n the old monotony was all. Just a notion, you might say, that come over me. I'm just a neighborhood kid, Captain."

He stopped as though he had finished the story. Kozak glanced over the boy's shoulder at the arresting officers and Lefty began again hurriedly.

"Ever' once in a while he'd pull a little single-shot of Scotch out of his pocket, stop a second t' toss it down, 'n toss the bottle at the car tracks. I picked up a bottle that didn't bust but there wasn't a spider left in 'er, the boobatch'd drunk her dry. 'N do you know, he had his pockets *full* of them little bottles? 'Stead of buyin' hisself a fifth in the first place. Can't understand a man who'll buy liquor that way. Right before the corner of Walton 'n Noble he popped into a hallway. That was Chiney-Eye-the-Princinct-Captain's hallway, so I popped right in after him. Me'n Chiney-Eye 'r just like that." The boy crossed two fingers of his left hand and asked innocently, "Has the alderman been in to straighten this out, Captain?"

"What time was all this, Lefty?"

"Well, some of the street lamps was lit awready 'n I didn't see nobody either way down Noble. It'd just started spitt'n a little snow 'n I couldn't see clear down Walton account of Wojciechowski's Tavern bein' in the way. He was a old guy, a dino you. He couldn't speak a word of English. But he started in cryin' about how every time he gets a little drunk the same old thing happens to him 'n he's gettin' fed up, he lost his last three checks in the very same hallway 'n it's gettin' so his family don't believe him no more . . ."

Lefty paused, realizing that his tongue was going faster than his brain. He unfolded his arms and shoved them down his pants pockets; the pants were turned up at the cuffs and the cuffs were frayed. He drew a colorless cap off his hip pocket and stood clutching it in his left hand.

"I didn't take him them other times, Captain," he anticipated Kozak.

"Who did?"

Silence.

"What's Benkowski doin' for a livin' these days, Lefty?"

"Just nutsin' around."

"What's Nowogrodski up to?"

"Goes wolfin' on roller skates by Riverview. The rink's open all year round."

"Does he have much luck?"

"Never turns up a hair. They go by too fast."

"What's that evil-eye up to?"

Silence.

"You know who I mean. Idzikowski."

"The Finger?"

"You know who I mean. Don't stall."

"He's hexin' fights, I heard."

"Seen Kodadek lately?"

"I guess. A week 'r two 'r a month ago."

"What was *he* up to?"

"Sir?"

"What was Kodadek doin' the last time you seen him?"

"You mean Dropkick? He was nutsin' around."

"Does he nuts around drunks in hallways?"

Somewhere in the room a small clock or wrist watch began ticking distinctly.

"Nutsin' around ain't jackrollin'."

"You mean Dropkick ain't a jackroller but you are."

The boy's blond lashes shuttered his eyes.

"All right, get ahead with your lyin' a little faster."

Kozak's head came down almost neckless onto his shoulders, and his face was molded like a flatiron, the temples narrow and the jaws rounded. Between the jaws and the open collar, against the graying hair of the chest, hung a tiny crucifix, slender and golden, a shade lighter than his tunic's golden buttons.

"I told him I wasn't gonna take his check, I just needed a little change, I'd pay it back someday. But maybe he didn't understand. He kept hollerin' how he lost his last check, please to let him keep this one. 'Why you drink'n it all up, then,' I put it to him, 'if you're that anxious to hold onto it?' He gimme a foxy grin then 'n pulls out four of them little bottles from four different pockets, 'n each one was a different kind of liquor. I could have one, he tells me in Polish, which do I want, 'n I slapped all four out of his hands. All four. I don't like to see no full-grown man drinkin' that way. A Polak hillbilly he was, 'n certain'y no citizen.

" 'Now let me have that change,' I asked him, 'n that wasn't so much t'ask. I don't go around just lookin' fer trouble, Captain. 'N my feet was slop-full of water 'n snow. I'm just a neighborhood fella. But he acted like I was gonna kill him 'r somethin'. I got one hand over his mouth 'n a half nelson behind him 'n talked polite-like in Polish in his ear, 'n he begun sweatin' 'n tryin' t' wrench away on me. 'Take it easy,' I asked him. 'Be reas'nable, we're both in this up to our necks now.' 'N he wasn't drunk no more then, 'n he was plenty t' hold onto. You wouldn't think a old boobatch like that'd have so much stren'th left in him, boozin' down Division night after night, year after year, like he didn't have no home to go to. He pulled my hand off his mouth 'n started hollerin', *Mlody bandyta! Mlody bandyta!* 'n I could feel him slippin'. He was just too strong fer a kid like me to hold—"

"Because you were reach'n for his wallet with the other hand?"

"Oh no. The reason I couldn't hold him was my right hand had the nelson 'n I'm not so strong there like in my left 'n even my left ain't what it was before I thrun it out pitchin' that double-header."

"So you kept the rod in your left hand?"

The boy hesitated. Then: "Yes sir." And felt a single drop

of sweat slide down his side from under his armpit. Stop and slide again down to the belt.

"What did you get off him?"

"I tell you, I had my hands too full to get *anythin'*—that's just what I been tryin' to tell you. I didn't get so much as one of them little single-shots for all my trouble."

"How many slugs did you fire?"

"Just one, Captain. That was all there was in 'er. I didn't really fire, though. Just at his feet. T' scare him so's he wouldn't jump me. I fired in self-defense. I just wanted to get out of there." He glanced helplessly around at Comiskey and Adamovitch. "You do crazy things sometimes, fellas—well, that's all I was doin'."

The boy caught his tongue and stood mute. In the silence of the query room there was only the scraping of the reporter's pencil and the unseen wrist watch. "I'll ask Chiney-Eye if it's legal, a reporter takin' down a confession, that's my out," the boy thought desperately, and added aloud, before he could stop himself: " 'N beside I had to show him—"

"Show him what, son?"

Silence.

"Show him what, Left-hander?"

"That I wasn't just another greenhorn sprout like he thought."

"Did he say you were just a sprout?"

"No. But I c'd tell. Lot of people think I'm just a green kid. I show 'em. I guess I showed 'em now all right." He felt he should be apologizing for something and couldn't tell whether it was for strong-arming a man or for failing to strong-arm him.

"I'm just a neighborhood kid. I belonged to the Keep-Our-City-Clean Club at St. John Cant'us. I told him polite-like, like a Polish-American citizen, this was Chiney-Eye-a-Friend-of-Mine's hallway. 'No more after this one,' I told him. 'This is your last time gettin' rolled, old man. After this I'm pertectin' you, I'm seein' to it nobody touches you—but the people who live here don't like this sort of thing goin' on any more'n you 'r I do. There's gotta be a stop to it, old man—'n we all gotta live, don't we?' That's what I told him in Polish."

Kozak exchanged glances with the prim-faced reporter from the *Chicagoski,* who began cleaning his black tortoise-shell spectacles hurriedly yet delicately, with the fringed tip of his cravat. They depended from a black ribbon; he snapped them back onto his beak.

"You shot him in the groin, Lefty. He's dead."

The reporter leaned slightly forward, but perceived no special reaction and so relaxed. A pretty comfy old chair for a dirty old police station, he thought lifelessly. Kozak shaded his eyes with his gloved hand and looked down at his charge sheet. The night lamp on the desk was still lit, as though he had been working all night; as the morning grew lighter behind him lines came out below his eyes, black as though packed with soot, and a curious droop came to the St. Bernard mouth.

"You shot him through the groin—zip." Kozak's voice came, flat and unemphatic, reading from the charge sheet as though without understanding. "Five children. Stella, Mary, Grosha, Wanda, Vincent. Thirteen, ten, six, six, and one two months. Mother invalided since last birth, name of Rose. WPA fifty-five dollars. You told the truth about *that,* at least."

Lefty's voice came in a shout: "You know *what?* That bullet must of bounced, that's what!"

"Who was along?"

"I was singlin'. Lone-wolf stuff." His voice possessed the first faint touch of fear.

"You said, 'We seen the man.' Was he a big man? How big a man was he?"

"I'd judge two hunerd twenty pounds," Comiskey offered, "at least. Fifty pounds heavier 'n this boy, just about. 'N half a head taller."

"Who's 'we,' Left-hander?"

"Captain, I said, 'We seen.' Lots of people, fellas, seen him is all I meant, cashin' his check by Stachula's when the place was crowded. Konstanty cashes checks if he knows you. Say, I even know the project that old man was on, far as that goes, because my old lady wanted we should give up the store so's I c'd get on it. But it was just me done it, Captain."

The raccoon coat readjusted his glasses. He would say something under a by-line like "This correspondent has never seen a colder gray than that in the eye of the wanton killer who arrogantly styles himself the *Lone Wolf of Potomac Street*." He shifted uncomfortably, wanting to get farther from the wall radiator but disliking to rise and push the heavy chair.

"Where was that bald-headed pal of yours all this time?"

"Don't know the fella, Captain. Nobody got hair any more around the neighborhood, it seems. The whole damn Triangle went 'n got army haircuts by Stachula's."

"Just you 'n Benkowski, I mean. Don't be afraid, son— we're not tryin' to ring in anythin' you done afore this. Just this one you were out cowboyin' with Benkowski on; were you help'n him 'r was he help'n you? Did you 'r him have the rod?"

Lefty heard a Ford V-8 pull into the rear of the station, and a moment later the splash of the gas as the officers refueled. Behind him he could hear Milano's heavy breathing. He looked down at his shoes, carefully buttoned all the way up and tied with a double bowknot. He'd have to have new laces mighty soon or else start tying them with a single bow.

"That Benkowski's sort of a toothless monkey used to go on at the City Garden at around a hundred an' eighteen pounds, ain't he?"

"Don't know the fella well enough t' say."

"Just from seein' him fight once 'r twice is all. 'N he wore a mouthpiece, I couldn't tell about his teeth. Seems to me he came in about one thirty-three, if he's the same fella you're thinkin' of, Captain."

"I guess you fought at the City Garden once 'r twice yourself, ain't you?"

"Oh, once 'r twice."

"How'd you make out, Left'?"

"Won 'em both on K.O.s. Stopped both fights in the first. One was against that boogie from the Savoy. If he woulda got up I woulda killed him fer life. Fer Christ I would. I didn't know I could hit like I can."

"With Benkowski in your corner both times?"

"Oh no, sir."

"That's a bloodsuck'n lie. I seen him in your corner with my own eyes the time you won off Cooney from the C.Y.O. He's your manager, jackroller."

"I didn't say he wasn't."

"You said he wasn't secondin' you."

"He don't."

"Who does?"

"The Finger."

"You told me the Finger was your hex-man. Make up your mind."

"He does both, Captain. He handles the bucket 'n sponge 'n in between he fingers the guy I'm fightin', 'n if it's close he fingers the ref 'n judges. Finger, he never losed a fight. He waited for the boogie outside the dressing room 'n pointed him clear to the ring. He win that one for me awright." The boy spun the frayed greenish cap in his hand in a concentric circle about his index finger, remembering a time when the cap was new and had earlaps. The bright checks were all faded now, to the color of worn pavement, and the earlaps were tatters.

"What possessed your mob to get their heads shaved, Lefty?"

"I strong-armed him myself, I'm rugged as a bull." The boy began to swell his chest imperceptibly; when his lungs were quite full he shut his eyes, like swimming under water at the Oak Street beach, and let his breath out slowly, ounce by ounce.

"I didn't ask you that. I asked you what happened to your hair."

Lefty's capricious mind returned abruptly to the word

"possessed" that Kozak had employed. That had a randy ring, sort of: "What possessed you boys?"

"I forgot what you just asked me."

"I asked you why you didn't realize it'd be easier for us to catch up with your mob when all of you had your heads shaved."

"I guess we figured there'd be so many guys with heads shaved it'd be harder to catch a finger than if we all had hair. But that was some accident all the same. A fella was gonna lend Ma a barber chair 'n go fifty-fifty with her shavin' all the Polaks on P'tom'c Street right back of the store, for relief tickets. So she started on me, just to show the fellas, but the hair made her sicker 'n ever 'n back of the store's the only place she got to lie down 'n I hadda finish the job myself.

"The fellas begun giv'n me a Christ-awful razzin' then, ever' day. God oh God, wherever I went around the Triangle, all the neighborhood fellas 'n little niducks 'n oldtime hoods by the Broken Knuckle, whenever they seen me they was pointin' 'n laughin' 'n sayin', 'Hi, Baldy Bicek!' So I went home 'n got the clippers 'n the first guy I seen w~~ Bibleback Watrobinski, you wouldn't know him. I jun~~ him 'n pushes the clip right through the middle of his hair—he ain't had a haircut since the alderman got indicted you—'n then he took one look at what I done in the drugstore window 'n we both bust out laughin' 'n laughin', 'n fin'lly Bible says I better finish what I started. So he set down on the curb 'n I finished him. When I got all I could off that way I took him back to the store 'n heated water 'n shaved him close 'n Ma couldn't see the point at all.

"Me 'n Bible prowled around a couple days 'n here come Catfoot Nowogrodski from Fry Street you, out of Stachula's with a spanty-new sideburner haircut 'n a green tie. I grabbed his arms 'n let Bible run it through the middle just like I done him. Then it was Catfoot's turn, 'n we caught Chester Chekhovka fer *him*, 'n fer Chester we got Cowboy Okulanis from by the Nort'western Viaduct you, 'n fer him we got Mustang, 'n fer Mustang we got John from the Joint, 'n fer

John we got Snake Baranowski, 'n we kep' right on goin'
that way till we was doin' guys we never seen before even,
Wallios 'n Greeks 'n a Flip from Clark Street he musta
been, walkin' with a white girl we done it to. 'N fin'lly all
the sprouts in the Triangle start comin' around with their
heads shaved, they want to join up with the Baldheads
A.C., they called it. They thought it was a club you.

"It got so a kid with his head shaved could beat up on a
bigger kid because the big one'd be a-scared to fight back
hard, he thought the Baldheads'd get him. So that's why we
changed our name then, that's why we're not the Warriors
any more, we're the Baldhead True American Social 'n
Athletic Club.

"I played first for the Warriors when I wasn't on the
mound," he added cautiously, " 'n I'm enterin' the Gold'n
Gloves next year 'less I go to collitch instead. I went to St.
John Cant'us all the way through. Eight' grade, that is. If I
keep on gainin' weight I'll be a hunerd ninety-eight this
time next year 'n be five-foot-ten—I'm a fair-size light-heavy
right this minute. That's what in England they call a cruiser
weight you."

He shuffled a step and made as though to unbutton his
shirt to show his proportions. But Adamovitch put one hand
on his shoulder and slapped the boy's hand down. He
didn't like this kid. This was a low-class Polak. He himself
was a high-class Polak because his name was Adamovitch
and not Adamowski. This sort of kid kept spoiling things for
the high-class Polaks by always showing off instead of just
being good citizens like the Irish. That was why the Irish
ran the City Hall and Police Department and the Board of
Education and the Post Office while the Polaks stayed on
relief and got drunk and never got anywhere and had everybody down on them. All they could do like the Irish, old
Adamovitch reflected bitterly, was to fight under Irish names
to get their ears knocked off at the City Garden.

"That's why I want to get out of this jam," this one was
saying beside him. "So's it don't ruin my career in the rope'

arena. I'm goin' straight. This has sure been one good lesson fer me. Now I'll go to a big-ten collitch 'n make good you."

Now, if the college-coat asked him, "What big-ten college?" he'd answer something screwy like "The Boozological Stoodent-Collitch." That ought to set Kozak back awhile, they might even send him to a bug doc. He'd have to be careful—not *too* screwy. Just screwy enough to get by without involving Benkowski.

He scuffed his shoes and there was no sound in the close little room save his uneasy scuffling; square-toed boy's shoes, laced with a button-hook. He wanted to look more closely at the reporter but every time he caught the glint of the fellow's glasses he felt awed and would have to drop his eyes; he'd never seen glasses on a string like that before and would have given a great deal to wear them a moment. He took to looking steadily out of the barred window behind Kozak's head, where the January sun was glowing sullenly, like a flame held steadily in a fog. Heard an empty truck clattering east on Chicago, sounding like either a '38 Chevvie or a '37 Ford dragging its safety chain against the car tracks; closed his eyes and imagined sparks flashing from the tracks as the iron struck, bounced, and struck again. The bullet had bounced too. Wow.

"What do you think we ought to do with a man like you, Bicek?"

The boy heard the change from the familiar "Lefty" to "Bicek" with a pang; and the dryness began in his throat again.

"One to fourteen is all I can catch fer manslaughter." He appraised Kozak as coolly as he could.

"You like farm work the next fourteen years? Is that okay with you?"

"I said that's all I could get, at the most. This is a first offense 'n self-defense too. I'll plead the unwritten law."

"Who give you *that* idea?"

"Thought of it myself. Just now. You ain't got a chance to send me over the road 'n you know it."

"We can send you to St. Charles, Bicek. 'N transfer you

when you come of age. Unless we can make it first-degree murder."

The boy ignored the latter possibility.

"Why, a few years on a farm'd true me up fine. I planned t' cut out cigarettes 'n whisky anyhow before I turn pro—a farm'd be just the place to do that."

"By the time you're released you'll be thirty-two, Bicek —too late to turn pro then, ain't it?"

"I wouldn't wait that long. Hungry Piontek-from-by-the-Warehouse you, he lammed twice from that St. Charles farm. 'N Hungry don't have all his marbles even. He ain't even a citizen."

"Then let's talk about somethin' you couldn't lam out of so fast 'n easy. Like the chair. Did you know that Bogatski from Noble Street, Bicek? The boy that burned last summer, I mean."

A plain-clothes man stuck his head in the door and called confidently: "That's the man, Captain. That's the man."

Bicek forced himself to grin good-naturedly. He was getting pretty good, these last couple days, at grinning under pressure. When a fellow got sore he couldn't think straight, he reflected anxiously. And so he yawned in Kozak's face with deliberateness, stretching himself as effortlessly as a cat.

"Captain, I ain't been in serious trouble like this before . . ." he acknowledged, and paused dramatically. He'd let them have it straight from the shoulder now: "So I'm mighty glad to be so close to the alderman. Even if he is indicted."

There. Now they know. He'd told them.

"You talkin' about my brother, Bicek?"

The boy nodded solemnly. Now they knew who they had hold of at last.

The reporter took the cigarette off his ear and hung it on his lower lip. And Adamovitch guffawed.

The boy jerked toward the officer: Adamovitch was laughing openly at him. Then they were all laughing openly at him. He heard their derision, and a red rain danced one moment before his eyes; when the red rain was past, Kozak

was sitting back easily, regarding him with the expression of
a man who has just been swung at and missed and plans to
use the provocation without undue haste. The captain didn't
look like the sort who'd swing back wildly or hurriedly. He
didn't look like the sort who missed. His complacency for a
moment was as unbearable to the boy as Adamovitch's
guffaw had been. He heard his tongue going, trying to
regain his lost composure by provoking them all.

"Hey, Stingywhiskers!" He turned on the reporter. "Get
your Eversharp goin' there, write down I plugged the old
rumpot, write down Bicek carries a rod night 'n day 'n don't
care where he points it. You, I go around slappin' the crap
out of whoever I feel like—"

But they all remained mild, calm, and unmoved: for a
moment he feared Adamovitch was going to pat him on the
head and say something fatherly in Polish.

"Take it easy, Fad," Adamovitch suggested. "You're in
the query room. We're here to help you, boy. We want to
see you through this thing so's you can get back to pugging.
You just ain't letting us help you, son."

Kozak blew his nose as though that were an achievement
in itself, and spoke with the false friendliness of the insurance man urging a fleeced customer toward the door.

"Want to tell us where you got that rod now, Lefty?"

"I don't want to tell you anything." His mind was setting
hard now, against them all. Against them all in here and all
like them outside. And the harder it set, the more things
seemed to be all right with Kozak: he dropped his eyes to
his charge sheet now and everything was all right with
everybody. The reporter shoved his notebook into his pocket
and buttoned the top button of his coat as though the
questioning were over.

It was all too easy. They weren't going to ask him anything more, and he stood wanting them to. He stood wishing them to threaten, to shake their heads ominously, wheedle
and cajole and promise him mercy if he'd just talk about the
rod.

"I ain't mad, Captain. I don't blame you men either. It's

your job, it's your bread 'n butter to talk tough to us neighborhood fellas—ever'body got to have a racket, 'n yours is talkin' tough." He directed this last at the captain, for Comiskey and Milano had left quietly. But Kozak was studying the charge sheet as though Bruno Lefty Bicek were no longer in the room. Nor anywhere at all.

"I'm still here," the boy said wryly, his lip twisting into a dry and bitter grin.

Kozak looked up, his big, wind-beaten, impassive face looking suddenly to the boy like an autographed pitcher's mitt he had once owned. His glance went past the boy and no light of recognition came into his eyes. Lefty Bicek felt a panic rising in him: a desperate fear that they weren't going to press him about the rod, about the old man, about his feelings. "Don't look at me like I ain't nowheres," he asked. And his voice was struck flat by fear.

Something else! The time he and Dropkick had broken into a slot machine! The time he and Casey had played the attention racket and made four dollars! Something! Anything else!

The reporter lit his cigarette.

"Your case is well disposed of," Kozak said, and his eyes dropped to the charge sheet forever.

"I'm born in this country. I'm educated here—"

But no one was listening to Bruno Lefty Bicek any more.

He watched the reporter leaving with regret—at least the guy could have offered him a drag—and stood waiting for someone to tell him to go somewhere now, shifting uneasily from one foot to the other. Then he started slowly, backward, toward the door: he'd make Kozak tell Adamovitch to grab him. Halfway to the door he turned his back on Kozak.

There was no voice behind him. Was this what "well disposed of" meant? He turned the knob and stepped confidently into the corridor; at the end of the corridor he saw the door that opened into the courtroom, and his heart began shaking his whole body with the impulse to make a run for it. He glanced back and Adamovitch was five yards behind, coming up catfooted like only an old man who has been a citizen-dress man can come up catfooted, just far enough behind and just casual enough to make it appear unimportant whether the boy made a run for it or not.

The Lone Wolf of Potomac Street waited miserably, in the long unlovely corridor, for the sergeant to thrust two fingers through the back of his belt. Didn't they realize that he might have Dropkick and Catfoot and Benkowski with a sub-machine gun in a streamlined cream-colored roadster right down front, that he'd zigzag through the courtroom onto the courtroom fire escape and—swish—down off the courtroom roof three stories with the chopper still under his arm and through the car's roof and into the driver's seat? Like that George Raft did that time he was innocent at the Chopin, and cops like Adamovitch had better start ducking when Lefty Bicek began making a run for it. He felt the fingers thrust overfamiliarly between his shirt and his belt.

A cold draft came down the corridor when the door at the far end opened; with the opening of the door came the smell of disinfectant from the basement cells. Outside, far overhead, the bells of St. John Cantius were beginning. The boy felt the winding steel of the staircase to the basement beneath his feet and heard the whining screech of a Chicago Avenue streetcar as it paused on Ogden for the traffic lights and then screeched on again, as though a cat were caught beneath its back wheels. Would it be snowing out there still? he wondered, seeing the whitewashed basement walls.

"Feel all right, son?" Adamovitch asked in his most fatherly voice, closing the cell door while thinking to himself: "The kid don't *feel* guilty is the whole trouble. You got to make them *feel* guilty or they'll never go to church at all. A man who goes to church without feeling guilty for *something* is wasting his time, I say." Inside the cell he saw the boy pause and go down on his knees in the cell's gray light. The boy's head turned slowly toward him, a pious oval in the dimness. Old Adamovitch took off his hat.

"This place'll rot down 'n mold over before Lefty Bicek starts prayin', boobatch. Prays, squeals, 'r bawls. So run

along 'n I'll see you in hell with yer back broke. I'm lookin'
for my cap I dropped is all."

Adamovitch watched him crawling forward on all fours,
groping for the pavement-colored cap; when he saw Bicek
find it he put his own hat back on and left feeling vaguely
dissatisfied.

He did not stay to see the boy, still on his knees, put his
hands across his mouth and stare at the shadowed wall.

Shadows were there within shadows.

"I knew I'd never get to be twenty-one anyhow," Lefty
told himself softly at last.

◆ ———————————————————————— ◆

THE EGG

Sherwood Anderson

My father was, I am sure, intended by nature to be a
cheerful, kindly man. Until he was thirty-four years old he
worked as a farm hand for a man named Thomas But-
terworth whose place lay near the town of Bidwell, Ohio.
He had then a horse of his own and on Saturday evenings
drove into town to spend a few hours in social intercourse
with other farm hands. In town he drank several glasses of
beer and stood about in Ben Head's saloon—crowded on
Saturday evenings with visiting farm hands. Songs were
sung and glasses thumped on the bar. At ten o'clock father
drove home along a lonely country road, made his horse
comfortable for the night and himself went to bed, quite
happy in his position in life. He had at that time no notion
of trying to rise in the world.

It was in the spring of his thirty-fifth year that father

married my mother, then a country school teacher, and in the following spring I came wriggling and crying into the world. Something happened to the two people. They became ambitious. The American passion for getting up in the world took possession of them.

It may have been that mother was responsible. Being a school teacher she had no doubt read books and magazines. She had, I presume, read of how Garfield, Lincoln, and other Americans rose from poverty to fame and greatness and as I lay beside her—in the days of her lying-in—she may have dreamed that I would some day rule men and cities. At any rate she induced father to give up his place as a farm hand, sell his horse and embark on an independent enterprise of his own. She was a tall silent woman with a long nose and troubled gray eyes. For herself she wanted nothing. For father and myself she was incurably ambitious.

The first venture into which the two people went turned out badly. They rented ten acres of poor stony land on Griggs's Road, eight miles from Bidwell, and launched into chicken raising. I grew into boyhood on the place and got my first impressions of life there. From the beginning they were impressions of disaster and if, in my turn, I am a gloomy man inclined to see the darker side of life, I attribute it to the fact that what should have been for me the happy joyous days of childhood were spent on a chicken farm.

One unversed in such matters can have no notion of the many and tragic things that can happen to a chicken. It is born out of an egg, lives for a few weeks as a tiny fluffy thing such as you will see pictured on Easter cards, then becomes hideously naked, eats quantities of corn and meal bought by the sweat of your father's brow, gets diseases called pip, cholera, and other names, stands looking with stupid eyes at the sun, becomes sick and dies. A few hens and now and then a rooster, intended to serve God's mysterious ends, struggle through to maturity. The hens lay eggs out of which come other chickens and the dreadful cycle is thus made complete. It is all unbelievably complex. Most philosophers must have been raised on chicken farms. One hopes for so much from a chicken and is so dreadfully disillusioned. Small chickens, just setting out on the journey of life, look so bright and alert and they are in fact so dreadfully stupid. They are so much like people they mix one up in one's judgments of life. If disease does not kill them they wait until your expectations are thoroughly aroused and then walk under the wheels of a wagon—to go squashed and dead back to their maker. Vermin infest their youth, and fortunes must be spent for curative powders. In later life I have seen how a literature has been built up on the subject of fortunes to be made out of the raising of chickens. It is intended to be read by the gods who have just eaten of the tree of the knowledge of good and evil. It is a hopeful literature and declares that much may be done by simple ambitious people who own a few hens. Do not be led astray by it. It was not written for you. Go hunt for gold on the frozen hills of Alaska, put your faith in the honesty of a politician, believe if you will that the world is daily growing better and that good will triumph over evil, but do not read and believe the literature that is written concerning the hen. It was not written for you.

I, however, digress. My tale does not primarily concern itself with the hen. If correctly told it will center on the egg. For ten years my father and mother struggled to make our chicken farm pay and then they gave up that struggle and began another. They moved into the town of Bidwell, Ohio, and embarked in the restaurant business. After ten years of worry with incubators that did not hatch, and with tiny— and in their own way lovely—balls of fluff that passed on into semi-naked pullethood and from that into dead henhood, we threw all aside and packing our belongings on a wagon drove down Griggs's Road toward Bidwell, a tiny caravan of hope looking for a new place from which to start on our upward journey through life.

We must have been a sad looking lot, not, I fancy, unlike refugees fleeing from a battlefield. Mother and I walked in the road. The wagon that contained our goods had been

borrowed for the day from Mr. Albert Griggs, a neighbor.
Out of its sides stuck the legs of cheap chairs and at the back
of the pile of beds, tables, and boxes filled with kitchen
utensils was a crate of live chickens, and on top of that the
baby carriage in which I had been wheeled about in my
infancy. Why we stuck to the baby carriage I don't know. It
was unlikely other children would be born and the wheels
were broken. People who have few possessions cling tightly
to those they have. That is one of the facts that make life so
discouraging.

Father rode on top of the wagon. He was then a bald-
headed man of forty-five, a little fat and from long association with mother and the chickens he had become habitually
silent and discouraged. All during our ten years on the
chicken farm he had worked as a laborer on neighboring
farms and most of the money he had earned had been spent
for remedies to cure chicken diseases, on Wilmer's White
Wonder Cholera Cure or Professor Bidlow's Egg Producer
or some other preparations that mother found advertised in
the poultry papers. There were two little patches of hair on
father's head just above his ears. I remember that as a child
I used to sit looking at him when he had gone to sleep in a
chair before the stove on Sunday afternoons in the winter. I
had at that time already begun to read books and have
notions of my own and the bald path that led over the top of
his head was, I fancied, something like a broad road, such a
road as Caesar might have made on which to lead his
legions out of Rome and into the wonders of an unknown
world. The tufts of hair that grew above father's ears were, I
thought, like forests. I fell into a half-sleeping, half-waking
state and dreamed I was a tiny thing going along the road
into a far beautiful place where there were no chicken farms
and where life was a happy eggless affair.

One might write a book concerning our flight from the
chicken farm into town. Mother and I walked the entire
eight miles—she to be sure that nothing fell from the wagon
and I to see the wonders of the world. On the seat of the

wagon beside father was his greatest treasure. I will tell you of that.

On a chicken farm where hundreds and even thousands of chickens come out of eggs surprising things sometimes happen. Grotesques are born out of eggs as out of people. The accident does not often occur—perhaps once in a thousand births. A chicken is, you see, born that has four legs, two pairs of wings, two heads or what not. The things do not live. They go quickly back to the hand of their maker that has for a moment trembled. The fact that the poor little things could not live was one of the tragedies of life to father. He had some sort of notion that if he could but bring into henhood or roosterhood a five-legged hen or a two-headed rooster his fortune would be made. He dreamed of taking the wonder about to county fairs and of growing rich by exhibiting it to other farm hands.

At any rate he saved all the little monstrous things that had been born on our chicken farm. They were preserved in alcohol and put each in its own glass bottle. These he had carefully put into a box and on our journey into town it was carried on the wagon seat beside him. He drove the horses with one hand and with the other clung to the box. When we got to our destination the box was taken down at once and the bottles removed. All during our days as keepers of a restaurant in the town of Bidwell, Ohio, the grotesques in their little glass bottles sat on a shelf back of the counter. Mother sometimes protested but father was a rock on the subject of his treasure. The grotesques were, he declared, valuable. People, he said, liked to look at strange and wonderful things.

Did I say that we embarked in the restaurant business in the town of Bidwell, Ohio? I exaggerated a little. The town itself lay at the foot of a low hill and on the shore of a small river. The railroad did not run through the town and the station was a mile away to the north at a place called Pickleville. There had been a cider mill and pickle factory at the station, but before the time of our coming they had both gone out of business. In the morning and in the evening busses came down to the station along a road called Turner's Pike from the hotel on the main street of Bidwell. Our going to the out-of-the-way place to embark in the restaurant business was mother's idea. She talked of it for a year and then one day went off and rented an empty store building opposite the railroad station. It was her idea that the restaurant would be profitable. Traveling men, she said, would be always waiting around to take trains out of town and town people would come to the station to await incoming trains. They would come to the restaurant to buy pieces of pie and drink coffee. Now that I am older I know that she had another motive in going. She was ambitious for me. She wanted me to rise in the world, to get into a town school and become a man of the towns.

At Pickleville father and mother worked hard as they always had done. At first there was the necessity of putting our place into shape to be a restaurant. That took a month. Father built a shelf on which he put tins of vegetables. He painted a sign on which he put his name in large red letters. Below his name was the sharp command—"EAT HERE"—that was so seldom obeyed. A showcase was bought and filled with cigars and tobacco. Mother scrubbed the floor and the walls of the room. I went to school in the town and was glad to be away from the farm and from the presence of the discouraged, sad-looking chickens. Still I was not very joyous. In the evening I walked home from school along Turner's Pike and remembered the children I had seen playing in the town school yard. A troop of little girls had gone hopping about and singing. I tried that. Down along the frozen road I went hopping solemnly on one leg. "Hippity Hop To The Barber Shop," I sang shrilly. Then I stopped and looked doubtfully about. I was afraid of being seen in my gay mood. It must have seemed to me that I was doing a thing that should not be done by one who, like myself, had been raised on a chicken farm where death was a daily visitor.

Mother decided that our restaurant should remain open at night. At ten in the evening a passenger train went north past our door followed by a local freight. The freight crew had switching to do in Pickleville and when the work was done they came to our restaurant for hot coffee and food. Sometimes one of them ordered a fried egg. In the morning at four they returned north-bound and again visited us. A little trade began to grow up. Mother slept at night and during the day tended the restaurant and fed our boarders while father slept. He slept in the same bed mother had occupied during the night and I went off to the town of Bidwell and to school. During the long nights, while mother and I slept, father cooked meats that were to go into sandwiches for the lunch baskets of our boarders. Then an idea in regard to getting up in the world came into his head. The American spirit took hold of him. He also became ambitious.

In the long nights when there was little to do father had time to think. That was his undoing. He decided that he had in the past been an unsuccessful man because he had not been cheerful enough and that in the future he would adopt a cheerful outlook on life. In the early morning he came upstairs and got into bed with mother. She woke and the two talked. From my bed in the corner I listened.

It was father's idea that both he and mother should try to entertain the people who came to eat at our restaurant. I cannot now remember his words, but he gave the impression of one about to become in some obscure way a kind of public entertainer. When people, particularly young people from the town of Bidwell, came into our place, as on very rare occasions they did, bright entertaining conversation was to be made. From father's words I gathered that something of the jolly innkeeper effect was to be sought. Mother must have been doubtful from the first, but she said nothing discouraging. It was father's notion that a passion for the company of himself and mother would spring up in the breasts of the younger people of the town of Bidwell. In the evening bright happy groups would come singing down Turner's Pike. They would troop shouting with joy and laughter into our place. There would be song and festivity. I do not mean to give the impression that father spoke so elaborately of the matter. He was as I have said an uncommunicative man. "They want some place to go. I tell you they want some place to go," he said over and over. That was as far as he got. My own imagination has filled in the blanks.

For two or three weeks this notion of father's invaded our house. We did not talk much, but in our daily lives tried earnestly to make smiles take the place of glum looks. Mother smiled at the boarders and I, catching the infection, smiled at our cat. Father became a little feverish in his anxiety to please. There was no doubt, lurking somewhere in him, a touch of the spirit of the showman. He did not waste much of his ammunition on the railroad men he served at night but seemed to be waiting for a young man or woman from Bidwell to come in to show what he could do. On the counter in the restaurant there was a wire basket kept always filled with eggs, and it must have been before his eyes when the idea of being entertaining was born in his brain. There was something pre-natal about the way eggs kept themselves connected with the development of his idea. At any rate an egg ruined his new impulse in life. Late one night I was awakened by a roar of anger coming from father's throat. Both mother and I sat upright in our beds. With trembling hands she lighted a lamp that stood on a table by her head. Downstairs the front door of our restaurant went shut with a bang and in a few minutes father tramped up the stairs. He held an egg in his hand and his hand trembled as though he were having a chill. There was a half-insane light in his eyes. As he stood glaring at us I was sure he intended throwing the egg at either mother or me. Then he laid it gently on the table beside the lamp and dropped on his knees beside mother's bed. He began to cry like a boy and I, carried away by his grief, cried with him. The two of us filled the little upstairs room with our wailing voices. It is ridiculous, but of the picture we made I can remember only the fact that mother's hand continually stroked the bald path that ran across the top of his head. I have forgotten what mother said to him and how she induced him to tell her of what had happened downstairs. His explanation also has gone out of my mind. I remember only my own grief and fright and the shiny path over father's head glowing in the lamp light as he knelt by the bed.

As to what happened downstairs. For some unexplainable reason I know the story as well as though I had been a witness to my father's discomfiture. One in time gets to know many unexplainable things. On that evening young Joe Kane, son of a merchant of Bidwell, came to Pickleville to meet his father, who was expected on the ten o'clock evening train from the South. The train was three hours late and Joe came into our place to loaf about and to wait for its arrival. The local freight train came in and the freight crew were fed. Joe was left alone in the restaurant with father.

From the moment he came into our place the Bidwell young man must have been puzzled by my father's actions. It was his notion that father was angry at him for hanging around. He noticed that the restaurant keeper was apparently disturbed by his presence and he thought of going out. However, it began to rain and he did not fancy the long walk to town and back. He bought a five-cent cigar and ordered a cup of coffee. He had a newspaper in his pocket and took it out and began to read. "I'm waiting for the evening train. It's late," he said apologetically.

For a long time father, whom Joe Kane had never seen before, remained silently gazing at his visitor. He was no doubt suffering from an attack of stage fright. As so often happens in life he had thought so much and so often of the situation that now confronted him that he was somewhat nervous in its presence.

For one thing, he did not know what to do with his hands. He thrust one of them nervously over the counter and shook hands with Joe Kane. "How-de-do," he said. Joe Kane put his newspaper down and stared at him. Father's eye lighted on the basket of eggs that sat on the counter and he began to talk. "Well," he began hesitatingly, "well, you have heard of Christopher Columbus, eh?" He seemed to be angry. "That Christopher Columbus was a cheat," he declared emphatically. "He talked of making an egg stand on its end. He talked, he did, and then he went and broke the end of the egg."

My father seemed to his visitor to be beside himself at the duplicity of Christopher Columbus. He muttered and swore. He declared it was wrong to teach children that Christopher Columbus was a great man when, after all, he cheated at the critical moment. He had declared he would make an egg stand on end and then when his bluff had been called he had done a trick. Still grumbling at Columbus, father took an egg from the basket on the counter and began to walk up and down. He rolled the egg between the palms of his hands. He smiled genially. He began to mumble words regarding the effect to be produced on an egg by the electricity that comes out of the human body. He declared that without breaking its shell and by virtue of rolling it back and forth in his hands he could stand the egg on its end. He explained that the warmth of his hands and the gentle rolling movement he gave the egg created a new center of gravity, and Joe Kane was mildly interested. "I have handled thousands of eggs," father said. "No one knows more about eggs than I do."

He stood the egg on the counter and it fell on its side. He tried the trick again and again, each time rolling the egg between the palms of his hands and saying the words regarding the wonders of electricity and the laws of gravity. When after a half hour's effort he did succeed in making the egg stand for a moment he looked up to find that his visitor was no longer watching. By the time he had succeeded in calling Joe Kane's attention to the success of his effort the egg had again rolled over and lay on its side.

Afire with the showman's passion and at the same time a good deal disconcerted by the failure of his first effort, father now took the bottles containing the poultry monstrosities down from their place on the shelf and began to show them to his visitor. "How would you like to have seven legs and two heads like this fellow?" he asked, exhibiting the most remarkable of his treasures. A cheerful smile played over his face. He reached over the counter and tried to slap Joe Kane on the shoulder as he had seen men do in Ben Head's saloon when he was a young farm hand and drove to town on Saturday evenings. His visitor was made a little ill by the sight of the body of the terribly deformed bird floating in the alcohol in the bottle and got up to go. Coming from behind the counter father took hold of the young man's arm and led him back to his seat. He grew a little angry and for a moment had to turn his face away and force himself to smile. Then he put the bottles back on the shelf. In an outburst of generosity he fairly compelled Joe Kane to have a fresh cup of coffee and another cigar at his expense. Then he took a pan and filling it with vinegar, taken from a jug that sat beneath the counter, he declared himself about to do a new trick. "I will heat this egg in this pan of vinegar," he said. "Then I will put it through the neck of a bottle without breaking the shell. When the egg is inside the bottle it will resume its normal shape and the shell will become hard again. Then I will give the bottle with the egg in it to you. You can take it about with you wherever you go. People will want to know how you got the egg in the bottle. Don't tell them. Keep them guessing. That is the way to have fun with this trick."

Father grinned and winked at his visitor. Joe Kane decided that the man who confronted him was mildly insane but harmless. He drank the cup of coffee that had been given him and began to read his paper again. When the egg had been heated in vinegar father carried it on a spoon to the counter and going into a back room got an empty bottle. He was angry because his visitor did not watch him as he began to do his trick, but nevertheless went cheerfully to work. For a long time he struggled, trying to get the egg to go through the neck of the bottle. He put the pan of vinegar back on the stove, intending to reheat the egg, then picked it up and burned his fingers. After a second bath in the hot vinegar the shell of the egg had been softened a little but not enough for his purpose. He worked and worked and a spirit of desperate determination took possession of him. When he thought that at last the trick was about to be

consummated the delayed train came in at the station and
Joe Kane started to go nonchalantly out at the door. Father
made a last desperate effort to conquer the egg and make it
do the thing that would establish his reputation as one who
knew how to entertain guests who came into his restaurant.
He worried the egg. He attempted to be somewhat rough
with it. He swore and the sweat stood out on his forehead.
The egg broke under his hand. When the contents spurted
over his clothes, Joe Kane, who had stopped at the door,
turned and laughed.

A roar of anger rose from my father's throat. He danced
and shouted a string of inarticulate words. Grabbing another
egg from the basket on the counter, he threw it, just missing the head of the young man as he dodged through the
door and escaped.

Father came upstairs to mother and me with an egg in his
hand. I do not know what he intended to do. I imagine he
had some idea of destroying it, of destroying all eggs, and
that he intended to let mother and me see him begin.
When, however, he got into the presence of mother something happened to him. He laid the egg gently on the table
and dropped on his knees by the bed as I have already
explained. He later decided to close the restaurant for the
night and to come upstairs and get into bed. When he did
so he blew out the light and after much muttered conversation both he and mother went to sleep. I suppose I went to
sleep also, but my sleep was troubled. I awoke at dawn and
for a long time looked at the egg that lay on the table. I
wondered why eggs had to be and why from the egg came
the hen who again laid the egg. The question got into my
blood. It has stayed there, I imagine, because I am the son
of my father. At any rate, the problem remains unsolved in
my mind. And that, I conclude, is but another evidence of
the complete and final triumph of the egg—at least as far as
my family is concerned.

TORCH SONG

John Cheever

After Jack Lorey had known Joan Harris in New York for a
few years, he began to think of her as The Widow. She
always wore black, and he was always given the feeling, by a
curious disorder in her apartment, that the undertakers had
just left. This impression did not stem from malice on his
part, for he was fond of Joan. They came from the same city
in Ohio and had reached New York at about the same time
in the middle thirties. They were the same age, and during
their first summer in the city they used to meet after work
and drink Martinis in places like the Brevoort and Charles',
and have dinner and play checkers at the Lafayette.

Joan went to a school for models when she settled in the
city, but it turned out that she photographed badly, so after
spending six weeks learning how to walk with a book on her
head she got a job as a hostess in a Longchamps. For the
rest of the summer she stood by the hatrack, bathed in an
intense pink light and the string music of heartbreak, swinging her mane of dark hair and her black skirt as she moved
forward to greet the customers. She was then a big, handsome girl with a wonderful voice, and her face, her whole
presence, always seemed infused with a gentle and healthy
pleasure at her surroundings, whatever they were. She was
innocently and incorrigibly convivial, and would get out of
bed and dress at three in the morning if someone called her
and asked her to come out for a drink, as Jack often did. In
the fall, she got some kind of freshman executive job in a
department store. They saw less and less of each other and

then for quite a while stopped seeing each other altogether. Jack was living with a girl he had met at a party, and it never occurred to him to wonder what had become of Joan.

Jack's girl had some friends in Pennsylvania, and in the spring and summer of his second year in town he often went there with her for weekends. All of this—the shared apartment in the Village, the illicit relationship, the Friday-night train to a country house—were what he had imagined life in New York to be, and he was intensely happy. He was returning to New York with his girl one Sunday night on the Lehigh line. It was one of those trains that move slowly across the face of New Jersey, bringing back to the city hundreds of people, like the victims of an immense and strenuous picnic, whose faces are blazing and whose muscles are lame. Jack and his girl, like most of the other passengers, were overburdened with vegetables and flowers. When the train stopped in Pennsylvania Station, they moved with the crowd along the platform, toward the escalator. As they were passing the wide, lighted windows of the diner, Jack turned his head and saw Joan. It was the first time he had seen her since Thanksgiving, or since Christmas. He couldn't remember.

Joan was with a man who had obviously passed out. His head was in his arms on the table, and an overturned highball glass was near one of his elbows. Joan was shaking his shoulders gently and speaking to him. She seemed to be vaguely troubled, vaguely amused. The waiters had cleared off all the other tables and were standing around Joan, waiting for her to resurrect her escort. It troubled Jack to see in these straits a girl who reminded him of the trees and the lawns of his home town, but there was nothing he could do to help. Joan continued to shake the man's shoulders, and the crowd pressed Jack past one after another of the diner's windows, past the malodorous kitchen, and up the escalator.

He saw Joan again, later that summer, when he was having dinner in a Village restaurant. He was with a new girl, a Southerner. There were many Southern girls in the

city that year. Jack and his belle had wandered into the
restaurant because it was convenient, but the food was
terrible and the place was lighted with candles. Halfway
through dinner, Jack noticed Joan on the other side of the
room, and when he had finished eating, he crossed the
room and spoke to her. She was with a tall man who was
wearing a monocle. He stood, bowed stiffly from the waist,
and said to Jack, "We are very pleased to meet you." Then
he excused himself and headed for the toilet. "He's a count,
he's a Swedish count," Joan said. "He's on the radio, Friday
afternoons at four-fifteen. Isn't it exciting?" She seemed to
be delightd with the count and the terrible restaurant.

Sometime the next winter, Jack moved from the Village
to an apartment in the East Thirties. He was crossing Park
Avenue one cold morning on his way to the office when he
noticed, in the crowd, a woman he had met a few times at
Joan's apartment. He spoke to her and asked about his
friend. "Haven't you heard?" she said. She pulled a long
face. "Perhaps I'd better tell you. Perhaps you can help."
She and Jack had breakfast in a drugstore on Madison
Avenue and she unburdened herself of the story.

The count had a program called "The Song of the Fiords,"
or something like that, and he sang Swedish folk songs.
Everyone suspected him of being a fake, but that didn't
bother Joan. He had met her at a party and, sensing a soft
touch, had moved in with her the following night. About a
week later, he complained of pains in his back and said he
must have some morphine. Then he needed morphine all
the time. If he didn't get morphine, he was abusive and
violent. Joan began to deal with those doctors and druggists
who peddle dope, and when they wouldn't supply her, she
went down to the bottom of the city. Her friends were
afraid she would be found some morning stuffed in a drain.
She got pregnant. She had an abortion. The count left her
and moved to a flea bag near Times Square, but she was so
impressed by then with his helplessness, so afraid that he
would die without her, that she followed him there and
shared his room and continued to buy his narcotics. He

abandoned her again, and Joan waited a week for him to return before she went back to her place and her friends in the Village.

It shocked Jack to think of the innocent girl from Ohio having lived with a brutal dope addict and traded with criminals, and when he got to his office that morning, he telephoned her and made a date for dinner that night. He met her at Charles'. When she came into the bar, she seemed as wholesome and calm as ever. Her voice was sweet, and reminded him of elms, of lawns, of those glass arrangements that used to be hung from porch ceilings to tinkle in the summer wind. She told him about the count. She spoke of him charitably and with no trace of bitterness, as if her voice, her disposition, were incapable of registering anything beyond simple affection and pleasure. Her walk, when she moved ahead of him toward their table, was light and graceful. She ate a large dinner and talked enthusiastically about her job. They went to a movie and said goodbye in fromt of her apartment house.

That winter, Jack met a girl he decided to marry. Their engagement was announced in January and they planned to marry in July. In the spring, he received, in his office mail, an invitation to cocktails at Joan's. It was for a Saturday when his fiancée was going to Massachusetts to visit her parents, and when the time came and he had nothing better to do, he took a bus to the Village. Joan had the same apartment. It was a walkup. You rang the bell above the mailbox in the vestibule and were answered with a death rattle in the lock. Joan lived on the third floor. Her calling card was in a slot on the mailbox, and above her name was written the name Hugh Bascomb.

Jack climbed the two flights of carpeted stairs, and when he reached Joan's apartment, she was standing by the open door in a black dress. After she greeted Jack, she took his arm and guided him across the room. "I want you to meet Hugh, Jack," she said.

Hugh was a big man with a red face and pale-blue eyes. His manner was courtly and his eyes were inflamed with drink. Jack talked with him for a little while and then went over to speak to someone he knew, who was standing by the mantelpiece. He noticed then, for the first time, the indescribable disorder of Joan's apartment. The books were in their shelves and the furniture was reasonably good, but the place was all wrong, somehow. It was as if things had been put in place without thought or real interest, and for the first time, too, he had the impression that there had been a death there recently.

As Jack moved around the room, he felt that he had met the ten or twelve guests at other parties. There was a woman executive with a fancy hat, a man who could imitate Roosevelt, a grim couple whose play was in rehearsal, and a newspaperman who kept turning on the radio for news of the Spanish Civil War. Jack drank Martinis and talked with the woman in the fancy hat. He looked out of the window at the back yards and the ailanthus trees and heard, in the distance, thunder exploding off the cliffs of the Hudson.

Hugh Bascomb got very drunk. He began to spill liquor, as if drinking, for him, were a kind of jolly slaughter and he enjoyed the bloodshed and the mess. He spilled whiskey from a bottle. He spilled a drink on his shirt and then tipped over someone else's drink. The party was not quiet, but Hugh's hoarse voice began to dominate the others. He attacked a photographer who was sitting in a corner explaining camera techniques to a homely woman. "What did you come to the party for if all you wanted to do was to sit there and stare at your shoes?" Hugh shouted. "What did you come for? Why don't you stay at home?"

The photographer didn't know what to say. He was not staring at his shoes. Joan moved lightly to Hugh's side. "Please don't get into a fight now, darling," she said. "Not this afternoon."

"Shut up," he said. "Let me alone. Mind your own business." He lost his balance, and in struggling to steady himself he tipped over a lamp.

"Oh, your lovely lamp, Joan," a woman sighed.

"Lamps!" Hugh roared. He threw his arms into the air

and worked them around his head as if he were bludgeoning
himself. "Lamps. Glasses. Cigarette boxes. Dishes. They're
killing me. They're killing me, for Christ's sake. Let's all go
up to the mountains, for Christ's sake. Let's all go up to the
mountains and hunt and fish and live like men, for Christ's
sake."

People were scattering as if a rain had begun to fall in the
room. It had, as a matter of fact, begun to rain outside.
Someone offered Jack a ride uptown, and he jumped at the
chance. Joan stood at the door, saying goodbye to her
routed friends. Her voice remained soft, and her manner,
unlike that of those Christian women who in the face of
disaster can summon new and formidable sources of composure, seemed genuinely simple. She appeared to be oblivious of the raging drunk at her back, who was pacing up
and down, grinding glass into the rug, and haranguing one
of the survivors of the party with a story of how he, Hugh,
had once gone without food for three weeks.

In July, Jack was married in an orchard in Duxbury, and
he and his wife went to West Chop for a few weeks. When
they returned to town, their apartment was cluttered with
presents, including a dozen after-dinner coffee cups from
Joan. His wife sent her the required note, but they did
nothing else.

Later in the summer, Joan telephoned Jack at his office
and asked if he wouldn't bring his wife to see her; she
named an evening the following week. He felt guilty about
not having called her, and accepted the invitation. This
made his wife angry. She was an ambitious girl who liked a
social life that offered rewards, and she went unwillingly to
Joan's Village apartment with him.

Written above Joan's name on the mailbox was the name
Franz Denzel. Jack and his wife climbed the stairs and were
met by Joan at the open door. They went into her apartment and found themselves among a group of people for
whom Jack, at least, was unable to find any bearings.
Franz Denzel was a middle-aged German. His face was

pinched with bitterness or illness. He greeted Jack and his wife with that elaborate and clever politeness that is intended to make guests feel that they have come too early or too late. He insisted sharply upon Jack's sitting in the chair in which he himself had been sitting, and then went and sat on a radiator. There were five other Germans sitting around the room, drinking coffee. In a corner was another American couple, who looked uncomfortable. Joan passed Jack and his wife small cups of coffee with whipped cream. "These cups belonged to Franz's mother," she said. "Aren't they lovely? They were the only things he took from Germany when he escaped from the Nazis."

Franz turned to Jack and said, "Perhaps you will give us your opinion on the American educational system. That is what we were discussing when you arrived."

Before Jack could speak, one of the German guests opened an attack on the American educational system. The other Germans joined in, and went on from there to describe every vulgarity that had impressed them in American life and to contrast German and American culture generally. Where, they asked one another passionately, could you find in America anything like the Mitropa dining cars, the Black Forest, the pictures in Munich, the music in Bayreuth? Franz and his friends began speaking in German. Neither Jack nor his wife nor Joan could understand German, and the other American couple had not opened their mouths since they were introduced. Joan went happily around the room, filling everyone's cup with coffee, as if the music of a foreign language were enough to make an evening for her.

Jack drank five cups of coffee. He was desperately uncomfortable. Joan went into the kitchen while the Germans were laughing at their German jokes, and he hoped she would return with some drinks, but when she came back, it was with a tray of ice cream and mulberries.

"Isn't this pleasant?" Franz asked, speaking in English again.

Joan collected the coffee cups, and as she was about to take them back to the kitchen, Franz stopped her.

"Isn't one of those cups chipped?"

"No, darling," Joan said. "I never let the maid touch them. I wash them myself."

"What's that?" he asked, pointing at the rim of one of the cups.

"That's the cup that's always been chipped, darling. It was chipped when you unpacked it. You noticed it then."

"These things were perfect when they arrived in this country," he said.

Joan went into the kitchen and he followed her.

Jack tried to make conversation with the Germans. From the kitchen there was the sound of a blow and a cry. Franz returned and began to eat his mulberries greedily. Joan came back with her dish of ice cream. Her voice was gentle. Her tears, if she had been crying, had dried as quickly as the tears of a child. Jack and his wife finished their ice cream and made their escape. The wasted and unnerving evening enraged Jack's wife, and he supposed that he would never see Joan again.

Jack's wife got pregnant early in the fall, and she seized on all the prerogatives of an expectant mother. She took long naps, ate canned peaches in the middle of the night, and talked about the rudimentary kidney. She chose to see only other couples who were expecting children, and the parties that she and Jack gave were temperate. The baby, a boy, was born in May, and Jack was very proud and happy. The first party he and his wife went to after her convalescence was the wedding of a girl whose family Jack had known in Ohio.

The wedding was at St. James', and afterward there was a big reception at the River Club. There was an orchestra dressed like Hungarians, and a lot of champagne and Scotch. Toward the end of the afternoon, Jack was walking down a dim corridor when he heard Joan's voice. "Please don't, darling," she was saying. "You'll break my arm. *Please* don't, darling." She was being pressed against the wall by a man who seemed to be twisting her arm. As soon as they saw Jack, the struggle stopped. All three of them were intensely embarrassed. Joan's face was wet and she made an effort to smile through her tears at Jack. He said hello and went on without stopping. When he returned, she and the man had disappeared.

When Jack's son was less than two years old, his wife flew with the baby to Nevada to get a divorce. Jack gave her the apartment and all its furnishings and took a room in a hotel near Grand Central. His wife got her decree in due course, and the story was in the newspapers. Jack had a telephone call from Joan a few days later.

"I'm awfully sorry to hear about your divorce, Jack," she said. "She seemed like *such* a nice girl. But that wasn't what I called you about. I want your help, and I wondered if you could come down to my place tonight around six. It's something I don't want to talk about over the phone."

He went obediently to the Village that night and climbed the stairs. Her apartment was a mess. The pictures and the curtains were down and the books were in boxes. "You moving, Joan?" he asked.

"That's what I wanted to see you about, Jack. First, I'll give you a drink." She made two Old-Fashioneds. "I'm being evicted, Jack," she said. "I'm being evicted because I'm an immoral woman. The couple who have the apartment downstairs—they're charming people, I've always thought—have told the real-estate agent that I'm a drunk and a prostitute and all kinds of things. Isn't that fantastic? This real-estate agent has always been so nice to me that I didn't think he'd believe them, but he's cancelled my lease, and if I make any trouble, he's threatened to take the matter up with the store, and I don't want to lose my job. This nice real-estate agent won't even talk with me any more. When I go over to the office, the receptionist leers at me as if I were some kind of dreadful woman. Of course, there have been a lot of men here and we sometimes are noisy, but I can't be expected to go to bed at ten every night. Can I? Well, the agent who manages this building has apparently told all the other agents in the neighborhood

that I'm an immoral and drunken woman, and none of them
will give me an apartment. I went in to talk with one
man—he seemed to be such a nice old gentleman—and he
made me an indecent proposal. Isn't it fantastic? I have to
be out of here on Thursday and I'm literally being turned
out into the street."

Joan seemed as serene and innocent as ever while she
described this scourge of agents and neighbors. Jack listened carefully for some sign of indignation or bitterness or
even urgency in her recital, but there was none. He was
reminded of a torch song, of one of those forlorn and touching ballads that had been sung neither for him nor for her
but for their older brothers and sisters by Marion Harris.
Joan seemed to be singing her wrongs.

"They've made my life miserable," she went on quietly.
"If I keep the radio on after ten o'clock, they telephone the
agent in the morning and tell him I had some kind of orgy
here. One night when Phillip—I don't think you've met
Phillip; he's in the Royal Air Force; he's gone back to
England—one night when Phillip and some other people
were here, they called the police. The police came bursting
in the door and talked to me as if I were I don't know what
and then looked in the bedroom. If they think there's a man
up here after midnight, they call me on the telephone and
say all kinds of disgusting things. Of course, I can put my
furniture into storage and go to a hotel, I guess. I guess a
hotel will take a woman with my kind of reputation, but I
thought perhaps you might know of an apartment. I
thought—"

It angered Jack to think of this big, splendid girl's being
persecuted by her neighbors, and he said he would do what
he could. He asked her to have dinner with him, but she
said she was busy.

Having nothing better to do, Jack decided to walk uptown to his hotel. It was a hot night. The sky was overcast.
On his way, he saw a parade in a dark side street off
Broadway near Madison Square. All the buildings in the
neighborhood were dark. It was so dark that he could not

see the placards the marchers carried until he came to a street light. Their signs urged the entry of the United States into the war, and each platoon represented a nation that had been subjugated by the Axis powers. They marched up Broadway, as he watched, to no music, to no sound but their own steps on the rough cobbles. It was for the most part an army of elderly men and women—Poles, Norwegians, Danes, Jews, Chinese. A few idle people like himself lined the sidewalks, and the marchers passed between them with all the self-consciousness of enemy prisoners. There were children among them dressed in the costumes in which they had, for the newsreels, presented the Mayor with a package of tea, a petition, a protest, a constitution, a check, or a pair of tickets. They hobbled through the darkness of the loft neighborhood like a mortified and destroyed people, toward Greeley Square.

In the morning, Jack put the problem of finding an apartment for Joan up to his secretary. She started phoning real-estate agents, and by afternoon she had found a couple of available apartments in the West Twenties. Joan called Jack the next day to say that she had taken one of the apartments and to thank him.

Jack didn't see Joan again until the following summer. It was a Sunday evening; he had left a cocktail party in a Washington Square apartment and had decided to walk a few blocks up Fifth Avenue before he took a bus. As he was passing the Brevoort, Joan called to him. She was with a man at one of the tables on the sidewalk. She looked cool and fresh, and the man appeared to be respectable. His name, it turned out, was Pete Bristol. He invited Jack to sit down and join in a celebration. Germany had invaded Russia that weekend, and Joan and Pete were drinking champagne to celebrate Russia's changed position in the war. The three of them drank champagne until it got dark. They had dinner and drank champagne with their dinner. They drank more champagne afterward and then went over to the Lafayette and then to two or three other places. Joan had always been tireless in her gentle way. She hated to see the night

end, and it was after three o'clock when Jack stumbled into
his apartment. The following morning he woke up haggard
and sick, and with no recollection of the last hour or so of
the previous evening. His suit was soiled and he had lost his
hat. He didn't get to his office until eleven. Joan had already called him twice, and she called him again soon after
he got in. There was no hoarseness at all in her voice. She
said that she had to see him, and he agreed to meet her for
lunch in a seafood restaurant in the Fifties.

He was standing at the bar when she breezed in, looking
as though she had taken no part in that calamitous night.
The advice she wanted concerned selling her jewelry. Her
grandmother had left her some jewelry, and she wanted to
raise money on it but didn't know where to go. She took
some rings and bracelets out of her purse and showed them
to Jack. He said that he didn't know anything about jewelry
but that he could lend her some money. "Oh, I couldn't
borrow money from you, Jack," she said. "You see, I want
to get the money for Pete. I want to help him. He wants to
open an advertising agency, and he needs quite a lot to
begin with." Jack didn't press her to accept his offer of a
loan after that, and the project wasn't mentioned again
during lunch.

He next heard about Joan from a young doctor who was a
friend of theirs. "Have you seen Joan recently?" the doctor
asked Jack one evening when they were having dinner
together. He said no. "I gave her a checkup last week," the
doctor said, "and while she's been through enough to kill
the average mortal—and you'll never know what she's been
through—she still has the constitution of a virtuous and
healthy woman. Did you hear about the last one? She sold
her jewelry to put him into some kind of a business, and as
soon as he got the money, he left her for another girl, who
had a car—a convertible."

Jack was drafted into the Army in the spring of 1942. He
was kept at Fort Dix for nearly a month, and during this
time he came to New York in the evening whenever he
could get permission. Those nights had for him the intense

keenness of a reprieve, a sensation that was heightened by the fact that on the train in from Trenton women would often press upon him dog-eared copies of *Life* and half-eaten boxes of candy, as though the brown clothes he wore were surely cerements. He telephoned Joan from Pennsylvania Station one night. "Come right over, Jack," she said. "Come right over. I want you to meet Ralph."

She was living in that place in the West Twenties that Jack had found for her. The neighborhood was a slum. Ash cans stood in front of her house, and an old woman was there picking out bits of refuse and garbage and stuffing them into a perambulator. The house in which Joan's apartment was located was shabby, but the apartment itself seemed familiar. The furniture was the same. Joan was the same big, easy-going girl. "I'm so glad you called me," she said. "It's so good to see you. I'll make you a drink. I was having one myself. Ralph ought to be here by now. He promised to take me to dinner." Jack offered to take her to Cavanagh's, but she said that Ralph might come while she was out. "If he doesn't come by nine, I'm going to make myself a sandwich. I'm not really hungry."

Jack talked about the Army. She talked about the store. She had been working in the same place for—how long was it? He didn't know. He had never seen her at her desk and he couldn't imagine what she did. "I'm terribly sorry Ralph isn't here," she said. "I'm sure you'd like him. He's not a young man. He's a heart specialist who loves to play the viola." She turned on some lights, for the summer sky had got dark. "He has this dreadful wife on Riverside Drive and four ungrateful children. He—"

The noise of an air-raid siren, lugubrious and seeming to spring from pain, as if all the misery and indecision in the city had been given a voice, cut her off. Other sirens, in distant neighborhoods, sounded, until the dark air was full of their noise. "Let me fix you another drink before I have to turn out the lights," Joan said, and took his glass. She brought the drink back to him and snapped off the lights. They went to the windows, and, as children watch a thun-

derstorm, they watched the city darken. All the lights nearby
went out but one. Air-raid wardens had begun to sound
their whistles in the street. From a distant yard came a
hoarse shriek of anger. "Put out your lights, you Fascists!" a
woman screamed. "Put out your lights, you Nazi Fascist
Germans. Turn out your lights. Turn out your lights." The
last light went off. They went away from the window and sat
in the lightless room.

In the darkness, Joan began to talk about her departed
lovers, and from what she said Jack gathered that they had
all had a hard time. Nils, the suspect count, was dead.
Hugh Bascomb, the drunk, had joined the Merchant Ma-
rine and was missing in the North Atlantic. Franz, the
German, had taken poison the night the Nazis bombed
Warsaw. "We listened to the news on the radio," Joan said,
"and then he went back to his hotel and took poison. The
maid found him dead in the bathroom the next morning."
When Jack asked her about the one who was going to open
an advertising agency, she seemed at first to have forgotten
him. "Oh, Pete," she said after a pause. "Well, he was
always very sick, you know. He was supposed to go to
Saranac, but he kept putting it off and putting it off and—"
She stopped talking when she heard steps on the stairs,
hoping, he supposed, that it was Ralph, but whoever it was
turned at the landing and continued to the top of the house.
"I wish Ralph would come," she said, with a sigh. "I want
you to meet him." Jack asked her again to go out, but she
refused, and when the all-clear sounded, he said goodbye.

Jack was shipped from Dix to an infantry training camp in
the Carolinas and from there to an infantry division sta-
tioned in Georgia. He had been in Georgia three months
when he married a girl from the Augusta boarding-house
aristocracy. A year or so later, he crossed the continent in a
day coach and thought sententiously that the last he might
see of the country he loved was the desert towns like
Barstow, that the last he might hear of it was the ringing of
the trolleys on the Bay Bridge. He was sent into the Pacific
and returned to the United States twenty months later,

uninjured and apparently unchanged. As soon as he received his furlough, he went to Augusta. He presented his wife with the souvenirs he had brought from the islands, quarrelled violently with her and all her family, and, after making arrangements for her to get an Arkansas divorce, left for New York.

Jack was discharged from the Army at a camp in the East a few months later. He took a vacation and then went back to the job he had left in 1942. He seemed to have picked up his life at approximately the moment when it had been interrupted by the war. In time, everything came to look and feel the same. He saw most of his old friends. Only two of the men he knew had been killed in the war. He didn't call Joan, but he met her one winter afternoon on a crosstown bus.

Her fresh face, her black clothes, and her soft voice instantly destroyed the sense—if he had ever had such a sense—that anything had changed or intervened since their last meeting, three or four years ago. She asked him up for cocktails and he went to her apartment the next Saturday afternoon. Her room and her guests reminded him of the parties she had given when she had first come to New York. There was a woman with a fancy hat, an elderly doctor, and a man who stayed close to the radio, listening for news from the Balkans. Jack wondered which of the men belonged to Joan and decided on an Englishman who kept coughing into a handkerchief that he pulled out of his sleeve. Jack was right. "Isn't Stephen brilliant?" Joan asked him a little later, when they were alone in a corner. "He knows more about the Polynesians than anyone else in the world."

Jack had returned not only to his old job but to his old salary. Since living costs had doubled and since he was paying alimony to two wives, he had to draw on his savings. He took another job, which promised more money, but it didn't last long and he found himself out of work. This didn't bother him at all. He still had money in the bank, and anyhow it was easy to borrow from friends. His indifference was the consequence not of lassitude or despair but

rather of an excess of hope. He had the feeling that he had
only recently come to New York from Ohio. The sense that
he was very young and that the best years of his life still lay
before him was an illusion that he could not seem to escape.
There was all the time in the world. He was living in hotels
then, moving from one to another every five days.

In the spring, Jack moved to a furnished room in the
badlands west of Central Park. He was running out of
money. Then, when he began to feel that a job was a
desperate necessity, he got sick. At first, he seemed to have
only a bad cold, but he was unable to shake it and he began
to run a fever and to cough blood. The fever kept him
drowsy most of the time, but he roused himself occasionally
and went out to a cafeteria for a meal. He felt sure that none
of his friends knew where he was, and he was glad of this.
He hadn't counted on Joan.

Late one morning, he heard her speaking in the hall with
his landlady. A few moments later, she knocked on his door.
He was lying on the bed in a pair of pants and a soiled
pajama top, and he didn't answer. She knocked again and
walked in. "I've been looking everywhere for you, Jack,"
she said. She spoke softly. "When I found out that you were
in a place like this I thought you must be broke or sick. I
stopped at the bank and got some money, in case you're
broke. I've brought you some Scotch. I thought a little
drink wouldn't do you any harm. Want a little drink?"

Joan's dress was black. Her voice was low and serene.
She sat in a chair beside his bed as if she had been coming
there every day to nurse him. Her features had coarsened,
he thought, but there were still very few lines in her face.
She was heavier. She was nearly fat. She was wearing black
cotton gloves. She got two glasses and poured Scotch into
them. He drank his whiskey greedily. "I didn't get to bed
until three last night," she said. Her voice had once before
reminded him of a gentle and despairing song, but now,
perhaps because he was sick, her mildness, the mourning
she wore, her stealthy grace, made him uneasy. "It was one
of those nights," she said. "We went to the theatre. After-

ward, someone asked us up to his place. I don't know who he was. It was one of those places. They're so strange. There were some meat-eating plants and a collection of Chinese snuff bottles. Why do people collect Chinese snuff bottles? We all autographed a lampshade, as I remember, but I can't remember much."

Jack tried to sit up in bed, as if there were some need to defend himself, and then fell back again, against the pillows. "How did you find me, Joan?" he asked.

"It was simple," she said. "I called that hotel. The one you were staying in. They gave me this address. My secretary got the telephone number. Have another little drink."

"You know you've never come to a place of mine before—never," he said. "Why did you come now?"

"Why did I come, darling?" she asked. "What a question! I've known you for thirty years. You're the oldest friend I have in New York. Remember that night in the Village when it snowed and we stayed up until morning and drank whiskey sours for breakfast? That doesn't seem like twelve years ago. And that night—"

"I don't like to have you see me in a place like this," he said earnestly. He touched his face and felt his beard.

"And all the people who used to imitate Roosevelt," she said, as if she had not heard him, as if she were deaf. "And that place on Staten Island where we all used to go for dinner when Henry had a car. Poor Henry. He bought a place in Connecticut and went out there by himself, one weekend. He fell asleep with a lighted cigarette and the house, the barn, everything burned. Ethel took the children out to California." She poured more Scotch into his glass and handed it to him. She lighted a cigarette and put it between his lips. The intimacy of this gesture, which made it seem not only as if he were deathly ill but as if he were her lover, troubled him.

"As soon as I'm better," he said, "I'll take a room at a good hotel. I'll call you then. It was nice of you to come."

"Oh, don't be ashamed of this room, Jack," she said. "Rooms never bother me. It doesn't seem to matter to me where I am. Stanley had a filthy room in Chelsea. At least, other people told me it was filthy. I never noticed it. Rats used to eat the food I brought him. He used to have to hang the food from the ceiling, from the light chain."

"I'll call you as soon as I'm better," Jack said. "I think I can sleep now if I'm left alone. I seem to need a lot of sleep."

"You really *are* sick, darling," she said. "You must have a fever." She sat on the edge of his bed and put a hand on his forehead.

"How is that Englishman, Joan?" he asked. "Do you still see him?"

"What Englishman?" she said.

"You know. I met him at your house. He kept a handkerchief up his sleeve. He coughed all the time. You know the one I mean."

"You must be thinking of someone else," she said. "I haven't had an Englishman at my place since the war. Of course, I can't remember everyone." She turned and, taking one of his hands, linked her fingers in his.

"He's dead, isn't he?" Jack said. "That Englishman's dead." He pushed her off the bed, and got up himself. "Get out," he said.

"You're sick, darling," she said. "I can't leave you alone here."

"Get out," he said again, and when she didn't move, he shouted, "What kind of an obscenity are you that you can smell sickness and death the way you do?"

"You poor darling."

"Does it make you feel young to watch the dying?" he shouted. "Is that the lewdness that keeps you young? Is that why you dress like a crow? Oh, I know there's nothing I can say that will hurt you. I know there's nothing filthy or corrupt or depraved or brutish or base that the others haven't tried, but this time you're wrong. I'm not ready. My life isn't ending. My life's beginning. There are wonderful years ahead of me. There are, there are wonderful, wonderful, wonderful years ahead of me, and when they're over, when it's time, then I'll call you. Then, as an old friend, I'll call you and give you whatever dirty pleasure you take in watching the dying, but until then, you and your ugly and misshapen forms will leave me alone."

She finished her drink and looked at her watch. "I guess I'd better show up at the office," she said. "I'll see you later. I'll come back tonight. You'll feel better then, you poor darling." She closed the door after her, and he heard her light step on the stairs.

Jack emptied the whiskey bottle into the sink. He began to dress. He stuffed his dirty clothes into a bag. He was trembling and crying with sickness and fear. He could see the blue sky from his window, and in his fear it seemed miraculous that the sky would be blue, that the white clouds should remind him of snow, that from the sidewalk he could hear the shrill voices of children shrieking, "I'm the king of the mountain, I'm the king of the mountain, I'm the king of the mountain." He emptied the ashtray containing his nail parings and cigarette butts into the toilet, and swept the floor with a shirt, so that there would be no trace of his life, of his body, when that lewd and searching shape of death came there to find him in the evening.

◆ ———————————————————————— ◆

WITCH'S MONEY

John Collier

Foiral had taken a load of cork up to the high road, where he met the motor truck from Perpignan. He was on his way back to the village, walking harmlessly beside his mule, and thinking of nothing at all, when he was passed by a striding madman, half naked, and of a type never seen before in this district of the Pyrénées-Orientales.

He was not of the idiot sort, with the big head, like two or three of them down in the village. Nor was he a lean, raving creature, like Barilles's old father after the house burned down. Nor had he a little, tiny, shrunken-up, chattering head, like the younger Lloubes. He was a new sort altogether.

Foiral decided he was a kind of *bursting* madman, all blare and racket, as bad as the sun. His red flesh burst out of his little bits of coloured clothes; red arms, red knees, red neck, and a great round red face bursting with smiles, words, laughter.

Foiral overtook him at the top of the ridge. He was staring down into the valley like a man thunderstruck. "My God!" he said to Foiral. "Just look at it!" Foiral looked at it. There was nothing wrong.

"Here have I," said the mad Jack, "been walking up and down these goddam Pyrénées for weeks—meadows, birch trees, pine trees, waterfalls—green as a dish of *haricots verts!* And here's what I've been looking for all the time. Why did no one tell me?"

There's a damned question to answer! However, madmen answer themselves. Foiral thumped his mule and started off down the track, but the mad fellow fell in step beside him.

"What is it, for God's sake?" said he. "A bit of Spain strayed over the frontier, or what? Might be a crater in the moon. No water, I suppose? God, look at that ring of red hills! Look at that pink and yellow land! Are those villages down there? Or the bones of some creatures that have died?

"I like it," he said. "I like the way the fig trees burst out of the rock. I like the way the seeds are bursting out of the figs. Ever heard of surrealism? This is surrealism come to life. What are those? Cork forests? They look like petrified ogres. Excellent ogres, who bleed when these impudent mortals flay you, with my little brush, on my little piece of canvas, I shall restore to you an important part of your life!"

Foiral, by no means devout, took the sensible precaution of crossing himself. The fellow went on and on, all the way down, two or three kilometres, Foiral answering with a "yes," a "no," and a grunt. "This is *my* country!" cried the lunatic. "It's *made* for me. Glad I didn't go to Morocco! Is this your village? Wonderful! Look at those houses—three, four stories. Why do they look as if they'd been piled up by cave-dwellers, cave-dwellers who couldn't find a cliff? Or are they caves from which the cliff has crumbled away, leaving them uneasy in the sunlight, huddling together? Why don't you have any windows? I like that yellow belfry. Sort of Spanish. I like the way the bell hangs in that iron cage. Black as your hat. Dead. Maybe that's why it's so quiet here. Dead noise, gibbeted against the blue! Ha! Ha! You're not amused, eh? You don't care for surrealism? So much the worse, my friend, because you're the stuff that sort of dream is made of. I like the black clothes all you people wear. Spanish touch again, I suppose? It makes you look like holes in the light."

"Goodbye," said Foiral.

"Wait a minute," said the stranger. "Where can I put up in this village? Is there an inn?"

"No," said Foiral, turning into his yard.

"Hell!" said the stranger. "I suppose someone has a room I can sleep in?"

"No," said Foiral.

That set the fellow back a bit. "Well," said he at last, "I'll have a look around, anyway."

So he went up the street. Foiral saw him talking to Madame Arago, and she was shaking her head. Then he saw him trying it on at the baker's, and the baker shook his head as well. However, he bought a loaf there, and some cheese and wine from Barilles. He sat down on the bench outside and ate it; then he went pottering off up the slope.

Foiral thought he'd keep an eye on him, so he followed to the top of the village, where he could see all over the hillside. The fellow was just mooning about; he picked up nothing, he did nothing. Then he began to drift over to the little farm-house, where the well is, a few hundred yards above the rest of the houses.

This happened to be Foiral's property, through his wife: a

good place, if they'd had a son to live in it. Seeing the stranger edging that way, Foiral followed, not too fast, you understand, and not too slow either. Sure enough, when he got there, there was the fellow peering through the chinks in the shutters, even trying the door. He might have been up to anything.

He looked round as Foiral came up. "Nobody lives here?" he said.

"No," said Foiral.

"Who does it belong to?" said the stranger.

Foiral hardly knew what to say. In the end he had to admit it was his.

"Will you rent it to me?" said the stranger.

"What's that?" said Foiral.

"I want the house for six months," said the stranger.

"What for?" said Foiral.

"Damn it!" said the stranger. "To live in."

"Why?" said Foiral.

The stranger holds up his hand. He picks hold of the thumb. He says, very slowly, "I am an artist, a painter."

"Yes," says Foiral.

Then the stranger lays hold of his forefinger. "I can work here. I like it. I like the view. I like those two ilex trees."

"Very good," says Foiral.

Then the stranger takes hold of his middle finger. "I want to stay here six months."

"Yes," says Foiral.

Then the stranger takes hold of his third finger. "In this house. Which, I may say, on this yellow ground, looks interestingly like a die on a desert. Or does it look like a skull?"

"Ah!" says Foiral.

Then the stranger takes hold of his little finger, and he says, "How much—do you want—to let me—live and work—in this house—for six months?"

"Why?" said Foiral.

At this the stranger began to stamp up and down. They had quite an argument. Foiral clinched the matter by saying that people didn't rent houses in that part of the world; everyone had his own.

"It is necessary," said the stranger, grinding his teeth, "for me to paint pictures here."

"So much the worse," said Foiral.

The stranger uttered a number of cries in some foreign gibberish, possibly that of hell itself. "I see your soul," said he, "as a small and exceedingly sterile black marble, on a waste of burning white alkali."

Foiral, holding his two middle fingers under his thumb, extended the first and fourth in the direction of the stranger, careless of whether he gave offence.

"What will you take for the shack?" said the stranger. "Maybe I'll buy it."

It was quite a relief to Foiral to find that after all he was just a plain, simple, ordinary lunatic. Without a proper pair of pants to his back-side, he was offering to buy this excellent sound house, for which Foiral would have asked twenty thousand francs, had there been anyone of whom to ask it.

"Come on," said the stranger. "How much?"

Foiral, thinking he had wasted enough time, and not objecting to an agreeable sensation, said, "Forty thousand."

Said the stranger, "I'll give you thirty-five."

Foiral laughed heartily.

"That's a good laugh," said the stranger. "I should like to paint a laugh like that. I should express it by a *mélange* of the roots of recently extracted teeth. Well, what about it? Thirty-five? I can pay you a deposit right now." And, pulling out a wallet, this Croesus among madmen rustled one, two, three, four, five thousand-franc notes under Foiral's nose.

"It'll leave me dead broke," he said. "Still, I expect I can sell it again?"

"If God wills," said Foiral.

"Anyway, I could come here now and then," said the other. "My God! I can paint a showful of pictures here in six months. New York'll go crazy. Then I'll come back here and paint another show."

Foiral, ravished with joy, ceased attempting to understand. He began to praise his house furiously: he dragged the man inside, showed him the oven, banged the walls, made him look up the chimney, into the shed, down the well—"All right. All right," said the stranger. "That's grand. Everything's grand. Whitewash the walls. Find me some woman to come and clean and cook. I'll go back to Perpignan and turn up in a week with my things. Listen, I want that table chucked in, two or three of the chairs, and the bedstead. I'll get the rest. Here's your deposit."

"No, no," said Foiral. "Everything must be done properly, before witnesses. Then, when the lawyer comes, he can make out the papers. Come back with me. I'll call Arago, he's a very honest man. Guis, very honest. Vigné, honest as the good earth. And a bottle of old wine. I have it. It shall cost nothing."

"Fine!" said the blessed madman, sent by God.

Back they went. In came Arago, Guis, Vigné, all as honest as the day. The deposit was paid, the wine was opened, the stranger called for more, others crowded in; those who were not allowed in stood outside to listen to the laughter. You'd have thought there was a wedding going on, or some wickedness in the house. In fact, Foiral's old woman went and stood in the doorway every now and then, just to let people see her.

There was no doubt about it, there was something very magnificent about this madman. Next day, after he had gone, they talked him over thoroughly. "To listen," said little Guis, "is to be drunk without spending a penny. You think you understand; you seem to fly through the air; you have to burst out laughing."

"I somehow had the delectable impression that I was rich," said Arago. "Not, I mean, with something in the chimney, but as if I—well, as if I were to spend it. And more."

"I like him," said little Guis. "He is my friend."

"Now you speak like a fool," said Foiral. "He is mad. And it is I who deal with him."

"I thought maybe he was not so mad when he said the

house was like an old skull looking out of the ground," said Guis, looking sideways, as well he might.

"Nor a liar, perhaps?" said Foiral. "Let me tell you, he said also it was like a die on a desert. Can it be both?"

"He said in one breath," said Arago, "that he came from Paris. In the next, that he was an American."

"Oh, yes. Unquestionably a great liar," said Quès. "Perhaps one of the biggest rogues in the whole world, going up and down. But, fortunately, mad as well."

"So he buys a house," said Lafago. "If he had his wits about him, a liar of that size, he'd take it—like that. As it is, he buys it. Thirty-five thousand francs!"

"Madness turns a great man inside out, like a sack," said Arago. "And if he is rich as well—"

"—money flies in all directions," said Guis.

Nothing could be more satisfactory. They waited impatiently for the stranger's return. Foiral whitewashed the house, cleaned the chimneys, put everything to rights. You may be sure he had a good search for anything that his wife's old man might have left hidden there years ago, and which this fellow might have heard of. They say they're up to anything in Paris.

The stranger came back, and they were all day with the mules getting his stuff from where the motor truck had left it. By the evening they were in the house, witnesses, helpers, and all—there was just the little matter of paying up the money.

Foiral indicated this with the greatest delicacy in the world. The stranger, all smiles and readiness, went into the room where his bags were piled up, and soon emerged with a sort of book in his hand, full of little *billets*, like those they try to sell for the lottery in Perpignan. He tore off the top one. "Here you are," he said to Foiral, holding it out. "Thirty thousand francs."

"No," said Foiral.

"What the hell now?" asked the stranger.

"I've seen that sort of thing," said Foiral. "And not for thirty thousand francs, my friend, but for three million. And afterwards—they tell you it hasn't won. I should prefer the money."

"This is the money," said the stranger. "It's as good as money anyway. Present this, and you'll get thirty thousand-franc notes, just like those I gave you."

Foiral was rather at a loss. It's quite usual in these parts to settle a sale at the end of a month. Certainly he wanted to run no risk of crabbing the deal. So he pocketed the piece of paper, gave the fellow good-day, and went off with the rest of them to the village.

The stranger settled in. Soon he got to know everybody. Foiral, a little uneasy, cross-examined him whenever they talked. It appeared, after all, that he *did* come from Paris, having lived there, and he *was* an American, having been born there. "Then you have no relations in this part of the world?" said Foiral.

"No relations at all."

Well! Well! Well! Foiral hoped the money was all right. Yet there was more in it than that. No relations! It was quite a thought. Foiral put it away at the back of his mind: he meant to extract the juice from it some night when he couldn't sleep.

At the end of the month, he took out his piece of paper, and marched up to the house again. There was the fellow, three parts naked, sitting under one of the ilex trees, painting away on a bit of canvas. And what do you think he had chosen to paint? Roustand's mangy olives, that haven't borne a crop in living memory!

"What is it?" said the mad fellow. "I'm busy."

"This," said Foiral, holding out the bit of paper. "I need the money."

"Then why, in the name of the devil," said the other, "don't you go and get the money, instead of coming here bothering me?"

Foiral had never seen him in this sort of mood before. But a lot of these laughers stop laughing when it comes to hard cash. "Look here," said Foiral. "This is a very serious matter."

"Look here," said the stranger. "That's what's called a cheque. I give it to you. You take it to a bank. The bank gives you the money."

"Which bank?" said Foiral.

"Your bank. Any bank. The bank in Perpignan," said the stranger. "You go there. They'll do it for you."

Foiral, still hankering after the cash, pointed out that he was a very poor man, and it took a whole day to get to Perpignan, a considerable thing to such an extremely poor man as he was.

"Listen," said the stranger. "You know goddam well you've made a good thing out of this sale. Let me get on with my work. Take the cheque to Perpignan. It's worth the trouble. I've paid you plenty."

Foiral knew then that Guis had been talking about the price of the house. "All right, my little Guis, I'll think that over some long evening when the rains begin." However, there was nothing for it, he had to put on his best black, take the mule to Estagel, and there get the bus, and the bus took him to Perpignan.

In Perpignan they are like so many monkeys. They push you, look you up and down, snigger in your face. If a man has business—with a bank, let us say—and he stands on the pavement opposite to have a good look at it, he gets elbowed into the roadway half a dozen times in five minutes, and he's lucky if he escapes with his life.

Nevertheless, Foiral got into the bank at last. As a spectacle it was tremendous. Brass rails, polished wood, a clock big enough for a church, little cotton-backs sitting among heaps of money like mice in a cheese.

He stood at the back for about half an hour, waiting, and no one took any notice of him at all. In the end one of the little cotton-backs beckoned him up to the brass railing. Foiral delved in his pocket, and produced the cheque. The cotton-back looked at it as if it were a mere nothing. "Holy Virgin!" thought Foiral.

"I want the money for it," said he.

"Are you a client of the bank?"

"No."

"Do you wish to be?"

"Shall I get the money?"

"But naturally. Sign this. Sign this. Sign on the back of the cheque. Take this. Sign this. Thank you. Good-day."

"But the thirty thousand francs?" cried Foiral.

"For that, my dear sir, we must wait till the cheque is cleared. Come back in about a week."

Foiral, half-dazed, went home. It was a bad week. By day he felt reasonably sure of the cash, but at night, as soon as he closed his eyes, he could see himself going into that bank, and all the cotton-backs swearing they'd never seen him before. Still, he got through it, and as soon as the time was up, he presented himself at the bank again.

"Do you want a cheque-book?"

"No. Just the money. The money."

"All of it? You want to close the account? Well! Well! Sign here. Sign here."

Foiral signed.

"There you are. Twenty-nine thousand eight hundred and ninety."

"But, sir, it was thirty thousand."

"But, my dear sir, the charges."

Foiral found it was no good arguing. He went off with his money. That was good. But the other hundred and ten! That sticks in a man's throat.

As soon as he got home, Foiral interviewed the stranger. "I am a poor man," said he.

"So am I," said the stranger. "A damned sight too poor to pay you extra because you can't get a cheque cashed in a civilized way."

This was a peculiarly villainous lie. Foiral had, with his own eyes, seen a whole block of these extraordinary thirty-thousand-franc *billets* in the little book from which the stranger had torn this one. But once more there was nothing to be done about it; a plain honest man is always being baffled and defeated. Foiral went home, and put his crippled twenty-nine thousand-odd into the little box behind the stone in the chimney. How different, if it had been a round thirty thousand! What barbarous injustice!

Here was something to think about in the evenings. Foiral thought about it a lot. In the end he decided it was impossible to act alone, and called in Arago, Quès, Lafago, Vigné, Barilles. Not Guis. It was Guis who had told the fellow he had paid too much for the house, and put his back up. Let Guis stay out of it.

To the rest he explained everything very forcefully. "Not a relation in the whole countryside. And in that book, my dear friends—you have seen it yourselves—ten, twelve, fifteen, maybe twenty of these extraordinary little *billets*."

"And if somebody comes after him? Somebody from America?"

"He has gone off, walking, mad, just as he came here. Anything can happen to a madman, walking about, scattering money."

"It's true. Anything can happen."

"But it should happen before the lawyer comes."

"That's true. So far even the curé hasn't seen him."

"There must be justice, my good friends, society cannot exist without it. A man, an honest man, is not to be robbed of a hundred and ten francs."

"No, that is intolerable."

The next night, these very honest men left their houses, those houses whose tall uprights of white plaster and black shadow appear, in moonlight even more than in sunlight, like a heap of bleached ribs lying in the desert. Without much conversation they made their way up the hill and knocked upon the stranger's door.

After a brief interval they returned, still without much conversation, and slipped one by one into their extremely dark doorways, and that was all.

For a whole week there was no perceptible change in the village. If anything, its darks and silences, those holes in the fierce light, were deeper. In every black interior sat a man who had two of these excellent *billets*, each of which commanded thirty thousand francs. Such a possession brightens

the eyes, and enhances the savour of solitude, enabling a
man, as the artist would have said, to partake of the nature
of Fabre's tarantula, motionless at the angle of her tunnel.
But they found it no longer easy to remember the artist. His
jabbering, his laughter, even his final yelp, left no echo at
all. It was all gone, like the rattle and flash of yesterday's
thunderstorm.

So apart from the tasks of the morning and the evening,
performing which they were camouflaged by habit, they sat
in their houses alone. Their wives scarcely dared to speak to
them, and they were too rich to speak to each other. Guis
found it out, for it was no secret except to the world outside, and Guis was furious. But his wife rated him from
morning till night, and left him no energy for reproaching
his neighbours.

At the end of the week, Barilles sprang into existence in
the doorway of his house. His thumbs were stuck in his
belt, his face was flushed from lead colour to plum colour,
his bearing expressed an irritable resolution.

He crossed to Arago's, knocked, leaned against a door-
post. Arago, emerging, leaned against the other. They talked
for some little time of nothing at all. Then Barilles, throwing
away the stump of his cigarette, made an oblique and sympathetic reference to a certain small enclosure belonging to
Arago, on which there was a shed, a few vines, a considerable grove of olives. "It is the very devil," said Barilles,
"how the worm gets into the olive in these days. Such a
grove as that, at one time, might have been worth something."

"It is worse than the devil," said Arago. "Believe me or
not, my dear friend, in some years I get no more than three
thousand francs from that grove."

Barilles burst into what passes for laughter in this part of
the world. "Forgive me!" he said. "I thought you said three
thousand. Three hundred—yes. I suppose in a good year
you might make that very easily."

This conversation continued through phases of civility,
sarcasm, rage, fury and desperation until it ended with a
cordial handshake, and a sale of the enclosure to Barilles for

twenty-five thousand francs. The witnesses were called in; Barilles handed over one of his *billets*, and received five thousand in cash from the box Arago kept in his chimney. Everyone was delighted by the sale: it was felt that things were beginning to move in the village.

They were. Before the company separated, *pourparlers* were already started for the sale of Vigné's mules to Quès for eight thousand, the transfer of Lloubes's cork concession to Foiral for fifteen thousand, the marriage of Roustand's daughter to Vigné's brother with a dowry of twenty thousand, and the sale of a miscellaneous collection of brass objects belonging to Madame Arago for sixty-five francs, after some very keen bargaining.

Only Guis was left out in the cold, but on the way home, Lloubes, with his skin full of wine, ventured to step inside the outcast's doorway, and looked his wife Filomena up and down, from top to toe, three times. A mild interest, imperfectly concealed, softened the bitter and sullen expression upon the face of Guis.

This was a mere beginning. Soon properties began to change hands at a bewildering rate and at increasing prices. It was a positive boom. Change was constantly being dug out from under flagstones, from the strawy interiors of mattresses, from hollows in beams, and from holes in walls. With the release of these frozen credits the village blossomed like an orchid sprung from a dry stick. Wine flowed with every bargain. Old enemies shook hands. Elderly spinsters embraced young suitors. Wealthy widowers married young brides. Several of the weaker sort wore their best black every day. One of these was Lloubes, who spent his evenings in the house of Guis. Guis in the evenings would wander round the village, no longer sullen, and was seen cheapening a set of harness at Lafago's, a first-rate gun at Roustand's. There was talk of something very special by way of a fiesta after the grape harvest, but this was only whispered, lest the curé should hear of it on one of his visits.

Foiral, keeping up his reputation as leader, made a staggering proposal. It was nothing less than to improve the

mule track all the way from the metalled road on the rim of
the hills, so that motor trucks could visit the village. It was
objected that the wage bill would be enormous. "Yes," said
Foiral, "but we shall draw the wages ourselves. We shall get
half as much again for our produce."

The proposal was adopted. The mere boys of the village
now shared the prosperity. Barilles now called his little
shop "Grand Café Glacier de l'Univers et des Pyrénées."
The widow Loyau offered room, board, and clothing to
certain unattached young women, and gave select parties in
the evenings.

Barilles went to Perpignan and returned with a sprayer
that would double the yield of his new olive grove. Lloubes
went and returned with a positive bale of ladies' under-
clothing, designed, you would say, by the very devil himself.
Two or three keen card players went and returned with new
packs of cards, so lustrous that your hand seemed to be all
aces and kings. Vigné went, and returned with a long face.

The bargaining, increasing all the time, called for more
and more ready money. Foiral made a new proposal. "We
will all go to Perpignan, the whole damned lot of us, march
to the bank, thump down our *billets*, and show the little
cotton-backs whom the money belongs to. Boys, we'll leave
them without a franc."

"They will have the hundred and ten," said Quès.

"To hell with the hundred and ten!" said Foiral. "And,
boys, after that—well—ha! ha!—all men sin once. They say
the smell alone of one of those creatures is worth fifty
francs. Intoxicating! Stair carpets, red hair, every sort of
wickedness! Tomorrow!"

"Tomorrow!" they all cried, and on the morrow they went
off, in their stiffest clothes, their faces shining. Every man was
smoking like a chimney, and every man had washed his feet.

The journey was tremendous. They stopped the bus at
every café on the road, and saw nothing they didn't ask the
price of. In Perpignan they kept together in a close phalanx;
if the townspeople stared, our friends stared back twice as
hard. As they crossed over to the bank, "Where is Guis?"

said Foiral, affecting to look for him among their number. "Has he nothing due to him?" That set them all laughing. Try as they might, they couldn't hold their faces straight. They were still choking with laughter when the swing doors closed behind them.

◆ ──────────────────────────────── ◆

AN OUTPOST OF PROGRESS

Joseph Conrad

There were two white men in charge of the trading station. Kayerts, the chief, was short and fat; Carlier, the assistant, was tall, with a large head and a very broad trunk perched upon a long pair of thin legs. The third man on the staff was a Sierra Leone nigger, who maintained that his name was Henry Price. However, for some reason or other, the natives down the river had given him the name of Makola, and it stuck to him through all his wanderings about the country. He spoke English and French with a warbling accent, wrote a beautiful hand, understood bookkeeping, and cherished in his innermost heart the worship of evil spirits. His wife was a negress from Loanda, very large and very noisy. Three children rolled about in sunshine before the door of his low, shed-like dwelling. Makola, taciturn and impenetrable, despised the two white men. He had charge of a small clay storehouse with a dried-grass roof, and pretended to keep a correct account of beads, cotton cloth, red kerchiefs, brass wire, and other trade goods it contained. Be-

sides the storehouse and Makola's hut, there was only one
large building in the cleared ground of the station. It was
built neatly of reeds, with a veranda on all the four sides.
There were three rooms in it. The one in the middle was
the living room, and had two rough tables and a few stools
in it. The other two were the bedrooms for the white men.
Each had a bedstead and a mosquito net for all furniture.
The plank floor was littered with the belongings of the
white men; open half-empty boxes, torn wearing apparel,
old boots; all the things dirty, and all the things broken, that
accumulate mysteriously round untidy men. There was also
another dwelling place some distance away from the buildings. In it, under a tall cross much out of the perpendicular,
slept the man who had seen the beginning of all this; who
had planned and had watched the construction of this out-
post of progress. He had been, at home, an unsuccessful
painter who, weary of pursuing fame on an empty stomach,
had gone out there through high protections. He had been
the first chief of that station. Makola had watched the energetic artist die of fever in the just finished house with his
usual kind of "I told you so" indifference. Then, for a time,
he dwelt alone with his family, his account books, and the
Evil Spirit that rules the lands under the equator. He got on
very well with his god. Perhaps he had propitiated him by a
promise of more white men to play with, by and by. At any
rate the director of the Great Trading Company, coming up
in a steamer that resembled an enormous sardine box with a
flat-roofed shed erected on it, found the station in good
order, and Makola as usual quietly diligent. The director
had the cross put up over the first agent's grave, and ap-
pointed Kayerts to the post. Carlier was told off as second in
charge. The director was a man ruthless and efficient, who
at times, but very imperceptibly, indulged in grim humor.
He made a speech to Kayerts and Carlier, pointing out to
them the promising aspect of their station. The nearest
trading post was about three hundred miles away. It was an
exceptional opportunity for them to distinguish themselves
and to earn percentages on the trade. This appointment was

a favor done to beginners. Kayerts was moved almost to tears by his director's kindness. He would, he said, by doing his best, try to justify the flattering confidence, etc., etc. Kayerts had been in the Administration of the Telegraphs, and knew how to express himself correctly. Carlier, an ex-noncommissioned officer of cavalry in an army guaranteed from harm by several European powers, was less impressed. If there were commissions to get, so much the better; and, trailing a sulky glance over the river, the forests, the impenetrable bush that seemed to cut off the station from the rest of the world, he muttered between his teeth, "We shall see, very soon."

Next day, some bales of cotton goods and a few cases of provisions having been thrown on shore, the sardine-box steamer went off, not to return for another six months. On the deck the director touched his cap to the two agents, who stood on the bank waving their hats, and turning to an old servant of the Company on his passage to headquarters, said, "Look at those two imbeciles. They must be mad at home to send me such specimens. I told those fellows to plant a vegetable garden, build new storehouses and fences, and construct a landing stage. I bet nothing will be done! They won't know how to begin. I always thought the station on this river useless, and they just fit the station!"

"They will form themselves there," said the old stager with a quiet smile.

"At any rate, I am rid of them for six months," retorted the director.

The two men watched the steamer round the bend, then, ascending arm in arm the slope of the bank, returned to the station. They had been in this vast and dark country only a very short time, and as yet always in the midst of other white men, under the eye and guidance of their superiors. And now, dull as they were to the subtle influences of surroundings, they felt themselves very much alone, when suddenly left unassisted to face the wilderness; a wilderness rendered more strange, more incomprehensible by the mysterious glimpses of the vigorous life it contained. They were

two perfectly insignificant and incapable individuals, whose
existence is only rendered possible through the high organi-
zation of civilized crowds. Few men realize that their life,
the very essence of their character, their capabilities and
their audacities, are only the expression of their belief in the
safety of their surroundings. The courage, the composure,
the confidence; the emotions and principles; every great
and every insignificant thought belongs not to the individual
but to the crowd: to the crowd that believes blindly in the
irresistible force of its institutions and of its morals, in the
power of its police and of its opinion. But the contact with
pure unmitigated savagery, with primitive nature and primitive man, brings sudden and profound trouble into the
heart. To the sentiment of being alone of one's kind, to the
clear perception of the loneliness of one's thoughts, of one's
sensations—to the negation of the habitual, which is safe,
there is added the affirmation of the unusual, which is
dangerous; a suggestion of things vague, uncontrollable, and
repulsive, whose discomposing intrusion excites the imagination and tries the civilized nerves of the foolish and the
wise alike.

Kayerts and Carlier walked arm in arm, drawing close to
one another as children do in the dark, and they had the
same, not altogether unpleasant, sense of danger which one
half suspects to be imaginary. They chatted persistently in
familiar tones. "Our station is prettily situated," said one.
The other assented with enthusiasm, enlarging volubly on
the beauties of the situation. Then they passed near the
grave. "Poor devil!" said Kayerts. "He died of fever, didn't
he?" muttered Carlier, stopping short. "Why," retorted
Kayerts, with indignation, "I've been told that the fellow
exposed himself recklessly to the sun. The climate here,
everybody says, is not at all worse than at home, as long as
you keep out of the sun. Do you hear that, Carlier? I am
chief here, and my orders are that you should not expose
yourself to the sun!" He assumed his superiority jocularly,
but his meaning was serious. The idea that he would, perhaps, have to bury Carlier and remain alone, gave him an

inward shiver. He felt suddenly that this Carlier was more precious to him here, in the center of Africa, than a brother could be anywhere else. Carlier, entering into the spirit of the thing, made a military salute and answered in a brisk tone, "Your orders shall be attended to, chief!" Then he burst out laughing, slapped Kayerts on the back and shouted, "We shall let life run easily here! Just sit still and gather in the ivory those savages will bring. This country has its good points, after all!" They both laughed loudly while Carlier thought: "That poor Kayerts; he is so fat and unhealthy. It would be awful if I had to bury him here. He is a man I respect." . . . Before they reached the veranda of their house they called one another "my dear fellow."

The first day they were very active, pottering about with hammers and nails and red calico, to put up curtains, make their house habitable and pretty; resolved to settle down comfortably to their new life. For them an impossible task. To grapple effectually with even purely material problems requires more serenity of mind and more lofty courage than people generally imagine. No two beings could have been more unfitted for such a struggle. Society, not from any tenderness, but because of its strange needs, had taken care of those two men, forbidding them all independent thought, all initiative, all departure from routine; and forbidding it under pain of death. They could only live on condition of being machines. And now, released from the fostering care of men with pens behind the ears, or of men with gold lace on the sleeves, they were like those life-long prisoners who, liberated after many years, do not know what use to make of their freedom. They did not know what use to make of their faculties, being both, through want of practice, incapable of independent thought.

At the end of two months Kayerts often would say, "If it was not for my Melie, you wouldn't catch me here." Melie was his daughter. He had thrown up his post in the Admin-stration of the Telegraphs, though he had been for seven-een years perfectly happy there, to earn a dowry for his girl. His wife was dead, and the child was being brought up by his sisters. He regretted the streets, the pavements, the cafés, his friends of many years; all the things he used to see, day after day; all the thoughts suggested by familiar things—the thoughts effortless, monotonous, and soothing of a Government clerk; he regretted all the gossip, the small enmities, the mild venom, and the little jokes of Government offices. "If I had had a decent brother-in-law," Carlier would remark, "a fellow with a heart, I would not be here." He had left the army and had made himself so obnoxious to his family by his laziness and impudence, that an exasperated brother-in-law had made superhuman efforts to procure him an appointment in the Company as a second-class agent. Having not a penny in the world he was compelled to accept this means of livelihood as soon as it became quite clear to him that there was nothing more to squeeze out of his relations. He, like Kayerts, regretted his old life. He regretted the clink of saber and spurs on a fine afternoon, the barrack-room witticisms, the girls of garrison towns; but, besides, he had also a sense of grievance. He was evidently a much ill-used man. This made him moody, at times. But the two men got on well together in the fellowship of their stupidity and laziness. Together they did nothing, absolutely nothing, and enjoyed the sense of the idleness for which they were paid. And in time they came to feel something resembling affection for one another.

They lived like blind men in a large room, aware only of what came in contact with them (and of that only imperfectly), but unable to see the general aspect of things. The river, the forest, all the great land throbbing with life, were like a great emptiness. Even the brilliant sunshine disclosed nothing intelligible. Things appeared and disappeared before their eyes in an unconnected and aimless kind of way. The river seemed to come from nowhere and flow nowhither. It flowed through a void. Out of that void, at times, came canoes, and men with spears in their hands would suddenly crowd the yard of the station. They were naked, glossy black, ornamented with snowy shells and glistening brass wire, perfect of limb. They made an uncouth babbling noise when they spoke, moved in a stately manner, and sent quick, wild glances out of their startled, never-resting eyes. Those warriors would squat in long rows, four or more deep, before the veranda, while their chiefs bargained for hours with Makola over an elephant tusk. Kayerts sat on his chair and looked down on the proceedings, understanding nothing. He stared at them with his round blue eyes, called out to Carlier, "Here, look! look at that fellow there—and that other one, to the left. Did you ever see such a face? Oh, the funny brute!"

Carlier, smoking native tobacco in a short wooden pipe, would swagger up twirling his mustaches, and surveying the warriors with haughty indulgence, would say:

"Fine animals. Brought any bone? Yes? It's not any too soon. Look at the muscles of that fellow—third from the end. I wouldn't care to get a punch on the nose from him. Fine arms, but legs no good below the knee. Couldn't make cavalry men of them." And after glancing down complacently at his own shanks, he always concluded, "Pah! Don't they stink! You, Makola! Take that herd over to the fetish" (the storehouse was in every station called the fetish, perhaps because of the spirit of civilization it contained) "and give them up some of the rubbish you keep there. I'd rather see it full of bone than full of rags."

Kayerts approved.

"Yes, yes! Go and finish that palaver over there, Mr. Makola. I will come round when you are ready, to weigh the tusk. We must be careful." Then turning to his companion: "This is the tribe that lives down the river; they are rather aromatic. I remember, they had been once before here. D'ye hear that row? What a fellow has got to put up with in this dog of a country! My head is split."

Such profitable visits were rare. For days the two pioneers of trade and progress would look on their empty courtyard in the vibrating brilliance of vertical sunshine. Below the high bank, the silent river flowed on glittering and steady. On the sands in the middle of the stream, hippos and alligators sunned themselves side by side. And stretching away in all directions, surrounding the insignificant cleared spot of the trading post, immense forests, hiding fateful complications of fantastic life, lay in the eloquent silence of mute greatness. The two men understood nothing, cared for nothing but for the passage of days that separated them from the steamer's return. Their predecessor had left some torn books. They took up these wrecks of novels, and, as they had never read anything of the kind before, they were surprised and amused. Then during long days there were interminable and silly discussions about plots and personages. In the center of Africa they made acquaintance of Richelieu and of d'Artagnan, of Hawk's Eye and of Father Goriot, and of many other people. All these imaginary personages became subjects for gossip as if they had been living friends. They discounted their virtues, suspected their motives, decried their successes; were scandalized at their duplicity or were doubtful about their courage. The accounts of crimes filled them with indignation, while tender or pathetic passages moved them deeply. Carlier cleared his throat and said in a soldierly voice, "What nonsense!" Kayerts, his round eyes suffused with tears, his fat cheeks quivering, rubbed his bald head, and declared, "This is a splendid book. I had no idea there were such clever fellows in the world." They also found some old copies of a home paper. That print discussed what it was pleased to call "Our Colonial Expansion" in high-flown language. It spoke much of the rights and duties of civilization, of the sacredness of the civilizing work, and extolled the merits of those who went about bringing light, and faith and commerce to the dark places of the earth. Carlier and Kayerts read, wondered, and began to think better of themselves. Carlier said one evening, waving his hand about, "In a hundred years, there will be perhaps a town here. Quays, and warehouses, and barracks, and—and—billiard rooms. Civilization, my boy, and virtue—and all. And then, chaps will read that two good fellows, Kayerts and Carlier, were the first civilized men to live in this very spot!" Kayerts nodded,

"Yes, it is a consolation to think of that." They seemed to forget their dead predecessor; but, early one day, Carlier went out and replanted the cross firmly. "It used to make me squint whenever I walked that way," he explained to Kayerts over the morning coffee. "It made me squint, leaning over so much. So I just planted it upright. And solid, I promise you! I suspended myself with both hands to the cross-piece. Not a move. Oh, I did that properly."

At times Gobila came to see them. Gobila was the chief of the neighboring villages. He was a gray-headed savage, thin and black, with a white cloth round his loins and a mangy panther skin hanging over his back. He came up with long strides of his skeleton legs, swinging a staff as tall as himself, and, entering the common room of the station, would squat on his heels to the left of the door. There he sat, watching Kayerts, and now and then making a speech which the other did not understand. Kayerts, without interrupting his occupation, would from time to time say in a friendly manner: "How goes it, you old image?" and they would smile at one another. The two whites had a liking for that old and incomprehensible creature, and called him Father Gobila. Gobila's manner was paternal, and he seemed really to love all white men. They all appeared to him very young, indistinguishably alike (except for stature), and he knew that they were all brothers, and also immortal. The death of the artist, who was the first white man whom he knew intimately, did not disturb this belief, because he was firmly convinced that the white stranger had pretended to die and got himself buried for some mysterious purpose of his own, into which it was useless to inquire. Perhaps it was his way of going home to his own country? At any rate, these were his brothers, and he transferred his absurd affection to them. They returned it in a way. Carlier slapped him on the back, and recklessly struck off matches for his amusement. Kayerts was always ready to let him have a sniff at the ammonia bottle. In short, they behaved just like that other white creature that had hidden itself in a hole in the ground. Gobila considered them attentively. Perhaps they were the same being with the other—or one of them was. He couldn't decide—clear up that mystery; but he remained always very friendly. In consequence of that friendship the women of Gobila's village walked in single file through the reedy grass, bringing every morning to the station, fowls, and sweet potatoes, and palm wine, and sometimes a goat. The Company never provisions the stations fully, and the agents required those local supplies to live. They had them through the good will of Gobila, and lived well. Now and then one of them had a bout of fever, and the other nursed him with gentle devotion. They did not think much of it. It left them weaker, and their appearance changed for the worse. Carlier was hollow-eyed and irritable. Kayerts showed a drawn, flabby face above the rotundity of his stomach, which gave him a weird aspect. But being constantly together, they did not notice the change that took place gradually in their appearance, and also in their dispositions.

Five months passed in that way.

Then, one morning, as Kayerts and Carlier, l   nging in their chairs under the veranda, talked about the approaching visit of the steamer, a knot of armed men came out of the forest and advanced towards the station. They were strangers to that part of the country. They were tall, slight, draped classically from neck to heel in blue fringed cloths, and carried percussion muskets over their bare right shoulders. Makola showed signs of excitement, and ran out of the storehouse (where he spent all his days) to meet these visitors. They came into the courtyard and looked about them with steady, scornful glances. Their leader, a powerful and determined-looking Negro with bloodshot eyes, stood in front of the veranda and made a long speech. He gesticulated much, and ceased very suddenly.

There was something in his intonation, in the sounds of the long sentences he used, that startled the two whites. It was like a reminiscence of something not exactly familiar, and yet resembling the speech of civilized men. It sounded like one of those impossible languages which sometimes we hear in our dreams.

"What lingo is that?" said the amazed Carlier. "In the first moment I fancied the fellow was going to speak French. Anyway, it is a different kind of gbberish to what we ever heard."

"Yes," replied Kayerts. "Hey, Makola, what does he say? Where do they come from? Who are they?"

But Makola, who seemed to be standing on hot bricks, answered hurriedly, "I don't know. They come from very far. Perhaps Mrs. Price will understand. They are perhaps bad men."

The leader, after waiting for a while, said something sharply to Makola, who shook his head. Then the man, after looking round, noticed Makola's hut and walked over there. The next moment Mrs. Makola was heard speaking with great volubility. The other strangers—they were six in all—strolled about with an air of ease, put their heads through the door of the storeroom, congregated round the grave, pointed understandingly at the cross, and generally made themselves at home.

"I don't like those chaps—and, I say, Kayerts, they must be from the coast; they've got firearms," observed the sagacious Carlier.

Kayerts also did not like those chaps. They both, for the first time, became aware that they lived in conditions where the unusual may be dangerous, and that there was no power on earth outside of themselves to stand between them and the unusual. They became uneasy, went in and loaded their revolvers. Kayerts said, "We must order Makola to tell them to go away before dark."

The strangers left in the afternoon, after eating a meal prepared for them by Mrs. Makola. The immense woman was excited, and talked much with the visitors. She rattled away shrilly, pointing here and there at the forests and at the river. Makola sat apart and watched. At times he got up and whispered to his wife. He accompanied the strangers across the ravine at the back of the station-ground, and returned slowly looking very thoughtful. When questioned by the white men he was very strange, seemed not to understand, seemed to have forgotten French—seemed to have forgotten how to speak altogether. Kayerts and Carlier agreed that the nigger had had too much palm wine.

There was some talk about keeping a watch in turn, but in the evening everything seemed so quiet and peaceful that they retired as usual. All night they were disturbed by a lot of drumming in the villages. A deep, rapid roll near by would be followed by another far off—then all ceased. Soon short appeals would rattle out here and there, then all mingle together, increase, become vigorous and sustained, would spread out over the forest, roll through the night, unbroken and ceaseless, near and far, as if the whole land had been one immense drum booming out steadily an appeal to heaven. And through the deep and tremendous noise sudden yells that resembled snatches of songs from a madhouse darted shrill and high in discordant jets of sound which seemed to rush far above the earth and drive all peace from under the stars.

Carlier and Kayerts slept badly. They both thought they had heard shots fired during the night—but they could not agree as to the direction. In the morning Makola was gone somewhere. He returned about noon with one of yesterday's strangers, and eluded all Kayerts' attempts to close with him: had become deaf apparently. Kayerts wondered. Carlier, who had been fishing off the bank, came back and remarked while he showed his catch, "The niggers seem to be in a deuce of a stir; I wonder what's up. I saw about fifteen canoes cross the river during the two hours I was there fishing." Kayerts, worried, said, "Isn't this Makola very queer today?" Carlier advised, "Keep all our men together in case of some trouble."

II

There were ten station men who had been left by the Director. Those fellows, having engaged themselves to the Company for six months (without having any idea of a month in particular and only a very faint notion of time in general), had been serving the cause of progress for upwards of two years. Belonging to a tribe from a very distant part of the land of darkness and sorrow, they did not run away, naturally supposing that as wandering strangers they would be killed by the inhabitants of the country; in which they were right. They lived in straw huts on the slope of a ravine overgrown with reedy grass, just behind the station buildings. They were not happy, regretting the festive incantations, the sorceries, the human sacrifices of their own land; where they also had parents, brothers, sisters, admired chiefs, respected magicians, loved friends, and other ties supposed generally to be human. Besides, the rice rations served out by the Company did not agree with them, being a food unknown to their land, and to which they could not get used. Consequently they were unhealthy and miserable. Had they been of any other tribe they would have made up their minds to die—for nothing is easier to certain savages than suicide—and so have escaped from the puzzling difficulties of existence. But belonging, as they did, to a warlike tribe with filed teeth, they had more grit, and went on stupidly living through disease and sorrow. They did very little work, and had lost their splendid physique. Carlier and Kayerts doctored them assiduously without being able to bring them back into condition again. They were mustered every morning and told off to different tasks—grass-cutting, fence-building, tree-felling, etc., etc., which no power on earth could induce them to execute efficiently. The two whites had practically very little control over them.

In the afternoon Makola came over to the big house and found Kayerts watching three heavy columns of smoke rising above the forests. "What is that?" asked Kayerts. "Some villages burn," answered Makola, who seemed to have regained his wits. Then he said abruptly: "We have got very little ivory; bad six months' trading. Do you like get a little more ivory?"

"Yes," said Kayerts, eagerly. He thought of percentages which were low.

"Those men who came yesterday are traders from Loanda

who have got more ivory than they can carry home. Shall I buy? I know their camp."

"Certainly," said Kayerts. "What are those traders?"

"Bad fellows," said Makola, indifferently. "They fight with people, and catch women and children. They are bad men, and got guns. There is a great disturbance in the country. Do you want ivory?"

"Yes," said Kayerts. Makola said nothing for a while. Then: "Those workmen of ours are no good at all," he muttered, looking round. "Station in very bad order, sir. Director will growl. Better get a fine lot of ivory, then he say nothing."

"I can't help it; the men won't work," said Kayerts. "When will you get that ivory?"

"Very soon," said Makola. "Perhaps tonight. You leave it to me, and keep indoors, sir. I think you had better give some palm wine to our men to make a dance this evening. Enjoy themselves. Work better tomorrow. There's plenty palm wine—gone a little sour."

Kayerts said "yes," and Makola, with his own hands carried big calabashes to the door of his hut. They stood there till the evening, and Mrs. Makola looked into every one. The men got them at sunset. When Kayerts and Carlier retired, a big bonfire was flaring before the men's huts. They could hear their shouts and drumming. Some men from Gobila's village had joined the station hands, and the entertainment was a great success.

In the middle of the night, Carlier waking suddenly, heard a man shout loudly; then a shot was fired. Only one. Carlier ran out and met Kayerts on the veranda. They were both startled. As they went across the yard to call Makola, they saw shadows moving in the night. One of them cried, "Don't shoot! It's me, Price." Then Makola appeared close to them. "Go back, go back, please," he urged, "you spoil all." "There are strange men about," said Carlier. "Never mind; I know," said Makola. Then he whispered, "All right. Bring ivory. Say nothing! I know my business." The two white men reluctantly went back to the house, but did not sleep. They heard footsteps, whispers, some groans. It seemed as if a lot of men came in, dumped heavy things on the ground, squabbled a long time, then went away. They lay on their hard beds and thought: "This Makola is invaluable." In the morning Carlier came out, very sleepy, and pulled at the cord of the big bell. The station hands mustered every morning to the sound of the bell. That morning nobody came. Kayerts turned out also, yawning. Across the yard they saw Makola come out of his hut, a tin basin of soapy water in his hand. Makola, a civilized nigger, was very neat in his person. He threw the soapsuds skillfully over a wretched little yellow cur he had, then turning his face to the agent's house, he shouted from the distance, "All the men gone last night!"

They heard him plainly, but in their surprise they both yelled out together: "What!" Then they stared at one another. "We are in a proper fix now," growled Carlier. "It's incredible!" muttered Kayerts. "I will go to the huts and see," said Carlier, striding off. Makola coming up found Kayerts standing alone.

"I can hardly believe it," said Kayerts tearfully. "We took care of them as if they had been our children."

"They went with the coast people," said Makola after a moment of hesitation.

"What do I care with whom they went—the ungrateful brutes!" exclaimed the other. Then with sudden suspicion, and looking hard at Makola, he added: "What do you know about it?"

Makola moved his shoulders, looking down on the ground. "What do I know? I think only. Will you come and look at the ivory I've got there? It is a fine lot. You never saw such."

He moved towards the store. Kayerts followed him mechanically, thinking about the incredible desertion of the men. On the ground before the door of the fetish lay six splendid tusks.

"What did you give for it?" asked Kayerts, after surveying the lot with satisfaction.

"No regular trade," said Makola. "They brought the ivory and gave it to me. I told them to take what they most wanted in the station. It is a beautiful lot. No station can show such tusks. Those traders wanted carriers badly, and our men were no good here. No trade, no entry in books; all correct."

Kayerts nearly burst with indignation. "Why!" he shouted, "I believe you have sold our men for these tusks!" Makola stood impassive and silent. "I—I—will—I," stuttered Kayerts. "You fiend!" he yelled out.

"I did the best for you and the Company," said Makola, imperturbably. "Why you shout so much? Look at this tusk."

"I dismiss you! I will report you—I won't look at the tusk. I forbid you to touch them. I order you to throw them into the river. You—you!"

"You very red, Mr. Kayerts. If you are so irritable in the sun, you will get fever and die—like the first chief!" pronounced Makola impressively.

They stood still, contemplating one another with intense eyes, as if they had been looking with effort across immense distances. Kayerts shivered. Makola had meant no more than he said, but his words seemed to Kayerts full of ominous menace! He turned sharply and went away to the house. Makola retired into the bosom of his family; and the tusks, left lying before the store, looked very large and valuable in the sunshine.

Carlier came back on the veranda. "They're all gone, hey?" asked Kayerts from the far end of the common room in a muffled voice. "You did not find anybody?"

"Oh, yes," said Carlier, "I found one of Gobila's people lying dead before the huts—shot through the body. We heard that shot last night."

Kayerts came out quickly. He found his companion staring grimly over the yard at the tusks, away by the store. They both sat in silence for a while. Then Kayerts related his conversation with Makola. Carlier said nothing. At the midday meal they ate very little. They hardly exchanged a word that day. A great silence seemed to lie heavily over the station and press on their lips. Makola did not open the store; he spent the day playing with his children. He lay full-length on a mat outside his door, and the youngsters sat on his chest and clambered all over him. It was a touching picture. Mrs. Makola was busy cooking all day as usual. The white men made a somewhat better meal in the evening. Afterwards, Carlier smoking his pipe strolled over to the store; he stood for a long time over the tusks, touched one or two with his foot, even tried to lift the largest one by its small end. He came back to his chief, who had not stirred from the veranda, threw himself in the chair and said:

"I can see it! They were pounced upon while they slept heavily after drinking all that palm wine you've allowed Makola to give them. A put-up job! See? The worst is, some of Gobila's people were there, and got carried off too, no doubt. The least drunk woke up, and got shot for his sobriety. This is a funny country. What will you do now?"

"We can't touch it, of course," said Kayerts.

"Of course not," assented Carlier.

"Slavery is an awful thing," stammered out Kayerts in an unsteady voice.

"Frightful—the sufferings," grunted Carlier with conviction.

They believed their words. Everybody shows a respectful deference to certain sounds that he and his fellows can make. But about feelings people really know nothing. We talk with indignation or enthusiasm; we talk about oppression, cruelty, crime, devotion, self-sacrifice, virtue, and we know nothing real beyond the words. Nobody knows what suffering or sacrifice mean—except, perhaps the victims of the mysterious purpose of these illusions.

Next morning they saw Makola very busy setting up in the yard the big scales used for weighing ivory. By and by Carlier said: "What's that filthy scoundrel up to?" and lounged out into the yard. Kayerts followed. They stood watching. Makola took no notice. When the balance was swung true, he tried to lift a tusk into the scale. It was too heavy. He looked up helplessly without a word, and for a minute they stood round that balance as mute and still as three statues. Suddenly Carlier said: "Catch hold of the other end, Makola— you beast!" and together they swung the tusk up. Kayerts trembled in every limb. He muttered, "I say! O! I say!" and putting his hand in his pocket found there a dirty bit of paper and the stump of a pencil. He turned his back on the others, as if about to do something tricky, and noted stealthily the weights which Carlier shouted out to him with unnecessary loudness. When all was over Makola whispered to himself: "The sun's very strong here for the tusks." Carlier said to Kayerts in a careless tone: "I say, chief, I might just as well give him a lift with this lot into the store."

As they were going back to the house Kayerts observed with a sigh: "It had to be done." And Carlier said: "It's deplorable, but, the men being Company's men the ivory is Company's ivory. We must look after it." "I will report to the Director, of course," said Kayerts. "Of course; let him decide," approved Carlier.

At midday they made a hearty meal. Kayerts sighed from time to time. Whenevr they mentioned Makola's name they always added to it an opprobrious epithet. It eased their conscience. Makola gave himself a half-holiday, and bathed his children in the river. No one from Gobila's villages came near the station that day. No one came the next day, and the next, nor for a whole week. Gobila's people might have been dead and buried for any sign of life they gave. But they were only mourning for those they had lost by the witchcraft of white men, who had brought wicked people into their country. The wicked people were gone, but fear remained. Fear always remains. A man may destroy everything within himself, love and hate and belief, and even doubt; but as long as he clings to life he cannot destroy fear: the fear, subtle, indestructible, and terrible, that pervades his being; that tinges his thoughts; that lurks in his heart; that watches on his lips the struggle of his last breath. In his fear, the mild old Gobila offered extra human sacrifices to all the Evil Spirits that had taken possession of his white friends. His heart was heavy. Some warriors spoke about burning and killing, but the cautious old savage dissuaded them. Who could foresee the woe those mysterious creatures, if irritated, might bring? They should be left alone. Perhaps in time they would disappear into the earth as the first one had disappeared. His people must keep away from them, and hope for the best.

Kayerts and Carlier did not disappear, but remained above on this earth, that, somehow, they fancied had become bigger and very empty. It was not the absolute and dumb solitude of the post that impressed them so much as an inarticulate feeling that something from within them was gone, something that worked for their safety, and had kept the wilderness from interfering with their hearts. The images of home; the memory of people like them, of men that thought and felt as they used to think and feel, receded into distances made indistinct by the glare of unclouded sunshine. And out of the great silence of the surrounding wilderness, its very hopelessness and savagery seemed to approach them nearer, to draw them gently, to look upon them, to envelop them with a solicitude irresistible, familiar, and disgusting.

Days lengthened into weeks, then into months. Gobila's people drummed and yelled to every new moon, as of yore, but kept away from the station. Makola and Carlier tried once in a canoe to open communications, but were received with a shower of arrows, and had to fly back to the station for dear life. That attempt set the country up and down the river into an uproar that could be very distinctly heard for days. The steamer was late. At first they spoke of delay jauntily, then anxiously, then gloomily. The matter was becoming serious. Stores were running short. Carlier cast his lines off the bank, but the river was low, and the fish kept out in the stream. They dared not stroll far away from the station to shoot. Moreover, there was no game in the impenetrable forest. Once Carlier shot a hippo in the river. They had no boat to secure it, and it sank. When it floated up it drifted away, and Gobila's people secured the carcass. It was the occasion for a national holiday, but Carlier had a

fit of rage over it and talked about the necessity of extermi-
nating all the niggers before the country could be made
habitable. Kayerts mooned about silently; spent hours looking at the portrait of his Melie. It represented a little girl
with long bleached tresses and a rather sour face. His legs
were much swollen, and he could hardly walk. Carlier,
undermined by fever, could not swagger any more, but kept
tottering about, still with a devil-may-care air, as became a
man who remembered his crack regiment. He had become
hoarse, sarcastic, and inclined to say unpleasant things. He
called it "being frank with you." They had long ago reck-
oned their percentages on trade, including in them that last
deal of "this infamous Makola." They had also concluded not
to say anything about it. Kayerts hesitated at first—was
afraid of the Director.

"He has seen worse things done on the quiet," maintained Carlier, with a hoarse laugh. "Trust him! He won't
thank you if you blab. He is no better than you or me. Who
will talk if we hold our tongues? There is nobody here."

That was the root of the trouble! There was nobody there;
and being left there alone with their weakness, they became
daily more like a pair of accomplices than like a couple of
devoted friends. They had heard nothing from home for
eight months. Every evening they said, "Tomorrow we shall
see the steamer." But one of the Company's steamers had
been wrecked, and the Director was busy with the other,
relieving very distant and important stations on the main
river. He thought that the useless station, and the useless
men, could wait. Meantime Kayerts and Carlier lived on
rice boiled without salt, and cursed the Company, all Africa,
and the day they were born. One must have lived on such
diet to discover what ghastly trouble the necessity of swallowing one's food may become. There was literally nothing
else in the station but rice and coffee; they drank the coffee
without sugar. The last fifteen lumps Kayerts had solemnly
locked away in his box, together with a half-bottle of cognac,
"in case of sickness," he explained. Carlier approved. "When
one is sick," he said, "any little extra like that is cheering."

They waited. Rank grass began to sprout over the court-yard. The bell never rang now. Days passed, silent, exasperating, and slow. When the two men spoke, they snarled; and their silences were bitter, as if tinged by the bitterness of their thoughts.

One day afer a lunch of boiled rice, Carlier put down his cup untasted, and said: "Hang it all! Let's have a decent cup of coffee for once. Bring out that sugar, Kayerts!"

"For the sick," muttered Kayerts, without looking up.

"For the sick," mocked Carlier. "Bosh! . . . Well! I am sick."

"You are no more sick than I am, and I go without," said Kayerts in a peaceful tone.

"Come! Out with that sugar, you stingy old slave dealer."

Kayerts looked up quickly. Carlier was smiling with marked insolence. And suddenly it seemed to Kayerts that he had never seen that man before. Who was he? He knew nothing about him. What was he capable of? There was a surprising flash of violent emotion within him, as if in the presence of something undreamt-of, dangerous, and final. But he managed to pronounce with composure:

"That joke is in very bad taste. Don't repeat it."

"Joke!" said Carlier, hitching himself forward on his seat. "I am hungry—I am sick—I don't joke! I hate hypocrites. You are a hypocrite. You are a slave dealer. I am a slave dealer. There's nothing but slave dealers in this cursed country. I mean to have sugar in my coffee today, anyhow!"

"I forbid you to speak to me in that way," said Kayerts with a fair show of resolution.

"You!—What?" shouted Carlier, jumping up.

Kayerts stood up also. "I am your chief," he began, trying to master the shakiness of his voice.

"What?" yelled the other. "Who's chief? There's no chief here. There's nothing here: there's nothing but you and I. Fetch the sugar—you pot-bellied ass."

"Hold your tongue. Go out of this room," screamed Kayerts. "I dismiss you—you scoundrel!"

Carlier swung a stool. All at once he looked dangerously

in earnest. "You flabby, good-for-nothing civilian—take that!" he howled.

Kayerts dropped under the table, and the stool struck the grass inner wall of the room. Then, as Carlier was trying to upset the table, Kayerts in desperation made a blind rush, head low, like a cornered pig would do, and overturning his friend, bolted along the veranda, and into his room. He locked the door, snatched his revolver, and stood panting. In less than a minute Carlier was kicking at the door furiously, howling, "If you don't bring out that sugar, I will shoot you at sight, like a dog. Now then—one—two—three. You won't? I will show you who's the master."

Kayerts thought the door would fall in, and scrambled through the square hole that served for a window in his room. There was then the whole breadth of the house between them. But the other was apparently not strong enough to break in the door, and Kayerts heard him running round. Then he also began to run laboriously on his swollen legs. He ran as quickly as he could, grasping the revolver, and unable yet to understand what was happening to him. He saw in succession Makola's house, the store, the river, the ravine, and the low bushes; and he saw all those things again as he ran for the second time round the house. Then again they flashed past him. That morning he could not have walked a yard without a groan.

And now he ran. He ran fast enough to keep out of sight of the other man.

Then as, weak and desperate, he thought, "Before I finish the next round I shall die," he heard the other man stumble heavily, then stop. He stopped also. He had the back and Carlier the front of the house, as before. He heard him drop into a chair cursing, and suddenly his own legs gave way, and he slid down into a sitting posture with his back to the wall. His mouth was as dry as a cinder, and his face was wet with perspiration—and tears. What was it all about? He thought it must be a horrible illusion; he thought he was dreaming; he thought he was going mad! After a while he collected his senses. What did they quarrel about? That sugar! How absurd! He would give it to him—didn't want it himself. And he began scrambling to his feet with a sudden feeling of security. But before he had fairly stood upright, a common-sense reflection occurred to him and drove him back into despair. He thought: "If I give way now to that brute of a soldier, he will begin this horror again tomorrow— and the day after—every day—raise other pretensions, trample on me, torture me, make me his slave—and I will be lost! Lost! The steamer may not come for days—may never come." He shook so that he had to sit down on the floor again. He shivered forlornly. He felt he could not, would not move any more. He was completely distracted by the sudden perception that the position was without issue—that death and life had in a moment become equally difficult and terrible.

All at once he heard the other push his chair back; and he leaped to his feet with extreme facility. He listened and got confused. Must run again! Right or left? He heard footsteps. He darted to the left, grasping his revolver, and at the very same instant, as it seemed to him, they came into violent collision. Both shouted with surprise. A loud explosion took place between them; a roar of red fire, thick smoke; and Kayerts, deafened and blinded, rushed back thinking: "I am hit—it's all over." He expected the other to come round—to gloat over his agony. He caught hold of an upright of the roof—"All over!" Then he heard a crashing fall on the other side of the house, as if somebody had tumbled headlong over a chair—then silence. Nothing more happened. He did not die. Only his shoulder felt as if it had been badly wrenched, and he had lost his revolver. He was disarmed and helpless! He waited for his fate. The other man made no sound. It was a stratagem. He was stalking him now! Along what side? Perhaps he was taking aim this very minute!

After a few moments of an agony frightful and absurd, he decided to go and meet his doom. He was prepared for every surrender. He turned the corner, steadying himself with one hand on the wall; made a few paces, and nearly swooned. He had seen on the floor, protruding past the other corner, a pair of turned-up feet. A pair of white naked feet in red slippers. He felt deadly sick, and stood for a time in profound darkness. Then Makola appeared before him, saying quietly: "Come along, Mr. Kayerts. He is dead." He burst into tears of gratitude; a loud, sobbing fit of crying. After a time he found himself sitting in a chair and looking at Carlier, who lay stretched on his back. Makola was kneeling over the body.

"Is this your revolver?" asked Makola, getting up.

"Yes," said Kayerts; then he added very quickly, "He ran after me to shoot me—you saw!"

"Yes, I saw," said Makola. 'There is only one revolver; where's his?"

"Don't know," whispered Kayerts in a voice that had become suddenly very faint.

"I will go and look for it," said the other, gently. He made the round along the veranda, while Kayerts sat still and looked at the corpse. Makola came back empty-handed, stood in deep thought, then stepped quietly into the dead man's room, and came out directly with a revolver, which he held up before Kayerts. Kayerts shut his eyes. Everything was going round. He found life more terrible and difficult than death. He had shot an unarmed man.

After meditating for a while, Makola said softly, pointing at the dead man who lay there with his right eye blown out:

"He died of fever." Kayerts looked at him with a stony stare. "Yes," repeated Makola, thoughtfully, stepping over the corpse, "I think he died of fever. Bury him tomorrow."

And he went away slowly to his expectant wife, leaving the two white men alone on the veranda.

Night came, and Kayerts sat unmoving on his chair. He sat quiet as if he had taken a dose of opium. The violence of the emotions he had passed through produced a feeling of exhausted serenity. He had plumbed in one short afternoon the depths of horror and despair, and now found repose in the conviction that life had no more secrets for him: neither had death! He sat by the corpse thinking; thinking very actively, thinking very new thoughts. He seemed to have broken loose from himself altogether. His old thoughts, convictions, likes and dislikes, things he respected and things he abhorred, appeared in their true light at last! Appeared contemptible and childish, false and ridiculous. He reveled in his new wisdom while he sat by the man he had killed. He argued with himself about all things under heaven with that kind of wrongheaded lucidity which may be observed in some lunatics. Incidentally he reflected that the fellow dead there had been a noxious beast anyway; that men died every day in thousands; perhaps in hundreds of thousands— who could tell?—and that in the number, that one death could not possibly make any difference; couldn't have any importance, at least to a thinking creature. He, Kayerts, was a thinking creature. He had been all his life, till that moment, a believer in a lot of nonsense like the rest of mankind—who are fools; but now he thought! He knew! He was at peace; he was familiar with the highest wisdom! Then he tried to imagine himself dead, and Carlier sitting in his chair watching him; and his attempt met with such unexpected success, that in a very few moments he became not at all sure who was dead and who was alive. This extraordinary achievement of his fancy startled him, however, and by a clever and timely effort of mind he saved himself just in time from becoming Carlier. His heart thumped, and he felt hot all over at the thought of that danger. Carlier! What a beastly thing! To compose his now disturbed nerves—and no wonder!—he tried to whistle a little. Then, suddenly, he fell asleep, or thought he had slept; but at any rate there was a fog, and somebody had whistled in the fog.

He stood up. The day had come, and a heavy mist had descended upon the land: the mist penetrating, enveloping, and silent; the morning mist of tropical lands; the mist that clings and kills; the mist white and deadly, immaculate and poisonous. He stood up, saw the body, and threw his arms above his head with a cry like that of a man who, waking from a trance, finds himself immured forever in a tomb. *"Help! . . . My God!"*

A shriek inhuman, vibrating and sudden, pierced like a sharp dart the white shroud of that land of sorrow. Three short, impatient screeches followed, and then, for a time, the fog-wreaths rolled on, undisturbed, through a formidable silence. Then many more shrieks, rapid and piercing, like the yells of some exasperated and ruthless creature, rent the air. Progress was calling to Kayerts from the river. Progress and civilization and all the virtues. Society was calling to its accomplished child to come, to be taken care of, to be instructed, to be judged, to be condemned; it called him to return to that rubbish heap from which he had wandered away, so that justice could be done.

Kayerts heard and understood. He stumbled out of the veranda, leaving the other man quite alone for the first time since they had been thrown there together. He groped his way through the fog, calling in his ignorance upon the invisible heaven to undo its work. Makola flitted by in the mist, shouting as he ran:

"Steamer! Steamer! They can't see. They whistle for the station. I go ring the bell. Go down to the landing, sir. I ring."

He disappeared, Kayerts stood still. He looked upwards; the fog rolled low over his head. He looked round like a man who has lost his way; and he saw a dark smudge, a cross-shaped stain, upon the shifting purity of the mist. As he began to stumble towards it, the station bell rang in a tumultuous peal its answer to the impatient clamor of the steamer.

The Managing Director of the Great Civilizing Company (since we know that civilization follows trade) landed first, and incontinently lost sight of the steamer. The fog down by the river was exceedingly dense; above, at the station, the bell rang unceasing and brazen.

The Director shouted loudly to the steamer:

"There is nobody down to meet us; there may be something wrong, though they are ringing. You had better come, too!"

And he began to toil up the steep bank. The captain and the engine-driver of the boat followed behind. As they scrambled up the fog thinned, and they could see their

Director a good way ahead. Suddenly they saw him start forward, calling to them over his shoulder: "Run! Run to the house! I've found one of them. Run, look for the other!"

He had found one of them! And even he, the man of varied and startling experience, was somewhat discomposed by the manner of this finding. He stood and fumbled in his pockets (for a knife) while he faced Kayerts, who was hanging by a leather strap from the cross. He had evidently climbed the grave, which was high and narrow, and after tying the end of the strap to the arm, had swung himself off. His toes were only a couple of inches above the ground; his arms hung stiffly down; he seemed to be standing rigidly at attention, but with one purple cheek playfully posed on the shoulder. And, irreverently, he was putting out a swollen tongue at his Managing Director.

◆ ——————————————————————— ◆

THE THIRD PRIZE

A. E. Coppard

Naboth Bird and George Robins were very fond of footracing. Neither of them was a champion runner, but each loved to train and to race; that was their pastime, their passion, their principal absorption and topic of conversation; occasionally it brought one or the other of them some sort of trophy.

One August bank holiday in the late nineties they travelled fifty miles to compete in a town where prizes of solid cash were to be given instead of the usual objects of glittering inutility. The town was a big town with a garrison and a dockyard. It ought to have been a city, and it would have been a city had not the only available cathedral been just inside an annoying little snob of a borough that kept itself (and its cathedral: admission sixpence) to itself just outside the boundaries of the real and proper town. On their arrival they found almost the entire populace wending to the carnival of games in a long stream of soldiers, sailors, and quite ordinary people, harried by pertinacious and vociferous little boys who yelled: "Program?" and blind beggars who just stood in the way and said nothing. Out of this crowd two jolly girls, Margery and Minnie, by some pleasant alchemy soon attached themselves to our two runners. Margery and Minnie were very different from each other. Why young maidens who hunt in couples and invariably dress alike should differ as much in character and temperament as Boadicea and Mrs. Hemans affords a speculation as fantastic as it is futile. They were different from each other, as different as a sherry cobbler and pineapple syrup, but they were not more different than were the two lads. The short snub one was Nab Bird; a mechanic by trade, with the ambition of a bus-conductor, he sold bicycle tires and did odd things to perambulators in a shed at the corner of a street; the demure Minnie became his friend. George Robins, a cute good-looking clerk, devoted his gifts of gallantry to Margery, and none the less readily because she displayed some qualities not commonly asscociated with demureness.

"From London you come!" exclaimed George. "How'd you get here?"

The young lady crisply testified that she came in a train— did the fathead think she had swum? They were jolly glad when they got here, too and all. Carriage full, and ructions all the way.

"Ructions! What ructions?"

"Boozy men! Half of 'em trying to cuddle you."

Mr. Robins intimated that he could well understand such desires. Miss Margery retorted that then he was understanding much more than was good for him. Mr. Robins thought not, he hoped not. Miss Margery indicated that he could hope for much more than he was likely to get. Mr.

Robins replied that, he would do that, and then double it. And he asserted, with all respect, that had he but happily been in that train he too might have, etc. and so on. Whereupon Miss Margery snapped, Would he? and Mr. Robins felt bound to say Sure!

"Would you—well, I'll tell you what I did to one of them." And she told him. It was quite unpleasant.

"Lady!" cried George sternly, "I hope you won't serve me like that."

" 'Pends on how you behave."

"How do you want me to behave?"

"Well, how *should* you behave to a lady?"

" 'Pends on what's expected of me." George delivered it with a flash of satisfaction.

"Oh, go on," she retorted, "you're as bad as the rest of 'em. It depends really on what is expected of me, don't it?"

"Oh, you're all right," he replied, "you're as good as they make 'em."

"How do you know?"

"Well, ain't you?"

"I'm as good as I *can* be. Is that good enough for you?"

" 'Pends on how good that is."

Margery declared her unqualified abhorrence of his sort of goodness.

"I'm all right when I *am* all right," George assured her.

"I know all about you!" There was a twinkle in her eyes.

"Do you!" interjected Nab; "then you know more than he'd like his mother to know."

They arrived at the sports field. Already there were ten thousand people there, and the bookmakers, having assembled their easels, cards, and boxes, were surrounded by betting men. The space adjacent to the arena was occupied by a gala fair with roundabouts, shies, booths, swings, and other uproarious seductions. The track was encircled by a wedge of onlookers ironic or enthusiastic, the sports began, runners came and went, the bookmakers stayed and roared, the hurdy gurdies lamented or rejoiced, the vanquished explained their defeats in terms that brought grins of commiseration to the faces of the victors, who explained their successes in terms that brought gleams of pride and triumph into the eyes of all who attended them. Very beautiful and bright the day was; the air smelt of grass, fusees, and cokernuts. Amongst those scantily garbed figures on the track Margery and Minnie scarcely recognized the young men they had accompanied, and for a long time they were unaware that George had won the third prize in a mile race.

Like all the other prize-winners he was subjected to the extravagant cajoleries of Jerry Chambers, a cockney ruffian living by his wits, a calling that afforded him no very great margin of security. He had lost his money, he was without a penny, and in the dressing-room he fastened himself upon Robins and Bird in an effort to obtain something or other, little or much, from each or either.

"I tell you," he darkly whispered, "the winner of the mile is a stiff un."

"What's a stiff un?" inquired Nab Bird.

"A stiff un! What a stiff un is!" Chambers's amusement at this youth's boundless ignorance was shrill and genuine. "Why, he's run under an assumed name and got about sixty yards the best of the handicap. You was third in that race, Robins, and the winner was a stiff un. Make it worth my while and I'll get him pinched for impersonation. Know him!—I knew his father! I'll tell you what I'll do, I'll get the second man disqualified as well—how will that stand you? Give me a dollar now so I can lodge the objection at once and the first prize must be awarded to you, it must. A five-pound note ain't it? I backed you to win myself and I don't like losing my money to a stiff un—I took ten pound to two about you. Now half a dollar won't hurt you. You won't! Well, good God Almighty!"—Chambers tilted his hat over one eye and scratched his neck—"don't let me try to persuade you. Lend us a tanner."

"To hell with you!"

"Make it eighteen pence, then."

They did not. At the distribution of the prize money, there was much ringing of a bell, shouting of names, and some factitious applause as a pert and portly lady of title appeared at a table in front of the pavilion to perform the ceremony. It was the only titled person our friends had ever seen, and the announcement of her grand name and the sound of her voice despite her appearance—for though she was a countess she had a stomach like a publican's wife—affected them occultly. A very gentlemanly steward, in private life a vendor of fish, bawled out the names of the prize-winners, and when it came to the turn of George Robins he was surprised to hear:

"Third prize in the mile race: W. Ballantyne."

He hesitated.

"It's wrong, O George!" gasped Nab Bird, "it's a mistake."

Nobody responding to the call for W. Ballantyne, George suddenly exchanged hats with his friend. Giving Nab his tweed cap he seized Nab's bowler hat and, although it was far too small, put it on his own head, where it looked much as it would have done on the bust of Homer.

"What—George, what?" asked his bewildered friend amid the chuckles of the two girls, but without stopping to explain, George Robins pushed his way through the crowd, advanced to the table, and received in the name of W. Ballantyne his own prize of a sovereign, which he acknowledged by just raising his terrible headgear and blowing his nose with a large handkerchief.

"Thanks, Nab," said he, returning to his friends. "I'll have my cap again."

The presentation concluded, the lady of title shook hands with the gentleman fishmonger and they went, presumably, their separate ways, while part of the crowd drifted gaily over to the fair booths and the rest went home to tea. With a mysterious preoccupied air George directed Nab to take the girls into a tent for tea and await him there.

"We'll look after him," declared Minnie, linking her arm with Nab's.

"But where you going, O George?" exclaimed the puzzled one, as Margery, too, linked an arm in his.

"See you later, five minutes, only five minutes. Take him

away," shouted the departing George to the girls, "give him a bun and don't let him make his face jammy."

So Nab went to tea with the girls, and says he:

"I wonder what he's up to."

"Didn't he run well?" said Minnie.

"Beautiful," agreed Margery.

"I don't want no tea." declared Nab, "I'm 'ot, but I'll have a couple of them saveloys, and then for a glass of ice cream-o. But you have just what you like, Minnie and Margery."

They had what they could get, and then, as Nab for the twentieth time was audibly wondering what George was "up to" and Margery for the dozenth time was realizing how splendidly he had run, George himself reappeared beaming with satisfaction.

"Where you been to, O George?"

"Been to get my prize."

"What prize?"

"In the mile."

"Third prize?"

"Didn't I win it?"

"But you got that before, didn't you?"

"Did I?"

"Well, 'aven't you?"

"Have I?"

Nab was mystified, George was triumphant: "I'll explain it to you. Listen, O Little Naboth. That third prize was awarded by some mischance to a chap the name of Ballantyne. Well, there wasn't any Ballantyne won that prize. That winner was G. Robins, that's me."

"Yes."

"So I go to the secretary of the sports and I say to him: 'Excuse me, sir, I'm George Robins, I won third prize in the mile, but there has been a mistake, and the prize has been given to someone called Ballantyne. What am I to do?' Well, there was a lot of palavering and running about and seeing stewards, but at last they found out that what I said was absolutely true and so they gave me another sovereign."

"Two lots of prize money you got, then!" ejaculated Nab, "two quid!"

George nodded modestly. "And they apologized for the mistake!"

"My goodness, isn't he—!" remarked Margery admiringly to Minnie, and Minnie too appeared to think he was—! But Nab was perturbed. Margery's observation—"All's fair in love and war!"—did not seem very pertinent to Nab and he corrected her:

"Love and war's one thing, sport's another."

"Sport!" exclaimed George. "But you know what these professionals are, you daren't trust 'em. Jerry Chambers, now, how about him if you met him on a dark night, eh? Any of these professionals would cut your throat for five-pence. They'd bag your boots and bone your bag and your skin too if you wasn't chained up inside it."

"Yes, O George, I know, but it wasn't them you done it to, it's the committee."

"Their look-out, ain't it? Their own mistake, not mine! It wasn't my mistake, now was it?"

"Well, no, but it's a bit like what Jerry Chambers might have done himself."

Margery interposed: "I think it was jolly smart, but you were a confederate—you lent him your hat."

"Of course! I borrowed that for disguise, see! But you shall share the swag, little Naboth, so don't keep grumbling and grumbling. Here's your half-a-james." Saying which, George stretched out a hand to his friend, who saw lying upon his palm a glittering sovereign. "Give me change for half of that!"

The girls sparklingly approved this offer of the magnanimous one, but Nab, a little confused, turned away saying:

"No, thanks, George O man, no, thanks."

Although they all surrounded Nab and tried to cajole him into acceptance, the little man was adamant—very kind of George, but he'd rather not. However, they all went away very amiably together, and it was apparent to Naboth Bird that his friend's questionable manoeuvre was acclaimed by the girls as an admirable exploit, while his own qualms were regarded as an indecent exhibition of an honesty no less questionable.

Moving idly down a hill amongst the stream of people, they were brought to a standstill at the edge of a crowd surrounding an old blind beggar and his wife. The man was playing a hymn tune on a tin pipe. Tall and ragged, with white thin beard and clerical hat, there was the strange dignity inseparable from blindness in his erect figure, but his shuffling wife, older, and very feeble, held his arm with one hand and outstretched the other for the few pitying pence that came to them. George and his friends were astonished to perceive the ruffian Jerry Chambers standing mockingly in front of the beggars. His arms were spread out to the halting people, his hat had been flung upon the ground before him, he was making excruciating gestures and noises with his hands and mouth, yodelling like a costermonger and performing ridiculous antics to gain their attention. He was entirely successful; the good-natured holiday folk assembled and stretched across the road in a great crowd. With an ironical gesture of the hand Chambers directed the attention of the onlookers to the forlorn couple behind him.

"Look at 'em," he yelled, "look at 'em—roll, bowl, or pitch—but look at 'em! Did ever you see such a thing in your lives?"

He paused for a moment and then recommenced very gently: "People, men of my own fraternity! I ain't doing this bit of a job for myself—nor for no barney—nor for no bank-holiday rag. I'm a-doing this—just five minutes—for my compatriarch and his noble consort. Look at 'em, I say. I bin a-looking at 'em—I 'ad to—and it just breaks my heart. Well, you're not a brass-bellied lot—you don't look it—*your* hearts ain't made of tripe. So that's where I've pushed in."

The old man had forborne his solemn piping; he blinked the sightless eyes unobjectively upon the people, while his partner clung to him with both arms, bewildered and a little terrified.

"I am going," Chambers began to roar again, "to sing you a comical song. Shall then, if my old compatriarch will oblige with a tootle on his bangalorum, shall then dance you a jig. Shall then crawl upon my hands and knees, barking like a tiger, with my cady in me mouth to collect bullion for this suffering fambly. Look at 'em, lord alive, look at 'em!"

After singing so raucous and ridiculous a song that his kindly intentions were nearly defeated Chambers poised himself for the jig:

"Righto, play up, uncle!"

But the old beggar could only repeat the one tune, his hymn called *Marching to Zion*.

"God A'mighty! 'ark at 'im!" cried the baffled Chambers. "Well, you people, men of my own fraternity, it's no go; 'ere's my cadging 'at—give us a good whip round for those two old bits of mutton!"

So the old man piped his hymn while the cockney ruffian begged and bullied a handful of money for them. Chaffing and scolding, he approached George; Margery was searching for a coin.

"It's all right," whispered George to her, "it's all right." He showed her the coin already in his fingers, the glittering questionable sovereign. She clutched his arm to prevent such a sacrifice, but she was too late, George dropped the coin into Chambers's hat and then, curiously shamefaced, at once walked away in a little drift of pleased excitement.

"Min, Min, d'you know what he's done!" cried Margery to the friends as they all followed after him, "he's given 'em that sovereign."

In the eyes of the dazzled girls the gesture crowned George with the last uttermost grace, and even Nab was mute before its sublimity. They hurried away as if the devil himself might be coming to thrust the sovereign back upon them.

And Chambers? His triumph, too, was great, the well-used occasion had won its well-devised reward, and his pleasure, though modestly expressed, was sincere.

"Ladies and gennermen," cried the jolly ruffian a few minutes later as he counted up the coin. "I thank you one and

all for your kindness to this old couple and the very handsome
collection (here y'are, uncle," he whispered, "it's splendid,
eight shillings and fo'pence). All correct, thank you, ladies
and gennermen. God bless the lot of yer," and then, leaving
the delighted beggars to their gains, and murmuring to
himself "Beau-tiful beautiful Zi-on!" he hurried rapidly away.

◆ ──────────────────────────── ◆

THE BRIDE COMES TO YELLOW SKY

Stephen Crane

The great pullman was whirling onward with such dignity of
motion that a glance from the window seemed simply to
prove that the plains of Texas were pouring eastward. Vast
flats of green grass, dull-hued spaces of mesquit and cactus,
little groups of frame houses, woods of light and tender
trees, all were sweeping into the east, sweeping over the
horizon, a precipice.

A newly married pair had boarded this coach at San
Antonio. The man's face was reddened from many days in
the wind and sun, and a direct result of his new black
clothes was that his brick-colored hands were constantly
performing in a most conscious fashion. From time to time
he looked down respectfully at his attire. He sat with a hand
on each knee, like a man waiting in a barber's shop. The
glances he devoted to other passengers were furtive and shy.

The bride was not pretty, nor was she very young. She
wore a dress of blue cashmere, with small reservations of

velvet here and there, and with steel buttons abounding. She continually twisted her head to regard her puff sleeves, very stiff, straight, and high. They embarrassed her. It was quite apparent that she had cooked, and that she expected to cook, dutifully. The blushes caused by the careless scrutiny of some passengers as she had entered the car were strange to see upon this plain, under-class countenance, which was drawn in placid, almost emotionless lines.

They were evidently very happy. "Ever been in a parlour-car before?" he asked, smiling with delight.

"No," she answered; "I never was. It's fine, ain't it?"

"Great! And then after a while we'll go forward to the diner, and get a big lay-out. Finest meal in the world. Charge a dollar."

"Oh, do they?" cried the bride. "Charge a dollar? Why, that's too much—for us—ain't it, Jack?"

"Not this trip, anyhow," he answered bravely. "We're going to go the whole thing."

Later he explained to her about the trains. "You see, it's a thousand miles from one end of Texas to the other; and this train runs right across it, and never stops but four times." He had the pride of an owner. He pointed out to her the dazzling fittings of the coach; and in truth her eyes opened wider as she contemplated the sea-green figured velvet, the shining brass, silver, and glass, the wood that gleamed as darkly brilliant as the surface of a pool of oil. At one end a bronze figure sturdily held a support for a separated chamber, and at convenient places on the ceiling were frescos in olive and silver.

To the minds of the pair, their surroundings reflected the glory of their marriage that morning in San Antonio; this was the environment of their new estate; and the man's face in particular beamed with an elation that made him appear ridiculous to the negro porter. This individual at times surveyed them from afar with an amused and superior grin. On other occasions he bullied them with skill in ways that did not make it exactly plain to them that they were being bullied. He subtly used all the manners of the most unconquerable kind of snobbery. He oppressed them; but of this oppression they had small knowledge, and they speedily forgot that infrequently a number of travellers covered them with stares of derisive enjoyment. Historically there was supposed to be something infinitely humorous in their situation.

"We are due in Yellow Sky at 3:42," he said, looking tenderly into her eyes.

"Oh, are we?" she said, as if she had not been aware of it. To evince surprise at her husband's statement was part of her wifely amiability. She took from a pocket a little silver watch; and as she held it before her, and stared at it with a frown of attention, the new husband's face shone.

"I bought it in San Anton' from a friend of mine," he told her gleefully.

"It's seventeen minutes past twelve," she said, looking up at him with a kind of shy and clumsy coquetry. A passenger, noting this play, grew excessively sardonic, and winked at himself in one of the numerous mirrors.

At last they went to the dining-car. Two rows of negro waiters, in glowing white suits, surveyed their entrance with the interest, and also the equanimity, of men who had been forewarned. The pair fell to the lot of a waiter who happened to feel pleasure in steering them through their meal. He viewed them with the manner of a fatherly pilot, his countenance radiant with benevolence. The patronage, entwined with the ordinary deference, was not plain to them. And yet, as they returned to their coach, they showed in their faces a sense of escape.

To the left, miles down a long purple slope, was a little ribbon of mist where moved the keening Rio Grande. The train was approaching it at an angle, and the apex was Yellow Sky. Presently it was apparent that, as the distance from Yellow Sky grew shorter, the husband became commensurately restless. His brick-red hands were more insistent in their prominence. Occasionally he was even rather absent-minded and far-away when the bride leaned forward and addressed him.

As a matter of truth, Jack Potter was beginning to find the

shadow of a deed weigh upon him like a leaden slab. He, the town marshal of Yellow Sky, a man known, liked, and feared in his corner, a prominent person, had gone to San Antonio to meet a girl he believed he loved, and there, after the usual prayers, had actually induced her to marry him, without consulting Yellow Sky for any part of the transaction. He was now bringing his bride before an innocent and unsuspecting community.

Of course people in Yellow Sky married as it pleased them, in accordance with a general custom; but such was Potter's thought of his duty to his friends, or of their idea of his duty, or of an unspoken form which does not control men in these matters, that he felt he was heinous. He had committed an extraordinary crime. Face to face with this girl in San Antonio, and spurred by his sharp impulse, he had gone headlong over all the social hedges. At San Antonio he was like a man hidden in the dark. A knife to sever any friendly duty, any form, was easy to his hand in that remote city. But the hour of Yellow Sky—the hour of daylight—was approaching.

He knew full well that his marriage was an important thing to his town. It could only be exceeded by the burning of the new hotel. His friends could not forgive him. Frequently he had reflected on the advisability of telling them by telegraph, but a new cowardice had been upon him. He feared to do it. And now the train was hurrying him toward a scene of amazement, glee, and reproach. He glanced out of the window at the line of haze swinging slowly in toward the train.

Yellow Sky had a kind of brass band, which played painfully, to the delight of the populace. He laughed without heart as he thought of it. If the citizens could dream of his prospective arrival with his bride, they would parade the band at the station and escort them, amid cheers and laughing congratulations, to his adobe home.

He resolved that he would use all the devices of speed and plainscraft in making the journey from the station to his house. Once within that safe citadel, he could issue some sort of vocal bulletin, and then not go among the citizens until they had time to wear off a little of their enthusiasm.

The bride looked anxiously at him. "What's worrying you, Jack?"

He laughed again. "I'm not worrying, girl; I'm only thinking of Yellow Sky."

She flushed in comprehension.

A sense of mutual guilt invaded their minds and developed a finer tenderness. They looked at each other with eyes softly aglow. But Potter often laughed the same nervous laugh; the flush upon the bride's face seemed quite permanent.

The traitor to the feelings of Yellow Sky narrowly watched the speeding landscape. "We're nearly there," he said.

Presently the porter came and announced the proximity of Potter's home. He held a brush in his hand, and, with all his airy superiority gone, he brushed Potter's new clothes as the latter slowly turned this way and that way. Potter fumbled out a coin and gave it to the porter, as he had seen others do. It was a heavy and muscle-bound business, as that of a man shoeing his first horse.

The porter took their bag, and as the train began to slow they moved forward to the hooded platform of the car. Presently the two engines and their long string of coaches rushed into the station of Yellow Sky.

"They have to take water here," said Potter, from a constricted throat and in mournful cadence, as one announcing death. Before the train stopped his eye had swept the length of the platform, and he was glad and astonished to see there was none upon it but the station-agent, who, with a slightly hurried and anxious air, was walking toward the water-tanks. When the train had halted, the porter alighted first, and placed in position a little temporary step.

"Come on, girl," said Potter, hoarsely. As he helped her down they each laughed on a false note. He took the bag from the negro, and bade his wife cling to his arm. As they slunk rapidly away, his hang-dog glance perceived that they were unloading the two trunks, and also that the station-agent, far ahead near the baggage-car, had turned and was running toward him, making gestures. He laughed, and groaned as he laughed, when he noted the first effect of his marital bliss upon Yellow Sky. He gripped his wife's arm firmly to his side, and they fled. Behind them the porter stood, chuckling fatuously.

II

The California express on the Southern Railway was due at Yellow Sky in twenty-one minutes. There were six men at the bar of the Weary Gentleman saloon. One was a drummer who talked a great deal and rapidly; three were Texans who did not care to talk at that time; and two were Mexican sheep-herders, who did not talk as a general practice in the Weary Gentleman saloon. The barkeeper's dog lay on the board walk that crossed in front of the door. His head was on his paws, and he glanced drowsily here and there with the constant vigilance of a dog that is kicked on occasion. Across the sandy street were some vivid green grass-plots, so wonderful in appearance, amid the sands that burned near them in a blazing sun, that they caused a doubt in the mind. They exactly resembled the grass mats used to represent lawns on the stage. At the cooler end of the railway station, a man without a coat sat in a tilted chair and smoked his pipe. The fresh-cut bank of the Rio Grande circled near the town, and there could be seen beyond it a great plum-coloured plain of mesquit.

Save for the busy drummer and his companions in the saloon, Yellow Sky was dozing. The new-comer leaned gracefully upon the bar, and recited many tales with the confidence of a bard who has come upon a new field.

"—and at the moment that the old man fell downstairs with the bureau in his arms, the old woman was coming up with two scuttles of coal, and of course—"

The drummer's tale was interrupted by a young man who suddenly appeared in the open door. He cried: "Scratchy Wilson's drunk, and has turned loose with both hands." The two Mexicans at once set down their glasses and faded out of the rear entrance of the saloon.

The drummer, innocent and jocular, answered: "All right, old man. S'pose he has? Come in and have a drink, anyhow."

But the information had made such an obvious cleft in every skull in the room that the drummer was obliged to see its importance. All had become instantly solemn. "Say," said he, mystified, "what is this?" His three companions made the introductory gesture of eloquent speech; but the young man at the door forestalled them.

"It means, my friend," he answered, as he came into the saloon, "that for the next two hours this town won't be a health resort."

The barkeeper went to the door, and locked and barred it; reaching out of the window, he pulled in heavy wooden shutters, and barred them. Immediately a solemn, chapel-like gloom was upon the place. The drummer was looking from one to another.

"But say," he cried, "what is this, anyhow? You don't mean there is going to be a gun-fight?"

"Don't know whether there'll be a fight or not," answered one man, grimly; "but there'll be some shootin'—some good shootin'."

The young man who had warned them waved his hand. "Oh, there'll be a fight fast enough, if any one wants it. Anybody can get a fight out there in the street. There's a fight just waiting."

The drummer seemed to be swayed between the interest of a foreigner and a perception of personal danger.

"What did you say his name was?" he asked.

"Scratchy Wilson," they answered in chorus.

"And will he kill anybody? What are you going to do? Does this happen often? Does he rampage around like this once a week or so? Can he break in that door?"

"No; he can't break down that door," replied the barkeeper. "He's tried it three times. But when he comes you'd better lay down on the floor, stranger. He's dead sure to shoot at it, and a bullet may come through."

Thereafter the drummer kept a strict eye upon the door. The time had not yet been called for him to hug the floor, but, as a minor precaution, he sidled near to the wall. "Will he kill anybody?" he said again.

The men laughed low and scornfully at the question.

"He's out to shoot, and he's out for trouble. Don't see any good in experimentin' with him."

"But what do you do in a case like this? What do you do?"

A man responded: "Why, he and Jack Potter—"

"But," in chorus the other men interrupted, "Jack Potter's in San Anton'."

"Well, who is he? What's he got to do with it?"

"Oh, he's the town marshal. He goes out and fights Scratchy when he gets on one of these tears."

"Wow!" said the drummer, mopping his brow. "Nice job he's got."

The voices had toned away to mere whisperings. The drummer wished to ask further questions, which were born of an increasing anxiety and bewilderment; but when he attempted them, the men merely looked at him in irritation and motioned him to remain silent. A tense waiting hush was upon them. In the deep shadows of the room their eyes shone as they listened for sounds from the street. One man made three gestures at the barkeeper; and the latter, moving like a ghost, handed him a glass and a bottle. The man poured a full glass of whisky, and set down the bottle noiselessly. He gulped the whisky in a swallow, and turned again toward the door in immovable silence. The drummer saw that the barkeeper, without a sound, had taken a Winchester from beneath the bar. Later he saw this individual beckoning to him, so he tiptoed across the room.

"You better come with me back of the bar."

"No, thanks," said the drummer, perspiring; "I'd rather be where I can make a break for the back door."

Whereupon the man of bottles made a kindly but peremptory gesture. The drummer obeyed it, and, finding himself seated on a box with his head below the level of the bar, balm was laid upon his soul at sight of various zinc and copper fittings that bore a resemblance to armourplate. The barkeeper took a seat comfortably upon an adjacent box.

"You see," he whispered, "this here Scratchy Wilson is a wonder with a gun—a perfect wonder; and when he goes on the war-trail, we hunt our holes—naturally. He's about the last one of the old gang that used to hang out along the river here. He's a terror when he's drunk. When he's sober he's all right—kind of simple—wouldn't hurt a fly—nicest fellow in town. But when he's drunk—whoo!"

There were periods of stillness. "I wish Jack Potter was back from San Anton'," said the barkeeper. "He shot Wilson up once—in the leg—and he would sail in and pull out the kinks in this thing."

Presently they heard from a distance the sound of a shot, followed by three wild yowls. It instantly removed a bond from the men in the darkened saloon. There was a shuffling of feet. They looked at each other. "Here he comes," they said.

III

A man in a maroon-coloured flannel shirt, which had been purchased for purposes of decoration, and made principally by some Jewish women on the East Side of New York, rounded a corner and walked into the middle of the main street of Yellow Sky. In either hand the man held a long, heavy, blue-black revolver. Often he yelled, and these cries rang through a semblance of a deserted village, shrilly flying over the roofs in a volume that seemed to have no relation to the ordinary vocal strength of a man. It was as if the surrounding stillness formed the arch of a tomb over him. These cries of ferocious challenge rang against walls of silence. And his boots had red tops with gilded imprints, of the kind beloved in winter by little sledding boys on the hillsides of New England.

The man's face flamed in a rage begot of whisky. His eyes, rolling, and yet keen for ambush, hunted the still doorways and windows. He walked with the creeping movement of the midnight cat. As it occurred to him, he roared menacing information. The long revolvers in his hands were as easy as straws; they were moved with an electric swiftness. The little fingers of each hand played sometimes in a musician's way. Plain from the low collar of the shirt, the cords of his neck straightened and sank, straightened and sank, as passion moved him. The only sounds were his terrible invitations. The calm adobes preserved their demeanour at the passing of this small thing in the middle of the street.

There was no offer of fight—no offer of fight. The man called to the sky. There were no attractions. He bellowed and fumed and swayed his revolvers here and everywhere.

The dog of the barkeeper of the Weary Gentleman saloon had not appreciated the advance of events. He yet lay dozing in front of his master's door. At sight of the dog, the man paused and raised his revolver humorously. At sight of the man, the dog sprang up and walked diagonally away, with a sullen head, and growling. The man yelled, and the dog broke into a gallop. As it was about to enter an alley, there was a loud noise, a whistling, and something spat the ground directly before it. The dog screamed, and, wheeling in terror, galloped headlong in a new direction. Again there was a noise, a whistling, and sand was kicked viciously before it. Fear-stricken, the dog turned and flurried like an animal in a pen. The man stood laughing, his weapons at his hips.

Ultimately the man was attracted by the closed door of the Weary Gentleman saloon. He went to it and, hammering with a revolver, demanded drink.

The door remaining imperturbable, he picked a bit of paper from the walk, and nailed it to the framework with a knife. He then turned his back contemptuously upon this popular resort and, walking to the opposite side of the street and spinning there on his heel quickly and lithely, fired at the bit of paper. He missed it by a half-inch. He swore at himself, and went away. Later he comfortably fusilladed the windows of his most intimate friend. The man was playing with this town; it was a toy for him.

But still there was no offer of fight. The name of Jack
Potter, his ancient antagonist, entered his mind, and he
concluded that it would be a glad thing if he should go to
Potter's house, and by bombardment induce him to come
out and fight. He moved in the direction of his desire,
chanting Apache scalp-music.

When he arrived at it, Potter's house presented the same
still front as had the other adobes. Taking up a strategic
position, the man howled a challenge. But this house regarded him as might a great stone god. It gave no sign.
After a decent wait, the man howled further challenges,
mingling with them wonderful epithets.

Presently there came the spectacle of a man churning
himself into deepest rage over the immobility of a house.
He fumed at it as the winter wind attacks a prairie cabin in
the North. To the distance there should have gone the
sound of a tumult like the fighting of two hundred Mexicans. As necessity bade him, he paused for breath or to
reload his revolvers.

IV

Potter and his bride walked sheepishly and with speed.
Sometimes they laughed together shamefacedly and low.

"Next corner, dear," he said finally.

They put forth the efforts of a pair walking bowed against
a strong wind. Potter was about to raise a finger to point the
first appearance of the new home when, as they circled the
corner, they came face to face with a man in a maroon-
coloured shirt, who was feverishly pushing cartridges into a
large revolver. Upon the instant the man dropped his revolver to the ground and, like lightning, whipped another
from its holster. The second weapon was aimed at the
bridegroom's chest.

There was a silence. Potter's mouth seemed to be merely
a grave for his tongue. He exhibited an instinct to at once
loosen his arm from the woman's grip, and he dropped the
bag to the sand. As for the bride, her face had gone as

yellow as old cloth. She was a slave to hideous rites, gazing at the apparitional snake.

The two men faced each other at a distance of three paces. He of the revolver smiled with a new and quiet ferocity.

"Tried to sneak up on me," he said. "Tried to sneak up on me!" His eyes grew more baleful. As Potter made a slight movement, the man thrust his revolver venomously forward. "No; don't you do it, Jack Potter. Don't you move a finger toward a gun just yet. Don't you move an eyelash. The time has come for me to settle with you, and I'm goin' to do it my own way, and loaf along with no interferin'. So if you don't want a gun bent on you, just mind what I tell you."

Potter looked at his enemy. "I ain't got a gun on me Scratchy," he said. "Honest, I ain't." He was stiffening and steadying, but yet somewhere at the back of his mind a vision of the Pullman floated: the sea-green figured velvet, the shining brass, silver, and glass, the wood that gleamed as darkly brilliant as the surface of a pool of oil—all the glory of the marriage, the environment of the new estate. "You know I fight when it comes to fighting, Scratchy Wilson; but I ain't got a gun on me. You'll have to do all the shootin' yourself."

His enemy's face went livid. He stepped forward, and lashed his weapon to and fro before Potter's chest. "Don't you tell me you ain't got no gun on you, you whelp. Don't tell me no lie like that. There ain't a man in Texas ever seen you without no gun. Don't take me for no kid." His eyes blazed with light, and his throat worked like a pump.

"I ain't takin' you for no kid," answered Potter. His heels had not moved an inch backward. "I'm takin' you for a damn fool. I tell you I ain't got a gun, and I ain't. If you're goin' to shoot me up, you better begin now; you'll never get a chance like this again."

So much enforced reasoning had told on Wilson's rage; he was calmer. "If you ain't got a gun, why ain't you got a gun?" he sneered. "Been to Sunday-school?"

"I ain't got a gun because I've just come from San Anton' with my wife. I'm married," said Potter. "And if I'd thought there was going to be any galoots like you prowling around when I brought my wife home, I'd had a gun, and don't you forget it."

"Married!" said Scratchy, not at all comprehending.

"Yes, married. I'm married," said Potter, distinctly.

"Married?" said Scratchy. Seemingly for the first time, he saw the drooping, drowning woman at the other man's side. "No!" he said. He was like a creature allowed a glimpse of another world. He moved a pace backward, and his arm, with the revolver, dropped to his side. "Is this the lady?" he asked.

"Yes; this is the lady," answered Potter.

There was another period of silence.

"Well," said Wilson at last, slowly, "I s'pose it's all off now."

"It's all off if you say so, Scratchy. You know I didn't make the trouble." Potter lifted his valise.

"Well, I 'low it's off, Jack," said Wilson. He was looking at the ground. "Married!" He was not a student of chivalry; it was merely that in the presence of this foreign condition he was a simple child of the earlier plains. He picked up his starboard revolver, and, placing both weapons in their holsters, he went away. His feet made funnel-shaped tracks in the heavy sand.

◆ ————————————————————————————————— ◆

OPEN WINTER

H. L. Davis

The drying east wind, which always brought hard luck to Eastern Oregon at whatever season it blew, had combed down the plateau grasslands through so much of the winter that it was hard to see any sign of grass ever having grown

on them. Even though March had come, it still blew, drying
the ground deep, shrinking the watercourses, beating back
the clouds that might have delivered rain, and grinding
coarse dust against the fifty-odd head of work horses that
Pop Apling, with young Beech Cartwright helping, had
brought down from his homestead to turn back into their
home pasture while there was still something left of them.

The two men, one past sixty and the other around sixteen, shouldered the horses through the gate of the home
pasture about dark, with lights beginning to shine out
from the little freighting town across Three Notch Valley,
and then they rode for the ranch house, knowing even
before they drew up outside the yard that they had picked
the wrong time to come. The house was too dark, and the
corrals and outbuildings too still, for a place that anybody
lived in.

There were sounds, but they were of shingles flapping in
the wind, a windmill running loose and sucking noisily at a
well that it had already pumped empty, a door that kept
banging shut and dragging open again. The haystacks were
gone, the stackyard fence had dwindled to a few naked
posts, and the entire pasture was as bare and as hard as a
floor all the way down into the valley.

The prospect looked so hopeless that the herd horses
refused even to explore it, and merely stood with their tails
turned to the wind, waiting to see what was to happen to
them next.

Old Apling went poking inside the house, thinking somebody might have left a note or that the men might have run
down to the saloon in town for an hour or two. He came
back, having used up all his matches and stopped the door
from banging, and said the place appeared to have been
handed back to the Government, or maybe the mortgage
company.

"You can trust old Ream Gervais not to be any place
where anybody wants him," Beech said. He had hired out
to herd for Ream Gervais over the winter. That entitled him
to be more critical than old Apling, who had merely con-

tracted to supply the horse herd with feed and pasture for the season at so much per head. "Well, my job was to help herd these steeds while you had 'em, and to help deliver 'em back when you got through with 'em, and here they are. I've put in a week on 'em that I won't ever git paid for, and it won't help anything to set around and watch 'em try to live on fence pickets. Let's git out."

Old Apling looked at the huddle of horses, at the naked slope with a glimmer of light still on it, and at the lights of the town twinkling in the wind. He said it wasn't his place to tell any man what to do, but that he wouldn't feel quite right to dump the horses and leave.

"I agreed to see that they got delivered back here, and I'd feel better about it if I could locate somebody to deliver 'em to," he said. "I'd like to ride across to town yonder, and see if there ain't somebody that knows something about 'em. You could hold 'em together here till I git back. We ought to look the fences over before we pull out, and you can wait here as well as anywhere else."

"I can't, but go ahead," Beech said. "I don't like to have 'em stand around and look at me when I can't do anything to help 'em out. They'd have been better off if we'd turned 'em out of your homestead and let 'em run loose on the country. There was more grass up there than there is here."

"There wasn't enough to feed 'em, and I'd have had all my neighbors down on me for it," old Apling said. "You'll find out one of these days that if a man aims to live in this world he's got to git along with the people in it. I'd start a fire and thaw out a little and git that pack horse unloaded, if I was you."

He rode down the slope, leaning low and forward to ease the drag of the wind on his tired horse. Beech heard the sound of the road gate being let down and put up again, the beat of hoofs in the hard road, and then nothing but the noises around him as the wind went through its usual process of easing down for the night to make room for the frost. Loose boards settled into place, the windmill clacked to a stop and began to drip water into a puddle, and the herd horses shifted around facing Beech, as if anxious not to miss anything he did.

He pulled off some fence pickets and built a fire, unsaddled his pony and unloaded the pack horse, and got out what was left of a sack of grain and fed them both, standing the herd horses off with a fence picket until they had finished eating.

That was strictly fair, for the pack horse and the saddle pony had worked harder and carried more weight than any of the herd animals, and the grain was little enough to even them up for it. Nevertheless, he felt mean at having to club animals away from food when they were hungry, and they crowded back and eyed the grain sack so wistfully that he carried it inside the yard and stored it down in the root cellar behind the house, so it wouldn't prey on their minds. Then he dumped another armload of fence pickets onto the fire and sat down to wait for old Apling.

The original mistake, he reflected, had been when old Apling took the Gervais horses to feed at the beginning of winter. Contracting to feed them had been well enough, for he had nursed up a stand of bunch grass on his homestead that would have carried an ordinary pack of horses with only a little extra feeding to help out in the roughest weather. But the Gervais horses were all big harness stock, they had pulled in half starved, and they had taken not much over three weeks to clean off the pasture that old Apling had expected would last them at least two months. Nobody would have blamed him for backing out on his agreement then, since he had only undertaken to feed the horses, not to treat them for malnutrition.

Beech wanted him to back out of it, but he refused to, said the stockmen had enough troubles without having that added to them, and started feeding out his hay and insisting that the dry wind couldn't possibly keep up much longer, because it wasn't in Nature.

By the time it became clear that Nature had decided to take in a little extra territory, the hay was all fed out, and, since there couldn't be any accommodation about letting the horses starve to death, he consented to throw the contract over and bring them back where they belonged.

The trouble with most of old Apling's efforts to be accommodating was that they did nobody any good. His neighbors would have been spared all their uneasiness if he had never brought in the horses to begin with. Gervais wouldn't have been any worse off, since he stood to lose them anyway; the horses could have starved to death as gracefully in November as in March, and old Apling would have been ahead a great deal of carefully accumulated bunch grass and two big stacks of extortionately valuable hay. Nobody had gained by his chivalrousness; he had lost by it, and yet he liked it so well that he couldn't stand to leave the horses until he had raked the country for somebody to hand the worthless brutes over to.

Beech fed sticks into the fire and felt out of patience with a man who could stick to his mistakes even after he had been cleaned out by them. He heard the road gate open and shut, and he knew by the draggy-sounding plod of old Apling's horse that the news from town was going to be bad.

Old Apling rode past the fire and over to the picket fence, got off as if he was trying to make it last, tied his horse carefully as if he expected the knot to last a month, and unsaddled and did up his latigo and folded his saddle blanket as if he was fixing them to put in a show window. He remarked that his horse had been given a bait of grain in town and wouldn't need feeding again, and then he began to work down to what he had found out.

"If you think things look bad along this road, you ought to see that town," he said. "All the sheep gone and all the ranches deserted and no trade to run on and their water threatenin' to give out. They've got a little herd of milk cows that they keep up for their children, and to hear 'em talk you'd think it was an ammunition supply that they expected to stand off hostile Indians with. They said Gervais pulled out of here around a month ago. All his men quit him, so he bunched his sheep and took 'em down to the railroad where he could ship in hay for 'em. Sheep will be a price this year, and you won't be able to buy a lamb for under twelve dollars except at a fire sale. Horses ain't in much demand. There's been a lot of 'em turned out wild, and everybody wants to git rid of 'em."

"I didn't drive this bunch of pelters any eighty miles against the wind to git a market report," Beech said. "You didn't find anybody to turn 'em over to, and Gervais didn't leave any word about what he wanted done with 'em. You've probably got it figured out that you ought to trail 'em a hundred and eighty miles to the railroad, so his feelings won't be hurt, and you're probably tryin' to study how you can work me in on it, and you might as well save your time. I've helped you with your accommodation jobs long enough. I've quit, and it would have been a whole lot better for you if I'd quit sooner."

Old Apling said he could understand that state of feeling, which didn't mean that he shared it.

"It wouldn't be as much of a trick to trail down to the railroad as a man might think," he said, merely to settle a question of fact. "We couldn't make it by the road in a starve-out year like this, but there's old Indian trails back on the ridge where any man has got a right to take livestock whenever he feels like it. Still, as long as you're set against it, I'll meet you halfway. We'll trail these horses down the ridge to a grass patch where I used to corral cattle when I was in the business, and we'll leave 'em there. It'll be enough so they won't starve, and I'll ride on down and notify Gervais where they are, and you can go where you please. It wouldn't be fair to do less than that, to my notion."

"Ream Gervais triggered me out of a week's pay," Beech said. "It ain't much, but he swindled you on that pasture contract too. If you expect me to trail his broken-down horses ninety miles down this ridge when they ain't worth anything, you've turned in a poor guess. You'll have to think of a better argument than that if you aim to gain any ground with me."

"Ream Gervais don't count in this," old Apling said. "What does he care about these horses, when he ain't even

left word what he wants done with 'em? What counts is you,
and I don't have to think up any better argument, because
I've already got one. You may not realize it, but you and me
are responsible for these horses till they're delivered to
their owner, and if we turn 'em loose here to bust fences
and overrun that town and starve to death in the middle of
it, we'll land in the pen. It's against the law to let horses
starve to death, did you know that? If you pull out of here
I'll pull out right along with you, and I'll have every man in
that town after you before the week's out. You'll have a
chance to git some action on that pistol of yours, if you're
careful."

Beech said he wasn't intimidated by that kind of talk, and
threw a couple of handfuls of dirt on the fire, so it wouldn't
look so conspicuous. His pistol was an old single-action relic
with its grips tied on with fish line and no trigger, so that it
had to be operated by flipping the hammer. The spring was
weak, so that sometimes it took several flips to get off one
shot. Suggesting that he might use such a thing to stand off
any pack of grim-faced pursuers was about the same as
saying that he was simple-minded. As far as he could see,
his stand was entirely sensible, and even humane.

"It ain't that I don't feel sorry for these horses, but they
ain't fit to travel," he said. "They wouldn't last twenty
miles. I don't see how it's any worse to let 'em stay here
than to walk 'em to death down that ridge."

"They make less trouble for people if you keep 'em on the
move," old Apling said. "It's something you can't be cinched
for in court, and it makes you feel better afterwards to know
that you tried everything you could. Suit yourself about it,
though. I ain't beggin' you to do it. If you'd sooner pull out
and stand the consequences, it's you for it. Before you go,
what did you do with that sack of grain?"

Beech had half a notion to leave, just to see how much of
that dark threatening would come to pass. He decided that
it wouldn't be worth it. "I'll help you trail the blamed skates
as far as they'll last, if you've got to be childish about it," he
said. "I put the grain in a root cellar behind the house, so

the rats wouldn't git into it. It looked like the only safe place
around here. There was about a half a ton of old sprouted
potatoes ricked up in it that didn't look like they'd been
bothered for twenty years. They had sprouts on 'em—" He
stopped, noticing that old Apling kept staring at him as if
something was wrong. "Good Lord, potatoes ain't good for
horse feed, are they? They had sprouts on 'em a foot long!"

Old Apling shook his head resignedly and got up. "We
wouldn't ever find anything if it wasn't for you," he said.
"We wouldn't ever git any good out of it if it wasn't for me,
so maybe we make a team. Show me where that root cellar
is, and we'll pack them spuds out and spread 'em around so
the horses can git started on 'em. We'll git this herd through
to grassland yet, and it'll be something you'll never be
ashamed of. It ain't everybody your age gits a chance to do a
thing like this, and you'll thank me for holdin' you to it
before you're through."

II

They climbed up by an Indian trail onto a high stretch of
tableland, so stony and scored with rock breaks that nobody
had ever tried to cultivate it, but so high that it sometimes
caught moisture from the atmosphere that the lower eleva-
tions missed. Part of it had been doled out among the
Indians as allotment lands, which none of them ever bothered to lay claim to, but the main spread of it belonged to
the nation, which was too busy to notice it.

The pasture was thin, though reliable, and it was so
scantily watered and so rough and broken that in ordinary
years nobody bothered to bring stock onto it. The open
winter had spoiled most of that seclusion. There was no part
of the trail that didn't have at least a dozen new bed grounds
for lambed ewes in plain view, easily picked out of the
landscape because of the little white flags stuck up around
them to keep sheep from straying out and coyotes from
straying in during the night. The sheep were pasturing
down the draws out of the wind, where they couldn't be

seen. There were no herders visible, not any startling amount
of grass, and no water except a mud tank thrown up to catch
a little spring for one of the camps.

They tried to water the horses in it, but it had taken up
the flavor of sheep, so that not a horse in the herd would
touch it. It was too near dark to waste time reasoning with
them about it, so old Apling headed them down into a long
rock break and across it to a tangle of wild cherry and
mountain mahogany that lasted for several miles and ended
in a grass clearing among some dwarf cottonwoods with a
mud puddle in the center of it.

The grass had been grazed over, though not closely, and
there were sheep tracks around the puddle that seemed to
be fresh, for the horses, after sniffing the water, decided
that they could wait a while longer. They spread out to
graze, and Beech remarked that he couldn't see where it
was any improvement over the tickle-grass homesteads.

"The grass may be better, but there ain't as much of it,
and the water ain't any good if they won't drink it," he said.
"Well, do you intend to leave 'em here, or have you got
some wrinkle figured out to make me help trail 'em on
down to the railroad?"

Old Apling stood the sarcasm unresistingly. "It would be
better to trail 'em to the railroad, now that we've got this
far," he said. "I won't ask you to do that much, because it's
outside of what you agreed to. This place has changed since
I was here last, but we'll make it do, and that water ought to
clear up fit to drink before long. You can settle down here
for a few days while I ride around and fix it up with the
sheep camps to let the horses stay here. We've got to do
that, or they're liable to think it's some wild bunch and start
shootin' 'em. Somebody's got to stay with 'em, and I can git
along with these herders better than you can."

"If you've got any sense, you'll let them sheep outfits
alone," Beech said. "They don't like tame horses on this
grass any better than they do wild ones, and they won't
make any more bones about shootin' 'em if they find out
they're in here. It's a hard place to find, and they'll stay

close on account of the water, and you'd better pull out and let 'em have it to themselves. That's what I aim to do."

"You've done what you agreed to, and I ain't got any right to hold you any longer," old Apling said. "I wish I could. You're wrong about them sheep outfits. I've got as much right to pasture this ridge as they have, and they know it, and nobody ever lost anything by actin' sociable with people."

"Somebody will before very long," Beech said. "I've got relatives in the sheep business, and I know what they're like. You'll land yourself in trouble, and I don't want to be around when you do it. I'm pullin' out of here in the morning, and if you had any sense you'd pull out along with me."

There were several things that kept Beech from getting much sleep during the night. One was the attachment that the horses showed for his sleeping place; they stuck so close that he could almost feel their breath on him, could hear the soft breaking sound that the grass made as they pulled it, the sound of their swallowing, the jar of the ground under him when one of the horses changed ground, the peaceful regularity of their eating, as if they didn't have to bother about anything so long as they kept old Apling in sight.

Another irritating thing was old Apling's complete freedom from uneasiness. He ought by rights to have felt more worried about the future than Beech did, but he slept, with the hard ground for a bed and his hard saddle for a pillow and the horses almost stepping on him every minute or two, as soundly as if the entire trip had come out exactly to suit him and there was nothing ahead but plain sailing.

His restfulness was so hearty and so unjustifiable that Beech couldn't sleep for feeling indignant about it, and got up and left about daylight to keep from being exposed to any more of it. He left without waking old Apling, because he saw no sense in a leave-taking that would consist merely in repeating his common-sense warnings and having them ignored, and he was so anxious to get clear of the whole layout that he didn't even take along anything to eat. The only thing he took from the pack was his ramshackle old pistol; there was no holster for it, and, in the hope that he

might get a chance to use it on a loose quail or prairie
chicken, he stowed it in an empty flour sack and hung it on
his saddle horn, a good deal like an old squaw heading for
the far blue distances with a bundle of diapers.

III

There was never anything recreational about traveling a
rock desert at any season of the year, and the combination
of spring gales, winter chilliness and summer drought all
striking at once brought it fairly close to hard punishment.
Beech's saddle pony, being jaded at the start with overwork
and underfeeding and no water, broke down in the first
couple of miles, and got so feeble and tottery that Beech
had to climb off and lead him, searching likely-looking thick-
ets all the way down the gully in the hope of finding some
little trickle that he wouldn't be too finicky to drink.

The nearest he came to it was a fair-sized rock sink under
some big half-budded cottonwoods that looked, by its dampness and the abundance of fresh animal tracks around it, as
if it might have held water recently, but of water there was
none, and even digging a hole in the center of the basin
failed to fetch a drop.

The work of digging, hill climbing and scrambling through
brush piles raised Beech's appetite so powerfully that he
could scarcely hold up, and, a little above where the gully
opened into the flat sagebrush plateau, he threw away his
pride, pistoled himself a jack rabbit, and took it down into
the sagebrush to cook, where his fire wouldn't give away
which gully old Apling was camped in.

Jack rabbit didn't stand high as a food. It was considered
an excellent thing to give men in the last stages of famine,
because they weren't likely to injure themselves by eating
too much of it, but for ordinary occasions it was looked
down on, and Beech covered his trail out of the gully and
built his cooking fire in the middle of a high stand of
sagebrush, so as not to be embarrassed by inquisitive visitors.

The meat cooked up strong, as it always did, but he ate

what he needed of it, and he was wrapping the remainder in
his flour sack to take along with him when a couple of men
rode past, saw his pony, and turned in to look him over.

They looked him over so closely and with so little concern
for his privacy that he felt insulted before they even spoke.

He studied them less openly, judging by their big gallon
canteens that they were out on some long scout.

One of them was some sort of hired hand, by his looks; he
was broad-faced and gloomy-looking, with a fine white horse,
a flower-stamped saddle, an expensive rifle scabbarded under his knee, and a fifteen-dollar saddle blanket, while his
own manly form was set off by a yellow hotel blanket and a
ninety-cent pair of overalls.

The other man had on a store suit, a plain black hat, fancy
stitched boots, and a white shirt and necktie, and rode a
burr-tailed Indian pony and an old wrangling saddle with
a loose horn. He carried no weapons in sight, but there was
a narrow strap across the lower spread of his necktie which
indicated the presence of a shoulder holster somewhere
within reach.

He opened the conversation by inquiring where Beech
had come from, what his business was, where he was going
and why he hadn't taken the county road to go there, and
why he had to eat jack rabbit when the country was littered
with sheep camps where he could get a decent meal by
asking for it?

"I come from the upper country," Beech said, being
purposely vague about it. "I'm travelin', and I stopped here
because my horse give out. He won't drink out of any place
that's had sheep in it, and he's gone short of water till he
breaks down easy."

"There's a place corralled in for horses to drink at down at
my lower camp," the man said, and studied Beech's pony.
"There's no reason for you to bum through the country on
jack rabbit in a time like this. My herder can take you down
to our water hole and see that you get fed and put to work
till you can make a stake for yourself. I'll give you a note.
That pony looks like he had Ream Gervais' brand on him.

Do you know anything about that herd of old work horses he's been pasturing around?"

"I don't know anything about him," Beech said, side-stepping the actual question while he thought over the offer of employment. He could have used a stake, but the location didn't strike him favorably. It was too close to old Apling's camp, he could see trouble ahead over the horse herd, and he didn't want to be around when it started. "If you'll direct me how to find your water, I'll ride on down there, but I don't need anybody to go with me, and I don't need any stake. I'm travelin'."

The man said there wasn't anybody so well off that he couldn't use a stake, and that it would be hardly any trouble at all for Beech to get one. "I want you to understand how we're situated around here, so you won't think we're any bunch of stranglers," he said. "You can see what kind of a year this has been, when we have to run lambed ewes in a rock patch like this. We've got five thousand lambs in here that we're trying to bring through, and we've had to fight the blamed wild horses for this pasture since the day we moved in. A horse that ain't worth hell room will eat as much as two dozen sheep worth twenty dollars, with the lambs, so you can see how it figures out. We've got 'em pretty well thinned out, but one of my packers found a trail of a new bunch that came up from around Three Notch within the last day or two, and we don't want them to feel as if we'd neglected them. We'd like to find out where they lit. You wouldn't have any information about 'em?"

"None that would do you any good to know," Beech said. "I know the man with that horse herd, and it ain't any use to let on that I don't, but it wouldn't be any use to try to deal with him. He don't sell out on a man he works for."

"He might be induced to," the man said. "We'll find him anyhow, but I don't like to take too much time to it. Just for instance, now, suppose you knew that pony of yours would have to go thirsty till you gave us a few directions about that horse herd? You'd be stuck here for quite a spell, wouldn't you?"

He was so pleasant about it that it took Beech a full minute to realize that he was being threatened. The heavy-set herder brought that home to him by edging out into a flank position and hoisting his rifle scabbard so it could be reached in a hurry. Beech removed the cooked jack rabbit from his flour sack carefully, a piece at a time, and, with the same mechanical thoughtfulness, brought out his triggerless old pistol, cut down on the pleasant-spoken man, and hauled back on the hammer and held it poised.

"That herder of yours had better go easy on his rifle," he said, trying to keep his voice from trembling. "This pistol shoots if I don't hold back the hammer, and if he knocks me out I'll have to let go of it. You'd better watch him, if you don't want your tack drove. I won't give you no directions about that horse herd, and this pony of mine won't go thirsty for it, either. Loosen them canteens of yours and let 'em drop on the ground. Drop that rifle scabbard back where it belongs, and unbuckle the straps and let go of it. If either of you tries any funny business, there'll be one of you to pack home, heels first."

The quaver in his voice sounded childish and undignified to him, but it had a more businesslike ring to them than any amount of manly gruffness. The herder unbuckled his rifle scabbard, and they both cast loose their canteen straps, making it last as long as they could while they argued with him, not angrily, but as if he was a dull stripling whom they wanted to save from some foolishness that he was sure to regret. They argued ethics, justice, common sense, his future prospects, and the fact that what he was doing amounted to robbery by force and arms and that it was his first fatal step into a probably unsuccessful career of crime. They worried over him, they explained themselves to him, and they ridiculed him.

They managed to make him feel like several kinds of a fool, and they were so pleasant and concerned about it that they came close to breaking him down. What held him steady was the thought of old Apling waiting up the gully.

"That herder with the horses never sold out on any man,

and I won't sell out on him," he said. "You've said your say
and I'm tired of holdin' this pistol on cock for you, so move
along out of here. Keep to open ground, so I can be sure
you're gone, and don't be in too much of a hurry to come
back. I've got a lot of things I want to think over, and I want
to be let alone while I do it."

IV

He did have some thinking that needed tending to, but
he didn't take time for it. When the men were well out of
range, he emptied their canteens into his hat and let his
pony drink. Then he hung the canteens and the scabbarded
rifle on a bush and rode back up the gully where the horse
camp was, keeping to shaly ground so as not to leave any
tracks. It was harder going up than it had been coming
down.

He had turned back from the scene of his run-in with the
two sheepmen about noon, and he was still a good two miles
from the camp when the sun went down, the wind lulled
and the night frost began to bite at him so hard that he
dismounted and walked to get warm. That raised his appetite again, and, as if by some special considerateness of
Nature, the cottonwoods around him seemed to be alive
with jack rabbits heading down into the pitch-dark gully
where he had fooled away valuable time trying to find water
that morning.

They didn't stimulate his hunger much; for a time they
even made him feel less like eating anything. Then his pony
gave out and had to rest, and, noticing that the cottonwoods
around him were beginning to bud out, he remembered
that peeling the bark off in the budding season would fetch
out a foamy, sweet-tasting sap which, among children of the
plateau country, was considered something of a delicacy.

He cut a blaze on a fair-sized sapling, waited ten minutes
or so, and touched his finger to it to see how much sap had
accumulated. None had; the blaze was moist to his touch,
but scarcely more so than when he had whittled it.

It wasn't important enough to do any bothering about, and yet a whole set of observed things began to draw together in his mind and form themselves into an explanation of something he had puzzled over: the fresh animal tracks he had seen around the rock sink when there wasn't any water; the rabbits going down into the gully; the cottonwoods in which the sap rose enough during the day to produce buds and got driven back at night when the frost set in. During the day, the cottonwoods had drawn the water out of the ground for themselves; at night they stopped drawing it, and it drained out into the rock sink for the rabbits.

It all worked out so simply that he led his pony down into the gully to see how much there was in it, and, losing his footing on the steep slope, coasted down into the rock sink in the dark and landed in water and thin mud up to his knees. He led his pony down into it to drink, which seemed little enough to get back for the time he had fooled away on it, and then he headed for the horse camp, which was all too easily discernible by the plume of smoke rising, white and ostentatious, against the dark sky from old Apling's campfire.

He made the same kind of entrance that old Apling usually affected when bringing some important item of news. He rode past the campfire and pulled up at a tree, got off deliberately, knocked an accumulation of dead twigs from his hat, took off his saddle and bridle and balanced them painstakingly in the tree fork, and said it was affecting to see how widespread the shortage of pasture was.

"It generally is," old Apling said. "I had a kind of a notion you'd be back after you'd had time to study things over. I suppose you got into some kind of a rumpus with some of them sheep outfits. What was it? Couldn't you git along with them, or couldn't they hit it off with you?"

"There wasn't any trouble between them and me," Beech said. "The only point we had words over was you. They wanted to know where you was camped, so they could shoot you up, and I didn't think it was right to tell 'em. I had to put a gun on a couple of 'em before they'd believe I meant

business, and that was all there was to it. They're out after
you now, and they can see the smoke of this fire of yours for
twenty miles, so they ought to be along almost any time
now. I thought I'd come back and see you work your socia-
bility on 'em."

"You probably kicked up a squabble with 'em yourself,"
old Apling said. He looked a little uneasy. "You talked right
up to 'em, I'll bet, and slapped their noses with your hat to
show 'em that they couldn't run over you. Well, what's
done is done. You did come back, and maybe they'd have
jumped us anyway. There ain't much that we can do. The
horses have got to have water before they can travel, and
they won't touch that seep. It ain't cleared up a particle."

"You can put that fire out, not but what the whole country has probably seen the smoke from it already," Beech
said. "If you've got to tag after these horses, you can run
'em off down the draw and keep 'em to the brush where
they won't leave a trail. There's some young cottonwood
bark that they can eat if they have to, and there's water in a
rock sink under some big cottonwood trees. I'll stay here
and hold off anybody that shows up, so you'll have time to
git your tracks covered."

Old Apling went over and untied the flour-sacked pistol
from Beech's saddle, rolled it into his blankets, and sat
down on it. "If there's any holdin' off to be done, I'll do it,"
he said. "You're a little too high-spirited to suit me, and a
little too hasty about your conclusions. I looked over that
rock sink down the draw today, and there wasn't anything in
it but mud, and blamed little of that. Somebody had dug for
water, and there wasn't none."

"There is now," Beech said. He tugged off one of his wet
boots and poured about a pint of the disputed fluid on the
ground. "There wasn't any in the daytime because the cottonwoods took it all. They let up when it turns cold, and it
runs back in. I waded in it."

He started to put his boot back on. Old Apling reached
out and took it, felt of it inside and out, and handed it over
as if performing some ceremonial presentation.

"I'd never have figured out a thing like that in this world," he said. "If we git them horses out of here, it'll be you that done it. We'll bunch 'em and work 'em down there. It won't be no picnic, but we'll make out to handle it somehow. We've got to, after a thing like this."

Beech remembered what had occasioned the discovery, and said he would have to have something to eat first. "I want you to keep in mind that it's you I'm doin' this for," he said. "I don't owe that old groundhog of a Ream Gervais anything. The only thing I hate about this is that it'll look like I'd done him a favor."

"He won't take it for one, I guess," old Apling said. "We've got to git these horses out because it'll be a favor to you. You wouldn't want to have it told around that you'd done a thing like findin' that water, and then have to admit that we'd lost all the horses anyhow. We can't lose 'em. You've acted like a man tonight, and I'll be blamed if I'll let you spoil it for any childish spite."

They got the horses out none too soon. Watering them took a long time, and when they finally did consent to call it enough and climb back up the side hill, Beech and old Apling heard a couple of signal shots from the direction of their old camping place, and saw a big glare mount up into the sky from it as the visitors built up their campfire to look the locality over. The sight was almost comforting; if they had to keep away from a pursuit, it was at least something to know where it was.

V

From then on they followed a grab-and-run policy, scouting ahead before they moved, holding to the draws by day and crossing open ground only after dark, never pasturing over a couple of hours in any one place, and discovering food value in outlandish substances—rock lichens, the sprouts of wild plum and serviceberry, the moss of old trees and the bark of some young ones—that neither they nor the horses had ever considered fit to eat before. When they struck

Boulder River Canyon they dropped down and toenailed their way along one side of it where they could find grass and water with less likelihood of having trouble about it.

The breaks of the canyon were too rough to run new-lambed sheep in, and they met with so few signs of occupancy that old Apling got overconfident, neglected his scouting to tie back a break they had been obliged to make in a line fence, and ran the horse herd right over the top of a camp where some men were branding calves, tearing down a cook tent and part of a corral and scattering cattle and bedding from the river all the way to the top of the canyon.

By rights, they should have sustained some damage for that piece of carelessness, but they drove through fast, and they were out of sight around a shoulder of rimrock before any of the men could get themselves picked up. Somebody did throw a couple of shots after them as they were pulling into a thicket of mock orange and chokecherry, but it was only with a pistol, and he probably did it more to relieve his feelings than with any hope of hitting anything.

They were so far out of range that they couldn't even hear where the bullets landed.

Neither of them mentioned that unlucky run-in all the rest of that day. They drove hard, punished the horses savagely when they lagged, and kept them at it until, a long time after dark, they struck an old rope ferry that crossed Boulder River at a place called, in memory of its original founders, Robbers' Roost.

The ferry wasn't a public carrier, and there was not even any main road down to it. It was used by the ranches in the neighborhood as the only means of crossing the river for fifty miles in either direction, and it was tied in to a log with a good solid chain and padlock. It was a way to cross, and neither of them could see anything else but to take it.

Beech favored waiting for daylight for it, pointing out that there was a ranch light half a mile up the slope, and that if anybody caught them hustling a private ferry in the dead of night they would probably be taken for criminals on the dodge. Old Apling said it was altogether likely, and drew Beech's pistol and shot the padlock apart with it.

"They could hear that up at that ranch house," Beech said. "What if they come pokin' down here to see what we're up to?"

Old Apling tossed the fragments of padlock into the river and hung the pistol in the waistband of his trousers. "Let 'em come," he said. "They'll go back again with their fingers in their mouths. This is your trip, and you put in good work on it, and I like to ruined the whole thing stoppin' to patch an eighty-cent fence so some scissorbill wouldn't have his feelings hurt, and that's the last accommodation anybody gits out of me till this is over with. I can take about six horses at a trip, it looks like. Help me to bunch 'em."

Six horses at a trip proved to be an overestimate. The best they could do was five, and the boat rode so deep with them that Beech refused to risk handling it. He stayed with the herd, and old Apling cut it loose, let the current sweep it across into slack water, and hauled it in to the far bank by winding in its cable on an old homemade capstan. Then he turned the horses into a counting pen and came back for another load.

He worked at it fiercely, as if he had a bet up that he could wear the whole ferry rig out, but it went with infernal slowness, and when the wind began to move for daylight there were a dozen horses still to cross and no place to hide them in case the ferry had other customers.

Beech waited and fidgeted over small noises until, hearing voices and the clatter of hoofs on shale far up the canyon behind him, he gave way, drove the remaining horses into the river, and swam them across, letting himself be towed along by his saddle horn and floating his clothes ahead of him on a board.

He paid for that flurry of nervousness before he got out. The water was so cold it paralyzed him, and so swift it whisked him a mile downstream before he could get his pony turned to breast it. He grounded on a gravel bar in a thicket of dwarf willows, with numbness striking clear to the center of his diaphragm and deadening his arms so he couldn't pick his clothes loose from the bundle to put on. He managed it, by using his teeth and elbows, and warmed himself a little by driving the horses afoot through the brush till he struck the ferry landing.

It had got light enough to see things in outline, and old Apling was getting ready to shove off for another crossing when the procession came lumbering at him out of the shadows. He came ashore, counted the horses into the corral to make sure none had drowned, and laid Beech under all the blankets and built up a fire to limber him out by. He got breakfast and got packed to leave, and he did some rapid expounding about the iniquity of risking the whole trip on such a wild piece of foolhardiness.

"That was the reason I wanted you to work this boat," he said. "I could have stood up to anybody that come projectin' around, and if they wanted trouble I could have filled their order for 'em. They won't bother us now, anyhow; it don't matter how bad they want to."

"I could have stood up to 'em if I'd had anything to do it with," Beech said. "You've got that pistol of mine, and I couldn't see to throw rocks. What makes you think they won't bother us? You know it was that brandin' crew comin' after us, don't you?"

"I expect that's who it was," old Apling agreed. "They ought to be out after the cattle we scattered, but you can trust a bunch of cowboys to pick out the most useless things to tend to first. I've got that pistol of yours because I don't aim for you to git in trouble with it while this trip is on. There won't anybody bother us because I've cut all the cables on the ferry, and it's lodged downstream on a gravel spit. If anybody crosses after us within fifty miles of here, he'll swim, and the people around here ain't as reckless around cold water as you are."

Beech sat up. "We got to git out of here," he said. "There's people on this side of the river that use that ferry, you old fool, and they'll have us up before every grand jury in the country from now on. The horses ain't worth it."

"What the horses is worth ain't everything," old Apling said. "There's a part of this trip ahead that you'll be glad you went through. You're entitled to that much out of it, after the work you've put in, and I aim to see that you git it. It ain't any use tryin' to explain to you what it is. You'll notice it when the time comes."

VI

They worked north, following the breaks of the river canyon, finding the rock breaks hard to travel, but easy to avoid observation in, and the grass fair in stand, but so poor and washy in body that the horses had to spend most of their time eating enough to keep up their strength so they could move.

They struck a series of gorges, too deep and precipitous to be crossed at all, and had to edge back into milder country where there were patches of plowed ground, some being harrowed over for summer fallow and others venturing out with a bright new stand of dark-green wheat.

The pasture was patchy and scoured by the wind, and all the best parts of it were under fence, which they didn't dare cut for fear of getting in trouble with the natives. Visibility was high in that section; the ground lay open to the north as far as they could see, the wind kept the air so clear that it hurt to look at the sky, and they were never out of sight of wheat ranchers harrowing down summer fallow.

A good many of the ranchers pulled up and stared after the horse herd as it went past, and two or three times they waved and rode down toward the road, as if they wanted to make it an excuse for stopping work. Old Apling surmised that they had some warning they wanted to deliver against respassing, and he drove on without waiting to hear it.

They were unable to find a camping place anywhere among those wheat fields, so they drove clear through to open country and spread down for the night alongside a shallow pond in the middle of some new grass not far enough along to be pastured, though the horses made what

they could out of it. There were no trees or shrubs anywhere
around, not even sagebrush. Lacking fuel for a fire, they
camped without one, and since there was no grass anywhere
except around the pond, they left the horses unguarded,
rolled in to catch up sleep, and were awakened about daylight by the whole herd stampeding past them at a gallop.

They both got up and moved fast. Beech ran for his pony,
which was trying to pull loose from its picket rope to go
with the bunch. Old Apling ran out into the dust afoot,
waggling the triggerless old pistol and trying to make out
objects in the half-light by hard squinting. The herd horses
fetched a long circle and came back past him, with a couple
of riders clouting along behind trying to turn them back into
open country. One of the riders opened up a rope and
swung it, the other turned in and slapped the inside flank-
ers with his hat, and old Apling hauled up the old pistol,
flipped the hammer a couple of rounds to get it warmed up,
and let go at them twice.

The half darkness held noise as if it had been a cellar. The
two shots banged monstrously, Beech yelled to old Apling to
be careful who he shot at, and the two men shied off sideways
and rode away into the open country. One of them yelled
something that sounded threatening in tone as they went out
of sight, but neither of them seemed in the least inclined to
bring on any general engagement. The dust blew clear, the
herd horses came back to grass, old Apling looked at the pistol
and punched the two exploded shells out of it, and Beech
ordered him to hand it over before he got in trouble with it.

"How do you know but what them men had a right
here?" he demanded sternly. "We'd be in a fine jack pot if
you'd shot one of 'em and it turned out he owned this land
we're on, wouldn't we?"

Old Apling looked at him, holding the old pistol poised as
if he was getting ready to lead a band with it. The light
strengthened and shed a rose-colored radiance over him, so
he looked flushed and joyous and lifted up. With some of
the dust knocked off him, he could have filled in easily as a
day star and son of the morning, whiskers and all.

"I wouldn't have shot them men for anything you could buy me!" he said, and faced north to a blue line of bluffs that came up out of the shadows, a blue gleam of water that moved under them, a white steamboat that moved upstream, glittering as the first light struck it. "Them men wasn't here because we was trespassers. Them was horse thieves, boy! We've brought these horses to a place where they're worth stealin', and we've brought 'em through! The railroad is under them bluffs, and that water down there is the old Columbia River!"

They might have made it down to the river that day, but having it in sight and knowing that nothing could stop them from reaching it, there no longer seemed any object in driving so unsparingly. They ate breakfast and talked about starting, and they even got partly packed up for it. Then they got occupied with talking to a couple of wheat ranchers who pulled in to inquire about buying some of the horse herd; the drought had run up wheat prices at a time when the country's livestock had been allowed to run down, and so many horses had been shot and starved out that they were having to take pretty much anything they could get.

Old Apling swapped them a couple of the most jaded herd horses for part of a haystack, referred other applicants to Gervais down at the railroad, and spent the remainder of the day washing, patching clothes and saddlery, and watching the horses get acquainted once more with a conventional diet.

The next morning a rancher dropped off a note from Gervais urging them to come right on down, and adding a kind but firm admonition against running up any feed bills without his express permission. He made it sound as if there might be some hurry about catching the horse market on the rise, so they got ready to leave, and Beech looked back over the road they had come, thinking of all that had happened on it.

"I'd like it better if old Gervais didn't have to work himself in on the end of it," he said. "I'd like to step out on the whole business right now."

"You'd be a fool to do that," old Apling said. "This is outside your work contract, so we can make the old gopher pay you what it's worth. I'll want to go in ahead and see about that and about the money that he owes me and about corral space and feed and one thing and another, so I'll want you to bring 'em in alone. You ain't seen everything there is to a trip like this, and you won't unless you stay with it."

VII

There would be no ending to this story without an understanding of what that little river town looked like at the hour, a little before sundown of a windy spring day, when Beech brought the desert horse herd down into it. On the wharf below town, some men were unloading baled hay from a steamboat, with some passengers watching from the saloon deck, and the river beyond them hoisting into white-capped peaks that shone and shed dazzling spray over the darkening water.

A switch engine was handling stock cars on a spur track, and the brakeman flagged it to a stop and stood watching the horses, leaning into the wind to keep his balance while the engineer climbed out on the tender to see what was going on.

The street of the town was lined with big leafless poplars that looked as if they hadn't gone short of moisture a day of their lives; the grass under them was bright green, and there were women working around flower beds and pulling up weeds, enough of them so that a horse could have lived on them for two days.

There was a Chinaman clipping grass with a pair of sheep shears to keep it from growing too tall, and there were lawn sprinklers running clean water on the ground in streams. There were stores with windows full of new clothes, and stores with bright hardware, and stores with strings of bananas and piles of oranges, bread and crackers and candy and rows of hams, and there were groups of anxious-faced men sitting around stoves inside who came out to watch

Beech pass and told one another hopefully that the back country might make a good year out of it yet, if a youngster could bring that herd of horses through it.

There were women who hauled back their children and cautioned them not to get in the man's way, and there were boys and girls, some near Beech's own age, who watched him and stood looking after him, knowing that he had been through more than they had ever seen and not suspecting that it had taught him something that they didn't know about the things they saw every day. None of them knew what it meant to be in a place where there were delicacies to eat and new clothes to wear and look at, what it meant to be warm and out of the wind for a change, what it could mean merely to have water enough to pour on the ground and grass enough to cut down and throw away.

For the first time, seeing how the youngsters looked at him, he understood what that amounted to. There wasn't a one of them who wouldn't have traded places with him. There wasn't one that he would have traded places with, for all the haberdashery and fancy groceries in town. He turned down to the corrals, and old Apling held the gate open for him and remarked that he hadn't taken much time to it.

"You're sure you had enough of that ridin' through town?" he said. "It ain't the same when you do it a second time, remember."

"It'll last me," Beech said. "I wouldn't have missed it, and I wouldn't want it to be the same again. I'd sooner have things the way they run with us out in the high country. I'd sooner not have anything be the same a second time."

Barn Burning

William Faulkner

The store in which the Justice of the Peace's court was sitting smelled of cheese. The boy, crouched on his nail keg at the back of the crowded room, knew he smelled cheese, and more: from where he sat he could see the ranked shelves close-packed with the solid, squat, dynamic shapes of tin cans whose labels his stomach read, not from the lettering which meant nothing to his mind but from the scarlet devils and the silver curve of fish—this, the cheese which he knew he smelled and the hermetic meat which his intestines believed he smelled coming in intermittent gusts momentary and brief between the other constant one, the smell and sense just a little of fear because mostly of despair and grief, the old fierce pull of blood. He could not see the table where the Justice sat and before which his father and his father's enemy (*our enemy* he thought in that despair; *ourn! mine and hisn both! He's my father!*) stood, but he could hear them, the two of them that is: because his father had said no word yet:

"But what proof have you, Mr. Harris?"

"I told you. The hog got into my corn. I caught it up and sent it back to him. He had no fence that would hold it. I told him so, warned him. The next time I put the hog in my pen. When he came to get it I gave him enough wire to patch up his pen. The next time I put the hog up and kept it. I rode down to his house and saw the wire I gave him still rolled on to the spool in his yard. I told him he could have the hog when he paid me a dollar pound fee. That evening a nigger came with the dollar and got the hog. He was a strange nigger. He said, 'He say to tell you wood and hay kin burn.' I said, 'What?' 'That whut he say to tell you,' the nigger said, 'Wood and hay kin burn.' That night my barn burned. I got the stock out but I lost the barn."

"Where is the nigger? Have you got him?"

"He was a strange nigger, I tell you. I don't know what became of him."

"But that's not proof. Don't you see that's not proof?"

"Get that boy up here. He knows." For a moment the boy thought too that the man meant his older brother until Harris said, "Not him. The little one. The boy," and, crouching, small for his age, small and wiry like his father, in patched and faded jeans even too small for him, with straight, uncombed, brown hair and eyes gray and wild as storm scud, he saw the men between himself and the table part and become a lane of grim faces, at the end of which he saw the Justice, a shabby, collarless, graying man in spectacles, beckoning him. He felt no floor under his bare feet; he seemed to walk beneath the palpable weight of the grim turning faces. His father, stiff in his black Sunday coat donned not for the trial but for the moving, did not even look at him. *He aims for me to lie*, he thought, again with that frantic grief and despair. *And I will have to do hit*.

"What's your name, boy?" the Justice said.

"Colonel Sartoris Snopes," the boy whispered.

"Hey?" the Justice said. "Talk louder. Colonel Sartoris? I reckon anybody named for Colonel Sartoris in this country can't help but tell the truth, can they?" The boy said nothing. *Enemy! Enemy!* he thought; for a moment he could not even see, could not see that the Justice's face was kindly nor discern that his voice was troubled when he spoke to the man named Harris: "Do you want me to question this boy?" But he could hear, and during those subsequent long seconds while there was absolutely no sound in the crowded little room save that of quiet and intent breathing it was as if he had swung outward at the end of a grape vine, over a ravine, and at the top of the swing had been caught in a prolonged instant of mesmerized gravity, weightless in time.

"No!" Harris said violently, explosively. "Damnation! Send him out of here!" Now time, the fluid world, rushed beneath him again, the voices coming to him again through the smell of cheese and sealed meat, the fear and despair and the old grief of blood:

"This case is closed. I can't find against you, Snopes, but I can give you advice. Leave this country and don't come back to it."

His father spoke for the first time, his voice cold and harsh, level, without emphasis: "I aim to. I don't figure to stay in a country among people who . . ." he said something unprintable and vile, addressed to no one.

"That'll do," the Justice said. "Take your wagon and get out of this country before dark. Case dismissed."

His father turned, and he followed the stiff black coat, the wiry figure walking a little stiffly from where a Confederate provost's man's musket ball had taken him in the heel on a stolen horse thirty years ago, followed the two backs now, since his older brother had appeared from somewhere in the crowd, no taller than the father but thicker, chewing tobacco steadily, between the two lines of grim-faced men and out of the store and across the worn gallery and down the sagging steps and among the dogs and half-grown boys in the mild May dust, where as he passed a voice hissed:

"Barn burner!"

Again he could not see, whirling; there was a face in a red haze, moonlike, bigger than the full moon, the owner of it half again his size, he leaping in the red haze toward the face, feeling no blow, feeling no shock when his head struck the earth, scrabbling up and leaping again, feeling no blow this time either and tasting no blood, scrabbling up to see the other boy in full flight and himself already leaping into pursuit as his father's hand jerked him back, the harsh, cold voice speaking above him: "Go get in the wagon."

It stood in a grove of locusts and mulberries across the road. His two hulking sisters in their Sunday dresses and his

mother and her sister in calico and sunbonnets were already
in it, sitting on and among the sorry residue of the dozen
and more movings which even the boy could remember—
the battered stove, the broken beds and chairs, the clock
inlaid with mother-of-pearl, which would not run, stopped
at some fourteen minutes past two o'clock of a dead and
forgotten day and time, which had been his mother's dowry.
She was crying, though when she saw him she drew her
sleeve across her face and began to descend from the wagon.
"Get back," the father said.

"He's hurt. I got to get some water and wash his . . ."

"Get back in the wagon," his father said. He got in too,
over the tail-gate. His father mounted to the seat where the
older brother already sat and struck the gaunt mules two
savage blows with the peeled willow, but without heat. It
was not even sadistic; it was exactly that same quality which
in later years would cause his descendants to overrun the
engine before putting a motor car into motion, striking and
reining back in the same movement. The wagon went on,
the store with its quiet crowd of grimly watching men
dropped behind; a curve in the road hid it. *Forever* he
thought. *Maybe he's done satisfied now, now that he has
. . .* stopping himself, not to say it aloud even to himself. His
mother's hand touched his shoulder.

"Does hit hurt?" she said.

"Naw," he said. "Hit don't hurt. Lemme be."

"Can't you wipe some of the blood off before hit dries?"

"I'll wash to-night," he said. "Lemme be, I tell you."

The wagon went on. He did not know where they were
going. None of them ever did or ever asked, because it was
always somewhere, always a house of sorts waiting for them
a day or two days or even three days away. Likely his father
had already arranged to make a crop on another farm before
he . . . Again he had to stop himself. He (the father) always
did. There was something about his wolflike independence
and even courage when the advantage was at least neutral
which impressed strangers, as if they got from his latent
ravening ferocity not so much a sense of dependability as a

feeling that his ferocious conviction in the rightness of his own actions would be of advantage to all whose interest lay with his.

That night they camped, in a grove of oaks and beeches where a spring ran. The nights were still cool and they had a fire against it, of a rail lifted from a nearby fence and cut into lengths—a small fire, neat, niggard almost, a shrewd fire; such fires were his father's habit and custom always, even in freezing weather. Older, the boy might have remarked this and wondered why not a big one; why should not a man who had not only seen the waste and extravagance of war, but who had in his blood an inherent voracious prodigality with material not his own, have burned everything in sight? Then he might have gone a step farther and thought that that was the reason: that niggard blaze was the living fruit of nights passed during those four years in the woods hiding from all men, blue or gray, with his strings of horses (captured horses, he called them). And older still, he might have divined the true reason: that the element of fire spoke to some deep mainspring of his father's being, as the element of steel or of powder spoke to other men, as the one weapon for the preservation of integrity, else breath were not worth the breathing, and hence to be regarded with respect and used with discretion.

But he did not think this now and he had seen those same niggard blazes all his life. He merely ate his supper beside it and was already half asleep over his iron plate when his father called him, and once more he followed the stiff back, the stiff and ruthless limp, up the slope and on to the starlit road where, turning, he could see his father against the stars but without face or depth—a shape black, flat, and bloodless as though cut from tin in the iron folds of the frockcoat which had not been made for him, the voice harsh like tin and without heat like tin:

"You were fixing to tell them. You would have told him." He didn't answer. His father struck him with the flat of his hand on the side of the head, hard but without heat, exactly as he had struck the two mules at the store, exactly as he would strike either of them with any stick in order to kill a horse fly, his voice still without fear or anger: "You're getting to be a man. You got to learn. You got to learn to stick to your own blood or you ain't going to have any blood to stick to you. Do you think either of them, any man there this morning, would? Don't you know all they wanted was a chance to get at me because they knew I had them beat? Eh?" Later, twenty years later, he was to tell himself, "If I had said they wanted only truth, justice, he would have hit me again." But now he said nothing. He was not crying. He just stood there. "Answer me," his father said.

"Yes," he whispered. His father turned.

"Get on to bed. We'll be there to-morrow."

To-morrow they were there. In the early afternoon the wagon stopped before a paintless two-room house identical almost with the dozen others it had stopped before even in the boy's ten years, and again, as on the other dozen occasions, his mother and aunt got down and began to unload the wagon, although his two sisters and his father and brother had not moved.

"Likely hit ain't fitten for hawgs," one of the sisters said.

"Nevertheless, fit it will and you'll hog it and like it," his father said. "Get out of them chairs and help your Ma unload."

The two sisters got down, big, bovine, in a flutter of cheap ribbons; one of them drew from the jumbled wagon bed a battered lantern, the other a worn broom. His father handed the reins to the older son and began to climb stiffly over the wheel. "When they get unloaded, take the team to the barn and feed them." Then he said, and at first the boy thought he was still speaking to his brother: "Come with me."

"Me?" he said.

"Yes," his father said. "You."

"Abner," his mother said. His father paused and looked back—the harsh level stare beneath the shaggy, graying, irascible brows.

"I reckon I'll have a word with the man that aims to begin to-morrow owning me body and soul for the next eight months."

They went back up the road. A week ago—or before last night, that is—he would have asked where they were going, but not now. His father had struck him before last night but never before had he paused afterward to explain why it was as if the blow and the following calm, outrageous voice still rang, repercussed, divulging nothing to him save the terrible handicap of being young, the light weight of his few years, just heavy enough to prevent his soaring free of the world as it seemed to be ordered but not heavy enough to keep him footed solid in it, to resist it and try to change the course of its events.

Presently he could see the grove of oaks and cedars and the other flowering trees and shrubs where the house would be, though not the house yet. They walked beside a fence massed with honeysuckle and Cherokee roses and came to a gate swinging open between two brick pillars, and now, beyond a sweep of drive, he saw the house for the first time and at that instant he forgot his father and the terror and despair both, and even when he remembered his father again (who had not stopped) the terror and despair did not return. Because, for all the twelve movings, they had sojourned until now in a poor country, a land of small farms and fields and houses, and he had never seen a house like this before. *Hit's big as a courthouse* he thought quietly, with a surge of peace and joy whose reason he could not have thought into words, being too young for that: *They are safe from him. People whose lives are a part of this peace and dignity are beyond his touch, he no more to them than a buzzing wasp: capable of stinging for a little moment but that's all; the spell of this peace and dignity rendering even the barns and stable and cribs which belong to it impervious to the puny flames he might contrive* . . . this, the peace and joy, ebbing for an instant as he looked again at the stiff black back, the stiff and implacable limp of the figure which was not dwarfed by the house, for the reason that it had never looked big anywhere and which now, against the serene columned backdrop, had more than ever that impervious quality of something cut ruthlessly from tin, depthless, as though, sidewise to the sun, it would cast no shadow. Watching him, the boy remarked the absolutely undeviating course which his father held and saw the stiff foot come squarely down in a pile of fresh droppings where a horse had stood in the drive and which his father could have avoided by a simple change of stride. But it ebbed only for a moment, though he could not have thought this into words either, walking on in the spell of the house, which he could even want but without envy, without sorrow, certainly never with that ravening and jealous rage which unknown to him walked in the ironlike black coat before him: *Maybe he will feel it too. Maybe it will even change him now from what maybe he couldn't help but be.*

They crossed the portico. Now he could hear his father's stiff foot as it came down on the boards with clocklike finality, a sound out of all proportion to the displacement of the body it bore and which was not dwarfed either by the white door before it, as though it had attained to a sort of vicious and ravening minimum not to be dwarfed by anything—the flat, wide, black hat, the formal coat of broadcloth which had once been black but which had now that friction-glazed greenish cast of the bodies of old house flies, the lifted sleeve which was too large, the lifted hand like a curled claw. The door opened so promptly that the boy knew the Negro must have been watching them all the time, an old man with neat grizzled hair, in a linen jacket, who stood barring the door with his body, saying, "Wipe yo foots, white man, fo you come in here. Major ain't home nohow."

"Get out of my way, nigger," his father said, without heat too, flinging the door back and the Negro also and entering, his hat still on his head. And now the boy saw the prints of the stiff foot on the doorjamb and saw them appear on the pale rug behind the machinelike deliberation of the foot which seemed to bear (or transmit) twice the weight which the body compassed. The Negro was shouting "Miss Lula! Miss Lula!" somewhere behind them, then the boy, deluged as though by a warm wave by a suave turn of carpeted stair and a pendant glitter of chandeliers and a mute gleam of gold frames, heard the swift feet and saw her too, a lady—perhaps he had never seen her like before either—in a gray, smooth gown with lace at the throat and an apron tied at the waist and the sleeves turned back, wiping cake or biscuit dough from her hands with a towel as she came up the hall, looking not at his father at all but at the tracks on the blond rug with an expression of incredulous amazement.

"I tried," the Negro cried. "I tole him to . . ."

"Will you please go away?" she said in a shaking voice. "Major de Spain is not at home. Will you please go away?"

His father had not spoken again. He did not speak again. He did not even look at her. He just stood stiff in the center of the rug, in his hat, the shaggy iron-gray brows twitching slightly above the pebble-colored eyes as he appeared to examine the house with brief deliberation. Then with the same deliberation he turned; the boy watched him pivot on the good leg and saw the stiff foot drag round the arc of the turning, leaving a final long and fading smear. His father never looked at it, he never once looked down at the rug. The Negro held the door. It closed behind them, upon the hysteric and indistinguishable woman-wail. His father stopped at the top of the steps and scraped his boot clean on the edge of it. At the gate he stopped again. He stood for a moment, planted stiffly on the stiff foot, looking back at the house. "Pretty and white, ain't it?" he said. "That's sweat. Nigger sweat. Maybe it ain't white enough yet to suit him. Maybe he wants to mix some white sweat with it."

Two hours later the boy was chopping wood behind the house within which his mother and aunt and the two sisters (the mother and aunt, not the two girls, he knew that; even at this distance and muffled by walls the flat loud voices of the two girls emanated an incorrigible idle inertia) were setting up the stove to prepare a meal, when he heard the hooves and saw the linen-clad man on a fine sorrel mare, whom he recognized even before he saw the rolled rug in front of the Negro youth following on a fat bay carriage horse—a suffused, angry face vanishing, still at full gallop, beyond the corner of the house where his father and brother were sitting in the two tilted chairs; and a moment later, almost before he could have put the axe down, he heard the hooves again and watched the sorrel mare go back out of the yard, already galloping again. Then his father began to shout one of the sisters' names, who presently emerged backward from the kitchen door dragging the rolled rug along the ground by one end while the other sister walked behind it.

"If you ain't going to tote, go on and set up the wash pot," the first said.

"You, Sarty!" the second shouted. "Set up the wash pot!" His father appeared at the door, framed against that shabbiness, as he had been against that other bland perfection, impervious to either, the mother's anxious face at his shoulder.

"Go on," the father said. "Pick it up." The two sisters stooped, broad, lethargic; stooping, they presented an incredible expanse of pale cloth and a flutter of tawdry ribbons.

"If I thought enough of a rug to have to git hit all the way from France I wouldn't keep hit where folks coming in would have to tromp on hit," the first said. They raised the rug.

"Abner," the mother said. "Let me do it."

"You go back and git dinner," his father said. "I'll tend to this."

From the woodpile through the rest of the afternoon the boy watched them, the rug spread flat in the dust beside the bubbling wash-pot, the two sisters stooping over it with that profound and lethargic reluctance, while the father stood over them in turn, implacable and grim, driving them though never raising his voice again. He could smell the harsh homemade lye they were using: he saw his mother come to the door once and look toward them with an expression not anxious now but very like despair; he saw his father turn, and he fell to with the axe and saw from the corner of his eye his father raise from the ground a flattish fragment of field stone and examine it and return to the pot, and this time his mother actually spoke: "Abner. Abner. Please don't. Please, Abner."

Then he was done too. It was dusk; the whippoorwills had already begun. He could smell coffee from the room where they would presently eat the cold food remaining from the mid-afternoon meal, though when he entered the house he realized they were having coffee again probably because there was a fire on the hearth, before which the rug now lay spread over the backs of the two chairs. The tracks of his father's foot were gone. Where they had been were now long, water-cloudy scoriations resembling the sporadic course of a Lilliputian mowing machine.

It still hung there while they ate the cold food and then went to bed, scattered without order or claim up and down the two rooms, his mother in one bed, where his father would later lie, the older brother in the other, himself, the aunt, and the two sisters on pallets on the floor. But his father was not in bed yet. The last thing the boy remembered was the depthless, harsh silhouette of the hat and coat bending over the rug and it seemed to him that he had not even closed his eyes when the silhouette was standing over him, the fire almost dead behind it, the stiff foot prodding him awake. "Catch up the mule," his father said.

When he returned with the mule his father was standing in the black door, the rolled rug over his shoulder. "Ain't you going to ride?" he said.

"No. Give me your foot."

He bent his knee into his father's hand, the wiry, surprising power flowed smoothly, rising, he rising with it, on to the mule's bare back (they had owned a saddle once; the boy could remember it though not when or where) and with the same effortlessness his father swung the rug up in front of him. Now in the starlight they retraced the afternoon's path, up the dusty road rife with honeysuckle, through the gate and up the black tunnel of the drive to the lightless house, where he sat on the mule and felt the rough warp of the rug drag across his thighs and vanish.

"Don't you want me to help?" he whispered. His father did not answer and now he heard again that stiff foot striking the hollow portico with that wooden and clocklike deliberation, that outrageous overstatement of the weight it carried. The rug, hunched, not flung (the boy could tell that even in the darkness) from his father's shoulder struck the angle of wall and floor with a sound unbelievably loud, thunderous, then the foot again, unhurried and enormous; a light came on in the house and the boy sat, tense, breathing steadily and quietly and just a little fast, though the foot itself did not increase its beat at all, descending the steps now; now the boy could see him.

"Don't you want to ride now?" he whispered. "We kin both ride now," the light within the house altering now, flaring up and sinking. *He's coming down the stairs now*, he thought. He had already ridden the mule up beside the horse block; presently his father was up behind him and he doubled the reins over and slashed the mule across the neck, but before the animal could begin to trot the hard, thin arm came round him, the hard, knotted hand jerking the mule back to a walk.

In the first red rays of the sun they were in the lot, putting plow gear on the mules. This time the sorrel mare was in the lot before he heard it at all, the rider collarless and even bareheaded, trembling, speaking in a shaking voice as the woman in the house had done, his father merely looking up once before stooping again to the hame he was buckling, so that the man on the mare spoke to his stooping back:

"You must realize you have ruined that rug. Wasn't there anybody here, any of your women . . ." he ceased, shaking, the boy watching him, the older brother leaning now in the stable door, chewing, blinking slowly and steadily at nothing apparently. "It cost a hundred dollars. But you never had a hundred dollars. You never will. So I'm going to charge you twenty bushels of corn against your crop. I'll add it in your contract and when you come to the commissary you can sign it. That won't keep Mrs. de Spain quiet but maybe it will teach you to wipe your feet off before you enter her house again."

Then he was gone. The boy looked at his father, who still

had not spoken or even looked up again, who was now adjusting the logger-head in the hame.

"Pap," he said. His father looked at him—the inscrutable face, the shaggy brows beneath which the gray eyes glinted coldly. Suddenly the boy went toward him, fast, stopping as suddenly. "You done the best you could!" he cried. "If he wanted hit done different why didn't he wait and tell you how? He won't git no twenty bushels! He won't git none! We'll gether hit and hide hit! I kin watch . . ."

"Did you put the cutter back in that straight stock like I told you?"

"No, sir," he said.

"Then go do it."

That was Wednesday. During the rest of that week he worked steadily, at what was within his scope and some which was beyond it, with an industry that did not need to be driven nor even commanded twice; he had this from his mother, with the difference that some at least of what he did he liked to do, such as splitting wood with the half-size axe which his mother and aunt had earned, or saved money somehow, to present him with at Christmas. In company with the two older women (and on one afternoon, even one of the sisters), he built pens for the shoat and the cow which were a part of his father's contract with the landlord, and one afternoon, his father being absent, gone somewhere on one of the mules, he went to the field.

They were running a middle buster now, his brother holding the plow straight while he handled the reins, and walking beside the straining mule, the rich black soil shearing cool and damp against his bare ankles, he thought *Maybe this is the end of it. Maybe even that twenty bushels that seems hard to have to pay for just a rug will be a cheap price for him to stop forever and always from being what he used to be;* thinking, dreaming now, so that his brother had to speak sharply to him to mind the mule: *Maybe he even won't collect the twenty bushels. Maybe it will all add up and balance and vanish—corn, rug, fire; the terror and*

grief, the being pulled two ways like between two teams of
horses—gone, done with for ever and ever.

Then it was Saturday; he looked up from beneath the
mule he was harnessing and saw his father in the black coat
and hat. "Not that," his father said. "The wagon gear." And
then, two hours later, sitting in the wagon bed behind his
father and brother on the seat, the wagon accomplished a
final curve, and he saw the weathered paintless store with
its tattered tobacco- and patent-medicine posters and the
tethered wagons and saddle animals below the gallery. He
mounted the gnawed steps behind his father and brother,
and there again was the lane of quiet, watching faces for the
three of them to walk through. He saw the man in spectacles sitting at the plank table and he did not need to be told
this was a Justice of the Peace; he sent one glare of fierce,
exultant, partisan defiance at the man in collar and cravat
now, whom he had seen but twice before in his life, and
that on a galloping horse, who now wore on his face an
expression not of rage but of amazed unbelief which the boy
could not have known was at the incredible circumstance of
being sued by one of his own tenants, and came and stood
against his father and cried at the Justice: "He ain't done it!
He ain't burnt . . ."

"Go back to the wagon," his father said.

"Burnt?" the Justice said. "Do I understand this rug was
burned too?"

"Does anybody here claim it was?" his father said. "Go
back to the wagon." But he did not, he merely retreated to
the rear of the room, crowded as that other had been, but
not to sit down this time, instead, to stand pressing among
the motionless bodies, listening to the voices:

"And you claim twenty bushels of corn is too high for the
damage you did to the rug?"

"He brought the rug to me and said he wanted the tracks
washed out of it. I washed the tracks out and took the rug
back to him."

"But you didn't carry the rug back to him in the same
condition it was in before you made the tracks on it."

His father did not answer, and now for perhaps half a minute there was no sound at all save that of breathing, the faint, steady suspiration of complete and intent listening.

"You decline to answer that, Mr. Snopes?" Again his father did not answer. "I'm going to find against you, Mr. Snopes. I'm going to find that you were responsible for the injury to Major de Spain's rug and hold you liable for it. But twenty bushels of corn seems a little high for a man in your circumstances to have to pay. Major de Spain claims it cost a hundred dollars. October corn will be worth about fifty cents. I figure that if Major de Spain can stand a ninety-five dollar loss on something he paid cash for, you can stand a five-dollar loss you haven't earned yet. I hold you in damages to Major de Spain to the amount of ten bushels of corn over and above your contract with him, to be paid to him out of your crop at gathering time. Court adjourned."

It had taken no time hardly, the morning was but half begun. He thought they would return home and perhaps back to the field, since they were late, far behind all other farmers. But instead his father passed on behind the wagon, merely indicating with his hand for the older brother to follow with it, and crossed the road toward the blacksmith shop opposite, pressing on after his father, overtaking him, speaking, whispering up at the harsh, calm face beneath the weathered hat: "He won't git no ten bushels neither. He won't git one. We'll . . ." until his father glanced for an instant down at him, the face absolutely calm, the grizzled eyebrows tangled above the cold eyes, the voice almost pleasant, almost gentle:

"You think so? Well, we'll wait till October anyway."

The matter of the wagon—the setting of a spoke or two and the tightening of the tires—did not take long either, the business of the tires accomplished by driving the wagon into the spring branch behind the shop and letting it stand there, the mules nuzzling into the water from time to time, and the boy on the seat with the idle reins, looking up the slope and through the sooty tunnel of the shed where the slow hammer rang and where his father sat on an upended cypress bolt, easily, either talking or listening, still sitting there when the boy brought the dripping wagon up out of the branch and halted it before the door.

"Take them on to the shade and hitch," his father said. He did so and returned. His father and the smith and a third man squatting on his heels inside the door were talking, about crops and animals; the boy, squatting too in the ammoniac dust and hoof-parings and scales of rust, heard his father tell a long and unhurried story out of the time before the birth of the older brother even when he had been a professional horsetrader. And then his father came up beside him where he stood before a tattered last year's circus poster on the other side of the store, gazing rapt and quiet at the scarlet horses, the incredible poisings and convolutions of tulle and tights and the painted leers of comedians, and said, "It's time to eat."

But not at home. Squatting beside his brother against the front wall, he watched his father emerge from the store and produce from a paper sack a segment of cheese and divide it carefully and deliberately into three with his pocket knife and produce crackers from the same sack. They all three squatted on the gallery and ate, slowly, without talking; then in the store again, they drank from a tin dipper tepid water smelling of the cedar bucket and of living beech trees. And still they did not go home. It was a horse lot this time, a tall rail fence upon and along which men stood and sat and out of which one by one horses were led, to be walked and trotted and then cantered back and forth along the road while the slow swapping and buying went on and the sun began to slant westward, they—the three of them—watching and listening, the older brother with his muddy eyes and his steady, inevitable tobacco, the father commenting now and then on certain of the animals, to no one in particular.

It was after sundown when they reached home. They ate supper by lamplight, then, sitting on the doorstep, the boy watched the night fully accomplish, listening to the whippoorwills and the frogs, when he heard his mother's voice: "Abner! No! No! Oh, God. Oh, God. Abner!" and he rose, whirled, and saw the altered light through the door where a candle stub now burned in a bottle neck on the table and his father, still in the hat and coat, at once formal and burlesque as though dressed carefully for some shabby and ceremonial violence, emptying the reservoir of the lamp back into the five-gallon kerosene can from which it had been filled, while the mother tugged at his arm until he shifted the lamp to the other hand and flung her back, not savagely or viciously, just hard, into the wall, her hands flung out against the wall for balance, her mouth open and in her face the same quality of hopeless despair as had been in her voice. Then his father saw him standing in the door.

"Go to the barn and get that can of oil we were oiling the wagon with," he said. The boy did not move. Then he could speak.

"What . . ." he cried. "What are you . . ."

"Go get that oil," his father said. "Go."

Then he was moving, running, outside the house, toward the stable: this the old habit, the old blood which he had not been permitted to choose for himself, which had been bequeathed him willy nilly and which had run for so long (and who knew where, battening on what of outrage and savagery and lust) before it came to him. *I could keep on*, he thought. *I could run on and on and never look back, never need to see his face again. Only I can't. I can't,* the rusted can in his hand now, the liquid sploshing in it as he ran back to the house and into it, into the sound of his mother's weeping in the next room, and handed the can to his father.

"Ain't you going to even send a nigger?" he cried. "At least you sent a nigger before!"

This time his father didn't strike him. The hand came even faster than the blow had, the same hand which had set the can on the table with almost excruciating care flashing from the can toward him too quick for him to follow it, gripping him by the back of his shirt and on to tiptoe before he had seen it quit the can, the face stooping at him in breathless and frozen ferocity, the cold, dead voice speaking

over him to the older brother who leaned aganst the table,
chewing with that steady, curious, sidewise motion of cows:

"Empty the can into the big one and go on. I'll catch up
with you."

"Better tie him up to the bedpost," the brother said.

"Do like I told you," the father said. Then the boy was
moving, his bunched shirt and the hard, bony hand between his shoulder-blades, his toes just touching the floor,
across the room and into the other one, past the sisters
sitting with spread heavy thighs in the two chairs over the
cold hearth, and to where his mother and aunt sat side by
side on the bed, the aunt's arms about his mother's shoulders.

"Hold him," the father said. The aunt made a startled
movement. "Not you," the father said. "Lennie. Take hold
of him. I want to see you do it." His mother took him by the
wrist. "You'll hold him better than that. If he gets loose
don't you know what he is going to do? He will go up
yonder." He jerked his head toward the road. "Maybe I'd
better tie him."

"I'll hold him," his mother whispered.

"See you do then." Then his father was gone, the stiff foot
heavy and measured upon the boards, ceasing at last.

Then he began to struggle. His mother caught him in
both arms, he jerking and wrenching at them. He would be
stronger in the end, he knew that. But he had no time to
wait for it. "Lemme go!" he cried. "I don't want to have to
hit you!"

"Let him go!" the aunt said. "If he don't go, before God, I
am going up there myself!"

"Don't you see I can't?" his mother cried. "Sarty! Sarty!
No! No! Help me, Lizzie!"

Then he was free. His aunt grasped at him but it was too
late. He whirled, running, his mother stumbled forward on
to her knees behind him, crying to the nearer sister: "Catch
him, Net! Catch him!" But that was too late too, the sister
(the sisters were twins, born at the same time, yet either of
them now gave the impression of being, encompassing as
much living meat and volume and weight as any other two

of the family) not yet having begun to rise from the chair, her head, face, alone merely turned, presenting to him in the flying instant an astonishing expanse of young female features untroubled by any surprise even, wearing only an expression of bovine interest. Then he was out of the room, out of the house, in the mild dust of the starlit road and the heavy rifeness of honeysuckle, the pale ribbon unspooling with terrific slowness under his running feet, reaching the gate at last and turning in, running, his heart and lungs drumming, on up the drive toward the lighted house, the lighted door. He did not knock, he burst in, sobbing for breath, incapable for the moment of speech; he saw the astonished face of the Negro in the linen jacket without knowing when the Negro had appeared.

"De Spain!" he cried, panted. "Where's . . ." then he saw the white man too emerging from a white door down the hall. "Barn!" he cried. "Barn!"

"What?" the white man said. "Barn?"

"Yes!" the boy cried. "Barn!"

"Catch him!" the white man shouted.

But it was too late this time too. The Negro grasped his shirt, but the entire sleeve, rotten with washing, carried away, and he was out that door too and in the drive again, and had actually never ceased to run even while he was screaming into the white man's face.

Behind him the white man was shouting, "My horse! Fetch my horse!" and he thought for an instant of cutting across the park and climbing the fence into the road, but he did not know the park nor how high the vine-massed fence might be and he dared not risk it. So he ran on down the drive, blood and breath roaring; presently he was in the road again though he could not see it. He could not hear either: the galloping mare was almost upon him before he heard her, and even then he held his course, as if the very urgency of his wild grief and need must in a moment more find him wings, waiting until the ultimate instant to hurl himself aside and into the weed-choked roadside ditch as the horse thundered past and on, for an instant in furious silhouette against the stars, the tranquil early summer night sky which, even before the shape of the horse and rider vanished, stained abruptly and violently upward: a long, swirling roar incredible and soundless, blotting the stars, and he springing up and into the road again, running again, knowing it was too late yet still running even after he heard the shot and, an instant later, two shots, pausing now without knowing he had ceased to run, crying "Pap! Pap!", running again before he knew he had begun to run, stumbling, tripping over something and scrabbling up again without ceasing to run, looking backward over his shoulder at the glare as he got up, running on among the invisible trees, panting, sobbing, "Father! Father!"

At midnight he was sitting on the crest of a hill. He did not know it was midnight and he did not know how far he had come. But there was no glare behind him now and he sat now, his back toward what he had called home for four days anyhow, his face toward the dark woods which he would enter when breath was strong again, small, shaking steadily in the chill darkness, hugging himself into the remainder of his thin, rotten shirt, the grief and despair now no longer terror and fear but just grief and despair. *Father. My father*, he thought. "He was brave!" he cried suddenly, aloud but not loud, no more than a whisper: "He was! He was in the war! He was in Colonel Sartoris' cav'ry!" not knowing that his father had gone to that war a private in the fine old European sense, wearing no uniform, admitting the authority of and giving fidelity to no man or army or flag, going to war as Malbrouck himself did: for booty—it meant nothing and less than nothing to him if it were enemy booty or his own.

The slow constellations wheeled on. It would be dawn and then sun-up after a while and he would be hungry. But that would be to-morrow and now he was only cold, and walking would cure that. His breathing was easier now and he decided to get up and go on, and then he found that he had been asleep because he knew it was almost dawn, the night almost over. He could tell that from the whippoorwills. They were everywhere now among the dark trees below him, constant and inflectioned and ceaseless, so that, as the instant for giving over to the day birds drew nearer and nearer, there was no interval at all between them. He got up. He was a little stiff, but walking would cure that too as it would the cold, and soon there would be the sun. He went on down the hill, toward the dark woods within which the liquid silver voices of the birds called unceasing—the rapid and urgent beating of the urgent and quiring heart of the late spring night. He did not look back.

◆ ———————————————————————— ◆

WINTER DREAMS

F. Scott Fitzgerald

Some of the caddies were poor as sin and lived in one-room houses with a neurasthenic cow in the front yard, but Dexter Green's father owned the second best grocery-store in Black Bear—the best one was "The Hub," patronized by the wealthy people from Sherry Island—and Dexter caddied only for pocket-money.

In the fall when the days became crisp and gray, and the long Minnesota winter shut down like the white lid of a box, Dexter's skis moved over the snow that hid the fairways of the golf course. At these times the country gave him a feeling of profound melancholy—it offended him that the links should lie in enforced fallowness, haunted by ragged sparrows for the long season. It was dreary, too, that on the tees where the gay colors fluttered in summer there were now only the desolate sand-boxes knee-deep in crusted ice. When he crossed the hills the wind blew cold as misery, and if the sun was out he tramped with his eyes squinted up against the hard dimensionless glare.

In April the winter ceased abruptly. The snow ran down into Black Bear Lake scarcely tarrying for the early golfers to brave the season with red and black balls. Without elation, without an interval of moist glory, the cold was gone.

Dexter knew that there was something dismal about this Northern spring, just as he knew there was something gorgeous about the fall. Fall made him clinch his hands and tremble and repeat idiotic sentences to himself, and make brisk abrupt gestures of command to imaginary audiences and armies. October filled him with hope which November raised to a sort of ecstatic triumph, and in this mood the fleeting brilliant impressions of the summer at Sherry Island were ready grist to his mill. He became a golf champion and defeated Mr. T. A. Hedrick in a marvellous match played a hundred times over the fairways of his imagination, a match each detail of which he changed about untiringly—sometimes he won with almost laughable ease, sometimes he came up magnificently from behind. Again, stepping from a Pierce-Arrow automobile, like Mr. Mortimer Jones, he strolled frigidly into the lounge of the Sherry Island Golf Club—or perhaps, surrounded by an admiring crowd, he gave an exhibition of fancy diving from the spring-board of the club raft. . . . Among those who watched him in open-mouthed wonder was Mr. Mortimer Jones.

And one day it came to pass that Mr. Jones—himself and not his ghost—came up to Dexter with tears in his eyes and said that Dexter was the —— best caddy in the club, and wouldn't he decide not to quit if Mr. Jones made it worth his while, because every other —— caddy in the club lost one ball a hole for him—regularly—

"No, sir," said Dexter decisively, "I don't want to caddy any more." Then, after a pause: "I'm too old."

"You're not more than fourteen. Why the devil did you decide just this morning that you wanted to quit? You promised that next week you'd go over to the state tournament with me."

"I decided I was too old."

Dexter handed in his "A Class" badge, collected what money was due him from the caddy-master, and walked home to Black Bear Village.

"The best — — caddy I ever saw," shouted Mr. Mortimer Jones over a drink that afternoon. "Never lost a ball! Willing! Intelligent! Quiet! Honest! Grateful!"

The little girl who had done this was eleven—beautifully ugly as little girls are apt to be who are destined after a few years to be inexpressibly lovely and bring no end of misery to a great number of men. The spark, however, was perceptible. There was a general ungodliness in the way her lips twisted down at the corners when she smiled, and in the—Heaven help us!—in the almost passionate quality of her eyes. Vitality is born early in such women. It was utterly in evidence now, shining through her thin frame in a sort of glow.

She had come eagerly out on to the course at nine o'clock with a white linen nurse and five small new golf-clubs in a white canvas bag which the nurse was carrying. When Dexter first saw her she was standing by the caddy house, rather ill at ease and trying to conceal the fact by engaging her nurse in an obviously unnatural conversation graced by startling and irrelevant grimaces from herself.

"Well, it's certainly a nice day, Hilda," Dexter heard her say. She drew down the corners of her mouth, smiled, and glanced furtively around, her eyes in transit falling for an instant on Dexter.

Then to the nurse:

"Well, I guess there aren't very many people out here this morning, are there?"

The smile again—radiant, blatantly artificial—convincing.

"I don't know what we're supposed to do now," said the nurse, looking nowhere in particular.

"Oh, that's all right. I'll fix it up."

Dexter stood perfectly still, his mouth slightly ajar. He knew that if he moved forward a step his stare would be in her line of vision—if he moved backward he would lose his full view of her face. For a moment he had not realized how young she was. Now he remembered having seen her several times the year before—in bloomers.

Suddenly, involuntarily, he laughed, a short abrupt laugh— then, startled by himself, he turned and began to walk quickly away.

"Boy!"

Dexter stopped.

"Boy—"

Beyond question he was addressed. Not only that, but he was treated to that absurd smile, that preposterous smile— the memory of which at least a dozen men were to carry into middle age.

"Boy, do you know where the golf teacher is?"

"He's giving a lesson."

"Well, do you know where the caddy-master is?"

"He isn't here yet this morning."

"Oh." For a moment this baffled her. She stood alternately on her right and left foot.

"We'd like to get a caddy," said the nurse. "Mrs. Mortimer Jones sent us out to play golf, and we don't know how without we get a caddy."

Here she was stopped by an ominous glance from Miss Jones, followed immediately by the smile.

"There aren't any caddies here except me," said Dexter to the nurse, "and I got to stay here in charge until the caddy-master gets here."

"Oh."

Miss Jones and her retinue now withdrew, and at a proper distance from Dexter became involved in a heated conversation, which was concluded by Miss Jones taking one of the clubs and hitting it on the ground with violence. For further emphasis she raised it again and was about to bring it down smartly upon the nurse's bosom, when the nurse seized the club and twisted it from her hands.

"You damn little mean old *thing!*" cried Miss Jones wildly.

Another argument ensued. Realizing that the elements of the comedy were implied in the scene, Dexter several times began to laugh, but each time restrained the laugh before it reached audibility. He could not resist the monstrous conviction that the little girl was justified in beating the nurse.

The situation was resolved by the fortuitous appearance of the caddy-master, who was appealed to immediately by the nurse.

"Miss Jones is to have a little caddy, and this one says he can't go."

"Mr. McKenna said I was to wait here till you came," said Dexter quickly.

"Well, he's here now." Miss Jones smiled cheerfully at the caddy-master. Then she dropped her bag and set off at a haughty mince toward the first tee.

"Well?" The caddy-master turned to Dexter. "What you standing there like a dummy for? Go pick up the young lady's clubs."

"I don't think I'll go out to-day," said Dexter.

"You don't—"

"I think I'll quit."

The enormity of his decision frightened him. He was a favorite caddy, and the thirty dollars a month he earned through the summer were not to be made elsewhere around the lake. But he had received a strong emotional shock, and his perturbation required a violent and immediate outlet.

It is not so simple as that, either. As so frequently would be the case in the future, Dexter was unconsciously dictated to by his winter dreams.

II

Now, of course, the quality and the seasonability of these winter dreams varied, but the stuff of them remained. They persuaded Dexter several years later to pass up a business course at the State university—his father, prospering now, would have paid his way—for the precarious advantage of attending an older and more famous university in the East, where he was bothered by his scanty funds. But do not get the impression, because his winter dreams happened to be concerned at first with musings on the rich, that there was anything merely snobbish in the boy. He wanted not association with glittering things and glittering people—he wanted the glittering things themselves. Often he reached out for the best without knowing why he wanted it—and sometimes he ran up against the mysterious denials and prohibitions in which life indulges. It is with one of those denials and not with his career as a whole that this story deals.

He made money. It was rather amazing. After college he went to the city from which Black Bear Lake draws its wealthy patrons. When he was only twenty-three and had been there not quite two years, there were already people who liked to say: "Now *there's* a boy—" All about him rich men's sons were peddling bonds precariously, or investing patrimonies precariously, or plodding through the two dozen volumes of the "George Washington Commercial Course," but Dexter borrowed a thousand dollars on his college degree and his confident mouth, and bought a partnership in a laundry.

It was a small laundry when he went into it, but Dexter made a specialty of learning how the English washed fine woolen golf-stockings without shrinking them, and within a year he was catering to the trade that wore knickerbockers. Men were insisting that their Shetland hose and sweaters go to his laundry, just as they had insisted on a caddy who could find golf-balls. A little later he was doing their wives' lingerie as well—and running five branches in different parts of the city. Before he was twenty-seven he owned the largest string of laundries in his section of the country. It was then that he sold out and went to New York. But the part of his story that concerns us goes back to the days when he was making his first big success.

When he was twenty-three Mr. Hart—one of the grayhaired men who like to say "Now there's a boy"—gave him a guest card to the Sherry Island Golf Club for a week-end. So he signed his name one day on the register, and that afternoon played golf in a foursome with Mr. Hart and Mr. Sandwood and Mr. T. A. Hedrick. He did not consider it necessary to remark that he had once carried Mr. Hart's bag over this same links, and that he knew every trap and gully with his eyes shut—but he found himself glancing at the four caddies who trailed them, trying to catch a gleam or gesture that would remind him of himself, that would lessen the gap which lay between his present and his past.

It was a curious day, slashed abruptly with fleeting, familiar impressions. One minute he had the sense of being a trespasser—in the next he was impressed by the tremendous superiority he felt toward Mr. T. A. Hedrick, who was a bore and not even a good golfer any more.

Then, because of a ball Mr. Hart lost near the fifteenth green, an enormous thing happened. While they were searching the stiff grasses of the rough there was a clear call of "Fore!" from behind a hill in their rear. And as they all turned abruptly from their search a bright new ball sliced abruptly over the hill and caught Mr. T. A. Hedrick in the abdomen.

"By Gad!" cried Mr. T. A. Hedrick, "they ought to put some of these crazy women off the course. It's getting to be outrageous."

A head and a voice came up together over the hill:

"Do you mind if we go through?"

"You hit me in the stomach!" declared Mr. Hedrick wildly.

"Did I?" The girl approached the group of men. "I'm sorry. I yelled 'Fore!' "

Her glance fell casually on each of the men—then scanned the fairway for her ball.

"Did I bounce into the rough?"

It was impossible to determine whether this question was ingenuous or malicious. In a moment, however, she left no doubt, for as her partner came up over the hill she called cheerfully:

"Here I am! I'd have gone on the green except that I hit something."

As she took her stance for a short mashie shot, Dexter looked at her closely. She wore a blue gingham dress, rimmed at throat and shoulders with a white edging that accentuated her tan. The quality of exaggeration, of thinness, which had made her passionate eyes and down-turning mouth absurd at eleven, was gone now. She was arrestingly beautiful. The color in her cheeks was centred like the color in a picture—it was not a "high" color, but a sort of fluctuating and feverish warmth, so shaded that it seemed at any moment it would recede and disappear. This color and the mobility of her mouth gave a continual impression of flux, of intense life, of passionate vitality—balanced only partially by the sad luxury of her eyes.

She swung her mashie impatiently and without interest, pitching the ball into a sand-pit on the other side of the green. With a quick, insincere smile and a careless "Thank you!" she went on after it.

"That Judy Jones!" remarked Mr. Hedrick on the next tee, as they waited—some moments—for her to play on ahead. "All she needs is to be turned up and spanked for six months and then to be married off to an old-fashioned cavalry captain."

"My God, she's good-looking!" said Mr. Sandwood, who was just over thirty.

"Good-looking!" cried Mr. Hedrick contemptuously, "she always looks as if she wanted to be kissed! Turning those big cow-eyes on every calf in town!"

It was doubtful if Mr. Hedrick intended a reference to the maternal instinct.

"She'd play pretty good golf if she'd try," said Mr. Sandwood.

"She has no form," said Mr. Hedrick solemnly.

"She has a nice figure," said Mr. Sandwood.

"Better thank the Lord she doesn't drive a swifter ball," said Mr. Hart, winking at Dexter.

Later in the afternoon the sun went down with a riotous swirl of gold and varying blues and scarlets, and left the dry, rustling night of Western summer. Dexter watched from the veranda of the Golf Club, watched the even overlap of the waters in the little wind, silver molasses under the harvest-moon. Then the moon held a finger to her lips and the lake became a clear pool, pale and quiet. Dexter put on his bathing-suit and swam out to the farthest raft, where he stretched dripping on the wet canvas of the springboard.

There was a fish jumping and a star shining and the lights around the lake were gleaming. Over on a dark peninsula a piano was playing the songs of last summer and of summers before that—songs from "Chin-Chin" and "The Count of Luxembourg" and "The Chocolate Soldier" —and because the sound of a piano over a stretch of water had always seemed beautiful to Dexter he lay perfectly quiet and listened.

The tune the piano was playing at that moment had been gay and new five years before when Dexter was a sophomore at college. They had played it at a prom once when he could not afford the luxury of proms, and he had stood outside the gymnasium and listened. The sound of the tune precipitated in him a sort of ecstasy and it was with that ecstasy he viewed what happened to him now. It was a mood of intense appreciation, a sense that, for once, he was magnificently attuned to life and that everything about him was radiating a brightness and a glamour he might never know again.

A low, pale oblong detached itself suddenly from the darkness of the Island, spitting forth the reverberate sound of a racing motor-boat. Two white streamers of cleft water rolled themselves out behind it and almost immediately the boat was beside him, drowning out the hot tinkle of the piano in the drone of its spray. Dexter raising himself on his arms was aware of a figure standing at the wheel, of two dark eyes regarding him over the lengthening space of water—then the boat had gone by and was sweeping in an immense and purposeless circle of spray round and round in the middle of the lake. With equal eccentricity one of the circles flattened out and headed back toward the raft.

"Who's that?" she called, shutting off her motor. She was so near now that Dexter could see her bathing-suit, which consisted apparently of pink rompers.

The nose of the boat bumped the raft, and as the latter tilted rakishly he was precipitated toward her. With different degrees of interest they recognized each other.

"Aren't you one of those men we played through this afternoon?" she demanded.

He was.

"Well, do you know how to drive a motor-boat? Because if you do I wish you'd drive this one so I can ride on the surf-board behind. My name is Judy Jones"—she favored him with an absurd smirk—rather, what tried to be a smirk, for, twist her mouth as she might, it was not grotesque, it was merely beautiful—"and I live in a house over there on the Island, and in that house there is a man waiting for me. When he drove up at the door I drove out of the dock because he says I'm his ideal."

There was a fish jumping and a star shining and the lights around the lake were gleaming. Dexter sat beside Judy Jones and she explained how her boat was driven. Then she was in the water, swimming to the floating surfboard with a sinuous crawl. Watching her was without effort to the eye, watching a branch waving or a sea-gull flying. Her arms, burned to butternut, moved sinuously among the dull platinum ripples, elbow appearing first, casting the forearm back with a cadence of falling water, then reaching out and down, stabbing a path ahead.

They moved out into the lake; turning, Dexter saw that she was kneeling on the low rear of the now uptilted surfboard.

"Go faster," she called, "fast as it'll go."

Obediently he jammed the lever forward and the white spray mounted at the bow. When he looked around again the girl was standing up on the rushing board, her arms spread wide, her eyes lifted toward the moon.

"It's awful cold," she shouted. "What's your name?"

He told her.

"Well, why don't you come to dinner to-morrow night?"

His heart turned over like the fly-wheel of the boat, and, for the second time, her casual whim gave a new direction to his life.

III

Next evening while he waited for her to come downstairs, Dexter peopled the soft deep summer room and the sun-porch that opened from it with the men who had already loved Judy Jones. He knew the sort of men they were—the men who when he first went to college had entered from the great prep schools with graceful clothes and the deep tan of healthy summers. He had seen that, in one sense, he was better than these men. He was newer and stronger. Yet in acknowledging to himself that he wished his children to be like them he was admitting that he was but the rough, strong stuff from which they eternally sprang.

When the time had come for him to wear good clothes, he had known who were the best tailors in America, and the best tailors in America had made him the suit he wore this evening. He had acquired that particular reserve peculiar to his university, that set it off from other universities. He recognized the value to him of such a mannerism and he had adopted it; he knew that to be careless in dress and manner required more confidence than to be careful. But carelessness was for his children. His mother's name had been Krimelich. She was a Bohemian of the peasant class and she had talked broken English to the end of her days. Her son must keep to the set patterns.

At a little after seven Judy Jones came down-stairs. She wore a blue silk afternoon dress, and he was disappointed at first that she had not put on something more elaborate. This feeling was accentuated when, after a brief greeting, she went to the door of a butler's pantry and pushing it open called: "You can serve dinner, Martha." He had rather expected that a butler would announce dinner, that there would be a cocktail. Then he put these thoughts behind him as they sat down side by side on a lounge and looked at each other.

"Father and mother won't be here," she said thoughtfully.

He remembered the last time he had seen her father, and he was glad the parents were not to be here to-night—they might wonder who he was. He had been born in Keeble, a Minnesota village fifty miles farther north, and he always gave Keeble as his home instead of Black Bear Village. Country towns were well enough to come from if they weren't inconveniently in sight and used as footstools by fashionable lakes.

They talked of his university, which she had visited frequently during the past two years, and of the near-by city which supplied Sherry Island with its patrons, and whither Dexter would return next day to his prospering laundries.

During dinner she slipped into a moody depression which gave Dexter a feeling of uneasiness. Whatever petulance she uttered in her throaty voice worried him. Whatever she smiled at—at him, at a chicken liver, at nothing—it disturbed him that her smile could have no root in mirth, or even in amusement. When the scarlet corners of her lips curved down, it was less a smile than an invitation to a kiss.

Then, after dinner, she led him out on the dark sun-porch and deliberately changed the atmosphere.

"Do you mind if I weep a little?" she said.

"I'm afraid I'm boring you," he responded quickly.

"You're not. I like you. But I've just had a terrible afternoon. There was a man I cared about, and this afternoon he told me out of a clear sky that he was poor as a churchmouse. He'd never even hinted it before. Does this sound horribly mundane?"

"Perhaps he was afraid to tell you."

"Suppose he was," she answered. "He didn't start right. You see, if I'd thought of him as poor—well, I've been mad about loads of poor men, and fully intended to marry them all. But in this case, I hadn't thought of him that way, and my interest in him wasn't strong enough to survive the shock. As if a girl calmly informed her fiancé that she was a widow. He might not object to widows, but—

"Let's start right," she interrupted herself suddenly. "Who are you, anyhow?"

For a moment Dexter hesitated. Then:

"I'm nobody," he announced. "My career is largely a matter of futures."

"Are you poor?"

"No," he said frankly, "I'm probably making more money than any man my age in the Northwest. I know that's an obnoxious remark, but you advised me to start right."

There was a pause. Then she smiled and the corners of her mouth drooped and an almost imperceptible sway brought her closer to him, looking up into his eyes. A lump rose in Dexter's throat, and he waited breathless for the experiment, facing the unpredictable compound that would form mysteriously from the elements of their lips. Then he saw— she communicated her excitement to him, lavishly, deeply, with kisses that were not a promise but a fulfillment. They aroused in him not hunger demanding renewal but surfeit that would demand more surfeit . . . kisses that were like charity, creating want by holding back nothing at all.

It did not take him many hours to decide that he had wanted Judy Jones ever since he was a proud, desirous little boy.

IV

It began like that—and continued, with varying shades of intensity, on such a note right up to the dénouement. Dexter surrendered a part of himself to the most direct and unprincipled personality with which he had ever come in contact. Whatever Judy wanted, she went after with the full pressure of her charm. There was no divergence of method, no jockeying for position or premeditation of effects—there was a very little mental side to any of her affairs. She simply made men conscious to the highest degree of her physical loveliness. Dexter had no desire to change her. Her deficiencies were knit up with a passionate energy that transcended and justified them.

When, as Judy's head lay against his shoulder that first night, she whispered, "I don't know what's the matter with me. Last night I thought I was in love with a man and to-night I think I'm in love with you—"—it seemed to him a beautiful and romantic thing to say. It was the exquisite excitability that for the moment he controlled and owned. But a week later he was compelled to view this same quality in a different light. She took him in her roadster to a picnic supper, and after supper she disappeared, likewise in her roadster, with another man. Dexter became enormously upset and was scarcely able to be decently civil to the other people present. When she assured him that she had not kissed the other man, he knew she was lying—yet he was glad that she had taken the trouble to lie to him.

He was, as he found before the summer ended, one of a varying dozen who circulated about her. Each of them had at one time been favored above all others—about half of them still basked in the solace of occasional sentimental revivals. Whenever one showed signs of dropping out through long neglect, she granted him a brief honeyed hour, which encouraged him to tag along for a year or so longer. Judy made these forays upon the helpless and defeated without malice, indeed half unconscious that there was anything mischievous in what she did.

When a new man came to town every one dropped out—dates were automatically cancelled.

The helpless part of trying to do anything about it was that she did it all herself. She was not a girl who could be "won" in the kinetic sense—she was proof against cleverness, she was proof against charm; if any of these assailed her too strongly she would immediately resolve the affair to a physical basis, and under the magic of her physical splendor the strong as well as the brilliant played her game and not their own. She was entertained only by the gratification of her desires and by the direct exercise of her own charm. Perhaps from so much youthful love, so many youthful lovers, she had come, in self-defense, to nourish herself wholly from within.

Succeeding Dexter's first exhilaration came restlessness and dissatisfaction. The helpless ecstasy of losing himself in her was opiate rather than tonic. It was fortunate for his work during the winter that those moments of ecstasy came infrequently. Early in their acquaintance it had seemed for a while that there was a deep and spontaneous mutual attraction—that first August, for example—three days of long evenings on her dusky veranda, of strange wan kisses through the late afternoon, in shadowy alcoves or behind the protecting trellises of the garden arbors, of mornings when she was fresh as a dream and almost shy at meeting him in the clarity of the rising day. There was all the ecstasy of an engagement about it, sharpened by his realization that there was no engagement. It was during those three days that, for the first time, he had asked her to marry him. She said "maybe some day," she said "kiss me," she said "I'd like to marry you," she said "I love you"—she said—nothing.

The three days were interrupted by the arrival of a New York man who visited at her house for half September. To Dexter's agony, rumor engaged them. The man was the son of the president of a great trust company. But at the end of a month it was reported that Judy was yawning. At a dance one night she sat all evening in a motor-boat with a local beau, while the New Yorker searched the club for her frantically. She told the local beau that she was bored with her visitor, and two days later he left. She was seen with him at the station, and it was reported that he looked very mournful indeed.

On this note the summer ended. Dexter was twenty-four, and he found himself increasingly in a position to do as he wished. He joined two clubs in the city and lived at one of them. Though he was by no means an integral part of the stag-lines at these clubs, he managed to be on hand at dances where Judy Jones was likely to appear. He could have gone out socially as much as he liked—he was an eligible young man, now, and popular with down-town fathers. His confessed devotion to Judy Jones had rather solidified his position. But he had no social aspirations and rather despised the dancing men who were always on tap for the Thursday or Saturday parties and who filled in at dinners with the younger married set. Already he was playing

with the idea of going East to New York. He wanted to take
Judy Jones with him. No disillusion as to the world in which
she had grown up could cure his illusion as to her desirability.

Remember that—for only in the light of it can what he
did for her be understood.

Eighteen months after he first met Judy Jones he became
engaged to another girl. Her name was Irene Scheerer, and
her father was one of the men who had always believed in
Dexter. Irene was light-haired and sweet and honorable,
and a little stout, and she had two suitors whom she pleasantly relinquished when Dexter formally asked her to marry
him.

Summer, fall, winter, spring, another summer, another
fall—so much he had given of his active life to the incorrigible lips of Judy Jones. She had treated him with interest,
with encouragement, with malice, with indifference, with
contempt. She had inflicted on him the innumerable little
slights and indignities possible in such a case—as if in
revenge for having ever cared for him at all. She had beckoned him and yawned at him and beckoned him again and
he had responded often with bitterness and narrowed eyes.
She had brought him ecstatic happiness and intolerable
agony of spirit. She had caused him untold inconvenience
and not a little trouble. She had insulted him, and she had
ridden over him, and she had played his interest in her
against his interest in his work—for fun. She had done
everything to him except to criticise him—this she had not
done—it seemed to him only because it might have sullied
the utter indifference she manifested and sincerely felt
toward him.

When autumn had come and gone again it occurred to
him that he could not have Judy Jones. He had to beat this
into his mind but he convinced himself at last. He lay awake
at night for a while and argued it over. He told himself the
trouble and the pain she had caused him, he enumerated
her glaring deficiencies as a wife. Then he said to himself
that he loved her, and after a while he fell asleep. For a
week, lest he imagine her husky voice over the telephone or

her eyes opposite him at lunch, he worked hard and late, and at night he went to his office and plotted out his years.

At the end of a week he went to a dance and cut in on her once. For almost the first time since they had met he did not ask her to sit out with him or tell her that she was lovely. It hurt him that she did not miss these things—that was all. He was not jealous when he saw that there was a new man to-night. He had been hardened against jealousy long before.

He stayed late at the dance. He sat for an hour with Irene Scheerer and talked about books and about music. He knew very little about either. But he was beginning to be master of his own time now, and he had a rather priggish notion that he—the young and already fabulously successful Dexter Green—should know more about such things.

That was in October, when he was twenty-five. In January, Dexter and Irene became engaged. It was to be announced in June, and they were to be married three months later.

The Minnesota winter prolonged itself interminably, and it was almost May when the winds came soft and the snow ran down into Black Bear Lake at last. For the first time in over a year Dexter was enjoying a certain tranquillity of spirit. Judy Jones had been in Florida, and afterward in Hot Springs, and somewhere she had been engaged, and somewhere she had broken it off. At first, when Dexter had definitely given her up, it had made him sad that people still linked them together and asked for news of her, but when he began to be placed at dinner next to Irene Scheerer people didn't ask him about her any more—they told him about her. He ceased to be an authority on her.

May at last. Dexter walked the streets at night when the darkness was damp as rain, wondering that so soon, with so little done, so much of ecstasy had gone from him. May one year back had been marked by Judy's poignant, unforgivable, yet forgiven turbulence—it had been one of those rare times when he fancied she had grown to care for him. That old penny's worth of happiness he had spent for this bushel of content. He knew that Irene would be no more than a curtain spread behind him, a hand moving among gleaming teacups, a voice calling to children . . . fire and loveliness were gone, the magic of nights and the wonder of the varying hours and seasons . . . slender lips, down-turning, dropping to his lips and bearing him up into a heaven of eyes. . . . The thing was deep in him. He was too strong and alive for it to die lightly.

In the middle of May when the weather balanced for a few days on the thin bridge that led to deep summer he turned in one night at Irene's house. Their engagement was to be announced in a week now—no one would be surprised at it. And to-night they would sit together on the lounge at the University Club and look on for an hour at the dancers. It gave him a sense of solidity to go with her—she was so sturdily popular, so intensely "great."

He mounted the steps of the brownstone house and stepped inside.

"Irene," he called.

Mrs. Scheerer came out of the living-room to meet him.

"Dexter," she said, "Irene's gone up-stairs with a splitting headache. She wanted to go with you but I made her go to bed."

"Nothing serious, I—"

"Oh, no. She's going to play golf with you in the morning. You can spare her for just one night, can't you, Dexter?"

Her smile was kind. She and Dexter liked each other. In the living-room he talked for a moment before he said good-night.

Returning to the University Club, where he had rooms, he stood in the doorway for a moment and watched the dancers. He leaned against the door-post, nodded at a man or two—yawned.

"Hello, darling."

The familiar voice at his elbow startled him. Judy Jones had left a man and crossed the room to him—Judy Jones, a slender enamelled doll in cloth of gold: gold in a band at her head, gold in two slipper points at her dress's hem. The fragile glow of her face seemed to blossom as she smiled at him. A breeze of warmth and light blew through the room. His hands in the pockets of his dinner-jacket tightened spasmodically. He was filled with a sudden excitement.

"When did you get back?" he asked casually.

"Come here and I'll tell you about it."

She turned and he followed her. She had been away—he could have wept at the wonder of her return. She had passed through enchanted streets, doing things that were like provocative music. All mysterious happenings, all fresh and quickening hopes, had gone away with her, come back with her now.

She turned in the doorway.

"Have you a car here? If you haven't, I have."

"I have a coupé."

In then, with a rustle of golden cloth. He slammed the door. Into so many cars she had stepped—like this—like that—her back against the leather, so—her elbow resting on the door—waiting. She would have been soiled long since had there been anything to soil her—except herself—but this was her own self outpouring.

With an effort he forced himself to start the car and back into the street. This was nothing, he must remember. She had done this before, and he had put her behind him, as he would have crossed a bad account from his books.

He drove slowly down-town and, affecting abstraction, traversed the deserted streets of the business section, peopled here and there where a movie was giving out its crowd or where consumptive or pugilistic youth lounged in front of pool halls. The clink of glasses and the slap of hands on the bars issued from saloons, cloisters of glazed glass and dirty yellow light.

She was watching him closely and the silence was embarrassing, yet in this crisis he could find no casual word with which to profane the hour. At a convenient turning he began to zigzag back toward the University Club.

"Have you missed me?" she asked suddenly.

"Everybody missed you."

He wondered if she knew of Irene Scheerer. She had been back only a day—her absence had been almost contemporaneous with his engagement.

"What a remark!" Judy laughed sadly—without sadness. She looked at him searchingly. He became absorbed in the dashboard.

"You're handsomer than you used to be," she said thoughtfully. "Dexter, you have the most rememberable eyes."

He could have laughed at this, but he did not laugh. It was the sort of thing that was said to sophomores. Yet it stabbed at him.

"I'm awfully tired of everything, darling." She called everyone darling, endowing the endearment with careless, individual comraderie. "I wish you'd marry me."

The directness of this confused him. He should have told her now that he was going to marry another girl, but he could not tell her. He could as easily have sworn that he had never loved her.

"I think we'd get along," she continued, on the same note, "unless probably you've forgotten me and fallen in love with another girl."

Her confidence was obviously enormous. She had said, in effect, that she found such a thing impossible to believe, that if it were true he had merely committed a childish indiscretion—and probably to show off. She would forgive him, because it was not a matter of any moment but rather something to be brushed aside lightly.

"Of course you could never love anybody but me," she continued, "I like the way you love me. Oh, Dexter, have you forgotten last year?"

"No, I haven't forgotten."

"Neither have I!"

Was she sincerely moved—or was she carried along by the wave of her own acting?

"I wish we could be like that again," she said, and he forced himself to answer:

"I don't think we can."

"I suppose not. . . . I hear you're giving Irene Scheerer a violent rush."

There was not the faintest emphasis on the name, yet Dexter was suddenly ashamed.

"Oh, take me home," cried Judy suddenly; "I don't want to go back to that idiotic dance—with those children."

Then, as he turned up the street that led to the residence district, Judy began to cry quietly to herself. He had never seen her cry before.

The dark street lightened, the dwellings of the rich loomed up around them, he stopped his coupé in front of the great white bulk of the Mortimer Joneses' house, somnolent, gorgeous, drenched with the splendor of the damp moonlight. Its solidity startled him. The strong walls, the steel of the girders, the breadth and beam and pomp of it were there only to bring out the contrast with the young beauty beside him. It was sturdy to accentuate her slightness—as if to show what a breeze could be generated by a butterfly's wing.

He sat perfectly quiet, his nerves in wild clamor, afraid that if he moved he would find her irresistibly in his arms. Two tears had rolled down her wet face and trembled on her upper lip.

"I'm more beautiful than anybody else," she said brokenly, "why can't I be happy?" Her moist eyes tore at his stability—her mouth turned slowly downward with an exquisite sadness: "I'd like to marry you if you'll have me, Dexter. I suppose you think I'm not worth having, but I'll be so beautiful for you, Dexter."

A million phrases of anger, pride, passion, hatred, tenderness fought on his lips. Then a perfect wave of emotion washed over him, carrying off with it a sediment of wisdom, of convention, of doubt, of honor. This was his girl who was speaking, his own, his beautiful, his pride.

"Won't you come in?" He heard her draw in her breath sharply.

Waiting.

"All right," his voice was trembling, "I'll come in."

V

It was strange that neither when it was over nor a long time afterward did he regret that night. Looking at it from the perspective of ten years, the fact that Judy's flare for him endured just one month seemed of little importance. Nor did it matter that by his yielding he subjected himself to a deeper agony in the end and gave serious hurt to Irene Scheerer and to Irene's parents, who had befriended him. There was nothing sufficiently pictorial about Irene's grief to stamp itself on his mind.

Dexter was at bottom hard-minded. The attitude of the city on his action was of no importance to him, not because he was going to leave the city, but because any outside attitude on the situation seemed superficial. He was completely indifferent to popular opinion. Nor, when he had seen that it was no use, that he did not possess in himself the power to move fundamentally or to hold Judy Jones, did he bear any malice toward her. He loved her, and he would love her until the day he was too old for loving—but he could not have her. So he tasted the deep pain that is reserved only for the strong, just as he had tasted for a little while the deep happiness.

Even the ultimate falsity of the grounds upon which Judy terminated the engagement that she did not want to "take him away" from Irene—Judy who had wanted nothing else— did not revolt him. He was beyond any revulsion or any amusement.

He went East in February with the intention of selling out his laundries and settling in New York—but the war came to America in March and changed his plans. He returned to the West, handed over the management of the business to his partner, and went into the first officers' training-camp in late April. He was one of those young thousands who greeted the war with a certain amount of relief, welcoming the liberation from webs of tangled emotion.

VI

This story is not his biography, remember, although things creep into it which have nothing to do with those dreams he had when he was young. We are almost done with them and with him now. There is only one more incident to be related here, and it happens seven years farther on.

It took place in New York, where he had done well—so well that there were no barriers too high for him. He was thirty-two years old, and, except for one flying trip immediately after the war, he had not been West in seven years. A man named Devlin from Detroit came into his office to see him in a business way, and then and there this incident occurred, and closed out, so to speak, this particular side of his life.

"So you're from the Middle West," said the man Devlin with careless curiosity. "That's funny—I thought men like you were probably born and raised on Wall Street. You know—wife of one of my best friends in Detroit came from your city. I was an usher at the wedding."

Dexter waited with no apprehension of what was coming.

"Judy Simms," said Devlin with no particular interest; "Judy Jones she was once."

"Yes, I knew her." A dull impatience spread over him. He had heard, of course, that she was married—perhaps deliberately he had heard no more.

"Awfully nice girl," brooded Devlin meaninglessly, "I'm sort of sorry for her."

"Why?" Something in Dexter was alert, receptive, at once.

"Oh, Lud Simms has gone to pieces in a way. I don't mean he ill-uses her, but he drinks and runs around—"

"Doesn't she run around?"

"No. Stays at home with her kids."

"Oh."

"She's a little too old for him," said Devlin.

"Too old!" cried Dexter. "Why, man, she's only twenty-seven."

He was possessed with a wild notion of rushing out into the streets and taking a train to Detroit. He rose to his feet spasmodically.

"I guess you're busy," Devlin apologized quickly. "I didn't realize—"

"No, I'm not busy," said Dexter, steadying his voice. "I'm not busy at all. Not busy at all. Did you say she was— twenty-seven? No, I said she was twenty-seven."

"Yes, you did," agreed Devlin dryly.

"Go on, then. Go on."

"What do you mean?"

"About Judy Jones."

Devlin looked at him helplessly.

"Well, that's—I told you all there is to it. He treats her like the devil. Oh, they're not going to get divorced or anything. When he's particularly outrageous she forgives him. In fact, I'm inclined to think she loves him. She was a pretty girl when she first came to Detroit."

A pretty girl! The phrase struck Dexter as ludicrous.

"Isn't she—a pretty girl, any more?"

"Oh, she's all right."

"Look here," said Dexter, sitting down suddenly. "I don't understand. You say she was a 'pretty girl' and now you say she's 'all right.' I don't understand what you mean—Judy Jones wasn't a pretty girl, at all. She was a great beauty. Why, I knew her, I knew her. She was—"

Devlin laughed pleasantly.

"I'm not trying to start a row," he said. "I think Judy's a nice girl and I like her. I can't understand how a man like Lud Simms could fall madly in love with her, but he did." Then he added: "Most of the women like her."

Dexter looked closely at Devlin, thinking wildly that there must be a reason for this, some insensitivity in the man or some private malice.

"Lots of women fade just like *that*," Devlin snapped his fingers. "You must have seen it happen. Perhaps I've forgotten how pretty she was at her wedding. I've seen her so much since then, you see. She has nice eyes."

A sort of dullness settled down upon Dexter. For the first time in his life he felt like getting very drunk. He knew that he was laughing loudly at something Devlin had said, but he did not know what it was or why it was funny. When, in a few minutes, Devlin went he lay down on his lounge and looked out the window at the New York sky-line into which the sun was sinking in dull lovely shades of pink and gold.

He had thought that having nothing else to lose he was invulnerable at last—but he knew that he had just lost something more, as surely as if he had married Judy Jones and seen her fade away before his eyes.

The dream was gone. Something had been taken from him. In a sort of panic he pushed the palms of his hands into his eyes and tried to bring up a picture of the waters lapping on Sherry Island and the moonlit veranda, and gingham on the golf-links and the dry sun and the gold color of her neck's soft down. And her mouth damp to his kisses and her eyes plaintive with melancholy and her freshness like new fine linen in the morning. Why, these things were no longer in the world! They had existed and they existed no longer.

For the first time in years the tears were streaming down his face. But they were for himself now. He did not care about mouth and eyes and moving hands. He wanted to care, and he could not care. For he had gone away and he could never go back any more. The gates were closed, the sun was gone down, and there was no beauty but the gray beauty of steel that withstands all time. Even the grief he could have borne was left behind in the country of illusion, of youth, of the richness of life, where his winter dreams had flourished.

"Long ago," he said, "long ago, there was something in me, but now that thing is gone. Now that thing is gone, that thing is gone. I cannot cry. I cannot care. That thing will come back no more."

SOLDIER'S HOME

Ernest Hemingway

Krebs went to the war from a Methodist college in Kansas. There is a picture which shows him among his fraternity brothers, all of them wearing exactly the same height and style collar. He enlisted in the Marines in 1917 and did not return to the United States until the second division returned from the Rhine in the summer of 1919.

There is a picture which shows him on the Rhine with two German girls and another corporal. Krebs and the corporal look too big for their uniforms. The German girls are not beautiful. The Rhine does not show in the picture.

By the time Krebs returned to his home town in Oklahoma the greeting of heroes was over. He came back much too late. The men from the town who had been drafted had all been welcomed elaborately on their return. There had been a great deal of hysteria. Now the reaction had set in. People seemed to think it was rather ridiculous for Krebs to be getting back so late, years after the war was over.

At first Krebs, who had been at Belleau Wood, Soissons, the Champagne, St. Mihiel and in the Argonne did not want to talk about the war at all. Later he felt the need to talk but no one wanted to hear about it. His town had heard too many atrocity stories to be thrilled by actualities. Krebs found that to be listened to at all he had to lie, and after he had done this twice he, too, had a reaction against the war and against talking about it. A distaste for everything that had happened to him in the war set in because of the lies he had told. All of the times that had been able to make him feel cool and clear inside himself when he thought of them; the times so long back when he had done the one thing, the only thing for a man to do, easily and naturally, when he might have done something else, now lost their cool, valuable quality and then were lost themselves.

His lies were quite unimportant lies and consisted in attributing to himself things other men had seen, done or heard of, and stating as facts certain apocryphal incidents familiar to all soldiers. Even his lies were not sensational at the pool room. His acquaintances, who had heard detailed accounts of German women found chained to machine guns in the Argonne forest and who could not comprehend, or were barred by their patriotism from interest in, any German machine gunners who were not chained, were not thrilled by his stories.

Krebs acquired the nausea in regard to experience that is the result of untruth or exaggeration, and when he occasionally met another man who had really been a soldier and they talked a few minutes in the dressing room at a dance he fell into the easy pose of the old soldier among other soldiers: that he had been badly, sickeningly frightened all the time. In this way he lost everything.

During this time, it was late summer, he was sleeping late in bed, getting up to walk down town to the library to get a book, eating lunch at home, reading on the front porch until he became bored and then walking down through the town to spend the hottest hours of the day in the cool dark of the pool room. He loved to play pool.

In the evening he practised on his clarinet, strolled down town, read and went to bed. He was still a hero to his two young sisters. His mother would have given him breakfast in bed if he had wanted it. She often came in when he was in bed and asked him to tell her about the war, but her attention always wandered. His father was non-committal.

Before Krebs went away to the war he had never been allowed to drive the family motor car. His father was in the real estate business and always wanted the car to be at his command when he required it to take clients out into the country to show them a piece of farm property. The car always stood outside the First National Bank building where his father had an office on the second floor. Now, after the war, it was still the same car.

Nothing was changed in the town except that the young girls had grown up. But they lived in such a complicated world of already defined alliances and shifting feuds that Krebs did not feel the energy or the courage to break into it. He liked to look at them, though. There were so many good-looking young girls. Most of them had their hair cut short. When he went away only little girls wore their hair like that or girls that were fast. They all wore sweaters and shirt waists with round Dutch collars. It was a pattern. He liked to look at them from the front porch as they walked on the other side of the street. He liked to watch them walking under the shade of the trees. He liked the round Dutch collars above their sweaters. He liked their silk stockings and flat shoes. He liked their bobbed hair and the way they walked.

When he was in town their appeal to him was not very strong. He did not like them when he saw them in the Greek's ice cream parlor. He did not want them themselves really. They were too complicated. There was something else. Vaguely he wanted a girl but he did not want to have to work to get her. He would have liked to have a girl but he did not want to have to spend a long time getting her. He did not want to get into the intrigue and the politics. He did not want to have to do any courting. He did not want to tell any more lies. It wasn't worth it.

He did not want any consequences. He did not want any consequences ever again. He wanted to live along without consequences. Besides he did not really need a girl. The army had taught him that. It was all right to pose as though you had to have a girl. Nearly everybody did that. But it wasn't true. You did not need a girl. That was the funny thing. First a fellow boasted how girls mean nothing to him, that he never thought of them, that they could not touch him. Then a fellow boasted that he could not get along without girls, that he had to have them all the time, that he could not go to sleep without them.

That was all a lie. It was all a lie both ways. You did not need a girl unless you thought about them. He learned that in the army. Then sooner or later you always got one. When you were really ripe for a girl you always got one. You did not have to think about it. Sooner or later it would come. He had learned that in the army.

Now he would have liked a girl if she had come to him and not wanted to talk. But here at home it was all too complicated. He knew he could never get through it all again. It was not worth the trouble. That was the thing about French girls and German girls. There was not all this talking. You couldn't talk much and you did not need to talk. It was simple and you were friends. He thought about France and then he began to think about Germany. On the whole he had liked Germany better. He did not want to leave Germany. He did not want to come home. Still, he had come home. He sat on the front porch.

He liked the girls that were walking along the other side of the street. He liked the look of them much better than the French girls or the German girls. But the world they were in was not the world he was in. He would like to have one of them. But it was not worth it. They were such a nice pattern. He liked the pattern. It was exciting. But he would not go through all the talking. He did not want one badly enough. He liked to look at them all, though. It was not worth it. Not now when things were getting good again.

He sat there on the porch reading a book on the war. It was a history and he was reading about all the engagements he had been in. It was the most interesting reading he had ever done. He wished there were more maps. He looked forward with a good feeling to reading all the really good histories when they would come out with good detail maps. Now he was really learning about the war. He had been a good soldier. That made a difference.

One morning after he had been home about a month his

mother came into his bedroom and sat on the bed. She smoothed her apron.

"I had a talk with your father last night, Harold," she said, "and he is willing for you to take the car out in the evenings."

"Yeah?" said Krebs, who was not fully awake. "Take the car out? Yeah?"

"Yes. Your father has felt for some time that you should be able to take the car out in the evenings whenever you wished but we only talked it over last night."

"I'll bet you made him," Krebs said.

"No. It was your father's suggestion that we talk the matter over."

"Yeah. I'll bet you made him." Krebs sat up in bed.

"Will you come down to breakfast, Harold?" his mother said.

"As soon as I get my clothes on," Krebs said.

His mother went out of the room and he could hear her frying something downstairs while he washed, shaved and dressed to go down into the dining-room for breakfast. While he was eating breakfast his sister brought in the mail.

"Well, Hare," she said. "You old sleepy-head. What do you ever get up for?"

Krebs looked at her. He liked her. She was his best sister.

"Have you got the paper?" he asked.

She handed him *The Kansas City Star* and he shucked off its brown wrapper and opened it to the sporting page. He folded *The Star* open and propped it against the water pitcher with his cereal dish to steady it, so he could read while he ate.

"Harold," his mother stood in the kitchen doorway, "Harold, please don't muss up the paper. Your father can't read his *Star* if it's been mussed."

"I won't muss it," Krebs said.

His sister sat down at the table and watched him while he read.

"We're playing indoor over at school this afternoon," she said. "I'm going to pitch."

"Good," said Krebs. "How's the old wing?"

"I can pitch better than lots of the boys. I tell them all you taught me. The other girls aren't much good."

"Yeah?" said Krebs.

"I tell them all you're my beau. Aren't you my beau, Hare?"

"You bet."

"Couldn't your brother really be your beau just because he's your brother?"

"I don't know."

"Sure you know. Couldn't you be my beau, Hare, if I was old enough and if you wanted to?"

"Sure. You're my girl now."

"Am I really your girl?"

"Sure."

"Do you love me?"

"Uh, huh."

"Will you love me always?"

"Sure."

"Will you come over and watch me play indoor?"

"Maybe."

"Aw, Hare, you don't love me. If you loved me, you'd want to come over and watch me play indoor."

Krebs's mother came into the dining-room from the kitchen. She carried a plate with two fried eggs and some crisp bacon on it and a plate of buckwheat cakes.

"You run along, Helen," she said. "I want to talk to Harold."

She put the eggs and bacon down in front of him and brought in a jug of maple syrup for the buckwheat cakes. Then she sat down across the table from Krebs.

"I wish you'd put down the paper a minute, Harold," she said.

Krebs took down the paper and folded it.

"Have you decided what you are going to do yet, Harold?" his mother said, taking off her glasses.

"No," said Krebs.

"Don't you think it's about time?" His mother did not say this in a mean way. She seemed worried.

"I hadn't thought about it," Krebs said.

"God has some work for everyone to do," his mother said. "There can be no idle hands in His Kingdom."

"I'm not in His Kingdom," Krebs said.

"We are all of us in His Kingdom."

Krebs felt embarrassed and resentful as always.

"I've worried about you so much, Harold," his mother went on. "I know the temptations you must have been exposed to. I know how weak men are. I know what your own dear grandfather, my own father, told us about the Civil War and I have prayed for you. I pray for you all day long, Harold."

Krebs looked at the bacon fat hardening on his plate.

"Your father is worried, too," his mother went on. "He thinks you have lost your ambition, that you haven't got a definite aim in life. Charley Simmons, who is just your age, has a good job and is going to be married. The boys are all settling down; they're all determined to get somewhere; you can see that boys like Charley Simmons are on their way to being really a credit to the community."

Krebs said nothing.

"Don't look that way, Harold," his mother said. "You know we love you and I want to tell you for your own good how matters stand. Your father does not want to hamper your freedom. He thinks you should be allowed to drive the car. If you want to take some of the nice girls out riding with you, we are only too pleased. We want you to enjoy yourself. But you are going to have to settle down to work, Harold. Your father doesn't care what you start in at. All work is honorable as he says. But you've got to make a start at something. He asked me to speak to you this morning and then you can stop in and see him at his office."

"Is that all?" Krebs said.

"Yes. Don't you love your mother, dear boy?"

"No," Krebs said.

His mother looked at him across the table. Her eyes were shiny. She started crying.

"I don't love anybody," Krebs said.

It wasn't any good. He couldn't tell her, he couldn't make her see it. It was silly to have said it. He had only hurt her. He went over and took hold of her arm. She was crying with her head in her hands.

"I didn't mean it," he said. "I was just angry at something. I didn't mean I didn't love you."

His mother went on crying. Krebs put his arm on her shoulder.

"Can't you believe me, mother?"

His mother shook her head.

"Please, please, mother. Please believe me."

"All right," his mother said chokily. She looked up at him. "I believe you, Harold."

Krebs kissed her hair. She put her face up to him.

"I'm your mother," she said. "I held you next to my heart when you were a tiny baby."

Krebs felt sick and vaguely nauseated.

"I know, Mummy," he said. "I'll try and be a good boy for you."

"Would you kneel and pray with me, Harold?" his mother asked.

They knelt down beside the dining-room table and Krebs's mother prayed.

"Now, you pray, Harold," she said.

"I can't," Krebs said.

"Try, Harold."

"I can't."

"Do you want me to pray for you?"

"Yes."

So his mother prayed for him and then they stood up and Krebs kissed his mother and went out of the house. He had tried so to keep his life from being complicated. Still, none of it had touched him. He had felt sorry for his mother and she had made him lie. He would go to Kansas City and get a job and she would feel all right about it. There would be one more scene maybe before he got away. He would not go down to his father's office. He would miss that one. He wanted his life to go smoothly. It had just gotten going that way. Well, that was all over now, anyway. He would go over to the schoolyard and watch Helen play indoor baseball.

◆ ———————————————————————————— ◆

THE TREE OF KNOWLEDGE

Henry James

It was one of the secret opinions, such as we all have, of Peter Brench that his main success in life would have consisted in his never having committed himself about the work, as it was called, of his friend Morgan Mallow. This was a subject on which it was, to the best of his belief, impossible with veracity to quote him, and it was nowhere on record that he had, in the connexion, on any occasion and in any embarrassment, either lied or spoken the truth. Such a triumph had its honour even for a man of other triumphs—a man who had reached fifty, who had escaped marriage, who had lived within his means, who had been in love with Mrs. Mallow for years without breathing it, and who, last but not least, had judged himself once for all. He had so judged himself in fact that he felt an extreme and general humility to be his proper portion; yet there was nothing that made him think so well of his parts as the course he had steered so often through the shallows just mentioned. It became thus a real wonder that the friends in

whom he had most confidence were just those with whom
he had most reserves. He couldn't tell Mrs. Mallow—or at
least he supposed, excellent man, he couldn't—that she was
the one beautiful reason he had never married; any more
than he could tell her husband that the sight of the multi-
plied marbles in that gentleman's studio was an affliction of
which even time had never blunted the edge. His victory,
however, as I have intimated, in regard to these productions, was not simply in his not having let it out that he
deplored them; it was, remarkably, in his not having kept it
in by anything else.

The whole situation, among these good people, was verily
a marvel, and there was probably not such another for a
long way from the spot that engages us—the point at which
the soft declivity of Hampstead began at that time to confess
in broken accents to Saint John's Wood. He despised Mallow's statues and adored Mallow's wife, and yet was distinctly fond of Mallow, to whom, in turn, he was equally
dear. Mrs. Mallow rejoiced in the statues—though she preferred, when pressed, the busts; and if she was visibly
attached to Peter Brench it was because of his affection for
Morgan. Each loved the other moreover for the love borne
in each case to Lancelot, whom the Mallows respectively
cherished as their only child and whom the friend of their
fireside identified as the third—but decidedly the handsomest—of his godsons. Already in the old years it had
come to that—that no one, for such a relation, could possibly have occurred to any of them, even to the baby itself,
but Peter. There was luckily a certain independence, of the
pecuniary sort, all round: the Master could never otherwise
have spent his solemn *Wanderjahre* in Florence and Rome,
and continued by the Thames as well as by the Arno and the
Tiber to add unpurchased group to group and model, for
what was too apt to prove in the event mere love, fancy-
heads of celebrities either too busy or too buried—too much
of the age or too little of it—to sit. Neither could Peter,
lounging in almost daily, have found time to keep the whole
complicated tradition so alive by his presence. He was

massive but mild, the depositary of these mysteries—large and loose and ruddy and curly, with deep tones, deep eyes, deep pockets, to say nothing of the habit of long pipes, soft hats and brownish greyish weather-faded clothes, apparently always the same.

He had "written," it was known, but had never spoken, never spoken in particular of that; and he had the air (since, as was believed, he continued to write) of keeping it up in order to have something more—as if he hadn't at the worst enough—to be silent about. Whatever his air, at any rate, Peter's occasional unmentioned prose and verse were quite truly the result of an impulse to maintain the purity of his taste by establishing still more firmly the right relation of fame to feebleness. The little green door of his domain was in a garden-wall on which the discoloured stucco made patches, and in the small detached villa behind it everything was old, the furniture, the servants, the books, the prints, the immemorial habits and the new improvements. The Mallows, at Carrara Lodge, were within ten minutes, and the studio there was on their little land, to which they had added, in their happy faith, for building it. This was the good fortune, if it was not the ill, of her having brought him in marriage a portion that put them in a manner at their ease and enabled them thus, on their side, to keep it up. And they did keep it up—they always had—the infatuated sculptor and his wife, for whom nature had refined on the impossible by relieving them of the sense of the difficult. Morgan had at all events everything of the sculptor but the spirit of Phidias—the brown velvet, the becoming *beretto,* the "plastic" presence, the fine fingers, the beautiful accent in Italian and the old Italian factotum. He seemed to make up for everything when he addressed Egidio with the "tu" and waved him to turn one of the rotary pedestals of which the place was full. They were tremendous Italians at Carrara Lodge, and the secret of the part played by this fact in Peter's life was in a large degree that it gave him, sturdy Briton as he was, just the amount of "going abroad" he could bear. The Mallows were all his Italy, but it was in a measure for Italy he liked them. His one worry was that Lance—to which they had shortened his godson—was, in spite of a public school, perhaps a shade too Italian. Morgan meanwhile looked like somebody's flattering idea of somebody's own person as expressed in the great room provided at the Uffizi Museum for the general illustration of that idea by eminent hands. The Master's sole regret that he hadn't been born rather to the brush than to the chisel sprang from his wish that he might have contributed to that collection.

It appeared with time at any rate to be to the brush that Lance had been born; for Mrs. Mallow, one day when the boy was turning twenty, broke it to their friend, who shared, to the last delicate morsel, their problems and pains, that it seemed as if nothing would really do but that he should embrace the career. It had been impossible longer to remain blind to the fact that he was gaining no glory at Cambridge, where Brench's own college had for a year tempered its tone to him as for Brench's own sake. Therefore why renew the vain form of preparing him for the impossible? The impossible—it had become clear—was that he should be anything but an artist.

"Oh dear, dear!" said poor Peter.

"Don't you believe in it?" asked Mrs. Mallow, who still, at more than forty, had her violet velvet eyes, her creamy satin skin and her silken chestnut hair.

"Believe in what?"

"Why in Lance's passion."

"I don't know what you mean by 'believing in it.' I've never been unaware, certainly, of his disposition, from his earliest time, to daub and draw; but I confess I've hoped it would burn out."

"But why should it," she sweetly smiled, "with his wonderful heredity? Passion is passion—though of course indeed *you*, dear Peter, know nothing of that. Has the Master's ever burned out?"

Peter looked off a little and, in his familiar formless way, kept up for a moment, a sound between a smothered whistle and a subdued hum. "Do you think he's going to be another Master?"

She seemed scarce prepared to go that length, yet she had on the whole a marvellous trust. "I know what you mean by that. Will it be a career to incur the jealousies and provoke the machinations that have been at times almost too much for his father? Well—say it may be, since nothing but clap-trap, in these dreadful days, *can*, it would seem, make its way, and since, with the curse of refinement and distinction, one may easily find one's self begging one's bread. Put it at the worst—say he *has* the misfortune to wing his flight further than the vulgar taste of his stupid countrymen can follow. Think, all the same, of the happiness—the same the Master has had. He'll *know*."

Peter looked rueful. "Ah but *what* will he know?"

"Quiet joy!" cried Mrs. Mallow, quite impatient and turning away.

II

He had of course before long to meet the boy himself on it and to hear that practically everything was settled. Lance was not to go up again, but to go instead to Paris where, since the die was cast, he would find the best advantages. Peter had always felt he must be taken as he was, but had never perhaps found him so much of that pattern as on this occasion. "You chuck Cambridge then altogether? Doesn't that seem rather a pity?"

Lance would have been like his father, to his friend's sense, had he had less humour, and like his mother had he had more beauty. Yet it was a good middle way for Peter that, in the modern manner, he was, to the eye, rather the young stockbroker than the young artist. The youth reasoned that it was a question of time—there was such a mill to go through, such an awful lot to learn. He had talked with fellows and had judged. "One has got, today," he said, "don't you see? to know."

His interlocutor, at this, gave a groan. "Oh hang it, *don't* know!"

Lance wondered. " 'Don't'? Then what's the use—?"

"The use of what?"

"Why of anything. Don't you think I've talent?"

Peter smoked away for a little in silence; then went on: "It isn't knowledge, it's ignorance that—as we've been beautifully told—is bliss."

"Don't you think I've talent?" Lance repeated.

Peter, with his trick of queer kind demonstrations, passed his arm round his godson and held him a moment. "How do I know?"

"Oh," said the boy, "if it's your own ignorance you're defending—!"

Again, for a pause, on the sofa, his godfather smoked. "It isn't. I've the misfortune to be omniscient."

"Oh well," Lance laughed again, "if you know *too* much—!"

"That's what I do, and it's why I'm so wretched."

Lance's gaiety grew. "Wretched? Come, I say!"

"But I forgot," his companion went on—"you're not to know about that. It would indeed for you too make the too much. Only I'll tell you what I'll do." And Peter got up from the sofa. "If you'll go up again I'll pay your way at Cambridge."

Lance stared, a little rueful in spite of being still more amused. "Oh Peter! You disapprove so of Paris?"

"Well, I'm afraid of it."

"Ah I see!"

"No, you don't see—yet. But you will—that is you would. And you mustn't."

The young man thought more gravely. "But one's innocence, already—!"

"Is considerably damaged? Ah that won't matter," Peter persisted—"we'll patch it up here."

"Here? Then you want me to stay at home?"

Peter almost confessed to it. "Well, we're so right—we four together—just as we are. We're so safe. Come, don't spoil it."

The boy, who had turned to gravity, turned from this, on the real pressure in his friend's tone, to consternation. "Then what's a fellow to be?"

"My particular care. Come, old man"—and Peter now fairly pleaded—"*I'll* look out for you."

Lance, who had remained on the sofa with his legs out and his hands in his pockets, watched him with eyes that showed suspicion. Then he got up. "You think there's something the matter with me—that I can't make a success."

"Well, what do you call a success?"

Lance thought again. "Why the best sort, I suppose, is to please one's self. Isn't that the sort that, in spite of cabals and things, is—in his own peculiar line—the Master's?"

There were so much too many things in this question to be answered at once that they practically checked the discussion, which became particularly difficult in the light of such renewed proof that, though the young man's innocence might, in the course of his studies, as he contended, somewhat have shrunken, the finer essence of it still remained. That was indeed exactly what Peter had assumed and what above all he desired; yet perversely enough it gave him a chill. The boy believed in the cabals and things, believed in the peculiar line, believed, to be brief, in the Master. What happened a month or two later wasn't that he went up again at the expense of his godfather, but that a fortnight after he had got settled in Paris this personage sent him fifty pounds.

He had meanwhile at home, this personage, made up his mind to the worst; and what that might be had never yet grown quite so vivid to him as when, on his presenting himself one Sunday night, as he never failed to do, for supper, the mistress of Carrara Lodge met him with an appeal as to—of all things in the world—the wealth of the Canadians. She was earnest, she was even excited. "Are many of them *really* rich?"

He had to confess he knew nothing about them, but he often thought afterwards of that evening. The room in which they sat was adorned with sundry specimens of the Master's genius, which had the merit of being, as Mrs. Mallow herself frequently suggested, of an unusually convenient size. They were indeed of dimensions not customary in the products of the chisel, and they had the singularity that, if

the objects and features intended to be small looked too
large, the objects and features intended to be large looked
too small. The Master's idea, either in respect to this matter
or to any other, had in almost any case, even after years,
remained undiscoverable to Peter Brench. The creations
that so failed to reveal it stood about on pedestals and
brackets, on tables and shelves, a little staring white population, heroic, idyllic, allegoric, mythic, symbolic, in which
"scale" had so strayed and lost itself that the public square
and the chimney-piece seemed to have changed places, the
monumental being all diminutive and the diminutive all
monumental; branches at any rate, markedly, of a family in
which stature was rather oddly irrespective of function, age
and sex. They formed, like the Mallows themselves, poor
Brench's own family—having at least to such a degree the
note of familiarity. The occasion was one of those he had
long ago learnt to know and to name—short flickers of the
faint flame, soft gusts of a kinder air. Twice a year regularly
the Master believed in his fortune, in addition to believing
all the year round in his genius. This time it was to be made
by a bereaved couple from Toronto, who had given him the
handsomest order for a tomb to three lost children, each of
whom they desired to see, in the composition, emblemati-
cally and characteristically represented.

Such was naturally the moral of Mrs. Mallow's question: if
their wealth was to be assumed, it was clear, from the
nature of their admiration, as well as from mysterious hints
thrown out (they were a little odd!) as to other possibilities
of the same mortuary sort, that their further patronage
might be; and not less evident that should the Master
become at all known in those climes nothing would be more
inevitable than a run of Canadian custom. Peter had been
present before at runs of custom, colonial and domestic—
present at each of those of which the aggregation had left so
few gaps in the marble company round him; but it was his
habit never at these junctures to prick the bubble in advance. The fond illusion, while it lasted, eased the wound of
elections never won, the long ache of medals and diplomas

carried off, on every chance, by every one but the Master; it moreover lighted the lamp that would glimmer through the next eclipse. They lived, however, after all—as it was always beautiful to see—at a height scarce susceptible of ups and downs. They strained a point at times charmingly, strained it to admit that the public was here and there not too bad to buy; but they would have been nowhere without their attitude that the Master was always too good to sell. They were at all events deliciously formed, Peter often said to himself, for their fate; the Master had a vanity, his wife had a loyalty, of which success, depriving these things of innocence, would have diminished the merit and the grace. Any one could be charming under a charm, and as he looked about him at a world of prosperity more void of proportion even than the Master's museum he wondered if he knew another pair that so completely escaped vulgarity.

"What a pity Lance isn't with us to rejoice!" Mrs. Mallow on this occasion sighed at supper.

"We'll drink to the health of the absent," her husband replied, filling his friend's glass and his own and giving a drop to their companion; "but we must hope he's preparing himself for a happiness much less like this of ours this evening—excusable as I grant it to be!—than like the comfort we have always (whatever has happened or has not happened) been able to trust ourselves to enjoy. The comfort," the Master explained, leaning back in the pleasant lamplight and firelight, holding up his glass and looking round at his marble family, quartered more or less, a monstrous brood, in every room—"the comfort of art in itself!"

Peter looked a little shyly at his wine. "Well—I don't care what you may call it when a fellow doesn't—but Lance must learn to *sell*, you know. I drink to his acquisition of the secret of a base popularity!"

"Oh, yes, *he* must sell," the boy's mother, who was still more, however, this seemed to give out, the Master's wife, father artlessly allowed.

"Ah," the sculptor after a moment confidently pronounced, "Lance *will*. Don't be afraid. He'll have learnt."

"Which is exactly what Peter," Mrs. Mallow gaily returned—"why in the world were you so perverse, Peter?—wouldn't when he told him hear of."

Peter, when this lady looked at him with accusatory affection—a grace on her part not infrequent—could never find a word; but the Master, who was always all amenity and tact, helped him out now as he had often helped him before. "That's his old idea, you know—on which we've so often differed: his theory that the artist should be all impulse and instinct. *I* go in of course for a certain amount of school. Not too much—but a due proportion. There's where his protest came in," he continued to explain to his wife, "as against what *might*, don't you see? be in question for Lance."

"Ah well"—and Mrs. Mallow turned the violet eyes across the table at the subject of this discourse—"he's sure to have meant of course nothing but good. Only that wouldn't have prevented him, if Lance *had* taken his advice, from being in effect horribly cruel."

They had a sociable way of talking of him to his face as if he had been in the clay or—at most—in the plaster, and the Master was unfailingly generous. He might have been waving Egidio to make him revolve. "Ah but poor Peter wasn't so wrong as to what it may after all come to that he *will* learn.

"Oh but nothing artistically bad," she urged—still, for poor Peter, arch and dewy.

"Why just the little French tricks," said the Master: on which their friend had to pretend to admit, when pressed by Mrs. Mallow, that these aesthetic vices had been the objects of his dread.

III

"I know now," Lance said to him the next year, "why you were so much against it." He had come back supposedly for a mere interval and was looking about him at Carrara Lodge, where indeed he had already on two or three occasions since his expatriation briefly reappeared. This had the air of a longer holiday. "Something rather awful has happened to me. It *isn't* so very good to know."

"I'm bound to say high spirits don't show in your face," Peter was rather ruefully forced to confess. "Still, are you very sure you do know?"

"Well, I at least know about as much as I can bear." These remarks were exchanged in Peter's den, and the young man, smoking cigarettes, stood before the fire with his back against the mantel. Something of his bloom seemed really to have left him.

Poor Peter wondered. "You're clear then as to what in particular I wanted you not to go for?"

"In particular?" Lance thought. "It seems to me that in particular there can have been only one thing."

They stood for a little sounding each other. "Are you quite sure?"

"Quite sure I'm a beastly duffer? Quite—by this time."

"Oh!"—and Peter turned away as if almost with relief.

"It's *that* that isn't pleasant to find out."

"Oh I don't care for 'that,' " said Peter, presently coming round again. "I mean I personally don't."

"Yet I hope you can understand a little that I myself should!"

"Well, what do you mean by it?" Peter sceptically asked.

And on this Lance had to explain—how the upshot of his studies in Paris had inexorably proved a mere deep doubt of his means. These studies had so waked him up that a new light was in his eyes; but what the new light did was really to show him too much. "Do you know what's the matter with me? I'm too horribly intelligent. Paris was really the last place for me. I've learnt what I can't do."

Poor Peter stared—it was a staggerer; but even after they had had, on the subject, a longish talk in which the boy brought out to the full the hard truth of his lesson, his friend betrayed less pleasure than usually breaks into a face to the happy tune of "I told you so!" Poor Peter himself made now indeed so little a point of having told him so that Lance broke ground in a different place a day or two after.

"What was it then that—before I went—you were afraid I
should find out?" This, however, Peter refused to tell him—on
the ground that if he hadn't yet guessed perhaps he never
would, and that in any case nothing at all for either of them
was to be gained by giving the thing a name. Lance eyed
him on this an instant with the bold curiosity of youth—with
the air indeed of having in his mind two or three names, of
which one or other would be right. Peter nevertheless,
turning his back again, offered no encouragement, and when
they parted afresh it was with some show of impatience on
the side of the boy. Accordingly on their next encounter
Peter saw at a glance that he had now, in the interval,
divined and that, to sound his note, he was only waiting till
they should find themselves alone. This he had soon arranged and he then broke straight out. "Do you know your
conundrum has been keeping me awake? But in the watches
of the night the answer came over me—so that, upon my
honour, I quite laughed out. Had you been supposing I had
to go to Paris to learn *that?*" Even now, to see him still so
sublimely on his guard, Peter's young friend had to laugh
afresh. "You won't give a sign till you're sure? Beautiful old
Peter!" But Lance at last produced it. "Why, hang it, the
truth about the Master."

It made between them for some minutes a lively passage,
full of wonder for each at the wonder of the other. "Then
how long have you understood—"

"The true value of his work? I understood it," Lance
recalled, "as soon as I began to understand anything. But I
didn't begin fully to do that, I admit, till I got *là-bas*."

"Dear, dear!"—Peter gasped with retrospective dread.

"But for what have you taken me? I'm a hopeless muff—
that I *had* to have rubbed in. But I'm not such a muff as the
Master!" Lance declared.

"Then why did you never tell me—?"

"That I hadn't, after all"—the boy took him up—"remained
such an idiot? Just because I never dreamed *you* knew. But
I beg your pardon. I only wanted to spare you. And what I

don't now understand is how the deuce then for so long you've managed to keep bottled."

Peter produced his explanation, but only after some delay and with a gravity not void of embarrassment. "It was for your mother."

"Oh!" said Lance.

"And that's the great thing now—since the murder *is* out. I want a promise from you. I mean"—and Peter almost feverishly followed it up—"a vow from you, solemn and such as you owe me here on the spot, that you'll sacrifice anything rather than let her ever guess—"

"That *I've* guessed?"—Lance took it in. "I see." He evidently after a moment had taken in much. "But what is it you've in mind that I may have a chance to sacrifice?"

"Oh one has always something."

Lance looked at him hard. "Do you mean that *you've* had—?" The look he received back, however, so put the question by that he found soon enough another. "Are you really sure my mother doesn't know?"

Peter, after renewed reflexion, was really sure. "If she does she's too wonderful."

"But aren't we all too wonderful?"

"Yes," Peter granted—"but in different ways. The thing's so desperately important because your father's little public consists only, as you know then," Peter developed—"well, of how many?"

"First of all," the Master's son risked, "of himself. And last of all too. I don't quite see of whom else."

Peter had an approach to impatience. "Of your mother, I say—*always*."

Lance cast it all up. "You absolutely feel that?"

"Absolutely."

"Well then with yourself that makes three."

"Oh *me!*"—and Peter, with a wag of his kind old head, modestly excused himself. "The number's at any rate small enough for any individual dropping out to be too dreadfully missed. Therefore, to put it in a nutshell, take care, my boy—that's all—that *you're* not!"

"I've got to keep on humbugging?" Lance wailed.

"It's just to warn you of the danger of your failing of that that I've seized this opportunity."

"And what do you regard in particular," the young man asked, "as the danger?"

"Why this certainty: that the moment your mother, who feels so strongly, should suspect your secret—well," said Peter desperately, "the fat would be on the fire."

Lance for a moment seemed to stare at the blaze. "She'd throw me over?"

"She'd throw *him* over."

"And come round to us?"

Peter, before he answered, turned away. "Come round to *you*." But he had said enough to indicate—and, as he evidently trusted, to avert—the horrid contingency.

IV

Within six months again, none the less, his fear was on more occasions than one all before him. Lance had returned to Paris for another trial; then had reappeared at home and had had, with his father, for the first time in his life, one of the scenes that strike sparks. He described it with much expression to Peter, touching whom (since they had never done so before) it was the sign of a new reserve on the part of the pair at Carrara Lodge that they at present failed, on a matter of intimate interest, to open themselves—if not in joy then in sorrow—to their good friend. This produced perhaps practically between the parties a shade of alienation and a slight intermission of commerce—marked mainly indeed by the fact that to talk at his ease with his old playmate Lance had in general to come to see him. The closest if not quite the gayest relation they had yet known together was thus ushered in. The difficulty for poor Lance was a tension at home—begotten by the fact that his father wished him to be at least the sort of success he himself had been. He hadn't "chucked" Paris—though nothing appeared more vivid to him than that Paris had chucked him: he would go back

again because of the fascination in trying, in seeing, in
sounding the depths—in learning one's lesson, briefly, even
if the lesson were simply that of one's impotence in the
presence of one's larger vision. But what did the Master, all
aloft in his senseless fluency, know of impotence, and what
vision—to be called such—had he in all his blind life ever
had? Lance, heated and indignant, frankly appealed to his
godparent on this score.

His father, it appeared, had come down on him for having, after so long, nothing to show, and hoped that on his
next return this deficiency would be repaired. *The* thing,
the Master complacently set forth was—for any artist, however inferior to himself—at least to "do" something. "What
can you do? That's all I ask!" *He* had certainly done enough,
and there was no mistake about what he had to show. Lance
had tears in his eyes when it came thus to letting his old
friend know how great the strain might be on the "sacrifice"
asked of him. It wasn't so easy to continue humbugging—as
from son to parent—after feeling one's self despised for not
grovelling in mediocrity. Yet a noble duplicity was what, as
they intimately faced the situation, Peter went on requiring;
and it was still for a time what his young friend, bitter and
sore, managed loyally to comfort him with. Fifty pounds
more than once again, it was true, rewarded both in London
and in Paris the young friend's loyalty; none the less sensi-
bly, doubtless, at the moment, that the money was a direct
advance on a decent sum for which Peter had long since
privately prearranged an ultimate function. Whether by
these arts or others, at all events, Lance's just resentment
was kept for a season—but only for a season—at bay. The
day arrived when he warned his companion that he could
hold out—or hold in—no longer. Carrara Lodge had had to
listen to another lecture delivered from a great height—an
infliction really heavier at last than, without striking back or
in some way letting the Master have the truth, flesh and
blood could bear.

"And what I don't see is," Lance observed with a certain
irritated eye for what was after all, if it came to that, owing

to himself too; "what I don't see is, upon my honour, how *you*, as things are going, can keep the game up."

"Oh the game for me is only to hold my tongue," said placid Peter. "And I have my reason."

"Still my mother?"

Peter showed a queer face as he had often shown it before—that is by turning it straight away. "What will you have? I haven't ceased to like her."

"She's beautiful—she's a dear of course," Lance allowed; "but what is she to you, after all, and what is it to you that, as to anything whatever, she should or she shouldn't?"

Peter, who had turned red, hung fire a little. "Well—it's all simply what I make of it."

There was now, however, in his young friend a strange, an adopted insistence. "What are you after all to *her*?"

"Oh nothing. But that's another matter."

"She cares only for my father," said Lance the Parisian.

"Naturally—and that's just why."

"Why you've wished to spare her?"

"Because she cares so tremendously much."

Lance took a turn about the room, but with his eyes still on his host. "How awfully—always—you must have liked her!"

"Awfully. Always," said Peter Brench.

The young man continued for a moment to muse—then stopped again in front of him. "Do you know how much she cares?" Their eyes met on it, but Peter, as if his own found something new in Lance's, appeared to hesitate, for the first time in an age, to say he did know. "*I've* only just found out," said Lance. "She came to my room last night, after being present, in silence and only with her eyes on me, at what I had had to take from him; she came—and she was with me an extraordinary hour."

He had paused again and they had again for a while sounded each other. Then something—and it made him suddenly turn pale—came to Peter. "She *does* know?"

"She does know. She let it all out to me—so as to demand of me no more than 'that,' as she said, of which she herself had been capable. She has always, always known," said Lance without pity.

Peter was silent a long time; during which his companion might have heard him gently breathe, and on touching him might have felt within him the vibration of a long low sound suppressed. By the time he spoke at last he had taken everything in. "Then I do see how tremendously much."

"Isn't it wonderful?" Lance asked.

"Wonderful," Peter mused.

"So that if your original effort to keep me from Paris was to keep me from knowledge—!" Lance exclaimed as if with a sufficient indication of this futility.

It might have been at the futility. Peter appeared for a little to gaze. "I think it must have been—without my quite at the time knowing it—to keep *me!*" he replied at last as he turned away.

◆ ─────────────────────────── ◆

THE BOARDING HOUSE

James Joyce

Mrs. Mooney was a butcher's daughter. She was a woman who was quite able to keep things to herself: a determined woman. She had married her father's foreman and opened a butcher's shop near Spring Gardens. But as soon as his father-in-law was dead Mr. Mooney began to go to the devil. He drank, plundered the till, ran head-long into debt. It was no use making him take the pledge: he was sure to break out again a few days after. By fighting his wife in the presence of customers and by buying bad meat he ruined his business. One night he went for his wife with the cleaver and she had to sleep in a neighbour's house.

After that they lived apart. She went to the priest and got a separation from him with care of the children. She would give him neither money nor food nor house-room; and so he was obliged to enlist himself as a sheriff's man. He was a shabby stooped little drunkard with a white face and a white moustache and white eyebrows, pencilled above his little eyes, which were pink-veined and raw; and all day long he sat in the bailiff's room, waiting to be put on a job. Mrs. Mooney, who had taken what remained of her money out of the butcher business and set up a boarding house in Hardwicke Street, was a big imposing woman. Her house had a floating population made up of tourists from Liverpool and the Isle of Man and, occasionally, *artistes* from the music halls. Its resident population was made up of clerks from the city. She governed the house cunningly and firmly, knew when to give credit, when to be stern and when to let things pass. All the resident young men spoke of her as *The Madam*.

Mrs. Mooney's young men paid fifteen shillings a week for board and lodgings (beer or stout at dinner excluded). They shared in common tastes and occupations and for this reason they were very chummy with one another. They discussed with one another the chances of favourites and outsiders. Jack Mooney, the Madam's son, who was clerk to a commission agent in Fleet Street, had the reputation of being a hard case. He was fond of using soldiers' obscenities: usually he came home in the small hours. When he met his friends he had always a good one to tell them and he was always sure to be on to a good thing—that is to say, a likely horse or a likely *artiste*. He was also handy with the mits and sang comic songs. On Sunday nights there would often be a reunion in Mrs. Mooney's front drawing-room. The music-hall *artistes* would oblige; and Sheridan played waltzes and polkas and vamped accompaniments. Polly Mooney, the Madam's daughter, would also sing. She sang:

> *"I'm a . . . naughty girl.*
> *You needn't sham:*
> *You know I am."*

Polly was a slim girl of nineteen; she had light soft hair and a small full mouth. Her eyes, which were grey with a shade of green through them, had a habit of glancing upwards when she spoke with anyone, which made her look like a little perverse madonna. Mrs. Mooney had first sent her daughter to be a typist in a corn-factor's office but, as a disreputable sheriff's man used to come every other day to the office, asking to be allowed to say a word to his daughter, she had taken her daughter home again and set her to do housework. As Polly was very lively the intention was to give her the run of the young men. Besides, young men like to feel that there is a young woman not very far away. Polly, of course, flirted with the young men but Mrs. Mooney, who was a shrewd judge, knew that the young men were only passing the time away: none of them meant business. Things went on so for a long time and Mrs. Mooney began to think of sending Polly back to typewriting when she noticed that something was going on between Polly and one of the young men. She watched the pair and kept her own counsel.

Polly knew that she was being watched, but still her mother's persistent silence could not be misunderstood. There had been no open complicity between mother and daughter, no open understanding but, though people in the house began to talk of the affair, still Mrs. Mooney did not intervene. Polly began to grow a little strange in her manner and the young man was evidently perturbed. At last, when she judged it to be the right moment, Mrs. Mooney intervened. She dealt with moral problems as a cleaver deals with meat: and in this case she had made up her mind.

It was a bright Sunday morning of early summer, promising heat, but with a fresh breeze blowing. All the windows of the boarding house were open and the lace curtains

ballooned gently towards the street beneath the raised sashes.
The belfry of George's Church sent out constant peals and
worshippers, singly or in groups, traversed the little circus
before the church, revealing their purpose by their self-
contained demeanour no less than by the little volumes in
their gloved hands. Breakfast was over in the boarding
house and the table of the breakfast-room was covered with
plates on which lay yellow streaks of eggs with morsels of
bacon-fat and bacon-rind. Mrs. Mooney sat in the straw
arm-chair and watched the servant Mary remove the breakfast things. She made Mary collect the crusts and pieces of
broken bread to help to make Tuesday's bread-pudding.
When the table was cleared, the broken bread collected,
the sugar and butter safe under lock and key, she began to
reconstruct the interview which she had had the night before with Polly. Things were as she had suspected: she had
been frank in her questions and Polly had been frank in her
answers. Both had been somewhat awkward, of course. She
had been made awkward by her not wishing to receive the
news in too cavalier a fashion or to seem to have connived and
Polly had been made awkward not merely because allusions
of that kind always made her awkward but also because she
did not wish it to be thought that in her wise innocence
she had divined the intention behind her mother's tolerance.

Mrs. Mooney glanced instinctively at the little gilt clock
on the mantelpiece as soon as she had become aware through
her revery that the bells of George's Church had stopped
ringing. It was seventeen minutes past eleven: she would
have lots of time to have the matter out with Mr. Doran and
then catch short twelve at Marlborough Street. She was
sure she would win. To begin with she had all the weight of
social opinion on her side: she was an outraged mother. She
had allowed him to live beneath her roof, assuming that he
was a man of honour, and he had simply abused her hospitality. He was thirty-four or thirty-five years of age, so that
youth could not be pleaded as his excuse; nor could ignorance be his excuse since he was a man who had seen
something of the world. He had simply taken advantage of

Polly's youth and inexperience: that was evident. The question was: What reparation would he make?

There must be reparation made in such cases. It is all very well for the man: he can go his ways as if nothing had happened, having had his moment of pleasure, but the girl has to bear the brunt. Some mothers would be content to patch up such an affair for a sum of money; she had known cases of it. But she would not do so. For her only one reparation could make up for the loss of her daughter's honour: marriage.

She counted all her cards again before sending Mary up to Mr. Doran's room to say that she wished to speak with him. She felt sure she would win. He was a serious young man, not rakish or loud-voiced like the others. If it had been Mr. Sheridan or Mr. Meade or Bantam Lyons her task would have been much harder. She did not think he would face publicity. All the lodgers in the house knew something of the affair; details had been invented by some. Besides, he had been employed for thirteen years in a great Catholic wine-merchant's office and publicity would mean for him, perhaps, the loss of his job. Whereas if he agreed all might be well. She knew he had a good screw for one thing and she suspected he had a bit of stuff put by.

Nearly the half-hour! She stood up and surveyed herself in the pier-glass. The decisive expression of her great florid face satisfied her and she thought of some mothers she knew who could not get their daughters off their hands.

Mr. Doran was very anxious indeed this Sunday morning. He had made two attempts to shave but his hand had been so unsteady that he had been obliged to desist. Three days' reddish beard fringed his jaws and every two or three minutes a mist gathered on his glasses so that he had to take them off and polish them with his pocket-handkerchief. The recollection of his confession of the night before was a cause of acute pain to him; the priest had drawn out every ridiculous detail of the affair and in the end had so magnified his sin that he was almost thankful at being afforded a loophole of reparation. The harm was done. What could he do now but marry her or run away? He could not brazen it out. The affair would be sure to be talked of and his employer would be certain to hear of it. Dublin is such a small city: everyone knows everyone else's business. He felt his heart leap warmly in his throat as he heard in his excited imagination old Mr. Leonard calling out in his rasping voice: "Send Mr. Doran here, please."

All his long years of service gone for nothing! All his industry and diligence thrown away! As a young man he had sown his wild oats, of course; he had boasted of his free-thinking and denied the existence of God to his companions in public-houses. But that was all passed and done with . . . nearly. He still bought a copy of *Reynolds's Newspaper* every week but he attended to his religious duties and for nine-tenths of the year lived a regular life. He had money enough to settle down on; it was not that. But the family would look down on her. First of all there was her disreputable father and then her mother's boarding house was beginning to get a certain fame. He had a notion that he was being had. He could imagine his friends talking of the affair and laughing. She *was* a little vulgar; some times she said "I seen" and "If I had've known." But what would grammar matter if he really loved her? He could not make up his mind whether to like her or despise her for what she had done. Of course he had done it too. His instinct urged him to remain free, not to marry. Once you are married you are done for, it said.

While he was sitting helplessly on the side of the bed in shirt and trousers she tapped lightly at his door and entered. She told him all, that she had made a clean breast of it to her mother and that her mother would speak with him that morning. She cried and threw her arms round his neck, saying:

"O Bob! Bob! What am I to do? What am I to do at all?" She would put an end to herself, she said.

He comforted her feebly, telling her not to cry, that it would be all right, never fear. He felt against his shirt the agitation of her bosom.

It was not altogether his fault that it had happened. He remembered well, with the curious patient memory of the celibate, the first casual caresses her dress, her breath, her fingers had given him. Then late one night as he was undressing for bed she had tapped at his door, timidly. She wanted to relight her candle at his for hers had been blown out by a gust. It was her bath night. She wore a loose open combing jacket of printed flannel. Her white instep shone in the opening of her furry slippers and the blood glowed warmly behind her perfumed skin. From her hands and wrists too as she lit and steadied her candle a faint perfume arose.

On nights when he came in very late it was she who warmed up his dinner. He scarcely knew what he was eating feeling her beside him alone, at night, in the sleeping house. And her thoughtfulness! If the night was anyway cold or wet or windy there was sure to be a little tumbler of punch ready for him. Perhaps they could be happy together. . . .

They used to go upstairs together on tiptoe, each with a candle, and on the third landing exchange reluctant goodnights. They used to kiss. He remembered well her eyes, the touch of her hand and his delirium. . . .

But delirium passes. He echoed her phrase, applying it to himself: *"What am I to do?"* The instinct of the celibate warned him to hold back. But the sin was there; even his sense of honour told him that reparation must be made for such a sin.

While he was sitting with her on the side of the bed Mary came to the door and said that the missus wanted to see him in the parlour. He stood up to put on his coat and waistcoat, more helpless than ever. When he was dressed he went over to her to comfort her. It would be all right, never fear. He left her crying on the bed and moaning softly: *"O my God!"*

Going down the stairs his glasses became so dimmed with moisture that he had to take them off and polish them. He longed to ascend through the roof and fly away to another country where he would never hear again of his trouble, and yet a force pushed him downstairs step by step. The implacable faces of his employer and of the Madam stared upon his discomfiture. On the last flight of stairs he passed Jack Mooney who was coming up from the pantry nursing two bottles of *Bass*. They saluted coldly; and the lover's eyes rested for a second or two on a thick bulldog face and a pair of thick short arms. When he reached the foot of the staircase he glanced up and saw Jack regarding him from the door of the return-room.

Suddenly he remembered the night when one of the music-hall *artistes*, a little blond Londoner, had made a rather free allusion to Polly. The reunion had been almost broken up on account of Jack's violence. Everyone tried to quiet him. The music-hall *artiste*, a little paler than usual, kept smiling and saying that there was no harm meant: but Jack kept shouting at him that if any fellow tried that sort of a game on with *his* sister he'd bloody well put his teeth down his throat, so he would.

Polly sat for a little time on the side of the bed, crying. Then she dried her eyes and went over to the looking-glass. She dipped the end of the towel in the water-jug and refreshed her eyes with the cool water. She looked at herself in profile and readjusted a hairpin above her ear. Then she went back to the bed again and sat at the foot. She regarded the pillows for a long time and the sight of them awakened in her mind secret, amiable memories. She rested the nape of her neck against the cool iron bed-rail and fell into a revery. There was no longer any perturbation visible on her face.

She waited on patiently, almost cheerfully, without alarm, her memories gradually giving place to hopes and visions of the future. Her hopes and visions were so intricate that she no longer saw the white pillows on which her gaze was fixed or remembered that she was waiting for anything.

At last she heard her mother calling. She started to her feet and ran to the banisters.

"Polly! Polly!"

"Yes, mamma?"

"Come down, dear. Mr. Doran wants to speak to you."

Then she remembered what she had been waiting for.

◆ ———————————————————————————— ◆

LIBERTY HALL

Ring Lardner

My husband is in Atlantic City, where they are trying out "Dear Dora," the musical version of "David Copperfield." My husband wrote the score. He used to take me along for these out-of-town openings, but not any more.

He, of course, has to spend almost all his time in the theater and that leaves me alone in the hotel, and pretty soon people find out whose wife I am and introduce themselves, and the next thing you know they are inviting us for a week or a weekend at Dobbs Ferry or Oyster Bay. Then it is up to me to think of some legitimate-sounding reason why we can't come.

In lots of cases they say, "Well, if you can't make it the twenty-second, how about the twenty-ninth?" and so on till you simply have to accept. And Ben gets mad and stays mad for days.

He absolutely abhors visiting and thinks there ought to be a law against invitations that go beyond dinner and bridge. He doesn't mind hotels where there is a decent light for reading in bed and one for shaving, and where you can order meals, with coffee, any time you want them. But I really believe he would rather spend a week in the death house at Sing Sing than in somebody else's home.

Three or four years ago we went around quite a lot with a couple whom I will call the Buckleys. We liked them and they liked us. We had dinner together at least twice a week and after dinner we played bridge or went to a show or just sat and talked.

Ben never turned down their invitations and often actually called them up himself and suggested parties. Finally they moved to Albany on account of Mr. Buckley's business. We missed them a great deal, and when Mrs. Buckley wrote for us to come up there for the holidays we were tickled pink.

Well, their guest-room was terribly cold; it took hours to fill the bathtub; there was no reading-lamp by the bed; three reporters called to interview Ben, two of them kittenish young girls; the breakfasts were just fruit and cereal and toast; coffee was not served at luncheon; the faucets in the wash-basin were the kind that won't run unless you keep pressing them; four important keys on the piano were stuck and people were invited in every night to hear Ben play, and the Buckley family had been augmented by a tremendous police dog, who was "just a puppy and never growled or snapped at anyone he knew," but couldn't seem to remember that Ben was not an utter stranger.

On the fourth awful day Ben gave out the news—news to him and to me as well as to our host and hostess—that he had lost a filling which he would not trust any but his own New York dentist to replace. We came home and we have never seen the Buckleys since. If we do see them it will be an accident. They will hardly ask us there unless we ask them here, and we won't ask them here for fear they would ask us there. And they were honestly the most congenial people we ever met.

It was after our visit to the Craigs at Stamford that Ben originated what he calls his "emergency exit." We had such a horrible time at the Craigs' and such a worse time getting away that Ben swore he would pay no more visits until he could think up a graceful method of curtailing them in the event they proved unbearable.

Here is the scheme he hit on: He would write himself a telegram and sign it with the name Ziegfeld or Gene Buck or Dillingham or George M. Cohan. The telegram would say that he must return to New York at once, and it would give a reason. Then, the day we started out, he would leave it with Irene, the girl at Harms', his publishers, with instructions to have it sent to him twenty-four hours later.

When it arrived at whatever town we were in, he would either have the host or hostess take it over the telephone or ask the telegraph company to deliver it so he could show it around. We would put on long faces and say how sorry we were, but of course business was business, so goodby and so forth. There was never a breath of suspicion even when the telegram was ridiculous, like the one Ben had sent to himself at Spring Lake, where we were staying with the Marshalls just after "Betty's Birthday" opened at the Globe. The Marshalls loved musical shows, but knew less than nothing about music and swallowed this one whole:

Shaw and Miss Miller both suffering from laryngitis Stop Entire score must be rewritten half tone lower Stop Come at once Stop.

> *C. B. Dillingham.*

If, miraculously, Ben had ever happened to be enjoying himself, he would, of course, have kept the contents of his message a secret or else displayed it and remarked swaggeringly that he guessed he wasn't going to let any so-and-so theatrical producer spoil his fun.

Ben is in Atlantic City now and I have read every book in the house and am writing this just because there doesn't seem to be anything else to do. And also because we have a friend, Joe Frazier, who is a magazine editor and the other day I told him I would like to try my hand at a short story, but I was terrible at plots, and he said plots weren't essential; look at Ernest Hemingway; most of his stories have hardly any plot; it's his style that counts. And he—I mean Mr. Frazier—suggested that I write about our visit to Mr.

and Mrs. Thayer in Lansdowne, outside of Philadelphia,
which Mr. Frazier said, might be termed the visit that
ended visits and which is the principal reason why I am here
alone.

Well, it was a beautiful night a year ago last September.
Ben was conducting the performance—"Step Lively"—and
I was standing at the railing of the Boardwalk in front of the
theater, watching the moonlight on the ocean. A couple
whom I had noticed in the hotel dining-room stopped alongside of me and pretty soon the woman spoke to me, something
about how pretty it was. Then came the old question, wasn't
I Mrs. Ben Drake? I said I was, and the woman went on:

"My name is Mrs. Thayer—Hilda Thayer. And this is my
husband. We are both simply crazy about Mr. Drake's
music and just dying to meet him personally. We wondered
if you and he would have supper with us after the performance tonight."

"Oh, I'm afraid that's impossible," I replied. "You see
when they are having a tryout, he and the librettists and the
lyric writers work all night every night until they get everything in shape for the New York opening. They never have
time for more than a sandwich and they eat that right in the
theater."

"Well, how about luncheon tomorrow?"

"He'll be rehearsing all day."

"How about dinner tomorrow evening?"

"Honestly, Mrs. Thayer, it's out of the question. Mr.
Drake never makes engagements during a tryout week."

"And I guess he doesn't want to meet us anyway," put in
Mr. Thayer. "What use would a genius like Ben Drake have
for a couple of common-no-account admirers like Mrs. Thayer
and myself! If we were 'somebody' too, it would be different!"

"Not at all!" said I. "Mr. Drake is perfectly human. He
loves to have his music praised and I am sure he would be
delighted to meet you if he weren't so terribly busy."

"Can you lunch with us yourself?"

"Tomorrow?"

"Any day."

Well, whatever Ben and other husbands may think, there is no decent way of turning down an invitation like that. And besides I was lonesome and the Thayers looked like awfully nice people.

I lunched with them and I dined with them, not only the next day but all the rest of the week. And on Friday I got Ben to lunch with them and he liked them, too; they were not half as gushing and silly as most of his "fans."

At dinner on Saturday night, they cross-examined me about our immediate plans. I told them that as soon as the show was "over" in New York, I was going to try to make Ben stay home and do nothing for a whole month.

"I should think," said Mrs. Thayer, "it would be very hard for him to rest there in the city, with the producers and publishers and phonograph people calling him up all the time."

I admitted that he was bothered a lot.

"Listen, dearie," said Mrs. Thayer. "Why don't you come to Lansdowne and spend a week with us? I'll promise you faithfully that you won't be disturbed at all. I won't let anyone know you are there and if any of our friends call on us I'll pretend we're not at home. I won't allow Mr. Drake to even touch the piano. If he wants exercise, there are miles of room in our yard to walk around in, and nobody can see him from the street. All day and all night, he can do nothing or anything, just as he pleases. It will be 'Liberty Hall' for you both. He needn't tell anybody where he is, but if some of his friends or business acquaintances find out and try to get in touch with him, I'll frighten them away. How does that sound?"

"It sounds wonderful," I said, "but—"

"It's settled then," said Mrs. Thayer, "and we'll expect you on Sunday, October eleventh."

"Oh, but the show may not be 'set' by that time," I remonstrated.

"How about the eighteenth?" said Mr. Thayer.

Well, it ended by my accepting for the week of the twenty-fifth and Ben took it quite cheerfully.

"If they stick to their promise to keep us under cover," he said, "it may be a lot better than staying in New York. I know that Buck and the Shuberts and Ziegfeld want me while I'm 'hot' and they wouldn't give me a minute's peace if they could find me. And of course if things aren't as good as they look, Irene's telegram will provide us with an easy out."

On the way over to Philadelphia he hummed me an awfully pretty melody which had been running through his head since we left the apartment. "I think it's sure fire," he said. "I'm crazy to get to a piano and fool with it."

"That isn't resting, dear."

"Well, you don't want me to throw away a perfectly good tune! They aren't so plentiful that I can afford to waste one. It won't take me five minutes at a piano to get it fixed in my mind."

The Thayers met us in an expensive-looking limousine.

"Ralph," said Mrs. Thayer to her husband, "you sit in one of the little seats and Mr. and Mrs. Drake will sit back here with me."

"I'd really prefer one of the little seats myself," said Ben and he meant it, for he hates to get his clothes mussed and being squeezed in beside two such substantial objects as our hostess and myself was bound to rumple him.

"No, sir!" said Mrs. Thayer positively. "You came to us for a rest and we're not going to start you off uncomfortable."

"But I'd honestly rather—"

It was no use. Ben was wedged between us and throughout the drive maintained a morose silence, unable to think of anything but how terrible his coat would look when he got out.

The Thayers had a very pretty home and the room assigned to us was close to perfection. There were comfortable twin beds with a small stand and convenient reading-lamp between; a big dresser and chiffonier; an ample closet with plenty of hangers; a bathroom with hot water that was hot, towels that were not too new and faucets that stayed on when turned on, and an ash-tray within reach of wherever you happened to be. If only we could have spent all our time in that guest-room, it would have been ideal.

But presently we were summoned downstairs to luncheon. I had warned Mrs. Thayer in advance and Ben was served with coffee. He drinks it black.

"Don't you take cream, Mr. Drake?"

"No. Never."

"But that's because you don't get good cream in New York."

"No. It's because I don't like cream in coffee."

"You would like our cream. We have our own cows and the cream is so rich that it's almost like butter. Won't you try just a little?"

"No, thanks."

"But just a little, to see how rich it is."

She poured about a tablespoonful of cream into his coffee-cup and for a second I was afraid he was going to pick up the cup and throw it in her face. But he kept hold of himself, forced a smile and declined a second chop.

"You haven't tasted your coffee," said Mrs. Thayer.

"Yes, I have," lied Ben. "The cream is wonderful. I'm sorry it doesn't agree with me."

"I don't believe coffee agrees with anyone," said Mrs. Thayer. "While you are here, not doing any work, why don't you try to give it up?"

"I'd be so irritable you wouldn't have me in the house. Besides, it isn't plain coffee that disagrees with me; it's coffee with cream."

"Pure, rich cream like ours couldn't hurt you," said Mrs. Thayer, and Ben, defeated, refused to answer.

He started to light a Jaguar cigaret, the brand he had been smoking for years.

"Here! Wait a minute!" said Mr. Thayer. "Try one of mine."

"What are they?" asked Ben.

"Trumps," said our host, holding out his case. "They're mild and won't irritate the throat."

"I'll sample one later," said Ben.

"You've simply got to try one now," said Mrs. Thayer. "You may as well get used to them because you'll have to smoke them all the time you're here. We can't have guests providing their own cigarets." So Ben had to discard his Jaguar and smoke a Trump, and it was even worse than he had anticipated.

After luncheon we adjourned to the living-room and Ben went straight to the piano.

"Here! Here! None of that!" said Mrs. Thayer. "I haven't forgotten my promise."

"What promise?" asked Ben.

"Didn't your wife tell you? I promised her faithfully that if you visited us, you wouldn't be allowed to touch the piano."

"But I want to," said Ben. "There's a melody in my head that I'd like to try."

"Oh, yes, I know all about that," said Mrs. Thayer. "You just think you've got to entertain us! Nothing doing! We invited you here for yourself, not to enjoy your talent. I'd be a fine one to ask you to my home for a rest and then make you perform."

"You're not making me," said Ben. "Honestly I want to play for just five or ten minutes. I've got a tune that I might do something with and I'm anxious to run it over."

"I don't believe you, you naughty man!" said our hostess. "Your wife has told you how wild we are about your music and you're determined to be nice to us. But I'm just as stubborn as you are. Not one note do you play as long as you're our guest!"

Ben favored me with a stricken look, mumbled something about unpacking his suitcase—it was already unpacked—and went up to our room, where he stayed nearly an hour, jotting down his new tune, smoking Jaguar after Jaguar and wishing that black coffee flowed from bathtub faucets.

About a quarter of four Mr. Thayer insisted on taking him around the place and showing him the shrubbery, something that held in Ben's mind a place of equal importance to the grade of wire used in hairpins.

"I'll have to go to business tomorrow," said Mr. Thayer, "and you will be left to amuse yourself. I thought you might enjoy this planting more if you knew a little about it. Of course it's much prettier in the spring of the year."

"I can imagine so."

"You must come over next spring and see it."

"I'm usually busy in the spring," said Ben.

"Before we go in," said Mr. Thayer, "I'd like to ask you one question: Do tunes come into your mind and then you write them down, or do you just sit at the piano and improvise until you strike something good?"

"Sometimes one way and sometimes the other," said Ben.

"That's very interesting," said Mr. Thayer. "I've often wondered how it was done. And another question: Do you write the tunes first and then give them to the men who write the words, or do the men write the words first and then give them to you to make up the music to them?"

"Sometimes one way and sometimes the other," said Ben.

"That's very interesting," said Mr. Thayer. "It's something I'm glad to know. And now we'd better join the ladies or my wife will say I'm monopolizing you."

They joined us, much to my relief. I had just reached a point where I would either have had to tell "Hilda" exactly how much Ben earned per annum or that it was none of her business.

"Well!" said Mrs. Thayer to Ben. "I was afraid Ralph had kidnaped you."

"He was showing me the shrubbery," said Ben.

"What did you think of it?"

"It's great shrubbery," said Ben, striving to put some warmth into his voice.

"You must come and see it in the spring."

"I'm usually busy in the spring."

"Ralph and I are mighty proud of our shrubbery."

"You have a right to be."

Ben was taking a book out of the bookcase.

"What book is that?" asked Mrs. Thayer.

" 'The Great Gatsby,' " said Ben. "I've always wanted to read it but never got around to it."

"Heavens!" said Mrs. Thayer as she took it away from him. "That's old! You'll find the newest ones there on the table. We keep pretty well up to date. Ralph and I are both great readers. Just try any one of those books in that pile. They're all good."

Ben glanced them over and selected "Chevrons." He sat down and opened it.

"Man! Man!" exclaimed Mrs. Thayer. "You've picked the most uncomfortable chair in the house!"

"He likes straight chairs," I said.

"That's on the square," said Ben.

"But you mustn't sit there," said Mrs. Thayer. "It makes me uncomfortable just to look at you. Take this chair here. It's the softest, nicest chair you've ever sat in."

"I like hard straight chairs," said Ben, but he sank into the soft, nice one and again opened his book.

"Oh, you never can see there!" said Mrs. Thayer. "You'll ruin your eyes! Get up just a minute and let Ralph move your chair by that lamp."

"I can see perfectly well."

"I know better! Ralph, move his chair so he can see."

"I don't believe I want to read just now anyway," said Ben, and went to the phonograph. "Bess," he said, putting on a record, "here's that 'Oh! Miss Hannah!' by the Revelers."

Mrs. Thayer fairly leaped to his side, and herded Miss Hannah back into her stall.

"We've got lots later ones than that," she said. "Let me play you the new Gershwins."

It was at this juncture that I began to suspect our hostess of a lack of finesse. After all, Gershwin is a rival of my husband's and, in some folks' opinion, a worthy one. However, Ben had a word of praise for each record as it ended and did not even hint that any of the tunes were based on melodies of his own.

"Mr. Drake," said our host at length, "would you like a gin cocktail or a Bacardi?"

"I don't like Bacardi at all," said Ben.

"I'll bet you will like the kind I've got," said Mr. Thayer. "It was brought to me by a friend of mine who just got back from Cuba. It's the real stuff!"

"I don't like Bacardi," said Ben.

"Wait till you taste this," said Mr. Thayer.

Well, we had Bacardi cocktails. I drank mine and it wasn't so good. Ben took a sip of his and pretended it was all right. But he had told the truth when he said he didn't like Bacardi.

I won't go into details regarding the dinner except to relate that three separate items were highly flavored with cheese, and Ben despises cheese.

"Don't you care for cheese, Mr. Drake?" asked Mr. Thayer, noticing that Ben was not exactly bolting his food.

"No," replied the guest of honor.

"He's spoofing you, Ralph," said Mrs. Thayer. "Everybody likes cheese."

There was coffee, and Ben managed to guzzle a cup before it was desecrated with pure cream.

We sat down to bridge.

"Do you like to play families or divide up?"

"Oh, we like to play together," said I.

"I'll bet you don't," said Mrs. Thayer. "Suppose Ralph and you play Mr. Drake and me. I think it's a mistake for husbands and wives to be partners. They're likely to criticize one another and say things that leave a scar."

Well, Mr. Thayer and I played against Ben and Mrs. Thayer and I lost sixty cents at a tenth of a cent a point. Long before the evening was over I could readily see why Mrs. Thayer thought it was a mistake to play with her husband and if it had been possible I'd have left him a complete set of scars.

Just as we were getting to sleep, Mrs. Thayer knocked on our door.

"I'm afraid you haven't covers enough," she called. "There are extra blankets on the shelf in your closet."

"Thanks," I said. "We're as warm as toast."

"I'm afraid you aren't," said Mrs. Thayer.

"Lock the door," said Ben, "before she comes in and feels our feet."

All through breakfast next morning we waited in vain for the telephone call that would yield Irene's message. The phone rang once and Mrs. Thayer answered, but we couldn't hear what she said. At noon Ben signaled me to meet him upstairs and there he stated grimly that I might do as I choose, but he was leaving Liberty Hall ere another sun had set.

"You haven't any excuse," I reminded him.

"I'm a genius," he said, "and geniuses are notoriously eccentric."

"Geniuses' wives sometimes get eccentric, too," said I, and began to pack up.

Mr. Thayer had gone to Philadelphia and we were alone with our hostess at luncheon.

"Mrs. Thayer," said Ben, "do you ever have premonitions or hunches?"

She looked frightened. "Why, no. Do you?"

"I had one not half an hour ago. Something told me that I positively must be in New York tonight. I don't know whether it's business or illness or what, but I've just got to be there!"

"That's the strangest thing I ever heard of," said Mrs. Thayer. "It scares me to death!"

"It's nothing you need be scared of," said Ben. "It only concerns me."

"Yes, but listen," said Mrs. Thayer. "A telegram came for you at breakfast time this morning. I wasn't going to tell you about it because I had promised that you wouldn't be disturbed. And it didn't seem so terribly important. But this hunch of yours puts the matter in a different light. I'm sorry now that I didn't give you the message when I got it, but I memorized it and can repeat it word for word: 'Mr. Ben Drake, care of Mr. Ralph Thayer, Lansdowne, Pennsylvania. In Nile song, second bar of refrain, bass drum part reads A flat which makes discord. Should it be A natural? Would appreciate your coming to theater tonight to straighten this out as harmony must be restored in orchestra if troupe is to be success. Regards, Gene Buck.' "

"It sounds silly, doesn't it?" said Ben. "And yet I have known productions to fail and lose hundreds of thousands of dollars just because an author or composer left town too soon. I can well understand that you considered the message trivial. At the same time I can thank my stars that this instinct, or divination, or whatever you want to call it, told me to go home."

Just as the trainmen were shouting "Board!" Mrs. Thayer said:

"I have one more confession to make. I answered Mr. Buck's telegram. I wired him. 'Mr. Ben Drake resting at my home. Must not be bothered. Suggest that you keep bass drums still for a week.' And I signed my name. Please forgive me if I have done something terrible. Remember, it was for you."

Small wonder that Ben was credited at the Lambs' Club with that month's most interesting bender.

◆ —————————————————— ◆

THE HORSE DEALER'S
DAUGHTER

D. H. Lawrence

"Well, Mabel, and what are you going to do with yourself?" asked Joe, with foolish flippancy. He felt quite safe himself. Without listening for an answer, he turned aside, worked a grain of tobacco to the tip of his tongue, and spat it out. He did not care about anything, since he felt safe himself.

The three brothers and the sister sat round the desolate breakfast table, attempting some sort of desultory consultation. The morning's post had given the final tap to the family fortune, and all was over. The dreary dining-room itself, with its heavy mahogany furniture, looked as if it were waiting to be done away with.

But the consultation amounted to nothing. There was a strange air of ineffectuality about the three men, as they sprawled at table, smoking and reflecting vaguely on their own condition. The girl was alone, a rather short, sullen-looking young woman of twenty-seven. She did not share the same life as her brothers. She would have been good-looking, save for the impassive fixity of her face, "bulldog," as her brothers called it.

There was a confused tramping of horses' feet outside. The three men all sprawled round in their chairs to watch. Beyond the dark holly-bushes that separated the strip of lawn from the highroad, they could see a cavalcade of shire horses swinging out of their own yard, being taken for exercise. This was the last time. These were the last horses that would go through their hands. The young men watched with critical, callous look. They were all frightened at the collapse of their lives, and the sense of disaster in which they were involved left them no inner freedom.

Yet they were three fine, well-set fellows enough. Joe, the eldest, was a man of thirty-three, broad and handsome in a hot, flushed way. His face was red, he twisted his black moustache over a thick finger, his eyes were shallow and restless. He had a sensual way of uncovering his teeth when he laughed, and his bearing was stupid. Now he watched the horses with a glazed look of helplessness in his eyes, a certain stupor of downfall.

The great draught-horses swung past. They were tied head to tail, four of them, and they heaved along to where a lane branched off from the highroad, planting their great hoofs floutingly in the fine black mud, swinging their great rounded haunches sumptuously, and trotting a few sudden steps as they were led into the lane, round the corner.

Every movement showed a massive, slumbrous strength, and a stupidity which held them in subjection. The groom at the head looked back, jerking the leading rope. And the cavalcade moved out of sight up the lane, the tail of the last horse, bobbed up tight and stiff, held out taut from the swinging great haunches as they rocked behind the hedges in a motion like sleep.

Joe watched with glazed hopeless eyes. The horses were almost like his own body to him. He felt he was done for now. Luckily he was engaged to a woman as old as himself, and therefore her father, who was steward of a neighbouring estate, would provide him with a job. He would marry and go into harness. His life was over, he would be a subject animal now.

He turned uneasily aside, the retreating steps of the horses echoing in his ears. Then, with foolish restlessness, he reached for the scraps of bacon-rind from the plates, and making a faint whistling sound, flung them to the terrier that lay against the fender. He watched the dog swallow them, and waited till the creature looked into his eyes. Then a faint grin came on his face, and in a high, foolish voice he said:

"You won't get much more bacon, shall you, you little bitch?"

The dog faintly and dismally wagged its tail, then lowered its haunches, circled round, and lay down again.

There was another helpless silence at the table. Joe sprawled uneasily in his seat, not willing to go till the family conclave was dissolved. Fred Henry, the second brother, was erect, clean-limbed, alert. He had watched the passing of the horses with more sang-froid. If he was an animal, like Joe, he was an animal which controls, not one which is controlled. He was master of any horse, and he carried himself with a well-tempered air of mastery. But he was not master of the situations of life. He pushed his coarse brown moustache upwards, off his lip, and glanced irritably at his sister, who sat impassive and inscrutable.

"You'll go and stop with Lucy for a bit, shan't you?" he asked. The girl did not answer.

"I don't see what else you can do," persisted Fred Henry.

"Go as a skivvy," Joe interpolated laconically.

The girl did not move a muscle.

"If I was her, I should go in for training for a nurse," said Malcolm, the youngest of them all. He was the baby of the family, a young man of twenty-two, with a fresh, jaunty *museau*.

But Mabel did not take any notice of him. They had talked at her and round her for so many years, that she hardly heard them at all.

The marble clock on the mantelpiece softly chimed the half-hour, the dog rose uneasily from the hearthrug and looked at the party at the breakfast table. But still they sat on in ineffectual conclave.

"Oh, all right," said Joe suddenly, apropos of nothing. "I'll get a move on."

He pushed back his chair, straddled his knees with a downward jerk, to get them free, in horsey fashion, and went to the fire. Still he did not go out of the room; he was curious to know what the others would do or say. He began to charge his pipe, looking down at the dog and saying, in a high, affected voice:

"Going wi' me? Going wi' me are ter? Tha'rt goin' further tha that counts on just now, dost hear?"

The dog faintly wagged its tail, the man stuck out his jaw and covered his pipe with his hands, and puffed intently, losing himself in the tobacco, looking down all the while at the dog with an absent brown eye. The dog looked up at him in mournful distrust. Joe stood with his knees stuck out, in real horsey fashion.

"Have you had a letter from Lucy?" Fred Henry asked of his sister.

"Last week," came the neutral reply.

"And what does she say?"

There was no answer.

"Does she *ask* you to go and stop there?" persisted Fred Henry.

"She says I can if I like."

"Well, then, you'd better. Tell her you'll come on Monday."

This was received in silence.

"That's what you'll do then, is it?" said Fred Henry, in some exasperation.

But she made no answer. There was a silence of futility and irritation in the room. Malcolm grinned fatuously.

"You'll have to make up your mind between now and next Wednesday," said Joe loudly, "or else find yourself lodgings on the kerbstone."

The face of the young woman darkened, but she sat on immutable.

"Here's Jack Fergusson!" exclaimed Malcolm, who was looking aimlessly out of the window.

"Where?" exclaimed Joe, loudly.

"Just gone past."

"Coming in?"

Malcolm craned his neck to see the gate.

"Yes," he said.

There was a silence. Mabel sat on like one condemned, at the head of the table. Then a whistle was heard from the kitchen. The dog got up and barked sharply. Joe opened the door and shouted:

"Come on."

After a moment a young man entered. He was muffled up in overcoat and a purple woollen scarf, and his tweed cap, which he did not remove, was pulled down on his head. He was of medium height, his face was rather long and pale, his eyes looked tired.

"Hello, Jack! Well, Jack!" exclaimed Malcolm and Joe. Fred Henry merely said, "Jack."

"What's doing?" asked the newcomer, evidently addressing Fred Henry.

"Same. We've got to be out by Wednesday. Got a cold?"

"I have—got it bad, too."

"Why don't you stop in?"

"*Me* stop in? When I can't stand on my legs, perhaps I shall have a chance." The young man spoke huskily. He had a slight Scotch accent.

"It's a knock-out, isn't it," said Joe, boisterously, "if a doctor goes round croaking with a cold. Looks bad for the patients, doesn't it?"

The young doctor looked at him slowly.

"Anything the matter with *you*, then?" he asked sarcastically.

"Not as I know of. Damn your eyes, I hope not. Why?"

"I thought you were very concerned about the patients, wondered if you might be one yourself."

"Damn it, no, I've never been patient to no flaming doctor, and I hope I never shall be," returned Joe.

At this point Mabel rose from the table, and they all seemed to become aware of her existence. She began putting the dishes together. The young doctor looked at her, but did not address her. He had not greeted her. She went out of the room with the tray, her face impassive and unchanged.

"When are you off then, all of you?" asked the doctor.

"I'm catching the eleven-forty," replied Malcolm. "Are you goin' down wi' th' trap, Joe?"

"Yes, I've told you I'm going down wi' th' trap, haven't I?"

"We'd better be getting her in then. So long, Jack, if I don't see you before I go," said Malcolm, shaking hands.

He went out, followed by Joe, who seemed to have his tail between his legs.

"Well, this is the devil's own," exclaimed the doctor, when he was left alone with Fred Henry. "Going before Wednesday, are you?"

"That's the orders," replied the other.

"Where, to Northampton?"

"That's it."

"The devil!" exclaimed Fergusson, with quiet chagrin.

And there was silence between the two.

"All settled up, are you?" asked Fergusson.

"About."

There was another pause.

"Well, I shall miss yer, Freddy, boy," said the young doctor.

"And I shall miss thee, Jack," returned the other.

"Miss you like hell," mused the doctor.

Fred Henry turned aside. There was nothing to say. Mabel came in again, to finish clearing the table.

"What are *you* going to do, then, Miss Pervin?" asked Fergusson. "Going to your sister's, are you?"

Mabel looked at him with her steady, dangerous eyes, that always made him uncomfortable, unsettling his superficial ease.

"No," she said.

"Well, what in the name of fortune *are* you going to do? Say what you mean to do," cried Fred Henry, with futile intensity.

But she only averted her head, and continued her work. She folded the white table-cloth, and put on the chenille cloth.

"The sulkiest bitch that ever trod!" muttered her brother.

But she finished her task with perfectly impassive face, the young doctor watching her interestedly all the while. Then she went out.

Fred Henry stared after her, clenching his lips, his blue eyes fixing in sharp antagonism, as he made a grimace of sour exasperation.

"You could bray her into bits, and that's all you'd get out of her," he said in a small, narrowed tone.

The doctor smiled faintly.

"What's she *going* to do, then?" he asked.

"Strike me if *I* know!" returned the other.

There was a pause. Then the doctor stirred.

"I'll be seeing you to-night, shall I?" he said to his friend.

"Ay—where's it to be? Are we going over to Jessdale?"

"I don't know. I've got a cold on me. I'll come round to the Moon and Stars, anyway."

"Let Lizzie and May miss their night for once, eh?"

"That's it—if I feel as I do now."

"All's one—"

The two young men went through the passage and down to the back door together. The house was large, but it was servantless now, and desolate. At the back was a small bricked house-yard, and beyond that a big square, gravelled fine and red, and having stables on two sides. Sloping, dank, winter-dark fields stretched away on the open sides.

But the stables were empty. Joseph Pervin, the father of the family, had been a man of no education, who had become a fairly large horse dealer. The stables had been full of horses, there was a great turmoil and come-and-go of horses and of dealers and grooms. Then the kitchen was full of servants. But of late things had declined. The old man had married a second time, to retrieve his fortunes. Now he was dead and everything was gone to the dogs, there was nothing but debt and threatening.

For months, Mabel had been servantless in the big house, keeping the home together in penury for her ineffectual brothers. She had kept house for ten years. But previously it was with unstinted means. Then, however brutal and coarse everything was, the sense of money had kept her proud, confident. The men might be foulmouthed, the women in the kitchen might have bad reputations, her brothers might have illegitimate children. But so long as there was money, the girl felt herself established, and brutally proud, reserved.

No company came to the house, save dealers and coarse men. Mabel had no associates of her own sex, after her sister went away. But she did not mind. She went regularly to church, she attended to her father. And she lived in the memory of her mother, who had died when she was fourteen, and whom she had loved. She had loved her father, too, in a different way, depending upon him, and feeling secure in him, until at the age of fifty-four he married again. And then she had set hard against him. Now he had died and left them all hopelessly in debt.

She had suffered badly during the period of poverty. Nothing, however, could shake the curious sullen, animal pride that dominated each member of the family. Now, for Mabel, the end had come. Still she would not cast about her. She would follow her own way just the same. She would always hold the keys of her own situation. Mindless and persistent, she endured from day to day. Why should she think? Why should she answer anybody? It was enough that this was the end, and there was no way out. She need not pass any more darkly along the main street of the small town, avoiding every eye. She need not demean herself any more, going into the shops and buying the cheapest food. This was at an end. She thought of nobody, not even of herself. Mindless and persistent, she seemed in a sort of ecstasy to be coming nearer to her fulfilment, her own glorification, approaching her dead mother, who was glorified.

In the afternoon she took a little bag, with shears and sponge and a small scrubbing brush, and went out. It was a grey, wintry day, with saddened, dark green fields and an atmosphere blackened by the smoke of foundries not far off. She went quickly, darkly along the causeway, heeding nobody, through the town to the churchyard.

There she always felt secure, as if no one could see her, although as a matter of fact she was exposed to the stare of every one who passed along under the churchyard wall. Nevertheless, once under the shadow of the great looming church, among the graves, she felt immune from the world, reserved within the thick churchyard wall as in another country.

Carefully she clipped the grass from the grave, and arranged the pinky white, small chrysanthemums in the tin cross. When this was done, she took an empty jar from a neighbouring grave, brought water, and carefully, most scrupulously sponged the marble headstone and the coping-stone.

It gave her sincere satisfaction to do this. She felt in immediate contact with the world of her mother. She took minute pains, went through the park in a state bordering on pure happiness, as if in performing this task she came into a subtle, intimate connection with her mother. For the life she followed here in the world was far less real than the world of death she inherited from her mother.

The doctor's house was just by the church. Fergusson, being a mere hired assistant, was slave to the country-side.

As he hurried now to attend to the outpatients in the surgery, glancing across the graveyard with his quick eye, he saw the girl at her task at the grave. She seemed so intent and remote, it was like looking into another world. Some mystical element was touched in him. He slowed down as he walked, watching her as if spell-bound.

She lifted her eyes, feeling him looking. Their eyes met. And each looked away again at once, each feeling, in some way, found out by the other. He lifted his cap and passed on down the road. There remained distinct in his consciousness, like a vision, the memory of her face, lifted from the tombstone in the churchyard, and looking at him with slow, large, portentous eyes. It *was* portentous, her face. It seemed to mesmerize him. There was a heavy power in her eyes which laid hold of his whole being, as if he had drunk some powerful drug. He had been feeling weak and done before. Now the life came back into him, he felt delivered from his own fretted, daily self.

He finished his duties at the surgery as quickly as might be, hastily filling up the bottle of the waiting people with cheap drugs. Then, in perpetual haste, he set off again to visit several cases in another part of his round, before tea-time. At all times he preferred to walk if he could, but particularly when he was not well. He fancied the motion restored him.

The afternoon was falling. It was grey, deadened, and wintry, with a slow, moist, heavy coldness sinking in and deadening all the faculties. But why should he think or notice? He hastily climbed the hill and turned across the dark green fields, following the black cinder-track. In the distance, across a shallow dip in the country, the small town was clustered like smouldering ash, a tower, a spire, a heap of low, raw, extinct houses. And on the nearest fringe of the town, sloping into the dip, was Oldmeadow, the Pervins' house. He could see the stables and the outbuildings distinctly, as they lay towards him on the slope. Well, he would not go there many more times! Another resource would be lost to him, another place gone: the only company he cared for in the alien, ugly little town he was losing. Nothing but work, drudgery, constant hastening from dwelling to dwelling among the colliers and the iron-workers. It wore him out, but at the same time he had a craving for it. It was a stimulant to him to be in the homes of the working people, moving as it were through the innermost body of their life. His nerves were excited and gratified. He could come so near, into the very lives of the rough, inarticulate, powerfully emotional men and women. He grumbled, he said he hated the hellish hole. But as a matter of fact it excited him, the contact with the rough, strongly-feeling people was a stimulant applied direct to his nerves.

Below Oldmeadow, in the green, shallow, soddened hollow of fields, lay a square, deep pond. Roving across the landscape, the doctor's quick eye detected a figure in black passing through the gate of the field, down towards the pond. He looked again. It would be Mabel Pervin. His mind suddenly became alive and attentive.

Why was she going down there? He pulled up on the path on the slope above, and stood staring. He could just make sure of the small black figure moving in the hollow of the failing day. He seemed to see her in the midst of such obscurity, that he was like a clairvoyant, seeing rather with the mind's eye than with ordinary sight. Yet he could see her positively enough, whilst he kept his eye attentive. He felt, if he looked away from her, in the thick, ugly falling dusk, he would lose her altogether.

He followed her minutely as she moved, direct and intent, like something transmitted rather than stirring in voluntary activity, straight down the field towards the pond. There she stood on the bank for a moment. She never raised her head. Then she waded slowly into the water.

He stood motionless as the small black figure walked slowly and deliberately towards the centre of the pond, very slowly, gradually moving deeper into the motionless water, and still moving forward as the water got up to her breast. Then he could see her no more in the dusk of the dead afternoon.

"There!" he exclaimed. "Would you believe it?"

And he hastened straight down, running over the wet, soddened fields, rushing through the hedges, down into the depression of callous wintry obscurity. It took him several minutes to come to the pond. He stood on the bank, breathing heavily. He could see nothing. His eyes seemed to penetrate the dead water. Yes, perhaps that was the dark shadow of her black clothing beneath the surface of the water.

He slowly ventured into the pond. The bottom was deep, soft clay, he sank in, and the water clasped dead cold round his legs. As he stirred he could smell the cold, rotten clay that fouled up into the water. It was objectionable in his lungs. Still, repelled and yet not heeding, he moved deeper into the pond. The cold water rose over his thighs, over his loins, upon his abdomen. The lower part of his body was all sunk in the hideous cold element. And the bottom was so deeply soft and uncertain he was afraid of pitching with his mouth underneath. He could not swim, and was afraid.

He crouched a little, spreading his hands under the water and moving them round, trying to feel for her. The dead cold pond swayed upon his chest. He moved again, a little deeper, and again, with his hands underneath, he felt all around under the water. And he touched her clothing. But it evaded his fingers. He made a desperate effort to grasp it.

And so doing he lost his balance and went under, horribly, suffocating in the foul earthy water, struggling madly for a few moments. At last, after what seemed an eternity, he got his footing, rose again into the air and looked around. He gasped, and knew he was in the world. Then he looked at the water. She had risen near him. He grasped her clothing, and drawing her nearer, turned to take his way to land again.

He went very slowly, carefully, absorbed in the slow progress. He rose higher, climbing out of the pond. The water was now only about his legs; he was thankful, full of relief to be out of the clutches of the pond. He lifted her and staggered on to the bank, out of the horror of wet, grey clay.

He laid her down on the bank. She was quite unconscious and running with water. He made the water come from her mouth, he worked to restore her. He did not have to work very long before he could feel the breathing begin again in her; she was breathing naturally. He worked a little longer. He could feel her live beneath his hands; she was coming back. He wiped her face, wrapped her in his overcoat, looked round into the dim, dark grey world, then lifted her and staggered down the bank and across the fields.

It seemed an unthinkably long way, and his burden so heavy he felt he would never get to the house. But at last he was in the stable-yard, and then in the house-yard. He opened the door and went into the house. In the kitchen he laid her down on the hearthrug, and called. The house was empty. But the fire was burning in the grate.

Then again he kneeled to attend to her. She was breathing regularly, her eyes were wide open and as if conscious, but there seemed something missing in her look. She was conscious in herself, but unconscious of her surroundings.

He ran upstairs, took blankets from a bed, and put them before the fire to warm. Then he removed her saturated, earthy-smelling clothing, rubbed her dry with a towel, and wrapped her naked in the blankets. Then he went into the dining-room, to look for spirits. There was a little whisky. He drank a gulp himself, and put some into her mouth.

The effect was instantaneous. She looked full into his face, as if she had been seeing him for some time, and yet had only just become conscious of him.

"Dr. Fergusson?" she said.

"What?" he answered.

He was divesting himself of his coat, intending to find some dry clothing upstairs. He could not bear the smell of the dead, clayey water, and he was mortally afraid for his own health.

"What did I do?" she asked.

"Walked into the pond," he replied. He had begun to shudder like one sick, and could hardly attend to her. Her eyes remained full on him, he seemed to be going dark in his mind, looking back at her helplessly. The shuddering became quieter in him, his life came back in him dark and unknowing, but strong again.

"Was I out of my mind?" she asked, while her eyes were fixed on him all the time.

"Maybe, for the moment," he replied. He felt quiet, because his strength had come back. The strange fretful strain had left him.

"Am I out of my mind now?" she asked.

"Are you?" he reflected a moment. "No," he answered truthfully, "I don't see that you are." He turned his face aside. He was afraid now, because he felt dazed, and felt dimly that her power was stronger than his, in this issue. And she continued to look at him fixedly all the time. "Can you tell me where I shall find some dry things to put on?" he asked.

"Did you dive into the pond for me?" she asked.

"No," he answered. "I walked in. But I went in overhead as well."

There was silence for a moment. He hesitated. He very much wanted to go upstairs to get into dry clothing. But there was another desire in him. And she seemed to hold him. His will seemed to have gone to sleep, and left him, standing there slack before her. But he felt warm inside himself. He did not shudder at all, though his clothes were sodden on him.

"Why did you?" she asked.

"Because I didn't want you to do such a foolish thing," he said.

"It wasn't foolish," she said, still gazing at him as she lay on the floor, with a sofa cushion under her head. "It was the right thing to do. I knew best, then."

"I'll go and shift these wet things," he said. But still he had not the power to move out of her presence, until she sent him. It was as if she had the life of his body in her hands, and he could not extricate himself. Or perhaps he did not want to.

Suddenly she sat up. Then she became aware of her own

immediate condition. She felt the blankets about her, she knew her own limbs. For a moment it seemed as if her reason were going. She looked round, with wild eye, as if seeking something. He stood still with fear. She saw her clothing lying scattered.

"Who undressed me?" she asked, her eyes resting full and inevitable on his face.

"I did," he replied, "to bring you round."

For some moments she sat and gazed at him awfully, her lips parted.

"Do you love me, then?" she asked.

He only stood and stared at her, fascinated. His soul seemed to melt.

She shuffled forward on her knees, and put her arms round him, round his legs, as he stood there, pressing her breasts against his knees and thighs, clutching him with strange, convulsive certainty, pressing his thighs against her, drawing him to her face, her throat, as she looked up at him with flaring, humble eyes of transfiguration, triumphant in first possession.

"You love me," she murmured, in strange transport, yearning and triumphant and confident. "You love me. I know you love me, I know."

And she was passionately kissing his knees, through the wet clothing, passionately and indiscriminately kissing his knees, his legs, as if unaware of everything.

He looked down at the tangled wet hair, the wild, bare, animal shoulders. He was amazed, bewildered, and afraid. He had never thought of loving her. He had never wanted to love her. When he rescued her and restored her, he was a doctor, and she was a patient. He had had no single personal thought of her. Nay, this introduction of the personal element was very distasteful to him, a violation of his professional honour. It was horrible to have her there embracing his knees. It was horrible. He revolted from it, violently. And yet—and yet—he had not the power to break away.

She looked at him again, with the same supplication of

powerful love, and that same transcendent, frightening light
of triumph. In view of the delicate flame which seemed to
come from her face like a light, he was powerless. And yet
he had never intended to love her. He had never intended.
And something stubborn in him could not give way.

"You love me," she repeated, in a murmur of deep,
rhapsodic assurance. "You love me."

Her hands were drawing him, drawing him down to her.
He was afraid, even a little horrified. For he had, really, no
intention of loving her. Yet her hands were drawing him
towards her. He put out his hand quickly to steady himself,
and grasped her bare shoulder. A flame seemed to burn the
hand that grasped her soft shoulder. He had no intention of
loving her: his whole will was against his yielding. It was
horrible. And yet wonderful was the touch of her shoulders,
beautiful the shining of her face. Was she perhaps mad? He
had a horror of yielding to her. Yet something in him ached
also.

He had been staring away at the door, away from her.
But his hand remained on her shoulder. She had gone
suddenly very still. He looked down at her. Her eyes were
now wide with fear, with doubt, the light was dying from
her face, a shadow of terrible greyness was returning. He
could not bear the touch of her eyes' question upon him,
and the look of death behind the question.

With an inward groan he gave way, and let his heart yield
towards her. A sudden gentle smile came on his face. And
her eyes, which never left his face, slowly, slowly filled with
tears. He watched the strange water rise in her eyes, like
some slow fountain coming up. And his heart seemed to
burn and melt away in his breast.

He could not bear to look at her any more. He dropped
on his knees and caught her head with his arms and pressed
her face against his throat. She was very still. His heart,
which seemed to have broken, was burning with a kind of
agony in his breast. And he felt her slow, hot tears wetting
his throat. But he could not move.

He felt the hot tears wet his neck and the hollows of his

neck, and he remained motionless, suspended through one of man's eternities. Only now it had become indispensable to him to have her face pressed close to him; he could never let her go again. He could never let her head go away from the close clutch of his arm. He wanted to remain like that for ever, with his heart hurting him in a pain that was also life to him. Without knowing, he was looking down on her damp, soft brown hair.

Then, as it were suddenly, he smelt the horrid stagnant smell of that water. And at the same moment she drew away from him and looked at him. Her eyes were wistful and unfathomable. He was afraid of them, and he fell to kissing her, not knowing what he was doing. He wanted her eyes not to have that terrible, wistful, unfathomable look.

When she turned her face to him again, a faint delicate flush was glowing, and there was again dawning that terrible shining of joy in her eyes, which really terrified him, and yet which he now wanted to see, because he feared the look of doubt still more.

"You love me?" she said, rather faltering.

"Yes." The word cost him a painful effort. Not because it wasn't true. But because it was too newly true, the *saying* seemed to tear open again his newly-torn heart. And he hardly wanted it to be true, even now.

She lifted her face to him, and he bent forward and kissed her on the mouth, gently, with the one kiss that is an eternal pledge. And as he kissed her his heart strained again in his breast. He never intended to love her. But now it was over. He had crossed over the gulf to her, and all that he had left behind had shrivelled and become void.

After the kiss, her eyes again slowly filled with tears. She sat still, away from him, with her face drooped aside, and her hands folded in her lap. The tears fell very slowly. There was complete silence. He too sat there motionless and silent on the hearthrug. The strange pain of his heart that was broken seemed to consume him. That he should love her? That this was love! That he should be ripped open in this way! Him, a doctor! How they would all jeer if they knew! It was agony to him to think they might know.

In the curious naked pain of the thought he looked again to her. She was sitting there drooped into a muse. He saw a tear fall, and his heart flared hot. He saw for the first time that one of her shoulders was quite uncovered, one arm bare, he could see one of her small breasts; dimly, because it had become almost dark in the room.

"Why are you crying?" he asked, in an altered voice.

She looked up at him, and behind her tears the consciousness of her situation for the first time brought a dark look of shame to her eyes.

"I'm not crying, really," she said, watching him half frightened.

He reached his hand, and softly closed it on her bare arm.

"I love you! I love you!" he said in a soft, low vibrating voice, unlike himself.

She shrank, and dropped her head. The soft, penetrating grip of his hand on her arm distressed her. She looked up at him.

"I want to go," she said. "I want to go and get you some dry things."

"Why?" he said. "I'm all right."

"But I want to go," she said. "And I want you to change your things."

He released her arm, and she wrapped herself in the blanket, looking at him rather frightened. And still she did not rise.

"Kiss me," she said wistfully.

He kissed her, but briefly, half in anger.

Then, after a second, she rose nervously, all mixed up in the blanket. He watched her in her confusion, as she tried to extricate herself and wrap herself up so that she could walk. He watched her relentlessly, as she knew. And as she went, the blanket trailing, and as he saw a glimpse of her feet and her white leg, he tried to remember her as she was when he had wrapped her in the blanket. But then he didn't want to remember, because she had been nothing to him then, and his nature revolted from remembering her as she was when she was nothing to him.

A tumbling, muffled noise from within the dark house startled him. Then he heard her voice:—"There are clothes." He rose and went to the foot of the stairs, and gathered up the garments she had thrown down. Then he came back to the fire, to rub himself down and dress. He grinned at his own appearance when he had finished.

The fire was sinking, so he put on coal. The house was now quite dark, save for the light of a street-lamp that shone in faintly from beyond the holly trees. He lit the gas with matches he found on the mantelpiece. Then he emptied the pockets of his own clothes, and threw all his wet things in a heap into the scullery. After which he gathered up her sodden clothes, gently, and put them in a separate heap on the copper-top in the scullery.

It was six o'clock on the clock. His own watch had stopped. He ought to go back to the surgery. He waited, and still she did not come down. So he went to the foot of the stairs and called:

"I shall have to go."

Almost immediately he heard her coming down. She had on her best dress of black voile, and her hair was tidy, but still damp. She looked at him—and in spite of herself, smiled.

"I don't like you in those clothes," she said.

"Do I look a sight?" he answered.

They were shy of one another.

"I'll make you some tea," she said.

"No, I must go."

"Must you?" And she looked at him again with the wide, strained, doubtful eyes. And again, from the pain of his breast, he knew how he loved her. He went and bent to kiss her, gently, passionately, with his heart's painful kiss.

"And my hair smells so horrible," she murmured in distraction. "And I'm so awful, I'm so awful! Oh, no, I'm too awful." And she broke into bitter, heart-broken sobbing. "You can't want to love me, I'm horrible."

"Don't be silly, don't be silly," he said, trying to comfort her, kissing her, holding her in his arms. "I want you, I want to marry you, we're going to be married, quickly, quickly—tomorrow if I can."

But she only sobbed terribly, and cried:

"I feel awful. I feel awful. I feel I'm horrible to you."

"No, I want you, I want you," was all he answered, blindly, with that terrible intonation which frightened her almost more than her horror lest he should *not* want her.

◆ ——————————————————— ◆

VIRGA VAY &
ALLAN CEDAR

Sinclair Lewis

Orlo Vay, the Chippewa Avenue Optician, Smart-Art Harlequin Tinted-Tortus Frames Our Specialty, was a public figure, as public as a cemetery. He was resentful that his profession, like that of an undertaker, a professor of art, or a Mormon missionary, was not appreciated for its patience and technical skill, as are the callings of wholesale grocer or mistress or radio-sports-commentator, and he tried to make up for the professional injustice by developing his personal glamour.

He wanted to Belong. He was a speaker. He was hearty and public about the local baseball and hockey teams, about the Kiwanis Club, about the Mayflower Congregational Church, and about all war drives. At forty-five he was bald, but the nobly glistening egg of his face and forehead, whose arc was broken only by a pair of Vay Li-Hi-Bifocals, was an adornment to all fund-raising rallies.

He urged his wife, Virga, to co-operate in his spiritual efforts, but she was a small, scared, romantic woman, ten years his junior; an admirer of passion in Technicolor, a clipper-out of newspaper lyrics about love and autumn smoke upon the hills. He vainly explained to her, "In these modern days, a woman can't fritter away her time daydreaming. She has to push her own weight, and not hide it under a bushel."

Her solace was in her lover, Dr. Allan Cedar, the dentist. Together, Virga and Allan would have been a most gentle pair, small, clinging, and credulous. But they could never be openly together. They were afraid of Mr. Vay and of Allan's fat and vicious wife, Bertha, and they met at soda counters in outlying drug stores and lovingly drank black-and-whites together or Jumbo Malteds and, giggling, ate ferocious banana splits; or, till wartime gasoline-rationing prevented, they sped out in Allan's coupé by twilight, and made shy, eager love in mossy pastures or, by the weak dashlight of the car, read aloud surprisingly good recent poets: Wallace Stevens, Sandburg, Robert Frost, Jeffers, T. S. Eliot, Lindsay.

Allan was one of the best actors in the Masquers, and though Virga could not act, she made costumes and hung about at rehearsals, and thus they were able to meet, and to stir the suspicions of Bertha Cedar.

Mrs. Cedar was a rare type of the vicious woman; she really hated her husband, though she did not so much scold him as mock him for his effeminate love of acting, for his verses, for his cherubic mustache, and even for his skill with golden bridge-work. She jeered, in the soap-reeking presence of her seven sisters and sisters-in-law, all chewing gum and adjusting their plates, that as a lover "Ally" had no staying-powers. That's what *she* thought.

She said to her mother, "Ally is a bum dentist; he hasn't got a single rich patient," and when they were at an evening party, she communicated to the festal guests, "Ally can't even pick out a necktie without asking my help," and on everything her husband said she commented, "Oh, don't be silly!"

She demanded, and received, large sympathy from all the females she knew, and as he was fond of golf and backgammon, she refused to learn either of them.

Whenever she had irritated him into jumpiness, she said judiciously, "You seem to be in a very nervous state." She picked at him about his crossword puzzles, about his stamp-collection, until he screamed, invariably, "Oh, let me *alone!*" and then she was able to say smugly, "I don't know what's the matter with you, so touchy about every little thing. You better go to a mind-doctor and have your head examined."

Then Bertha quite unexpectedly inherited seven thousand dollars and a house in San Jose, California, from a horrible aunt. She did not suggest to her husband but told him that they would move out to that paradise for chilled Minnesotans, and he would practise there.

It occurred to Allan to murder her, but not to refuse to go along. Many American males confuse their wives and the policeman on the beat.

But he knew that it would be death for him to leave Virga Vay, and that afternoon, when Virga slipped into his office at three o'clock in response to his code telephone call of "This is the Superba Market and we're sending you three bunches of asparagus," she begged, "Couldn't we elope some place together? Maybe we could get a little farm."

"She'd find us. She has a cousin who's a private detective in Duluth."

"Yes, I guess she would. Can't we *ever* be together always?'"

"There is one way—if you wouldn't be afraid."

He explained the way.

"No, I wouldn't be afraid, if you stayed right with me," she said.

Dr. Allan Cedar was an excellent amateur machinist. On a Sunday afternoon when Bertha was visiting her mother, he cut a hole through the steel bottom of the luggage compartment of his small dark-gray coupé. This compartment opened into the body of the car. That same day he stole the hose of their vacuum-cleaner and concealed it up on the rafters of their galvanized-iron garage.

On Tuesday—this was in February—he bought a blue ready-made suit at Goldenkron Brothers', on Ignatius Street. He was easy to fit, and no alterations were needed. They wanted to deliver the suit that afternoon, but he insisted, "No, hold it here for me and I'll come in and put it on tomorrow morning. I want to surprise somebody."

"Your Missus will love it, Doc," said Monty Goldenkron.

"I hope she will—when she sees it!"

He also bought three white-linen shirts and a red bow-tie, and paid cash for the lot.

"Your credit is good here, Doc—none better," protested Monty.

Allan puzzled him by the triumphant way in which he answered, "I want to keep it good, just now!"

From Goldenkrons' he walked perkily to the Emporium, to the Golden Rule drug store, to the Co-operative Dairy, paying his bills in full at each. On his way he saw a distinguished fellow-townsman, Judge Timberlane, and his pretty wife. Allan had never said ten words to either of them, but he thought affectionately, "There's a couple who are intelligent enough and warm-hearted enough to know what love is worth."

That evening he said blandly to his wife, "Strangest thing happened today. The University school of dentistry telephoned me."

"Long distance?"

"Surely."

"Well!" Her tone was less of disbelief than of disgust.

"They're having a special brush-up session for dentists and they want me to come down to Minneapolis first thing tomorrow morning to stay for three days and give instruction in bridge-work. And of course you must come along. It's too bad I'll have to work from nine in the morning till midnight— they do rush those special courses so—but you can go to the movies by yourself, or just sit comfortably in the hotel."

"No—thank—*you!*" said Bertha. "I prefer to sit here at home. Why you couldn't have been an M.D. doctor and take out gallbladders and make some real money! And I'll thank you to be home not later than Sunday morning. You know we have Sunday dinner with Mother."

He knew.

"I hope that long before that I'll be home," he said.

He told her that he would be staying at the Flora Hotel, in Minneapolis. But on Wednesday morning, after putting on the new suit at Goldenkrons', he drove to St. Paul, through light snowflakes which he thought of as fairies. "But I haven't a bit of real poet in me. Just second-rate and banal," he sighed. He tried to make a poem, and got no farther than:

> *It is snowing,*
> *The wind is blowing,*
> *But I am happy to be going.*

In St. Paul he went to the small, clean Hotel Orkness, registered as "Mr. A. M. Romeo & wife," asked for a room with a double bed, and explained to the clerk, "My wife is coming by train. She should be here in about seventeen minutes now, I figure it."

He went unenthusiastically to the palsied elevator, up to their room. It was tidy, and on the wall was an Adolph Dehn lithograph instead of the fake English-hunting-print that he had dreaded. He kneaded the bed with his fist. He was pleased.

Virga Vay arrived nineteen minutes later, with a bellboy carrying her new imitation-leather bag.

"So you're here, husband. Not a bad room," she said indifferently.

The bellboy knew from her indifference and from her calling the man "husband" that she was not married to him, but unstintingly in love. Such paradoxes are so common in his subterranean business that he had forgotten about Virga by the time he reached his bench in the lobby. Six stories above him, Virga and Allan were lost and blind and quivering in their kiss.

Presently she said, "Oh, you have a new suit! Turn around. Why, it fits beautifully! And such a nice red tie. You do look so young and cute in a bow-tie. Did you get it for me?"

"Of course. And then—I kind of hate to speak of it now, but I want us to get so used to the idea that we can just forget it—I don't want us to look frowsy when they find us. As if we hadn't been happy. And we *will* be—we are!"

"Yes."

"You're still game for it?"

"With you? For anything."

He was taking off the new suit; she was tenderly lifting from her bag a nightgown which she had made and embroidered this past week.

They had all their meals in the room; they did not leave it till afternoon of the next day. The air became a little close, thick from perfume and cigarette smoke and the bubble baths they took together.

Late the next afternoon they dressed and packed their bags, completely. He laid on the bureau two ten-dollar bills. They left the luggage at the foot of their bed, which she had made up. She took nothing from the room, and he nothing except a paper bag containing a bottle of Bourbon whisky, with the cork loosened, and a pocket anthology of new poetry. At the door she looked back, and said to him, "I shall remember this dear room as long as we live."

"Yes. . . . As long as we live."

He took his dark-gray coupé out of the hotel garage, tipping an amazed attendant one dollar, and they drove to Indian Mounds Park, overlooking the erratic Mississippi. He stopped in the park, at dusk, and said, "Think of the Indians that came along here, and Pike and Lewis Cass!"

"They were brave," she mused.

"Brave, *too!*" They nervously laughed. Indeed, after a moment of solemnity when they had left the hotel, they had been constantly gay, laughing at everything, even when she sneezed and he piped, "No more worry about catching pneumonia!"

He drove into a small street near by and parked the car, distant from any house. Working in the half-darkness, leav-

ing the engine running, he pushed the vacuum-cleaner hose
through the hole in the bottom of the luggage compartment,
wired it to the exhaust pipe, and hastily got back into the
car. The windows were closed. Already the air in the car
was sick-sweet with carbon monoxide.

He slipped the whisky bottle out of the paper bag and
tenderly urged, "Take a swig of this. Keep your courage up."

"Dearest, I don't need anything to keep it up."

"I do, by golly. I'm not a big he-man like you, Virg!"

They both laughed, and drank from the bottle, and kissed
lingeringly.

"I wonder if I could smoke a cigarette. I don't *think* C_2O_2
is explosive," he speculated.

"Oh, sweet, be careful! It *might* explode!"

"Yes, it—" Then he shouted. "Listen at us! As if we cared
if we got blown up now!"

"Oh, I am too brainless, Allan! I don't know if you'll be
able to stand me much longer."

"As long as we live, my darling, my very dear, oh, my
dear love!"

"As long as we live. Together now. Together."

His head aching, his throat sore, he forgot to light the
cigarette. He switched on the tiny dashlight, he lifted up
the book as though it were a bar of lead, and from Conrad
Aiken's "Sea Holly" he began to read to her:

> *It was for this*
> *Barren beauty, barrenness of rock that aches*
> *On the seaward path, seeing the fruitful sea,*
> *Hearing the lark of rock that sings—*

He was too drowsy to read more than just the ending:

> *Stone pain in the stony heart,*
> *The rock loved and labored; and all is lost.*

The book fell to the seat, his head drooped, and his
arm groped drowsily about her. She rested contentedly,
in vast dreams, her head secure upon his shoulder.

Harsh screaming snatched them back from paradise. The car windows were smashed, someone was dragging them out . . . and Bertha was slapping Virga's face, while Bertha's cousin, the detective, was beating Allan's shoulders with a blackjack, to bring him to. In doing so, he broke Allan's jaw.

Bertha drove him back to Grand Republic and nursed him while he was in bed, jeering to the harpies whom she had invited in, "Ally tried to—you know—with a woman, but he was no good, and he was so ashamed he tried to kill himself."

He kept muttering, "Please go away and don't torture me."

She laughed.

Later, Bertha was able to intercept every one of the letters that Virga sent to him from Des Moines, where she had gone to work in a five-and-ten-cent store after Orlo had virtuously divorced her.

"Love! Ally is learning what that kind of mush gets you," Bertha explained to her attentive women friends.

◆ —————————————————————————————— ◆

MARRIAGE À LA MODE

Katherine Mansfield

On his way to the station William remembered with a fresh pang of disappointment that he was taking nothing down to the kiddies. Poor little chaps! It was hard lines on them. Their first words always were as they ran to greet him, "What have you got for me, daddy?" and he had nothing. He would have to buy them some sweets at the station. But that was what he had done for the past four Saturdays; their faces had fallen last time when they saw the same old boxes produced again.

And Paddy had said, "I had red ribbing on mine *bee-fore!*'

And Johnny had said, "It's always pink on mine, I hate pink."

But what was William to do? The affair wasn't so easily settled. In the old days, of course, he would have taken a taxi off to a decent toyshop and chosen them something in five minutes. But nowadays they had Russian toys, French toys, Serbian toys—toys from God knows where. It was over a year since Isabel had scrapped the old donkeys and engines and so on because they were so "dreadfully senti-mental" and "so appallingly bad for the babies' sense of form."

"It's so important," the new Isabel had explained, "that they should like the right things from the very beginning. It saves so much time later on. Really, if the poor pets have to spend their infant years staring at these horrors, one can imagine them growing up and asking to be taken to the Royal Academy."

And she spoke as though a visit to the Royal Academy was certain immediate death to any one. . . .

"Well, I don't know," said William slowly. "When I was their age I used to go to bed hugging an old towel with a knot in it."

The new Isabel looked at him, her eyes narrowed, her lips apart.

"*Dear* William! I'm sure you did!" She laughed in the new way.

Sweets it would have to be, however, thought William gloomily, fishing in his pocket for change for the taxi-man. And he saw the kiddies handing the boxes round—they were awfully generous little chaps—while Isabel's precious friends didn't hesitate to help themselves. . . .

What about fruit? William hovered before a stall just inside the station. What about a melon each? Would they

have to share that, too? Or a pineapple for Pad, and a melon
for Johnny? Isabel's friends could hardly go sneaking up to
the nursery at the children's meal-times. All the same, as he
bought the melon William had a horrible vision of one of
Isabel's young poets lapping up a slice, for some reason,
behind the nursery door.

With his two very awkward parcels he strode off to his
train. The platform was crowded, the train was in. Doors
banged open and shut. There came such a loud hissing from
the engine that people looked dazed as they scurried to and
fro. William made straight for a first-class smoker, stowed
away his suit-case and parcels, and taking a huge wad of
papers out of his inner pocket, he flung down in the corner
and began to read.

"Our client moreover is positive. . . . We are inclined to
reconsider . . . in the event of—" Ah, that was better. William pressed back his flattened hair and stretched his legs
across the carriage floor. The familiar dull gnawing in his
breast quietened down. "With regard to our decision—" He
took out a blue pencil and scored a paragraph slowly.

Two men came in, stepped across him, and made for the
farther corner. A young fellow swung his golf clubs into the
rack and sat down opposite. The train gave a gentle lurch,
they were off. William glanced up and saw the hot, bright
station slipping away. A red-faced girl raced along by the
carriages, there was something strained and almost desperate in the way she waved and called. "Hysterical!" thought
William dully. Then a greasy, blackfaced workman at the
end of the platform grinned at the passing train. And William thought, "A filthy life!" and went back to his papers.

When he looked up again there were fields, and beasts
standing for shelter under the dark trees. A wide river, with
naked children splashing in the shallows, glided into sight
and was gone again. The sky shone pale, and one bird
drifted high like a dark fleck in a jewel.

"We have examined our client's correspondence files. . . ."
The last sentence he had read echoed in his mind. "We
have examined . . ." William hung on to that sentence, but

it was no good; it snapped in the middle, and the fields, the sky, the sailing bird, the water, all said, "Isabel." The same thing happened every Saturday afternoon. When he was on his way to meet Isabel there began those countless imaginary meetings. She was at the station, standing just a little apart from everybody else; she was sitting in the open taxi outside; she was at the garden gate; walking across the parched grass; at the door, or just inside the hall.

And her clear, light voice said, "It's William," or "Hillo, William!" or "So William has come!" He touched her cool hand, her cool cheek.

The exquisite freshness of Isabel! When he had been a little boy, it was his delight to run into the garden after a shower of rain and shake the rosebush over him. Isabel was that rosebush, petal-soft, sparkling and cool. And he was still that little boy. But there was no running into the garden now, no laughing and shaking. The dull, persistent gnawing in his breast started again. He drew up his legs, tossed the papers aside, and shut his eyes.

"What is it, Isabel? What is it?" he said tenderly. They were in their bedroom in the new house. Isabel sat on a painted stool before the dressing-table that was strewn with little black and green boxes.

"What is what, William?" And she bent forward, and her fine light hair fell over her cheeks.

"Ah, you know!" He stood in the middle of the strange room and he felt a stranger. At that Isabel wheeled round quickly and faced him.

"Oh, William!" she cried imploringly, and she held up the hair-brush: "Please! Please don't be so dreadfully stuffy and—tragic. You're always saying or looking or hinting that I've changed. Just because I've got to know really congenial people, and go about more, and am frightfully keen on—on everything, you behave as though I'd—" Isabel tossed back her hair and laughed—"killed our love or something. It's so awfully absurd"—she bit her lip—"and it's so maddening, William. Even this new house and the servants you grudge me."

"Isabel!"

"Yes, yes, it's true in a way," said Isabel quickly. "You think they are another bad sign. Oh, I know you do. I feel it," she said softly, "every time you come up the stairs. But we couldn't have gone on living in that other poky little hole, William. Be practical, at least! Why, there wasn't enough room for the babies even."

No, it was true. Every morning when he came back from chambers it was to find the babies with Isabel in the back drawing-room. They were having rides on the leopard skin thrown over the sofa back, or they were playing shops with Isabel's desk for a counter, or Pad was sitting on the hearthrug rowing away for dear life with a little brass fire shovel, while Johnny shot at pirates with the tongs. Every evening they each had a pick-a-back up the narrow stairs to their fat old Nanny.

Yes, he supposed it was a poky little house. A little white house with blue curtains and a windowbox of petunias. William met their friends at the door with "Seen our petunias? Pretty terrific for London, don't you think?"

But the imbecile thing, the absolutely extraordinary thing was that he hadn't the slightest idea that Isabel wasn't as happy as he. God, what blindness! He hadn't the remotest notion in those days that she really hated that inconvenient little house, that she thought the fat Nanny was ruining the babies, that she was desperately lonely, pining for new people and new music and pictures and so on. If they hadn't gone to that studio party at Moira Morrison's—if Moira Morrison hadn't said as they were leaving, "I'm going to rescue your wife, selfish man. She's like an exquisite little Titania"—if Isabel hadn't gone with Moira to Paris—if— if . . .

The train stopped at another station. Bettingford. Good heavens! They'd be there in ten minutes. William stuffed the papers back into his pockets; the young man opposite had long since disappeared. Now the other two got out. The late afternoon sun shone on women in cotton frocks and little sunburnt, barefoot children. It blazed on a silky yellow

flower with coarse leaves which sprawled over a bank of
rock. The air ruffling through the window smelled of the
sea. Had Isabel the same crowd with her this weekend,
wondered William?

And he remembered the holidays they used to have, the
four of them, with a little farm girl, Rose, to look after the
babies. Isabel wore a jersey and her hair in a plait; she
looked about fourteen. Lord! how his nose used to peel!
And the amount they ate, and the amount they slept in that
immense feather bed with their feet locked together. . . . William couldn't help a grim smile as he thought of Isabel's
horror if she knew the full extent of his sentimentality.

"Hillo, William!" She was at the station after all, standing
just as he had imagined, apart from the others, and—William's heart leapt—she was alone.

"Hallo, Isabel!" William stared. He thought she looked so
beautiful that he had to say something, "You look very cool."

"Do I?" said Isabel. "I don't feel very cool. Come along,
your horrid old train is late. The taxi's outside." She put her
hand lightly on his arm as they passed the ticket collector.
"We've all come to meet you," she said. "But we've left
Bobby Kane at the sweet shop, to be called for."

"Oh!" said William. It was all he could say for the moment.

There in the glare waited the taxi, with Bill Hunt and
Dennis Green sprawling on one side, their hats tilted over
their faces, while on the other, Moira Morrison, in a bonnet
like a huge strawberry, jumped up and down.

"No ice! No ice! No ice!" she shouted gaily.

And Dennis chimed in from under his hat. "*Only* to be
had from the fishmonger's."

And Bill Hunt, emerging, added, "With *whole* fish in it."

"Oh, what a bore!" wailed Isabel. And she explained to
William how they had been chasing round the town for ice
while she waited for him. "Simply everything is running
down the steep cliffs into the sea, beginning with the butter."

"We shall have to anoint ourselves with the butter," said
Dennis. "May thy head, William, lack not ointment."

"Look here," said William, "how are we going to sit? I'd better get up by the driver.

"No, Bobby Kane's by the driver," said Isabel. "You're to sit between Moira and me." The taxi started. "What have you got in those mysterious parcels?"

"De-cap-it-ated heads!" said Bill Hunt, shuddering beneath his hat.

"Oh, fruit!" Isabel sounded very pleased. "Wise William! A melon and a pineapple. How too nice!"

"No, wait a bit," said William, smiling. But he really was anxious. "I brought them down for the kiddies."

"Oh, my dear!" Isabel laughed, and slipped her hand through his arm. "They'd be rolling in agonies if they were to eat them. No"—she patted his hand—"you must bring them something next time. I refuse to part with my pineapple."

"Cruel Isabel! Do let me smell it!" said Moira. She flung her arms across William appealingly. "Oh!" The strawberry bonnet fell forward: she sounded quite faint.

"A Lady in Love with a Pineapple," said Dennis, as the taxi drew up before a little shop with a striped blind. Out came Bobby Kane, his arms full of little packets.

"I do hope they'll be good. I've chosen them because of the colours. There are some round things which really look too divine. And just look at this nougat," he cried ecstatically, "just look at it! It's a perfect little ballet."

But at that moment the shopman appeared. "Oh, I forgot. They're none of them paid for," said Bobby, looking frightened. Isabel gave the shopman a note, and Bobby was radiant again. "Hallo, William! I'm sitting by the driver." And bareheaded, all in white, with his sleeves rolled up to the shoulders, he leapt into his place. "Avanti!" he cried. . . .

After tea the others went off to bathe, while William stayed and made his peace with the kiddies. But Johnny and Paddy were asleep, the rose-red glow had paled, bats were flying, and still the bathers had not returned. As William wandered downstairs, the maid crossed the hall carrying a lamp. He followed her into the sitting-room. It was a long room, coloured yellow. On the wall opposite William some one had painted a young man, over life-size, with very wobbly legs, offering a wide-eyed daisy to a young woman who had one very short arm and one very long, thin one. Over the chairs and sofa there hung strips of black material, covered with big splashes like broken eggs, and everywhere one looked there seemed to be an ash-tray full of cigarette ends. William sat down in one of the arm-chairs. Nowadays, when one felt with one hand down the sides, it wasn't to come upon a sheep with three legs or a cow that had lost one horn, or a very fat dove out of the Noah's Ark. One fished up yet another little paper-covered book of smudged-looking poems. . . . He thought of the wad of papers in his pocket, but he was too hungry and tired to read. The door was open; sounds came from the kitchen. The servants were talking as if they were alone in the house. Suddenly there came a loud screech of laughter and an equally loud "Sh!" They had remembered him. William got up and went through the French windows into the garden, and as he stood there in the shadow he heard the bathers coming up the sandy road; their voices rang through the quiet.

"I think it's up to Moira to use her little arts and wiles."

A tragic moan from Moira.

"We ought to have a gramophone for the week-ends that played 'The Maid of the Mountains.'"

"Oh no! Oh no!" cried Isabel's voice. "That's not fair to William. Be nice to him, my children! He's only staying until to-morrow evening."

"Leave him to me," cried Bobby Kane. "I'm awfully good at looking after people."

The gate swung open and shut. William moved on the terrace; they had seen him. "Hallo, William!" And Bobby Kane, flapping his towel, began to leap and pirouette on the parched lawn. "Pity you didn't come, William. The water was divine. And we all went to a little pub afterwards and had sloe gin."

The others had reached the house. "I say, Isabel," called Bobby, "would you like me to wear my Nijinsky dress to-night?"

"No," said Isabel, "nobody's going to dress. We're all starving. William's starving, too. Come along, *mes amis*, let's begin with sardines."

"I've found the sardines," said Moira, and she ran into the hall, holding a box high in the air.

"A Lady with a Box of Sardines," said Dennis gravely.

"Well, William, and how's London?" asked Bill Hunt, drawing the cork out of a bottle of whisky.

"Oh, London's not much changed," answered William.

"Good old London," said Bobby, very hearty, spearing a sardine.

But a moment later William was forgotten. Moira Morrison began wondering what colour one's legs really were under water.

"Mine are the palest, palest mushroom colour."

Bill and Dennis ate enormously. And Isabel filled glasses, and changed plates, and found matches, smiling blissfully. At one moment she said, "I do wish, Bill, you'd paint it."

"Paint what?" said Bill loudly, stuffing his mouth with bread.

"Us," said Isabel, "round the table. It would be so fascinating in twenty years' time."

Bill screwed up his eyes and chewed. "Light's wrong," he said rudely, "far too much yellow"; and went on eating. And that seemed to charm Isabel, too.

But after supper they were all so tired they could do nothing but yawn until it was late enough to go to bed. . . .

It was not until William was waiting for his taxi the next afternoon that he found himself alone with Isabel. When he brought his suit-case down into the hall, Isabel left the others and went over to him. She stooped down and picked up the suit-case. "What a weight!" she said, and she gave a little awkward laugh. "Let me carry it! To the gate."

"No, why should you?" said William. "Of course, not. Give it to me."

"Oh, please do let me," said Isabel. "I want to, really." They walked together silently. William felt there was nothing to say now.

"There," said Isabel triumphantly, setting the suit-case down, and she looked anxiously along the sandy road. "I hardly seem to have seen you this time," she said breathlessly. "It's so short, isn't it? I feel you've only just come. Next time—" The taxi came into sight. "I hope they look after you properly in London. I'm so sorry the babies have been out all day, but Miss Neil had arranged it. They'll hate missing you. Poor William, going back to London." The taxi turned. "Good-bye!" She gave him a little hurried kiss; she was gone.

Fields, trees, hedges streamed by. They shook through the empty, blind-looking little town, ground up the steep pull to the station.

The train was in. William made straight for a first-class smoker, flung back into the corner, but this time he let the papers alone. He folded his arms against the dull, persistent gnawing, and began in his mind to write a letter to Isabel.

The post was late as usual. They sat outside the house in long chairs under coloured parasols. Only Bobby Kane lay on the turf at Isabel's feet. It was dull, stifling; the day drooped like a flag.

"Do you think there will be Mondays in Heaven?" asked Bobby childishly.

And Dennis murmured, "Heaven will be one long Monday."

But Isabel couldn't help wondering what had happened to the salmon they had for supper last night. She had meant to have fish mayonnaise for lunch and now . . .

Moira was asleep. Sleeping was her latest discovery. "It's *so* wonderful. One simply shuts one's eyes, that's all. It's *so* delicious."

When the old ruddy postman came beating along the sandy road on his tricycle one felt the handle-bars ought to have been oars.

Bill Hunt put down his book. "Letters," he said complacently, and they all waited. But, heartless postman—O malignant world! There was only one, a fat one for Isabel. Not even a paper.

"And mine's only from William," said Isabel mournfully.

"From William—already?"

"He's sending you back your marriage lines as a gentle reminder."

"Does everybody have marriage lines? I thought they were only for servants."

"Pages and pages! Look at her! A Lady reading a Letter," said Dennis.

My darling, precious Isabel. Pages and pages there were. As Isabel read on her feeling of astonishment changed to a stifled feeling. What on earth had induced William . . . ? How extraordinary it was. . . . What could have made him . . . ? She felt confused, more and more excited, even frightened. It was just like William. Was it? It was absurd, of course, it must be absurd, ridiculous. "Ha, ha, ha! Oh dear!" What was she to do? Isabel flung back in her chair and laughed till she couldn't stop laughing.

"Do, do tell us," said the others. "You must tell us."

"I'm longing to," gurgled Isabel. She sat up, gathered the letter, and waved it at them. "Gather round," she said. "Listen, it's too marvellous. A love-letter!"

"A love-letter! But how divine!" *Darling, precious Isabel.* But she had hardly begun before their laughter interrupted her.

"Go on, Isabel, it's perfect."

"It's the most marvellous find."

"Oh, do go on, Isabel!"

God forbid, my darling, that I should be a drag on your happiness.

"Oh! oh! oh!"

"Sh! sh! sh!"

And Isabel went on. When she reached the end they were hysterical: Bobby rolled on the turf and almost sobbed.

"You must let me have it just as it is, entire, for my new book," said Dennis firmly. "I shall give it a whole chapter."

"Oh, Isabel," moaned Moira, "that wonderful bit about holding you in his arms!"

"I always thought those letters in divorce cases were made up. But they pale before this."

"Let me hold it. Let me read it, mine own self," said Bobby Kane.

But, to their surprise, Isabel crushed the letter in her hand. She was laughing no longer. She glanced quickly at them all; she looked exhausted. "No, not just now. Not just now," she stammered.

And before they could recover she had run into the house, through the hall, up the stairs into her bedroom. Down she sat on the side of the bed. "How vile, odious, abominable, vulgar," muttered Isabel. She pressed her eyes with her knuckles and rocked to and fro. And again she saw them, but not four, more like forty, laughing, sneering, jeering, stretching out their hands while she read them William's letter. Oh, what a loathsome thing to have done. How could she have done it! *God forbid, my darling, that I should be a drag on your happiness.* William! Isabel pressed her face into the pillow. But she felt that even the grave bedroom knew her for what she was, shallow, tinkling, vain. . . .

Presently from the garden below there came voices.

"Isabel, we're all going for a bathe. Do come!"

"Come, thou wife of William!"

"Call her once before you go, call once yet!"

Isabel sat up. Now was the moment, now she must decide. Would she go with them, or stay here and write to William. Which, which should it be? "I must make up my mind." Oh, but how could there be any question? Of course she would stay here and write.

"Titania!" piped Moira.

"Isa-bel?"

No, it was too difficult. "I'll—I'll go with them, and write to William later. Some other time. Later. Not now. But I shall *certainly* write," thought Isabel hurriedly.

And, laughing in the new way, she ran down the stairs.

THE OUTSTATION

W. Somerset Maugham

The new assistant arrived in the afternoon. When the Resident, Mr. Warburton, was told that the prahu was in sight he put on his solar topee and went down to the landing-stage. The guard, eight little Dyak soldiers, stood to attention as he passed. He noted with satisfaction that their bearing was martial, their uniforms neat and clean, and their guns shining. They were a credit to him. From the landing-stage he watched the bend of the river round which in a moment the boat would sweep. He looked very smart in his spotless ducks and white shoes. He held under his arm a gold-headed Malacca cane which had been given him by the Sultan of Perak. He awaited the newcomer with mingled feelings. There was more work in the district than one man could properly do, and during his periodical tours of the country under his charge it had been inconvenient to leave the station in the hands of a native clerk, but he had been so long the only white man there that he could not face the arrival of another without misgiving. He was accustomed to loneliness. During the war he had not seen an English face for three years: and once when he was instructed to put up an afforestation officer he was seized with panic, so that when the stranger was due to arrive, having arranged everything for his reception, he wrote a note telling him he was obliged to go up-river, and fled; he remained away till he was informed by a messenger that his guest had left.

Now the prahu appeared in the broad reach. It was

manned by prisoners, Dyaks under various sentences, and a
couple of warders were waiting on the landing-stage to take
them back to jail. They were sturdy fellows, used to the
river, and they rowed with a powerful stroke. As the boat
reached the side a man got out from under the attap awning
and stepped on shore. The guard presented arms.

"Here we are at last. By God, I'm as cramped as the
devil. I've brought you your mail."

He spoke with exuberant joviality. Mr. Warburton politely held out his hand.

"Mr. Cooper, I presume?"

"That's right. Were you expecting any one else?"

The question had a facetious intent, but the Resident did
not smile.

"My name is Warburton. I'll show you your quarters.
They'll bring your kit along."

He preceded Cooper along the narrow pathway and they
entered a compound in which stood a small bungalow.

"I've had it made as habitable as I could, but of course no
one has lived in it for a good many years."

It was built on piles. It consisted of a long living-room
which opened on to a broad verandah, and behind, on each
side of a passage, were two bedrooms.

"This'll do me all right," said Cooper.

"I daresay you want to have a bath and a change. I shall
be very much pleased if you'll dine with me to-night. Will
eight o'clock suit you?"

"Any old time will do for me."

The Resident gave a polite, but slightly disconcerted,
smile and withdrew. He returned to the Fort where his own
residence was. The impression which Allen Cooper had
given him was not very favourable, but he was a fair man,
and he knew that it was unjust to form an opinion on so
brief a glimpse. Cooper seemed to be about thirty. He was
a tall, thin fellow, with a sallow face in which there was not
a spot of colour. It was a face all in one tone. He had a
large, hooked nose and blue eyes. When, entering the
bungalow, he had taken off his topee and flung it to a

waiting boy, Mr. Warburton noticed that his large skull, covered with short, brown hair, contrasted somewhat oddly with a weak, small chin. He was dressed in khaki shorts and a khaki shirt, but they were shabby and soiled; and his battered topee had not been cleaned for days. Mr. Warburton reflected that the young man had spent a week on a coasting steamer and had passed the last forty-eight hours lying in the bottom of a prahu.

"We'll see what he looks like when he comes in to dinner."

He went into his room where his things were as neatly laid out as if he had an English valet, undressed, and, walking down the stairs to the bath-house, sluiced himself with cool water. The only concession he made to the climate was to wear a white dinner-jacket; but otherwise, in a boiled shirt and a high collar, silk socks and patent-leather shoes, he dressed as formally as though he were dining at his club in Pall Mall. A careful host, he went into the dining-room to see that the table was properly laid. It was gay with orchids and the silver shone brightly. The napkins were folded into elaborate shapes. Shaded candles in silver candlesticks shed a soft light. Mr. Warburton smiled his approval and returned to the sitting-room to await his guest. Presently he appeared. Cooper was wearing the khaki shorts, the khaki shirt, and the ragged jacket in which he had landed. Mr. Warburton's smile of greeting froze on his face.

"Hulloa, you're all dressed up," said Cooper. "I didn't know you were going to do that. I very nearly put on a sarong."

"It doesn't matter at all. I daresay your boys were busy."

"You needn't have bothered to dress on my account, you know."

"I didn't. I always dress for dinner."

"Even when you're alone?"

"Especially when I'm alone," replied Mr. Warburton, with a frigid stare.

He saw a twinkle of amusement in Cooper's eyes, and he flushed an angry red. Mr. Warburton was a hot-tempered man; you might have guessed that from his red face with its

pugnacious features and from his red hair, now growing
white; his blue eyes, cold as a rule and observing, could
flush with sudden wrath; but he was a man of the world and
he hoped a just one. He must do his best to get on with this
fellow.

"When I lived in London I moved in circles in which it
would have been just as eccentric not to dress for dinner
every night as not to have a bath every morning. When I
came to Borneo I saw no reason to discontinue so good a
habit. For three years, during the war, I never saw a white
man. I never omitted to dress on a single occasion on which
I was well enough to come in to dinner. You have not been
very long in this country; believe me, there is no better way
to maintain the proper pride which you should have in
yourself. When a white man surrenders in the slightest
degree to the influences that surround him he very soon
loses his self-respect, and when he loses his self-respect you
may be quite sure that the natives will soon cease to respect
him."

"Well, if you expect me to put on a boiled shirt and a stiff
collar in this heat I'm afraid you'll be disappointed."

"When you are dining in your own bungalow you will, of
course, dress as you think fit, but when you do me the
pleasure of dining with me, perhaps you will come to the
conclusion that it is only polite to wear the costume usual in
civilized society."

Two Malay boys, in sarongs and songkoks, with smart
white coats and brass buttons, came in, one bearing gin
pahits, and the other a tray on which were olives and
anchovies. Then they went in to dinner. Mr. Warburton
flattered himself that he had the best cook, a Chinese, in
Borneo, and he took great trouble to have as good food as in
the difficult circumstances was possible. He exercised much
ingenuity in making the best of his materials.

"Would you care to look at the menu?" he said, handing
it to Cooper.

It was written in French and the dishes had resounding
names. They were waited on by the two boys. In opposite

corners of the room two more waved immense fans, and so gave movement to the sultry air. The fare was sumptuous and the champagne excellent.

"Do you do yourself like this every day?" said Cooper.

Mr. Warburton gave the menu a careless glance.

"I have not noticed that the dinner is any different from usual," he said. "I eat very little myself, but I make a point of having a proper dinner served to me every night. It keeps the cook in practice and it's good discipline for the boys."

The conversation proceeded with effort. Mr. Warburton was elaborately courteous, and it may be that he found a slightly malicious amusement in the embarrassment which he thereby occasioned in his companion. Cooper had not been more than a few months in Sembulu, and Mr. Warburton's enquiries about friends of his in Kuala Solor were soon exhausted.

"By the way," he said presently, "did you meet a lad called Hennerley? He's come out recently, I believe."

"Oh, yes, he's in the police. A rotten bounder."

"I should hardly have expected him to be that. His uncle is my friend Lord Barraclough. I had a letter from Lady Barraclough only the other day asking me to look out for him."

"I heard he was related to somebody or other. I suppose that's how he got the job. He's been to Eton and Oxford and he doesn't forget to let you know it."

"You surprise me," said Mr. Warburton. "All his family have been at Eton and Oxford for a couple of hundred years. I should have expected him to take it as a matter of course."

"I thought him a damned prig."

"To what school did you go?"

"I was born in Barbadoes. I was educated there."

"Oh, I see."

Mr. Warburton managed to put so much offensiveness into his brief reply that Cooper flushed. For a moment he was silent.

"I've had two or three letters from Kuala Solor," continued Mr. Warburton, "and my impression was that young Hennerley was a great success. They say he's a first-rate sportsman."

"Oh, yes, he's very popular. He's just the sort of fellow they would like in K.S. I haven't got much use for the first-rate sportsman myself. What does it amount to in the long run that a man can play golf and tennis better than other people? And who cares if he can make a break of seventy-five at billiards? They attach a damned sight too much importance to that sort of thing in England."

"Do you think so? I was under the impression that the first-rate sportsman had come out of the war certainly no worse than any one else."

"Oh, if you're going to talk of the war then I do know what I'm talking about. I was in the same regiment as Hennerley and I can tell you that the men couldn't stick him at any price."

"How do you know?"

"Because I was one of the men."

"Oh, you hadn't got a commission."

"A fat chance I had of getting a commission. I was what was called a Colonial. I hadn't been to a public school and I had no influence. I was in the ranks the whole damned time."

Cooper frowned. He seemed to have difficulty in preventing himself from breaking into violent invective. Mr. Warburton watched him, his little blue eyes narrowed, watched him and formed his opinion. Changing the conversation, he began to speak to Cooper about the work that would be required of him, and as the clock struck ten he rose.

"Well, I won't keep you any more. I daresay you're tired by your journey."

They shook hands.

"Oh, I say, look here," said Cooper, "I wonder if you can find me a boy. The boy I had before never turned up when I was starting from K.S. He took my kit on board and all that and then disappeared. I didn't know he wasn't there till we were out of the river."

"I'll ask my head-boy. I have no doubt he can find you some one."

"All right. Just tell him to send the boy along and if I like the look of him I'll take him."

There was a moon, so that no lantern was needed. Cooper walked across from the Fort to his bungalow.

"I wonder why on earth they've sent me a fellow like that?" reflected Mr. Warburton. "If that's the kind of man they're going to get out now I don't think much of it."

He strolled down his garden. The Fort was built on the top of a little hill and the garden ran down to the river's edge; on the bank was an arbour, and hither it was his habit to come after dinner to smoke a cheroot. And often from the river that flowed below him a voice was heard, the voice of some Malay too timorous to venture into the light of day, and a complaint or an accusation was softly wafted to his ears, a piece of information was whispered to him or a useful hint, which otherwise would never have come into his official ken. He threw himself heavily into a long rattan chair. Cooper! An envious, ill-bred fellow, bumptious, self-assertive and vain. But Mr. Warburton's irritation could not withstand the silent beauty of the night. The air was scented with the sweet-smelling flowers of a tree that grew at the entrance to the arbour, and the fireflies, sparkling dimly, flew with their slow and silvery flight. The moon made a pathway on the broad river for the light feet of Siva's bride, and on the further bank a row of palm trees was delicately silhouetted against the sky. Peace stole into the soul of Mr. Warburton.

He was a queer creature and he had had a singular career. At the age of twenty-one he had inherited a considerable fortune, a hundred thousand pounds, and when he left Oxford he threw himself into the gay life which in those days (now Mr. Warburton was a man of four and fifty) offered itself to the young man of good family. He had his flat in Mount Street, his private hansom, and his hunting-

box in Warwickshire. He went to all the places where the
fashionable congregate. He was handsome, amusing and
generous. He was a figure in the society of London in the
early nineties, and society then had not lost its exclusive-
ness nor its brilliance. The Boer War which shook it was
unthought of; the Great War which destroyed it was proph-
esied only by the pessimists. It was no unpleasant thing to
be a rich young man in those days, and Mr. Warburton's
chimney-piece during the season was packed with cards for
one great function after another. Mr. Warburton displayed
them with complacency. For Mr. Warburton was a snob.
He was not a timid snob, a little ashamed of being impressed by his betters, nor a snob who sought the intimacy
of persons who had acquired celebrity in politics or notori-
ety in the arts, nor the snob who was dazzled by riches; he
was the naked, unadulterated common snob who dearly
loved a lord. He was touchy and quick-tempered, but he
would much rather have been snubbed by a person of quality than flattered by a commoner. His name figured insignif-
icantly in Burke's Peerage, and it was marvellous to watch
the ingenuity he used to mention his distant relationship to
the noble family he belonged to; but never a word did he
say of the honest Liverpool manufacturer from whom, through
his mother, a Miss Gubbins, he had come by his fortune. It
was the terror of his fashionable life that at Cowes, maybe,
or at Ascot, when he was with a duchess or even with a
prince of the blood, one of these relatives would claim
acquaintance with him.

His failing was too obvious not soon to become notorious,
but its extravagance saved it from being merely despicable.
The great whom he adored laughed at him, but in their
hearts felt his adoration not unnatural. Poor Warburton was
a dreadful snob, of course, but after all he was a good
fellow. He was always ready to back a bill for an impecu-
nious nobleman, and if you were in a tight corner you could
safely count on him for a hundred pounds. He gave good
dinners. He played whist badly, but never minded how
much he lost if the company was select. He happened to be

a gambler, an unlucky one, but he was a good loser, and it was impossible not to admire the coolness with which he lost five hundred pounds at a sitting. His passion for cards, almost as strong as his passion for titles, was the cause of his undoing. The life he led was expensive and his gambling losses were formidable. He began to plunge more heavily, first on horses, and then on the Stock Exchange. He had a certain simplicity of character and the unscrupulous found him an ingenuous prey. I do not know if he ever realized that his smart friends laughed at him behind his back, but I think he had an obscure instinct that he could not afford to appear other than careless of his money. He got into the hands of money-lenders. At the age of thirty-four he was ruined.

He was too much imbued with the spirit of his class to hesitate in the choice of his next step. When a man in his set had run through his money he went out to the colonies. No one heard Mr. Warburton repine. He made no complaint because a noble friend had advised a disastrous speculation; he pressed nobody to whom he had lent money to repay it, he paid his debts (if he had only known it, the despised blood of the Liverpool manufacturer came out in him there), sought help from no one, and, never having done a stroke of work in his life, looked for a means of livelihood. He remained cheerful, unconcerned and full of humour. He had no wish to make any one with whom he happened to be uncomfortable by the recital of his misfortune. Mr. Warburton was a snob, but he was also a gentleman.

The only favour he asked of any of the great friends in whose daily company he had lived for years was a recommendation. The able man who was at that time Sultan of Sembulu took him into his service. The night before he sailed he dined for the last time at his club.

"I hear you're going away, Warburton," the old Duke of Hereford said to him.

"Yes, I'm going to Borneo."

"Good God, what are you going there for?"

"Oh, I'm broke."

"Are you? I'm sorry. Well, let us know when you come back. I hope you have a good time."

"Oh, yes. Lots of shooting, you know."

The Duke nodded and passed on. A few hours later Mr. Warburton watched the coast of England recede into the mist, and he left behind everything which to him made life worth living.

Twenty years had passed since then. He kept up a busy correspondence with various great ladies and his letters were amusing and chatty. He never lost his love for titled persons and paid careful attention to the announcements in The Times (which reached him six weeks after publication) of their comings and goings. He perused the column which records births, deaths, and marriages, and he was always ready with his letter of congratulation or condolence. The illustrated papers told him how people looked and on his periodical visits to England, able to take up the threads as though they had never been broken, he knew all about any new person who might have appeared on the social surface. His interest in the world of fashion was as vivid as when himself had been a figure in it. It still seemed to him the only thing that mattered.

But insensibly another interest had entered into his life. The position he found himself in flattered his vanity; he was no longer the sycophant craving the smiles of the great, he was the master whose word was law. He was gratified by the guard of Dyak soldiers who presented arms as he passed. He liked to sit in judgment on his fellow men. It pleased him to compose quarrels between rival chiefs. When the head-hunters were troublesome in the old days he set out to chastise them with a thrill of pride in his own behaviour. He was too vain not to be of dauntless courage, and a pretty story was told of his coolness in adventuring single-handed into a stockaded village and demanding the surrender of a bloodthirsty pirate. He became a skillful administrator. He was strict, just and honest.

And little by little he conceived a deep love for the

Malays. He interested himself in their habits and customs. He was never tired of listening to their talk. He admired their virtues, and with a smile and a shrug of the shoulders condoned their vices.

"In my day," he would say, "I have been on intimate terms with some of the greatest gentlemen in England, but I have never known finer gentlemen than some well-born Malays whom I am proud to call my friends."

He liked their courtesy and their distinguished manners, their gentleness and their sudden passions. He knew by instinct exactly how to treat them. He had a genuine tenderness for them. But he never forgot that he was an English gentleman and he had no patience with the white men who yielded to native customs. He made no surrenders. And he did not imitate so many of the white men in taking a native woman to wife, for an intrigue of this nature, however sanctified by custom, seemed to him not only shocking but undignified. A man who had been called George by Albert Edward, Prince of Wales, could hardly be expected to have any connection with a native. And when he returned to Borneo from his visits to England it was now with something like relief. His friends, like himself, were no longer young, and there was a new generation which looked upon him as a tiresome old man. It seemed to him that the England of to-day had lost a good deal of what he had loved in the England of his youth. But Borneo remained the same. It was home to him now. He meant to remain in the service as long as was possible, and the hope in his heart was that he would die before at last he was forced to retire. He had stated in his will that wherever he died he wished his body to be brought back to Sembulu and buried among the people he loved within sound of the softly flowing river.

But these emotions he kept hidden from the eyes of men; and no one, seeing this spruce, stout, well-set-up man, with his clean-shaven strong face and his whitening hair, would have dreamed that he cherished so profound a sentiment.

He knew how the work of the station should be done, and during the next few days he kept a suspicious eye on his assistant. He saw very soon that he was painstaking and competent. The only fault he had to find with him was that he was brusque with the natives.

"The Malays are shy and very sensitive," he said to him. "I think you will find that you will get much better results if you take care always to be polite, patient and kindly."

Cooper gave a short, grating laugh.

"I was born in Barbadoes and I was in Africa in the war. I don't think there's much about niggers that I don't know."

"I know nothing," said Mr. Warburton acidly. "But we were not talking of them. We were talking of Malays."

"Aren't they niggers?"

"You are very ignorant," replied Mr. Warburton.

He said no more.

On the first Sunday after Cooper's arrival he asked him to dinner. He did everything ceremoniously, and though they had met on the previous day in the office and later, on the Fort verandah where they drank a gin and bitters together at six o'clock, he sent a polite note across to the bungalow by a boy. Cooper, however unwillingly, came in evening dress and Mr. Warburton, though gratified that his wish was respected, noticed with disdain that the young man's clothes were badly cut and his shirt ill-fitting. But Mr. Warburton was in a good temper that evening.

"By the way," he said to him, as he shook hands, "I've talked to my head-boy about finding you some one and he recommends his nephew. I've seen him and he seems a bright and willing lad. Would you like to see him?"

"I don't mind."

"He's waiting now."

Mr. Warburton called his boy and told him to send for his nephew. In a moment a tall, slender youth of twenty appeared. He had large dark eyes and a good profile. He was very neat in his sarong, a little white coat, and a fez, without a tassel, of plum-coloured velvet. He answered to the name of Abas. Mr. Warburton looked on him with approval, and his manner insensibly softened as he spoke to him in fluent and idiomatic Malay. He was inclined to be

sarcastic with white people, but with the Malays he had a
happy mixture of condescension and kindliness. He stood in
the place of the Sultan. He knew perfectly how to preserve
his own dignity, and at the same time put a native at his
ease.

"Will he do?" said Mr. Warburton, turning to Cooper.

"Yes, I daresay he's no more of a scoundrel than any of
the rest of them."

Mr. Warburton informed the boy that he was engaged
and dismissed him.

"You're very lucky to get a boy like that," he told Cooper.
"He belongs to a very good family. They came over from
Malacca nearly a hundred years ago."

"I don't much mind if the boy who cleans my shoes and
brings me a drink when I want it has blue blood in his veins
or not. All I ask is that he should do what I tell him and look
sharp about it."

Mr. Warburton pursed his lips, but made no reply.

They went in to dinner. It was excellent, and the wine
was good. Its influence presently had its effect on them and
they talked not only without acrimony, but even with friendliness. Mr. Warburton liked to do himself well, and on
Sunday night he made it a habit to do himself even a little
better than usual. He began to think he was unfair to Cooper.
Of course he was not a gentleman, but that was not his fault,
and when you got to know him it might be that he would turn
out a very good fellow. His faults, perhaps, were faults of
manner. And he was certainly good at his work, quick, con-
scientious and thorough. When they reached the dessert Mr.
Warburton was feeling kindly disposed towards all mankind.

"This is your first Sunday and I'm going to give you a very
special glass of port. I've only got about two dozen of it left
and I keep it for special occasions."

He gave his boy instructions and presently the bottle was
brought. Mr. Warburton watched the boy open it.

"I got this port from my old friend Charles Hollington.
He'd had it for forty years and I've had it for a good many.
He was well known to have the best cellar in England."

"Is he a wine merchant?"

"Not exactly," smiled Mr. Warburton. "I was speaking of Lord Hollington of Castle Reagh. He's one of the richest peers in England. A very old friend of mine. I was at Eton with his brother."

This was an opportunity that Mr. Warburton could never resist and he told a little anecdote of which the only point seemed to be that he knew an earl. The port was certainly very good; he drank a glass and then a second. He lost all caution. He had not talked to a white man for months. He began to tell stories. He showed himself in the company of the great. Hearing him you would have thought that at one time ministries were formed and policies decided on his suggestion whispered into the ear of a duchess or thrown over the dinner-table to be gratefully acted on by the confidential adviser of the sovereign. The old days at Ascot, Goodwood and Cowes lived again for him. Another glass of port. There were the great house-parties in Yorkshire and in Scotland to which he went every year.

"I had a man called Foreman then, the best valet I ever had, and why do you think he gave me notice? You know in the Housekeeper's Room the ladies' maids and the gentlemen's gentlemen sit according to the precedence of their masters. He told me he was sick of going to party after party at which I was the only commoner. It meant that he always had to sit at the bottom of the table and all the best bits were taken before a dish reached him. I told the story to the old Duke of Hereford and he roared. 'By God, sir,' he said, 'if I were King of England I'd make you a viscount just to give your man a chance.' 'Take him yourself, Duke,' I said. 'He's the best valet I've ever had.' 'Well, Warburton,' he said, 'if he's good enough for you he's good enough for me. Send him along.'"

Then there was Monte Carlo where Mr. Warburton and the Grand Duke Fyodor, playing in partnership, had broken the bank one evening; and there was Marienbad. At Marienbad Mr. Warburton had played baccarat with Edward VII.

"He was only Prince of Wales then, of course. I remember him saying to me, 'George, if you draw on a five you'll lose your shirt.' He was right; I don't think he ever said a truer word in his life. He was a wonderful man. I always said he was the greatest diplomatist in Europe. But I was a young fool in those days, I hadn't the sense to take his advice. If I had, if I'd never drawn on a five, I daresay I shouldn't be here to-day."

Cooper was watching him. His blue eyes, deep in their sockets, were hard and supercilious, and on his lips was a mocking smile. He had heard a good deal about Mr. Warburton in Kuala Solor. Not a bad sort, and he ran his district like clockwork, they said, but by heaven, what a snob! They laughed at him good-naturedly, for it was impossible to dislike a man who was so generous and so kindly, and Cooper had already heard the story of the Prince of Wales and the game of baccarat. But Cooper listened without indulgence. From the beginning he had resented the Resident's manner. He was very sensitive and he writhed under Mr. Warburton's polite sarcasms. Mr. Warburton had a knack of receiving a remark of which he disapproved with a devastating silence. Cooper had lived little in England and he had a peculiar dislike of the English. He resented especially the public-school boy since he always feared that he was going to patronize him. He was so much afraid of others putting on airs with him that, in order as it were to get in first, he put on such airs as to make every one think him insufferably conceited.

"Well, at all events the war has done one good thing for us," he said at last. "It's smashed up the power of the aristocracy. The Boer War started it, and 1914 put the lid on."

"The great families of England are doomed," said Mr. Warburton with the complacent melancholy of an *émigré* who remembered the court of Louis XV. "They cannot afford any longer to live in their splendid palaces and their princely hospitality will soon be nothing but a memory."

"And a damned good job too in my opinion."

"My poor Cooper, what can you know of the glory that was Greece and the grandeur that was Rome?"

Mr. Warburton made an ample gesture. His eyes for an instant grew dreamy with a vision of the past.

"Well, believe me, we're fed up with all that rot. What we want is a business government by business men. I was born in a Crown Colony and I've lived practically all my life in the colonies. I don't give a row of pins for a lord. What's wrong with England is snobbishness. And if there's anything that gets my goat it's a snob."

A snob! Mr. Warburton's face grew purple and his eyes blazed with anger. That was a word that had pursued him all his life. The great ladies whose society he had enjoyed in his youth were not inclined to look upon his appreciation of themselves as unworthy, but even great ladies are sometimes out of temper and more than once Mr. Warburton had had the dreadful word flung in his teeth. He knew, he could not help knowing, that there were odious people who called him a snob. How unfair it was! Why, there was no vice he found so detestable as snobbishness. After all, he liked to mix with people of his own class, he was only at home in their company, and how in heaven's name could any one say that was snobbish? Birds of a feather.

"I quite agree with you," he answered. "A snob is a man who admires or despises another because he is of a higher social rank than his own. It is the most vulgar failing of our English middle class."

He saw a flicker of amusement in Cooper's eyes. Cooper put up his hand to hide the broad smile that rose to his lips, and so made it more noticeable. Mr. Warburton's hands trembled a little.

Probably Cooper never knew how greatly he had offended his chief. A sensitive man himself he was strangely insensitive to the feelings of others.

Their work forced them to see one another for a few minutes now and then during the day, and they met at six to have a drink on Mr. Warburton's verandah. This was an old-established custom of the country which Mr. Warburton would not for the world have broken. But they ate their meals separately, Cooper in his bungalow and Mr. Warburton at the Fort. After the office work was over they walked till dusk fell, but they walked apart. There were but few paths in this country, where the jungle pressed close upon the plantations of the village, and when Mr. Warburton caught sight of his assistant passing along with his loose stride, he would make a circuit in order to avoid him. Cooper, with his bad manners, his conceit in his own judgment and his intolerance, had already got on his nerves; but it was not till Cooper had been on the station for a couple of months that an incident happened which turned the Resident's dislike into bitter hatred.

Mr. Warburton was obliged to go up-country on a tour of inspection, and he left the station in Cooper's charge with more confidence, since he had definitely come to the conclusion that he was a capable fellow. The only thing he did not like was that he had no indulgence. He was honest, just and painstaking, but he had no sympathy for the natives. It bitterly amused Mr. Warburton to observe that this man, who looked upon himself as every man's equal, should look upon so many men as his own inferiors. He was hard, he had no patience with the native mind, and he was a bully. Mr. Warburton very quickly realized that the Malays disliked and feared him. He was not altogether displeased. He would not have liked it very much if his assistant had enjoyed a popularity which might rival his own. Mr. Warburton made his elaborate preparations, set out on his expedition, and in three weeks returned. Meanwhile the mail had arrived. The first thing that struck his eyes when he entered his sitting-room was a great pile of open newspapers. Cooper had met him, and they went into the room together. Mr. Warburton turned to one of the servants who had been left behind and sternly asked him what was the meaning of those open papers. Cooper hastened to explain.

"I wanted to read all about the Wolverhampton murder and so I borrowed your Times. I brought them back again. I knew you wouldn't mind."

Mr. Warburton turned on him, white with anger.

"But I do mind. I mind very much."

"I'm sorry," said Cooper, with composure. "The fact is, I simply couldn't wait till you came back."

"I wonder you didn't open my letters as well."

Cooper, unmoved, smiled at his chief's exasperation.

"Oh, that's not quite the same thing. After all, I couldn't imagine you'd mind my looking at your newspapers. There's nothing private in them."

"I very much object to any one reading my paper before me." He went up to the pile. There were nearly thirty numbers there. "I think it extremely impertinent of you. They're all mixed up."

"We can easily put them in order," said Cooper, joining him at the table.

"Don't touch them," cried Mr. Warburton.

"I say, it's childish to make a scene about a little thing like that."

"How dare you speak to me like that?"

"Oh go to hell," said Cooper, and he flung out of the room.

Mr. Warburton, trembling with passion, was left contemplating his papers. His greatest pleasure in life had been destroyed by those callous, brutal hands. Most people living in out-of-the-way places when the mail comes tear open impatiently their papers and taking the last ones first glance at the latest news from home. Not so Mr. Warburton. His newsagent had instructions to write on the outside of the wrapper the date of each paper he despatched and when the great bundle arrived Mr. Warburton looked at these dates and with his blue pencil numbered them. His head-boy's orders were to place one on the table every morning in the verandah with the early cup of tea, and it was Mr. Warburton's especial delight to break the wrapper as he sipped his tea, and read the morning paper. It gave him the illusion of living at home. Every Monday morning he read the Monday Times of six weeks back and so went through the week. On Sunday he read The Observer. Like his habit of dressing for dinner it was a tie to civilization. And it was his pride that no matter how exciting the news was he had never yielded to the temptation of opening a paper before its allotted time. During the war the suspense sometimes had been intolerable, and when he read one day that a push was begun he had undergone agonies of suspense which he might have saved himself by the simple expedient of opening a later paper which lay waiting for him on a shelf. It had been the severest trial to which he had ever exposed himself, but he victoriously surmounted it. And that clumsy fool had broken open those neat tight packages because he wanted to know whether some horrid woman had murdered her odious husband.

Mr. Warburton sent for his boy and told him to bring wrappers. He folded up the papers as neatly as he could, placed a wrapper round each and numbered it. But it was a melancholy task.

"I shall never forgive him," he said. "Never."

Of course his boy had been with him on his expedition; he never travelled without him, for his boy knew exactly how he liked things, and Mr. Warburton was not the kind of jungle traveller who was prepared to dispense with his comforts; but in the interval since their arrival he had been gossiping in the servants' quarters. He had learnt that Cooper had had trouble with his boys. All but the youth Abas had left him. Abas had desired to go too, but his uncle had placed him there on the instructions of the Resident, and he was afraid to leave without his uncle's permission.

"I told him he had done well, Tuan," said the boy. "But he is unhappy. He says it is not a good house and he wishes to know if he may go as the others have gone."

"No, he must stay. The tuan must have servants. Have those who went been replaced?"

"No, Tuan, no one will go."

Mr. Warburton frowned. Cooper was an insolent fool, but he had an official position and must be suitably provided with servants. It was not seemly that his house should be improperly conducted.

"Where are the boys who ran away?"

"They are in the kampong, Tuan."

"Go and see them to-night and tell them that I expect them to be back at Tuan Cooper's house at dawn tomorrow."

"They say they will not go, Tuan."

"On my order?"

The boy had been with Mr. Warburton for fifteen years, and he knew every intonation of his master's voice. He was not afraid of him, they had gone through too much together, once in the jungle the Resident had saved his life and once, upset in some rapids, but for him the Resident would have been drowned; but he knew when the Resident must be obeyed without question.

"I will go to the kampong," he said.

Mr. Warburton expected that his subordinate would take the first opportunity to apologize for his rudeness, but Cooper had the ill-bred man's inability to express regret; and when they met next morning in the office he ignored the incident. Since Mr. Warburton had been away for three weeks it was necessary for them to have a somewhat prolonged interview. At the end of it Mr. Warburton dismissed him.

"I don't think there's anything else, thank you." Cooper turned to go, but Mr. Warburton stopped him. "I understand you've been having some trouble with your boys."

Cooper gave a harsh laugh.

"They tried to blackmail me. They had the damned cheek to run away, all except that incompetent fellow Abas—he knew when he was well off—but I just sat tight. They've all come to heel again."

"What do you mean by that?"

"This morning they were all back on their jobs, the Chinese cook and all. There they were, as cool as cucumbers; you would have thought they owned the place. I suppose they'd come to the conclusion that I wasn't such a fool as I looked."

"By no means. They came back on my express order."

Cooper flushed slightly.

"I should be obliged if you wouldn't interfere with my private concerns."

"They're not your private concerns. When your servants run away it makes you ridiculous. You are perfectly free to make a fool of yourself, but I cannot allow you to be made a fool of. It is unseemly that your house should not be properly staffed. As soon as I heard that your boys had left you, I had them told to be back in their place at dawn. That'll do."

Mr. Warburton nodded to signify that the interview was at an end. Cooper took no notice.

"Shall I tell you what I did? I called them and gave the whole bally lot the sack. I gave them ten minutes to get out of the compound."

Mr. Warburton shrugged his shoulders.

"What makes you think you can get others?"

"I've told my own clerk to see about it."

Mr. Warburton reflected for a moment.

"I think you behaved very foolishly. You will do well to remember in future that good masters make good servants."

"Is there anything else you want to teach me?"

"I should like to teach you manners, but it would be an arduous task, and I have not the time to waste. I will see that you get boys."

"Please don't put yourself to any trouble on my account. I'm quite capable of getting them for myself."

Mr. Warburton smiled acidly. He had an inkling that Cooper disliked him as much as he disliked Cooper, and he knew that nothing is more galling than to be forced to accept the favours of a man you detest.

"Allow me to tell you that you have no more chance of getting Malay or Chinese servants here now than you have of getting an English butler or a French chef. No one will come to you except on an order from me. Would you like me to give it?"

"No."

"As you please. Good morning."

Mr. Warburton watched the development of the situation with acrid humour. Cooper's clerk was unable to persuade

Malay, Dyak or Chinese to enter the house of such a master. Abas, the boy who remained faithful to him, knew how to cook only native food, and Cooper, a coarse feeder, found his gorge rise against the everlasting rice. There was no water-carrier, and in that great heat he needed several baths a day. He cursed Abas, but Abas opposed him with sullen resistance and would not do more than he chose. It was galling to know that the lad stayed with him only because the Resident insisted. This went on for a fortnight and then, one morning, he found in his house the very servants whom he had previously dismissed. He fell into a violent rage, but he had learnt a little sense, and this time, without a word, he let them stay. He swallowed his humiliation, but the impatient contempt he had felt for Mr. Warburton's idiosyncrasies changed into a sullen hatred; the Resident with this malicious stroke had made him the laughing-stock of all the natives.

The two men now held no communication with one another. They broke the time-honoured custom of sharing, notwithstanding personal dislike, a drink at six o'clock with any white man who happened to be at the station. Each lived in his own house as though the other did not exist. Now that Cooper had fallen into the work, it was necessary for them to have little to do with one another in the office. Mr. Warburton used his orderly to send any message he had to give his assistant, and his instructions he sent by formal letter. They saw one another constantly, that was inevitable, but did not exchange half a dozen words in a week. The fact that they could not avoid catching sight of one another got on their nerves. They brooded over their antagonism and Mr. Warburton, taking his daily walk, could think of nothing but how much he detested his assistant.

And the dreadful thing was that in all probability they would remain thus, facing each other in deadly enmity, till Mr. Warburton went on leave. It might be three years. He had no reason to send in a complaint to headquarters: Cooper did his work very well, and at that time men were hard to get. True, vague complaints reached him and hints

that the natives found Cooper harsh. There was certainly a
feeling of dissatisfaction among them. But when Mr.
Warburton looked into specific cases, all he could say was
that Cooper had shown severity where mildness would not
have been misplaced and had been unfeeling when himself
would have been sympathetic. He had done nothing for
which he could be taken to task. But Mr. Warburton watched
him. Hatred will often make a man clear-sighted, and he
had a suspicion that Cooper was using the natives without
consideration, yet keeping within the law, because he felt
that thus he could exasperate his chief. One day perhaps he
would go too far. None knew better than Mr. Warburton
how irritable the incessant heat could make a man and how
difficult it was to keep one's self-control after a sleepless
night. He smiled softly to himself. Sooner or later Cooper
would deliver himself into his hand.

When at last the opportunity came Mr. Warburton laughed
aloud. Cooper had charge of the prisoners; they made roads,
built sheds, rowed when it was necessary to send the prahu
up- or down-stream, kept the town clean and otherwise
usefully employed themselves. If well-behaved they even
on occasion served as house-boys. Cooper kept them hard at
it. He liked to see them work. He took pleasure in devising
tasks for them; and seeing quickly enough that they were
being made to do useless things the prisoners worked badly.
He punished them by lengthening their hours. This was
contrary to the regulations, and as soon as it was brought to
the attention of Mr. Warburton, without referring the matter back to his subordinate, he gave instructions that the old
hours should be kept; Cooper, going out for his walk, was
astounded to see the prisoners strolling back to the jail; he
had given instructions that they were not to knock off till
dusk. When he asked the warder in charge why they had
left off work he was told that it was the Resident's bidding.

White with rage he strode to the Fort. Mr. Warburton, in
his spotless white ducks and his neat topee, with a walking-
stick in his hand, followed by his dogs, was on the point of
starting out on his afternoon stroll. He had watched Cooper

go and knew that he had taken the road by the river. Cooper jumped up the steps and went straight up to the Resident.

"I want to know what the hell you mean by countermanding my order that the prisoners were to work till six," he burst out, beside himself with fury.

Mr. Warburton opened his cold blue eyes very wide and assumed an expression of great surprise.

"Are you out of your mind? Are you so ignorant that you do not know that that is not the way to speak to your official superior?"

"Oh go to hell. The prisoners are my pidgin and you've got no right to interfere. You mind your business and I'll mind mine. I want to know what the devil you mean by making a damned fool of me. Every one in the place will know that you've countermanded my order."

Mr. Warburton kept very cool.

"You had no power to give the order you did. I countermanded it because it was harsh and tyrannical. Believe me, I have not made half such a damned fool of you as you have made of yourself."

"You disliked me from the first moment I came here. You've done everything you could to make the place impossible for me because I wouldn't lick your boots for you. You got your knife into me because I wouldn't flatter you."

Cooper, spluttering with rage, was nearing dangerous ground, and Mr. Warburton's eyes grew on a sudden colder and more piercing.

"You are wrong. I thought you were a cad, but I was perfectly satisfied with the way you did your work."

"You snob. You damned snob. You thought me a cad because I hadn't been to Eton. Oh, they told me in K.S. what to expect. Why, don't you know that you're the laughing-stock of the whole country? I could hardly help bursting into a roar of laughter when you told your celebrated story about the Prince of Wales. My God, how they shouted at the club when they told it. By God, I'd rather be the cad I am than the snob you are."

He got Mr. Warburton on the raw.

"If you don't get out of my house this minute I shall knock you down," he cried.

The other came a little closer to him and put his face in his.

"Touch me, touch me," he said. "By God, I'd like to see you hit me. Do you want me to say it again? Snob. Snob."

Cooper was three inches taller than Mr. Warburton, a strong, muscular young man. Mr. Warburton was fat and fifty-four. His clenched fist shot out. Cooper caught him by the arm and pushed him back.

"Don't be a damned fool. Remember I'm not a gentleman, I know how to use my hands."

He gave a sort of hoot, and, grinning all over his pale, sharp face, jumped down the verandah steps. Mr. Warburton, his heart in his anger pounding against his ribs, sank exhausted into a chair. His body tingled as though he had prickly heat. For one horrible moment he thought he was going to cry. But suddenly he was conscious that his head-boy was on the verandah and instinctively regained control of himself. The boy came forward and filled him a glass of whisky and soda. Without a word Mr. Warburton took it and drank it to the dregs.

"What do you want to say to me?" asked Mr. Warburton, trying to force a smile on to his strained lips.

"Tuan, the assistant tuan is a bad man. Abas wishes again to leave him."

"Let him wait a little. I shall write to Kuala Solor and ask that Tuan Cooper should go elsewhere."

"Tuan Cooper is not good with the Malays."

"Leave me."

The boy silently withdrew. Mr. Warburton was left alone with his thoughts. He saw the club at Kuala Solor, the men sitting round the table in the window in their flannels, when the night had driven them in from golf and tennis, drinking whiskies and gin pahits and laughing when they told the celebrated story of the Prince of Wales and himself at Marienbad. He was hot with shame and misery. A snob!

They all thought him a snob. And he had always thought them very good fellows, he had always been gentleman enough to let it make no difference to him that they were of very second-rate position. He hated them now. But his hatred for them was nothing compared with his hatred for Cooper. And if it had come to blows Cooper could have thrashed him. Tears of mortification ran down his red, fat face. He sat there for a couple of hours smoking cigarette after cigarette, and he wished he were dead.

At last the boy came back and asked him if he would dress for dinner. Of course! He always dressed for dinner. He rose wearily from his chair and put on his stiff shirt and the high collar. He sat down at the prettily decorated table and was waited on as usual by the two boys while two others waved their great fans. Over there in the bungalow, two hundred yards away, Cooper was eating a filthy meal clad only in a sarong and a baju. His feet were bare and while he ate he probably read a detective story. After dinner Mr. Warburton sat down to write a letter. The Sultan was away, but he wrote, privately and confidentially, to his representative. Cooper did his work very well, he said, but the fact was that he couldn't get on with him. They were getting dreadfully on each other's nerves and he would look upon it as a very great favour if Cooper could be transferred to another post.

He despatched the letter next morning by special messenger. The answer came a fortnight later with the month's mail. It was a private note and ran as follows:

> My dear Warburton:—
> I do not want to answer your letter officially and so I am writing you a few lines myself. Of course if you insist I will put the matter up to the Sultan, but I think you would be much wiser to drop it. I know Cooper is a rough diamond, but he is capable, and he had a pretty thin time in the war, and I think he should be given every chance. I think you are a little too much inclined to attach importance to a man's

social position. You must remember that times have changed. Of course it's a very good thing for a man to be a gentleman, but it's better that he should be competent and hard-working. I think if you'll exercise a little tolerance you'll get on very well with Cooper.

Yours very sincerely
Richard Temple.

The letter dropped from Mr. Warburton's hand. It was easy to read between the lines. Dick Temple, whom he had known for twenty years, Dick Temple, who came from quite a good county family, thought him a snob and for that reason had no patience with his request. Mr. Warburton felt on a sudden discouraged with life. The world of which he was a part had passed away, and the future belonged to a meaner generation. Cooper represented it and Cooper he hated with all his heart. He stretched out his hand to fill his glass and at the gesture his head-boy stepped forward.

"I didn't know you were there."

The boy picked up the official letter. Ah, that was why he was waiting.

"Does Tuan Cooper go, Tuan?"

"No."

"There will be a misfortune."

For a moment the words conveyed nothing to his lassitude. But only for a moment. He sat up in his chair and looked at the boy. He was all attention.

"What do you mean by that?"

"Tuan Cooper is not behaving rightly with Abas."

Mr. Warburton shrugged his shoulders. How should a man like Cooper know how to treat servants? Mr. Warburton knew the type: he would be grossly familiar with them at one moment and rude and inconsiderate the next.

"Let Abas go back to his family."

"Tuan Cooper holds back his wages so that he may not run away. He has paid him nothing for three months. I tell him to be patient. But he is angry, he will not listen to reason. If the tuan continues to use him ill there will be a misfortune."

"You were right to tell me."

The fool! Did he know so little of the Malays as to think he could safely injure them? It would serve him damned well right if he got a kris in his back. A kris. Mr. Warburton's heart seemed on a sudden to miss a beat. He had only to let things take their course and one fine day he would be rid of Cooper. He smiled faintly as the phrase, a masterly inactivity, crossed his mind. And now his heart beat a little quicker, for he saw the man he hated lying on his face in a pathway of the jungle with a knife in his back. A fit end for the cad and the bully. Mr. Warburton sighed. It was his duty to warn him and of course he must do it. He wrote a brief and formal note to Cooper asking him to come to the Fort at once.

In ten minutes Cooper stood before him. They had not spoken to one another since the day when Mr. Warburton had nearly struck him. He did not now ask him to sit down.

"Did you wish to see me?" Cooper asked.

He was untidy and none too clean. His face and hands were covered with little red blotches where mosquitoes had bitten him and he had scratched himself till the blood came. His long, thin face bore a sullen look.

"I understand that you are again having trouble with your servants. Abas, my head-boy's nephew, complains that you have held back his wages for three months. I consider it a most arbitrary proceeding. The lad wishes to leave you, and I certainly do not blame him. I must insist on your paying what is due to him."

"I don't choose that he should leave me. I am holding back his wages as a pledge of his good behaviour."

"You do not know the Malay character. The Malays are very sensitive to injury and ridicule. They are passionate and revengeful. It is my duty to warn you that if you drive this boy beyond a certain point you run a great risk."

Cooper gave a contemptuous chuckle.

"What do you think he'll do?"

"I think he'll kill you."

"Why should you mind?"

"Oh, I wouldn't," replied Mr. Warburton, with a faint laugh. "I should bear it with the utmost fortitude. But I feel the official obligation to give you a proper warning."

"Do you think I'm afraid of a damned nigger?"

"It's a matter of entire indifference to me."

"Well, let me tell you this, I know how to take care of myself; that boy Abas is a dirty, thieving rascal, and if he tries any monkey tricks on me, by God, I'll wring his bloody neck."

"That was all I wished to say to you," said Mr. Warburton. "Good evening."

Mr. Warburton gave him a little nod of dismissal. Cooper flushed, did not for a moment know what to say or do, turned on his heel and stumbled out of the room. Mr. Warburton watched him go with an icy smile on his lips. He had done his duty. But what would he have thought had he known that when Cooper got back to his bungalow, so silent and cheerless, he threw himself down on his bed and in his bitter loneliness on a sudden lost all control of himself? Painful sobs tore his chest and heavy tears rolled down his thin cheeks.

After this Mr. Warburton seldom saw Cooper, and never spoke to him. He read his Times every morning, did his work at the office, took his exercise, dressed for dinner, dined and sat by the river smoking his cheroot. If by chance he ran across Cooper he cut him dead. Each, though never for a moment unconscious of the propinquity, acted as though the other did not exist. Time did nothing to assuage their animosity. They watched one another's actions and each knew what the other did. Though Mr. Warburton had been a keen shot in his youth, with age he had acquired a distaste for killing the wild things of the jungle, but on Sundays and holidays Cooper went out with his gun: if he got something it was a triumph over Mr. Warburton; if not, Mr. Warburton shrugged his shoulders and chuckled. These counter-jumpers trying to be sportsmen! Christmas was a bad time for both

of them: they ate their dinners alone, each in his own
quarters, and they got deliberately drunk. They were the
only white men within two hundred miles and they lived
within shouting distance of each other. At the beginning of
the year Cooper went down with fever, and when Mr.
Warburton caught sight of him again he was surprised to see
how thin he had grown. He looked ill and worn. The
solitude, so much more unnatural because it was due to no
necessity, was getting on his nerves. It was getting on Mr.
Warburton's too, and often he could not sleep at night. He
lay awake brooding. Cooper was drinking heavily and surely
the breaking point was near; but in his dealings with the
natives he took care to do nothing that might expose him to
his chief's rebuke. They fought a grim and silent battle with
one another. It was a test of endurance. The months passed,
and neither gave sign of weakening. They were like men
dwelling in regions of eternal night, and their souls were
oppressed with the knowledge that never would the day
dawn for them. It looked as though their lives would continue for ever in this dull and hideous monotony of hatred.

And when at last the inevitable happened it came upon
Mr. Warburton with all the shock of the unexpected. Cooper accused the boy Abas of stealing some of his clothes,
and when the boy denied the theft took him by the scruff of
the neck and kicked him down the steps of the bungalow.
The boy demanded his wages, and Cooper flung at his head
every word of abuse he knew. If he saw him in the compound in an hour he would hand him over to the police.
Next morning the boy waylaid him outside the Fort when
he was walking over to his office, and again demanded his
wages. Cooper struck him in the face with his clenched fist.
The boy fell to the ground and got up with blood streaming
from his nose.

Cooper walked on and set about his work. But he could
not attend to it. The blow had calmed his irritation, and he
knew that he had gone too far. He was worried. He felt ill,
miserable and discouraged. In the adjoining office sat Mr.
Warburton, and his impulse was to go and tell him what he

had done; he made a movement in his chair, but he knew with what icy scorn he would listen to the story. He could see his patronizing smile. For a moment he had an uneasy fear of what Abas might do. Warburton had warned him all right. He sighed. What a fool he had been! But he shrugged his shoulders impatiently. He did not care; a fat lot he had to live for. It was all Warburton's fault; if he hadn't put his back up nothing like this would have happened. Warburton had made life a hell for him from the start. The snob. But they were all like that: it was because he was a Colonial. It was a damned shame that he had never got his commission in the war; he was as good as any one else. They were a lot of dirty snobs. He was damned if he was going to knuckle under now. Of course Warburton would hear of what had happened; the old devil knew everything. He wasn't afraid. He wasn't afraid of any Malay in Borneo, and Warburton could go to blazes.

He was right in thinking that Mr. Warburton would know what had happened. His head-boy told him when he went in to tiffin.

"Where is your nephew now?"

"I do not know, Tuan. He has gone."

Mr. Warburton remained silent. After luncheon as a rule he slept a little, but today he found himself very wide awake. His eyes involuntarily sought the bungalow where Cooper was now resting.

The idiot! Hesitation for a little was in Mr. Warburton's mind. Did the man know in what peril he was? He supposed he ought to send for him. But each time he had tried to reason with Cooper, Cooper had insulted him. Anger, furious anger welled up suddenly in Mr. Warburton's heart, so that the veins on his temples stood out and he clenched his fists. The cad had had his warning. Now let him take what was coming to him. It was no business of his and if anything happened it was not his fault. But perhaps they would wish in Kuala Solor that they had taken his advice and transferred Cooper to another station.

He was strangely restless that night. After dinner he

walked up and down the verandah. When the boy went away to his own quarters, Mr. Warburton asked him whether anything had been seen of Abas.

"No, Tuan, I think maybe he has gone to the village of his mother's brother."

Mr. Warburton gave him a sharp glance, but the boy was looking down and their eyes did not meet. Mr. Warburton went down to the river and sat in his arbour. But peace was denied him. The river flowed ominously silent. It was like a great serpent gliding with sluggish movement towards the sea. And the trees of the jungle over the water were heavy with a breathless menace. No bird sang. No breeze ruffled the leaves of the cassias. All around him it seemed as though something waited.

He walked across the garden to the road. He had Cooper's bungalow in full view from there. There was a light in his sitting-room and across the road floated the sound of ragtime. Cooper was playing his gramophone. Mr. Warburton shuddered; he had never got over his instinctive dislike of that instrument. But for that he would have gone over and spoken to Cooper. He turned and went back to his own house. He read late into the night, and at last he slept. But he did not sleep very long, he had terrible dreams, and he seemed to be awakened by a cry. Of course that was a dream too, for no cry—from the bungalow for instance—could be heard in his room. He lay awake till dawn. Then he heard hurried steps and the sound of voices, his head-boy burst suddenly into the room without his fez, and Mr. Warburton's heart stood still.

"Tuan, Tuan."

Mr. Warburton jumped out of bed.

"I'll come at once."

He put on his slippers, and in his sarong and pyjama-jacket walked across his compound and into Cooper's. Cooper was lying in bed, with his mouth open, and a kris sticking in his heart. He had been killed in his sleep. Mr. Warburton started, but not because he had not expected to see just such a sight, he started because he felt in himself a sudden glow of exultation. A great burden had been lifted from his shoulders.

Cooper was quite cold. Mr. Warburton took the kris out of the wound, it had been thrust in with such force that he had to use an effort to get it out, and looked at it. He recognized it. It was a kris that a dealer had offered him some weeks before and which he knew Cooper had bought.

"Where is Abas?" he asked sternly.

"Abas is at the village of his mother's brother."

The sergeant of the native police was standing at the foot of the bed.

"Take two men and go to the village and arrest him."

Mr. Warburton did what was immediately necessary. With set face he gave orders. His words were short and peremptory. Then he went back to the Fort. He shaved and had his bath, dressed and went into the dining-room. By the side of his plate The Times in its wrapper lay waiting for him. He helped himself to some fruit. The headboy poured out his tea while the second handed him a dish of eggs. Mr. Warburton ate with a good appetite. The head-boy waited.

"What is it?" asked Mr. Warburton.

"Tuan, Abas, my nephew, was in the house of his mother's brother all night. It can be proved. His uncle will swear that he did not leave the kampong."

Mr. Warburton turned upon him with a frown.

"Tuan Cooper was killed by Abas. You know it as well as I know. Justice must be done."

"Tuan, you would not hang him?"

Mr. Warburton hesitated an instant, and though his voice remained set and stern a change came into his eyes. It was a flicker which the Malay was quick to notice and across his own eyes flashed an answering look of understanding.

"The provocation was very great. Abas will be sentenced to a term of imprisonment." There was a pause while Mr. Warburton helped himself to marmalade. "When he has served a part of his sentence in prison I will take him into this house as a boy. You can train him in his duties. I have no doubt that in the house of Tuan Cooper he got into bad habits."

"Shall Abas give himself up, Tuan?"

"It would be wise of him."

The boy withdrew. Mr. Warburton took his Times and neatly slit the wrapper. He loved to unfold the heavy, rustling pages. The morning, so fresh and cool, was delicious and for a moment his eyes wandered out over his garden with a friendly glance. A great weight had been lifted from his mind. He turned to the columns in which were announced the births, deaths, and marriages. That was what he always looked at first. A name he knew caught his attention. Lady Ormskirk had had a son at last. By George, how pleased the old dowager must be! He would write her a note of congratulation by the next mail.

Abas would make a very good house-boy.

That fool Cooper!

◆ ——————————————————————————— ◆

"CRUEL AND BARBAROUS TREATMENT"

Mary McCarthy

She could not bear to hurt her husband. She impressed this on the Young Man, on her confidantes, and finally on her husband himself. The thought of Telling Him actually made her heart turn over in a sudden and sickening way, she said. This was true, and yet she knew that being a potential divorcee was deeply pleasurable in somewhat the same way that being an engaged girl had been. In both cases, there was at first a subterranean courtship, whose significance it was necessary to conceal from outside observers. The concealment of the original, premarital courtship had, however, been a mere superstitious gesture, briefly sustained. It had also been, on the whole, a private secretiveness, not a partnership of silence. One put one's family and one's friends off the track because one was still afraid that the affair might not come out right, might not lead in a clean, direct line to the altar. To confess one's aspirations might be, in the end, to publicize one's failure. Once a solid understanding had been reached, there followed a short intermission of ritual bashfulness, in which both parties awkwardly participated, and then came the Announcement.

But with the extramarital courtship, the deception was prolonged where it had been ephemeral, necessary where it had been frivolous, conspiratorial where it had been lonely. It was, in short, serious where it had been dilettantish. That it was accompanied by feelings of guilt, by sharp and genuine revulsions, only complicated and deepened its delights, by abrading the sensibilities, and by imposing a sense of outlawry and consequent mutual dependence upon the lovers. But what this interlude of deception gave her, above all, she recognized, was an opportunity, unparalleled in her experience, for excercising feelings of superiority over others. For her husband she had, she believed, only sympathy and compunction. She got no fun, she told the Young Man, out of putting horns on her darling's head, and never for a moment, she said, did he appear to her as the comic figure of the cuckolded husband that one saw on the stage. (The Young Man assured her that his own sentiments were equally delicate, that for the wronged man he felt the most profound respect, tinged with consideration.) It was as if by the mere act of betraying her husband, she had adequately bested him; it was supererogatory for her to gloat, and, if she gloated at all, it was over her fine restraint in not-gloating, over the integrity of her moral sense, which al-

lowed her to preserve even while engaged in sinfulness the
acute realization of sin and shame. Her overt superiority
feelings she reserved for her friends. Lunches and teas,
which had been timekillers, matters of routine, now became
perilous and dramatic adventures. The Young Man's name
was a bright, highly explosive ball which she bounced casually back and forth in these feminine tête-à-têtes. She would
discuss him in his status of friend of the family, speculate on
what girls he might have, attack him or defend him, anato-
mize him, keeping her eyes clear and impersonal, her voice
empty of special emphasis, her manner humorously detached. *While all the time . . . !*

Three times a week or oftener, at lunch or tea, she would
let herself tremble thus on the exquisite edge of self-betrayal,
involving her companions in a momentous game whose
rules and whose risks only she herself knew. The Public
Appearances were even more satisfactory. To meet at a
friend's house by design and to register surprise, to strike
just the right note of young-matronly affection at cocktail
parties, to treat him formally as "my escort" at the theater
during intermissions—these were triumphs of stage management, more difficult of execution, more nerve-racking
than the lunches and teas, because *two* actors were involved. His overardent glance must be hastily deflected; his
too-self-conscious reading of his lines must be entered in
the debit side of her ledger of love, in anticipation of an
indulgent accounting in private.

The imperfections of his performance were, indeed, pleasing to her. Not, she thought, because his impetuosities, his
gaucheries, demonstrated the sincerity of his passion for
her, nor because they proved him a new hand at this game
of intrigue, but rather because the high finish of her own
acting showed off well in comparison. "I should have gone
on the stage," she could tell him gaily, "or been a diplomat's
wife or an international spy," while he would admiringly
agree. Actually, she doubted whether she could ever have
been an actress, acknowledging that she found it more

amusing and more gratifying to play herself than to inter-
pret any character conceived by a dramatist. In these private theatricals it was her own many-faceted nature that she
put on exhibit, and the audience, in this case unfortunately
limited to two, could applaud both her skill of projection
and her intrinsic variety. Furthermore, this was a play in
which the donnée was real, and the penalty for a missed cue
or an inopportune entrance was, at first anyway, unthinkable.

She loved him, she knew, for being a bad actor, for his
docility in accepting her tender, mock-impatient instruction. Those superiority feelings were fattening not only on
the gullibility of her friends, but also on the comic flaws of
her lover's character, and on the vulnerability of her lover's
position. In this particular hive she was undoubtedly queen
bee.

The Public Appearances were not exclusively duets. They
sometimes took the form of a trio. On these occasions the
studied and benevolent carefulness which she always showed
for her husband's feelings served a double purpose. She
would affect a conspicuous domesticity, an affectionate con-
jugal demonstrativeness, would sprinkle her conversation
with "Darlings," and punctuate it with pats and squeezes till
her husband would visibly expand and her lover plainly and
painfully shrink. For the Young Man no retaliation was
possible. These endearments of hers were sanctioned by
law, usage, and habit; they belonged to her rôle of wife and
could not be condemned or paralleled by a young man who
was himself unmarried. They were clear provocations, but
they could not be called so, and the Young Man preferred
not to speak of them. *But she knew*. . . . Though she was
aware of the sadistic intention of these displays, she was not
ashamed of them, as she was sometimes twistingly ashamed
of the hurt she was preparing to inflict on her husband.
Partly she felt that they were punishments which the Young
Man richly deserved for the wrong he was doing her husband, and that she herself in contriving them was acting,
quite fittingly, both as judge and accused. Partly, too, she
believed herself justified in playing the fond wife, whatever

the damage to her lover's ego, because, in a sense, she actually was a fond wife. She *did* have these feelings, she insisted, whether she was exploiting them or not.

Eventually, however, her reluctance to wound her husband and her solicitude for his pride were overcome by an inner conviction that her love affair must move on to its next preordained stage. The possibilities of the subterranean courtship had been exhausted; it was time for the Announcement. She and the Young Man began to tell each other in a rather breathless and literary style that the Situation Was Impossible, and Things Couldn't Go On This Way Any Longer. The ostensible meaning of these flurried laments was that, under present conditions, they were not seeing enough of each other, that their hours together were too short and their periods of separation too dismal, that the whole business of deception had become morally distasteful to them. Perhaps the Young Man really believed these things; she did not. For the first time, she saw that the virtue of marriage as an institution lay in its public character. Private cohabitation, long continued, was, she concluded, a bore. Whatever the coziness of isolation, the warm delights of having a secret, a love affair finally reached the point where it needed the glare of publicity to revive the interest of its protagonists. Hence, she thought, the engagement parties, the showers, the big church weddings, the presents, the receptions. These were simply socially approved devices by which the lovers got themselves talked about. The gosssip-value of a divorce and remarriage was obviously far greater than the gossip-value of a mere engagement, and she was now ready, indeed hungry, to hear What People Would Say.

The lunches, the teas, the Public Appearances were getting a little flat. It was not, in the end, enough to be a Woman With A Secret, if to one's friends one appeared to be a woman without a secret. The bliss of having a secret required, in short, the consummation of telling it, and she looked forward to the My-dear-I-had-no-idea's, the I-thought-you-and-Bill-were-so-happy-together's, the How-did-you-keep-it-so-dark's with which her intimates would greet her announcement. The audience of two no longer sufficed her; she required a larger stage. She tried it first, a little nervously, on two or three of her closest friends, swearing them to secrecy. "Bill must hear it first from me," she declared. "It would be too terrible for his pride if he found out afterwards that the whole town knew it before he did. So you mustn't tell, even later on, that I told you about this today. I felt I had to talk to someone." After these lunches she would hurry to a phone booth to give the Young Man the gist of the conversation, just as a reporter, sent to cover a fire, telephones in to the city desk. "She certainly was surprised," she could always say with a little gush of truimph. "But she thinks it's fine." *But did they actually?* She could not be sure. Was it possible that she sensed in these luncheon companions, her dearest friends, a certain reserve, a certain unexpressed judgment?

It was a pity, she reflected, that she was so sensitive to public opinion. "I couldn't really love a man," she murmured to herself once, "if everybody didn't think he was wonderful." Everyone seemed to like the Young Man, of course. *But still.* . . . She was getting panicky, she thought. Surely it was only common sense that nobody is admired by everybody. And even if a man were universally despised, would there not be a kind of defiant nobility in loving him in the teeth of the whole world? There would, certainly, but it was a type of heroism that she would scarcely be called upon to practice, for the Young Man was popular, he was invited everywhere, he danced well, his manners were ingratiating, he kept up intellectually. But was he not perhaps *too* amiable, *too* accommodating? Was it for this that her friends seemed silently to criticize him?

At this time a touch of acridity entered into her relations with the Young Man. Her indulgent scoldings had an edge to them now, and it grew increasingly difficult for her to keep her make-believe impatience from becoming real. She would look for dark spots in his character and drill away at them as relentlessly as a dentist at a cavity. A compulsive didacticism possessed her: no truism of his, no cliché, no ineffectual joke could pass the rigidity of her censorship. And, hard as she tried to maintain the character of charming schoolmistress, the Young Man, she saw, was taking alarm. She suspected that, frightened and puzzled, he contemplated flight. She found herself watching him with scientific interest, speculating as to what course he would take, and she was relieved but faintly disappointed when it became clear that he ascribed her sharpness to the tension of the situation and had decided to stick it out.

The moment had come for her to tell her husband. By this single, cathartic act, she would, she believed, rid herself of the doubts and anxieties that beset her. If her husband were to impugn the Young Man's character, she could answer his accusations and at the same time discount them as arising from jealousy. From her husband, at least, she might expect the favor of an open attack to which she could respond with the prepared defense that she carried, unspoken, about with her. Further, she had an intense, childlike curiosity as to How Her Husband Would Take It, a curiosity which she disguised for decency's sake as justifiable apprehension. The confidences already imparted to her friends seemed like pale dress rehearsals of the supreme confidence she was about to make. Perhaps it was toward this moment that the whole affair had been tending, for this moment that the whole affair had been designed. This would be the ultimate testing of her husband's love, its final, rounded, quintessential expression. Never, she thought, when you live with a man do you feel the full force of his love. It is gradually rationed out to you in an impure state, compounded with all the other elements of daily existence, so that you are hardly sensible of receiving it. There is no single point at which it is concentrated; it spreads out into the past and the future until it appears as a nearly imperceptible film over the surface of your life. Only face to face with its own annihilation could it show itself wholly, and, once shown, drop into the category of completed experiences.

She was not disappointed. She told him at breakfast in a

fashionable restaurant, because, she said, he would be better able to control his feelings in public. When he called at once for the check, she had a spasm of alarm lest in an access of brutality or grief he leave her there alone, conspicuous, and, as it were, unfulfilled. But they walked out of the restaurant together and through the streets, hand in hand, tears streaming, "unchecked," she whispered to herself, down their faces. Later they were in the Park, by an artificial lake, watching the ducks swim. The sun was very bright, and she felt a kind of superb pathos in the careful and irrelevant attention they gave to the pastoral scene. This was, she knew, the most profound, the most subtle, the most idyllic experience of her life. All the strings of her nature were, at last, vibrant. She was both doer and sufferer: she inflicted pain and participated in it. And she was, at the same time, physician, for, as she was the weapon that dealt the wound, she was also the balm that could assuage it. Only she could know the hurt that engrossed him, and it was to her that he turned for the sympathy she had ready for him. Finally, though she offered him his discharge slip with one hand, with the other she beckoned him to approach. She was wooing him all over again, but wooing him to a deeper attachment than he had previously experienced, to an unconditional surrender. She was demanding his total understanding of her, his compassion, and his forgiveness. When at last he answered her repeated and agonized I-love-you's by grasping her hand more tightly and saying gently, "I know," she saw that she had won him over. She had drawn him into a truly mystical union. Their marriage was complete.

Afterwards everything was more prosaic. The Young Man had to be telephoned and summoned to a conference à trois, a conference, she said, of civilized, intelligent people. The Young Man was a little awkward, even dropped a tear or two, which embarrassed everyone else, but what after all, she thought, could you expect? He was in a difficult position; his was a thankless part. With her husband behaving so well, indeed, so gallantly, the Young Man could not fail to look a trifle inadequate. The Young Man would have preferred it, of course, if her husband had made a scene, had bullied or threatened her, so that he himself might have acted the chivalrous protector. She, however, did not hold her husband's heroic courtesy against him: in some way, it reflected credit on herself. The Young Man, apparently, was expecting to Carry Her Off, but this she would not allow. "It would be too heartless," she whispered when they were alone for a moment. "We must all go somewhere together."

So the three went out for a drink, and she watched with a sort of desperation her husband's growing abstraction, the more and more perfunctory attention he accorded the conversation she was so bravely sustaining. "He is bored," she thought. "He is going to leave." The prospect of being left alone with the Young Man seemed suddenly unendurable. If her husband were to go now, he would take with him the third dimension that had given the affair depth, and abandon her to a flat and vulgar love scene. Terrified, she wondered whether she had not already prolonged the drama beyond its natural limits, whether the confession in the restaurant and the absolution in the Park had not rounded off the artistic whole, whether the sequel of divorce and remarriage would not, in fact, constitute an anticlimax. Already she sensed that behind her husband's good manners an ironical attitude toward herself had sprung up. Was it possible that he had believed that they would return from the Park and all would continue as before? It was conceivable that her protestations of love had been misleading, and that his enormous tenderness toward her had been based, not on the idea that he was giving her up, but rather on the idea that he was taking her back—with no questions asked. If that were the case, the telephone call, the conference, and the excursion had in his eyes been a monstrous gaffe, a breach of sensibility and good taste, for which he would never forgive her. She blushed violently. Looking at him again, she thought he was watching her with an expression which declared: I have found you out: now I know what you are like. For the first time, she felt him utterly alienated.

When he left them she experienced the let-down she had feared but also a kind of relief. She told herself that it was as well that he had cut himself off from her: it made her decision simpler. There was now nothing for her to do but to push the love affair to its conclusion, whatever that might be, and this was probably what she most deeply desired. Had the poignant intimacy of the Park persisted, she might have been tempted to drop the adventure she had begun and return to her routine. But that was, looked at coldly, unthinkable. For if the adventure would seem a little flat after the scene in the Park, the resumption of her marriage would seem even flatter. If the drama of the triangle had been amputated by her confession, the curtain had been brought down with a smack on the drama of wedlock.

And, as it turned out, the drama of the triangle was not quite ended by the superficial rupture of her marriage. Though she had left her husband's apartment and been offered shelter by a confidante, it was still necessary for her to see him every day. There were clothes to be packed, and possessions to be divided, love letters to be reread and mementos to be wept over in common. There were occasional passionate, unconsummated embraces; there were endearments and promises. And though her husband's irony remained, it was frequently vulnerable. It was not, as she had at first thought, an armor against her, but merely a sword, out of *Tristan and Isolde*, which lay permanently between them and enforced discretion.

They met often, also, at the houses of friends, for, as she said, "What can I do? I know it's not tactful, but we all know the same people. You can't expect me to give up my friends." These Public Appearances were heightened in interest by the fact that these audiences, unlike the earlier ones, had, as it were, purchased librettos, and were in full possession of the intricacies of the plot. She preferred, she decided, the evening parties to the cocktail parties, for there she could dance alternately with her lover and her husband to the accompaniment of subdued gasps on the part of the bystanders.

This interlude was at the same time festive and heart-rending: her only dull moments were the evenings she spent alone with the Young Man. Unfortunately, the Post-Announcement period was only too plainly an interlude and its very nature demanded that it be followed by something else. She could not preserve her anomalous status indefinitely. It was not decent, and, besides, people would be bored. From the point of view of one's friends, it was all very well to entertain a Triangle as a novelty; to cope with it as a permanent problem was a different matter. Once they had all three gotten drunk, and there was a scene, and, though everyone talked about it afterwards, her friends were, she thought, a little colder, a little more critical. People began to ask her when she was going to Reno. Furthermore, she noticed that her husband was getting a slight edge in popularity over the Young Man. It was natural, of course, that everyone should feel sorry for him, and be especially nice. *But yet.* . . .

When she learned from her husband that he was receiving invitations from members of her own circle, invitations in which she and the Young Man were unaccountably not included, she went at once to the station and bought her ticket. Her good-bye to her husband, which she had privately allocated to her last hours in town, took place prematurely, two days before she was to leave. He was rushing off to what she inwardly feared was a Gay Weekend in the country; he had only a few minutes; he wished her a pleasant trip; and he would write, of course. His highball was drained while her glass still stood half full; he sat forward nervously on his chair; and she knew herself to be acting the Ancient Mariner, but her dignity would not allow her to hurry. She hoped that he would miss his train for her, but he did not. He left her sitting in the bar, and that night the Young Man could not, as he put it, do a thing with her. There was nowhere, absolutely nowhere, she said passionately, that she wanted to go, nobody she wanted to see, nothing she wanted to do. "You need a drink," he said with the air of a diagnostician. "A drink," she answered bitterly.

"I'm sick of the drinks we've been having. Gin, whiskey, rum, what else is there?" He took her into a bar, and she cried, but he bought her a fancy mixed drink, something called a Ramos gin fizz, and she was a little appeased because she had never had one before. Then some friends came in, and they all had another drink together, and she felt better. "There," said the Young Man, on the way home, "don't I know what's good for you? Don't I know how to handle you?" "Yes," she answered in her most humble and feminine tones, but she knew that they had suddenly dropped into a new pattern, that they were no longer the cynosure of a social group, but merely another young couple with an evening to pass, another young couple looking desperately for entertainment, wondering whether to call on a married couple or to drop in somewhere for a drink. This time the Young Man's prescription had worked, but it was pure luck that they had chanced to meet someone they knew. A second or a third time they would scan the faces of the other drinkers in vain, would order a second drink and surreptitiously watch the door, and finally go out alone, with a quite detectable air of being unwanted.

When, a day and a half later, the Young Man came late to take her to the train, and they had to run down the platform to catch it, she found him all at once detestable. He would ride to 125th Street with her, he declared in a burst of gallantry, but she was angry all the way because she was afraid there would be trouble with the conductor. At 125th Street, he stood on the platform blowing kisses to her and shouting something that she could not hear through the glass. She made a gesture of repugnance, but, seeing him flinch, seeing him weak and charming and incompetent, she brought her hand reluctantly to her lips and blew a kiss back. The other passengers were watching, she was aware, and though their looks were doting and not derisive, she felt herself to be humiliated and somehow vulgarized. When the train began to move, and the Young Man began to run down the platform after it, still blowing kisses and shouting alternately, she got up, turned sharply away from the win-

dow and walked back to the Club car. There she sat down
and ordered a whiskey and soda.

There were a number of men in the car, who looked up in
unison as she gave her order, but, observing that they were
all the middle-aged, small-business-men who "belonged" as
inevitably to the club car as the white-coated porter and the
leather-bound *Saturday Evening Post*, she paid them no
heed. She was now suddenly overcome by a sense of depression and loss that was unprecedented for being in no
way dramatic or pleasurable. In the last half hour she had
seen clearly that she would never marry the Young Man,
and she found herself looking into an insubstantial future
with no signpost to guide her. Almost all women, she thought,
when they are girls never believe that they will get married.
The terror of spinsterhood hangs over them from adoles-
cence on. Even if they are popular they think that no one
really interesting will want them enough to marry them.
Even if they get engaged they are afraid that something will
go wrong, something will intervene. When they do get
married it seems to them a sort of miracle, and, after they
have been married for a time, though in retrospect the
whole process looks perfectly natural and inevitable, they
retain a certain unarticulated pride in the wonder they have
performed. Finally, however, the terror of spinsterhood has
been so thoroughly exorcised that they forget ever having
been haunted by it, and it is at this stage that they contem-
plate divorce. "How could I have forgotten?" she said to
herself and began to wonder what she would do.

She could take an apartment by herself in the Village.
She would meet new people. She would entertain. But, she
thought, if I have people in for cocktails, there will always
come the moment when they have to leave, and I will be
alone and have to pretend to have another engagement in
order to save embarrassment. If I have them to dinner, it
will be the same thing, but at least I will not have to
pretend to have an engagement. I shall give dinners. Then,
she thought, there will be the cocktail parties, and, if I go
alone, I shall always stay a little too late, hoping that a

young man or even a party of people will ask me to dinner. And if I fail, if no one asks me, I shall have the ignominy of walking out alone, trying to look as if I had somewhere to go. Then there will be the evenings at home with a good book when there will be no reason at all for going to bed, and I shall perhaps sit up all night. And the mornings when there will be no point in getting up, and I shall perhaps stay in bed till dinnertime. There will be the dinners in tea rooms with other unmarried women, tea rooms because women alone look conspicuous and forlorn in good restaurants. And then, she thought, I shall get older.

She would never, she reflected angrily, have taken this step, had she felt that she was burning her bridges behind her. She would never have left one man unless she had had another to take his place. But the Young Man, she now saw, was merely a sort of mirage which she had allowed herself to mistake for an oasis. "If the Man," she muttered, "did not exist, the Moment would create him." This was what had happened to her. She had made herself the victim of an imposture. But, she argued, with an access of cheerfulness, if this were true, if out of the need of a second, a new, husband she had conjured up the figure of one, she had possibly been impelled by unconscious forces to behave more intelligently than appearances would indicate. She was perhaps acting out in a sort of hypnotic trance a ritual whose meaning had not yet been revealed to her, a ritual which required that, first of all, the Husband be eliminated from the cast of characters. Conceivably, she was designed for the rôle of *femme fatale*, and for such a personage considerations of safety, provisions against loneliness and old age, were not only Philistine but irrelevant. She might marry a second, a third, a fourth time, or she might never marry again. But, in any case, for the thrifty bourgeois love-insurance, with its daily payments of patience, forbearance, and resignation, she was no longer eligible. She would be, she told herself delightedly, a bad risk.

She was, or soon would be, a Young Divorcee, and the term still carried glamor. Her divorce decree would be a

passport conferring on her the status of citizeness of the
world. She felt gratitude toward the Young Man for having
unwittingly effected her transit into a new life. She looked
about her at the other passengers. Later she would talk to
them. They would ask, of course, where she was bound for;
that was the regulation opening move of train conversations.
But it was a delicate question what her reply should be. To
say "Reno" straight out would be vulgar; it would smack of
confidences too cheaply given. Yet to lie, to say "San Francisco" for instance, would be to cheat herself, to minimize
her importance, to mislead her interlocutor into believing
her an ordinary traveler with a commonplace destination.
There must be some middle course which would give information without appearing to do so, which would hint at a
vie galante yet indicate a barrier of impeccable reserve. It
would probably be best, she decided, to say "West" at first,
with an air of vagueness and hesitation. Then, when pressed,
she might go so far as to say "Nevada." But no farther.

◆ ──────────────────────────────────── ◆

THE SOJOURNER

Carson McCullers

The twilight border between sleep and waking was a Roman
one this morning: splashing fountains and arched, narrow
streets, the golden lavish city of blossoms and age-soft stone.
Sometimes in this semi-consciousness he sojourned again in
Paris, or war German rubble, or Swiss skiing and a snow
hotel. Sometimes, also, in a fallow Georgia field at hunting
dawn. Rome it was this morning in the yearless region of
dreams.

John Ferris awoke in a room in a New York hotel. He had the feeling that something unpleasant was awaiting him—what it was, he did not know. The feeling, submerged by matinal necessities, lingered even after he had dressed and gone downstairs. It was a cloudless autumn day and the pale sunlight sliced between the pastel skyscrapers. Ferris went into the next-door drugstore and sat at the end booth next to the window glass that overlooked the sidewalk. He ordered an American breakfast with scrambled eggs and sausage.

Ferris had come from Paris to his father's funeral which had taken place the week before in his home town in Georgia. The shock of death had made him aware of youth already passed. His hair was receding and the veins in his now naked temples were pulsing and prominent and his body was spare except for an incipient belly bulge. Ferris had loved his father and the bond between them had once been extraordinarily close—but the years had somehow unraveled this filial devotion; the death, expected for a long time, had left him with an unforseen dismay. He had stayed as long as possible to be near his mother and brothers at home. His plane for Paris was to leave the next morning.

Ferris pulled out his address book to verify a number. He turned the pages with growing attentiveness. Names and addresses from New York, the capitals of Europe, a few faint ones from his home state in the South. Faded, printed names, sprawled drunken ones. Betty Wills: a random love, married now. Charlie Williams: wounded in the Hürtgen Forest, unheard of since. Grand old Williams—did he live or die? Don Walker: a B.T.O. in television, getting rich. Henry Green: hit the skids after the war, in a sanitarium now, they say. Cozie Hall: he had heard that she was dead. Heedless, laughing Cozie—it was strange to think that she too, silly girl, could die. As Ferris closed the address book, he suffered a sense of hazard, transience, almost of fear.

It was then that his body jerked suddenly. He was staring out of the window when there on the sidewalk, passing by, was his ex-wife. Elizabeth passed quite close to him, walking slowly. He could not understand the wild quiver of his heart, nor the following sense of recklessness and grace that lingered after she was gone.

Quickly Ferris paid his check and rushed out to the sidewalk. Elizabeth stood on the corner waiting to cross Fifth Avenue. He hurried toward her meaning to speak, but the lights changed and she crossed the street before he reached her. Ferris followed. On the other side he could easily have overtaken her, but he found himself lagging unaccountably. Her fair brown hair was plainly rolled, and as he watched her Ferris recalled that once his father had remarked that Elizabeth had a 'beautiful carriage.' She turned at the next corner and Ferris followed, although by now his intention to overtake her had disappeared. Ferris questioned the bodily disturbance that the sight of Elizabeth aroused in him, the dampness of his hands, the hard heartstrokes.

It was eight years since Ferris had last seen his ex-wife. He knew that long ago she had married again. And there were children. During recent years he had seldom thought of her. But at first, after the divorce, the loss had almost destroyed him. Then after the anodyne of time, he had loved again, and then again. Jeannine, she was now. Certainly his love for his ex-wife was long since past. So why the unhinged body, the shaken mind? He knew only that his clouded heart was oddly dissonant with the sunny, candid autumn day. Ferris wheeled suddenly and, walking with long strides, almost running, hurried back to the hotel.

Ferris poured himself a drink, although it was not yet eleven o'clock. He sprawled out in an armchair like a man exhausted, nursing his glass of bourbon and water. He had a full day ahead of him as he was leaving by plane the next morning for Paris. He checked over his obligations: take luggage to Air France, lunch with his boss, buy shoes and an overcoat. And something—wasn't there something else? Ferris finished his drink and opened the telephone directory.

His decision to call his ex-wife was impulsive. The number was under Bailey, the husband's name, and he called before he had much time for self-debate. He and Elizabeth had exchanged cards at Christmastime, and Ferris had sent a carving set when he received the announcement of her wedding. There was no reason *not* to call. But as he waited, listening to the ring at the other end, misgiving fretted him.

Elizabeth answered; her familiar voice was a fresh shock to him. Twice he had to repeat his name, but when he was identified, she sounded glad. He explained he was only in town for that day. They had a theater engagement, she said—but she wondered if he would come by for an early dinner. Ferris said he would be delighted.

As he went from one engagement to another, he was still bothered at odd moments by the feeling that something necessary was forgotten. Ferris bathed and changed in the late afternoon, often thinking about Jeannine: he would be with her the following night. 'Jeannine,' he would say, 'I happened to run into my ex-wife when I was in New York. Had dinner with her. And her husband, of course. It was strange seeing her after all these years.'

Elizabeth lived in the East Fifties, and as Ferris taxied uptown he glimpsed at intersections the lingering sunset, but by the time he reached his destination it was already autumn dark. The place was a building with a marquee and a doorman, and the apartment was on the seventh floor.

'Come in, Mr. Ferris.'

Braced for Elizabeth or even the unimagined husband, Ferris was astonished by the freckled red-haired child; he had known of the children, but his mind had failed somehow to acknowledge them. Surprise made him step back awkwardly.

'This is our apartment,' the child said politely. 'Aren't you Mr. Ferris? I'm Billy. Come in.'

In the living room beyond the hall, the husband provided another surprise; he too had not been acknowledged emotionally. Bailey was a lumbering red-haired man with a deliberate manner. He rose and extended a welcoming hand.

'I'm Bill Bailey. Glad to see you. Elizabeth will be in, in a minute. She's finishing dressing.'

The last words struck a gliding series of vibrations, memories of the other years. Fair Elizabeth, rosy and naked before her bath. Half-dressed before the mirror of her dressing table, brushing her fine, chestnut hair. Sweet, casual intimacy, the soft-fleshed loveliness indisputably possessed. Ferris shrank from the unbidden memories and compelled himself to meet Bill Bailey's gaze.

'Billy, will you please bring that tray of drinks from the kitchen table?'

The child obeyed promptly, and when he was gone Ferris remarked conversationally, 'Fine boy you have there.'

'We think so.'

Flat silence until the child returned with a tray of glasses and a cocktail shaker of Martinis. With the priming drinks they pumped up conversation: Russia, they spoke of, and the New York rain-making, and the apartment situation in Manhattan and Paris.

'Mr. Ferris is flying all the way across the ocean tomorrow,' Bailey said to the little boy who was perched on the arm of his chair, quiet and well behaved. 'I bet you would like to be a stowaway in his suitcase.'

Billy pushed back his limp bangs. 'I want to fly in an airplane and be a newspaperman like Mr. Ferris.' He added with sudden assurance, 'That's what I would like to do when I am big.'

Bailey said, 'I thought you wanted to be a doctor.'

'I do!' said Billy. 'I would like to be both. I want to be a atom-bomb scientist too.'

Elizabeth came in carrying in her arms a baby girl.

'Oh, John!' she said. She settled the baby in the father's lap. 'It's grand to see you. I'm awfully glad you could come.'

The little girl sat demurely on Bailey's knees. She wore a pale pink crepe de Chine frock, smocked around the yoke with rose, and a matching silk hair ribbon tying back her pale soft curls. Her skin was summer tanned and her brown eyes flecked with gold and laughing. When she reached up and fingered her father's horn-rimmed glasses, he took them off and let her look through them a moment. 'How's my old Candy?'

Elizabeth was very beautiful, more beautiful perhaps than he had ever realized. Her straight clean hair was shining. Her face was softer, glowing and serene. It was a madonna loveliness, dependent on the family ambiance.

'You've hardly changed at all,' Elizabeth said, 'but it has been a long time.'

'Eight years.' His hand touched his thinning hair self-consciously while further amenities were exchanged.

Ferris felt himself suddenly a spectator—an interloper among these Baileys. Why had he come? He suffered. His own life seemed so solitary, a fragile column supporting nothing amidst the wreckage of the years. He felt he could not bear much longer to stay in the family room.

He glanced at his watch. 'You're going to the theater?'

'It's a shame,' Elizabeth said, 'but we've had this engagement for more than a month. But surely, John, you'll be staying home one of these days before long. You're not going to be an expatriate, are you?'

'Expatriate,' Ferris repeated. 'I don't much like the word.'

'What's a better word?' she asked.

He thought for a moment. 'Sojourner might do.'

Ferris glanced again at his watch, and again Elizabeth apologized. 'If only we had known ahead of time—'

'I just had this day in town. I came home unexpectedly. You see, Papa died last week.'

'Papa Ferris is dead?'

'Yes, at Johns-Hopkins. He had been sick there nearly a year. The funeral was down home in Georgia.'

'Oh, I'm so sorry, John. Papa Ferris was always one of my favorite people.'

The little boy moved from behind the chair so that he could look into his mother's face. He asked, 'Who is dead?'

Ferris was oblivious to apprehension; he was thinking of his father's death. He saw again the outstretched body on the quilted silk within the coffin. The corpse flesh was bizarrely rouged and the familiar hands lay massive and joined above a spread of funeral roses. The memory closed and Ferris awakened to Elizabeth's calm voice.

'Mr. Ferris's father, Billy. A really grand person. Somebody you didn't know.'

'But why did you call him *Papa* Ferris?'

Bailey and Elizabeth exchanged a trapped look. It was Bailey who answered the questioning child. 'A long time ago,' he said, 'your mother and Mr. Ferris were once married. Before you were born—a long time ago.'

'Mr. Ferris?'

The little boy stared at Ferris, amazed and unbelieving. And Ferris's eyes, as he returned the gaze, were somehow unbelieving too. Was it indeed true that at one time he had called this stranger, Elizabeth, Little Butterduck during nights of love, that they had lived together, shared perhaps a thousand days and nights and—finally—endured in the misery of sudden solitude the fiber by fiber (jealousy, alcohol and money quarrels) destruction of the fabric of married love.

Bailey said to the children, 'It's somebody's suppertime. Come on now.'

'But Daddy! Mama and Mr. Ferris—I—'

Billy's everlasting eyes—perplexed and with a glimmer of hostility—reminded Ferris of the gaze of another child. It was the young son of Jeannine—a boy of seven with a shadowed little face and knobby knees whom Ferris avoided and usually forgot.

'Quick march!' Bailey gently turned Billy toward the door. 'Say good night now, son.'

'Good night, Mr. Ferris.' He added resentfully, 'I thought I was staying up for the cake.'

'You can come in afterward for the cake,' Elizabeth said. 'Run along now with Daddy for your supper.'

Ferris and Elizabeth were alone. The weight of the situation descended on those first moments of silence. Ferris asked permission to pour himself another drink and Elizabeth set the cocktail shaker on the table at his side. He looked at the grand piano and noticed the music on the rack.

'Do you still play as beautifully as you used to?'

'I still enjoy it.'

'Please play, Elizabeth.'

Elizabeth arose immediately. Her readiness to perform when asked had always been one of her amiabilities; she never hung back, apologized. Now as she approached the piano there was the added readiness of relief.

She began with a Bach prelude and fugue. The prelude was as gaily iridescent as a prism in a morning room. The first voice of the fugue, an announcement pure and solitary, was repeated intermingling with a second voice, and again repeated within an elaborated frame, the multiple music, horizontal and serene, flowed with unhurried majesty. The principal melody was woven with two other voices, embellished with countless ingenuities—now dominant, again submerged, it had the sublimity of a single thing that does not fear surrender to the whole. Toward the end, the density of the material gathered for the last enriched insistence on the dominant first motif and with a chorded final statement the fugue ended. Ferris rested his head on the chair back and closed his eyes. In the following silence a clear, high voice came from the room down the hall.

'Daddy, how *could* Mama and Mr. Ferris—' A door was closed.

The piano began again—what was this music? Unplaced, familiar, the limpid melody had lain a long while dormant in his heart. Now it spoke to him of another time, another place—it was the music Elizabeth used to play. The delicate air summoned a wilderness of memory. Ferris was lost in the riot of past longings, conflicts, ambivalent desires. Strange that the music, catalyst for this tumultuous anarchy, was so serene and clear. The singing melody was broken off by the appearance of the maid.

'Miz Bailey, dinner is out on the table now.'

Even after Ferris was seated at the table between his host and hostess, the unfinished music still overcast his mood. He was a little drunk.

'L'improvisation de la vie humaine,' he said. 'There's noth-

ing that makes you so aware of the improvisation of human existence as a song unfinished. Or an old address book.'

'Address book?' repeated Bailey. Then he stopped, non-committal and polite.

'You're still the same old boy, Johnny,' Elizabeth said with a trace of the old tenderness.

It was a Southern dinner that evening, and the dishes were his old favorites. They had fried chicken and corn pudding and rich, glazed candied sweet potatoes. During the meal Elizabeth kept alive a conversation when the silences were overlong. And it came about that Ferris was led to speak of Jeannine.

'I first knew Jeannine last autumn—about this time of the year—in Italy. She's a singer and she had an engagement in Rome. I expect we will be married soon.'

The words seemed so true, inevitable, that Ferris did not at first acknowledge to himself the lie. He and Jeannine had never in that year spoken of marriage. And indeed, she was still married—to a White Russian moneychanger in Paris from whom she had been separated for five years. But it was too late to correct the lie. Already Elizabeth was saying: 'This really makes me glad to know. Congratulations, Johnny.'

He tried to make amends with truth. 'The Roman autumn is so beautiful. Balmy and blossoming.' He added, 'Jeannine has a little boy of six. A curious trilingual little fellow. We go to the Tuileries sometimes.'

A lie again. He had taken the boy once to the gardens. The sallow foreign child in shorts that bared his spindly legs had sailed his boat in the concrete pond and ridden the pony. The child had wanted to go in to the puppet show. But there was not time, for Ferris had an engagement at the Scribe Hotel. He had promised they would go to the guignol another afternoon. Only once had he taken Valentin to the Tuileries.

There was a stir. The maid brought in a white-frosted cake with pink candles. The children entered in their night clothes. Ferris still did not understand.

'Happy birthday, John,' Elizabeth said. 'Blow out the candles.'

Ferris recognized his birthday date. The candles blew out lingeringly and there was the smell of burning wax. Ferris was thirty-eight years old. The veins in his temples darkened and pulsed visibly.

'It's time you started for the theater.'

Ferris thanked Elizabeth for the birthday dinner and said the appropriate good-byes. The whole family saw him to the door.

A high, thin moon shone above the jagged, dark skyscrapers. The streets were windy, cold. Ferris hurried to Third Avenue and hailed a cab. He gazed at the nocturnal city with the deliberate attentiveness of departure and perhaps farewell. He was alone. He longed for flighttime and the coming journey.

The next day he looked down on the city from the air, burnished in sunlight, toylike, precise. Then America was left behind and there was only the Atlantic and the distant European shore. The ocean was milky pale and placid beneath the clouds. Ferris dozed most of the day. Toward dark he was thinking of Elizabeth and the visit of the previous evening. He thought of Elizabeth among her family with longing, gentle envy and inexplicable regret. He sought the melody, the unfinished air, that had so moved him. The cadence, some unrelated tones, were all that remained; the melody itself evaded him. He had found instead the first voice of the fugue that Elizabeth had played—it came to him, inverted mockingly and in a minor key. Suspended above the ocean the anxieties of transience and solitude no longer troubled him and he thought of his father's death with equanimity. During the dinner hour the plane reached the shore of France.

At midnight Ferris was in a taxi crossing Paris. It was a clouded night and mist wreathed the lights of the Place de la Concorde. The midnight bistros gleamed on the wet pavements. As always after a transocean flight the change of continents was too sudden. New York at morning, this midnight Paris. Ferris glimpsed the disorder of his life: the succession of cities, of transitory loves; and time, the sinister glissando of the years, time always.

'Vite! Vite!' he called in terror. 'Dépêchez-vous.'

Valentin opened the door to him. The little boy wore pajamas and an outgrown red robe. His grey eyes were shadowed and, as Ferris passed into the flat, they flickered momentarily.

'J'attends Maman.'

Jeannine was singing in a night club. She would not be home before another hour. Valentin returned to a drawing, squatting with his crayons over the paper on the floor. Ferris looked down at the drawing—it was a banjo player with notes and wavy lines inside a comic-strip balloon.

'We will go again to the Tuileries.'

The child looked up and Ferris drew him closer to his knees. The melody, the unfinished music that Elizabeth had played, came to him suddenly. Unsought, the load of memory jettisoned—this time bringing only recognition and sudden joy.

'Monsieur Jean,' the child said, 'did you see him?'

Confused, Ferris thought only of another child—the freckled, family-loved boy. 'See who, Valentin?'

'Your dead papa in Georgia.' The child added, 'Was he okay?'

Ferris spoke with rapid urgency: 'We will go often to the Tuileries. Ride the pony and we will go into the guignol. We will see the puppet show and never be in a hurry any more.'

'Monsieur Jean,' Valentin said. 'The guignol is now closed.'

Again, the terror the acknowledgment of wasted years and death. Valentin, responsive and confident, still nestled in his arms. His cheek touched the soft cheek and felt the brush of the delicate eyelashes. With inner desperation he pressed the child close—as though an emotion as protean as his love could dominate the pulse of time.

THE OPEN WINDOW

"Saki" (H. H. Munro)

"My aunt will be down presently, Mr. Nuttel," said a very self-possessed young lady of fifteen; "in the meantime you must try and put up with me."

Framton Nuttel endeavoured to say the correct some-thing which should duly flatter the niece of the moment without unduly discounting the aunt that was to come. Privately he doubted more than ever whether these formal visits on a succession of total strangers would do much towards helping the nerve cure which he was supposed to be undergoing.

"I know how it will be," his sister had said when he was preparing to migrate to this rural retreat; "you will bury yourself down there and not speak to a living soul, and your nerves will be worse than ever from moping. I shall just give you letters of introduction to all the people I know there. Some of them, as far as I can remember, were quite nice."

Framton wondered whether Mrs. Sappleton, the lady to whom he was presenting one of the letters of introduction, came into the nice division.

"Do you know many of the people round here?" asked the niece, when she judged that they had had sufficient silent communion.

"Hardly a soul," said Framton. "My sister was staying here, at the rectory, you know, some four years ago, and she gave me letters of introduction to some of the people here."

He made the last statement in a tone of distinct regret.

"Then you know practically nothing about my aunt?" pursued the self-possessed young lady.

"Only her name and address," admitted the caller. He was wondering whether Mrs. Sappleton was in the married or widowed state. An undefinable something about the room seemed to suggest masculine habitation.

"Her great tragedy happened just three years ago," said the child; "that would be since your sister's time."

"Her tragedy?" asked Framton; somehow in this restful country spot tragedies seemed out of place.

"You may wonder why we keep that window wide open on an October afternoon," said the niece, indicating a large French window that opened on to a lawn.

"It is quite warm for the time of the year," said Framton; "but has that window got anything to do with the tragedy?"

"Out through that window, three years ago to a day, her husband and her two young brothers went off for their day's shooting. They never came back. In crossing the moor to their favourite snipe-shooting ground they were all three engulfed in a treacherous piece of bog. It had been that dreadful wet summer, you know, and places that were safe in other years gave way suddenly without warning. Their bodies were never recovered. That was the dreadful part of it." Here the child's voice lost its self-possessed note and became falteringly human. "Poor aunt always thinks that they will come back some day, they and the little brown spaniel that was lost with them, and walk in at that window just as they used to do. That is why the window is kept open every evening till it is quite dusk. Poor dear aunt, she has often told me how they went out, her husband with his white waterproof coat over his arm, and Ronnie, her youngest brother, singing, 'Bertie, why do you bound?' as he always did to tease her, because she said it got on her nerves. Do you know, sometimes on still, quiet evenings like this, I almost get a creepy feeling that they will all walk in through that window—"

She broke off with a little shudder. It was a relief to

Framton when the aunt bustled into the room with a whirl of apologies for being late in making her appearance.

"I hope Vera has been amusing you?" she said.

"She has been very interesting," said Framton.

"I hope you don't mind the open window," said Mrs. Sappleton briskly; "my husband and brothers will be home directly from shooting, and they always come in this way. They've been out for snipe in the marshes today, so they'll make a fine mess over my poor carpets. So like you menfolk, isn't it?"

She rattled on cheerfully about the shooting and the scarcity of birds, and the prospects for duck in the winter. To Framton it was all purely horrible. He made a desperate but only partially successful effort to turn the talk on to a less ghastly topic; he was conscious that his hostess was giving him only a fragment of her attention, and her eyes were constantly straying past him to the open window and the lawn beyond. It was certainly an unfortunate coincidence that he should have paid his visit on this tragic anniversary.

"The doctors agree in ordering me complete rest, an absence of mental excitement, and avoidance of anything in the nature of violent physical exercise," announced Framton, who laboured under the tolerably wide-spread delusion that total strangers and chance acquaintances are hungry for the least detail of one's ailments and infirmities, their cause and cure. "On the matter of diet they are not so much in agreement," he continued.

"No?" said Mrs. Sappleton, in a voice which only replaced a yawn at the last moment. Then she suddenly brightened into alert attention—but not to what Framton was saying.

"Here they are at last!" she cried. "Just in time for tea, and don't they look as if they were muddy up to the eyes!"

Framton shivered slightly and turned towards the niece with a look intended to convey sympathetic comprehension. The child was staring out through the open window with dazed horror in her eyes. In a chill shock of nameless fear

Framton swung round in his seat and looked in the same direction.

In the deepening twilight three figures were walking across the lawn towards the window; they all carried guns under their arms, and one of them was additionally burdened with a white coat hung over his shoulders. A tired brown spaniel kept close at their heels. Noiselessly they neared the house, and then a hoarse young voice chanted out of the dusk: "I said, Bertie, why do you bound?"

Framton grabbed wildly at his stick and hat; the hall-door, the gravel-drive, and the front gate were dimly noted stages in his headlong retreat. A cyclist coming along the road had to run into the hedge to avoid imminent collision.

"Here we are, my dear," said the bearer of the white mackintosh, coming in through the window; "fairly muddy, but most of it's dry. Who was that who bolted out as we came up?"

"A most extraordinary man, a Mr. Nuttel," said Mrs. Sappleton; "could only talk about his illnesses, and dashed off without a word of good-bye or apology when you arrived. One would think he had seen a ghost."

"I expect it was the spaniel," said the niece calmly; "he told me he had a horror of dogs. He was once hunted into a cemetery somewhere on the banks of the Ganges by a pack of pariah dogs, and had to spend the night in a newly dug grave with the creatures snarling and grinning and foaming just above him. Enough to make any one lose their nerve."

Romance at short notice was her speciality.

MY OEDIPUS COMPLEX

Frank O'Connor

Father was in the army all through the war—the first war, I mean—so, up to the age of five, I never saw much of him, and what I saw did not worry me. Sometimes I woke and there was a big figure in khaki peering down at me in the candlelight. Sometimes in the early morning I heard the slamming of the front door and the clatter of nailed boots down the cobbles of the lane. These were Father's entrances and exits. Like Santa Claus he came and went mysteriously.

In fact, I rather liked his visits, though it was an uncomfortable squeeze between Mother and him when I got into the big bed in the early morning. He smoked, which gave him a pleasant musty smell, and shaved, an operation of astounding interest. Each time he left a trail of souvenirs—model tanks and Gurkha knives with handles made of bullet cases, and German helmets and cap badges and button-sticks, and all sorts of military equipment—carefully stowed away in a long box on top of the wardrobe, in case they ever came in handy. There was a bit of the magpie about Father; he expected everything to come in handy. When his back was turned, Mother let me get a chair and rummage through his treasures. She didn't seem to think so highly of them as he did.

The war was the most peaceful period of my life. The

window of my attic faced southeast. My mother had curtained it, but that had small effect. I always woke with the first light and, with all the responsibilities of the previous day melted, feeling myself rather like the sun, ready to illumine and rejoice. Life never seemed so simple and clear and full of possibilities as then. I put my feet out from under the clothes—I called them Mrs. Left and Mrs. Right—and invented dramatic situations for them in which they discussed the problems of the day. At least Mrs. Right did; she was very demonstrative, but I hadn't the same control of Mrs. Left, so she mostly contented herself with nodding agreement.

They discussed what Mother and I should do during the day, what Santa Claus should give a fellow for Christmas, and what steps should be taken to brighten the home. There was that little matter of the baby, for instance. Mother and I could never agree about that. Ours was the only house in the terrace without a new baby, and Mother said we couldn't afford one till Father came back from the war because they cost seventeen and six. That showed how simple she was. The Geneys up the road had a baby, and everyone knew they couldn't afford seventeen and six. It was probably a cheap baby, and Mother wanted something really good, but I felt she was too exclusive. The Geneys' baby would have done us fine.

Having settled my plans for the day, I got up, put a chair under the attic window, and lifted the frame high enough to stick out my head. The window overlooked the front gardens of the terrace behind ours, and beyond these it looked over a deep valley to the tall, red-brick houses terraced up the opposite hillside, which were all still in shadow, while those at our side of the valley were all lit up, though with long strange shadows that made them seem unfamiliar; rigid and painted.

After that I went into Mother's room and climbed into the big bed. She woke and I began to tell her of my schemes. By this time, though I never seem to have noticed it, I was petrified in my nightshirt, and I thawed as I talked until, the last frost melted, I fell asleep beside her and woke again only when I heard her below in the kitchen, making the breakfast.

After breakfast we went into town; heard Mass at St. Augustine's and said a prayer for Father, and did the shopping. If the afternoon was fine we either went for a walk in the country or a visit to Mother's great friend in the convent, Mother St. Dominic. Mother had them all praying for Father, and every night, going to bed, I asked God to send him back safe from the war to us. Little, indeed, did I know what I was praying for!

One morning, I got into the big bed, and there, sure enough, was Father in his usual Santa Claus manner, but later, instead of uniform, he put on his best blue suit, and Mother was as pleased as anything. I saw nothing to be pleased about, because, out of uniform, Father was altogether less interesting, but she only beamed, and explained that our prayers had been answered, and off we went to Mass to thank God for having brought Father safely home.

The irony of it! That very day when he came in to dinner he took off his boots and put on his slippers, donned the dirty old cap he wore about the house to save him from colds, crossed his legs, and began to talk gravely to Mother, who looked anxious. Naturally, I disliked her looking anxious, because it destroyed her good looks, so I interrupted him.

"Just a moment, Larry!" she said gently.

This was only what she said when we had boring visitors, so I attached no importance to it and went on talking.

"Do be quiet, Larry!" she said impatiently. "Don't you hear me talking to Daddy?"

This was the first time I had heard those ominous words, "talking to Daddy," and I couldn't help feeling that if this was how God answered prayers, he couldn't listen to them very attentively.

"Why are you talking to Daddy?" I asked with as great a show of indifference as I could muster.

"Because Daddy and I have business to discuss. Now, don't interrupt again!"

In the afternoon, at Mother's request, Father took me for a walk. This time we went into town instead of out the country, and I thought at first, in my usual optimistic way, that it might be an improvement. It was nothing of the sort. Father and I had quite different notions of a walk in town. He had no proper interest in trams, ships, and horses, and the only thing that seemed to divert him was talking to fellows as old as himself. When I wanted to stop he simply went on, dragging me behind him by the hand; when he wanted to stop I had no alternative but to do the same. I noticed that it seemed to be a sign that he wanted to stop for a long time whenever he leaned against a wall. The second time I saw him do it I got wild. He seemed to be settling himself forever. I pulled him by the coat and trousers, but, unlike Mother who, if you were too persistent, got into a wax and said: "Larry, if you don't behave yourself, I'll give you a good slap," Father had an extraordinary capacity for amiable inattention. I sized him up and wondered would I cry, but he seemed to be too remote to be annoyed even by that. Really, it was like going for a walk with a mountain! He either ignored the wrenching and pummeling entirely, or else glanced down with a grin of amusement from his peak. I had never met anyone so absorbed in himself as he seemed.

At teatime, "talking to Daddy" began again, complicated this time by the fact that he had an evening paper and every few minutes he put it down and told Mother something new out of it. I felt this was foul play. Man for man, I was prepared to compete with him any time for Mother's attention, but when he had it all made up for him by other people it left me no chance. Several times I tried to change the subject without success.

"You must be quiet while Daddy is reading, Larry," Mother said impatiently.

It was clear that she either genuinely liked talking to Father better than talking to me, or else that he had some terrible hold on her which made her afraid to admit the truth.

"Mummy," I said that night when she was tucking me up, "do you think if I prayed hard God would send Daddy back to the war?"

She seemed to think about that for a moment.

"No, dear," she said with a smile. "I don't think he would."

"Why wouldn't he, Mummy?"

"Because there isn't a war any longer, dear."

"But, Mummy, couldn't God make another war, if He liked?"

"He wouldn't like to, dear. It's not God who makes wars, but bad people."

"Oh!" I said.

I was disappointed about that. I began to think that God wasn't quite what he was cracked up to be.

Next morning I woke at my usual hour, feeling like a bottle of champagne. I put out my feet and invented a long conversation in which Mrs. Right talked of the trouble she had with her own father till she put him in the Home. I didn't quite know what the Home was but it sounded the right place for Father. Then I got my chair and stuck my head out of the attic window. Dawn was just breaking, with a guilty air that made me feel I had caught it in the act. My head bursting with stories and schemes, I stumbled in next door, and in the half-darkness scrambled into the big bed. There was no room at Mother's side so I had to get between her and Father. For the time being I had forgotten about him, and for several minutes I sat bolt upright, racking my brains to know what I could do with him. He was taking up more than his fair share of the bed, and I couldn't get comfortable, so I gave him several kicks that made him grunt and stretch. He made room all right, though. Mother waked and felt for me. I settled back comfortably in the warmth of the bed with my thumb in my mouth.

"Mummy!" I hummed, loudly and contentedly.

"Sssh! dear," she whispered. "Don't wake Daddy!"

This was a new development, which threatened to be even more serious than "talking to Daddy." Life without my early-morning conferences was unthinkable.

"Why?" I asked severely.

"Because poor Daddy is tired."

This seemed to me a quite inadequate reason, and I was sickened by the sentimentality of her "poor Daddy." I never liked that sort of gush; it always struck me as insincere.

"Oh!" I said lightly. Then in my most winning tone: "Do you know where I want to go with you today, Mummy?"

"No, dear," she sighed.

"I want to go down the Glen and fish for thornybacks with my new net, and then I want to go out to the Fox and Hounds, and—"

"Don't-wake-Daddy!" she hissed angrily, clapping her hand across my mouth.

But it was too late. He was awake, or nearly so. He grunted and reached for the matches. Then he stared incredulously at his watch.

"Like a cup of tea, dear?" asked Mother in a meek, hushed voice I had never heard her use before. It sounded almost as though she were afraid.

"Tea?" he exclaimed indignantly. "Do you know what the time is?"

"And after that I want to go up the Rathcooney Road," I said loudly, afraid I'd forget something in all those interruptions.

"Go to sleep at once, Larry!" she said sharply.

I began to snivel. I couldn't concentrate, the way that pair went on, and smothering my early-morning schemes was like burying a family from the cradle.

Father said nothing, but lit his pipe and sucked it, looking out into the shadows without minding Mother or me. I knew he was mad. Every time I made a remark Mother hushed me irritably. I was mortified. I felt it wasn't fair; there was even something sinister in it. Every time I had pointed out to her the waste of making two beds when we could both sleep in one, she had told me it was healthier like that, and now here was this man, this stranger, sleeping with her without the least regard for her health!

He got up early and made tea, but though he brought Mother a cup he brought none for me.

"Mummy," I shouted, "I want a cup of tea, too."

"Yes, dear," she said patiently. "You can drink from Mummy's saucer."

That settled it. Either Father or I would have to leave the house. I didn't want to drink from Mother's saucer; I wanted to be treated as an equal in my own home, so, just to spite her, I drank it all and left none for her. She took that quietly, too.

But that night when she was putting me to bed she said gently:

"Larry, I want you to promise me something."

"What is it?" I asked.

"Not to come in and disturb poor Daddy in the morning. Promise?"

"Poor Daddy" again! I was becoming suspicious of everything involving that quite impossible man.

"Why?" I asked.

"Because poor Daddy is worried and tired and he doesn't sleep well."

"Why doesn't he, Mummy?"

"Well, you know, don't you, that while he was at the war Mummy got the pennies from the Post Office?"

"From Miss MacCarthy?"

"That's right. But now, you see, Miss MacCarthy hasn't any more pennies, so Daddy must go out and find us some. You know what would happen if he couldn't?"

"No," I said, "tell us."

"Well, I think we might have to go out and beg for them like the poor old woman on Fridays. We wouldn't like that, would we?"

"No," I agreed. "We wouldn't."

"So you'll promise not to come in and wake him?"

"Promise."

Mind you, I meant that. I knew pennies were a serious

matter, and I was all against having to go out and beg like the old woman on Fridays. Mother laid out all my toys in a complete ring round the bed so that, whatever way I got out, I was bound to fall over one of them.

When I woke I remembered my promise all right. I got up and sat on the floor and played—for hours, it seemed to me. Then I got my chair and looked out the attic window for more hours. I wished it was time for Father to wake; I wished someone would make me a cup of tea. I didn't feel in the least like the sun; instead, I was bored and so very, very cold! I simply longed for the warmth and depth of the big featherbed.

At last I could stand it no longer. I went into the next room. As there was still no room at Mother's side I climbed over her and she woke with a start.

"Larry," she whispered, gripping my arm very tightly, "what did you promise?"

"But I did, Mummy," I wailed, caught in the very act. "I was quiet for ever so long."

"Oh, dear, and you're perished!" she said sadly, feeling me all over. "Now, if I let you stay will you promise not to talk?"

"But I want to talk, Mummy," I wailed.

"That has nothing to do with it," she said with a firmness that was new to me. "Daddy wants to sleep. Now, do you understand that?"

I understood it only too well. I wanted to talk, he wanted to sleep—whose house was it, anyway?

"Mummy," I said with equal firmness, "I think it would be healthier for Daddy to sleep in his own bed."

That seemed to stagger her, because she said nothing for a while.

"Now, once for all," she went on, "you're to be perfectly quiet or go back to your own bed. Which is it to be?"

The injustice of it got me down. I had convicted her out of her own mouth of inconsistency and unreasonableness, and she hadn't even attempted to reply. Full of spite, I gave

Father a kick, which she didn't notice but which made him grunt and open his eyes in alarm.

"What time is it?" he asked in a panic-stricken voice, not looking at Mother but at the door, as if he saw someone there.

"It's early yet," she replied soothingly. "It's only the child. Go to sleep again. . . . Now, Larry," she added, getting out of bed, "you've wakened Daddy and you must go back."

This time, for all her quiet air, I knew she meant it, and knew that my principal rights and privileges were as good as lost unless I asserted them at once. As she lifted me, I gave a screech, enough to wake the dead, not to mind Father. He groaned.

"That damn child! Doesn't he ever sleep?"

"It's only a habit, dear," she said quietly, though I could see she was vexed.

"Well, it's time he got out of it," shouted Father, beginning to heave in the bed. He suddenly gathered all the bedclothes about him, turned to the wall, and then looked back over his shoulder with nothing showing only two small, spiteful, dark eyes. The man looked very wicked.

To open the bedroom door, Mother had to let me down, and I broke free and dashed for the farthest corner, screeching. Father sat bolt upright in bed.

"Shut up, you little puppy!" he said in a choking voice.

I was so astonished that I stopped screeching. Never, never had anyone spoken to me in that tone before. I looked at him incredulously and saw his face convulsed with rage. It was only then that I fully realized how God had codded me, listening to my prayers for the safe return of this monster.

"Shut up, you!" I bawled, beside myself.

"What's that you said?" shouted Father, making a wild leap out of the bed.

"Mick, Mick!" cried Mother. "Don't you see the child isn't used to you?"

"I see he's better fed than taught," snarled Father, waving his arms wildly. "He wants his bottom smacked."

All his previous shouting was as nothing to these obscene words referring to my person. They really made my blood boil.

"Smack your own!" I screamed hysterically. "Smack your own! Shut up! Shut up!"

At this he lost his patience and let fly at me. He did it with the lack of conviction you'd expect of a man under Mother's horrified eyes, and it ended up as a mere tap, but the sheer indignity of being struck at all by a stranger, a total stranger who had cajoled his way back from the war into our big bed as a result of my innocent intercession, made me completely dotty. I shrieked and shrieked, and danced in my bare feet, and Father, looking awkward and hairy in nothing but a short grey army shirt, glared down at me like a mountain out for murder. I think it must have been then that I realized he was jealous too. And there stood Mother in her nightdress, looking as if her heart was broken between us. I hoped she felt as she looked. It seemed to me that she deserved it all.

From that morning out my life was a hell. Father and I were enemies, open and avowed. We conducted a series of skirmishes against one another, he trying to steal my time with Mother and I his. When she was sitting on my bed, telling me a story, he took to looking for some pair of old boots which he alleged he had left behind him at the beginning of the war. While he talked to Mother I played loudly with my toys to show my total lack of concern. He created a terrible scene one evening when he came in from work and found me at his box, playing with his regimental badges, Gurkha knives and button-sticks. Mother got up and took the box from me.

"You mustn't play with Daddy's toys unless he lets you, Larry," she said severely. "Daddy doesn't play with yours."

For some reason Father looked at her as if she had struck him and then turned away with a scowl.

"Those are not toys," he growled, taking down the box

again to see had I lifted anything. "Some of those curios are very rare and valuable."

But as time went on I saw more and more how he managed to alienate Mother and me. What made it worse was that I couldn't grasp his method or see what attraction he had for Mother. In every possible way he was less winning than I. He had a common accent and made noises at his tea. I thought for a while that it might be the newspapers she was interested in, so I made up bits of news of my own to read to her. Then I thought it might be the smoking, which I personally thought attractive, and took his pipes and went round the house dribbling into them till he caught me. I even made noises at my tea, but Mother only told me I was disgusting. It all seemed to hinge round that unhealthy habit of sleeping together, so I made a point of dropping into their bedroom and nosing round, talking to myself, so that they wouldn't know I was watching them, but they were never up to anything that I could see. In the end it beat me. It seemed to depend on being grown-up and giving people rings, and I realized I'd have to wait.

But at the same time I wanted him to see that I was only waiting, not giving up the fight. One evening when he was being particularly obnoxious, chattering away well above my head, I let him have it.

"Mummy," I said, "do you know what I'm going to do when I grow up?"

"No, dear," she replied. "What?"

"I'm going to marry you," I said quietly.

Father gave a great guffaw out of him, but he didn't take me in. I knew it must only be pretence. And Mother, in spite of everything, was pleased. I felt she was probably relieved to know that one day Father's hold on her would be broken.

"Won't that be nice?" she said with a smile.

"It'll be very nice," I said confidently. "Because we're going to have lots and lots of babies."

"That's right, dear," she said placidly. "I think we'll have one soon, and then you'll have plenty of company."

I was no end pleased about that because it showed that in spite of the way she gave in to Father she still considered my wishes. Besides, it would put the Geneys in their place.

It didn't turn out like that, though. To begin with, she was very preoccupied—I supposed about where she would get the seventeen and six—and though Father took to staying out late in the evenings it did me no particular good. She stopped taking me for walks, became as touchy as blazes, and smacked me for nothing at all. Sometimes I wished I'd never mentioned the confounded baby—I seemed to have a genius for bringing calamity on myself.

And calamity it was! Sonny arrived in the most appalling hullabaloo—even that much he couldn't do without a fuss—and from the first moment I disliked him. He was a difficult child—so far as I was concerned he was always difficult—and demanded far too much attention. Mother was simply silly about him, and couldn't see when he was only showing off. As company he was worse than useless. He slept all day, and I had to go round the house on tiptoe to avoid waking him. It wasn't any longer a question of not waking Father. The slogan now was "Don't-wake-Sonny!" I couldn't understand why the child wouldn't sleep at the proper time, so whenever Mother's back was turned I woke him. Sometimes to keep him awake I pinched him as well. Mother caught me at it one day and gave me a most unmerciful flaking.

One evening, when Father was coming in from work, I was playing trains in the front garden. I let on not to notice him; instead, I pretended to be talking to myself, and said in a loud voice: "If another bloody baby comes into this house, I'm going out."

Father stopped dead and looked at me over his shoulder.

"What's that you said?" he asked sternly.

"I was only talking to myself," I replied, trying to conceal my panic. "It's private."

He turned and went in without a word. Mind you, I intended it as a solemn warning, but its effect was quite different. Father started being quite nice to me. I could understand that, of course. Mother was quite sickening about Sonny. Even at mealtimes she'd get up and gawk at him in the cradle with an idiotic smile, and tell Father to do the same. He was always polite about it, but he looked so puzzled you could see he didn't know what she was talking about. He complained of the way Sonny cried at night, but she only got cross and said that Sonny never cried except when there was something up with him—which was a flaming lie, because Sonny never had anything up with him, and only cried for attention. It was really painful to see how simple-minded she was. Father wasn't attractive, but he had a fine intelligence. He saw through Sonny, and now he knew that I saw through him as well.

One night I woke with a start. There was someone beside me in the bed. For one wild moment I felt sure it must be Mother, having come to her senses and left Father for good, but then I heard Sonny in convulsions in the next room, and Mother saying: "There! There! There!" and I knew it wasn't she. It was Father. He was lying beside me, wide awake, breathing hard and apparently as mad as hell.

After a while it came to me what he was mad about. It was his turn now. After turnng me out of the big bed, he had been turned out himself. Mother had no consideration now for anyone but that poisonous pup, Sonny. I couldn't help feeling sorry for Father. I had been through it all myself, and even at that age I was magnanimous. I began to stroke him down and say: "There! There!" He wasn't exactly responsive.

"Aren't you asleep either?" he snarled.

"Ah, come on and put your arm around us, can't you?" I said, and he did, in a sort of way. Gingerly, I suppose, is how you'd describe it. He was very bony but better than nothing.

At Christmas he went out of his way to buy me a really nice model railway.

INNOCENCE

Seán O'Faoláin

All this month the nuns have been preparing my little boy for his first Confession. In a few days he will go in a crocodile from the school to the parish church; enter the strange-looking cabinet in the corner of the aisle and see in the dusk of this secretive box an old priest's face behind a grille. He will acknowledge his wickedness to this pale, criss-crossed face. He will be a little frightened but he will enjoy it too, because he does not really believe any of it—for him it is a kind of game that the nuns and the priest are playing between them.

How could he believe it? The nuns tell him that the Infant Jesus is sad when he is wicked. But he is never wicked, so what can it matter? If they told him instead of the sorrow he causes the Weasel, or Two Toes, or the Robin in the Cow's Ear, all of which live in the fields below our house, he would believe it in just the same way. To be sure he tells lies, he is a terrible liar, and when he plays Rummy with me he cheats as often as he can, and when he is slow and I flurry him he flies into furious rages and his eyes swim with tears and he dashes the cards down and calls me A Pig. For this I love him so much that I hug him, because it is so transparent and innocent; and at night if I remember his tears I want to go into his room and hold his fat, sweaty hand that lies on the coverlet clutching some such treasure as an empty reel. How, then, can he believe that God could be angry with him because he tells lies or calls his daddy A Pig?

Yet, I hate to see him being prepared for his first Confession because one day he will really do something wicked, and I know the fear that will come over him on that day—and I cannot prevent it.

I have never forgotten the first time I knew that I had committed sin. I had been going to Confession for years, ever since I was seven, as he is now, telling the same things time after time just as he will do. 'Father, I told a lie . . . Father, I forgot to say my morning prayers . . . Father, I was disobedient to my parents . . . And that is all, Father.' It was always quite true: I had done these things; but, as with him, it was only true as a fable or a mock-battle is true since none of these things were any more sinful than childish lies and rages. Until, one dim, wintry afternoon, not long after Christmas, when I went as usual to Confession in an old, dark, windy church called Saint Augustine's, down a side-lane, away from the city's traffic, a place as cold and damp and smelly as a tomb. It has since been pulled down and if they had not pulled it down it must soon have fallen down. It was the sort of church where there was always a beggar or two sheltering from the weather in the porch or in the dusky part under the back gallery; and always some poor shawled woman sighing her prayers in a corner like the wind fluttering in the slates. The paint was always clean and fresh, but the floor and the benches and the woodwork were battered and worn by the generations. The priests dressed in the usual black Augustinian garment with a cowl and a leather cincture. Altogether, a stranger would have found it a gloomy place. But I was familiar with it ever since my mother brought me there to dedicate me to Saint Monica, the mother of Augustine, and I loved the bright candles before her picture, and the dark nooks under the galleries, and the painted tondos on the ceiling, and the stuffy confessional boxes with their heavy purple curtains, underneath which the heels of the penitents stuck out when they knelt to the grille.

There I was, glad to be out of the January cold, kneeling before Saint Monica, brilliant with the candles of her mendicants. I was reading down through the lists of sins in my penny prayer-book, heeding the ones I knew, passing over the ones I didn't know, when I suddenly stopped at the name of a sin that I had hitherto passed by as having nothing to do with me.

As I write down these words I again feel the terror that crept into me like a snake as I realized that I knew that sin. I knew it well. No criminal who feels the sudden grip of a policeman on his arm can have felt more fear than I did as I stared at the horrible words. . . .

I joined the long silent queue of penitents seated against the wall. I went, at last, into the dark confessional. I told my usual innocent litany. I whispered the sin.

Now, the old priest inside the confessional was a very aged man. He was so old and feeble that the community rarely allowed him to do anything but say Mass and hear Confessions. Whenever they let him preach he would ramble on and on for an hour; people would get up and go away; the sacristan would peep out in despair through the sacristy door; and in the end an altar-boy would be sent out to ring the great gong on the altar-steps to make him stop. I have seen the boy come out three times to the gong before the old man could be lured down from the pulpit.

When this old priest heard what I said to him he gave a groan that must have been heard in the farthest corner of the church. He leaned his face against the wire and called me his 'child,' as all priests in the confessional call every penitent. Then he began to question me about the details. I had not counted on this. I had thought that I would say my sin and be forgiven: for up to this every priest had merely told me that I was a very good little boy and asked me to pray for him as if I were a little angel whose prayers had a special efficacy, and then I would be dismissed jumping with joy.

To his questions I replied tremulously that it had happened 'more than once'—How soon we begin to evade the truth!—and, I said, 'Yes, Father, it was with another.' At this he let out another groan so that I wanted to beg him to be quiet or the people outside would hear him. Then he asked me a question that made my clasped hands sweat and shake on the ledge of the grille. He asked me if any harm had been done to me. At first I didn't know what he meant. Then horrible shapes of understanding came creeping towards me along the dark road of my ignorance, as, in some indistinct manner, I recognized that he was mistaking me for a girl! I cried out that nothing at all had happened, Father. Nothing! Nothing! Nothing! But he only sighed like the south wind and said:

'Ah, my poor child, you won't know for several months.'

I now had no desire but to escape. I was ready to tell him any story, any lie, if he would only stop his questions. What I did say I don't know but in some fashion I must have made the old man understand that I was a male sinner. For his next question, which utterly broke me, was:

'I see, I see. Well, tell me, my poor child. Was she married or unmarried?'

I need hardly say that as I remember this now I laugh at it for an absurd misadventure, and I have sometimes made my friends laugh at his questions and his groans, and at me with my two skinny heels sticking out under the curtains and knocking like castanets, and the next penitents wondering what on earth was going on inside the box. But, then, I was like a pup caught in a bramble bush, recanting and retracting and trying to get to the point where he would say the blessed words 'Absolvo te . . .' and tell me what my penance would be.

What I said I cannot recall. All I remember distinctly is how I emerged under the eyes of the queue, walked up the aisle, as far away as I could get from the brightness of Saint Monica into the darkest corner under the gallery where the poorest of the poor crowd on Sundays. I saw everything through smoke. The scarlet eye of the sanctuary lamp—the only illumination apart from the candles before the shrine— stared at me. The shawled woman sighed at me. The wind under my bare knees crept away from me. A beggar in a corner, picking his nose and scratching himself, was Purity itself compared to me.

In the streets the building stood dark and wet against the after-Christmas pallor of the sky. High up over the city there was one tiny star. It was as bright and remote as lost innocence. The blank windows that held the winter sky were sullen. The wet cement walls were black. I walked around for hours. When I crept in home my mother demanded angrily where I had been all these hours and I told her lies that *were* lies, because I wanted to deceive her, and I knew that from this on I would always be deceiving everybody because I had something inside me that nobody must ever know. I was afraid of the dark night before me. And I still had to face another Confession when I would have to confess all these fresh lies that I had just told the old priest and my mother.

It's forty years ago, now: something long since put in its unimportant place. Yet, somehow, when I look across at this small kid clutching his penny prayer-book in his sweaty hands and wrinkling up his nose at the hard words—I cannot laugh. It does not even comfort me when I think of that second Confession, after I had carefully examined those lists of sins for the proper name of my sin. For, what I said to the next priest was: 'Father, I committed adultery.' With infinite tenderness he assured me that I was mistaken, and that I would not know anything about that sin for many years to come, indeed, that I would have to be married before I could commit it—and then asked me to pray for him, and said I was a very good little boy and sent me away jumping with joy. When I think of that and look at this small Adam he becomes like that indescribably remote and tender star, and I sigh like that old, dead priest, and it does not help to know that he is playing a fable of—'Father, I told lies . . . Father, I forgot to say my morning prayers. . . . Father, I called my daddy A Pig.'

THE NIGHTINGALES SING

Elizabeth Parsons

Through the fog the car went up the hill, whining in second gear, up the sandy road that ran between the highest and broadest stone walls that Joanna had ever seen. There were no trees at all, only the bright-green, cattle-cropped pastures sometimes visible above the walls, and sweetfern and juniper bushes, all dim in the opaque air and the wan light of an early summer evening. Phil, driving the creaking station wagon with dexterous recklessness, said to her, "I hope it's the right road. Nothing looks familiar in this fog and I've only been here once before."

"It was nice of him to ask us—me especially," said Joanna, who was young and shy and grateful for favors.

"Oh, he loves company," Phil said. "I wish we could have got away sooner to be here to help him unload the horses, though. Still, Chris will be there."

"Is Chris the girl who got thrown today?" Joanna asked, remembering the slight figure in the black coat going down in a spectacular fall with a big bay horse. Phil nodded, and brought the car so smartly around a bend that the two tack boxes in the back of it skidded across the floor. Then he stopped, at last on the level, at a five-barred gate that suddenly appeared out of the mist.

"I'll do the gate," said Joanna, and jumped out. It opened easily and she swung it back against the fence and held it while Phil drove through; then the engine stalled, and in the silence she stood for a moment, her head raised, sniffing the damp, clean air. There was no sound—not the sound of a bird, or a lamb, or the running of water over stones, or of wind in leaves; there was only a great stillness and a sense of height and strangeness and the smell of grass and dried dung. This was the top of the world, this lost hillside, green and bare, ruled across by enormous old walls—the work, so it seemed, of giants. In the air there was a faint movement as of a great wind far away, breathing through the fog. Joanna pulled the gate shut and got in again with Phil and they drove on along the smooth crest of the hill, the windshield wipers swinging slowly to and fro and Phil's sharp, red-headed profile drawn clearly against the gray background. She was grateful to him for taking her to the horse show that afternoon, but she was timid about the invitation to supper that it had led to. Still, there was no getting out of it now. Phil was the elder brother of a school friend of hers, Carol Watson—he was so old he might as well have been of another generation and there was about him, still incredibly unmarried at the age of thirty-one, the mysterious aura that bachelor elder brothers always possess. Carol was supposed to have come with them but she had developed chickenpox the day before. However, Phil had kindly offered to take Joanna just the same, since he had had to ride, and he had kept a fatherly eye on her whenever he could. Then a friend of his named Sandy Sheldon, a breeder of polo ponies, had asked him to stop at his farm for supper on the way home. Phil had asked Joanna if she wanted to go and she had said yes, knowing that he wanted to.

Being a good child, she had telephoned her family to tell them she would not be home until late.

"*Whose* place?" her mother's faraway voice had asked, doubtfully. "Well, don't be late, will you, dear? And call me up when you're leaving, won't you? It's a miserable night to be driving."

"I can't call you," Joanna had said. "There's no telephone."

"Couldn't you call up from somewhere after you've left?"

the faint voice had said. "You know how Father worries, and Phil's such a fast driver."

"I'll try to." Exasperation had made Joanna's voice stiff. What earthly good was *telephoning?* She hung up the receiver with a bang, showing a temper she would not have dared display in the presence of her parents.

Now, suddenly, out of the fog great buildings loomed close, and they drove through an open gate into a farmyard with gray wooden barns on two sides of it and stone walls on the other two sides. A few white hens rushed away across the dusty ground, and a gray cat sitting on the pole of a blue dump cart stared coldly at the car as Phil stopped it beside a battered horse van. The instant he stopped, a springer ran barking out of one of the barn doors, and a man appeared behind him and came quickly out to them, up to Joanna's side of the car, where he put both hands on the door and bent his head a little to look in at them.

"Sandy, this is Joanna Gibbs," said Phil.

Sandy looked at her without smiling, but not at all with unfriendliness, only with calm consideration. "Hello, Joanna," he said, and opened the door for her.

"Hello," she said, and then forgot to be shy, for, instead of uttering the kind of asinine, polite remarks she was accustomed to hearing from strangers, he did not treat her as a stranger at all, but said immediately, "You're just in time to help put the horses away. Chris keeled over the minute we got here and I had to send her to bed, and Jake's gone after one of the cows that's strayed off." He spoke in a light, slow, Western voice. He was a small man about Phil's age, with a flat freckled face, light-brown, intelligent eyes, and faded brown hair cut short all over his round head. He looked very sturdy and stocky, walking toward the van beside Phil's thin New England elegance, and he had a self-confidence that sprang simply from his own good nature.

"Quite a fog you greet us with," said Phil, taking off his coat and hanging it on the latch of the open door of the van. Inside in the gloom four long, shining heads were turned toward them, and one of the horses gave a gentle, anxious whinny.

"Yes, we get them once in a while," said Sandy. "I like 'em."

"So do I," said Joanna.

He turned to her and said, "Look, there's really no need in your staying out here. Run in the house, where it's warm, and see if the invalid's all right. You go through that gate." He pointed to a small sagging gate at a gap in the wall.

"All right, I will," she answered, and she started off across the yard toward the end gable of a house she could see rising dimly above some apple trees, the spaniel going with her.

"Joanna!" Sandy called after her, just as she reached the gate.

"Yes?" She turned back. The two men were standing by the runway of the van. They both looked at her, seeing a tall young girl in a blue dress and sweater, with her hair drawn straight back over her head and tied at the back of her neck in a chignon with a black bow and made more beautiful and airy than she actually was by the watery air.

"Put some wood on the kitchen fire as you go in, will you?" Sandy shouted to her. "The woodbox is right by the stove."

"All right," she answered again, and she and the spaniel went through the little gate in the wall.

A path led from the gate, under the apple trees where the grass was cut short and neat, to a door in the ell of the house. The house itself was big and old and plain, almost square, with a great chimney settled firmly across the ridge pole, and presumably it faced down the hill toward the sea. It was conventional and unimposing, with white painted trim and covered with gray old shingles. There was a lilac bush by the front door and a bed of unbudded red lilies around one of the apple trees, but except for these there was neither shrubbery nor flowers. It looked austere and pleasing to Joanna, and she went in through the door in the ell and saw the woodbox beside the black stove. As she poked some pieces of birch wood down into the snapping fire, a girl's voice called from upstairs, "Sandy?"

Joanna put the lid on the stove and went through a tiny hallway into a living room. An enclosed staircase went up out of one corner and she went to it and called up it, "Sandy's in the barn. Are you all right?"

"Oh, I'm fine," the voice answered, hard and clear. "Just a little shaky when I move around. Come on up."

Joanna climbed up. Immediately at the top of the stairs was a big square bedroom, papered in a beautiful faded paper with scrolls and wheat sheaves. On a four-posted bed lay a girl not many years older than Joanna, covered to the chin with a dark patchwork quilt. Her short black hair stood out against the pillow, and her face was colorless and expressionless and at the same time likeable and amusing. She did not sit up when Joanna came in; she clasped her hands behind her head and looked at her with blue eyes under lowered black lashes.

"You came with Phil, didn't you?" she asked.

"Yes," said Joanna, moving hesitantly up to the bed and leaning against one of the footposts. "They're putting the horses away and they thought I'd better come in and see how you were."

"Oh, I'm fine," said Chris again. "I'll be O.K. in a few minutes. I lit on my head, I guess, by the way it feels, but I don't remember a thing."

Joanna remembered. It had not seemed possible that that black figure could emerge, apparently from directly underneath the bay horse and, after sitting a minute on the grass with hanging head, could get up and walk grimly away, ignoring the animal who had made such a clumsy error and was being led out by an attendant in a long tan coat.

She also remembered that when people were ill or in pain you brought them weak tea and aspirin and hot water bottles, and that they were usually in bed, wishing to suffer behind partly lowered shades, not just lying under a quilt with the fog pressing against darkening windows. But there

was something here that did not belong in the land of tea
and hot water bottles—a land that, indeed, now seemed on
another planet. Joanna knew this, though she did not know
what alternatives to offer, so she made no suggestions but
just stood there, looking with shy politeness around the
room. It was a cold, sparsely furnished place and it looked
very bare to Joanna, most of whose life so far had been
spent in comfortable, chintz-warmed interiors, with carpets
that went from wall to wall. In this room, so obviously
untouched for the past hundred years or more, was only the
bed, a tall chest of drawers, a wash-hand-stand with a gold
and white bowl and pitcher, two plain painted chairs, and a
threadbare oval braided rug beside the bed. There were no
curtains at the four windows, and practically no paint left on
the uneven old floor. The fireplace was black and damp-
smelling and filled with ashes and charred paper that rose
high about the feet of the andirons. Joanna could not make
out whether it was a guest room, or whose room it was; here
and there were scattered possessions that might have been
male or female—a bootjack, some framed snapshots, a comb,
a dirty towel, some socks, a magazine on the floor. Chris's
black coat was lying on a chair, and her bowler stood on the
bureau. It was a blank room, bleak in the failing light.

Chris watched her from under her half-closed lids, waiting for her to speak, and presently Joanna said, "That was
really an awful spill you had."

Chris moved her head on the pillow and said, "He's a
brute of a horse. He'll never be fit to ride. I've schooled
him for Mrs. Whittaker for a year now and ridden him in
three shows and I thought he was pretty well over his
troubles." She shrugged, and wrapped herself tighter in the
quilt. "She's sunk so much money in him it's a crime, but
he's just a brute and I don't think I can do anything more
with him. Of course, if she wants to go on paying me to ride
him, O.K., and her other horses are tops, so I haven't any
kick, really. You can't have them all perfect."

"What does she bother with him for?" asked Joanna.

"Well, she's cracked, like most horse-show people," said

Chris. "They can't resist being spectacular—exhibitionists, or whatever they call it. Got to have something startling, and then more startling, and so on. And I must say this horse is something to see. He's beautiful." Her somewhat bored little voice died away.

Joanna contemplated all this seriously. It seemed to her an arduous yet dramatic way of earning one's living; she did not notice that there was nothing in the least dramatic about the girl on the bed beside her. Chris, for her part, was speculating more directly about Joanna, watching her, appreciating her looks, wondering what she was doing with Phil. Then, because she was not unkind and sensed that Joanna was at loose ends in the strange house, she said to her, suddenly leaving the world of horses for the domestic scene where women cozily collaborate over the comforts of their men, "Is there a fire in the living room? I was too queasy to notice when I came in. If there isn't one why don't you light it so it'll be warm when they come in?"

"I'll look," said Joanna. "I didn't notice either. Can I get you anything?"

"No, I'll be down pretty soon," Chris said. "I've got to start supper."

Joanna went back down the little stairs. There was no fire in the living room, but a broken basket beside the fireplace was half full of logs, and she carefully laid these on the andirons and stuffed in some twigs and old comics and lit them. The tall flames sprang up into the black chimney, shiny with creosote. As they roared up, she sat on the floor and looked around the room. It was the same size as the bedroom above it, but it was comfortable and snug, with plain gray walls and white woodwork. A fat sofa, covered with dirty flowered linen, stood in front of the fire. There were some big wicker chairs and four little carved Victorian chairs and a round table with big bowed legs, covered with a tablecloth; a high, handsome secretary stood against the wall opposite the fire—its veneer was peeling, and d with tarnished silver cups and ribbon rosettes. a chair. There were dog hairs on the sofa and the floor was dirty, and outside the windows there was nothingness. Joanna got up to look at the kitchen fire, put more wood on it, and returned to the living room. Overhead she heard Chris moving around quietly, and she pictured her walking about the barren, dusty bedroom, combing her short black hair, tying her necktie, folding up the quilt, looking in the gloom for a lipstick, and suddenly a dreadful, lonely sadness and longing came over her. The living room was growing dark too, and she would have lit the big nickel lamp standing on the table but she did not know how to, so she sat there dreaming in the hot golden firelight. Presently she heard the men's voices outside and they came into the kitchen and stopped there to talk, one of them rattling the stove lids. Sandy came to the door and, seeing Joanna, said to her, "Is Chris all right?"

"Yes, I think so," Joanna said. "She said she was, anyway."

"Guess I'll just see," he said, and went running up the stairs. The spaniel came in to the fire. Joanna stroked his back. His wavy coat was damp with fog and he smelled very strongly of dog; he sat down on the hearth facing the fire, raised his muzzle, and closed his eyes and gave a great sigh of comfort. Then all of a sudden he trotted away and went leaping up the stairs to the bedroom, and Joanna could hear his feet overhead.

Phil came in next, his hair sticking to his forehead. He hung his coat on a chair-back and said to Joanna, "How do you like it here?"

"It's wonderful," she said earnestly.

"It seems to me a queer place," he said, lifting the white fluted china shade off the lamp and striking a match. "Very queer—so far off. We're marooned. I don't feel there's any other place anywhere, do you?"

Joanna shook her head and watched him touch the match to the wick and stoop to settle the chimney on its base. When he put on the shade the soft yellow light ca[*] becomingly on his red head and his narrow face w[*] sharp cheekbones and the small, deep-set blue ey[*] had known him for years but she realized looki[*]

the yellow light, that she knew almost nothing about him.
Before this, he had been Carol's elder brother, but here in
the unfamiliar surroundings he was somebody real. She
looked away from his lighted face, surprised and wondering.
He took his pipe out of his coat pocket and came to the sofa
and sat down with a sigh of comfort exactly like the dog's,
sticking his long thin booted feet out to the fire, banishing
the dark, making the fog retreat.

Sandy came down the stairs and went toward the kitchen,
and Phil called after him, "Chris all right?"

"Yes," Sandy said, going out.

"She's a little crazy," Phil said. "Too much courage and
no sense. But she's young. She'll settle down, maybe."

"Are she and Sandy engaged?" Joanna asked.

"Well, no," said Phil. "Sandy's got a wife. She stays in
Texas." He paused to light his pipe, and then he said,
"That's where he raises his horses, you know—this place is
only sort of a salesroom. But he and Chris know each other
pretty well."

This seemed obvious to Joanna, who said, "Yes, I know."
Phil smoked in silence.

"Doesn't his wife *ever* come here?" Joanna asked after a
moment.

"I don't think so," Phil answered.

They could hear Sandy in the kitchen, whistling, and
occasionally rattling pans. They heard the pump squeak as
he worked the handle and the water splashed down into the
black iron sink. Then he too came in to the fire and said to
Joanna, smiling down at her, "Are you comfy, and all?"

"Oh, *yes*," she said and flushed with pleasure. "I love
your house," she managed to say.

"I'm glad you do. It's kind of a barn of a place, but fine for
the little I'm in it." He walked away, pulled the flowered
curtains across the windows, and came back to stand before
the fire. He looked very solid, small, and cheerful, with his
shirt-sleeves rolled up and his collar unbuttoned with the
gay printed tie loosened. He seemed to Joanna so smug and
kind, so, somehow, sympathetic, that she could have leaned

forward and hugged him round the knees—but at the idea
of doing any such thing she blushed again and bent to pat
the dog. Sandy took up the guitar and tuned it lazily.

As he began playing absent-mindedly, his stubby fingers
straying across the strings as he stared into the fire, Chris
came down the stairs. Instead of her long black boots she
had on a pair of dilapidated Indian moccasins with a few
beads remaining on the toes, and between these and the
ends of her breeches legs were gay blue socks. The breeches
were fawn-colored, and she had on a fresh white shirt with
the sleeves rolled up. Her curly hair, cropped nearly as
short as a boy's, was brushed and shining, and her hard,
sallow little face was carefully made up and completely
blank. Whether she was happy or disturbed, well or ill,
Joanna could see no stranger would be able to tell.

"What about supper?" she asked Sandy.

"Calm yourself," he said. "I'm cook tonight. It's all started."
He took her hand to draw her down on the sofa, but she
moved away and pulled a cushion off a chair and lay down
on the floor, her feet toward the fire and her hands folded
like a child's on her stomach. Phil had gone into the next
room and now he came back carrying a lighted lamp; it
dipped wildly in his hand as he set it on the round table
beside the other one. The room shone in the low, benefi-
cent light. Sandy, leaning his head against the high, carved
back of the sofa, humming and strumming, now sang aloud
in a light, sweet voice,

> "For I'd rather hear your fiddle
> And the tone of one string
> Than watch the waters a-gliding,
> Hear the nightingales sing."

The soft strumming went on, and the soft voice, accompanied by Chris's gentle crooning. The fire snapped. Phil
handed round some glasses and then went round with a bottle
of whisky he had found in the kitchen. He paused at Joanna's
glass, smiled at her, and poured her a very small portion.

"If I ever return,
It will be in the spring
To watch the waters a-gliding
Hear the nightingales sing."

The old air died on a trailing chord.

"That's a lovely song," said Joanna, and then shrank at her sentimentality.

But Sandy said, "Yes, it's nice. My mother used to sing it. She knew an awful lot of old songs." He picked out the last bars again on the guitar. Joanna, sitting beside him on the floor, was swept with warmth and comfort.

"My God, the peas!" Sandy said suddenly in horror, as a loud sound of hissing came from the kitchen. Throwing the guitar down on the sofa, he rushed to rescue the supper.

Joanna and Chris picked their way toward the privy that adjoined the end of the barn nearer the house. They moved in a little circle of light from the kerosene lantern that Chris carried, the batteries of Sandy's big flashlight having turned out to be dead. They were both very full of food, and sleepy, and just a little tipsy. Chris had taken off her socks and moccasins and Joanna her leather sandals, and the soaking grass was cold indeed to their feet that had so lately been stretched out to the fire. Joanna had never been in a privy in her life and when Chris opened the door she was astonished at the four neatly covered holes, two large and—on a lower level—two small. Everything was whitewashed; there were pegs to hang things on, and a very strong smell of disinfectant. A few flies woke up and buzzed. Chris set the lantern down on the path and partly closed the door behind them.

There was something cozy about the privy, and they were in no particular hurry to go back to the house. Chris lit a cigarette, and they sat there comfortably in the semidarkness, and Chris talked. She told Joanna about her two years in college, to which she had been made to go by her family. But Chris's love was horses, not gaining an education, and finally she had left and begun to support herself as a professional rider.

"I'd known Sandy ever since I was little," she said. "I used to hang around him when I was a kid, and he let me ride his horses and everything, and when I left college he got me jobs and sort of looked after me."

"He's a darling, isn't he?" Joanna said dreamily, watching the dim slice of light from the open door, and the mist that drifted past it.

"Well, sometimes he is," said Chris. "And sometimes I wish I'd never seen him."

"Oh, *no!*" cried Joanna. "Why?"

"Because he's got so he takes charge too much of the time—you know?" Chris said. "At first I was so crazy about him I didn't care, but now it's gone on so long I'm beginning to see I'm handicapped in a way—or that's what I think, anyway. Everybody just assumes I'm his girl. And he's got a wife, you know, and he won't leave her, ever. And then he's not here a lot of the time. But the worst of all is that he's spoiled me—everybody else seems kind of tame and young. So you see it's a mixed pleasure."

Joanna pondered, a little fuzzily. She was not at all sure what it was that Chris was telling her, but she felt she was being talked to as by one worldly soul to another. Now Chris was saying, "He said that would happen, and I didn't care then. He said, 'I'm too *old* for you, Chris, even if I was single, and this way it's hopeless for you.' But I didn't care. I didn't want anybody or anything else and I just plain chased him. And now I don't want anything else either. So it *is* hopeless. . . .I hope you don't ever love anybody more than he loves you," said Chris.

"I've never really been in love," said Joanna bravely.

"Well, you will be," Chris said, lighting a second cigarette. The little white interior and their two young, drowsy faces shone for a second in the flash of the match. "First I thought you were coming here because you were Phil's girl, but I soon saw you weren't."

"Oh *no!*" cried Joanna again. "He's just the brother of a friend of mine, that's all."

"Yes," said Chris, "he always picks racier types than you."

Racy, thought Joanna. I wish *I* was racy, but I'm too scared.

"I've seen some of his girls, and not one of them was as good-looking as you are," Chris went on. "But they were all very dizzy. He has to have that, I guess—he's so sort of restrained himself, with that family and all. I went to a cocktail party at his house once, and it was terrible. Jeepers!" She began to laugh.

Vulgarity is what he likes, then, said Joanna to herself. Perhaps I like it myself, though I don't know that I know what it is. Perhaps my mother would say Chris and Sandy were vulgar, but they don't seem vulgar to me, though I'm glad Mother isn't here to hear their language and some of Sandy's songs.

She gave it up, as Chris said with a yawn, "We'd better get back."

As they went toward the house it loomed up above them, twice its size, the kitchen windows throwing low beams of light out into the fog. Still there was no wind. In the heavy night air nothing was real, not even Chris and the lantern and the corner of a great wall near the house. Joanna was disembodied, moving through a dream on her bare, numb feet to a house of no substance.

"Let's walk around to the front," she said. "I love the fog."

"O.K.," said Chris, and they went around the corner and stopped by the lilac bushes to listen to the stillness.

But suddenly the dampness reached their bones, and they shivered and screeched and ran back to the back door, with the bobbing lantern smoking and smelling in Chris's hand.

When they came in, Phil looked at them fondly. "Dear little Joanna," he said. "She's all dripping and watery and vaporous, like Undine. What in God's name have you girls been doing?"

"Oh, talking," said Chris.

"Pull up to the fire," Sandy said. "What did you talk about? Us?"

"Yes, dear," said Chris. "We talked about you every single second."

"Joanna's very subdued," remarked Phil. "Did you talk her into a stupor, or what?"

"Joanna doesn't have to talk if she doesn't want to," said Sandy. "I like a quiet woman, myself."

"Do you now?" said Phil, laughing at Chris, who made a face at him and sat down beside Sandy and gave him a violent hug.

Joanna, blinking, sat on the floor with her wet feet tucked under her, and listened vaguely to the talk that ran to and fro above her. Her head was swimming, and she felt sleepy and wise, in the warm lamplight and with the sound of the bantering voices which she did not have to join unless she wanted to. Suddenly she heard Phil saying, "You know, Joanna, we've got to start along. It seems to me you made a rash promise to your family that you'd be home early and it's nearly ten now and we've got thirty miles to go." He yawned, stretched, and bent to knock out his pipe on the side of the fireplace.

"I don't want to go," said Joanna.

"Then stay," said Sandy. "There's plenty of room."

But Phil said, getting up, "No, we've got to go. They'd have the police out if we didn't come soon. Joanna's very carefully raised, you know."

"I *love* Joanna," said Chris, hugging Sandy again until he grunted. "I don't care how carefully she was raised, I love her."

"We all love her," Sandy said. "You haven't got a monopoly on her. Come again and stay longer, will you, Joanna? We love you, and you look so nice here in this horrible old house."

They really do like me, thought Joanna, pulling on her sandals. But not as much as I like them. They have a lot of fun all the time, so it doesn't mean as much to them to find somebody they like. But I'll remember this evening as long as I live.

Sadly she went out with them to the station wagon, following the lantern, and climbed in and sat on the clammy leather seat beside Phil. Calling back, and being called to, they drove away, bumping slowly over the little road, and in a second Chris and Sandy and the lantern were gone in the fog.

Joanna let herself in the front door and turned to wave to Phil, who waved back and drove off down the leafy street, misty in the midnight silence. Inland, the fog was not as bad as it had been near the sea, but the trees dripped with the wetness and the sidewalk shone under the street light. She listened to the faraway, sucking sound of Phil's tires die away; then she sighed and closed the door and moved sleepily into the still house, dropping her key into the brass bowl on the hall table. The house was cool, and dark downstairs except for the hall light, and it smelled of the earth in her mother's little conservatory.

Joanna started up the stairs, slowly unfastening the belt of the old trench coat she had borrowed from Phil. The drive back had been a meaningless interval swinging in the night, with nothing to remember but the glow of the headlights blanketed by the fog so that they had had to creep around the curves and down the hills, peering out until their eyes ached. Soon after they had left the farm they had stopped in a small town while Joanna telephoned her family; through the open door of the phone booth she had watched Phil sitting on a spindly stool at the little marble counter next to the shelves full of Westerns, drinking a Coke—she had a Coke herself and sipped it as the telephone rang far away in her parents' house, while back of the counter a radio played dance music. And twice after that Phil had pulled off the road, once to light his pipe, and once for Joanna to put on his coat. But now, moving up the shallow, carpeted stairs, she was back in the great, cold, dusty house with the sound of Sandy's guitar and the smell of the oil lamps, and the night, the real night, wide and black and empty, only a step away outside.

Upstairs, there was a light in her own room and one in her mother's dressing room. It was a family custom that when she came in late she should put out her mother's light, so now she went into the small, bright room. With her hand on the light-chain she looked around her, at the chintz-covered chaise longue, the chintz-skirted dressing table with family snapshots, both old and recent, arranged under its glass top, at the polished furniture, the long mirror, the agreeable clutter of many years of satisfactory married life. On the walls were more family pictures covering quite a long period of time—enlargements of picnic photographs, of boats, of a few pets. There was Joanna at the age of twelve on a cowpony in Wyoming, her father and uncle in snow goggles and climbing boots on the lower slopes of Mont Blanc heaven knows how long ago, her sister and brother-in-law looking very young and carefree with their bicycles outside Salisbury Cathedral sometime in the early thirties, judging by her sister's clothes. The world of the pictures was as fresh and good and simple as a May morning; the sun shone and everyone was happy. She stared at the familiar little scenes on the walls with love—and with a sympathy for them she had never felt before—and then she put out the light and went back along the hall.

In her own room she kicked off her sandals and dropped Phil's coat on a chair. A drawn window shade moved inward and fell back again in the night breeze that rustled the thick, wet trees close outside; her pajamas lay on the turned-down bed with its tall, fluted posts. Joanna did not stop to brush her teeth or braid her hair; she was in bed in less than two minutes.

In the darkness she heard the wind rising around Sandy's house, breathing over the open hill, whistling softly in the wet, rusted window screens, stirring in the apple trees. She heard the last burning log in the fireplace tumble apart, and a horse kick at his stall out in the barn. If I'd stayed all night, she thought, in the morning when the fog burned off

I'd have known how far you could see from the top of the hill.

For in the morning the hot sun would shine from a mild blue sky, the roofs would steam, the horses would gallop and squeal in the pastures between the great walls, and all the nightingales would rise singing out of the short, tough grass.

◆ ─── ◆

FLOWERING JUDAS

Katherine Anne Porter

Braggioni sits heaped upon the edge of a straight-backed chair much too small for him, and sings to Laura in a furry, mournful voice. Laura has begun to find reasons for avoiding her own house until the latest possible moment, for Braggioni is there almost every night. No matter how late she is, he will be sitting there with a surly, waiting expression, pulling at his kinky yellow hair, thumbing the strings of his guitar, snarling a tune under his breath. Lupe the Indian maid meets Laura at the door, and says with a flicker of a glance towards the upper room, "He waits."

Laura wishes to lie down, she is tired of her hairpins and the feel of her long tight sleeves, but she says to him, "Have you a new song for me this evening?" If he says yes, she asks him to sing it. If he says no, she remembers his favorite one, and asks him to sing it again. Lupe brings her a cup of chocolate and a plate of rice, and Laura eats at the small table under the lamp, first inviting Braggioni, whose answer is always the same: "I have eaten, and besides, chocolate thickens the voice."

Laura says, "Sing, then," and Braggioni heaves himself into song. He scratches the guitar familiarly as though it were a pet animal, and sings passionately off key, taking the high notes in a prolonged painful squeal. Laura, who haunts the markets listening to the ballad singers, and stops every day to hear the blind boy playing his reed-flute in Sixteenth of September Street, listens to Braggioni with pitiless courtesy, because she dares not smile at his miserable performance. Nobody dares to smile at him. Braggioni is cruel to everyone, with a kind of specialized insolence, but he is so vain of his talents, and so sensitive to slights, it would require a cruelty and vanity greater than his own to lay a finger on the vast cureless wound of his self-esteem. It would require courage, too, for it is dangerous to offend him, and nobody has this courage.

Braggioni loves himself with such tenderness and amplitude and eternal charity that his followers—for he is a leader of men, a skilled revolutionist, and his skin has been punctured in honorable warfare—warm themselves in the reflected glow, and say to each other: "He has a real nobility, a love of humanity raised above mere personal affections." The excess of this self-love has flowed out, inconveniently for her, over Laura, who, with so many others, owes her comfortable situation and her salary to him. When he is in a very good humor, he tells her, "I am tempted to forgive you for being a *gringa, Gringita!*" and Laura, burning, imagines herself leaning forward suddenly, and with a sound back-handed slap wiping the suety smile from his face. If he notices her eyes at these moments he gives no sign.

She knows what Braggioni would offer her, and she must resist tenaciously without appearing to resist, and if she could avoid it she would not admit even to herself the slow drift of his intention. During these long evenings which have spoiled a long month for her, she sits in her deep chair with an open book on her knees, resting her eyes on the consoling rigidity of the printed page when the sight and sound of Braggioni singing threaten to identify themselves with all her remembered afflictions and to add their weight to her

uneasy premonitions of the future. The gluttonous bulk of
Braggioni has become a symbol of her many disillusions, for
a revolutionist should be lean, animated by heroic faith, a
vessel of abstract virtues. This is nonsense, she knows it
now and is ashamed of it. Revolution must have leaders,
and leadership is a career for energetic men. She is, her
comrades tell her, full of romantic error, for what she de-
fines as cynicism in them is merely "a developed sense of
reality." She is almost too willing to say, "I am wrong, I
suppose I don't really understand the principles," and afterward she makes a secret truce with herself, determined not
to surrender her will to such expedient logic. But she cannot help feeling that she has been betrayed irreparably by
the disunion between her way of living and her feeling of
what life should be, and at times she is almost contented to
rest in this sense of grievance as a private store of consolation. Sometimes she wishes to run away, but she stays. Now
she longs to fly out of this room, down the narrow stairs,
and into the street where the houses lean together like
conspirators under a single mottled lamp, and leave Braggioni
singing to himself.

Instead she looks at Braggioni, frankly and clearly, like a
good child who understands the rules of behavior. Her
knees cling together under sound blue serge, and her round
white collar is not purposely nun-like. She wears the uniform of an idea, and has renounced vanities. She was born
Roman Catholic, and in spite of her fear of being seen by
someone who might make a scandal of it, she slips now and
again into some crumbling little church, kneels on the chilly
stone, and says a Hail Mary on the gold rosary she bought
in Tehuantepec. It is no good and she ends by examining
the altar with its tinsel flowers and ragged brocades, and
feels tender about the battered dollshape of some male saint
whose white, lace-trimmed drawers hang limply around his
ankles below the hieratic dignity of his velvet robe. She has
encased herself in a set of principles derived from her early
training, leaving no detail of gesture or of personal taste
untouched, and for this reason she will not wear lace made

on machines. This is her private heresy, for in her special
group the machine is sacred, and will be the salvation of the
workers. She loves fine lace, and there is a tiny edge of
fluted cobweb on this collar, which is one of twenty precisely alike, folded in blue tissue paper in the upper drawer
of her clothes chest.

Braggioni catches her glance solidly as if he had been
waiting for it, leans forward, balancing his paunch between
his spread knees, and sings with tremendous emphasis,
weighing his words. He has, the song relates, no father and
no mother, nor even a friend to console him; lonely as a
wave of the sea he comes and goes, lonely as a wave. His
mouth opens round and yearns sideways, his balloon cheeks
grow oily with the labor of song. He bulges marvelously in
his expensive garments. Over his lavender collar, crushed
upon a purple necktie, held by a diamond hoop: over his
ammunition belt of tooled leather worked in silver, buckled
cruelly around his gasping middle: over the tops of his
glossy yellow shoes Braggioni swells with ominous ripeness,
his mauve silk hose stretched taut, his ankles bound with
the stout leather thongs of his shoes.

When he stretches his eyelids at Laura she notes again
that his eyes are the true tawny yellow cat's eyes. He is
rich, not in money, he tells her, but in power, and this
power brings with it the blameless ownership of things, and
the right to indulge his love of small luxuries. "I have a taste
for the elegant refinements," he said once, flourishing a
yellow silk handkerchief before her nose. "Smell that? It is
Jockey Club, imported from New York." Nonetheless he is
wounded by life. He will say so presently. "It is true everything turns to dust in the hand, to gall on the tongue." He
sighs and his leather belt creaks like a saddle girth. "I am
disappointed in everything as it comes. Everything." He
shakes his head. "You, poor thing, you will be disappointed
too. You are born for it. We are more alike than you realize
in some things. Wait and see. Some day you will remember
what I have told you, you will know that Braggioni was your
friend."

Laura feels a slow chill, a purely physical sense of danger, a warning in her blood that violence, mutilation, a shocking death, wait for her with lessening patience. She has translated this fear into something homely, immediate, and sometimes hesitates before crossing the street. "My personal fate is nothing, except as the testimony of a mental attitude," she reminds herself, quoting from some forgotten philosophic primer, and is sensible enough to add, "Anyhow, I shall not be killed by an automobile if I can help it."

"It may be true I am as corrupt, in another way, as Braggioni," she thinks in spite of herself, "as callous, as incomplete," and if this is so, any kind of death seems preferable. Still she sits quietly, she does not run. Where could she go? Uninvited she has promised herself to this place; she can no longer imagine herself as living in another country, and there is no pleasure in remembering her life before she came here.

Precisely what is the nature of this devotion, its true motives, and what are its obligations? Laura cannot say. She spends part of her days in Xochimilco, near by, teaching Indian children to say in English, "The cat is on the mat." When she appears in the classroom they crowd about her with smiles on their wise, innocent, clay-colored faces, crying, "Good morning, my titcher!" in immaculate voices, and they make of her desk a fresh garden of flowers every day.

During her leisure she goes to union meetings and listens to busy important voices quarreling over tactics, methods, internal politics. She visits the prisoners of her own political faith in their cells, where they entertain themselves with counting cockroaches, repenting of their indiscretions, composing their memoirs, writing out manifestoes and plans for their comrades who are still walking about free, hands in pockets, sniffing fresh air. Laura brings them food and cigarettes and a little money, and she brings messages disguised in equivocal phrases from the men outside who dare not set foot in the prison for fear of disappearing into the cells kept empty for them. If the prisoners confuse night and day, and complain, "Dear little Laura, time doesn't pass in this infernal hole, and I won't know when it is time to sleep unless I have a reminder," she brings them their favorite narcotics, and says in a tone that does not wound them with pity, "Tonight will really be night for you," and though her Spanish amuses them, they find her comforting, useful. If they lose patience and all faith, and curse the slowness of their friends in coming to their rescue with money and influence, they trust her not to repeat everything, and if she inquires, "Where do you think we can find money, or influence?" they are certain to answer, "Well, there is Braggioni, why doesn't he do something?"

She smuggles letters from headquarters to men hiding from firing squads in back streets in mildewed houses, where they sit in tumbled beds and talk bitterly as if all Mexico were at their heels, when Laura knows positively they might appear at the band concert in the Alameda on Sunday morning, and no one would notice them. But Braggioni says, "Let them sweat a little. The next time they may be careful. It is very restful to have them out of the way for a while." She is not afraid to knock on any door in any street after midnight, and enter in the darkness, and say to one of these men who is really in danger: "They will be looking for you—seriously—tomorrow morning after six. Here is some money from Vicente. Go to Vera Cruz and wait."

She borrows money from the Roumanian agitator to give to his bitter enemy the Polish agitator. The favor of Braggioni is their disputed territory, and Braggioni holds the balance nicely, for he can use them both. The Polish agitator talks love to her over café tables, hoping to exploit what he believes is her secret sentimental preference for him, and he gives her misinformation which he begs her to repeat as the solemn truth to certain persons. The Roumanian is more adroit. He is generous with his money in all good causes, and lies to her with an air of ingenuous candor, as if he were her good friend and confidant. She never repeats anything they may say. Braggioni never asks questions. He has other ways to discover all that he wishes to know about them.

Nobody touches her, but all praise her gray eyes, and the soft, round under lip which promises gayety, yet is always grave, nearly always firmly closed: and they cannot understand why she is in Mexico. She walks back and forth on her errands, with puzzled eyebrows, carrying her little folder of drawings and music and school papers. No dancer dances more beautifully than Laura walks, and she inspires some amusing, unexpected ardors, which cause little gossip, because nothing comes of them. A young captain who had been a soldier in Zapata's army attempted, during a horseback ride near Cuernavaca, to express his desire for her with the noble simplicity befitting a rude folk-hero: but gently, because he was gentle. This gentleness was his defeat, for when he alighted, and removed her foot from the stirrup, and essayed to draw her down into his arms, her horse, ordinarily a tame one, shied fiercely, reared and plunged away. The young hero's horse careered blindly after his stable-mate, and the hero did not return to the hotel until rather late that evening. At breakfast he came to her table in full charro dress, gray buckskin jacket and trousers with strings of silver buttons down the leg, and he was in a humorous, careless mood. "May I sit with you?" and "You are a wonderful rider. I was terrified that you might be thrown and dragged. I should never have forgiven myself. But I cannot admire you enough for your riding!"

"I learned to ride in Arizona," said Laura.

"If you will ride with me again this morning, I promise you a horse that will not shy with you," he said. But Laura remembered that she must return to Mexico City at noon.

Next morning the children made a celebration and spent their playtime writing on the blackboard, "We lov ar ticher," and with tinted chalks they drew wreaths of flowers around the words. The young hero wrote her a letter: "I am a very foolish, wasteful, impulsive man. I should have first said I love you, and then you would not have run away. But you shall see me again." Laura thought, "I must send him a box of colored crayons," but she was trying to forgive herself for having spurred her horse at the wrong moment.

A brown, shock-haired youth came and stood in her patio one night and sang like a lost soul for two hours, but Laura could think of nothing to do about it. The moonlight spread a wash of gauzy silver over the clear spaces of the garden, and the shadows were cobalt blue. The scarlet blossoms of the Judas tree were dull purple, and the names of the colors repeated themselves automatically in her mind, while she watched not the boy, but his shadow, fallen like a dark garment across the fountain rim, trailing in the water. Lupe came silently and whispered expert counsel in her ear: "If you will throw him one little flower, he will sing another song or two and go away." Laura threw the flower, and he sang a last song and went away with the flower tucked in the band of his hat. Lupe said, "He is one of the organizers of the Typographers Union, and before that he sold corridos in the Merced market, and before that, he came from Guanajuato, where I was born. I would not trust any man, but I trust least those from Guanajuato."

She did not tell Laura that he would be back again the next night, and the next, nor that he would follow her at a certain fixed distance around the Merced market, through the Zócolo, up Francisco I. Madero Avenue, and so along the Paseo de la Reforma to Chapultepec Park, and into the Philosopher's Footpath, still with that flower withering in his hat, and an indivisible attention in his eyes.

Now Laura is accustomed to him, it means nothing except that he is nineteen years old and is observing a convention with all propriety, as though it were founded on a law of nature, which in the end it might well prove to be. He is beginning to write poems which he prints on a wooden press, and he leaves them stuck like handbills in her door. She is pleasantly disturbed by the abstract, unhurried watchfulness of his black eyes which will in time turn easily towards another object. She tells herself that throwing the flower was a mistake, for she is twenty-two years old and knows better; but she refuses to regret it, and persuades herself that her negation of all external events as they occur is a sign that she is gradually perfecting herself in the stoicism she strives to cultivate against that disaster she fears, though she cannot name it.

She is not at home in the world. Every day she teaches children who remain strangers to her, though she loves their tender round hands and their charming opportunist savagery. She knocks at unfamiliar doors not knowing whether a friend or a stranger shall answer, and even if a known face emerges from the sour gloom of that unknown interior, still it is the face of a stranger. No matter what this stranger says to her, nor what her message to him, the very cells of her flesh reject knowledge and kinship in one monotonous word. No. No. No. She draws her strength from this one holy talismanic word which does not suffer her to be led into evil. Denying everything, she may walk anywhere in safety, she looks at everything without amazement.

No, repeats this firm unchanging voice of her blood; and she looks at Braggioni without amazement. He is a great man, he wishes to impress this simple girl who covers her great round breasts with thick dark cloth, and who hides long, invaluably beautiful legs under a heavy skirt. She is almost thin except for the incomprehensible fullness of her breasts, like a nursing mother's, and Braggioni, who considers himself a judge of women, speculates again on the puzzle of her notorious virginity, and takes the liberty of speech which she permits without a sign of modesty, indeed, without any sort of sign, which is disconcerting.

"You think you are so cold, *gringita!* Wait and see. You will surprise yourself some day! May I be there to advise you!" He stretches his eyelids at her, and his ill-humored cat's eyes waver in a separate glance for the two points of light marking the opposite ends of a smoothly drawn path between the swollen curve of her breasts. He is not put off by that blue serge, nor by her resolutely fixed gaze. There is all the time in the world. His cheeks are bellying with the wind of song. "O girl with the dark eyes," he sings, and reconsiders. "But yours are not dark. I can change all that. O girl with the green eyes, you have stolen my heart away!" then his mind wanders to the song, and Laura feels the weight of his attention being shifted elsewhere. Singing thus, he seems harmless, he is quite harmless, there is nothing to do but sit patiently and say "No," when the moment comes. She draws a full breath, and her mind wanders also, but not far. She dares not wander too far.

Not for nothing has Braggioni taken pains to be a good revolutionist and a professional lover of humanity. He will never die of it. He has the malice, the cleverness, the wickedness, the sharpness of wit, the hardness of heart, stipulated for loving the world profitably. *He will never die of it*. He will live to see himself kicked out from his feeding trough by other hungry world-saviors. Traditionally he must sing in spite of his life which drives him to bloodshed, he tells Laura, for his father was a Tuscany peasant who drifted to Yucatan and married a Maya woman: a woman of race, an aristocrat. They gave him the love and knowledge of music, thus: and under the rip of his thumbnail, the strings of the instrument complain like exposed nerves.

Once he was called Delgadito by all the girls and married women who ran after him; he was so scrawny all his bones showed under his thin cotton clothing, and he could squeeze his emptiness to the very backbone with his two hands. He was a poet and the revolution was only a dream then; too many women loved him and sapped away his youth, and he could never find enough to eat anywhere, anywhere! Now he is a leader of men, crafty men who whisper in his ear, hungry men who wait for hours outside his office for a word with him, emaciated men with wild faces who waylay him at the street gate with a timid, "Comrade, let me tell you . . ." and they blow the foul breath from their empty stomachs in his face.

He is always sympathetic. He gives them handfuls of small coins from his own pocket, he promises them work, there will be demonstrations, they must join the unions and attend the meetings, above all they must be on the watch for spies. They are closer to him than his own brothers, without them he can do nothing—until tomorrow, comrade!

Until tomorrow. "They are stupid, they are lazy, they are

treacherous, they would cut my throat for nothing," he says to Laura. He has good food and abundant drink, he hires an automobile and drives in the Paseo on Sunday morning, and enjoys plenty of sleep in a soft bed beside a wife who dares not disturb him; and he sits pampering his bones in easy billows of fat, singing to Laura, who knows and thinks these things about him. When he was fifteen, he tried to drown himself because he loved a girl, his first love, and she laughed at him. "A thousand women have paid for that," and his tight little mouth turns down at the corners. Now he perfumes his hair with Jockey Club, and confides to Laura: "One woman is really as good as another for me, in the dark. I prefer them all."

His wife organizes unions among the girls in the cigarette factories, and walks in picket lines, and even speaks at meetings in the evening. But she cannot be brought to acknowledge the benefits of true liberty. "I tell her I must have my freedom, net. She does not understand my point of view." Laura has heard this many times. Braggioni scratches the guitar and meditates. "She is an instinctively virtuous woman, pure gold, no doubt of that. If she were not, I should lock her up, and she knows it."

His wife, who works so hard for the good of the factory girls, employs part of her leisure lying on the floor weeping because there are so many women in the world, and only one husband for her, and she never knows where nor when to look for him. He told her: "Unless you can learn to cry when I am not here, I must go away for good." That day he went away and took a room at the Hotel Madrid.

It is this month of separation for the sake of higher principles that has been spoiled not only for Mrs. Braggioni, whose sense of reality is beyond criticism, but for Laura, who feels herself bogged in a nightmare. Tonight Laura envies Mrs. Braggioni, who is alone, and free to weep as much as she pleases about a concrete wrong. Laura has just come from a visit to the prison, and she is waiting for tomorrow with a bitter anxiety as if tomorrow may not come, but time may be caught immovably in this hour, with herself transfixed, Braggioni singing on forever, and Eugenio's body not yet discovered by the guard.

Braggioni says: "Are you going to sleep?" Almost before she can shake her head, he begins telling her about the May-day disturbances coming on in Morelia, for the Catholics hold a festival in honor of the Blessed Virgin, and the Socialists celebrate their martyrs on that day. "There will be two independent processions, starting from either end of town, and they will march until they meet, and the rest depends . . ." He asks her to oil and load his pistols. Standing up, he unbuckles his ammunition belt, and spreads it laden across her knees. Laura sits with the shells slipping through the cleaning cloth dipped in oil, and he says again he cannot understand why she works so hard for the revolutionary idea unless she loves some man who is in it. "Are you not in love with someone?" "No," says Laura. "And no one is in love with you?" "No." "Then it is your own fault. No woman need go begging. Why, what is the matter with you? The legless beggar woman in the Alameda has a perfectly faithful lover. Did you know that?"

Laura peers down the pistol barrel and says nothing, but a long, slow faintness rises and subsides in her; Braggioni curves his swollen fingers around the throat of the guitar and softly smothers the music out of it, and when she hears him again he seems to have forgotten her, and is speaking in the hypnotic voice he uses when talking in small rooms to a listening, close-gathered crowd. Some day this world, now seemingly so composed and eternal, to the edges of every sea shall be merely a tangle of gaping trenches, of crashing walls and broken bodies. Everything must be torn from its accustomed place where it has rotted for centuries, hurled skyward and distributed, cast down again clean as rain, without separate identity. Nothing shall survive that the stiffened hands of poverty have created for the rich and no one shall be left alive except the elect spirits destined to procreate a new world cleansed of cruelty and injustice, ruled by benevolent anarchy: "Pistols are good, I love them, cannon are even better, but in the end I pin my faith to good dynamite," he concludes, and strokes the pistol lying in her hands. "Once I dreamed of destroying this city, in case it offered resistance to General Ortíz, but it fell into his hands like an overripe pear."

He is made restless by his own words, rises and stands waiting. Laura holds up the belt to him: "Put that on, and go kill somebody in Morelia, and you will be happier," she says softly. The presence of death in the room makes her bold. "Today, I found Eugenio going into a stupor. He refused to allow me to call the prison doctor. He had taken all the tablets I brought him yesterday. He said he took them because he was bored."

"He is a fool, and his death is his own business," says Braggioni, fastening his belt carefully.

"I told him if he had waited only a little while longer, you would have got him set free," says Laura. "He said he did not want to wait."

"He is a fool and we are well rid of him," says Braggioni, reaching for his hat.

He goes away. Laura knows his mood has changed, she will not see him any more for a while. He will send word when he needs her to go on errands into strange streets, to speak to the strange faces that will appear, like clay masks with the power of human speech, to mutter their thanks to Braggioni for his help. Now she is free, and she thinks, I must run while there is time. But she does not go.

Braggioni enters his own house where for a month his wife has spent many hours every night weeping and tangling her hair upon her pillow. She is weeping now, and she weeps more at the sight of him, the cause of all her sorrows. He looks about the room. Nothing is changed, the smells are good and familiar, he is well acquainted with the woman who comes toward him with no reproach except grief on her face. He says to her tenderly: "You are so good, please don't cry any more, you dear good creature." She says, "Are you tired, my angel? Sit here and I will wash your feet." She brings a bowl of water, and kneeling, unlaces his shoes, and when from her knees she raises her sad eyes under her blackened lids, he is sorry for everything, and bursts into tears. "Ah, yes, I am hungry, I am tired, let us eat something together," he says, between sobs. His wife leans her head on his arm and says, "Forgive me!" and this time he is refreshed by the solemn, endless rain of her tears.

Laura takes off her serge dress and puts on a white linen nightgown and goes to bed. She turns her head a little to one side, and lying still, reminds herself that it is time to sleep. Numbers tick in her brain like little clocks, soundless doors close of themselves around her. If you would sleep, you must not remember anything, the children will say tomorrow, good morning, my teacher, the poor prisoners who come every day bringing flowers to their jailor. 1-2-3-4-5—it is monstrous to confuse love with revolution, night with day, life with death—ah, Eugenio!

The tolling of the midnight bell is a signal, but what does it mean? Get up, Laura, and follow me: come out of your sleep, out of your bed, out of this strange house. What are you doing in this house? Without a word, without fear she rose and reached for Eugenio's hand, but he eluded her with a sharp, sly smile and drifted away. This is not all, you shall see—Murderer, he said, follow me, I will show you a new country, but it is far away and we must hurry. No, said Laura, not unless you take my hand, no; and she clung first to the stair rail, and then to the topmost branch of the Judas tree that bent down slowly and set her upon the earth, and then to the rocky ledge of a cliff, and then to the jagged wave of a sea that was not water but a desert of crumbling stone. Where are you taking me, she asked in wonder but without fear. To death, and it is a long way off, and we must hurry, said Eugenio. No, said Laura, not unless you take my hand. Then eat these flowers, poor prisoner, said Eugenio in a voice of pity, take and eat: and from the Judas tree he stripped the warm bleeding flowers, and held them to her lips. She saw that his hand was fleshless, a cluster of small white petrified branches, and his eye sockets were without light, but she ate the flowers greedily for they satisfied both hunger and thirst. Murderer! said Eugenio, and Cannibal! This is my body and my blood. Laura cried No! and at the sound of her own voice, she awoke trembling, and was afraid to sleep again.

◆ ————————————————————————————— ◆

THE VALIANT WOMAN

J. F. Powers

They had come to the dessert in a dinner that was a shambles. "Well, John," Father Nulty said, turning away from Mrs. Stoner and to Father Firman, long gone silent at his own table. "You've got the bishop coming for confirmations next week."

"Yes," Mrs. Stoner cut in, "and for dinner. And if he don't eat any more than he did last year—"

Father Firman, in a rare moment, faced it. "Mrs. Stoner, the bishop is not well. You know that."

"And after I fixed that fine dinner and all." Mrs. Stoner pouted in Father Nulty's direction.

"I wouldn't feel bad about it, Mrs. Stoner," Father Nulty said. "He never eats much anywhere."

"It's funny. And that new Mrs. Allers said he ate just fine when he was there," Mrs. Stoner argued, and then spit out, "but she's a damned liar!"

Father Nulty, unsettled but trying not to show it, said, "Who's Mrs. Allers?"

"She's at Holy Cross," Mrs. Stoner said.

"She's the housekeeper," Father Firman added, thinking Mrs. Stoner made it sound as though Mrs. Allers were the pastor there.

"I swear I don't know what to do about the dinner this year," Mrs. Stoner said.

Father Firman moaned. "Just do as you've always done, Mrs. Stoner."

"Huh! And have it all to throw out! Is that any way to do?"

"Is there any dessert?" Father Firman asked coldly.

Mrs. Stoner leaped up from the table and bolted into the kitchen, mumbling. She came back with a birthday cake. She plunged it in the center of the table. She found a big wooden match in her apron pocket and thrust it at Father Firman.

"I don't like this bishop," she said. "I never did. And the way he went and cut poor Ellen Kennedy out of Father Doolin's will!"

She went back into the kitchen.

"Didn't they talk a lot of filth about Doolin and the housekeeper?" Father Nulty asked.

"I should think they did," Father Firman said. "All because he took her to the movies on Sunday night. After he died and the bishop cut her out of the will, though I hear he gives her a pension privately, they talked about the bishop."

"I don't like this bishop at all," Mrs. Stoner said, appearing with a cake knife. "Bishop Doran—there was the man!"

"We know," Father Firman said. "All man and all priest."

"He did know real estate," Father Nulty said.

Father Firman struck the match.

"Not on the chair!" Mrs. Stoner cried, too late.

Father Firman set the candle burning—it was suspiciously large and yellow, like a blessed one, but he could not be sure. They watched the fluttering flame.

"I'm forgetting the lights!" Mrs. Stoner said, and got up to turn them off. She went into the kitchen again.

The priests had a moment of silence in the candle-light.

"Happy birthday, John," Father Nulty said softly. "Is it fifty-nine you are?"

"As if you didn't know, Frank," Father Firman said, "and you the same but one."

Father Nulty smiled, the old gold of his incisors shining in the flickering light, his collar whiter in the dark, and raised his glass of water, which would have been wine or better in the bygone days, and toasted Father Firman.

"Many of 'em, John."

"Blow it out," Mrs. Stoner said, returning to the room. She waited by the light switch for Father Firman to blow out the candle.

Mrs. Stoner, who ate no desserts, began to clear the dishes into the kitchen, and the priests, finishing their cake and coffee in a hurry, went to sit in the study.

Father Nulty offered a cigar.

"John?"

"My ulcers, Frank."

"Ah, well, you're better off." Father Nulty lit the cigar and crossed his long black legs. "Fish Frawley has got him a Filipino, John. Did you hear?"

Father Firman leaned forward, interested. "He got rid of the woman he had?"

"He did. It seems she snooped."

"Snooped, eh?"

"She did. And gossiped. Fish introduced two town boys to her, said, 'Would you think these boys were my nephews?' That's all, and the next week the paper had it that his two nephews were visiting him from Erie. After that, he let her believe he was going East to see his parents, though both are dead. The paper carried the story. Fish returned and made a sermon out of it. Then he got the Filipino."

Father Firman squirmed with pleasure in his chair. "That's like Fish, Frank. He can do that." He stared at the tips of his fingers bleakly. "You could never get a Filipino to come to a place like this."

"Probably not," Father Nulty said. "Fish is pretty close to

Minneapolis. Ah, say, do you remember the trick he played on us all in Marmion Hall!"

"That I'll not forget!" Father Firman's eyes remembered. "Getting up New Year's morning and finding the toilet seats all painted!

"Happy Circumcision! Hah!" Father Nulty had a coughing fit.

When he had got himself together again, a mosquito came and sat on his wrist. He watched it a moment before bringing his heavy hand down. He raised his hand slowly, viewed the dead mosquito, and sent it spinning with a plunk of his middle finger.

"Only the female bites," he said.

"I didn't know that," Father Firman said.

"Ah, yes . . ."

Mrs. Stoner entered the study and sat down with some sewing—Father Firman's black socks.

She smiled pleasantly at Father Nulty. "And what do you think of the atom bomb, Father?"

"Not much," Father Nulty said.

Mrs. Stoner had stopped smiling. Father Firman yawned.

Mrs. Stoner served up another: "Did you read about this communist convert, Father?"

"He's been in the Church before," Father Nulty said, "and so it's not a conversion, Mrs. Stoner."

"No? Well, I already got him down on my list of Monsignor's converts."

"It's better than a conversion, Mrs. Stoner, for there is more rejoicing in heaven over the return of . . .uh, he that was lost, Mrs. Stoner, is found."

"And that congresswoman, Father?"

"Yes. A convert—she."

"And Henry Ford's grandson, Father. I got him down."

"Yes, to be sure."

Father Firman yawned, this time audibly, and held his jaw.

"But he's one only by marriage, Father," Mrs. Stoner said. "I always say you got to watch those kind."

"Indeed you do, but a convert nonetheless, Mrs. Stoner. Remember, Cardinal Newman himself was one."

Mrs. Stoner was unimpressed. "I see where Henry Ford's making steering wheels out of soybeans, Father."

"I didn't see that."

"I read it in the *Reader's Digest* or some place."

"Yes, well . . ." Father Nulty rose and held his hand out to Father Firman. "John," he said. "It's been good."

"I heard Hirohito's next," Mrs. Stoner said, returning to converts.

"Let's wait and see, Mrs. Stoner," Father Nulty said.

The priests walked to the door.

"You know where I live, John."

"Yes. Come again, Frank. Good night."

Father Firman watched Father Nulty go down the walk to his car at the curb. He hooked the screen door and turned off the porch light. He hesitated at the foot of the stairs, suddenly moved to go to bed. But he went back into the study.

"Phew!" Mrs. Stoner said. "I thought he'd never go. Here it is after eight o'clock."

Father Firman sat down in his rocking chair. "I don't see him often," he said.

"I give up!" Mrs. Stoner exclaimed, flinging the holey socks upon the horsehair sofa. "I'd swear you had a nail in your shoe."

"I told you I looked."

"Well, you ought to look again. And cut your toenails, why don't you? Haven't I got enough to do?"

Father Firman scratched in his coat pocket for a pill, found one, swallowed it. He let his head sink back against the chair and closed his eyes. He could hear her moving about the room, making the preparations; and how he knew them—the fumbling in the drawer for a pencil with a point, the rip of the page from his daily calendar, and finally the leg of the card table sliding up against his leg.

He opened his eyes. She yanked the floor lamp alongside the table, setting the bead fringe tinkling on the shade, and pulled up her chair on the other side. She sat down and smiled at him for the first time that day. Now she was happy.

She swept up the cards and began to shuffle with the abandoned virtuosity of an old riverboat gambler, standing them on end, fanning them out, whirling them through her fingers, dancing them halfway up her arms, cracking the whip over them. At last they lay before him tamed into a neat deck.

"Cut?"

"Go ahead," he said. She liked to go first.

She gave him her faint, avenging smile and drew a card, cast it aside for another which he thought must be an ace from the way she clutched it face down.

She was getting all the cards, as usual, and would have been invincible if she had possessed his restraint and if her cunning had been of a higher order. He knew a few things about leading and lying back that she would never learn. Her strategy was attack, forever attack, with one baffling departure: she might sacrifice certain tricks as expendable if only she could have the last ones, the heartbreaking ones, if she could slap them down one after another, shatteringly.

She played for blood, no bones about it, but for her there was no other way; it was her nature, as it was the lion's, and for this reason he found her ferocity pardonable, more a defect of the flesh, venial, while his own trouble was all in the will, mortal. He did not sweat and pray over each card as she must, but he did keep an eye out for reneging and demanded a cut now and then just to aggravate her, and he was always secretly hoping for aces.

With one card left in her hand, the telltale trick coming next, she delayed playing it, showing him first the smile, the preview of defeat. She laid it on the table—so! She held one more trump than he had reasoned possible. Had she palmed it from somewhere? No, she would not go that far; that would not be fair, was worse than reneging, which so easily and often happened accidentally, and she believed in being fair. Besides he had been watching her.

God smote the vines with hail, the sycamore trees with frost, and offered up the flocks to the lightning—but Mrs. Stoner! What a cross Father Firman had from God in Mrs. Stoner! There were other housekeepers as bad, no doubt, walking the rectories of the world, yes, but . . . yes. He could name one and maybe two priests who were worse off. One, maybe two. Cronin. His scraggly blonde of sixty— take her, with her everlasting banging on the grand piano, the gift of the pastor; her proud talk about the goiter operation at the Mayo Brothers', also a gift; her honking the parish Buick at passing strange priests because they were all in the game together. She was worse. She was something to keep the home fires burning. Yes sir. And Cronin said she was not a bad person really, but what was he? He was quite a freak himself.

For that matter, could anyone say that Mrs. Stoner was a bad person? No. He could not say it himself, and he was no freak. She had her points, Mrs. Stoner. She was clean. And though she cooked poorly, could not play the organ, would not take up the collection in an emergency, and went to card parties, and told all—even so, she was clean. She washed everything. Sometimes her underwear hung down beneath her dress like a paratrooper's pants, but it and everything she touched was clean. She washed constantly. She was clean.

She had her other points, to be sure—her faults, you might say. She snooped—no mistake about it—but it was not snooping for snooping's sake; she had a reason. She did other things, always with a reason. She overcharged on rosaries and prayer books, but that was for the sake of the poor. She censored the pamphlet rack, but that was to prevent scandal. She pried into the baptismal and matrimonial records, but there was no other way if Father was out, and in this way she had once uncovered a bastard and flushed him out of the rectory, but that was the perverted decency of the times. She held her nose over bad marriages in the presence of the victims, but that was her sorrow and came from having her husband buried in a mine. And he had caught her telling a bewildered young couple that there was only one good reason for their wanting to enter into a mixed marriage—the child had to have a name, and that—that was what?

She hid his books, kept him from smoking, picked his friends (usually the pastors of her colleagues), bawled out people for calling after dark, had no humor, except at cards, and then it was grim, very grim, and she sat hatchet-faced every morning at Mass. But she went to Mass, which was all that kept the church from being empty some mornings. She did annoying things all day long. She said annoying things into the night. She said she had given him the best years of her life. Had she? Perhaps—for the miner had her only a year. It was too bad, sinfully bad, when he thought of it like that. But all talk of best years and life was nonsense. He had to consider the heart of the matter, the essence. The essence was that housekeepers were hard to get, harder to get than ushers, than willing workers, than organists, than secretaries—yes, harder to get than assistants or vocations.

And she was a *saver*—saved money, saved electricity, saved string, bags, sugar, saved—him. That's what she did. That's what she said she did, and she was right, in a way. In a way, she was usually right. In fact, she was always right—in a way. And you could never get a Filipino to come way out here and live. Not a young one anyway, and he had never seen an old one. Not a Filipino. They liked to dress up and live.

Should he let it drop about Fish having one, just to throw a scare into her, let her know he was doing some thinking? No. It would be a perfect cue for the one about a man needing a woman to look after him. He was not up to that again, not tonight.

Now she was doing what she liked most of all. She was making a grand slam, playing it out card for card, though it was in the bag, prolonging what would have been cut short out of mercy in gentle company. Father Firman knew the agony of losing.

She slashed down the last card, a miserable deuce trump, and did in the hapless king of hearts he had been saving.

"Skunked you!"

She was awful in victory. Here was the bitter end of their long day together, the final murderous hour in which all they wanted to say—all he wouldn't and all she couldn't —came out in the cards. Whoever won at honeymoon won the day, slept on the other's scalp, and God alone had to help the loser.

"We've been at it long enough, Mrs. Stoner," he said, seeing her assembling the cards for another round.

"Had enough, huh!"

Father Firman grumbled something.

"No?"

"Yes."

She pulled the table away and left it against the wall for the next time. She went out of the study carrying the socks, content and clucking. He closed his eyes after her and began to get under way in the rocking chair, the nightly trip to nowhere. He could hear her brewing a cup of tea in the kitchen and conversing with the cat. She made her way up the stairs, carrying the tea, followed by the cat, purring.

He waited, rocking out to sea, until she would be sure to be through in the bathroom. Then he got up and locked the front door (she looked after the back door) and loosened his collar going upstairs.

In the bathroom he mixed a glass of antiseptic, always afraid of pyorrhea, and gargled to ward off pharyngitis.

When he turned on the light in his room, the moths and beetles began to batter against the screens, the lighter insects humming. . . .

Yes, and she had the guest room. How did she come to get that? Why wasn't she in the back room, in her proper place? He knew, if he cared to remember. The screen in the back room—it let in mosquitoes, and if it didn't do that she'd love to sleep back there, Father, looking out at the steeple and the blessed cross on top, Father, if it just weren't for the screen, Father. Very well, Mrs. Stoner, I'll get it fixed or fix it myself. Oh, could you now, Father? I could, Mrs. Stoner, and I will. In the meantime you take the guest room.

Yes, Father, and thank you, Father, the house ringing with amenities then. Years ago, all that. She was a pie-faced girl then, not really a girl perhaps, but not too old to marry again. But she never had. In fact, he could not remember that she had even tried for a husband since coming to the rectory, but, of course, he could be wrong, not knowing how they went about it. God! God save us! Had she got her wires crossed and mistaken him all these years for *that? That!* Him! Suffering God! No. That was going too far. That was getting morbid. No. He must not think of that again, ever. No.

But just the same she had got the guest room and she had it yet. Well, did it matter? Nobody ever came to see him any more, nobody to stay overnight anyway, nobody to stay very long . . . not any more. He knew how they laughed at him. He had heard Frank humming all right—before he saw how serious and sad the situation was and took pity—humming, "Wedding Bells Are Breaking Up That Old Gang of Mine." But then they'd always laughed at him for something—for not being an athlete, for wearing glasses, for having kidney trouble . . . and mail coming addressed to Rev. and Mrs. Stoner.

Removing his shirt, he bent over the table to read the volume left open from last night. He read, translating easily, "Eisdem licet cum illis . . . Clerics are allowed to reside only with women about whom there can be no suspicion, either because of a natural bond (as mother, sister, aunt) or of advanced age, combined in both cases with good repute."

Last night he had read it, and many nights before, each time as though this time to find what was missing, to find what obviously was not in the paragraph, his problem considered, a way out. She was not mother, not sister, not aunt, and *advanced age* was a relative term (why, she was younger than he was) and so, eureka, she did not meet the letter of the law—but, alas, how she fulfilled the spirit! And besides it would be a slimy way of handling it after all her years of service. He could not afford to pension her off, either.

He slammed the book shut. He slapped himself fiercely on the back, missing the wily mosquito, and whirled to find it. He took a magazine and folded it into a swatter. Then he saw it—oh, the preternatural cunning of it!—poised in the beard of St. Joseph on the bookcase. He could not hit it there. He teased it away, wanting it to light on the wall, but it knew his thoughts and flew high away. He swung wildly, hoping to stun it, missed, swung back, catching St. Joseph across the neck. The statue fell to the floor and broke.

Mrs. Stoner was panting in the hall outside his door.

"What is it!"

"Mosquitoes!"

"What is it, Father? Are you hurt?"

"Mosquitoes—damn it! And only the female bites!"

Mrs. Stoner, after a moment, said, "Shame on you, Father. She needs the blood for her eggs."

He dropped the magazine and lunged at the mosquito with his bare hand.

She went back to her room, saying, "Pshaw, I thought it was burglars murdering you in your bed."

He lunged again.

◆ ─────────────── ◆

THE EIGHTY-YARD RUN

Irwin Shaw

The pass was high and wide and he jumped for it, feeling it slap flatly against his hands, as he shook his hips to throw off the halfback who was diving at him. The center floated by, his hands desperately brushing Darling's knee as Darling picked his feet up high and delicately ran over a blocker and an opposing linesman in a jumble on the ground near the scrimmage line. He had ten yards in the clear and picked up speed, breathing easily, feeling his thigh pads rising and falling against his legs, listening to the sound of cleats behind him, pulling away from them, watching the other backs heading him off toward the sideline, the whole picture, the men closing in on him, the blockers fighting for position, the ground he had to cross, all suddenly clear in his head, for the first time in his life not a meaningless confusion of men, sounds, speed. He smiled a little to himself as he ran, holding the ball lightly in front of him with his two hands, his knees pumping high, his hips twisting in the almost girlish run of a back in a broken field. The first halfback came at him and he fed him his leg, then swung at the last moment, took the shock of the man's shoulder without breaking stride, ran right through him, his cleats biting securely into the turf. There was only the safety man now, coming warily at him, his arms crooked, hands spread. Darling tucked the ball in, spurted at him, driving hard, hurling himself along, all two hundred pounds bunched into controlled attack. He was sure he was going to get past the safety man. Without thought, his arms and legs working beautifully together, he headed right for the safety man, stiff-armed him, feeling blood spurt instantaneously from the man's nose onto his hand, seeing his face go awry, head turned, mouth pulled to one side. He pivoted away, keeping the arm locked, dropping the safety man as he ran easily toward the goal line, with the drumming of cleats diminishing behind him.

How long ago? It was autumn then, and the ground was getting hard because the nights were cold and leaves from the maples around the stadium blew across the practice fields in gusts of wind, and the girls were beginning to put polo coats over their sweaters when they came to watch practice in the afternoons. . . . Fifteen years. Darling walked slowly over the same ground in the spring twilight, in his neat shoes, a man of thirty-five dressed in a double-breasted suit, ten pounds heavier in the fifteen years, but not fat, with the years between 1925 and 1940 showing in his face.

The coach was smiling quietly to himself and the assistant coaches were looking at each other with pleasure the way they always did when one of the second stringers suddenly did something fine, bringing credit to them, making their $2,000 a year a tiny bit more secure.

Darling trotted back, smiling, breathing deeply but easily, feeling wonderful, not tired, though this was the tail end of practice and he'd run eighty yards. The sweat poured off his face and soaked his jersey and he liked the feeling, the warm moistness lubricating his skin like oil. Off in a corner of the field some players were punting and the smack of leather against the ball came pleasantly through the afternoon air. The freshmen were running signals on the next field and the quarterback's sharp voice, the pound of the eleven pairs of cleats, the "Dig, now *dig!*" of the coaches, the laughter of the players all somehow made him feel happy as he trotted back to midfield, listening to the applause and shouts of the students along the sidelines, knowing that after that run the coach would have to start him Saturday against Illinois.

Fifteen years, Darling thought, remembering the shower after the workout, the hot water steaming off his skin and the deep soapsuds and all the young voices singing with the water streaming down and towels going and managers running in and out and the sharp sweet smell of oil of wintergreen and everybody clapping him on the back as he dressed and Packard, the captain, who took being captain very seriously, coming over to him and shaking his hand and saying, "Darling, you're going to go places in the next two years."

The assistant manager fussed over him, wiping a cut on his leg with alcohol and iodine, the little sting making him realize suddenly how fresh and whole and solid his body felt. The manager slapped a piece of adhesive tape over the cut, and Darling noticed the sharp clean white of the tape against the ruddiness of the skin, fresh from the shower.

He dressed slowly, the softness of his shirt and the soft

warmth of his wool socks and his flannel trousers a reward against his skin after the harsh pressure of the shoulder harness and thigh and hip pads. He drank three glasses of cold water, the liquid reaching down coldly inside of him, soothing the harsh dry places in his throat and belly left by the sweat and running and shouting of practice.

Fifteen years.

The sun had gone down and the sky was green behind the stadium and he laughed quietly to himself as he looked at the stadium, rearing above the trees, and knew that on Saturday when the 70,000 voices roared as the team came running out onto the field, part of that enormous salute would be for him. He walked slowly, listening to the gravel crunch satisfactorily under his shoes in the still twilight, feeling his clothes swing lightly against his skin, breathing the thin evening air, feeling the wind more softly in his damp hair, wonderfully cool behind his ears and at the nape of his neck.

Louise was waiting for him at the road, in her car. The top was down and he noticed all over again, as he always did when he saw her, how pretty she was, the rough blonde hair and the large, inquiring eyes and the bright mouth, smiling now.

She threw the door open. "Were you good today?" she asked.

"Pretty good," he said. He climbed in, sank luxuriously into the soft leather, stretched his legs far out. He smiled, thinking of the eighty yards. "Pretty damn good."

She looked at him seriously for a moment, then scrambled around, like a little girl, kneeling on the seat next to him, grabbed him, her hands along his ears, and kissed him as he sprawled, head back, on the seat cushion. She let go of him, but kept her head close to his, over his. Darling reached up slowly and rubbed the back of his hand against her cheek, lit softly by a street lamp a hundred feet away. They looked at each other, smiling.

Louise drove down to the lake and they sat there silently, watching the moon rise behind the hills on the other side.

Finally he reached over, pulled her gently to him, kissed her. Her lips grew soft, her body sank into his, tears formed slowly in her eyes. He knew, for the first time, that he could do whatever he wanted with her.

"Tonight," he said. "I'll call for you at seven-thirty. Can you get out?"

She looked at him. She was smiling, but the tears were still full in her eyes. "All right," she said. "I'll get out. How about you? Won't the coach raise hell?"

Darling grinned. "I got the coach in the palm of my hand," he said. "Can you wait till seven-thirty?"

She grinned back at him. "No," she said.

They kissed and she started the car and they went back to town for dinner. He sang on the way home.

Christian Darling, thirty-five years old, sat on the frail spring grass, greener now than it ever would be again on the practice field, looked thoughtfully up at the stadium, a deserted ruin in the twilight. He had started on the first team that Saturday and every Saturday after that for the next two years, but it had never been as satisfactory as it should have been. He never had broken away, the longest run he'd ever made was thirty-five yards, and that in a game that was already won, and then that kid had come up from the third team, Diederich, a blank-faced German kid from Wisconsin, who ran like a bull, ripping lines to pieces Saturday after Saturday, plowing through, never getting hurt, never changing his expression, scoring more points, gaining more ground than all the rest of the team put together, making everybody's All-American, carrying the ball three times out of four, keeping everybody else out of the headlines. Darling was a good blocker and he spent his Saturday afternoons working on the big Swedes and Polacks who played tackle and end for Michigan, Illinois, Purdue, hurling into huge pile-ups, bobbing his head wildly to elude the great raw hands swinging like meat-cleavers at him as he went charging in to open up holes for Diederich coming through like a locomotive behind him. Still, it wasn't so bad. Everybody liked him and he did his job and he was pointed out on the campus and boys always felt important when they introduced their girls to him at their proms, and Louise loved him and watched him faithfully in the games, even in the mud, when your own mother wouldn't know you, and drove him around in her car keeping the top down because she was proud of him and wanted to show everybody that she was Christian Darling's girl. She bought him crazy presents because her father was rich, watches, pipes, humidors, an icebox for beer for his room, curtains, wallets, a fifty-dollar dictionary.

"You'll spend every cent your old man owns," Darling protested once when she showed up at his rooms with seven different packages in her arms and tossed them onto the couch.

"Kiss me," Louise said, "and shut up."

"Do you want to break your poor old man?"

"I don't mind. I want to buy you presents."

"Why?"

"It makes me feel good. Kiss me. I don't know why. Did you know that you're an important figure?"

"Yes," Darling said gravely.

"When I was waiting for you at the library yesterday two girls saw you coming and one of them said to the other, 'That's Christian Darling. He's an important figure.' "

"You're a liar."

"I'm in love with an important figure."

"Still, why the hell did you have to give me a forty-pound dictionary?"

"I wanted to make sure," Louise said, "that you had a token of my esteem. I want to smother you in tokens of my esteem."

Fifteen years ago.

They'd married when they got out of college. There'd been other women for him, but all casual and secret, more for curiosity's sake, and vanity, women who'd thrown themselves at him and flattered him, a pretty mother at a summer camp for boys, an old girl from his home town who'd suddenly blossomed into a coquette, a friend of Louise's who had dogged him grimly for six months and had taken advantage of the two weeks that Louise went home when her mother died. Perhaps Louise had known, but she'd kept quiet, loving him completely, filling his rooms with presents, religiously watching him battling with the big Swedes and Polacks on the line of scrimmage on Saturday afternoons, making plans for marrying him and living with him in New York and going with him there to the night clubs, the theaters, the good restaurants, being proud of him in advance, tall, white-teethed, smiling, large, yet moving lightly, with an athlete's grace, dressed in evening clothes, approvingly eyed by magnificently dressed and famous women in theater lobbies, with Louise adoringly at his side.

Her father, who manufactured inks, set up a New York office for Darling to manage and presented him with three hundred accounts, and they lived on Beekman Place with a view of the river with fifteen thousand dollars a year between them, because everybody was buying everything in those days, including ink. They saw all the shows and went to all the speakeasies and spent their fifteen thousand dollars a year and in the afternoons Louise went to the art galleries and the matinees of the more serious plays that Darling didn't like to sit through and Darling slept with a girl who danced in the chorus of *Rosalie* and with the wife of a man who owned three copper mines. Darling played squash three times a week and remained as solid as a stone barn and Louise never took her eyes off him when they were in the same room together, watching him with a secret, miser's smile, with a trick of coming over to him in the middle of a crowded room and saying gravely, in a low voice, "You're the handsomest man I've ever seen in my whole life. Want a drink?"

Nineteen twenty-nine came to Darling and to his wife and father-in-law, the maker of inks, just as it came to everyone else. The father-in-law waited until 1933 and then blew his brains out and when Darling went to Chicago to see what the books of the firm looked like he found out all

that was left were debts and three or four gallons of un-
bought ink.

"Please, Christian," Louise said, sitting in their neat
Beekman Place apartment, with a view of the river and
prints of paintings by Dufy and Braque and Picasso on the
wall, "please, why do you want to start drinking at two
o'clock in the afternoon?"

"I have nothing else to do," Darling said, putting down
his glass, emptied of its fourth drink. "Please pass the
whisky."

Louise filled his glass. "Come take a walk with me," she
said. "We'll walk along the river."

"I don't want to walk along the river," Darling said,
squinting intensely at the prints of paintings by Dufy, Braque
and Picasso.

"We'll walk along Fifth Avenue."

"I don't want to walk along Fifth Avenue."

"Maybe," Louise said gently, "you'd like to come with me
to some art galleries. There's an exhibition by a man named
Klee. . . ."

"I don't want to go to any art galleries. I want to sit here
and drink Scotch whisky," Darling said. "Who the hell hung
these goddam pictures up on the wall?"

"I did," Louise said.

"I hate them."

"I'll take them down," Louise said.

"Leave them there. It gives me something to do in the
afternoon. I can hate them." Darling took a long swallow.
"Is that the way people paint these days?"

"Yes, Christian. Please don't drink any more."

"Do you like painting like that?"

"Yes dear."

"Really?"

"Really."

Darling looked carefully at the prints once more. "Little
Louise Tucker. The middle-western beauty. I like pictures
with horses in them. Why should you like pictures like
that?"

"I just happen to have gone to a lot of galleries in the last few years . . ."

"Is that what you do in the afternoon?"

"That's what I do in the afternoon," Louise said.

"I drink in the afternoon."

Louise kissed him lightly on the top of his head as he sat there squinting at the pictures on the wall, the glass of whisky held firmly in his hand. She put on her coat and went out without saying another word. When she came back in the early evening, she had a job on a woman's fashion magazine.

They moved downtown and Louise went out to work every morning and Darling sat home and drank and Louise paid the bills as they came up. She made believe she was going to quit work as soon as Darling found a job, even though she was taking over more responsibility day by day at the magazine, interviewing authors, picking painters for the illustrations and covers, getting actresses to pose for pictures, going out for drinks with the right people, making a thousand new friends whom she loyally introduced to Darling.

"I don't like your hat," Darling said, once, when she came in in the evening and kissed him, her breath rich with Martinis.

"What's the matter with my hat, Baby?" she asked, running her fingers through his hair. "Everybody says it's very smart."

"It's too damned smart," he said. "It's not for you. It's for a rich, sophisticated woman of thirty-five with admirers."

Louise laughed. "I'm practicing to be a rich, sophisticated woman of thirty-five with admirers," she said. He stared soberly at her. "Now, don't look so grim, Baby. It's still the same simple little wife under the hat." She took the hat off, threw it into a corner, sat on his lap. "See? Homebody Number One."

"Your breath could run a train," Darling said, not wanting to be mean, but talking out of boredom, and sudden shock at seeing his wife curiously a stranger in a new hat, with a new expression in her eyes under the little brim, secret, confident, knowing.

Louise tucked her head under his chin so he couldn't smell her breath. "I had to take an author out for cocktails," she said. "He's a boy from the Ozark Mountains and he drinks like a fish. He's a Communist."

"What the hell is a Communist from the Ozarks doing writing for a woman's fashion magazine?"

Louise chuckled. "The magazine business is getting all mixed up these days. The publishers want to have a foot in every camp. And anyway, you can't find an author under seventy these days who isn't a Communist."

"I don't think I like you to associate with all those people, Louise," Darling said. "Drinking with them."

"He's a very nice, gentle boy," Louise said. "He reads Ernest Dowson."

"Who's Ernest Dowson?"

Louise patted his arm, stood up, fixed her hair. "He's an English poet."

Darling felt that somehow he had disappointed her. "Am I supposed to know who Ernest Dowson is?"

"No, dear. I'd better go in and take a bath."

After she had gone, Darling went over to the corner where the hat was lying and picked it up. It was nothing, a scrap of straw, a red flower, a veil, meaningless on his big hand, but on his wife's head a signal of something . . . big city, smart and knowing women drinking and dining with men other than their husbands, conversation about things a normal man wouldn't know much about, Frenchmen who painted as though they used their elbows instead of brushes, composers who wrote whole symphonies without a single melody in them, writers who knew all about politics and women who knew all about writers, the movement of the proletariat, Marx, somehow mixed up with five-dollar dinners and the best-looking women in America and fairies who made them laugh and half-sentences immediately understood and secretly hilarious and wives who called their husbands "Baby." He put the hat down, a scrap of straw and a red flower, and a little veil. He drank some whisky straight and went into the bathroom where his wife was lying deep in her bath, singing to herself and smiling from time to time like a little girl, paddling the water gently with her hands, sending up a slight spicy fragrance from the bath salts she used.

He stood over her, looking down at her. She smiled up at him, her eyes half closed, her body pink and shimmering in the warm, scented water. All over again, with all the old suddenness, he was hit deep inside him with the knowledge of how beautiful she was, how much he needed her.

"I came in here," he said, "to tell you I wish you wouldn't call me 'Baby.' "

She looked up at him from the bath, her eyes quickly full of sorrow, half-understanding what he meant. He knelt and put his arms around her, his sleeves plunged heedlessly in the water, his shirt and jacket soaking wet as he clutched her wordlessly, holding her crazily tight, crushing her breath from her, kissing her desperately, searchingly, regretfully.

He got jobs after that, selling real estate and automobiles, but somehow, although he had a desk with his name on a wooden wedge on it, and he went to the office religiously at nine each morning, he never managed to sell anything and he never made any money.

Louise was made assistant editor, and the house was always full of strange men and women who talked fast and got angry on abstract subjects like mural painting, novelists, labor unions. Negro short-story writers drank Louise's liquor, and a lot of Jews, and big solemn men with scarred faces and knotted hands who talked slowly but clearly about picket lines and battles with guns and leadpipe at mine-shaft-heads and in front of factory gates. And Louise moved among them all, confidently, knowing what they were talking about, with opinions that they listened to and argued about just as though she were a man. She knew everybody, condescended to no one, devoured books that Darling had never heard of, walked along the streets of the city, excited, at home, soaking in all the million tides of New York without fear, with constant wonder.

Her friends liked Darling and sometimes he found a man who wanted to get off in the corner and talk about the new boy who played fullback for Princeton, and the decline of the double wing-back, or even the state of the stock market, but for the most part he sat on the edge of things, solid and quiet in the high storm of words. "The dialectics of the situation . . . The theater has been given over to expert jugglers . . . Picasso? What man has a right to paint old bones and collect ten thousand dollars for them? . . . I stand firmly behind Trotsky . . . Poe was the last American critic. When he died they put lilies on the grave of American criticism. I don't say this because they panned my last book, but . . ."

Once in a while he caught Louise looking soberly and consideringly at him through the cigarette smoke and the noise and he avoided her eyes and found an excuse to get up and go into the kitchen for more ice or to open another bottle.

"Come on," Cathal Flaherty was saying, standing at the door with a girl, "you've got to come down and see this. It's down on Fourteenth Street, in the old Civic Repertory, and you can only see it on Sunday nights and I guarantee you'll come out of the theater singing." Flaherty was a big young Irishman with a broken nose who was the lawyer for a longshoreman's union, and he had been hanging around the house for six months on and off, roaring and shutting everybody else up when he got in an argument. "It's a new play, *Waiting for Lefty*; it's about taxi-drivers."

"Odets," the girl with Flaherty said. "It's by a guy named Odets."

"I never heard of him," Darling said.

"He's a new one," the girl said.

"It's like watching a bombardment," Flaherty said. "I saw it last Sunday night. You've got to see it."

"Come on, Baby," Louise said to Darling, excitement in her eyes already. "We've been sitting in the Sunday *Times* all day, this'll be a great change."

"I see enough taxi-drivers every day," Darling said, not because he meant that, but because he didn't like to be around Flaherty, who said things that made Louise laugh a lot and whose judgment she accepted on almost every subject. "Let's go to the movies."

"You've never seen anything like this before," Flaherty said. "He wrote this play with a baseball bat."

"Come on," Louise coaxed, "I bet it's wonderful."

"He has long hair," the girl with Flaherty said. "Odets. I met him at a party. He's an actor. He didn't say a goddam thing all night."

"I don't feel like going down to Fourteenth Street," Darling said, wishing Flaherty and his girl would get out. "It's gloomy."

"Oh, hell!" Louise said loudly. She looked coolly at Darling, as though she'd just been introduced to him and was making up her mind about him, and not very favorably. He saw her looking at him, knowing there was something new and dangerous in her face and he wanted to say something, but Flaherty was there and his damned girl, and anyway, he didn't know what to say.

"I'm going," Louise said, getting her coat. "I don't think Fourteenth Street is gloomy."

"I'm telling you," Flaherty was saying, helping her on with her coat, "it's the Battle of Gettysburg, in Brooklynese."

"Nobody could get a word out of him," Flaherty's girl was saying as they went through the door. "He just sat there all night."

The door closed. Louise hadn't said good night to him. Darling walked around the room four times, then sprawled out on the sofa, on top of the Sunday *Times*. He lay there for five minutes looking at the ceiling, thinking of Flaherty walking down the street talking in that booming voice, between the girls, holding their arms.

Louise had looked wonderful. She'd washed her hair in the afternoon and it had been very soft and light and clung close to her head as she stood there angrily putting her coat on. Louise was getting prettier every year, partly because she knew by now how pretty she was, and made the most of it.

"Nuts," Darling said, standing up. "Oh, nuts."

He put on his coat and went down to the nearest bar and had five drinks off by himself in a corner before his money ran out.

The years since then had been foggy and downhill. Louise had been nice to him, and in a way, loving and kind, and they'd fought only once, when he said he was going to vote for Landon. ("Oh, Christ," she'd said, "doesn't *anything* happen inside your head? Don't you read the papers? The penniless Republican!") She'd been sorry later and apologized for hurting him, but apologized as she might to a child. He'd tried hard, had gone grimly to the art galleries, the concert halls, the bookshops, trying to gain on the trail of his wife, but it was no use. He was bored, and none of what he saw or heard or dutifully read made much sense to him and finally he gave it up. He had thought, many nights as he ate dinner alone, knowing that Louise would come home late and drop silently into bed without explanation, of getting a divorce, but he knew the loneliness, the hopelessness, of not seeing her again would be too much to take. So he was good, completely devoted, ready at all times to go any place with her, do anything she wanted. He even got a small job, in a broker's office and paid his own way, bought his own liquor.

Then he'd been offered the job of going from college to college as a tailor's representative. "We want a man," Mr. Rosenberg had said, "who as soon as you look at him, you say, 'There's a university man.'" Rosenberg had looked approvingly at Darling's broad shoulders and well-kept waist, at his carefully brushed hair and his honest, wrinkleless face. "Frankly, Mr. Darling, I am willing to make you a proposition. I have inquired about you, you are favorably known on your old campus, I understand you were in the backfield with Alfred Diederich."

Darling nodded. "Whatever happened to him?"

"He is walking around in a cast for seven years now. An iron brace. He played professional football and they broke his neck for him."

Darling smiled. That, at least, had turned out well.

"Our suits are an easy product to sell, Mr. Darling," Rosenberg said. "We have a handsome, custom-made garment. What has Brooks Brothers got that we haven't got? A name. No more."

"I can make fifty-sixty dollars a week," Darling said to Louise that night. "And expenses. I can save some money and then come back to New York and really get started here."

"Yes, Baby," Louise said.

"As it is," Darling said carefully, "I can make it back here once a month, and holidays and the summer. We can see each other often."

"Yes, Baby." He looked at her face, lovelier now at thirty-five than it had ever been before, but fogged over now as it had been for five years with a kind of patient, kindly, remote boredom.

"What do you say?" he asked. "Should I take it?" Deep within him he hoped fiercely, longingly, for her to say, "No, Baby, you stay right here," but she said, as he knew she'd say, "I think you'd better take it."

He nodded. He had to get up and stand with his back to her, looking out the window because there were things plain on his face that she had never seen in the fifteen years she'd known him. "Fifty dollars is a lot of money," he said. "I never thought I'd ever see fifty dollars again." He laughed. Louise laughed, too.

Christian Darling sat on the frail green grass of the practice field. The shadow of the stadium had reached out and covered him. In the distance the lights of the university shone a little mistily in the light haze of evening. Fifteen years. Flaherty even now was calling for his wife, buying her a drink, filling whatever bar they were in with that voice of his and that easy laugh. Darling half-closed his eyes, almost saw the boy fifteen years ago reach for the pass, slip the halfback, go skittering lightly down the field, his knees high and fast and graceful, smiling to himself because he knew he was going to get past the safety man. That was the high point, Darling thought, fifteen years ago, on an autumn afternoon, twenty years old and far from death, with the air coming easily into his lungs, and a deep feeling inside him that he could do anything, knock over anybody, outrun whatever had to be outrun. And the shower after and the three glasses of water and the cool night air on his damp head and Louise sitting hatless in the open car with a smile and the first kiss she ever really meant. The high point, an eighty-yard run in the practice, and a girl's kiss and everything after that a decline. Darling laughed. He had practiced the wrong thing, perhaps. He hadn't praticed for 1929 and New York City and a girl who would turn into a woman. Somewhere, he thought, there must have been a point where she moved up to me, was even with me for a moment, when I could have held her hand, if I'd known, held tight, gone with her. Well, he'd never known. Here he was on a playing field that was fifteen years away and his wife was in another city having dinner with another and better man, speaking with him a different, new language, a language nobody had ever taught him.

Darling stood up, smiled a little, because if he didn't smile he knew the tears would come. He looked around him. This was the spot. O'Connor's pass had come sliding out just to here . . . the high point. Darling put up his hands, felt all over again the flat slap of the ball. He shook his hips to throw off the halfback, cut back inside the center, picked his knees high as he ran gracefully over two men jumbled on the ground at the line of scrimmage, ran easily, gaining speed, for ten yards, holding the ball lightly in his two hands, swung away from the halfback diving at him, ran, swinging his hips in the almost girlish manner of a back in a broken field, tore into the safety man, his shoes drumming heavily on the turf, stiff-armed, elbow locked, pivoted, raced lightly and exultantly for the goal line.

It was only after he had sped over the goal line and slowed to a trot that he saw the boy and girl sitting together on the turf, looking at him wonderingly.

He stopped short, dropping his arms. "I . . ." he said, gasping a little, though his condition was fine and the run hadn't winded him. "I—once I played here."

The boy and the girl said nothing. Darling laughed embarrassedly, looked hard at them sitting there, close to each other, shrugged, turned and went toward his hotel, the sweat breaking out on his face and running down into his collar.

A COUNTRY LOVE STORY

Jean Stafford

An antique sleigh stood in the yard, snow after snow banked up against its eroded runners. Here and there upon the bleached and splintery seat were wisps of horsehair and scraps of the black leather that had once upholstered it. It bore, with all its jovial curves, an air not so much of desuetude as of slowed-down dash, as if weary horses, unable to go another step, had at last stopped here. The sleigh had come with the house. The former owner, a gifted business-woman from Castine who bought old houses and sold them again with all their pitfalls still intact, had said when she was showing them the place, "A picturesque detail, I think," and, waving it away, had turned to the well, which, with enthusiasm and at considerable length, she said had never gone dry. Actually, May and Daniel had found the detail more distracting than picturesque, so nearly kin was it to outdoor arts and crafts, and when the woman, as they departed in her car, gestured toward it again and said, "Paint that up a bit with something cheery and it will really add no end to your yard," simultaneous shudders coursed them. They had planned to remove the sleigh before they did anything else.

But partly because there were more important things to be done, and partly because they did not know where to put it (a sleigh could not, in the usual sense of the words, be thrown away), and partly because it seemed defiantly a part of the yard, as entitled to be there permanently as the trees, they did nothing about it. Throughout the summer, they saw birds briefly pause on its rakish front and saw the fresh rains wash the runners; in the autumn they watched the golden leaves fill the seat and nestle dryly down; and now, with the snow, they watched this new accumulation.

The sleigh was visible from the windows of the big, bright kitchen where they ate all their meals and, sometimes too bemused with country solitude to talk, they gazed out at it, forgetting their food in speculating on its history. It could have been driven cavalierly by the scion of some sea captain's family, or it could have been used soberly to haul the household's Unitarians to church or to take the womenfolk around the countryside on errands of good will. They did not speak of what its office might have been, and the fact of their silence was often nettlesome to May, for she felt they were silent too much of the time; a little morosely, she thought, If something as absurd and as provocative as this at which we look together—and which is, even though we didn't want it, our own property—cannot bring us to talk, what can? But she did not disturb Daniel in his private musings; she held her tongue, and out of the corner of her eye she watched him watch the winter cloak the sleigh, and, as if she were computing a difficult sum in her head, she tried to puzzle out what it was that had stilled tongues that earlier, before

Daniel's illness, had found the days too short to communicate all they were eager to say.

It had been Daniel's doctor's idea, not theirs, that had brought them to the solemn hinterland to stay after all the summer gentry had departed in their beach wagons. The Northern sun, the pristine air, the rural walks and soundless nights, said Dr. Tellenbach, perhaps pining for his native Switzerland, would do more for the "Professor's" convalescent lung than all the doctors and clinics in the world. Privately he had added to May that after so long a season in the sanitarium (Daniel had been there a year), where everything was tuned to a low pitch, it would be difficult and it might be shattering for "the boy" (not now the "Professor," although Daniel, nearly fifty, was his wife's senior by twenty years and Dr. Tellenbach's by ten) to go back at once to the excitements and the intrigues of the university, to what, with finicking humor, the Doctor called "the omnium-gatherum of the school master's life." The rigors of a country winter would be as nothing, he insisted, when compared to the strain of feuds and cocktail parties. All professors wanted to write books, didn't they? Surely Daniel, a historian with all the material in the world at his fingertips, must have something up his sleeve that could be the *raison d'être* for this year away? May said she supposed he had, she was not sure. She could hear the reluctance in her voice as she escaped the Doctor's eyes and gazed through his windows at the mountains behind the sanitarium. In the dragging months Daniel had been gone, she had taken solace in imagining the time when they *would* return to just that pandemonium the Doctor so deplored, and because it had been pandemonium on the smallest and most discreet scale, she smiled through her disappointment at the little man's Swiss innocence and explained that they had always lived quietly, seldom dining out or entertaining more than twice a week.

"Twice a week!" He was appalled.

"But I'm afraid," she had protested, "that he would find a second year of inactivity intolerable. He does intend to write a book, but he means to write it in England, and we can't go to England now."

"England!" Dr. Tellenbach threw up his hands. "Good *air* is my recommendation for your husband. Good air and little talk."

She said, "It's talk he needs, I should think, after all this time of communing only with himself except when I came to visit."

He had looked at her with exaggerated patience, and then, courtly but authoritative, he said, "I hope you will not think I importune when I tell you that I am very well acquainted with your husband, and, as his physician, I order this retreat. *He* quite agrees."

Stung to see that there was a greater degree of understanding between Daniel and Dr. Tellenbach than between Daniel and herself, May had objected further, citing an occasion when her husband had put his head in his hands and mourned, "I hear talk of nothing but sputum cups and X-rays. Aren't people interested in the state of the world any more?"

But Dr. Tellenbach had been adamant, and at the end, when she had risen to go, he said, "You are bound to find him changed a little. A long illness removes a thoughtful man from his fellow-beings. It is like living with an exacting mistress who is not content with half a man's attention but must claim it all." She had thought his figure of speech absurd and disdained to ask him what he meant.

Actually, when the time came for them to move into the new house and she found no alterations in her husband but found, on the other hand, much pleasure in their country life, she began to forgive Dr. Tellenbach. In the beginning, it was like a second honeymoon, for they had moved to a part of the North where they had never been and they explored it together, sharing its charming sights and sounds. Moreover, they had never owned a house before but had always lived in city apartments, and though the house they bought was old and derelict, its lines and doors and windowlights were beautiful, and they were obsessed with it. All through the summer, they reiterated, "To think that we own all of this! That it actually belongs to us!" And they wandered from room to room marveling at their windows, from none of which was it possible to see an ugly sight. They looked to the south upon a river, to the north upon a lake; to the west of them were pine woods where the wind forever sighed, voicing a vain entreaty; and to the east a rich man's long meadow that ran down a hill to his old, magisterial house. It was true, even in those bewitched days, that there were times on the lake, when May was gathering water lilies as Daniel slowly rowed, that she had seen on his face a look of abstraction and she had known that he was worlds away, in his memories, perhaps, of his illness and the sanitarium (of which he would never speak) or in the thought of the book he was going to write as soon, he said, as the winter set in and there was nothing to do but work. Momentarily the look frightened her and she remembered the Doctor's words, but then, immediately herself again in the security of married love, she caught at another water lily and pulled at its long stem. Companionably, they gardened, taking special pride in the nicotiana that sent its nighttime fragrance into their bedroom. Together, and with fascination, they consulted carpenters, plasterers, and chimney sweeps. In the blue evenings they read at ease, hearing no sound but that of the night birds—the loons on the lake and the owls in the tops of trees. When the days began to cool and shorten, a cricket came to bless their house, nightly singing behind the kitchen stove. They got two fat and idle tabby cats, who lay insensible beside the fireplace and only stirred themselves to purr perfunctorily.

Because they had not moved in until July and by that time the workmen of the region were already engaged, most of the major repairs of the house were to be postponed until the spring, and in October, when May and Daniel had done all they could by themselves and Daniel had begun his own work, May suddenly found herself without occupation. Whole days might pass when she did nothing more than cook three meals and walk a little in the autumn mist and pet the cats and wait for Daniel to come down from his upstairs study to talk to her. She began to think with longing of the crowded days in Boston before Daniel was sick, and even in the year past, when he had been away and she had gone to concerts and recitals and had done good deeds for crippled children and had endlessly shopped for presents to lighten the tedium of her husband's unwilling exile. And, longing, she was remorseful, as if by desiring another she betrayed this life, and, remorseful, she hid away in sleep. Sometimes she slept for hours in the daytime, imitating the cats, and when at last she got up, she had to push away the dense sleep as if it were a door.

One day at lunch, she asked Daniel to take a long walk with her that afternoon to a farm where the owner smoked his own sausages.

"You never go outdoors," she said, "and Dr. Tellenbach said you must. Besides, it's a lovely day."

"I can't," he said. "I'd like to, but I can't. I'm busy. You go alone."

Overtaken by a gust of loneliness, she cried, "Oh, Daniel, I have nothing to *do!*"

A moment's silence fell, and then he said, "I'm sorry to put you through this, my dear, but you must surely admit that it's not my fault I got sick."

In her shame, her rapid, overdone apologies, her insistence that nothing mattered in the world except his health and peace of mind, she made everything worse, and at last he said shortly to her, "Stop being a child, May. Let's just leave each other alone."

This outbreak, the very first in their marriage of five years, was the beginning of a series. Hardly a day passed that they did not bicker over something; they might dispute a question of fact, argue a matter of taste, catch each other out in an inaccuracy, and every quarrel ended with Daniel's saying to her, "Why don't you leave me alone?" Once he said, "I've been sick and now I'm busy and I'm no longer young enough to shift the focus of my mind each time it suits your whim." Afterward, there were always apologies, and then Daniel went back to his study and did not open the door of it again until the next meal. Finally, it seemed to her that love, the very center of their being, was choked off, overgrown, invisible. And silent with hostility or voluble with trivial reproach, they tried to dig it out impulsively and could not—could only maul it in its unkempt grave. Daniel, in his withdrawal from her and from the house, was preoccupied with his research, of which he never spoke except to say that it would bore her, and most of the time, so it appeared to May, he did not worry over what was happening to them. She felt the cold, old house somehow enveloping her as if it were their common enemy, maliciously bent on bringing them to disaster. Sunken in faithlessness, they stared, at mealtimes, atrophied within the present hour, at the irrelevant and whimsical sleigh that stood abandoned in the mammoth winter.

May found herself thinking, If we redeemed it and painted it, our house would have something in common with Henry Ford's Wayside Inn. And I might make this very observation to him and he might greet it with disdain and we might once again communicate. Perhaps we could talk of Williamsburg and how we disapproved of it. Her mind went toiling on. Williamsburg was part of our honeymoon trip; somewhere our feet were entangled in suckers as we stood kissing under a willow tree. Soon she found that she did not care for this line of thought, nor did she care what his response to it might be. In her imagined conversations with Daniel, she never spoke of the sleigh. To the thin, ill scholar whose scholarship and illness had usurped her place, she had gradually taken a weighty but unviolent dislike.

The discovery of this came, not surprising her, on Christmas Day. The knowledge sank like a plummet, and at the same time she was thinking about the sleigh, connecting it with the smell of the barn on damp days, and she thought perhaps it had been drawn by the very animals who had been stabled there and had pervaded the timbers with their odor. There must have been much life within this house once—but long ago. The earth immediately behind the barn was said by everyone to be extremely rich because of the horses, although there had been none there for over fifty years. Thinking of this soil, which earlier she had eagerly sifted through her fingers, May now realized that she had no wish for the spring to come, no wish to plant a garden, and, branching out at random, she found she had no wish to see the sea again, or children, or favorite pictures, or even her own face on a happy day. For a minute or two, she was almost enraptured in this state of no desire, but then, purged swiftly of her cynicism, she knew it to be false, knew that actually she did have a desire—the desire for a desire. And now she felt that she was stationary in a whirlpool, and at the very moment she conceived the notion a bit of wind brought to the seat of the sleigh the final leaf from the elm tree that stood beside it. It crossed her mind that she might consider the wood of the sleigh in its juxtaposition to the living tree and to the horses, who, although they were long since dead, reminded her of their passionate, sweating, running life every time she went to the barn for firewood.

They sat this morning in the kitchen full of sun, and, speaking not to him but to the sleigh, to icicles, to the dark, motionless pine woods, she said, "I wonder if on a day like this they used to take the pastor home after lunch." Daniel gazed abstractedly at the bright-silver drifts beside the well and said nothing. Presently a wagon went past hauled by two oxen with bells on their yoke. This was the hour they always passed, taking to an unknown destination an aged man in a fur hat and an aged woman in a shawl. May and Daniel listened.

Suddenly, with impromptu anger, Daniel said, "What did you just say?"

"Nothing," she said. And then, after a pause, "It would be lovely at Jamaica Pond today."

He wheeled on her and pounded the table with his fist. "I did not ask for this!" The color rose feverishly to his thin cheeks and his breath was agitated. "You are trying to make me sick again. It was wonderful, wasn't it, for you while I was gone?"

"Oh, no, no! Oh, no, Daniel, it was hell!"

"Then, by the same token, this must be heaven." He smiled, the professor catching out a student in a fallacy.

"Heaven." She said the word bitterly.

"Then why do you stay here?" he cried.

It was a cheap impasse, desolate, true, unfair. She did not answer him.

After a while he said, "I almost believe there's something you haven't told me."

She began to cry at once, blubbering across the table at him. "You have said that before. What am I to say? What have I done?"

He looked at her, impervious to her tears, without mercy and yet without contempt. "I don't know. But you've done something."

It was as if she were looking through someone else's scrambled closets and bureau drawers for an object that had not been named to her, but nowhere could she find her gross offense.

Domestically she asked him if he would have more coffee and he peremptorily refused and demanded, "Will you tell me why it is you must badger me? Is it a compulsion? Can't you control it? Are you going mad?"

From that day onward, May felt a certain stirring of life within her solitude, and now and again, looking up from a book to see if the damper on the stove was right, to listen to a rat renovating its house-within-a-house, to watch the belled oxen pass, she nursed her wound, hugged it, repeated his awful words exactly as he had said them, reproduced the way his wasted lips had looked and his bright, farsighted eyes. She could not read for long at any time, nor could she sew. She cared little now for planning changes in her house; she had meant to sand the painted floors to uncover the wood of the wide boards and she had imagined how the long, paneled windows of the drawing room would look when yellow velvet curtains hung there in the spring. Now, schooled by silence and indifference, she was immune to disrepair and to the damage done by the wind and snow,

and she looked, as Daniel did, without dislike upon the old
and nasty wallpaper and upon the shabby kitchen floor. One
day, she knew that the sleigh would stay where it was so
long as they stayed there. From every thought, she returned to her deep, bleeding injury. He had asked her if
she were going mad.

She repaid him in the dark afternoons while he was
closeted away in his study, hardly making a sound save
when he added wood to his fire or paced a little, deep in
thought. She sat at the kitchen table looking at the sleigh
and she gave Daniel insult for his injury by imagining a
lover. She did not imagine his face, but she imagined his
clothing, which would be costly and in the best of taste, and
his manner, which would be urbane and anticipatory of her
least whim, and his clever speech, and his adept courtship
that would begin the moment he looked at the sleigh and
said, "I must get rid of that for you at once." She might be a
widow, she might be divorced, she might be committing
adultery. Certainly there was no need to specify in an affair
so securely legal. There was no need, that is, up to a point,
and then the point came when she took in the fact that she
not only believed in this lover but loved him and depended
wholly on his companionship. She complained to him of
Daniel and he consoled her; she told him stories of her
girlhood, when she had gaily gone to parties, squired by
boys her own age; she dazzled him sometimes with the wise
comments she made on the books she read. It came to be
true that if she so much as looked at the sleigh, she was
weakened, failing with starvation.

Often, about her daily tasks of cooking food and washing
dishes and tending the fires and shopping in the general
store of the village, she thought she should watch her step,
that it was this sort of thing that *did* make one go mad; for a
while, then, she went back to Daniel's question, sharpening
its razor edge. But she could not corral her alien thoughts
and she trembled as she bought split peas, fearful that the
old men loafing by the stove could see the incubus of her
sins beside her. She could not avert such thoughts when

they rushed upon her sometimes at tea with one of the old religious ladies of the neighborhood, so that, in the middle of a conversation about a deaconess in Bath, she retired from them, seeking her lover, who came, faceless, with his arms outstretched, even as she sat up straight in a Boston rocker, even as she accepted another cup of tea. She lingered over the cake plates and the simple talk, postponing her return to her own house and to Daniel, whom she continually betrayed.

It was not long after she recognized her love that she began to wake up even before the dawn and to be all day quick to everything, observant of all the signs of age and eccentricity in her husband, and she compared him in every particular—to his humiliation, in her eyes—with the man whom now it seemed to her she had always loved at fever pitch.

Once when Daniel, in a rare mood, kissed her, she drew back involuntarily and he said gently, "I wish I knew what you had done, poor dear." He looked, as if for written words, in her face.

"You said you knew," she said, terrified.

"I do."

"Then why do you wish you knew?" Her baffled voice was high and frantic. "You don't talk sense!"

"I do," he said sedately. "I talk sense always. It is you who are oblique." Her eyes stole like a sneak to the sleigh. "But I wish I knew your motive," he said impartially.

For a minute, she felt that they were two maniacs answering each other questions that had not been asked, never touching the matter at hand because they did not know what the matter was. But in the next moment, when he turned back to her spontaneously and clasped her head between his hands and said, like a tolerant father, "I forgive you, darling, because you don't know how you persecute me. No one knows except the sufferer what this sickness is," she knew again, helplessly, that they were not harmonious even in their aberrations.

These days of winter came and went, and on each of them, after breakfast and as the oxen passed, he accused her of her concealed misdeed. She could no longer truthfully deny that she was guilty, for she was in love, and she heard the subterfuge in her own voice and felt the guilty fever in her veins. Daniel knew it, too, and watched her. When she was alone, she felt her lover's presence protecting her—when she walked past the stiff spiraea, with icy cobwebs hung between its twigs, down to the lake, where the black, unmeasured water was hidden beneath a lid of ice; when she walked, instead, to the salt river to see the tar-paper shacks where the men caught smelt through the ice; when she walked in the dead dusk up the hill from the store, catching her breath the moment she saw the sleigh. But sometimes this splendid being mocked her when, freezing with fear of the consequences of her sin, she ran up the stairs to Daniel's room and burrowed her head in his shoulder and cried, "Come downstairs! I'm lonely, please come down!" But he would never come, and at last, bitterly, calmed by his calmly inquisitive regard, she went back alone and stood at the kitchen window, coyly half hidden behind the curtains.

For months she lived with her daily dishonor, rattled, ashamed, stubbornly clinging to her secret. But she grew more and more afraid when, oftener and oftener, Daniel said, "Why do you lie to me? What does this mood of yours mean?" and she could no longer sleep. In the raw nights, she lay straight beside him as he slept, and she stared at the ceiling, as bright as the snow it reflected, and tried not to think of the sleigh out there under the elm tree but could think only of it and of the man, her lover, who was connected with it somehow. She said to herself, as she listened to his breathing, "If I confessed to Daniel, he would understand that I was lonely and he would comfort me, saying, 'I am here, May. I shall never let you be lonely again.'" At these times, she was so separated from the world, so far removed from his touch and his voice, so solitary, that she would have sued a stranger for companionship. Daniel slept deeply, having no guilt to make him toss. He slept, indeed, so well that he never even heard the ditcher on snowy nights rising with a groan over the hill, flinging the snow from the road and warning of its approach by lights that first flashed red, then blue. As it passed their house, the hurled snow swashed like flames. All night she heard the squirrels adding up their nuts in the walls and heard the spirit of the house creaking and softly clicking upon the stairs and in the attics.

In early spring, when the whippoorwills begged in the cattails and the marsh reeds, and the northern lights patinated the lake and the tidal river, and the stars were large, and the huge vine of Dutchman's-pipe had started to leaf out, May went to bed late. Each night she sat on the back steps waiting, hearing the snuffling of a dog as it hightailed it for home, the single cry of a loon. Night after night, she waited for the advent of her rebirth while upstairs Daniel, who had spoken tolerantly of her vigils, slept, keeping his knowledge of her to himself. "A symptom," he had said, scowling in concentration, as he remarked upon her new habit. "Let it run its course. Perhaps when this is over, you will know the reason why you torture me with these obsessions and will stop. You know, you may really have a slight disorder of the mind. It would be nothing to be ashamed of; you could go to a sanitarium."

One night, looking out the window, she clearly saw her lover sitting in the sleigh. His hand was over his eyes and his chin was covered by a red silk scarf. He wore no hat and his hair was fair. He was tall and his long legs stretched indolently along the floorboard. He was younger than she had imagined him to be and he seemed rather frail, for there was a delicate pallor on his high, intelligent forehead and there was an invalid's languor in his whole attitude. He wore a white blazer and gray flannels and there was a yellow rosebud in his lapel. Young as he was, he did not, even so, seem to belong to her generation; rather, he seemed to be the reincarnation of someone's uncle as he had been fifty years before. May did not move until he vanished, and then, even though she knew now that she was truly bedeviled, the only emotion she had was bashfulness, mingled with doubt; she was not sure, that is, that he loved her.

That night, she slept a while. She lay near to Daniel, who was smiling in the moonlight. She could tell that the sleep she would have tonight would be as heavy as a coma, and she was aware of the moment she was overtaken.

She was in a canoe in a meadow of water lilies and her lover was tranquilly taking the shell off a hard-boiled egg. "How intimate," he said, "to eat an egg with you." She was nervous lest the canoe tip over, but at the same time she was charmed by his wit and by the way he lightly touched her shoulder with the varnished paddle.

"May? May? I love you, May."

"Oh!" enchanted, she heard her voice replying. "Oh, I love you, too!"

"The winter is over, May. You must forgive the hallucinations of a sick man."

She woke to see Daniel's fair, pale head bending toward her. "He is old! He is ill!" she thought, but through her tears, to deceive him one last time, she cried, "Oh, thank God, Daniel!"

He was feeling cold and wakeful and he asked her to make him a cup of tea; before she left the room, he kissed her hands and arms and said, "If I am ever sick again, don't leave me, May."

Downstairs, in the kitchen, cold with shadows and with the obtrusion of dawn, she was belabored by a chill. "What time is it?" she said aloud, although she did not care. She remembered, not for any reason, a day when she and Daniel had stood in the yard last October wondering whether they should cover the chimneys that would not be used and he decided that they should not, but he had said, "I hope no birds get trapped." She had replied, "I thought they all left at about this time for the South," and he had answered, with an unintelligible reproach in his voice, "The starlings stay." And she remembered, again for no reason, a day when, in pride and excitement, she had burst into the house crying, "I saw an ermine. It was terribly poised and let me watch it quite a while." He had said categorically, "There are no ermines here."

She had not protested; she had sighed as she sighed now and turned to the window. The sleigh was livid in this light and no one was in it; nor had anyone been in it for many years. But at that moment the blacksmith's cat came guardedly across the dewy field and climbed into it, as if by careful plan, and curled up on the seat. May prodded the clinkers in the stove and started to the barn for kindling. But she thought of the cold and the damp and the smell of the horses, and she did not go but stood there, holding the poker and leaning upon it as if it were an umbrella. There was no place warm to go. "What time is it?" she whimpered, heartbroken, and moved the poker, stroking the lion foot of the fireless stove.

She knew now that no change would come, and that she would never see her lover again. Confounded utterly, like an orphan in solitary confinement, she went outdoors and got into the sleigh. The blacksmith's imperturbable cat stretched and rearranged his position, and May sat beside him with her hands locked tightly in her lap, rapidly wondering over and over again how she would live the rest of her life.

◆ ———————————————————————————— ◆

FLIGHT

John Steinbeck

About fifteen miles below Monterey, on the wild coast, the Torres family had their farm, a few sloping acres above a cliff that dropped to the brown reefs and to the hissing white waters of the ocean. Behind the farm the stone mountains stood up against the sky. The farm buildings huddled like little clinging aphids on the mountain skirts, crouched low to the ground as though the wind might blow them into the sea. The little shack, the rattling, rotting barn were gray-bitten with sea salt, beaten by the damp wind until they had taken on the color of the granite hills. Two horses, a red cow and a red calf, half a dozen pigs and a flock of lean, multi-colored chickens stocked the place. A little corn was raised on the sterile slope, and it grew short and thick under the wind, and all the cobs formed on the landward sides of the stalks.

Mama Torres, a lean, dry woman with ancient eyes, had ruled the farm for ten years, ever since her husband tripped over a stone in the field one day and fell full length on a rattlesnake. When one is bitten on the chest there is not much that can be done.

Mama Torres had three children, two undersized black ones of twelve and fourteen, Emilio and Rosy, whom Mama kept fishing on the rocks below the farm when the sea was kind and when the truant officer was in some distant part of Monterey County. And there was Pepé, the tall smiling son of nineteen, a gentle, affectionate boy, but very lazy. Pepé had a tall head, pointed at the top, and from its peak, coarse black hair grew down like a thatch all around. Over his smiling little eyes Mama cut a straight bang so he could see. Pepé had sharp Indian cheekbones and an eagle nose, but his mouth was as sweet and shapely as a girl's mouth, and his chin was fragile and chiseled. He was loose and gangling, all legs and feet and wrists, and he was very lazy. Mama thought him fine and brave, but she never told him so. She said, "Some lazy cow must have got into thy father's family, else how could I have a son like thee." And she said, "When I carried thee, a sneaking lazy coyote came out of the brush and looked at me one day. That must have made thee so."

Pepé smiled sheepishly and stabbed at the ground with his knife to keep the blade sharp and free from rust. It was his inheritance, that knife, his father's knife. The long heavy blade folded back into the black handle. There was a button on the handle. When Pepé pressed the button, the blade leaped out ready for use. The knife was with Pepé always, for it had been his father's knife.

One sunny morning when the sea below the cliff was glinting and blue and the white surf creamed on the reef, when even the stone mountains looked kindly, Mama Torres called out the door of the shack, "Pepé, I have a labor for thee."

There was no answer. Mama listened. From behind the barn she heard a burst of laughter. She lifted her full long skirt and walked in the direction of the noise.

Pepé was sitting on the ground with his back against a box. His white teeth glistened. On either side of him stood the two black ones, tense and expectant. Fifteen feet away a redwood post was set in the ground. Pepé's right hand lay limply in his lap, and in the palm the big black knife rested. The blade was closed back into the handle. Pepé looked smiling at the sky.

Suddenly Emilio cried, "Ya!"

Pepé's wrist flicked like the head of a snake. The blade seemed to fly open in mid-air, and with a thump the point dug into the redwood post, and the black handle quivered. The three burst into excited laughter. Rosy ran to the post and pulled out the knife and brought it back to Pepé. He closed the blade and settled the knife carefully in his listless palm again. He grinned self-consciously at the sky.

"Ya!"

The heavy knife lanced out and sunk into the post again. Mama moved forward like a ship and scattered the play.

"All day you do foolish things with the knife, like a toy-baby," she stormed. "Get up on thy huge feet that eat up shoes. Get up!" She took him by one loose shoulder and hoisted at him. Pepé grinned sheepishly and came half-heartedly to his feet. "Look!" Mama cried. "Big lazy, you must catch the horse and put on him thy father's saddle. You must ride to Monterey. The medicine bottle is empty. There is no salt. Go thou now, Peanut! Catch the horse."

A revolution took place in the relaxed figure of Pepé. "To Monterey, me? Alone? Sí, Mama."

She scowled at him. "Do not think, big sheep, that you will buy candy. No, I will give you only enough for the medicine and the salt."

Pepé smiled. "Mama, you will put the hatband on the hat?"

She relented then. "Yes, Pepé. You may wear the hatband."

His voice grew insinuating, "And the green handkerchief, Mama?"

"Yes, if you go quickly and return with no trouble, the silk green handkerchief will go. If you make sure to take off the handkerchief when you eat so no spot may fall on it. . . ."

"Sí, Mama. I will be careful. I am a man."

"Thou? A man? Thou art a peanut."

He went into the rickety barn and brought out a rope, and he walked agilely enough up the hill to catch the horse.

When he was ready and mounted before the door, mounted on his father's saddle that was so old that the oaken frame showed through torn leather in many places, then Mama brought out the round black hat with the tooled leather band, and she reached up and knotted the green silk handkerchief about his neck. Pepé's blue denim coat was much darker than his jeans, for it had been washed much less often.

Mama handed up the big medicine bottle and the silver coins. "That for the medicine," she said, "and that for the salt. That for a candle to burn for the papa. That for *dulces* for the little ones. Our friend Mrs. Rodriguez will give you dinner and maybe a bed for the night. When you go to the church say only ten Paternosters and only twenty-five Ave Marias. Oh! I know, big coyote. You would sit there flapping your mouth over Aves all day while you looked at the candles and the holy pictures. That is not good devotion to stare at the pretty things."

The black hat, covering the high pointed head and black thatched hair of Pepé, gave him dignity and age. He sat the rangy horse well. Mama thought how handsome he was, dark and lean and tall. "I would not send thee now alone, thou little one, except for the medicine," she said softly. "It is not good to have no medicine, for who knows when the toothache will come, or the sadness of the stomach. These things are."

"Adios, Mama," Pepé cried. "I will come back soon. You may send me often alone. I am a man."

"Thou art a foolish chicken."

He straightened his shoulders, flipped the reins against the horse's shoulder and rode away. He turned once and saw that they still watched him, Emilio and Rosy and Mama. Pepé grinned with pride and gladness and lifted the tough buckskin horse to a trot.

When he had dropped out of sight over a little dip in the road, Mama turned to the black ones, but she spoke to herself. "He is nearly a man now," she said. "It will be a nice thing to have a man in the house again." Her eyes sharpened on the children. "Go to the rocks now. The tide is going out. There will be abalones to be found." She put the iron hooks into their hands and saw them down the steep trail to the reefs. She brought the smooth stone *metate* to the doorway and sat grinding her corn to flour and looking occasionally at the road over which Pepé had gone. The noonday came and then the afternoon, when the little ones beat the abalones on a rock to make them tender and Mama patted the tortillas to make them thin. They ate their dinner as the red sun was plunging down toward the ocean. They sat on the doorsteps and watched the big white moon come over the mountaintops.

Mama said, "He is now at the house of our friend Mrs. Rodriguez. She will give him nice things to eat and maybe a present."

Emilio said, "Some day I too will ride to Monterey for medicine. Did Pepé come to be a man today?"

Mama said wisely, "A boy gets to be a man when a man is needed. Remember this thing. I have known boys forty years old because there was no need for a man."

Soon afterwards they retired, Mama in her big oak bed on one side of the room, Emilio and Rosy in their boxes full of straw and sheepskins on the other side of the room.

The moon went over the sky and the surf roared on the rocks. The roosters crowed the first call. The surf subsided to a whispering surge against the reef. The moon dropped toward the sea. The roosters crowed again.

*   *   *

The moon was near down to the water when Pepé rode on a winded horse to his home flat. His dog bounced out and circled the horse yelping with pleasure. Pepé slid off the saddle to the ground. The weathered little shack was silver in the moonlight and the square shadow of it was black to the north and east. Against the east the piling mountains were misty with light; their tops melted into the sky.

Pepé walked wearily up the three steps and into the house. It was dark inside. There was a rustle in the corner.

Mama cried out from her bed. "Who comes? Pepé, is it you?"

"Sí, Mama."

"Did you get the medicine?"

"Sí, Mama."

"Well, go to sleep, then. I thought you would be sleeping at the house of Mrs. Rodriguez." Pepé stood silently in the dark room. "Why do you stand there, Pepé? Did you drink wine?"

"Sí, Mama."

"Well, go to bed then and sleep out the wine."

His voice was tired and patient, but very firm. "Light the candle, Mama. I must go away into the mountains."

"What is this, Pepé? You are crazy." Mama struck a sulphur match and held the little blue burr until the flame spread up the stick. She set light to the candle on the floor beside her bed. "Now, Pepé, what is this you say?" She looked anxiously into his face.

He was changed. The fragile quality seemed to have gone from his chin. His mouth was less full than it had been, the lines of the lips were straighter, but in his eyes the greatest change had taken place. There was no laughter in them any more nor any bashfulness. They were sharp and bright and purposeful.

He told her in a tired monotone, told her everything just as it had happened. A few people came into the kitchen of Mrs. Rodriguez. There was wine to drink. Pepé drank wine. The little quarrel—the man started toward Pepé and then the knife—it went almost by itself. It flew, it darted before Pepé knew it. As he talked, Mama's face grew stern, and it seemed to grow more lean. Pepé finished. "I am a man now, Mama. The man said names to me I could not allow."

Mama nodded. "Yes, thou art a man, my poor little Pepé. Thou art a man. I have seen it coming on thee. I have watched you throwing the knife into the post, and I have been afraid." For a moment her face had softened, but now it grew stern again. "Come! We must get you ready. Go. Awaken Emilio and Rosy. Go quickly."

Pepé stepped over to the corner where his brother and sister slept among the sheepskins. He leaned down and shook them gently. "Come, Rosy! Come, Emilio! The mama says you must arise."

The little black ones sat up and rubbed their eyes in the candlelight. Mama was out of bed now, her long black skirt over her nightgown. "Emilio," she cried. "Go up and catch the other horse for Pepé. Quickly now! Quickly." Emilio put his legs in his overalls and stumbled sleepily out the door.

"You heard no one behind you on the road?" Mama demanded.

"No, Mama. I listened carefully. No one was on the road."

Mama darted like a bird about the room. From a nail on the wall she took a canvas water bag and threw it on the floor. She stripped a blanket from her bed and rolled it into a tight tube and tied the ends with string. From a box beside the stove she lifted a flour sack half full of black stringy jerky. "Your father's black coat, Pepé. Here, put it on."

Pepé stood in the middle of the floor watching her activity. She reached behind the door and brought out the rifle, a long 38-56, worn shiny the whole length of the barrel. Pepé took it from her and held it in the crook of his elbow. Mama brought a little leather bag and counted the cartridges into his hand. "Only ten left," she warned. "You must not waste them."

Emilio put his head in the door. " *'Qui 'st 'l caballo,* Mama."

"Put on the saddle from the other horse. Tie on the blanket. Here, tie the jerky to the saddle horn."

Still Pepé stood silently watching his mother's frantic activity. His chin looked hard, and his sweet mouth was drawn and thin. His little eyes followed Mama about the room almost suspiciously.

Rosy asked softly, "Where goes Pepé?"

Mama's eyes were fierce. "Pepé goes on a journey. Pepé is a man now. He has a man's thing to do."

Pepé straightened his shoulders. His mouth changed until he looked very much like Mama.

At last the preparation was finished. The loaded horse stood outside the door. The water bag dripped a line of moisture down the bay shoulder.

The moonlight was being thinned by the dawn and the big white moon was near down to the sea. The family stood by the shack. Mama confronted Pepé. "Look, my son! Do not stop until it is dark again. Do not sleep even though you are tired. Take care of the horse in order that he may not stop of weariness. Remember to be careful with the bullets— there are only ten. Do not fill thy stomach with jerky or it will make thee sick. Eat a little jerky and fill thy stomach with grass. When thou comest to the high mountains, if thou seest any of the dark watching men, go not near to them nor try to speak to them. And forget not thy prayers." She put her lean hands on Pepé's shoulders, stood on her toes and kissed him formally on both cheeks, and Pepé kissed her on both cheeks. Then he went to Emilio and Rosy and kissed both of their cheeks.

Pepé turned back to Mama. He seemed to look for a little softness, a little weakness in her. His eyes were searching, but Mama's face remained fierce. "Go now," she said. "Do not wait to be caught like a chicken."

Pepé pulled himself into the saddle. "I am a man," he said.

It was the first dawn when he rode up the hill toward the

little canyon which let a trail into the mountains. Moonlight and daylight fought with each other, and the two warring qualities made it difficult to see. Before Pepé had gone a hundred yards, the outlines of his figure were misty; and long before he entered the canyon, he had become a gray, indefinite shadow.

Mama stood stiffly in front of her doorstep, and on either side of her stood Emilio and Rosy. They cast furtive glances at Mama now and then.

When the gray shape of Pepé melted into the hillside and disappeared, Mama relaxed. She began the high, whining keen of the death wail. "Our beautiful—our brave," she cried. "Our protector, our son is gone." Emilio and Rosy moaned beside her. "Our beautiful—our brave, he is gone." It was the formal wail. It rose to a high piercing whine and subsided to a moan. Mama raised it three times and then she turned and went into the house and shut the door.

Emilio and Rosy stood wondering in the dawn. They heard Mama whimpering in the house. They went out to sit on the cliff above the ocean. They touched shoulders. "When did Pepé come to be a man?" Emilio asked.

"Last night," said Rosy. "Last night in Monterey. The ocean clouds turned red with the sun that was behind the mountains.

"We will have no breakfast," said Emilio. "Mama will not want to cook." Rosy did not answer him. "Where is Pepé gone?" he asked.

Rosy looked around at him. She drew her knowledge from the quiet air. "He has gone on a journey. He will never come back."

"Is he dead? Do you think he is dead?"

Rosy looked back at the ocean again. A little steamer, drawing a line of smoke sat on the edge of the horizon. "He is not dead," Rosy explained. "Not yet."

Pepé rested the big rifle across the saddle in front of him. He let the horse walk up the hill and he didn't look back. The stony slope took on a coat of short brush so that Pepé found the entrance to a trail and entered it.

When he came to the canyon opening, he swung once in his saddle and looked back, but the houses were swallowed in the misty light. Pepé jerked forward again. The high shoulder of the canyon closed in on him. His horse stretched out its neck and sighed and settled to the trail.

It was a well-worn path, dark soft leaf-mold earth strewn with broken pieces of sandstone. The trail rounded the shoulder of the canyon and dropped steeply into the bed of the stream. In the shallows the water ran smoothly, glinting in the first morning sun. Small round stones on the bottom were as brown as rust with sun moss. In the sand along the edges of the stream the tall, rich wild mint grew, while in the water itself the cress, old and tough, had gone to heavy seed.

The path went into the stream and emerged on the other side. The horse sloshed into the water and stopped. Pepé dropped his bridle and let the beast drink of the running water.

Soon the canyon sides became steep and the first giant sentinel redwoods guarded the trail, great round red trunks bearing foliage as green and lacy as ferns. Once Pepé was among the trees, the sun was lost. A perfumed and purple light lay in the pale green of the underbrush. Gooseberry bushes and blackberries and tall ferns lined the stream, and overhead the branches of the redwoods met and cut off the sky.

Pepé drank from the water bag, and he reached into the flour sack and brought out a black string of jerky. His white teeth gnawed at the string until the tough meat parted. He chewed slowly and drank occasionally from the water bag. His little eyes were slumberous and tired, but the muscles of his face were hard set. The earth of the trail was black now. It gave up a hollow sound under the walking hoofbeats.

The stream fell more sharply. Little waterfalls splashed on the stones. Five-fingered ferns hung over the water and dripped spray from their fingertips. Pepé rode half over in his saddle, dangling one leg loosely. He picked a bay leaf from a tree beside the way and put it into his mouth for a moment to flavor the dry jerky. He held the gun loosely across the pommel.

Suddenly he squared in his saddle, swung the horse from the trail and kicked it hurriedly up behind a big redwood tree. He pulled up the reins tight against the bit to keep the horse from whinnying. His face was intent and his nostrils quivered a little.

A hollow pounding came down the trail, and a horseman rode by, a fat man with red cheeks and a white stubble beard. His horse put down its head and blubbered at the trail when it came to the place where Pepé had turned off. "Hold up!" said the man and he pulled up his horse's head.

When the last sound of the hoofs died away, Pepé came back into the trail again. He did not relax in the saddle any more. He lifted the big rifle and swung the lever to throw a shell into the chamber, and then he let down the hammer to half cock.

The trail grew very steep. Now the redwood trees were smaller and their tops were dead, bitten dead where the wind reached them. The horse plodded on; the sun went slowly overhead and started down toward the afternoon.

Where the stream came out of a side canyon, the trail left it. Pepé dismounted and watered his horse and filled up his water bag. As soon as the trail had parted from the stream, the trees were gone and only the thick brittle sage and manzanita and chaparral edged the trail. And the soft black earth was gone, too, leaving only the light tan broken rock for the trail bed. Lizards scampered away into the brush as the horse rattled over the little stones.

Pepé turned in his saddle and looked back. He was in the open now: he could be seen from a distance. As he ascended the trail the country grew more rough and terrible and dry. The way wound about the bases of great square rocks. Little gray rabbits skittered in the brush. A bird made a monotonous high creaking. Eastward the bare rock mountaintops were pale and powder-dry under the dropping sun. The horse plodded up and up the trail toward a little V in the ridge which was the pass.

Pepé looked suspiciously back every minute or so, and his eyes sought the tops of the ridges ahead. Once, on a white barren spur, he saw a black figure for a moment, but he looked quickly away, for it was one of the dark watchers. No one knew who the watchers were, nor where they lived, but it was better to ignore them and never to show interest in them. They did not bother one who stayed on the trail and minded his own business.

The air was parched and full of light dust blown by the breeze from the eroding mountains. Pepé drank sparingly from his bag and corked it tightly and hung it on the horn again. The trail moved up the dry shale hillside, avoiding rocks, dropping under clefts, climbing in and out of old water scars. When he arrived at the little pass he stopped and looked back for a long time. No dark watchers were to be seen now. The trail behind was empty. Only the high tops of the redwoods indicated where the stream flowed.

Pepé rode on through the pass. His little eyes were nearly closed with weariness, but his face was stern, relentless and manly. The high mountain wind coasted sighing through the pass and whistled on the edges of the big blocks of broken granite. In the air, a red-tailed hawk sailed over close to the ridge and screamed angrily. Pepé went slowly through the broken jagged pass and looked down on the other side.

The trail dropped quickly, staggering among broken rock. At the bottom of the slope there was a dark crease, thick with brush, and on the other side of the crease a little flat, in which a grove of oak trees grew. A scar of green grass cut across the flat. And behind the flat another mountain rose, desolate with dead rocks and starving little black bushes. Pepé drank from the bag again for the air was so dry that it encrusted his nostrils and burned his lips. He put the horse down the trail. The hooves slipped and struggled on the steep way, starting little stones that rolled off into the brush. The sun was gone behind the westward mountain now, but still it glowed brilliantly on the oaks and on the grassy flat. The rocks and the hillsides still sent up waves of the heat they had gathered from the day's sun.

Pepé looked up to the top of the next dry withered ridge. He saw a dark form against the sky, a man's figure standing on top of a rock, and he glanced away quickly not to appear curious. When a moment later he looked up again, the figure was gone.

Downward the trail was quickly covered. Sometimes the horse floundered for footing, sometimes set his feet and slid a little way. They came at last to the bottom where the dark chaparral was higher than Pepé's head. He held up his rifle on one side and his arm on the other to shield his face from the sharp brittle fingers of the brush.

Up and out of the crease he rode, and up a little cliff. The grassy flat was before him, and the round comfortable oaks. For a moment he studied the trail down which he had come, but there was no movement and no sound from it. Finally he rode out over the flat, to the green streak, and at the upper end of the damp he found a little spring welling out of the earth and dropping into a dug basin before it seeped out over the flat.

Pepé filled his bag first, and then he let the thirsty horse drink out of the pool. He led the horse to the clump of oaks, and in the middle of the grove, fairly protected from sight on all sides, he took off the saddle and the bridle and laid them on the ground. The horse stretched his jaws sideways and yawned. Pepé knotted the lead rope about the horse's neck and tied him to a sapling among the oaks, where he could graze in a fairly large circle.

When the horse was gnawing hungrily at the dry grass, Pepé went to the saddle and took a black string of jerky from the sack and strolled to an oak tree on the edge of the grove, from under which he could watch the trail. He sat down in the crisp dry oak leaves and automatically felt for his big black knife to cut the jerky, but he had no knife. He leaned back on his elbow and gnawed at the tough strong meat. His face was blank, but it was a man's face.

The bright evening light washed the eastern ridge, but the valley was darkening. Doves flew down from the hills to the spring, and the quail came running out of the brush and joined them, calling clearly to one another.

Out of the corner of his eye Pepé saw a shadow grow out of the bushy crease. He turned his head slowly. A big spotted wildcat was creeping toward the spring, belly to the ground, moving like thought.

Pepé cocked his rifle and edged the muzzle slowly around. Then he looked apprehensively up the trail and dropped the hammer again. From the ground beside him he picked an oak twig and threw it toward the spring. The quail flew up with a roar and the doves whistled away. The big cat stood up: for a long moment he looked at Pepé with cold yellow eyes, and then fearlessly walked back into the gulch.

The dusk gathered quickly in the deep valley. Pepé muttered his prayers, put his head down on his arm and went instantly to sleep.

The moon came up and filled the valley with cold blue light, and the wind swept rustling down from the peaks. The owls worked up and down the slopes looking for rabbits. Down in the brush of the gulch a coyote gabbled. The oak trees whispered softly in the night breeze.

Pepé started up, listening. His horse had whinnied. The moon was just slipping behind the western ridge, leaving the valley in darkness behind it. Pepé sat tensely gripping his rifle. From far up the trail he heard an answering whinny and the crash of shod hooves on the broken rock. He jumped to his feet, ran to his horse and led it under the trees. He threw on the saddle and cinched it tight for the steep trail, caught the unwilling head and forced the bit into the mouth. He felt the saddle to make sure the water bag and the sack of jerky were there. Then he mounted and turned up the hill.

It was velvet dark. The horse found the entrance to the trail where it left the flat, and started up, stumbling and slipping on the rocks. Pepé's hand rose up to his head. His hat was gone. He had left it under the oak tree.

The horse had struggled far up the trail when the first change of dawn came into the air, a steel grayness as light mixed thoroughly with dark. Gradually the sharp snaggled edge of the ridge stood out above them, rotten granite tortured and eaten by the winds of time. Pepé had dropped his reins on the horn, leaving direction to the horse. The brush grabbed at his legs in the dark until one knee of his jeans was ripped.

Gradually the light flowed down over the ridge. The starved brush and rocks stood out in the half light, strange and lonely in high perspective. Then there came warmth into the light. Pepé drew up and looked back, but he could see nothing in the darker valley below. The sky turned blue over the coming sun. In the waste of the mountainside, the poor dry brush grew only three feet high. Here and there, big outcroppings of unrotted granite stood up like moldering houses. Pepé relaxed a little. He drank from his water bag and bit off a piece of jerky. A single eagle flew over, high in the light.

Without warning Pepé's horse screamed and fell on its side. He was almost down before the rifle crash echoed up from the valley. From a hole behind the struggling shoulder, a stream of bright crimson blood pumped and stopped and pumped and stopped. The hooves threshed on the ground. Pepé lay half stunned beside the horse. He looked slowly down the hill. A piece of sage clipped off beside his head and another crash echoed up from side to side of the canyon. Pepé flung himself frantically behind a bush.

He crawled up the hill on his knees and on one hand. His right hand held the rifle up off the ground and pushed it ahead of him. He moved with the instinctive care of an animal. Rapidly he wormed his way toward one of the big outcroppings of granite on the hill above him. Where the brush was high he doubled up and ran, but where the cover was slight he wriggled forward on his stomach, pushing the rifle ahead of him. In the last little distance there was no cover at all. Pepé poised and then he darted across the space and flashed around the corner of the rock.

He leaned panting against the stone. When his breath came easier he moved along behind the big rock until he came to a narrow split that offered a thin section of vision down the hill. Pepé lay on his stomach and pushed the rifle barrel through the slit and waited.

The sun reddened the western ridges now. Already the

buzzards were settling down toward the place where the
horse lay. A small brown bird scratched in the dead sage
leaves directly in front of the rifle muzzle. The coasting
eagle flew back toward the rising sun.

Pepé saw a little movement in the brush far below. His
grip tightened on the gun. A little brown doe stepped
daintily out on the trail and crossed it and disappeared into
the brush again. For a long time Pepé waited. Far below he
could see the little flat and the oak trees and the slash of
green. Suddenly his eyes flashed back at the trail again. A
quarter of a mile down there had been a quick movement in
the chaparral. The rifle swung over. The front sight nestled
in the V of the rear sight. Pepé studied for a moment
and then raised the rear sight a notch. The little movement
in the brush came again. The sight settled on it. Pepé
squeezed the trigger. The explosion crashed down the mountain and up the other side, and came rattling back. The
whole side of the slope grew still. No more movement. And
then a white streak cut into the granite of the slit and a
bullet whined away and a crash sounded up from below.
Pepé felt a sharp pain in his right hand. A sliver of granite
was sticking out from between his first and second knuckles
and the point protruded from his palm. Carefully he pulled
out the sliver of stone. The wound bled evenly and gently.
No vein nor artery was cut.

Pepé looked into a little dusty cave in the rock and
gathered a handful of spider web, and he pressed the mass
into the cut, plastering the soft web into the blood. The flow
stopped almost at once.

The rifle was on the ground. Pepé picked it up, levered a
new shell into the chamber. And then he slid into the brush
on his stomach. Far to the right he crawled, and then up
the hill, moving slowly and carefully, crawling to cover and
resting and then crawling again.

In the mountains the sun is high in its arc before it
penetrates the gorges. The hot face looked over the hill and
brought instant heat with it. The white light beat on the
rocks and reflected from them and rose up quivering from

the earth again, and the rocks and bushes seemed to quiver behind the air.

Pepé crawled in the general direction of the ridge peak, zig-zagging for cover. The deep cut between his knuckles began to throb. He crawled close to a rattlesnake before he saw it, and when it raised its dry head and made a soft beginning whirr, he backed up and took another way. The quick gray lizards flashed in front of him, raising a tiny line of dust. He found another mass of spider web and pressed it against his throbbing hand.

Pepé was pushing the rifle with his left hand now. Little drops of sweat ran to the ends of his coarse black hair and rolled down his cheeks. His lips and tongue were growing thick and heavy. His lips writhed to draw saliva into his mouth. His little dark eyes were uneasy and suspicious. Once when a gray lizard paused in front of him on the parched ground and turned its head sideways he crushed it flat with a stone.

When the sun slid past noon he had not gone a mile. He crawled exhaustedly a last hundred yards to a patch of high sharp manzanita, crawled desperately, and when the patch was reached he wriggled in among the tough gnarly trunks and dropped his head on his left arm. There was little shade in the meager brush, but there was cover and safety. Pepé went to sleep as he lay and the sun beat on his back. A few little birds hopped close to him and peered and hopped away. Pepé squirmed in his sleep and he raised and dropped his wounded hand again and again.

The sun went down behind the peaks and the cool evening came, and then the dark. A coyote yelled from the hillside, Pepé started awake and looked about with misty eyes. His hand was swollen and heavy; a little thread of pain ran up the inside of his arm and settled in a pocket in his armpit. He peered about and then stood up, for the mountains were black and the moon had not yet risen. Pepé stood up in the dark. The coat of his father pressed on his arm. His tongue was swollen until it nearly filled his mouth. He wriggled out of the coat and dropped it in the brush, and then he struggled up the hill, falling over rocks and tearing his way through the brush. The rifle knocked against stones as he went. Little dry avalanches of gravel and shattered stone went whispering down the hill behind him.

After a while the old moon came up and showed the jagged ridge top ahead of him. By moonlight Pepé traveled more easily. He bent forward so that his throbbing arm hung away from his body. The journey uphill was made in dashes and rests, a frantic rush up a few yards and then a rest. The wind coasted down the slope rattling the dry stems of the bushes.

The moon was at meridian when Pepé came at last to the sharp backbone of the ridge top. On the last hundred yards of the rise no soil had clung under the wearing winds. The way was on solid rock. He clambered to the top and looked down on the other side. There was a draw like the last below him, misty with moonlight, brushed with dry struggling sage and chaparral. On the other side the hill rose up sharply and at the top the jagged rotten teeth of the mountain showed against the sky. At the bottom of the cut the brush was thick and dark.

Pepé stumbled down the hill. His throat was almost closed with thirst. At first he tried to run, but immediately he fell and rolled. After that he went more carefully. The moon was just disappearing behind the mountains when he came to the bottom. He crawled into the heavy brush feeling with his fingers for water. There was no water in the bed of the stream, only damp earth. Pepé laid his gun down and scooped up a handful of mud and put it in his mouth, and then he spluttered and scraped the earth from his tongue with his finger, for the mud drew at his mouth like a poultice. He dug a hole in the stream bed with his fingers, dug a little basin to catch water; but before it was very deep his head fell forward on the damp ground and he slept.

The dawn came and the heat of the day fell on the earth, and still Pepé slept. Late in the afternoon his head jerked up. He looked slowly around. His eyes were slits of wariness. Twenty feet away in the heavy brush a big tawny mountain lion stood looking at him. Its long thick tail waved gracefully, its ears erect with interest, not laid back dangerously. The lion squatted down on its stomach and watched him.

Pepé looked at the hole he had dug in the earth. A half inch of muddy water had collected in the bottom. He tore the sleeve from his hurt arm, with his teeth ripped out a little square, soaked it in the water and put it in his mouth. Over and over he filled the cloth and sucked it.

Still the lion sat and watched him. The evening came down but there was no movement on the hills. No birds visited the dry bottom of the cut. Pepé looked occasionally at the lion. The eyes of the yellow beast drooped as though he were about to sleep. He yawned and his long thin red tongue curled out. Suddenly his head jerked around and his nostrils quivered. His big tail lashed. He stood up and slunk like a tawny shadow into the thick brush.

A moment later Pepé heard the sound, the faint far crash of horses' hooves on gravel. And he heard something else, a high whining yelp of a dog.

Pepé took his rifle in his left hand and he glided into the brush almost as quietly as the lion had. In the darkening evening he crouched up the hill toward the next ridge. Only when the dark came did he stand up. His energy was short. Once it was dark he fell over the rocks and slipped to his knees on the steep slope, but he moved on and on up the hill, climbing and scrabbling over the broken hillside.

When he was far up toward the top, he lay down and slept for a little while. The withered moon, shining on his face, awakened him. He stood up and moved up the hill. Fifty yards away he stopped and turned back, for he had forgotten his rifle. He walked heavily down and poked about in the brush, but he could not find his gun. At last he lay down to rest. The pocket of pain in his armpit had grown more sharp. His arm seemed to swell out and fall with every heartbeat. There was no position lying down where the heavy arm did not press against his armpit.

With the effort of a hurt beast, Pepé got up and moved again toward the top of the ridge. He held his swollen arm away from his body with his left hand. Up the steep hill he dragged himself, a few steps and a rest, and a few more steps. At last he was nearing the top. The moon showed the uneven sharp back of it against the sky.

Pepé's brain spun in a big spiral up and away from him. He slumped to the ground and lay still. The rock ridge top was only a hundred feet above him.

The moon moved over the sky. Pepé half turned on his back. His tongue tried to make words, but only a thick hissing came from between his lips.

When the dawn came, Pepé pulled himself up. His eyes were sane again. He drew his great puffed arm in front of him and looked at the angry wound. The black line ran up from his wrist to his armpit. Automatically he reached in his pocket for the big black knife, but it was not there. His eyes searched the ground. He picked up a sharp blade of stone and scraped at the wound, sawed at the proud flesh and then squeezed the green juice out in big drops. Instantly he threw back his head and whined like a dog. His whole right side shuddered at the pain, but the pain cleared his head.

In the gray light he struggled up the last slope to the ridge and crawled over and lay down behind a line of rocks. Below him lay a deep canyon exactly like the last, waterless and desolate. There was no flat, no oak trees, not even heavy brush in the bottom of it. And on the other side a sharp ridge stood up, thinly brushed with starving sage, littered with broken granite. Strewn over the hill there were giant outcroppings, and on the top the granite teeth stood out against the sky.

The new day was light now. The flame of sun came over the ridge and fell on Pepé where he lay on the ground. His coarse black hair was littered with twigs and bits of spider web. His eyes had retreated back into his head. Between his lips the tip of his black tongue showed.

He sat up and dragged his great arm into his lap and nursed it, rocking his body and moaning in his throat. He threw back his head and looked up into the pale sky. A big black bird circled nearly out of sight, and far to the left another was sailing near.

He lifted his head to listen, for a familiar sound had come to him from the valley he had climbed out of; it was the crying yelp of hounds, excited and feverish, on a trail.

Pepé bowed his head quickly. He tried to speak rapid words but only a thick hiss came from his lips. He drew a shaky cross on his breast with his left hand. It was a long struggle to get to his feet. He crawled slowly and mechanically to the top of a big rock on the ridge peak. Once there, he arose slowly, swaying to his feet, and stood erect. Far below he could see the dark brush where he had slept. He braced his feet and stood there, black against the morning sky.

There came a ripping sound at his feet. A piece of stone flew up and a bullet droned off into the next gorge. The hollow crash echoed up from below. Pepé looked down for a moment and then pulled himself straight again.

His body jarred back. His left hand fluttered helplessly toward his breast. The second crash sounded from below. Pepé swung forward and toppled from the rock. His body struck and rolled over and over, starting a little avalanche. And when at last he stopped against a bush, the avalanche slid slowly down and covered up his head.

◆ ———————————————————————— ◆

A RED-LETTER DAY

Elizabeth Taylor

The hedgerow was beaded with silver. In the English November fog, the leaves dripped with a deadly intensity, as if each falling drop were a drop of acid.

Through the mist, cabs came suddenly face to face with one another, passing and repassing between station and

school. Backing into the hedges—twigs, withered berries
striking the windows—the drivers leaned out to exchange
remarks incomprehensible to their passengers, who felt oddly
at their mercy. Town parents, especially, shrank from this
malevolent landscape—the wastes of rotting cabbages, flint
cottages with rakish privies, rubbish heaps, gray napkins
drooping on clotheslines, soil like plum cake. Even turning
in at the rather superior school gates, they were dismayed
by the mossy stone and the smell of fungus. Then, as the
building itself came into view, they could see Matron standing at the top of the steps, fantastically white, shaming Nature, her hands laid affectionately upon the shoulders of such
boys as could not resist her. The weather was put in its place.
The day would take its course. She had an air of professional
bonhomie, as if she shared in the gaiety of the occasion.
But, each term, Visiting Day to her was like Christmas Day
to a clergyman, a great climax of work and preparation.

Tory was one of the last to get a cab. Having no man to
exert authority for her, she must merely take her turn and
stand on the slimy pavement waiting for a car to come back
to the station empty. She stamped her feet, feeling the
damp creeping through her shoes. When she left home, she
had thought herself suitably dressed; even for such an early
hour, her hat was surely plain enough? One after another,
she had tried on every one she owned, and had come out,
in the end, leaving hats all over the bed, so that it resembled a new grave with its mound of wreathed flowers. But
the other mothers had hats of undreamed-of austerity, and
the most sensible of Tory's shoes could not withstand the
insidious damp.

One other woman was on her own. Tory eyed her with
distaste. Her sons (for surely there were more than one; she
looked as if she had what is often called a teeming womb,
like a woman symbolizing maternity in a pageant), her many
sons would never feel the lack of a father (as Tory's one boy
was bound to), for she was large enough to be both father
and mother to them. Yes, Tory thought, she would have
them out on the lawn and bowl at them by the hour, would

coach them in mathematics, oil their bats, dub their boots, tan their backsides. Tory was working herself up into a hatred of this woman, who seemed to be all that she herself was not, with only one love affair in her life, or, rather, one mating. She has probably eaten her husband now that her child-bearing days are over, Tory thought. He would never have dared to ask for a divorce, as mine did. The woman still carried her "mother's bag"—the vast thing that, full of diapers, bibs, bottles of orange juice, accompanies babies out to tea. Tory wondered what was in it now. Sensible things—a Bradshaw, ration books, a bag of biscuits, large, clean handkerchiefs, a tablet of soap, and aspirins?

A jolly manner. ("I love young people—I feed on them," Tory thought spitefully.) The furs on the woman's shoulders made her even larger; they clasped paws across her great, authoritative back, like hands across the ocean. Tory lifted her muff to hide her smile.

Nervous dread made her feel fretful and vicious. In *her* life, all was frail, precarious—emotions fleeting, relation-ships fragmentary. Her life with her husband had suddenly loosened and dissolved; her love for her son was painful, shadowed by guilt—the guilt of having nothing solid to offer, of having grown up and forgotten, of adventuring still, away from her child, of not being able to resist those emo-tional adventures, the tenuous grasping after life. He was threatened by the very look of her, attracting those deli-cious secret glances, glimpses, and whispers, by the chal-lenge she always felt, and the excitement—not deeply sexual, for she was merely flirtatious. But I am not, she thought, watching Mrs. Hay-Hardy (whose name she was soon to learn but did not yet know) rearranging her furs on her shoulders, I am not a great feather bed of oblivion. Between Edward and me there is no premise of love, none at all—nothing taken for granted, as between most sons and moth-ers, but all tentative and agonized. We are indeed amateurs, both of us; no tradition behind us, no gift for the job. All we achieve is too hard come by. We try too piteously to please one another, and if we do, feel frightened by the miracle of it. I do indeed love him above all others. Above all others, but not exclusively . . .

Here a taxi swerved against the station curb and palpitated as she stepped forward quickly, triumphantly, before Mrs. Hay-Hardy could do so, and settled herself in the back seat.

"Could we share?" Mrs. Hay-Hardy asked, her voice confident, melodious, and one foot definitely on the running board. Tory smiled and moved over much farther than was necessary, as if such a teeming womb could scarcely be accommodated on the seat beside her.

Shifting her furs on her shoulders, settling herself, Mrs. Hay-Hardy glanced out through the filming windows, undaunted by the weather, which, she said, would clear, would lift. Oh, she was confident that it would lift by midday!

"One has to get up so early it seems midday now," Tory complained.

But Mrs. Hay-Hardy explained that she had not risen until six, so, naturally, it still seemed only eleven to her, as it was.

She will share the fare, down to the last penny, Tory thought. There will be a loud and forthright women's argument. She will count out coppers and make a fuss.

This did happen. At the top of the steps, Matron still waited, with the three Hay-Hardy boys grouped about her, and Edward, who blushed and whitened alternately with terrible excitement, a little to one side. Yes, he had grown, Tory thought, and his shorts were high above his roughened knees. He looked more than eleven, but his complexion was peachy and downy still, like a younger child's, and his long lashes threw shadows across his eyes. As an only son, he had not the same claim to Matron's attention as the Hay-Hardys, and she had chosen them to encircle. Sensing this, perhaps, Edward stood apart.

To meet this wonderful customer, this profitable womb, the headmaster's wife herself came into the hall. Her husband had sent her, instructing her with deft cynicism from behind his detective novel. He himself, of course, was one of those gods who rarely descend, except, like Zeus, in a very private capacity.

This is the moment I marked off on the calendar, Edward thought. Here it is. Every night, he and the other boys had thrown one of their pebbles out of the window to mark a day gone. The little stones had dropped back onto the gravel under the window, quite lost, untraceable—the days of their lives.

As smooth as minnows were Mrs. Lancaster's phrases of welcome; she had soothed so many mothers, mothered so many boys. Her words swam all one way, in unison, but her heart never moved. Matron, on the other hand, was always nervous; the results of her work were so much on the surface, so easily checked. The rest of the staff could hide their inefficiency or shift their responsibility. She could not. If Mrs. Hay-Hardy cried, as she did today, "Dear boy, your teeth!" to her first-born, it was Matron's work she criticized, and Matron flushed. And Mrs. Lancaster flushed for Matron, and Derrick Hay-Hardy flushed for his mother.

"Perhaps I am not a born mother," Tory thought, going down the steps with Edward. They would walk back to the town and have lunch at the Crown, she said to him. Edward pressed her arm as a taxi, bulging with Hay-Hardys, went away down the drive.

"Do you mean you wanted to go with them?" Tory asked. They will get here long before us, she thought. They will have eaten everything.

"No."

"Don't you like them?"

"No."

"But why?"

"They don't like me."

Unbearable news for any mother, for surely all the world loves one's child, one's only child. Doubt set in, a little, nagging toothache of doubt. You *are* happy? she wanted to ask. "I've looked forward so much to this," she said instead. "*So* much."

He stared ahead. All around the gateposts, drops of moisture fell from one leaf to another, and the stone griffins were hunched up in misery.

"But I imagined it being a different day," Tory added. "Quite different."

"It will be nice to get something different to eat," Edward said.

They walked down the road toward the Crown in silence, as if they could not make any progress until they had reached that point.

"You *are* warm enough at night?" Tory asked when at last they were sitting in the hotel dining room.

"Yes," he said absently, and then, bringing himself back to the earlier, distant politeness, added, "Stifling hot."

"Stifling? But surely you have plenty of fresh air?" She could feel her questions sliding off him.

"*I* do," he said reassuringly. "My bed's just under the window. Perishing. I have to keep my head under the bed-clothes, or I get earache."

I am asking for all this, she thought. When the waiter brought her pink gin, she drank it quickly, conscious that Mrs. Hay-Hardy, across the hotel dining room, was pouring out a nice glass of water for herself, was so full of jokes that Tory felt she had perhaps brought a collection of them along with her in her shopping bag. Laughter ran around and around the Hay-Hardys' table, above the glasses of water. Edward turned once, and she glimpsed the faintest quiver under one eye, and an answering quiver on the middle Hay-Hardy's face.

She felt exasperated. Cold had settled in her; her mouth—her heart, too—felt stiff.

"What would you like to do after lunch?" she asked.

"We could look round the shops," Edward said, nibbling away at his bread, as if to keep hunger at arm's length.

The shops were in the market square. At the draper's, the hats were steadily coming around into fashion again. "I could astonish everyone with one of these," Tory thought, setting her own hat right by her reflection in the window. Bales of cotton apron print rose on both sides; a wax-faced boy wore a stiff suit, its price ticket dangling from his yellow, broken fingers, his painted blue eyes turned mildly upon the street. Edward gave him a look of contempt and went to the shop door. Breathing on the glass, peering in through a little space among suspended bibs and jabots and parlormaids' caps, he watched the cages flying overhead between cashier and counter.

The Hay-Hardys streamed by, heading for the open country.

Most minutely, Tory and Edward examined the windows of the draper's shop, the bicycle shop, the family grocer's. There was nothing to say. They were just reading the postcards in the news agent's window when Edward's best friend greeted them. His father, a clergyman, snatched off his hat and clapped it to his chest at the sight of Tory. When she turned back to the postcards, she could see how unsuitable they were—jokes about bloomers, about twins; a great sea-side world of fat men in striped bathing suits; enormous women trotted down to the sea's edge while crabs humorously nipped their behinds; farcical situations arose over bathing machines; and little boys had trouble with their water. She blushed.

The afternoon seemed to give a little sigh, stirred itself, and shook down a spattering of rain over the pavements. Beyond the market square, the countryside, which had absorbed the Hay-Hardys, lowered at them.

"Is there anything you want?" Tory asked desperately, coveting the warm interiors of the shops.

"I could do with a new puncture outfit for my bike," Edward said.

They went back to the bicycle shop. My God, it's only three o'clock, Tory thought in despair as she glanced secretly under her glove at her watch.

The Museum Room at the Guildhall was not gay, but at least there were Roman remains, a few instruments of torture, and half of a mammoth's jawbone. Tory sat down on a seat among all the broken terra cotta and took out a cigarette.

"No smoking, please," the attendant said, coming out from behind a case of stuffed deer.

"Oh, please!" Tory begged. She sat primly on the chair, her feet together, and when she looked up at him, her violet eyes flashed with tears. Edward wandered away.

The attendant struck a match for her, and his hand, curving around it, trembled.

"It's the insurance," he apologized. "I'll have this later, if I may," he said when she offered him a cigarette, and he put it very carefully in his breast pocket, as if it were a lock of her hair.

"Do you have to stay here all day long with these dull little broken jugs and things?" she asked, looking about.

He forgave her at once for belittling his life's work, only pointing out his pride, the fine mosaic on the wall.

"But floors should be lying down," she said naïvely, without innocence.

Edward came tiptoeing back.

"You see that quite delightful floor hanging up there?" she said to him. "This gentleman will tell you all about it. . . . My son adores Greek mythology," she explained to the attendant.

"Your son!" he repeated, affecting gallant disbelief, his glance stripping ten or fifteen years from her. Then, "This happens to be a Byzantine mosaic," he said, and looked reproachfully at it for not being what it could not be. Edward listened grudgingly. His mother had forced him into similar situations at other times—in the armory of the Tower of London and, once, at Kew. It was as if she kindled in men a flicker of interest and admiration that her son must keep fanned, for she would not. Boredom drew her away again, yet her charm must still hold sway. So now Edward listened crossly to the story of the Byzantine mosaic as, last holidays, he had minutely observed the chasing on Henry VIII's breastplate, and in utter exasperation, the holidays before, had watched curlews through field glasses ("Edward is so very keen on birds") for the whole of a hot day while Tory dozed elegantly in the heather.

Ordinary days perhaps are better, Edward thought. Sinking down through him were the lees of despair, which must at all costs be hidden from his mother. He glanced up at every clock they passed, and wondered about his friends. Alone with his mother, he felt unsafe, wounded and wounding, and, oppressed by responsibility, he saw himself in relation to the outside world. Thoughts of the future and even—as they stood in the church porch to shelter from another little gust of rain—of death seemed to brush against him, alight on him, and they disturbed him, as they would not do if he were at school, anonymous and safe.

Tory sat down on a seat and read a notice about missionaries, chafing her hands inside her muff, while all her bracelets jingled softly.

Flapping, black, in his cassock, a clergyman came hurrying through the graveyard, between the dripping umbrella trees. Edward stepped guiltily off the porch, as if he had been trespassing.

"Good afternoon," the vicar said.

"Good afternoon," Tory replied. She looked up from blowing the fur of her muff into divisions and her smile broke warmly, beautifully, over the dark afternoon.

Then, "The weather—" they both began ruefully, broke off, and hesitated, then laughed at one another.

It was wonderful; now they would soon be saying goodbye. It was over, The day they had longed for was almost over—the polite little tea among the chintz and the wheelback chairs of the Copper Kettle, Tory frosty and imperious with the waitress, and, once, Edward beginning, "Father . . . ," at which she looked up sharply before she could gather together the careful indifference she always assumed at this name. Edward faltered, "He sent me a parcel." "How nice!" said Tory, laying ice all over his heart. She called the waitress. Her cup was cracked. She could not drink tea from riveted china, however prettily painted. The waitress went sulkily away. All around them sat other small boys with their parents. Tory's bracelets tinkled as she clasped her hands tightly together and leaned forward. "And how is your father's wife?" she asked brightly, indifferently.

*   *   *

They took a taxi back to the school. Sullenly, the day withdrew; as they turned in at the gates, they could see lights in the ground-floor windows. She thought of going back in the train, of a lonely evening. She would take a drink up to her bedroom and sip it while she did her hair, the gas fire roaring in its white ribs, Edward's photograph beside her bed.

The Hay-Hardys were unloading at the foot of the school steps; flushed from their country walk and all their laughter, they seemed to swarm and shout.

Edward got out of the taxi and stood looking up at Tory, his new puncture outfit clasped tightly in his hand. Uncertainly, awaiting a cue from her, he tried to begin his goodbye.

Warm, musky-scented, softly rustling with the sound of her bracelets, the touch of her fur, she leaned and kissed him. "So lovely, darling!" she murmured. She had no cue to give him. Mrs. Hay-Hardy had gone into the school to have a word with Matron, so Tory must find her own way of saying farewell.

They smiled gaily, as if they were greeting one another.

"See you soon," she said.

"Yes, see you soon."

"Goodbye, then, darling."

"Goodbye," said Edward.

She slammed the door and, as the taxi moved off, leaned toward the window and waved. He stood there uncertainly, waving back, radiant with relief. Then, as she disappeared around the curve of the drive, he ran quickly up the steps to find his friends, and safety.

A SPINSTER'S TALE

Peter Taylor

My brother would often get drunk when I was a little girl, but that put a different sort of fear into me from what Mr. Speed did. With Brother it was a spiritual thing. And though it was frightening to know that he would have to burn for all that giggling and bouncing around on the stair at night, the truth was that he only seemed jollier to me when I would stick my head out of the hall door. It made him seem almost my age for him to act so silly, putting his white forefinger all over his flushed face and finally over his lips to say, "Sh-sh-sh-sh!" But the really frightening thing about seeing Brother drunk was what I always heard when I had slid back into bed. I could always recall my mother's words to him when he was sixteen, the year before she died, spoken in her greatest sincerity, in her most religious tone:

"Son, I'd rather see you in your grave."

Yet those nights put a scaredness into me that was clearly distinguishable from the terror that Mr. Speed instilled by stumbling past our house two or three afternoons a week. The most that I knew about Mr. Speed was his name. And this I considered that I had somewhat fabricated—by allowing him the "Mr."—in my effort to humannize and soften the monster that was forever passing our house on Church Street. My father would point him out through the wide parlor window in soberness and severity to my brother with: "There goes Old Speed, again." Or on Saturdays when Brother was with the Benton boys and my two uncles were over having toddies with Father in the parlor, Father would

refer to Mr. Speed's passing with a similar speech, but in a
blustering tone of merry tolerance: "There goes Old Speed,
again. The rascal!" These designations were equally awful,
both spoken in tones that were foreign to my father's manner of addressing me; and not unconsciously I prepared the
euphemism, Mister Speed, against the inevitable day when
I should have to speak of him to someone.

I was named Elizabeth, for my mother. My mother had
died in the spring before Mr. Speed first came to my notice
on that late afternoon in October. I had bathed at four with
the aid of Lucy, who had been my nurse and who was now
the upstairs maid; and Lucy was upstairs turning back the
covers of the beds in the rooms with their color schemes of
blue and green and rose. I wandered into the shadowy
parlor and sat first on one chair, then on another. I tried
lying down on the settee that went with the parlor set, but
my legs had got too long this summer to stretch out straight
on the settee. And my feet looked long in their pumps
against the wicker arm. I looked at the pictures around the
room blankly and at the stained-glass windows on either
side of the fireplace; and the winter light coming through
them was hardly bright enough to show the colors. I struck
a match on the mosaic hearth and lit the gas-logs.

Kneeling on the hearth I watched the flames till my face
felt hot. I stood up then and turned directly to one of the
full-length mirror-panels that were on each side of the front
window. This one was just to the right of the broad window
and my reflection in it stood out strangely from the rest of
the room in the dull light that did not penetrate beyond my
figure. I leaned closer to the mirror trying to discover a
resemblance between myself and the wondrous Alice who
walked through a looking-glass. But that resemblance I was
seeking I could not find in my sharp features, or in my
heavy, dark curls hanging like fragments of hosepipe to my
shoulders.

I propped my hands on the borders of the narrow mirror
and put my face close to watch my lips say, "Away." I would

hardly open them for the "a"; and then I would contort my face by the great opening I made for the "way." I whispered, "Away, away." I whispered it over and over, faster and faster, watching myself in the mirror: "A-way—a-way—a-way-away-awayaway." Suddenly I burst into tears and turned from the gloomy mirror to the daylight at the wide parlor window. Gazing tearfully through the expanse of plate glass there, I beheld Mr. Speed walking like a cripple with one foot on the curb and one in the street. And faintly I could hear him cursing the trees as he passed them, giving each a lick with his heavy walking cane.

Presently I was dry-eyed in my fright. My breath came short, and I clasped the black bow at the neck of my middy blouse.

When he had passed from view, I stumbled back from the window. I hadn't heard the houseboy enter the parlor, and he must not have noticed me there. I made no move of recognition as he drew the draperies across the wide front window for the night. I stood cold and silent before the gas-logs with a sudden inexplicable memory of my mother's cheek and a vision of her in her bedroom on a spring day.

That April day when spring had seemed to crowd itself through the windows into the bright upstairs rooms, the old-fashioned mahogany sick-chair had been brought down from the attic to my mother's room. Three days before, a quiet service had been held there for the stillborn baby, and I had accompanied my father and brother to our lot in the gray cemetery to see the box (large for so tiny a parcel) lowered and covered with mud. But in the parlor now by the gas-logs I remembered the day that my mother had sent for the sick-chair and for me.

The practical nurse, sitting in a straight chair busy at her needlework, looked over her glasses to give me some little instruction in the arrangement of my mother's pillows in the chair. A few minutes before, this practical nurse had lifted my sick mother bodily from the bed, and I had had the privilege of rolling my mother to the big bay window that looked out ideally over the new foliage of small trees in our side yard.

I stood self-consciously straight, close by my mother, a maturing little girl awkward in my curls and long-waisted dress. My pale mother, in her silk bed-jacket, with a smile leaned her cheek against the cheek of her daughter. Outside it was spring. The furnishings of the great blue room seemed to partake for that one moment of nature's life. And my mother's cheek was warm on mine. This I remembered when I sat before the gas-logs trying to put Mr. Speed out of my mind; but that a few moments later my mother beckoned to the practical nurse and sent me suddenly from the room, my memory did not dwell upon. I remembered only the warmth of the cheek and the comfort of that other moment.

I sat near the blue burning logs and waited for my father and my brother to come in. When they came saying the same things about office and school that they said every day, turning on lights beside chairs that they liked to flop into, I realized not that I was ready or unready for them but that there had been, within me, an attempt at a preparation for such readiness.

They sat so customarily in their chairs at first and the talk ran so easily that I thought that Mr. Speed could be forgotten as quickly and painlessly as a doubting of Jesus or a fear of death from the measles. But the conversation took insinuating and malicious twists this afternoon. My father talked about the possibilities of a general war and recalled opinions that people had had just before the Spanish-American. He talked about the hundreds of men in the Union Depot. Thinking of all those men there, that close together, was something like meeting Mr. Speed in the front hall. I asked my father not to talk about war, which seemed to him a natural enough request for a young lady to make.

"How is your school, my dear?" he asked me. "How are Miss Hood and Miss Herron? Have they found who's stealing the boarders' things, my dear?"

All of those little girls safely in Belmont School being called for by gentle ladies or warm-breasted Negro women were a pitiable sight beside the beastly vision of Mr. Speed which even they somehow conjured.

At dinner, with Lucy serving and sometimes helping my plate (because she had done so for so many years), Brother teased me first one way and then another. My father joined in on each point until I began to take the teasing very seriously, and then he told Brother that he was forever carrying things too far.

Once at dinner I was convinced that my preposterous fears that Brother knew what had happened to me by the window in the afternoon were not at all preposterous. He had been talking quietly. It was something about the meeting that he and the Benton boys were going to attend after dinner. But quickly, without reason, he turned his eyes on me across the table and fairly shouted in his new deep voice: "I saw three horses running away out on Harding Road today! They were just like the mules we saw at the mines in the mountains! They were running to beat hell and with little girls riding them!"

The first week after I had the glimpse of Mr. Speed through the parlor window, I spent the afternoons dusting the bureau and mantel and bedside table in my room, arranging on the chaise longue the dolls which at this age I never played with and rarely even talked to; or I would absent-mindedly assist Lucy in turning down the beds and maybe watch the houseboy set the dinner table. I went to the parlor only when Father came or when Brother came earlier and called me in to show me a shin bruise or a box of cigarettes which a girl had given him.

Finally I put my hand on the parlor doorknob just at four one afternoon and entered the parlor, walking stiffly as I might have done with my hands in a muff going into church. The big room with its heavy furniture and pictures showed no change since the last afternoon that I had spent there, unless possibly there were fresh antimacassars on the chairs.

I confidently pushed an odd chair over to the window and took my seat and sat erect and waited.

My heart would beat hard when, from the corner of my eye, I caught sight of some figure moving up Church Street. And as it drew nearer, showing the form of some Negro or neighbor or drummer, I would sigh from relief and from regret. I was ready for Mr. Speed. And I knew that he would come again and again, that he had been passing our house for inconceivable numbers of years. I knew that if he did not appear today, he would pass tomorrow. Not because I had had accidental, unavoidable glimpses of him from upstairs windows during the past week, nor because there were indistinct memories of such a figure, hardly noticed, seen on afternoons that preceded that day when I had seen him stumbling like a cripple along the curb and beating and cursing the trees did I know that Mr. Speed was a permanent and formidable figure in my life which I would be called upon to deal with; my knowledge, I was certain, was purely intuitive.

I was ready now not to face him with his drunken rage directed at me, but to look at him far off in the street and to appraise him. He didn't come that afternoon, but he came the next. I sat prim and straight before the window. I turned my head neither to the right to anticipate the sight of him nor to the left to follow his figure when it had passed. But when he was passing before my window, I put my eyes full on him and looked though my teeth chattered in my head. And now I saw his face heavy, red, fierce like his body. He walked with an awkward, stomping sort of stagger, carrying his gray top coat over one arm; and with his other hand he kept poking his walnut cane into the soft sod along the sidewalk. When he was gone, I recalled my mother's cheek again, but the recollection this time, though more deliberate, was dwelt less upon; and I could only think of watching Mr. Speed again and again.

There was snow on the ground the third time that I watched Mr. Speed pass our house. Mr. Speed spat on the

snow, and with his cane he aimed at the brown spot that his
tobacco made there. And I could see that he missed his aim.
The fourth time that I sat watching for him from the window, snow was actually falling outside; and I felt a sort of
anxiety to know what would ever drive him into my own
house. For a moment I doubted that he would really come
to my door; but I prodded myself with the thought of his
coming and finding me unprepared. And I continued to
keep my secret watch for him two or three times a week
during the rest of the winter.

Meanwhile my life with my father and brother and the
servants in the shadowy house went on from day to day. On
week nights the evening meal usually ended with petulant
arguing between the two men, the atlas or the encyclopedia
usually drawing them from the table to read out the statis-
tics. Often Brother was accused of having looked-them-up-
previously and of maneuvering the conversation toward the
particular subject, for topics were very easily introduced
and dismissed by the two. Once I, sent to the library to
fetch a cigar, returned to find the discourse shifted in two
minutes' time from the Kentucky Derby winners to the
languages in which the Bible was first written. Once I
actually heard the conversation slip, in the course of a small
dessert, from the comparative advantages of urban and agrar-
ian life for boys between the ages of fifteen and twenty to
the probable origin and age of the Icelandic parliament and
then to the doctrines of the Campbellite church.

That night I followed them to the library and beheld
them fingering the pages of the flimsy old atlas in the light
from the beaded lampshade. They paid no attention to me
and little to one another, each trying to turn the pages of
the book and mumbling references to newspaper articles
and to statements of persons of responsibility. I slipped
from the library to the front parlor across the hall where I
could hear the contentious hum. And I lit the gas-logs,
trying to warm my long legs before them as I examined my
own response to the unguided and remorseless bickering of
the masculine voices.

It was, I thought, their indifferent shifting from topic to topic that most disturbed me. Then I decided that it was the tremendous gaps that there seemed to be between the subjects that was bewildering to me. Still again I thought that it was the equal interest which they displayed for each subject that was dismaying. All things in the world were equally at home in their arguments. They exhibited equal indifference to the horrors that each topic might suggest; and I wondered whether or not their imperturbability was a thing that they had achieved.

I knew that I had got myself so accustomed to the sight of Mr. Speed's peregrinations, persistent, yet, withal, seemingly without destination, that I could view his passing with perfect equanimity. And from this I knew that I must extend my preparation for the day when I should have to view him at closer range. When the day would come, I knew that it must involve my father and my brother and that his existence therefore must not remain an unmentionable thing, the secrecy of which to explode at the moment of crisis, only adding to its confusion.

Now, the door to my room was the first at the top of the long red-carpeted stairway. A wall light beside it was left burning on nights when Brother was out, and, when he came in, he turned it off. The light shining through my transom was a comforting sight when I had gone to bed in the big room; and in the summertime I could see the reflection of light bugs on it, and often one would plop against it. Sometimes I would wake up in the night with a start and would be frightened in the dark, not knowing what had awakened me until I realized that Brother had just turned out the light. On other nights, however, I would hear him close the front door and hear him bouncing up the steps. When I then stuck my head out the door, usually he would toss me a piece of candy and he always signaled to me to be quiet.

I had never intentionally stayed awake till he came in until one night toward the end of February of that year, and I hadn't been certain then that I should be able to do it. Indeed, when finally the front door closed, I had dozed several times sitting up in the dark bed. But I was standing with my door half open before he had come a third of the way up the stair. When he saw me, he stopped still on the stairway resting his hand on the banister. I realized that purposefulness must be showing on my face, and so I smiled at him and beckoned. His red face broke into a fine grin, and he took the next few steps two at a time. But he stumbled on the carpeted steps. He was on his knees, yet with his hand still on the banister. He was motionless there for a moment with his head cocked to one side, listening. The house was quiet and still. He smiled again, sheepishly this time, and kept putting his white forefinger to his red face as he ascended on tiptoe the last third of the flight of steps.

At the head of the stair he paused, breathing hard. He reached his hand into his coat pocket and smiled confidently as he shook his head at me. I stepped backward into my room.

"Oh," he whispered. "Your candy."

I stood straight in my white nightgown with my black hair hanging over my shoulders, knowing that he could see me only indistinctly. I beckoned to him again. He looked suspiciously about the hall, then stepped into the room and closed the door behind him.

"What's the matter, Betsy?" he said.

I turned and ran and climbed between the covers of my bed.

"What's the matter, Betsy?" he said. He crossed to my bed and sat down beside me on it.

I told him that I didn't know what was the matter.

"Have you been reading something you shouldn't, Betsy?" he asked.

I was silent.

"Are you lonely, Betsy?" he said. "Are you a lonely little girl?"

I sat up on the bed and threw my arms about his neck. And as I sobbed on his shoulder I smelled for the first time the fierce odor of his cheap whisky.

"Yes, I'm always lonely," I said with directness, and I was then silent with my eyes open and my cheek on the shoul-

der of his overcoat which was yet cold from the February
night air.

He kept his face turned away from me and finally spoke,
out of the other corner of his mouth, I thought, "I'll come
home earlier some afternoons and we'll talk and play."

"Tomorrow."

When I had said this distinctly, I fell away from him back
on the bed. He stood up and looked at me curiously, as
though in some way repelled by my settling so comfortably
in the covers. And I could see his eighteen-year-old head
cocked to one side as though trying to see my face in the
dark. He leaned over me, and I smelled his whisky breath.
It was not repugnant to me. It was blended with the odor
that he always had. I thought that he was going to strike
me. He didn't, however, and in a moment was opening the
door to the lighted hall. Before he went out, again I said:

"Tomorrow."

The hall light dark and the sound of Brother's footsteps
gone, I naturally repeated the whole scene in my mind and
upon examination found strange elements present. One was
something like a longing for my brother to strike me when
he was leaning over me. Another was his bewilderment at
my procedure. On the whole I was amazed at the way I had
carried the thing off. Now I only wished that in the darkness
when he was leaning over me I had said languidly, "Oh,
Brother," had said it in a tone indicating that we had in
common some unmentionable trouble. Then I should have
been certain of his presence next day. As it was, though, I
had little doubt of his coming home early.

I would not let myself reflect further on my feelings for
my brother—my desire for him to strike me and my delight
in his natural odor. I had got myself in the habit of postponing such elucidations until after I had completely settled
with Mr. Speed. But, as after all such meetings with my
brother, I reflected upon the posthumous punishments in
store for him for his carousing and drinking and remembered
my mother's saying that she had rather see him in his grave.

*   *   *

The next afternoon at four I had the chessboard on the tea table before the front parlor window. I waited for my brother, knowing pretty well that he would come and feeling certain that Mr. Speed would pass. (For this was a Thursday afternoon; and during the winter months I had found that there were two days of the week on which Mr. Speed never failed to pass our house. These were Thursday and Saturday.) I led my brother into that dismal parlor chattering about the places where I had found the chessmen long in disuse. When I paused a minute, slipping into my seat by the chessboard, he picked up with talk of the senior class play and his chances for being chosen valedictorian. Apparently I no longer seemed an enigma to him. I thought that he must have concluded that I was just a lonely little girl named Betsy. But I doubted that his nature was so different from my own that he could sustain objective sympathy for another child, particularly a younger sister, from one day to another. And since I saw no favors that he could ask from me at this time, my conclusion was that he believed that he had never exhibited his drunkenness to me with all his bouncing about on the stair at night; but that he was not certain that talking from the other corner of his mouth had been precaution enough against his whisky breath.

We faced each other over the chessboard and set the men in order. There were only a few days before it would be March, and the light through the window was first bright and then dull. During my brother's moves I stared out the window at the clouds that passed before the sun and watched pieces of newspaper that blew about the yard. I was calm beyond my own credulity. I found myself responding to my brother's little jokes and showing real interest in the game. I tried to terrorize myself by imagining Mr. Speed's coming up to the very window this day. I even had him shaking his cane and his derby hat at us. But the frenzy which I expected at this step of my preparation did not come. And some part of Mr. Speed's formidability seemed to have vanished. I realized that by not hiding my face in my mother's bosom and by looking at him so regularly for so

many months, I had come to accept his existence as a
natural part of my life on Church Street, though something
to be guarded against, or, as I had put it before, to be
thoroughly prepared for when it came to my door.

The problem then, in relation to my brother, had suddenly resolved itself in something much simpler than the
conquest of my fear of looking upon Mr. Speed alone had
been. This would be only a matter of how I should act and
of what words I should use. And from the incident of the
night before, I had some notion that I'd find a suitable way
of procedure in our household.

Mr. Speed appeared in the street without his overcoat
but with one hand holding the turned-up lapels and collar of
his gray suit coat. He followed his cane, stomping like an
enraged blind man with his head bowed against the March
wind. I squeezed from between my chair and the table and
stood right at the great plate glass window, looking out.
From the corner of my eye I saw that Brother was intent
upon his play. Presently, in the wind, Mr. Speed's derby
went back on his head, and his hand grabbed at it, pulled it
back in place, then returned to hold his lapels. I took a
sharp breath, and Brother looked up. And just as he looked
out the window, Mr. Speed's derby did blow off and across
the sidewalk, over the lawn. Mr. Speed turned, holding his
lapels with his tremendous hand, shouting oaths that I could
hear ever so faintly, and tried to stumble after his hat.

Then I realized that my brother was gone from the room;
and he was outside the window with Mr. Speed chasing Mr.
Speed's hat in the wind.

I sat back in my chair, breathless; one elbow went down
on the chessboard disordering the black and white pawns
and kings and castles. And through the window I watched
Brother handing Mr. Speed his derby. I saw his apparent
indifference to the drunk man's oaths and curses. I saw him
coming back to the house while the old man yet stood
railing at him. I pushed the table aside and ran to the front
door lest Brother be locked outside. He met me in the hall
smiling blandly.

I said, "That's Mr. Speed."

He sat down on the bottom step of the stairway, leaning backward and looking at me inquisitively.

"He's drunk, Brother," I said. "Always."

My brother looked frankly into the eyes of this half-grown sister of his but said nothing for a while.

I pushed myself up on the console table and sat swinging my legs and looking seriously about the walls of the cavernous hallway at the expanse of oak paneling, at the inset canvas of the sixteenth-century Frenchman making love to his lady, at the hat rack, and at the grandfather's clock in the darkest corner. I waited for Brother to speak.

"You don't like people who get drunk?" he said.

I saw that he was taking the whole thing as a thrust at his own behavior.

"I just think Mr. Speed is very ugly, Brother."

From the detached expression of his eyes I knew that he was not convinced.

"I wouldn't mind him less if he were sober," I said. "Mr. Speed's like—a loose horse."

This analogy convinced him. He knew then what I meant.

"You mustn't waste your time being afraid of such things," he said in great earnestness. "In two or three years there'll be things that you'll have to be afraid of. Things you really can't avoid."

"What did he say to you?" I asked.

"He cussed and threatened to hit me with that stick."

"For no reason?"

"Old Mr. Speed's burnt out his reason with whisky."

"Tell me about him." I was almost imploring him.

"Everybody knows about him. He just wanders around town, drunk. Sometimes downtown they take him off in the Black Maria."

I pictured him on the main streets that I knew downtown and in the big department stores. I could see him in that formal neighborhood where my grandmother used to live. In the neighborhood of Miss Hood and Miss Herron's school.

Around the little houses out where my father's secretary
lived. Even in nigger town.

"You'll get used to him, for all his ugliness," Brother said.
Then we sat there till my father came in, talking almost
gaily about things that were particularly ugly in Mr. Speed's
clothes and face and in his way of walking.

Since the day that I watched myself say "away" in the
mirror, I had spent painful hours trying to know once more
that experience which I now regarded as something like
mystical. But the stringent course that I, motherless and
lonely in our big house, had brought myself to follow while
only thirteen had given me certain mature habits of thought.
Idle and unrestrained daydreaming I eliminated almost entirely from my experience, though I delighted myself with
fantasies that I quite consciously worked out and which,
when concluded, I usually considered carefully, trying to fix
them with some sort of childish symbolism.

Even idleness in my nightly dreams disturbed me. And
sometimes as I tossed half awake in my big bed I would try
to piece together my dreams into at least a form of logic.
Sometimes I would complete an unfinished dream and
wouldn't know in the morning what part I had dreamed and
what part pieced out. I would often smile over the ends that
I had plotted in half wakeful moments but found pride in
dreams that were complete in themselves and easy to fix
with allegory, which I called "meaning." I found that a
dream could start for no discoverable reason, with the sight
of a printed page on which the first line was, "Once upon a
time"; and soon could have me a character in a strange
story. Once upon a time there was a little girl whose hands
began to get very large. Grown men came for miles around
to look at the giant hands and to shake them, but the little
girl was ashamed of them and hid them under her skirt. It
seemed that the little girl lived in the stable behind my
grandmother's old house, and I watched her from the top of
the loft ladder. Whenever there was the sound of footsteps,
she trembled and wept; so I would beat on the floor above

her and laugh uproariously at her fear. But presently I was
the little girl listening to the noise. At first I trembled
and called out for my father, but then I recollected that it
was I who had made the noises and I felt that I had made a
very considerable discovery for myself.

I awoke one Saturday morning in early March at the
sound of my father's voice in the downstairs hall. He was
talking to the servants, ordering the carriage I think. I
believe that I awoke at the sound of the carriage horses'
names. I went to my door and called "good-bye" to him. He
was twisting his mustache before the hall mirror, and he
looked up the stairway at me and smiled. He was always
abashed to be caught before a looking-glass, and he called
out self-consciously and affectionately that he would be home
at noon.

I closed my door and went to the little dressing table that
he had had put in my room on my birthday. The card with
his handwriting on it was still stuck in the corner of the
mirror: "For my young lady daughter." I was so thoroughly
aware of the gentleness in his nature this morning that any
childish timidity before him would, I thought, seem an
injustice, and I determined that I should sit with him and
my uncles in the parlor that afternoon and perhaps tell them
all of my fear of the habitually drunken Mr. Speed and with
them watch him pass before the parlor window. That morning I sat before the mirror of my dressing table and put up
my hair in a knot on the back of my head for the first time.

Before Father came home at noon, however, I had taken
my hair down, and I was not now certain that he would be
unoffended by my mention of the neighborhood drunkard.
But I was resolute in my purpose, and when my two uncles
came after lunch, and the three men shut themselves up in
the parlor for the afternoon, I took my seat across the hall in
the little library, or den, as my mother had called it, and
spent the first of the afternoon skimming over the familiar
pages of *Tales of Ol' Virginny*, by Thomas Nelson Page.

My father had seemed tired at lunch. He talked very
little and drank only half his cup of coffee. He asked Brother

matter-of-fact questions about his plans for college in the fall
and told me once to try cutting my meat instead of pulling it
to pieces. And as I sat in the library afterward, I wondered
if he had been thinking of my mother. Indeed, I wondered
whether or not he ever thought of her. He never mentioned
her to us; and in a year I had forgotten exactly how he
treated her when she had been alive.

It was not only the fate of my brother's soul that I had
given thought to since my mother's death. Father had always had his toddy on Saturday afternoon with his two
bachelor brothers. But there was more than one round of
toddies served in the parlor on Saturday now. Throughout
the early part of this afternoon I could hear the tinkle of the
bell in the kitchen, and presently the houseboy would appear at the door of the parlor with a tray of ice-filled glasses.

As he entered the parlor each time, I would catch a
glimpse over my book of the three men. One was usually
standing, whichever one was leading the conversation. Once
they were laughing heartily; and as the Negro boy came out
with the tray of empty glasses, there was a smile on his face.

As their voices grew louder and merrier, my courage slackened. It was then I first put into words the thought that in my
brother and father I saw something of Mr. Speed. And I knew
that it was more than a taste of whisky they had in common.

At four o'clock I heard Brother's voice mixed with those
of the Benton boys outside the front door. They came into
the hall, and their voices were high and excited. First one,
then another would demand to be heard with: "No, listen
now; let me tell you what." In a moment I heard Brother on
the stairs. Then two of the Benton brothers appeared in the
doorway of the library. Even the youngest, who was not a
year older than I and whose name was Henry, wore long
pants, and each carried a cap in hand and a linen duster
over his arm. I stood up and smiled at them, and with my
right forefinger I pushed the black locks which hung loosely
about my shoulders behind my ears.

"We're going motoring in the Carltons' machine," Henry
said.

I stammered my surprise and asked if Brother were going to ride in it. One of them said that he was upstairs getting his hunting cap, since he had no motoring cap. The older brother, Gary Benton, went back into the hall. I walked toward Henry, who was standing in the doorway.

"But does Father know you're going?" I asked.

As I tried to go through the doorway, Henry stretched his arm across it and looked at me with a critical frown on his face.

"Why don't you put up your hair?" he said.

I looked at him seriously, and I felt the heat of the blush that came over my face. I felt it on the back of my neck. I stooped with what I thought considerable grace and slid under his arm and passed into the hall. There were the other two Benton boys listening to the voices of my uncles and my father through the parlor door. I stepped between them and threw open the door. Just as I did so, Henry Benton commanded, "Elizabeth, don't do that!" And I, swinging the door open, turned and smiled at him.

I stood for a moment looking blandly at my father and my uncles. I was considering what had made me burst in upon them in this manner. It was not merely that I had perceived the opportunity of creating this little disturbance and slipping in under its noise, though I was not unaware of the advantage. I was frightened by the boys' impending adventure in the horseless carriage but surely not so much as I normally should have been at breaking into the parlor at this forbidden hour. The immediate cause could only be the attention which Henry Benton had shown me. His insinuation had been that I remained too much a little girl, and I had shown him that at any rate I was a bold, or at least a naughty, little girl.

My father was on his feet. He put his glass on the mantelpiece. And it seemed to me that from the three men came in rapid succession all possible arrangements of the words, boys-come-in. Come-in-boys. Well-boys-come-in. Come-on-in. Boys-come-in-the-parlor. The boys went in, rather showing off their breeding and poise, I thought. The three men moved and talked clumsily before them, as the

three Benton brothers went each to each of the men carefully distinguishing between my uncles' titles: doctor and
colonel. I thought how awkward all of the members of my
own family appeared on occasions that called for grace.
Brother strode into the room with his hunting cap sideways
on his head, and he announced their plans, which the
tactful Bentons, uncertain of our family's prejudices regarding machines, had not mentioned. Father and my uncles
had a great deal to say about who was going-to-do-the-
driving, and Henry Benton without giving an answer gave a
polite invitation to the men to join them. To my chagrin
both my uncles accepted with-the-greatest-of-pleasure what
really had not been an invitation at all. And they persisted
in accepting it even after Brother in his rudeness raised the
question of room in the five-passenger vehicle.

Father said, "Sure. The more, the merrier." But he declined to go himself and declined for me Henry's invitation.

The plan was, then, as finally outlined by the oldest of the
Benton brothers, that the boys should proceed to the Carltons' and that Brother should return with the driver to take
our uncles out to the Carltons' house which was one of the
new residences across from Centennial Park, where the
excursions in the machine were to be made.

The four slender youths took their leave from the heavy
men with the gold watch chains across their stomachs, and I
had to shake hands with each of the Benton brothers. To
each I expressed my regret that Father would not let me
ride with them, emulating their poise with all my art.
Henry Benton was the last, and he smiled as though he
knew what I was up to. In answer to his smile I said,
"Games are *so* much fun."

I stood by the window watching the four boys in the
street until they were out of sight. My father and his brothers had taken their seats in silence, and I was aware of just
how unwelcome I was in the room. Finally my uncle who
had been a colonel in the Spanish War and who wore bushy
blond sideburns whistled under his breath and said, "Well,
there's no doubt about it, no doubt about it."

He winked at my father, and my father looked at me and then at my uncle. Then quickly in a ridiculously over-serious tone he asked, "What, sir? No doubt about what, sir?"

"Why, there's no doubt that this daughter of yours was flirting with the youngest of the Messrs. Benton."

My father looked at me and twisted his mustache and said with the same pomp that he didn't know what he'd do with me if I started that sort of thing. My two uncles threw back their heads, each giving a short laugh. My uncle the doctor took off his pince-nez and shook them at me and spoke in the same mock-serious tone of his brothers:

"Young lady, if you spend your time in such pursuits you'll only bring upon yourself and upon the young men about Nashville the greatest unhappiness. I, as a bachelor, must plead the cause of the young Bentons!"

I turned to my father in indignation that approached rage.

"Father," I shouted, "there's Mr. Speed out there!"

Father sprang from his chair and quickly stepped up beside me at the window. Then, seeing the old man staggering harmlessly along the sidewalk, he said in, I thought, affected easiness:

"Yes. Yes, dear."

"He's drunk," I said. My lips quivered, and I think I must have blushed at this first mention of the unmentionable to my father.

"Poor Old Speed," he said. I looked at my uncles, and they were shaking their heads, echoing my father's tone.

"What ever did happen to Speed's old maid sister?" my uncle the doctor said.

"She's still with him," Father said.

Mr. Speed appeared soberer today than I had ever seen him. He carried no overcoat to drag on the ground, and his stagger was barely noticeable. The movement of his lips and an occasional gesture were the only evidence of intoxication. I was enraged by the irony that his good behavior on this of all days presented. Had I been a little younger I might have suspected conspiracy on the part of all men against me, but I was old enough to suspect no person's being even interested enough in me to plot against my understanding, unless it be some vague personification of life itself.

The course which I took, I thought afterward, was the proper one. I do not think that it was because I was then really conscious that when one is determined to follow some course rigidly and is blockaded one must fire furiously, if blindly, into the blockade, but rather because I was frightened and in my fear forgot all logic of attack. At any rate, I fired furiously at the three immutable creatures.

"I'm afraid of him," I broke out tearfully. I shouted at them, "He's always drunk! He's always going by our house drunk!"

My father put his arms about me, but I continued talking as I wept on his shirt front, and I felt my father move one hand from my back to motion my uncles to go. And as they shut the parlor door after them, I felt that I had let them escape me.

I heard the sound of the motor fading out up Church Street, and Father led me to the settee. We sat there together for a long while, and neither of us spoke until my tears had dried.

I was eager to tell him just exactly how fearful I was of Mr. Speed's coming into our house. But he only allowed me to tell him that I *was* afraid; for when I had barely suggested that much, he said that I had no business watching Mr. Speed, that I must shut my eyes to some things. "After all," he said, nonsensically I thought, "you're a young lady now." And in several curiously twisted sentences he told me that I mustn't seek things to fear in this world. He said that it was most unlikely, besides, that Speed would ever have business at our house. He punched at his left side several times, gave a prolonged belch, settled a pillow behind his head, and soon was sprawled beside me on the settee, snoring.

But Mr. Speed did come to our house, and it was in less than two months after this dreary twilight. And he came as I had feared he might come, in his most extreme state of drunkenness and at a time when I was alone in the house with the maid Lucy. But I had done everything that a little girl, now fourteen, could do in preparation for such an eventuality. And the sort of preparation that I had been able to make, the clearance of all restraints and inhibitions regarding Mr. Speed in my own mind and in my relationship with my world, had necessarily, I think, given me a maturer view of my own limited experiences; though, too, my very age must be held to account for a natural step toward maturity.

In the two months following the day that I first faced Mr. Speed's existence with my father, I came to look at every phase of our household life with a more direct and more discerning eye. As I wandered about that shadowy and somehow brutally elegant house, sometimes now with a knot of hair on the back of my head, events and customs there that had repelled or frightened me I gave the closest scrutiny. In the daytime I ventured into such forbidden spots as the servants' and the men's bathrooms. The filth of the former became a matter of interest in the study of the servants' natures, instead of the object of ineffable disgust. The other became a fascinating place of wet shaving brushes and leather straps and red rubber bags.

There was an anonymous little Negro boy that I had seen many mornings hurrying away from our back door with a pail. I discovered that he was toting buttermilk from our icebox with the permission of our cook. And I sprang at him from behind a corner of the house one morning and scared him so that he spilled the buttermilk and never returned for more.

Another morning I heard the cook threatening to slash the houseboy with her butcher knife, and I made myself burst in upon them; and before Lucy and the houseboy I told her that if she didn't leave our house that day, I'd call my father and, hardly knowing what I was saying, I added, "And the police." She was gone, and Lucy had got a new cook before dinner time. In this way, from day to day, I began to take my place as mistress in our motherless household.

I could no longer be frightened by my brother with a mention of runaway horses. And instead of terrorized I felt only depressed by his long and curious arguments with my father. I was depressed by the number of the subjects to and from which they oscillated. The world as a whole still seemed unconscionably larger than anything I could comprehend. But I had learned not to concern myself with so general and so unreal a problem until I had cleared up more particular and real ones.

It was during these two months that I noticed the difference between the manner in which my father spoke before my uncles of Mr. Speed when he passed and that in which he spoke of him before my brother. To my brother it was the condemning, "There goes Old Speed again." But to my uncles it was, "There goes Old Speed," with the sympathetic addition, "the rascal." Though my father and his brothers obviously found me more agreeable because a pleasant spirit had replaced my old timidity, they yet considered me a child; and my father little dreamed that I discerned such traits in his character, or that I understood, if I even listened to, their anecdotes and their long funny stories, and it was an interest in the peculiar choice of subject and in the way that the men told their stories.

When Mr. Speed came, I was accustomed to thinking that there was something in my brother's and in my father's natures that was fully in sympathy with the very brutality of his drunkenness. And I knew that they would not consider my hatred for him and for that part of him which I saw in them. For that alone I was glad that it was on a Thursday afternoon, when I was in the house alone with Lucy, that one of the heavy sort of rains that come toward the end of May drove Mr. Speed onto our porch for shelter.

Otherwise I wished for nothing more than the sound of my father's strong voice when I stood trembling before the parlor window and watched Mr. Speed stumbling across our lawn in the flaying rain. I only knew to keep at the window and make sure that he was actually coming into our house. I believe that he was drunker than I had ever before seen him, and his usual ire seemed to be doubled by the raging weather.

Despite the aid of his cane, Mr. Speed fell to his knees once in the muddy sod. He remained kneeling there for a time with his face cast in resignation. Then once more he struggled to his feet in the rain. Though I was ever conscious that I was entering into young-womanhood at that age, I can only think of myself as a child at that moment; for it was the helpless fear of a child that I felt as I watched Mr. Speed approaching our door. Perhaps it was the last time I ever experienced the inconsolable desperation of childhood.

Next I could hear his cane beating on the boarding of the little porch before our door. I knew that he must be walking up and down in that little shelter. Then I heard Lucy's exasperated voice as she came down the steps. I knew immediately, what she confirmed afterward, that she thought it Brother, eager to get into the house, beating on the door.

I, aghast, opened the parlor door just as she pulled open the great front door. Her black skin ashened as she beheld Mr. Speed, his face crimson, his eyes bleary, and his gray clothes dripping water. He shuffled through the doorway and threw his stick on the hall floor. Between his oaths and profanities he shouted over and over in his broken, old man's voice, "Nigger, nigger." I could understand little of his rapid and slurred speech, but I knew his rage went round and round a man in the rain and the shelter of a neighbor's house.

Lucy fled up the long flight of steps and was on her knees at the head of the stair, in the dark upstairs hall, begging me to come up to her. I only stared, as though paralyzed and dumb, at him and then up the steps at her. The front door was still open; the hall was half in light; and I could hear the rain on the roof of the porch and the wind blowing the trees which were in full green foliage.

At last I moved. I acted. I slid along the wall past the hat rack and the console table, my eyes on the drunken old man who was swearing up the steps at Lucy. I reached for the telephone; and when I had rung for central, I called for the police station. I knew what they did with Mr. Speed downtown, and I knew with what I had threatened the cook. There was a part of me that was crouching on the top step with Lucy, vaguely longing to hide my face from this in my own mother's bosom. But there was another part which was making me deal with Mr. Speed, however wrongly, myself. Innocently I asked the voice to send "the Black Maria" to our house number on Church Street.

Mr. Speed had heard me make the call. He was still and silent for just one moment. Then he broke into tears, and he seemed to be chanting his words. He repeated the word "child" so many times that I felt I had acted wrongly, with courage but without wisdom. I saw myself as a little beast adding to the injury that what was bestial in man had already done him. He picked up his cane and didn't seem to be talking either to Lucy or to me, but to the cane. He started out the doorway, and I heard Lucy come running down the stairs. She fairly glided around the newel post and past me to the telephone. She wasn't certain that I had made the call. She asked if I had called my father. I simply told her that I had not.

As she rang the telephone, I watched Mr. Speed cross the porch. He turned to us at the edge of the porch and shouted one more oath. But his foot touched the wet porch step, and he slid and fell unconscious on the steps.

He lay there with the rain beating upon him and with Lucy and myself watching him, motionless from our place by the telephone. I was frightened by the thought of the cruelty which I found I was capable of, a cruelty which seemed inextricably mixed with what I had called courage. I looked at him lying out there in the rain and despised and pitied him at the same time, and I was afraid to go minister to the helpless old Mr. Speed.

Lucy had her arms about me and kept them there until two gray horses pulling their black coach had galloped up in front of the house and two policemen had carried the limp body through the rain to the dreadful vehicle.

Just as the policemen closed the doors in the back of the

coach, my father rode up in a closed cab. He jumped out
and stood in the rain for several minutes arguing with the
policemen. Lucy and I went to the door and waited for him
to come in. When he came, he looked at neither of us. He
walked past us saying only, "I regret that the bluecoats were
called." And he went into the parlor and closed the door.

I never discussed the events of that day with my father,
and I never saw Mr. Speed again. But, despite the surge of
pity I felt for the old man on our porch that afternoon, my
hatred and fear of what he had stood for in my eyes has
never left me. And since the day that I watched myself say
"away" in the mirror, not a week has passed but that he has
been brought to my mind by one thing or another. It was only
the other night that I dreamed I was a little girl on Church
Street again and that there was a drunk horse in our yard.

♦ ─────────────────── ♦

YOU COULD LOOK
IT UP

James Thurber

It all begun when we dropped down to C'lumbus, Ohio,
from Pittsburgh to play a exhibition game on our way out to
St. Louis. It was gettin' on into September, and though
we'd been leadin' the league by six, seven games most of
the season, we was now in first place by a margin you could
'a' got it into the eye of a thimble, bein' only a half a game
ahead of St. Louis. Our slump had given the boys the
leapin' jumps, and they was like a bunch a old ladies at a

lawn fete with a thunderstorm comin' up, runnin' around snarlin' at each other, eatin' bad and sleepin' worse, and battin' for a team average of maybe .186. Half the time nobody'd speak to nobody else, without it was to bawl 'em out.

Squawks Magrew was managin' the boys at the time, and he was darn near crazy. They called him "Squawks" 'cause when things was goin' bad he lost his voice, or perty near lost it, and squealed at you like a little girl you stepped on her doll or somethin'. He yelled at everybody and wouldn't listen to nobody, without maybe it was me. I'd been trainin' the boys for ten year, and he'd take more lip from me than from anybody else. He knowed I was smarter'n him, anyways, like you're goin' to hear.

This was thirty, thirty-one year ago; you could look it up, 'cause it was the same year C'lumbus decided to call itself the Arch City, on account of a lot of iron arches with electric-light bulbs into 'em which stretched acrost High Street. Thomas Albert Edison sent 'em a telegram, and they was speeches and maybe even President Taft opened the celebration by pushin' a button. It was a great week for the Buckeye capital, which was why they got us out there for this exhibition game.

Well, we just lose a double-header to Pittsburgh, 11 to 5 and 7 to 3, so we snarled all the way to C'lumbus, where we put up at the Chittaden Hotel, still snarlin'. Everybody was tetchy, and when Billy Klinger took a sock at Whitey Cott at breakfast, Whitey throwed marmalade all over his face.

"Blind each other, whatta I care?" says Magrew. "You can't see nothin' anyways."

C'lumbus win the exhibition game, 3 to 2, whilst Magrew set in the dugout, mutterin' and cursin' like a fourteen-year-old Scotty. He bad-mouthed everybody on the ball club and he bad-mouthed everybody offa the ball club, includin' the Wright brothers, who, he claimed, had yet to build a airship big enough for any of our boys to hit it with a ball bat.

"I wisht I was dead," he says to me. "I wisht I was in heaven with the angels."

I told him to pull hisself together, 'cause he was drivin'

the boys crazy, the way he was goin' on, sulkin' and bad-mouthin' and whinin'. I was older'n he was and smarter'n he was, and he knowed it. I was ten times smarter'n he was about this Pearl du Monville, first time I ever laid eyes on the little guy, which was one of the saddest days of my life.

Now, most people name of Pearl is girls, but this Pearl du Monville was a man, if you could call a fella a man who was only thirty-four, thirty-five inches high. Pearl du Monville was a midget. He was part French and part Hungarian, and maybe even part Bulgarian or somethin'. I can see him now, a sneer on his little pushed-in pan, swingin' a bamboo cane and smokin' a big cigar. He had a gray suit with a big black check into it, and he had a gray felt hat with one of them rainbow-colored hatbands onto it, like the young fellas wore in them days. He talked like he was talkin' into a tin can, but he didn't have no foreign accent. He might 'a' been fifteen or he might 'a' been a hundred, you couldn't tell. Pearl du Monville.

After the game with C'lumbus, Magrew headed straight for the Chittaden bar—the train for St. Louis wasn't goin' for three, four hours—and there he set, drinkin' rye and talkin' to this bartender.

"How I pity me, brother," Magrew was tellin' this bartender. "How I pity me." That was alwuz his favorite tune. So he was settin' there, tellin' this bartender how heartbreakin' it was to be manager of a bunch a blindfolded circus clowns, when up pops this Pearl du Monville outa nowheres.

It give Magrew the leapin' jumps. He thought at first maybe the D.T.'s had come back on him; he claimed he'd had 'em once, and little guys had popped up all around him, wearin' red, white and blue hats.

"Go on, now!" Magrew yells. "Get away from me!"

But the midget clumb up on a chair acrost the table from Magrew and says, "I seen that game today, Junior, and you ain't got no ball club. What you got there, Junior," he says, "is a side show."

"Whatta ya mean, 'Junior'?" says Magrew, touchin' the little guy to satisfy hisself he was real.

"Don't pay him no attention, mister," says the bartender.
"Pearl calls everybody 'Junior,' 'cause it alwuz turns out he's
a year older'n anybody else."

"Yeh?" says Magrew. "How old is he?"

"How old are you, Junior?" says the midget.

"Who, me? I'm fifty-three," says Magrew.

"Well, I'm fifty-four," says the midget.

Magrew grins and asts him what he'll have, and that was
the beginnin' of their beautiful friendship, if you don't care
what you say.

Pearl du Monville stood up on his chair and waved his
cane around and pretended like he was ballyhooin' for a
circus. "Right this way, folks!" he yells. "Come on in and
see the greatest collection of freaks in the world! See the
armless pitchers, see the eyeless batters, see the infielders
with five thumbs!" and on and on like that, feedin' Magrew
gall and handin' him a laugh at the same time, you might say.

You could hear him and Pearl du Monville hootin' and
hollerin' and singin' way up to the fourth floor of the Chittaden, where the boys was packin' up. When it come time
to go to the station, you can imagine how disgusted we was
when we crowded into the doorway of that bar and seen
them two singin' and goin' on.

"Well, well, well," says Magrew, lookin' up and spottin'
us. "Look who's here. . . . Clowns, this is Pearl du Monville, a monseer of the old, old school. . . . Don't shake
hands with 'em, Pearl, 'cause their fingers is made of chalk
and would bust right off in your paws," he says, and he
starts guffawin' and Pearl starts titterin' and we stand there
givin' 'em the iron eye, it bein' the lowest ebb a ball-club
manager'd got hisself down to since the national pastime
was started.

Then the midget begun givin' us the ballyhoo. "Come on
in!" he says, wavin' his cane. "See the legless base runners,
see the outfielders with the butter fingers, see the southpaw
with the arm of a little chee-ild!"

Then him and Magrew begun to hoop and holler and
nudge each other till you'd of thought this little guy was the

funniest guy than even Charlie Chaplin. The fellas filed outa the bar without a word and went on up to the Union Depot, leavin' me to handle Magrew and his newfound crony.

Well, I got 'em outa there finely. I had to take the little guy along, 'cause Magrew had a holt onto him like a vise and I couldn't pry him loose.

"He's comin' along as masket," says Magrew, holdin' the midget in the crouch of his arm like a football. And come along he did, hollerin' and protestin' and beatin' at Magrew with his little fists.

"Cut it out, will ya, Junior?" the little guy kept whinin'. "Come on, leave a man loose, will ya, Junior?"

But Junior kept a holt onto him and begun yellin', "See the guys with the glass arms, see the guys with the castiron brains, see the fielders with the feet on their wrists!"

So it goes, right through the whole Union Depot, with people starin' and catcallin', and he don't put the midget down till he gets him through the gates.

"How'm I goin' to go along without no toothbrush?" the midget asts. "What'm I goin' to do without no other suit?" he says.

"Doc here," says Magrew, meanin' me—"doc here will look after you like you was his own son, won't you, doc?"

I give him the iron eye, and he finely got on the train and prob'ly went to sleep with his clothes on.

This left me alone with the midget. "Lookit," I says to him. "Why don't you go on home now? Come mornin', Magrew'll forget all about you. He'll prob'ly think you was somethin' he seen in a nightmare maybe. And he ain't goin' to laugh so easy in the mornin', neither," I says. "So why don't you go on home?"

"Nix," he says to me. "Skiddoo," he says, "twenty-three for you," and he tosses his cane up into the vestibule of the coach and clam'ers on up after it like a cat. So that's the way Pearl du Monville come to go to St. Louis with the ball club.

I seen 'em first at breakfast the next day, settin' opposite each other; the midget playin' Turkey in the Straw on a harmonium and Magrew starin' at his eggs and bacon like they was a uncooked bird with its feathers still on.

"Remember where you found this?" I says, jerkin' my thumb at the midget. "Or maybe you think they come with breakfast on these trains," I says, bein' a good hand at turnin' a sharp remark in them days.

The midget puts down the harmonium and turns on me. "Sneeze," he says; "your brains is dusty." Then he snaps a couple drops of water at me from a tumbler. "Drown," he says, tryin' to make his voice deep.

Now, both them cracks is Civil War cracks, but you'd of thought they was brand new and the funniest than any crack Magrew'd ever heard in his whole life. He started hoopin' and hollerin', and the midget started hoopin' and hollerin', so I walked on away and set down with Bugs Courtney and Hank Metters, payin' no attention to this weak-minded Damon and Phidias acrost the aisle.

Well, sir, the first game with St. Louis was rained out, and there we was facin' a double-header next day. Like maybe I told you, we lose the last three double-headers we play, makin' maybe twenty-five errors in the six games, which is all right for the intimates of a school for the blind, but is disgraceful for the world's champions. It was too wet to go to the zoo, and Magrew wouldn't let us go to the movies, 'cause they flickered so bad in them days. So we just set around, stewin' and frettin'.

One of the newspaper boys come over to take a pitture of Billy Klinger and Whitey Cott shakin' hands—this reporter'd heard about the fight—and whilst they was standin' there, toe to toe, shakin' hands, Billy give a back lunge and a jerk, and throwed Whitey over his shoulder into a corner of the room, like a sack a salt. Whitey come back at him with a chair, and Bethlehem broke loose in that there room. The camera was tromped to pieces like a berry basket. When we finely got 'em pulled apart, I heard a laugh, and there was Magrew and the midget standin' in the doorway and givin' us the iron eye.

"Wrasslers," says Magrew, cold-like, "that's what I got for

a ball club, Mr. Du Monville, wrasslers—and not very good wrasslers at that, you ast me."

"A man can't be good at everythin'," says Pearl, "but he oughta be good at somethin'."

This sets Magrew guffawin' again, and away they go, the midget taggin' along by his side like a hound dog and handin' him a fast line of so-called comic cracks.

When we went out to face that battlin' St. Louis club in a double-header the next afternoon, the boys was jumpy as tin toys with keys in their back. We lose the first game, 7 to 2, and are trailin', 4 to 0, when the second game ain't but ten minutes old. Magrew set there like a stone statue, speakin' to nobody. Then, in their half a the fourth, somebody singled to center and knocked in two more runs for St. Louis.

That made Magrew squawk. "I wisht one thing," he says. "I wisht I was manager of a old ladies' sewin' circle 'stead of a ball club."

"You are, Junior, you are," says a familyer and disagreeable voice.

It was that Pearl du Monville again, poppin' up outa nowheres, swingin' his bamboo cane and smokin' a cigar that's three sizes too big for his face. By this time we'd finely got the other side out, and Hank Metters slithered a bat acrost the ground, and the midget had to jump to keep both his ankles from bein' broke.

I thought Magrew'd bust a blood vessel. "You hurt Pearl and I'll break your neck!" he yelled.

Hank muttered somethin' and went on up to the plate and struck out.

We managed to get a couple runs acrost in our half a the sixth, but they come back with three more in their half a the seventh, and this was too much for Magrew.

"Come on, Pearl," he says. "We're gettin' outa here."

"Where you think you're goin'?" I ast him.

"To the lawyer's again," he says cryptly.

"I didn't know you'd been to the lawyer's once, yet," I says.

"Which that goes to show how much you don't know," he says.

With that, they was gone, and I didn't see 'em the rest of the day, nor know what they was up to, which was a God's blessin'. We lose the nightcap, 9 to 3, and that puts us into second place plenty, and as low in our mind as a ball club can get.

The next day was a horrible day, like anybody that lived through it can tell you. Practice was just over and the St. Louis club was takin' the field, when I hears this strange sound from the stands. It sounds like the nervous whickerin' a horse gives when he smells somethin' funny on the wind. It was the fans ketchin' sight of Pearl du Monville, like you have prob'ly guessed. The midget had popped up onto the field all dressed up in a minacher club uniform, sox, cap, little letters sewed onto his chest, and all. He was swingin' a kid's bat and the only thing kept him from lookin' like a real ballplayer seen through the wrong end of a microscope was this cigar he was smokin'.

Bugs Courtney reached over and jerked it outa his mouth and throwed it away. "You're wearin' that suit on the playin' field," he says to him, severe as a judge. "You go insultin' it and I'll take you out to the zoo and feed you to the bears."

Pearl just blowed some smoke at him which he still has in his mouth.

Whilst Whitey was foulin' off four or five prior to strikin' out, I went on over to Magrew. "If I was as comic as you," I says, "I'd laugh myself to death," I says. "Is that any way to treat the uniform, makin' a mockery out of it?"

"It might surprise you to know I ain't makin' no mockery outa the uniform," says Magrew. "Pearl du Monville here has been made a bone-of-fida member of this so-called ball club. I fixed it up with the front office by long-distance phone."

"Yeh?" I says. "I can just hear Mr. Dillworth or Bart Jenkins agreein' to hire a midget for the ball club. I can just hear 'em." Mr. Dillworth was the owner of the club and Bart Jenkins was the secretary, and they never stood for no monkey business. "May I be so bold as to inquire," I says, "just what you told 'em?"

"I told 'em," he says, "I wanted to sign up a guy they ain't no pitcher in the league can strike him out."

"Uh-huh," I says, "and did you tell 'em what size of a man he is?"

"Never mind about that," he says. "I got papers on me, made out legal and proper, constitutin' one Pearl du Monville a bone-of-fida member of this former ball club. Maybe that'll shame them big babies into gettin' in there and swingin', knowin' I can replace any one of 'em with a midget, if I have a mind to. A St. Louis lawyer I seen twice tell me it's all legal and proper."

"A St. Louis lawyer would," I says, "seein' nothin' could make him happier than havin' you makin' a mockery outa this one-time baseball outfit," I says.

Well, sir, it'll all be there in the papers of thirty, thirty-one year ago, and you could look it up. The game went along without no scorin' for seven innings, and since they ain't nothin' much to watch but guys poppin' up or strikin' out, the fans pay most of their attention to the goin's-on of Pearl du Monville. He's out there in front a the dugout, turnin' handsprings, balancin' his bat on his chin, walkin' a imaginary line, and so on. The fans clapped and laughed at him, and he ate it up.

So it went up to the last a the eighth, nothin' to nothin', not more'n seven, eight hits all told, and no errors on neither side. Our pitcher gets the first two men out easy in the eighth. Then up come a fella name of Porter or Billings, or some such name, and he lammed one up against the tobacco sign for three bases. The next guy up slapped the first ball out into left for a base hit, and in come the fella from third for the only run of the ball game so far. The crowd yelled, the look a death come onto Magrew's face again, and even the midget quit his tomfoolin'. Their next man fouled out back a third, and we come up for our last bats like a bunch a schoolgirls steppin' into a pool of cold water. I was lower in my mind than I'd been since the day in Nineteen-four when Chesbro throwed the wild pitch in the ninth inning with a man on third and lost the pennant for the Highlanders. I knowed something just as bad was goin' to happen, which shows I'm a clairvoyun, or was then.

When Gordy Mills hit out to second, I just closed my eyes. I opened 'em up again to see Dutch Muller standin' on second, dustin' off his pants, him havin' got his first hit in maybe twenty times to the plate. Next up was Harry Loesing, battin' for our pitcher, and he got a base on balls, walkin' on a fourth one you could 'a' combed your hair with.

Then up come Whitey Cott, our lead-off man. He crotches down in what was prob'ly the most fearsome stanch in organized ball, but all he can do is pop out to short. That brung up Billy Klinger, with two down and a man on first and second. Billy took a cut at one you could 'a' knocked a plug hat offa this here Carnera with it, but then he gets sense enough to wait 'em out, and finely he walks, too, fillin' the bases.

Yes, sir, there you are; the tyin' run on third and the winnin, run on second, first a the ninth, two men down, and Hank Metters comin' to the bat. Hank was built like a Pope-Hartford and he couldn't run no faster'n President Taft, but he had five home runs to his credit for the season, and that wasn't bad in them days. Hank was still hittin' better'n anybody else on the ball club, and it was mighty heartenin', seein' him stridin' up towards the plate. But he never got there.

"Wait a minute!" yells Magrew, jumpin' to his feet. "I'm sendin' in a pinch hitter!" he yells.

You could 'a' heard a bomb drop. When a ball-club manager says he's sendin' in a pinch hitter for the best batter on the club, you know and I know and everybody knows he's lost his holt.

"They're goin' to be sendin' the funny wagon for you, if you don't watch out," I says, grabbin' a holt of his arm.

But he pulled away and run out towards the plate, yellin', "Du Monville battin' for Metters!"

All the fellas begun squawlin' at once, except Hank, and

he just stood there starin' at Magrew like he'd gone crazy and was claimin' to be Ty Cobb's grandma or somethin'. Their pitcher stood out there with his hands on his hips and a disagreeable look on his face, and the plate umpire told Magrew to go on and get a batter up. Magrew told him again Du Monville was battin' for Metters, and the St. Louis manager finely got the idea. It brung him outa his dugout, howlin' and bawlin' like he'd lost a female dog and her seven pups.

Magrew pushed the midget towards the plate and he says to him, he says, "Just stand up there and hold that bat on your shoulder. They ain't a man in the world can throw three strikes in there 'fore he throws four balls!" he says.

"I get it, Junior!" says the midget. "He'll walk me and force in the tyin' run!" And he starts on up to the plate as cocky as if he was Willie Keeler.

I don't need to tell you Bethlehem broke loose on that there ball field. The fans got onto their hind legs, yellin' and whistlin', and everybody on the field begun wavin' their arms and hollerin' and shovin'. The plate umpire stalked over to Magrew like a traffic cop, waggin' his jaw and pointin' his finger, and the St. Louis manager kept yellin' like his house was on fire. When Pearl got up to the plate and stood there, the pitcher slammed his glove down onto the ground and started stompin' on it, and they ain't nobody can blame him. He's just walked two normal-sized human bein's, and now here's a guy up to the plate they ain't more'n twenty inches between his knees and his shoulders.

The plate umpire called in the field umpire, and they talked a while, like a couple doctors seein' the bucolic plague or somethin' for the first time. Then the plate umpire come over to Magrew with his arms folded acrost his chest, and he told him to go on and get a batter up, or he'd forfeit the game to St. Louis. He pulled out his watch, but somebody batted it outa his hand in the scufflin', and I thought there'd be a free-for-all, with everybody yellin' and shovin' except Pearl du Monville, who stood up at the plate with his little bat on his shoulder, not movin' a muscle.

Then Magrew played his ace. I seen him pull some papers outa his pocket and show 'em to the plate umpire. The umpire begun lookin' at 'em like they was bills for somethin' he not only never bought it, he never even heard of it. The other umpire studied 'em like they was a death warren, and all this time the St. Louis manager and the fans and the players is yellin' and hollerin'.

Well, sir, they fought about him bein' a midget, and they fought about him usin' a kid's bat, and they fought about where'd he been all season. They was eight or nine rule books brung out and everybody was thumbin' through 'em, tryin' to find out what it says about midgets, but it don't say nothin' about midgets, 'cause this was somethin' never'd come up in the history of the game before, and nobody'd ever dreamed about it, even when they has nightmares. Maybe you can't send no midgets in to bat nowadays, 'cause the old game's changed a lot, mostly for the worst, but you could then, it turned out.

The plate umpire finely decided the contrack papers was all legal and proper, like Magrew said, so he waved the St. Louis players back to their places and he pointed his finger at their manager and told him to quit hollerin' and get on back in the dugout. The manager says the game is percedin' under protest, and the umpire bawls, "Play ball!" over 'n' above the yellin' and booin', him havin' a voice like a hog-caller.

The St. Louis pitcher picked up his glove and beat at it with his fist six or eight times, and then got set on the mound and studied the situation. The fans realized he was really goin' to pitch to the midget, and they went crazy, hoopin' and hollerin' louder'n ever, and throwin' pop bottles and hats and cushions down onto the field. It took five, ten minutes to get the fans quieted down again, whilst our fellas that was on base set down on the bags and waited. And Pearl du Monville kept standin' up there with the bat on his shoulder, like he'd been told to.

So the pitcher starts studyin' the setup again, and you got to admit it was the strangest setup in a ball game since the players cut off their beards and begun wearin' gloves. I wisht I could call the pitcher's name—it wasn't old Barney Pelty nor Nig Jack Powell nor Harry Howell. He was a big right-hander, but I can't call his name. You could look it up. Even in a crotchin' position, the ketcher towers over the midget like the Washington Monument.

The plate umpire tries standin' on his tiptoes, then he tries crotchin' down, and he finely gets hisself into a stanch nobody'd ever seen on a baseball field before, kinda squattin' down on his hanches.

Well, the pitcher is sore as a old buggy horse in fly time. He slams in the first pitch, hard and wild, and maybe two foot higher'n the midget's head.

"Ball one!" hollers the umpire over 'n' above the racket, 'cause everybody is yellin' worsten ever.

The ketcher goes on out towards the mound and talks to the pitcher and hands him the ball. This time the big right-hander tries a undershoot, and it comes in a little closer, maybe no higher'n a foot, foot and a half above Pearl's head. It would 'a' been a strike with a human bein' in there, but the umpire's got to call it, and he does.

"Ball two!" he bellers.

The ketcher walks on out to the mound again, and the whole infield comes over and gives advice to the pitcher about what they'd do in a case like this, with two balls and no strikes on a batter that oughta be in a bottle of alcohol 'stead of up there at the plate in a big-league game between the teams that is fightin' for first place.

For the third pitch, the pitcher stands there flat-footed and tosses up the ball like he's playin' ketch with a little girl.

Pearl stands there motionless as a hitchin' post, and the ball comes in big and slow and high—high for Pearl, that is, it bein' about on a level with his eyes, or a little higher'n a grown man's knees.

They ain't nothin' else for the umpire to do, so he calls, "Ball three!"

Everybody is onto their feet, hoopin' and hollerin', as the

pitcher sets to throw ball four. The St. Louis manager is makin' signs and faces like he was a contorturer, and the infield is givin' the pitcher some more advice about what to do this time. Our boys who was on base stick right onto the bag, runnin' no risk of bein' nipped for the last out.

Well, the pitcher decides to give him a toss again, seein' he come closer with that than with a fast ball. They ain't nobody ever seen a slower ball throwed. It come in big as a balloon and slower'n any ball ever throwed before in the major leagues. It come right in over the plate in front of Pearl's chest, lookin' prob'ly big as a full moon to Pearl. They ain't never been a minute like the minute that followed since the United States was founded by the pilgrim grandfathers.

Pearl du Monville took a cut at that ball, and he hit it! Magrew give a groan like a poleaxed steer as the ball rolls out in front a the plate into fair territory.

"Fair ball!" yells the umpire, and the midget starts runnin' for first, still carryin' that little bat, and makin' maybe ninety foot an hour. Bethlehem breaks loose on that ball field and in them stands. They ain't never been nothin' like it since creation was begun.

The ball's rollin' slow, on down towards third, goin' maybe eight, ten foot. The infield comes in fast and our boys break from their bases like hares in a brush fire. Everybody is standin' up, yellin' and hollerin', and Magrew is tearin' his hair outa his head, and the midget is scamperin' for first with all the speed of one of them little dash-hounds carryin' a satchel in his mouth.

The ketcher gets to the ball first, but he boots it on out past the pitcher's box, the pitcher fallin' on his face tryin' to stop it, the shortstop sprawlin' after it full length and zaggin' it on over towards the second baseman, whilst Muller is scorin' with the tyin' run and Loesing is roundin' third with the winnin' run. Ty Cobb could 'a' made a three-bagger outa that bunt, with everybody fallin' over theirself tryin' to pick the ball up. But Pearl is still maybe fifteen, twenty feet from the bag, toddlin' like a baby and yeepin' like a trapped rabbit, when the second baseman finely gets a holt of that ball and slams it over to first. The first baseman ketches it and stomps on the bag, the base umpire waves Pearl out, and there goes your old ball game, the craziest ball game ever played in the history of the organized world.

Their players start runnin' in, and then I see Magrew. He starts after Pearl, runnin' faster'n any man ever run before. Pearl sees him comin' and runs behind the base umpire's legs and gets a holt onto 'em. Magrew comes up, pantin' and roarin', and him and the midget plays ring-around-a-rosy with the umpire, who keeps shovin' at Magrew with one hand and tryin' to slap the midget loose from his legs with the other.

Finely Magrew ketches the midget, who is still yeepin' like a stuck sheep. He gets holt of that little guy by both his ankles and starts whirlin' him round and round his head like Magrew was a hammer thrower and Pearl was the hammer. Nobody can stop him without gettin' their head knocked off, so everybody just stands there and yells. Then Magrew lets the midget fly. He flies on out towards second, high and fast, like a human home run, headed for the soap sign in center field.

Their shortstop tries to get to him, but he can't make it, and I knowed the little fella was goin' to bust to pieces like a dollar watch on a asphalt street when he hit the ground. But it so happens their center fielder is just crossin' second, and he starts runnin' back, tryin' to get under the midget, who had took to spiralin' like a football 'stead of turnin' head over foot, which give him more speed and more distance.

I know you never seen a midget ketched, and you prob'ly never even seen one throwed. To ketch a midget that's been throwed by a heavy-muscled man and is flyin' through the air, you got to run under him and with him and pull your hands and arms back and down when you ketch him, to break the compact of his body, or you'll bust him in two like a matchstick. I seen Bill Lange and Willie Keeler and Tris Speaker make some wonderful ketches in my day, but I never seen nothin' like that center fielder. He goes back

and back and still further back and he pulls that midget
down outa the air like he was liftin' a sleepin' baby from a
cradle. They wasn't a bruise onto him, only his face was the
color of cat's meat and he ain't got no air in his chest. In his
excitement, the base umpire, who was runnin' back with
the center fielder when he ketched Pearl, yells, "Out!" and
that give hysteries to the Bethlehem which was ragin' like
Niagry on that ball field.

Everybody was hoopin' and hollerin' and yellin' and runnin',
with the fans swarmin' onto the field, and the cops tryin' to
keep order, and some guys laughin' and some of the women
fans cryin', and six or eight of us holdin' onto Magrew to
keep him from gettin' at that midget and finishin' him off.
Some of the fans picks up the St. Louis pitcher and the
center fielder, and starts carryin' 'em around on their shoulders, and they was the craziest goin's-on knowed to the
history of organized ball on this side of the 'Lantic Ocean.

I seen Pearl du Monville strugglin' in the arms of a lady
fan with a ample bosom, who was laughin' and cryin' at the
same time, and him beatin' at her with his little fists and
bawlin' and yellin'. He clawed his way loose finely and
disappeared in the forest of legs which made that ball field
look like it was Coney Island on a hot summer's day.

That was the last I ever seen of Pearl du Monville. I
never seen hide nor hair of him from that day to this, and
neither did nobody else. He just vanished into the thin of
the air, as the fella says. He was ketched for the final out of
the ball game and that was the end of him, just like it was
the end of the ball game, you might say, and also the end of
our losin' streak, like I'm goin' to tell you.

That night we piled onto a train for Chicago, but we wasn't
snarlin' and snappin' any more. No, sir, the ice was finely
broke and a new spirit come into that ball club. The old zip
come back with the disappearance of Pearl du Monville out
back a second base. We got to laughin' and talkin' and kiddin'
together, and 'fore long Magrew was laughin' with us. He got
a human look onto his pan again, and he quit whinin' and
complainin' and wishtin' he was in heaven with the angels.

Well, sir, we wiped up that Chicago series, winnin' all four games, and makin' seventeen hits in one of 'em. Funny thing was, St. Louis was so shook up by that last game with us, they never did hit their stride again. Their center fielder took to misjudgin' everything that come his way, and the rest a the fellas followed suit, the way a club'll do when one guy blows up.

'Fore we left Chicago, I and some of the fellas went out and bought a pair of them little baby shoes, which we had 'em golded over and give 'em to Magrew for a souvenir, and he took it all in good spirit. Whitey Cott and Billy Klinger made up and was fast friends again, and we hit our home lot like a ton of dynamite and they was nothin' could stop us from then on.

I don't recollect things as clear as I did thirty, forty year ago. I can't read no fine print no more, and the only person I got to check with on the golden days of the national pastime, as the fella says, is my friend, old Milt Kline, over in Springfield, and his mind ain't as strong as it once was.

He gets Rube Waddell mixed up with Rube Marquard, for one thing, and anybody does that oughta be put away where he won't bother nobody. So I can't tell you the exact margin we win the pennant by. Maybe it was two and a half games, or maybe it was three and a half. But it'll all be there in the newspapers and record books of thirty, thirty-one year ago and, like I was sayin', you could look it up.

WHY I LIVE AT THE P.O.

Eudora Welty

I was getting along fine with Mama, Papa-Daddy and Uncle
Rondo until my sister Stella-Rondo just separated from her
husband and came back home again. Mr. Whitaker! Of
course I went with Mr. Whitaker first, when he first appeared here in China Grove, taking "Pose Yourself photos,
and Stella-Rondo broke us up. Told him I was one-sided.
Bigger on one side than the other, which is a deliberate,
calculated falsehood: I'm the same. Stella-Rondo is exactly
twelve months to the day younger than I am and for that
reason she's spoiled.

She's always had anything in the world she wanted and
then she'd throw it away. Papa-Daddy gave her this gorgeous Add-a-Pearl necklace when she was eight years old
and she threw it away playing baseball when she was nine,
with only two pearls.

So as soon as she got married and moved away from home
the first thing she did was separate! From Mr. Whitaker!
This photographer with the popeyes she said she trusted.
Came home from one of those towns up in Illinois and to
our complete surprise brought this child of two.

Mama said she like to made her drop dead for a second.
"Here you had this marvelous blonde child and never so
much as wrote your mother a word about it," says Mama
"I'm thoroughly ashamed of you." But of course she wasn't.

Stella-Rondo just calmly takes off this *hat*, I wish you

could see it. She says, "Why, Mama, Shirley-T.'s adopted, I can prove it."

"How?" says Mama, but all I says was, "H'm!" There I was over the hot stove, trying to stretch two chickens over five people and a completely unexpected child into the bargain, without one moment's notice.

"What do you mean—'H'm!'?" says Stella-Rondo, and Mama says, "I heard that, Sister."

I said that oh, I didn't mean a thing, only that whoever Shirley-T. was, she was the spit-image of Papa-Daddy if he'd cut off his beard, which of course he'd never do in the world. Papa-Daddy's Mama's papa and sulks.

Stella-Rondo got furious! She said, "Sister, I don't need to tell you you got a lot of nerve and always did have and I'll thank you to make no future reference to my adopted child whatsoever."

"Very well," I said. "Very well, very well. Of course I noticed at once she looks like Mr. Whitaker's side too. That frown. She looks like a cross between Mr. Whitaker and Papa-Daddy."

"Well, all I can say is she isn't."

"She looks exactly like Shirley Temple to me," says Mama, but Shirley-T. just ran away from her.

So the first thing Stella-Rondo did at the table was turn Papa-Daddy against me.

"Papa-Daddy," she says. He was trying to cut up his meat. "Papa-Daddy!" I was taken completely by surprise. Papa-Daddy is about a million years old and's got this long-long beard. "Papa-Daddy, Sister says she fails to understand why you don't cut off your beard."

So Papa-Daddy l-a-y-s down his knife and fork! He's real rich. Mama says he is, he says he isn't. So he says, "Have I heard correctly? You don't understand why I don't cut off my beard?"

"Why," I says, "Papa-Daddy, of course I understand, I did not say any such of a thing, the idea!"

He says, "Hussy!"

I says, "Papa-Daddy, you know I wouldn't any more want

you to cut off your beard than the man in the moon. It was the farthest thing from my mind! Stella-Rondo sat there and made that up while she was eating breast of chicken."

But he says, "So the postmistress fails to understand why I don't cut off my beard. Which job I got you through my influence with the government. 'Bird's nest'—is that what you call it?"

Not that it isn't the next to smallest P.O. in the entire state of Mississippi.

I says, "Oh, Papa-Daddy," I says, "I didn't say any such of a thing, I never dreamed it was a bird's nest, I have always been grateful though this is the next to smallest P.O. in the state of Mississippi, and I do not enjoy being referred to as a hussy by my own grandfather."

But Stella-Rondo says, "Yes, you did say it too. Anybody in the world could of heard you, that had ears."

"Stop right there," says Mama, looking at *me*.

So I pulled my napkin straight back through the napkin ring and left the table.

As soon as I was out of the room Mama says, "Call her back, or she'll starve to death," but Papa-Daddy says, "This is the beard I started growing on the Coast when I was fifteen years old." He would of gone on till nightfall if Shirley-T. hadn't lost the Milky Way she ate in Cairo.

So Papa-Daddy says, "I am going out and lie in the hammock, and you can all sit here and remember my words: I'll never cut off my beard as long as I live, even one inch, and I don't appreciate it in you at all." Passed right by me in the hall and went straight out and got in the hammock.

It would be a holiday. It wasn't five minutes before Uncle Rondo suddenly appeared in the hall in one of Stella-Rondo's flesh-colored kimonos, all cut on the bias, like something Mr. Whitaker probably thought was gorgeous.

"Uncle Rondo!" I says. "I didn't know who that was! Where are you going?"

"Sister," he says, "get out of my way, I'm poisoned."

"If you're poisoned stay away from Papa-Daddy," I says. "Keep out of the hammock. Papa-Daddy will certainly beat you on the head if you come within forty miles of him. He thinks I deliberately said he ought to cut off his beard after he got me the P.O., and I've told him and told him and told him, and he acts like he just don't hear me. Papa-Daddy must of gone stone deaf."

"He picked a fine day to do it then," says Uncle Rondo, and before you could say "Jack Robinson" flew out in the yard.

What he'd really done, he'd drunk another bottle of that prescription. He does it every single Fourth of July as sure as shooting, and it's horribly expensive. Then he falls over in the hammock and snores. So he insisted on zigzagging right on out to the hammock, looking like a half-wit.

Papa-Daddy woke up with this horrible yell and right there without moving an inch he tried to turn Uncle Rondo against me. I heard every word he said. Oh, he told Uncle Rondo I didn't learn to read till I was eight years old and he didn't see how in the world I ever got the mail put up at the P.O., much less read it all, and he said if Uncle Rondo could only fathom the lengths he had gone to to get me that job! And he said on the other hand he thought Stella-Rondo had a brilliant mind and deserved credit for getting out of town. All the time he was just lying there swinging as pretty as you please and looping out his beard, and poor Uncle Rondo was *pleading* with him to slow down the hammock, it was making him as dizzy as a witch to watch it. But that's what Papa-Daddy likes about a hammock. So Uncle Rondo was too dizzy to get turned against me for the time being. He's Mama's only brother and is a good case of a one-track mind. Ask anybody. A certified pharmacist.

Just then I heard Stella-Rondo raising the upstairs window. While she was married she got this peculiar idea that it's cooler with the windows shut and locked. So she has to raise the window before she can make a soul hear her outdoors.

So she raises the window and says, "*Oh!*" You would have thought she was mortally wounded.

Uncle Rondo and Papa-Daddy didn't even look up, but kept right on with what they were doing. I had to laugh.

I flew up the stairs and threw the door open! I says,

"What in the wide world's the matter, Stella-Rondo? You mortally wounded?"

"No," she says, "I am not mortally wounded but I wish you would do me the favor of looking out that window there and telling me what you see."

So I shade my eyes and look out the window.

"I see the front yard," I says.

"Don't you see any human beings?" she says.

"I see Uncle Rondo trying to run Papa-Daddy out of the hammock," I says. "Nothing more. Naturally, it's so suffocating-hot in the house, with all the windows shut and locked, everybody who cares to stay in their right mind will have to go out and get in the hammock before the Fourth of July is over."

"Don't you notice anything different about Uncle Rondo?" asks Stella-Rondo.

"Why, no, except he's got on some terrible-looking flesh-colored contraption I wouldn't be found dead in, is all I can see," I says.

"Never mind, you won't be found dead in it, because it happens to be part of my trousseau, and Mr. Whitaker took several dozen photographs of me in it," says Stella-Rondo. "What on earth could Uncle Rondo *mean* by wearing part of my trousseau out in the broad open daylight without saying so much as 'Kiss my foot,' *knowing* I only got home this morning after my separation and hung my negligee up on the bathroom door, just as nervous as I could be?"

"I'm sure I don't know, and what do you expect me to do about it?" I says. "Jump out the window?"

"No, I expect nothing of the kind. I simply declare that Uncle Rondo looks like a fool in it, that's all," she says. "It makes me sick to my stomach."

"Well, he looks as good as he can," I says. "As good as anybody in reason could." I stood up for Uncle Rondo, please remember. And I said to Stella-Rondo, "I think I would do well not to criticize so freely if I were you and came home with a two-year-old child I had never said a word about, and no explanation whatever about my separation."

"I asked you the instant I entered this house not to refer one more time to my adopted child, and you gave me your word of honor you would not," was all Stella-Rondo would say, and started pulling out every one of her eyebrows with some cheap Kress tweezers.

So I merely slammed the door behind me and went down and made some green-tomato pickle. Somebody had to do it. Of course Mama had turned both the niggers loose; she always said no earthly power could hold one anyway on the Fourth of July, so she wouldn't even try. It turned out that Jaypan fell in the lake and came within a very narrow limit of drowning.

So Mama trots in. Lifts up the lid and says, "H'm! Not very good for your Uncle Rondo in his precarious condition, I must say. Or poor little adopted Shirley-T. Shame on you!"

That made me tired. I says, "Well, Stella-Rondo had better thank her lucky stars it was her instead of me came trotting in with that very peculiar-looking child. Now if it had been me that trotted in from Illinois and brought a peculiar-looking child of two, I shudder to think of the reception I'd of got, much less controlled the diet of an entire family."

"But you must remember, Sister, that you were never married to Mr. Whitaker in the first place and didn't go up to Illinois to live," says Mama, shaking a spoon in my face. "If you had I would of been just as overjoyed to see you and your little adopted girl as I was to see Stella-Rondo, when you wound up with your separation and came on back home."

"You would not," I says.

"Don't contradict me, I would," says Mama.

But I said she couldn't convince me though she talked till she was blue in the face. Then I said, "Besides, you know as well as I do that that child is not adopted."

"She most certainly is adopted," says Mama, stiff as a poker.

I says, "Why, Mama, Stella-Rondo had her just as sure as anything in this world, and just too stuck up to admit it."

"Why, Sister," said Mama. "Here I thought we were

going to have a pleasant Fourth of July, and you start right out not believing a word your own baby sister tells you!"

"Just like Cousin Annie Flo. Went to her grave denying the facts of life," I remind Mama.

"I told you if you ever mentioned Annie Flo's name I'd slap your face," says Mama, and slaps my face.

"All right, you wait and see," I says.

"I," says Mama, "*I* prefer to take my children's word for anything when it's humanly possible." You ought to see Mama, she weighs two hundred pounds and has real tiny feet.

Just then something perfectly horrible occurred to me.

"Mama," I says, "can that child talk?" I simply had to whisper! "Mama, I wonder if that child can be—you know—in any way? Do you realize," I says, "that she hasn't spoken one single, solitary word to a human being up to the minute? This is the way she looks," I says, and I looked like this.

Well, Mama and I just stood there and stared at each other. It was horrible!

"I remember well that Joe Whitaker frequently drank like a fish," says Mama. "I believed to my soul he drank *chemicals*." And without another word she marches to the foot of the stairs and calls Stella-Rondo.

"Stella-Rondo? O-o-o-o-o! Stella-Rondo!"

"What?" says Stella-Rondo from upstairs. Not even the grace to get up off the bed.

"Can that child of yours talk?" asks Mama.

Stella-Rondo says, "Can she what?"

"Talk! Talk!" says Mama. "Burdyburdyburdyburdy!"

So Stella-Rondo yells back, "Who says she can't talk?"

"Sister says so," says Mama.

"You didn't have to tell me, I know whose word of honor don't mean a thing in this house," says Stella-Rondo.

And in a minute the loudest Yankee voice I ever heard in my life yells out, "OE'm Pop-OE the Sailor-r-r-r Ma-a-an!" and then somebody jumps up and down in the upstairs hall. In another second the house would of fallen down.

"Not only talks, she can tap-dance!" calls Stella-Rondo. "Which is more than some people I won't name can do."

"Why, the little precious darling thing!" Mama says, so surprised. "Just as smart as she can be!" Starts talking baby talk right there. Then she turns on me. "Sister, you ought to be thoroughly ashamed! Run upstairs this instant and apologize to Stella-Rondo and Shirley-T."

"Apologize for what?" I says. "I merely wondered if the child was normal, that's all. Now that she's proved she is, why, I have nothing further to say."

But Mama just turned on her heel and flew out, furious. She ran right upstairs and hugged the baby. She believed it was adopted. Stella-Rondo hadn't done a thing but turn her against me from upstairs while I stood there helpless over the hot stove. So that made Mama, Papa-Daddy and the baby all on Stella-Rondo's side.

Next, Uncle Rondo.

I must say that Uncle Rondo has been marvelous to me at various times in the past and I was completely unprepared to be made to jump out of my skin, the way it turned out. Once Stella-Rondo did something perfectly horrible to him— broke a chain letter from Flanders Field—and he took the radio back he had given her and gave it to me. Stella-Rondo was furious! For six months we all had to call her Stella instead of Stella-Rondo, or she wouldn't answer. I always thought Uncle Rondo had all the brains of the entire family. Another time he sent me to Mammoth Cave, with all expenses paid.

But this would be the day he was drinking that prescription, the Fourth of July.

So at supper Stella-Rondo speaks up and says she thinks Uncle Rondo ought to try to eat a little something. So finally Uncle Rondo said he would try a little cold biscuits and ketchup, but that was all. So *she* brought it to him.

"Do you think it wise to disport with ketchup in Stella-Rondo's flesh-colored kimono?" I says. Trying to be considerate! If Stella-Rondo couldn't watch out for her trousseau, somebody had to.

"Any objections?" asks Uncle Rondo, just about to pour out all the ketchup.

"Don't mind what she says, Uncle Rondo," says Stella-Rondo. "Sister has been devoting this solid afternoon to sneering out my bedroom window at the way you look."

"What's that?" says Uncle Rondo. Uncle Rondo has got the most terrible temper in the world. Anything is liable to make him tear the house down if it comes at the wrong time.

So Stella-Rondo says, "Sister says, 'Uncle Rondo certainly does look like a fool in that pink kimono!'"

Do you remember who it was really said that?

Uncle Rondo spills out all the ketchup and jumps out of his chair and tears off the kimono and throws it down on the dirty floor and puts his foot on it. It had to be sent all the way to Jackson to the cleaners and re-pleated.

"So that's your opinion of your Uncle Rondo, is it?" he says. "I look like a fool, do I? Well, that's the last straw. A whole day in this house with nothing to do, and then to hear you come out with a remark like that behind my back!"

"I didn't say any such of a thing, Uncle Rondo," I says, "and I'm not saying who did, either. Why, I think you look all right. Just try to take care of yourself and not talk and eat at the same time," I says. "I think you better go lie down."

"Lie down my foot," says Uncle Rondo. I ought to of known by that he was fixing to do something perfectly horrible.

So he didn't do anything that night in the precarious state he was in—just played Casino with Mama and Stella-Rondo and Shirley-T. and gave Shirley-T. a nickel with a head on both sides. It tickled her nearly to death, and she called him "Papa." But at 6:30 A.M. the next morning, he threw a whole five-cent package of some unsold one-inch firecrackers from the store as hard as he could into my bedroom and they every one went off. Not one bad one in the string. Anybody else, there'd be one that wouldn't go off.

Well, I'm just terribly susceptible to noise of any kind, the doctor has always told me I was the most sensitive person he had ever seen in his whole life, and I was simply prostrated. I couldn't eat! People tell me they heard it as far as the cemetery, and old Aunt Jep Patterson, that had been holding her own so good, thought it was Judgment Day and she was going to meet her whole family. It's usually so quiet here.

And I'll tell you it didn't take me any longer than a minute to make up my mind what to do. There I was with the whole entire house on Stella-Rondo's side and turned against me. If I have anything at all I have pride.

So I just decided I'd go straight down to the P.O. There's plenty of room there in the back, I says to myself.

Well! I made no bones about letting the family catch on to what I was up to. I didn't try to conceal it.

The first thing they knew, I marched in where they were all playing Old Maid and pulled the electric oscillating fan out by the plug, and everything got real hot. Next I snatched the pillow I'd done the needlepoint on right off the davenport from behind Papa-Daddy. He went "Ugh!" I beat Stella-Rondo up the stairs and finally found my charm bracelet in her bureau drawer under a picture of Nelson Eddy.

"So that's the way the land lies," says Uncle Rondo. There he was, piecing on the ham. "Well, Sister, I'll be glad to donate my army cot if you got any place to set it up, providing you'll leave right this minute and let me get some peace." Uncle Rondo was in France.

"Thank you kindly for the cot and 'peace' is hardly the word I would select if I had to resort to firecrackers at 6:30 A.M. in a young girl's bedroom," I says back to him. "And as to where I intend to go, you seem to forget my position as postmistress of China Grove, Mississippi," I says. "I've always got the P.O."

Well, that made them all sit up and take notice.

I went out front and started digging up some four-o'clocks to plant around the P.O.

"Ah-ah-ah!" says Mama, raising the window. "Those happen to be my four-o'clocks. Everything planted in that star is mine. I've never known you to make anything grow in your life."

"Very well," I says. "But I take the fern. Even you,

Mama, can't stand there and deny that I'm the one watered that fern. And I happen to know where I can send in a box top and get a packet of one thousand mixed seeds, no two the same kind, free."

"Oh, where?" Mama wants to know.

But I says, "Too late. You 'tend to your house, and I'll 'tend to mine. You hear things like that all the time if you know how to listen to the radio. Perfectly marvelous offers. Get anything you want free."

So I hope to tell you I marched in and got that radio, and they could of all bit a nail in two, especially Stella-Rondo, that it used to belong to, and she well knew she couldn't get it back, I'd sue for it like a shot. And I very politely took the sewing-machine motor I helped pay the most on to give Mama for Christmas back in 1929, and a good big calendar, with the first-aid remedies on it. The thermometer and the Hawaiian ukulele certainly were rightfully mine, and I stood on the step-ladder and got all my watermelon-rind preserves and every fruit and vegetable I'd put up, every jar. Then I began to pull the tacks out of the bluebird wall vases on the archway to the dining room.

"Who told you you could have those, Miss Priss?" says Mama, fanning as hard as she could.

"I bought 'em and I'll keep track of 'em," I says. "I'll tack 'em up one on each side the post-office window, and you can see 'em when you come to ask me for your mail, if you're so dead to see 'em."

"Not I! I'll never darken the door to that post office again if I live to be a hundred," Mama says. "Ungrateful child! After all the money we spent on you at the Normal."

"Me either," says Stella-Rondo. "You can just let my mail lie there and *rot*, for all I care. I'll never come and relieve you of a single, solitary piece."

"I should worry," I says. "And who you think's going to sit down and write you all those big fat letters and post-cards, by the way? Mr. Whitaker? Just because he was the only man ever dropped down in China Grove and you got him—unfairly—is he going to sit down and write you a lengthy correspondence after you come home giving no rhyme nor reason whatsoever for your separation and no explanation for the presence of that child? I may not have your brilliant mind, but I fail to see it."

So Mama says, "Sister, I've told you a thousand times that Stella-Rondo simply got homesick, and this child is far too big to be hers," and she says, "Now, why don't you all just sit down and play Casino?"

Then Shirley-T. sticks out her tongue at me in this perfectly horrible way. She has no more manners than the man in the moon. I told her she was going to cross her eyes like that some day and they'd stick.

"It's too late to stop me now," I says. "You should have tried that yesterday. I'm going to the P.O. and the only way you can possibly see me is to visit me there."

So Papa-Daddy says, "You'll never catch me setting foot in that post office, even if I should take a notion into my head to write a letter some place." He says, "I won't have you reachin' out of that little old window with a pair of shears and cuttin' off any beard of mine. I'm too smart for you!"

"We all are," says Stella-Rondo.

But I said, "If you're so smart, where's Mr. Whitaker?"

So then Uncle Rondo says, "I'll thank you from now on to stop reading all the orders I get on postcards and telling everybody in China Grove what you think is the matter with them," but I says, "I draw my own conclusions and will continue in the future to draw them." I says, "If people want to write their inmost secrets on penny postcards, there's nothing in the wide world you can do about it, Uncle Rondo."

"And if you think we'll ever *write* another postcard you're sadly mistaken," says Mama.

"Cutting off your nose to spite your face then," I says. "But if you're all determined to have no more to do with the U. S. mail, think of this: What will Stella-Rondo do now, if she wants to tell Mr. Whitaker to come after her?"

"Wah!" says Stella-Rondo. I knew she'd cry. She had a conniption fit right there in the kitchen.

"It will be interesting to see how long she holds out," I says. "And now—I am leaving."

"Good-bye," says Uncle Rondo.

"Oh, I declare," says Mama, "to think that a family of mine should quarrel on the Fourth of July, or the day after, over Stella-Rondo leaving old Mr. Whitaker and having the sweetest little adopted child! It looks like we'd all be glad!"

"Wah!" says Stella-Rondo, and has a fresh conniption fit.

"*He* left *her*—you mark my words," I says. "That's Mr. Whitaker. I know Mr. Whitaker. After all, I knew him first. I said from the beginning he'd up and leave her. I foretold every single thing that's happened."

"Where did he go?" asks Mama.

"Probably to the North Pole, if he knows what's good for him," I says.

But Stella-Rondo just bawled and wouldn't say another word. She flew to her room and slammed the door.

"Now look what you've gone and done, Sister," says Mama. "You go apologize."

"I haven't got time, I'm leaving," I says.

"Well, what are you waiting around for?" asks Uncle Rondo.

So I just picked up the kitchen clock and marched off, without saying "Kiss my foot" or anything, and never did tell Stella-Rondo good-bye.

There was a nigger girl going along on a little wagon right in front.

"Nigger girl," I says, "come help me haul these things down the hill, I'm going to live in the post office."

Took her nine trips in her express wagon. Uncle Rondo came out on the porch and threw her a nickel.

And that's the last I've laid eyes on any of my family or my family laid eyes on me for five solid days and nights. Stella-Rondo may be telling the most horrible tales in the world about Mr. Whitaker, but I haven't heard them. As I tell everybody, I draw my own conclusions.

But oh, I like it here. It's ideal, as I've been saying. You see, I've got everything cater-cornered, the way I like it.

Hear the radio? All the war news. Radio, sewing machine, book ends, ironing board and that great big piano lamp— peace, that's what I like. Butter-bean vines planted all along the front where the strings are.

Of course, there's not much mail. My family are naturally the main people in China Grove, and if they prefer to vanish from the face of the earth, for all the mail they get or the mail they write, why, I'm not going to open my mouth. Some of the folks here in town are taking up for me and some turned against me. I know which is which. There are always people who will quit buying stamps just to get on the right side of Papa-Daddy.

But here I am, and here I'll stay. I want the world to know I'm happy.

And if Stella-Rondo should come to me this minute, on bended knees, and *attempt* to explain the incidents of her life with Mr. Whitaker, I'd simply put my fingers in both my ears and refuse to listen.

◆ ———————————————————————— ◆

THE USE OF FORCE

William Carlos Williams

They were new patients to me, all I had was the name, Olson. Please come down as soon as you can, my daughter is very sick.

When I arrived I was met by the mother, a big startled looking woman, very clean and apologetic who merely said, Is this the doctor? and let me in. In the back, she added. You must excuse us, doctor, we have her in the kitchen where it is warm. It is very damp here sometimes.

The child was fully dressed and sitting on her father's lap near the kitchen table. He tried to get up, but I motioned for him not to bother, took off my overcoat and started to look things over. I could see that they were all very nervous, eyeing me up and down distrustfully. As often, in such cases, they weren't telling me more than they had to, it was up to me to tell them; that's why they were spending three dollars on me.

The child was fairly eating me up with her cold, steady eyes, and no expression to her face whatever. She did not move and seemed, inwardly, quiet; an unusually attractive little thing, and as strong as a heifer in appearance. But her face was flushed, she was breathing rapidly, and I realized that she had a high fever. She had magnificent blonde hair, in profusion. One of those picture children often reproduced in advertising leaflets and the photogravure sections of the Sunday papers.

She's had a fever for three days, began the father and we don't know what it comes from. My wife has given her things, you know, like people do, but it don't do no good. And there's been a lot of sickness around. So we tho't you'd better look her over and tell us what is the matter.

As doctors often do I took a trial shot at it as a point of departure. Has she had a sore throat?

Both parents answered me together, No . . . No, she says her throat don't hurt her.

Does your throat hurt you? added the mother to the child. But the little girl's expression didn't change nor did she move her eyes from my face.

Have you looked?

I tried to, said the mother, but I couldn't see.

As it happens we had been having a number of cases of diphtheria in the school to which this child went during that month and we were all, quite apparently, thinking of that, though no one had as yet spoken of the thing.

Well, I said, suppose we take a look at the throat first. I smiled in my best professional manner and asking for the child's first name I said, come on, Mathilda, open your mouth and let's take a look at your throat.

Nothing doing.

Aw, come on, I coaxed, just open your mouth wide and let me take a look. Look, I said opening both hands wide, I haven't anything in my hands. Just open up and let me see.

Such a nice man, put in the mother. Look how kind he is to you. Come on, do what he tells you to. He won't hurt you.

At that I ground my teeth in disgust. If only they wouldn't use the word "hurt" I might be able to get somewhere. But I did not allow myself to be hurried or disturbed but speaking quietly and slowly I approached the child again.

As I moved my chair a little nearer suddenly with one catlike movement both her hands clawed instinctively for my eyes and she almost reached them too. In fact she knocked my glasses flying and they fell, though unbroken, several feet away from me on the kitchen floor.

Both the mother and father almost turned themselves inside out in embarrassment and apology. You bad girl, said the mother, taking her and shaking her by one arm. Look what you've done. The nice man . . .

For heaven's sake, I broke in. Don't call me a nice man to her. I'm here to look at her throat on the chance that she might have diphtheria and possibly die of it. But that's nothing to her. Look here, I said to the child, we're going to look at your throat. You're old enough to understand what I'm saying. Will you open it now by yourself or shall we have to open it for you?

Not a move. Even her expression hadn't changed. Her breaths however were coming faster and faster. Then the battle began. I had to do it. I had to have a throat culture for her own protection. But first I told the parents that it was entirely up to them. I explained the danger but said that I would not insist on a throat examination so long as they would take the responsibility.

If you don't do what the doctor says you'll have to go to the hospital, the mother admonished her severely.

Oh yeah? I had to smile to myself. After all, I had already

fallen in love with the savage brat, the parents were contemptible to me. In the ensuing struggle they grew more and more abject, crushed, exhausted while she surely rose to magnificent heights of insane fury of effort bred of her terror of me.

The father tried his best, and he was a big man but the fact that she was his daughter, his shame at her behavior and his dread of hurting her made him release her just at the critical times when I had almost achieved success, till I wanted to kill him. But his dread also that she might have diphtheria made him tell me to go on, go on though he himself was almost fainting, while the mother moved back and forth behind us raising and lowering her hands in an agony of apprehension.

Put her in front of you on your lap, I ordered, and hold both her wrists.

But as soon as he did the child let out a scream. Don't, you're hurting me. Let go of my hands. Let them go I tell you. Then she shrieked terrifyingly, hysterically. Stop it! Stop it! You're killing me!

Do you think she can stand it, doctor! said the mother.

You get out, said the husband to his wife. Do you want her to die of diphtheria?

Come on now, hold her, I said.

Then I grasped the child's head with my left hand and tried to get the wooden tongue depressor between her teeth. She fought, with clenched teeth, desperately! But now I also had grown furious—at a child. I tried to hold myself down but I couldn't. I know how to expose a throat for inspection. And I did my best. When finally I got the wooden spatula behind the last teeth and just the point of it into the mouth cavity, she opened up for an instant but before I could see anything she came down again and gripping the wooden blade between her molars she reduced it to splinters before I could get it out again.

Aren't you ashamed, the mother yelled at her. Aren't you ashamed to act like that in front of the doctor?

Get me a smooth-handled spoon of some sort, I told the

mother. We're going through with this. The child's mouth was already bleeding. Her tongue was cut and she was screaming in wild hysterical shrieks. Perhaps I should have desisted and come back in an hour or more. No doubt it would have been better. But I have seen at least two children lying dead in bed of neglect in such cases, and feeling that I must get a diagnosis now or never I went at it again. But the worst of it was that I too had got beyond reason. I could have torn the child apart in my own fury and enjoyed it. It was a pleasure to attack her. My face was burning with it.

The damned little brat must be protected against her own idiocy, one says to one's self at such times. Others must be protected against her. It is a social necessity. And all these things are true. But a blind fury, a feeling of adult shame, bred of a longing for muscular release are the operatives. One goes on to the end.

In a final unreasoning assault I overpowered the child's neck and jaws. I forced the heavy silver spoon back of her teeth and down her throat till she gagged. And there it was—both tonsils covered with membrane. She had fought valiantly to keep me from knowing her secret. She had been hiding that sore throat for three days at least and lying to her parents in order to escape just such an outcome as this.

Now truly she was furious. She had been on the defensive before but now she attacked. Tried to get off her father's lap and fly at me while tears of defeat blinded her eyes.

WORCESTER VOCATIONAL HIGH SCHOOL